PRAI[SE]
nationally [bestselling auth]ors:

Barbara Delinsky

"When you care to read the very best, the name of
Barbara Delinsky should come immediately to mind."
—*Rave Reviews*

"One of this generation's most gifted writers
of contemporary women's fiction."
—*Affaire de Coeur*

Anne Stuart

"One of the most original authors
in or out of the genre."
—*Romantic Times*

"Before I read an Anne Stuart book I make sure my
day is free, because once I start, she has me hooked!"
—bestselling author Debbie Macomber

Tara Taylor Quinn

"Tara Taylor Quinn's deeply felt stories of romance
and family will warm your heart."
—national bestselling author Jennifer Crusie

"Tara Taylor Quinn writes with wonderful
assurance...she manages to make her heroes both
intriguing and human, which isn't always easy.
She seems to genuinely like and understand men,
an attitude as refreshing as it is unusual."
—*New York Times* bestselling author Jennifer Blake

Barbara Delinsky was born and raised in suburban Boston. She worked as a researcher, photographer and reporter before turning to writing full-time in 1980. With more than fifty novels to her credit, she is truly one of the shining stars in contemporary romance fiction. This talented writer has received numerous awards and honors, and her involving stories have made her a *New York Times* bestselling author. There are over 12 million copies of her books in print worldwide—a testament to Barbara's universal appeal.

Anne Stuart has, in her more than twenty-five years as a published author, won every major award in the business, appeared on various bestseller lists, been quoted by *People, USA Today* and *Vogue,* appeared on *Entertainment Tonight* and warmed the hearts of readers worldwide. She has written more than thirty novels for Harlequin and Silhouette, plus another thirty or more suspense and historical titles for other publishers. When asked to describe herself, she has said, "Anne Stuart has written lots of books in lots of genres for lots of publishers. She lives with her splendid husband and two magnificent children in the hills of northern Vermont, where it snows so much, she hasn't much else to do but write."

Tara Taylor Quinn worked as a journalist and an English teacher before she finally realized her dream of becoming a Harlequin writer—a dream she'd nursed ever since buying her first Harlequin Romance novel at the age of fourteen. Her first novel, *Yesterday's Secrets,* was a finalist for the Romance Writers of America RITA Award. She has now written more than fifteen novels, including the popular Shelter Valley trilogy, and her contribution to the Trueblood, Texas continuity series, *The Rancher's Bride,* will appear in June.

BARBARA DELINSKY

ANNE STUART
TARA TAYLOR QUINN

LOST IN THE NIGHT

HARLEQUIN®

TORONTO • NEW YORK • LONDON
AMSTERDAM • PARIS • SYDNEY • HAMBURG
STOCKHOLM • ATHENS • TOKYO • MILAN • MADRID
PRAGUE • WARSAW • BUDAPEST • AUCKLAND

HARLEQUIN BOOKS
225 Duncan Mill Road, Don Mills,
Ontario, Canada M3B 3K9

ISBN 0-373-83537-X

LOST IN THE NIGHT

Copyright © 2002 by Harlequin Books S.A.

The publisher acknowledges the copyright holders
of the individual works as follows:

THE REAL THING
Copyright © 1986 by Barbara Delinsky.

HEAT LIGHTNING
Copyright © 1992 by Anne Kristine Stuart Ohlrogge.

FATHER: UNKNOWN
Copyright © 1998 by Tara Lee Reames.

This edition published by arrangement with Harlequin Books S.A.

® and TM are trademarks of the publisher. Trademarks indicated with ® are registered in the United States Patent and Trademark Office, the Canadian Trade Marks Office and in other countries.

Visit us at www.eHarlequin.com

Printed in U.S.A.

CONTENTS

THE REAL THING
Barbara Delinsky

CHAPTER ONE

IT WASN'T EARTH-SHATTERING in the overall scheme of things. Nor was it unexpected. Yet coming as it did topping six weeks' worth of unpleasantness, it was the final straw.

Neil Hersey glared out the window of his office. He saw neither Constitution Plaza below him, nor anything else of downtown Hartford. The anger that blinded him would have spilled into his voice had not frustration already staked its claim there.

"Okay, Bob. Let me have it. We've been friends for too long to beat around the bush." He kept his fists anchored in the pockets of his tailored slacks. "It's not just a question of preferring someone else. We both know I'm as qualified for the job as any man. And we both know that Ryoden's been courting me for the past year. For some reason there's been an eleventh-hour reversal." Very slowly he turned. "I have my suspicions. Confirm them."

Robert Balkan, executive vice president of the Ryoden Manufacturing conglomerate, eyed the ramrod-straight figure across from him. He and Neil Hersey went back a long way. Their friendship was based on mutual admiration and genuine affection, and Bob respected Neil far too much to lie.

"Word came directly from Wittnauer-Douglass," he stated defeatedly. "Your release as corporate counsel there was a compassionate move. It was either let you go or bring you to trial."

Neil swore softly and bowed his head. "Go on."

"They alleged you were responsible for some transactions that were unethical, some that were downright illegal. For your own protection, the details remain private. The corporation is taking internal measures to counter the damage."

"I'll bet."

"What can I say, Neil? The charge was totally unsubstantiated, but it was enough to get the chairman of our board up in arms.

One word in the old coot's ear and it became a crusade with him. Someone at Wittnauer-Douglass knew exactly what he was doing when he made that call. Then Ned Fallenworth got in on the act and that was that.''

Fallenworth was the president of Ryoden. Bob had had reason to regret that fact in the past, but never as vehemently as he did now. "I've been spitting bullets since Ned gave me his decision. Ned's always been a coward, and what he's doing is a sad reflection on Ryoden. I gave it all I had, but his mind was closed. Narrow minds, Neil. That's what we're dealing with. Narrow minds.''

Neil deliberately unclenched his jaw. "Narrow minds with a hell of a lot of power'' was his own bleak assessment of the situation.

Leaving the window, he prowled the room, moving from parquet floor to Oriental rug and back, continuing the circle until he reached his gleaming mahogany desk. He leaned against the edge, his long legs extended and crossed at the ankles. His arms were folded over his chest. The pose might have been one of casual confidence under other circumstances. "Six weeks, Bob,'' he gritted. "This hell's being going on for six weeks. I'm being blackballed and it's touched every blessed aspect of my life. Something's got to give!''

"Do you need money? If it's a question of finances, I'd be glad to—''

"No, no.'' Neil waved aside the suggestion, then gentled his expression into a half smile of thanks. "Money's no problem. Not for now, at least.'' With the measured breath he took, the remnants of his half smile vanished. "The way things stand, though,'' he resumed, unable to stem his irritation, "my future as a lawyer in this town is just about nil, which is exactly what Wittnauer-Douglass intended.''

"I think you should sue.''

"Are you kidding?'' Straightening his arms, he gripped the edge of the desk on either side of his lean hips. "Listen, I appreciate your vote of confidence, but you don't know that company as I do. A, they'd cover everything up. B, they'd drag the proceedings on so long that I would run out of money. C, *regardless* of the outcome, they'd make such a public issue of a suit that what little is left of my reputation would be shot to hell in the process. We're talking piranhas here, Bob.''

"So why did you represent them?"

"Because I didn't *know*, damn it!" His shoulders slumped. "And that's the worst of it, I think. I just...didn't...know." His gaze skittered to the floor, dark brows lowered to hide his expression of deep self-dismay.

"You're human. Like the rest of us."

"Not much by way of encouragement."

Bob rose. "I wish I could do more."

"But you've done what you came to do and it's time to leave." Neil heard the bitterness in his voice, and while he detested it, he couldn't bring himself to apologize.

"I have an appointment at three." Bob's tone verged on apologetic, and Neil was quickly wary. He'd witnessed six weeks of defections, of so-called friends falling by the wayside.

Testing the waters, he extended his hand. "I haven't seen Julie in months. Let's meet for dinner sometime soon?"

"Sure thing," Bob said, smiling a little too broadly as the two shook hands.

Bob was relieved, Neil mused. The dirty work was done. And a "sure thing" for dinner was as noncommittal as Neil had feared it might be.

Moments later he was alone with an anger that approached explosive levels. Slumping into the mate of the chair Bob had just left, he pressed a finger to the crease in the center of his forehead and rubbed up and down. His head was splitting; he had to keep it together somehow. But how to remain sane when everything else was falling apart... Where was justice? Where in the hell was the justice in life?

Okay, he could understand why his working relationship with Wittnauer-Douglass would be severed after the abysmal scene six weeks ago. There had been, and was a difference of opinion. A rather drastic difference of opinion. He wouldn't have wanted to continue serving as counsel for the corporation any more than they'd wanted him to. But should he be punished this way?

His entire life was twisted. Damn it, it wasn't right!

Okay, so he'd lost Ryoden. He could have lived with that if it hadn't been for the fact that he'd also lost three other major clients in as many weeks. He was being blackballed within the corporate community. How the hell could he counter it, when the enemy was so much larger, so much more powerful?

He took several slow, measured breaths, opened his eyes and looked around the office. Ceiling-high mahogany bookshelves filled with legal tomes; an impressive collection of diplomas and brass-framed citations; a state-of-the-art telephone system linking him to his secretary and the world beyond; a credenza filled with important forms and personal papers—all worthless. What counted was in his head. But if he couldn't practice law his mind was worthless, too; it was hammering at his skull now, hammering mercilessly.

Neil Hersey had never felt so furious, so bitter—so utterly help-less—in his entire life. He knew that something had to be done, and that he was the one who was going to have to do it. For the life of him, though, he didn't know what action to take. His thoughts were mired in that fury and bitterness. He couldn't think clearly.

Muttering a dark oath, he bolted from his seat. He needed a break, a change of scenery. More than anything at the moment, he needed out.

Rounding the desk, he snatched his personal phone book from the top right-hand drawer and flipped to the Ls. Landry. Lazuk. Lee. Lesser. He set the book down, marking the place with his finger. Lesser. Victoria Lesser. Within seconds he'd punched out the number that would connect him with the stylish Park Avenue co-op high above the hustle of Manhattan.

A very proper maid answered. "Lesser residence."

"This is Neil Hersey. Is Mrs. Lesser in?"

"Please hold the phone."

Neil waited, tapping his foot impatiently. He massaged the throb-bing spot on his forehead. He squeezed his eyes shut. Only when he pictured Victoria breezing toward the phone—wending her way through the most elegant of furnishings while, very likely, wearing jeans and an oversized work shirt—did he give a small smile.

Victoria Lesser was a character. Thanks to the husband she'd worshipped until his death six years earlier, she was extremely wealthy and influential. She was also a nonconformist, which was what Neil adored about her. Though never outrageous, she did what she wanted, thumbing her nose at the concept of a staid and proper fifty-two-year-old widow. She traveled. She entertained. She took up ballet dancing. She fantasized herself a painter. She was interesting and refreshing and generous to the core.

It was that generosity Neil was counting on.

"Neil Hersey...fine friend you are!" A good-natured tirade burst from the other end of the line. "Do you know how long it's been since I've heard from you? It's been months! *Months!*"

"I know, Victoria. And I'm sorry. How are you?"

"How I am is beside the point," Victoria said more softly. "The question is, how are *you*?"

Neil hadn't been sure how far word had spread, but he should have realized Victoria would have heard. The mutual friend through which they'd originally met was an executive at Wittnauer-Douglass.

"You're speaking to me," he answered cautiously, "which makes me feel better already."

"Of course I'm speaking to you. I know what happened there, Neil. I know that board of directors. That is, I know how to recognize snakes. I also know what kind of lawyer you are—I haven't forgotten what you did for my niece—and I know the bind you're in right now."

"Then you know I need to get away." He broached the topic quickly. He was in no mood, even with Victoria, to pussyfoot around. "I can't think here. I'm too angry. I need peace and quiet. And seclusion."

"Something like a remote and uninhabited island off the coast of Maine?"

Neil's mouth lifted slightly at the corners. "Something like that."

"It's yours."

"No one's there?"

"In October?" She snorted. "People nowadays are sissies. Once Labor Day's passed, you'd think going north to an island was tantamount to exploring the Arctic. It's yours, Neil, for as long as you want it."

"Two weeks should do it. If I can't come up with some solutions by then..." There wasn't much more he could say.

"You haven't called me before, and knowing you, you'll want

to work this out for yourself. But if there's anything I can do, will you let me know?''

Neil found solace in her words. She had the courage that others lacked. Not only was she unswayed by smear tactics, she would root for the underdog any day. "Use of the island is more than enough," he said gratefully.

"When were you thinking of going?"

"As soon as possible. Tomorrow, I guess. But you'll have to tell me how to get there."

Victoria did so. "Once you get to Spruce Head, ask for Thomas Nye. Big fellow. Bushy red beard. He lobsters from there. I'll call ahead and alert him. He'll take you out to the island."

With brief but heartfelt thanks, plus a promise to call her when he returned, Neil hung up the phone. He spent the rest of the afternoon working with his secretary to clear his calendar for the next two weeks. It was a relatively easy feat, given the amount of work he'd recently lost. He met in turn with each of his two young associates, giving them enough direction to keep them marginally occupied during his absence.

For the first time in his memory, when he left the office his briefcase remained behind. He carried nothing more than a handful of Havana cigars.

If he was going to escape it all, he decided belligerently, he'd go all the way.

DEIRDRE JOYCE glowered at the thick white cast that sheathed her left leg from thigh to toe. It was a diversionary tactic. If she looked into the urgent faces that circled her hospital bed, she was sure she'd explode.

"It was an act of fate, Deirdre," her mother was saying. "A message. I've been trying to get it across for months now, but you've refused to listen, so someone higher up is spelling it out. Your place is in the business with your sister, not teaching aerobics."

"My teaching aerobics had nothing to do with this, Mother," Deirdre declared. "I tripped on the stairs in my own town house. I fell. I broke my leg. I don't see any message there, except that I was careless. I left a magazine where it shouldn't have been and slipped on it. It could as easily have been *Forbes* as *Runner's World*."

"The message," Maria Joyce went on, undaunted, "is that physical fitness will only get you so far. For heaven's sake, Deirdre, you'll be sidelined for weeks. You can't teach your precious dance even if you want to. What better time is there to help Sandra out?"

Deirdre looked at her sister then. Once upon a time she'd have felt compassion for her, but that was before six months of nonstop pressure had taken its toll. "I'm sorry, Sandra. I can't."

"Why not, Dee?" Tall and dark-haired, Sandra took after their mother, while Deirdre was more fair and petite. She had been different from the start. "You have the same education I do, the same qualifications," Sandra pressed.

"I don't have the temperament. I never did."

Maria was scowling. "Temperament has nothing to do with it. You decided early on that you preferred to take the easy way out. Well, you have, and look where it's gotten you."

"Mother..." Deirdre closed her eyes and sank deeper into the pillows. Four days of confinement in a bed had left her weak, and that annoyed her. It had also left her craving a hot shower, but that was out of the question. To say that she was testy was putting it mildly.

Her voice was quiet, but there was clear conviction in her words. "We've been through this a hundred times. You and Dad may have shared the dream of a family corporation, but it's your dream, not mine. I don't want it. I'm not suited for it. It's too structured, too demanding. I gave it a try once and it was a disaster."

"Eight months," Maria argued, "years ago."

"Your mother's right, Deirdre." The deep, slightly gravelly voice belonged to Deirdre's uncle. He had been standing, silent and innocuous up to that point, at the foot of the bed. "You'd only just graduated from college, but even then you showed potential. You're a doer, like your father, but you were young and you let things overwhelm you. You left too soon. You didn't give it a fair shot."

Deirdre shook her head. "I knew myself then," she insisted, scrunching folds of the coarse white sheet between tense fingers, "and I know myself now. I'm not cut out for the business world. Having a technical aptitude for business is one thing. Maybe I do have that. But emotionally—what with board meetings, conferences, three-martini lunches, client dinners, being constantly *on*— I'd go stark raving mad!''

''You're being melodramatic,'' her mother scoffed.

''Right. That's the way I am, and there's no place for melodrama in Joyce Enterprises. So please,'' she begged, ''please leave me out of it.''

Sandra took a step closer. ''We need you, Dee. *I* need you. Do you think I'm any more suited to heading a corporation than you are?''

''At least you want to do it.''

''Whether I do or not is irrelevant. Things have been a mess since Dad died.''

Since Dad died. That was the crux of it. Six months before, Allan Joyce had died in his sleep, never knowing that what he'd done so peacefully had created utter havoc.

Deirdre closed her eyes. ''I think this conversation's going nowhere,'' she stated quietly. ''The only reason things have been a mess since Dad died is that not one of you—of us—has the overall vision necessary to head a corporation. What Joyce Enterprises needs is outside help. It's as simple as that.''

''We're a family-run company—'' her mother began, only to stop short when Deirdre's eyes flew open, flashing.

''And we've run out of family. You can't run a business, Mother. Apparently neither can Sandra. Uncle Peter is as helpless as Uncle Max, and I'm the only one who's willing to acknowledge that the time has come for a change.'' She gave an exasperated sigh. ''What astounds me most is that the corporation is still functioning. It's been running itself, coasting along on Dad's momentum. But without direction it's only a matter of time before it grinds to a halt. *Sell it*, Mother. And if you won't do that, hire a president and several vice presidents and—''

''We have a president and several vice presidents,'' Maria informed her unnecessarily. ''What we lack is someone to coordinate things. You're the organizer. You're what we need. You're the one who's put together all kinds of functions.''

''Charity functions, Mother. One, maybe two, a year. Benefit road races and sports days,'' she replied wearily. "We're not talking heavy business here.''

"You're your father's daughter.''

"I'm not my father.''

"But still—''

"Mother, I have a wicked headache and you're not helping. Uncle Peter, will you please take Mother home?''

Maria held her ground. "Now just a minute, Deirdre. I won't be dismissed. You're being selfish. You've always put your own needs first. Don't you have any sense of responsibility toward this family?''

The guilt trip. It had been inevitable. "I'm not up to this,'' Deirdre moaned.

"Fine.'' Maria straightened. "Then we'll discuss it tomorrow. You're being discharged in the morning. We'll be here to pick you up and drive you to the house—''

"I'm not going to the house. I'm going to my place.''

"With a broken leg? Don't be absurd, Deirdre. You can't climb those stairs.''

"If I can't handle a flight of stairs, how can I possibly run a multimillion-dollar corporation from a seventeenth-floor office?''

"There are elevators.''

"That's not the point, Mother!'' Deirdre threw an arm over her eyes. She felt tired and unbelievably frustrated. It was nothing new. Just worse. "All I know,'' she managed stiffly, "is that I'm checking out of here tomorrow morning and going to my own town house. Where I go from there is anyone's guess, but it won't be to Joyce Enterprises.''

"We'll discuss it tomorrow.''

"There's nothing to discuss. It's settled.''

Maria's chin gave a little twitch. It was a nervous gesture, one that appeared when she wasn't getting her way. Deirdre had caused it more times than either of them could count. "You're upset. It's understandable, given what you've been through.'' She patted her daughter's cheek. "Tomorrow. We'll talk tomorrow.''

Deirdre said nothing. Lips set in a grim line, she watched her visitors pass one by one through the door. Alone at last, she pressed her finger hard on the call button.

Her head throbbed. Her leg throbbed. She needed aspirin.

She also needed a magic carpet to sweep her up, up and away.

This time when she glowered at her cast, there was no diversion intended. How could she have been so careless as to slip on that magazine? Why hadn't she caught herself, grabbed the banister? Why hadn't she just sat down and bumped her way to the bottom of the stairs?

But that would have been too simple. Deirdre the athlete had had to tumble head over heels. She'd had to catch her ankle in the banister, breaking her leg in three places.

Given the picture of coordination she'd projected day in day out for the past five years, it was downright embarrassing. Given the physical exertion her body was used to, her body craved, her present state was downright stifling.

It was also depressing. Her future was a huge question mark. Rather than a simple break, what she'd done to her leg had required intricate surgery to repair. She'd been trussed up in the hospital for four days. She'd be in the cast for six weeks more. She'd have to work her way through several weeks of physical therapy after that, and only *then* would she learn whether she'd be able to teach again.

As if her own problems weren't enough to bear, there was the matter of her family...and Joyce Enterprises. That provoked anger. Ever since her initial eight-month fiasco of a professional introduction to the company, she'd insisted that she wanted no part of it.

While he'd been alive, her father had put in repeated plugs. *Try it again, Deirdre. You'll grow to like it, Deirdre. If the business isn't for my children, who is it for, Deirdre?* After his death, her mother had picked up the gauntlet. Her sister and her uncles in turn had joined in later. And as the company had begun to fray at the edges, the pressure had increased.

Deirdre loved her own career. It was an outlet—demanding, creative and rewarding. She took pride in the fact that she was a good teacher, that she'd developed a loyal following, that her classes were packed to overflowing and that she'd become known as the queen of aerobics at the health club.

Her career had also been a convenient excuse, and now she was without.

A pair of aspirin eased the pain in her leg and, to some extent, her headache. Unfortunately, it did nothing to ease her dilemma. The prospect of leaving the hospital in the morning, and by doing so putting herself at the mercy of her family, was dismal. She could see it now—the phone calls, the drop-in visits, the ongoing and relentless campaign to draft her. Dismal. Unfair. *Unbearable.* If only there were someplace quiet, distant, secluded...

Sparked by a sudden determination, she grabbed the phone, dealing first with the hospital operator, then New York City information, then the hospital operator once more. At last her call went through.

A very proper maid answered. "Lesser residence."

"This is Deirdre Joyce. Is Mrs. Lesser in?"

"Please hold the phone."

Deirdre waited, tapping her finger impatiently against the plastic receiver. She shifted her weight from one bed-weary hip to the other. She squeezed her eyes shut, relieving herself of the sight of the sickroom. And she pictured Victoria, dressed no doubt in an oversized shirt and jeans, wending her way through the most elegant of surroundings to pick up the phone. Would she be coming from the music room, having just set down her cello? Or from tending African violets in her rooftop greenhouse?

Victoria was neither a musician nor a gardener, if skill was the measure. But whatever she did she loved, which was more than enough measure for Deirdre. Of all the family friends Deirdre had come to know in her twenty-nine years, Victoria Lesser was the one she most admired. Victoria was a freethinker, an individual. Rather than withering when the husband she'd loved had died, she'd blossomed and grown. She shunned parochialism and put protocol in its place. She did what she wanted, yet was always within the boundaries of good taste.

Deirdre enjoyed and respected her. It had been far too long since they'd seen each other.

"Hey, stranger," came the ebullient voice from the other end of the line, "where *have* you been?"

Deirdre gave a wan half smile. "Providence, as always, Victoria. How are you?"

"Not bad, if I do say so myself."

"What were you doing just now? I've been trying to imagine. Was it music? Gardening? Tell me. Make me smile."

"Oh-oh. Something's wrong."

For an instant Deirdre's throat grew tight. She hadn't spoken with Victoria in months, yet they could pick up a conversation as though it had been left off the day before. Despite the more than twenty years separating them, their relationship was honest.

Deirdre swallowed the knot. "What were you doing?"

"Stenciling the bathroom ceiling... Are you smiling?"

"A little."

"What's wrong, Dee?"

"I've always hated that nickname. Did you know? The only people who use it are members of my family...and you. When they do it, I feel like a child. When you do it, I feel like...a friend."

"You are," Victoria said softly, "which is why I want you to tell me what's wrong. Are they at it again?"

Deirdre sighed and threw an arm across the mop of sandy hair on her forehead. "With a vengeance. Only this time I'm operating from a position of weakness. I broke my leg. Can you believe it? Super athlete hits the dust."

Silence.

Deirdre's voice dropped an octave. "If you're laughing at me, Victoria, so help me..."

"I'm not laughing, sweetheart. I'm not laughing."

"You're smiling. I can hear it."

"It's either that or cry. The irony of it is too much. Of all the people to break a leg, you can stand it the least...no pun intended. Are you going stir-crazy?"

"I can see it coming fast. It's bad enough that I can't work out. Lord only knows when—or if—I'll be able to teach again. But they're closing in on me, and they're not about to let up until I either give in and go to the office or flip out completely." She took an uneven breath. "I need to get away, Victoria. There'll be no peace here and I have to think about what I'm going to do if...if I can't..." She didn't need to finish; Victoria felt her fear.

There was a pause. "You're thinking of Maine."

"If it'd be all right with you. You've mentioned it so often, but the timing's never been right. It might be just what I need now—distant enough, quiet, undemanding.''

''And there's no phone.''

''You do understand.''

''Uh-huh.'' There was another pause, then a pensive, ''Mmmm. Maine might be just what you need. When were you thinking of going?''

For the first time since her fall down the stairs, Deirdre felt a glimmer of spirit. ''As soon as I can.'' Definitely. ''Tomorrow, I guess.'' Why not! ''But you'll have to tell me how to get there.''

Victoria did so, giving her route and exit numbers. ''Can you get someone to drive you?''

''I'll drive myself.''

''What about your broken leg?''

''It's my left one.''

''Ahhh. Be grateful for small favors.''

''Believe me, I am. Okay, once I get to Spruce Head, what do I do?''

''Look for Thomas Nye. Big fellow. Bushy red beard. He lobsters from there. I'll call ahead and alert him. He'll take you out to the island.''

Deirdre managed a smile then. ''You are a true friend, Victoria. A lifesaver.''

''I hope so,'' Victoria replied cautiously. ''Will you give me a call when you get back to let me know how things went?''

Deirdre agreed, adding heartfelt thanks before she finally hung up the phone and lay back on the bed.

Victoria, on the other hand, merely pressed the disconnect button. When the line was clear, she put through her second call in as many hours to Thomas Nye. She wore a distinct look of satisfaction when she finally returned the receiver to its cradle.

IT WAS STILL RAINING. Strike that, Neil amended sourly. It was pouring.

He scowled past his streaming windshield to the rain-spattered road ahead. The storm had followed him north, he decided. Just his luck. From Connecticut, through Massachusetts, to New Hampshire, then Maine—four-plus hours of nonstop rain. Leaden skies promised more of the same.

His windshield wipers flicked from left to right and back in double time, yet the passing landscape blurred. He hadn't minded the lack of visibility when he'd been on the superhighway—there hadn't been much to see. But he was well off the turnpike now, following Route 1 through towns such as Bath, Wiscasset and Damariscotta. He would have welcomed the diversion of an occasional "down east" sight.

But all he saw was the dappling and redappling sweep of grays and browns, in the middle of which—demanding his constant attention—was the road. The only sounds he heard were the steady beat of rain on the roof of the car and the more rhythmic, if frantic, pulse of the wipers. The world smelled wet. He was tired of sitting. And his mind... His mind persisted in rummaging through the baggage it had brought along on the trip.

Shortly before three in the afternoon, his mood as dark as the clouds overhead, Neil pulled his black LeBaron to a stop alongside the weathered wharf at Spruce Head. He should have been relieved that the arduous drive was over. He should have felt uplifted, filled with anticipation, eager to be nearing his destination.

What he felt was dismay. The docks were mucky. Visibility beyond the moored but wildly bobbing boats was practically nil. And the stench in the air, seeping steadily into the car, was nearly overpowering.

Distastefully he studied the large lobster tanks lined up on the wharf, then the nearby vats filled with dead fish, rotting for use as lobster bait. His own fondness for lobster meat in no way made the smell easier to take.

A gust of wind buffeted the car, driving the rain against it with renewed fury. Neil sat back in the seat and swore softly. What he needed, he decided, were a fisherman's oilskins. As far as he could see, though, not even the fishermen were venturing outside.

Unfortunately he had to venture. He had to find Thomas Nye.

Retrieving his Windbreaker from the back seat, he struggled into it. Then, on a single sucked-in breath, he opened the car door, bolted out, slammed the door behind him and raced to the nearest building.

The first door he came to opened with a groan. Three men sat inside what appeared to be a crude office, though Neil doubted he'd interrupted serious work. Each man held a mug filled with something steaming. Two of the chairs were tipped back on their hind legs; the third was being straddled backside-to.

All three men looked up at his entrance, and Neil was almost grateful for his disheveled appearance. His hair was damp and mussed; a day's worth of stubble darkened his cheeks. His Windbreaker and worn jeans were rain spattered, his running shoes mud spattered, as well. He felt right at home.

"I'm looking for Thomas Nye," he announced straightaway. Fishermen were laconic; that suited him fine. He was in no mood for polite chitchat. "Big fellow with a bushy red beard?"

One chair and one chair only hit the floor. Its occupant propped his elbows on his knees and gestured with a single hand. "Down a block...feust left...second house on y'or right."

Nodding, Neil left. Head ducked low against the torrent, he dashed back to the car and threw himself inside. Rain dripped from his Windbreaker onto the leather seats, but he paid no heed. In the short minutes since he'd arrived at Spruce Head, his focus had narrowed. Reaching Victoria's island and shutting himself inside her house to avail himself of that highly acclaimed master bedroom with its walls of glass, its huge stone fireplace and its quilt-covered king-size bed seemed all-important.

Taking a minute to decide which way was "down" the block, he started the car and set off. One left later he turned, then pulled up at the second house on the right. It was one of several in a row on the street, and he might have said it had charm had he been in a better mood. It was small, white with gray shutters and, with its paint peeling sadly, looked as aged as he felt.

Loath to waste time, he ran from the car and up the short front walk. Seeing no doorbell, he knocked loudly enough to make himself heard above the storm. Shortly the door was opened by a big fellow with a bushy red beard.

Neil sighed. "Thomas Nye."

The man nodded, held the door wide and cocked his head toward the inside of the house. Neil accepted his invitation instantly.

LESS THAN AN HOUR LATER, Deirdre pulled up at the same house. She looked in turn at the humble structure, then at the sporty black car parked in front of her. Even had she not seen the Connecticut license plate she would have bet it wasn't the car of a lobsterman.

Thomas Nye apparently had guests and the thought didn't thrill her. She wasn't exactly at her best—an assessment, she realized, that was decidedly kind.

She'd been lucky. A passerby at the wharf had given her directions, sparing her a dash from the car. Not that she could dash. Or even walk. Hobble was more like it.

But her luck had run out. She was at Thomas Nye's house and there was no way she could speak to the man without leaving the haven of her car. That meant hauling out her crutches, extricating her casted leg from the hollow to the left of the brake and maneuvering herself to a standing position. It also meant getting wet.

Well, why not! she snapped to herself. The day had been a nightmare from the start. What was a little more grief?

Tugging her hip-length Goretex parka from the back seat, she struggled into it. Then, taking a minute to work out the logistics of dealing with cast, crutches and rain, she opened the car door and set to it.

By the time she reached Thomas Nye's front door, she was gritting her teeth in frustration. What might have taken ten seconds, had she been operating on two strong legs, had taken nearly two minutes—long enough for the storm to drench her. Her hair was plastered to her head and dripping in her eyes. Her sweatpants were noticeably heavier. Her wet grip on the crutches was precarious. And her armpits ached.

Tamping down her irritation as best she could, she shifted her weight to one crutch and knocked. As the small porch overhang offered some protection from the gusting rain, she wedged herself closer to the door.

She twitched her nose. The rank odor that had hit her full force at the wharf was less pungent here, diluted by the fresh salty air and the rain.

She tugged at her collar. She was cold. Impatient, she knocked again, louder this time. Within seconds, the door was opened by a big fellow with a bushy red beard.

Deirdre sighed. "Thomas Nye."

Eyes skittering away, he nodded, held the door wide and cocked his head toward the inside of the house. She hitched her way into the narrow front hall, and at another silent gesture from the large man, into the small living room.

The first thing she saw was a low table spread with papers, charts and what looked to be bills. The second was the television set, broadcasting *Wheel of Fortune* in living color. The third was the dark, brooding figure of a man slouched in a chair in the far corner of the room.

The fourth thing she noticed, unfortunately, was that Thomas Nye had calmly settled into a seat by the table, returning to the work her knock had apparently interrupted.

She cleared her throat. "You were expecting me."

"That's right," he said. He had already lifted several papers, and didn't look up. "Want to sit?"

"Uh…are we…going?"

"Not now."

She ingested that information with as much aplomb as she could, given that the last thing she wanted was a delay. "It's the weather, I take it?" The possibility had been niggling at the back of her mind for the past hour. She'd done her best to ignore it.

The man in the corner grunted.

Thomas Nye nodded.

"Do you have any idea when we *will* be able to go?" she asked, discouraged; it seemed like forever since she'd awoken that morning. She now had to admit that making the trip on the same day as her discharge from the hospital may have been taking too much upon herself. But it was done. The best she could hope for was that the delay would be minimal.

In answer to her question, the bearded man shrugged. "As soon as it lets up."

"But it could rain for days," she returned. When a second grunt came from the man in the corner, she darted him a scowl. At the moment all she wanted was to be dry and warm beneath a heavy quilt on that king-size bed in the house on Victoria's island. Alone. With no one to stare at the sorry sight she made and no one to make her feel guilty about anything.

She willed her concentration on Nye. "I thought you went lobstering rain or no rain."

"The wind's the problem." At precisely that moment a gust howled around the house.

Deirdre shuddered. "I see." She paused. "Is there a forecast? Do you have any idea when it will let up?"

Nye shrugged. "An hour, maybe two, maybe twelve."

She leaned heavily on the crutches. An hour or two she could live with. But twelve? She doubted she could last twelve hours without that warm, dry bed and heavy quilt. And where would she be waiting out the time?

She glanced again at the man in the corner. He sat low in his chair, one leg stretched out, the other ankle crossed over his knee. His elbows were propped on the arms of the chair, his mouth pressed flush against knuckle-to-knuckle fists. His eyebrows were dark, the eyes beneath them even darker. He, too, was waiting. She could sense his frustration as clearly as she felt her own.

"Uh, Mr. Nye," she began, "I really have to get out there soon. If I don't get off this leg, I'm apt to be in trouble."

Nye was jotting something on the top of one of the papers that lay before him. He lifted his gaze to the game show and gestured with his pencil toward a faded sofa. "Please. Sit."

Deirdre watched as he resumed his work. She contemplated arguing further but sensed the futility of it. He looked calm, satisfied...and utterly immovable. With a grimace she plodded to the sofa. Jerking off her wet parka, she thrust it over the back of the worn cushion, coupled her crutches to one side of her and eased her way down.

When she lifted her eyes once more, she found the man in the corner staring at her. Irritated, she glared back. "Is something wrong?"

He arched a brow, lowered his fists and pursed his lips. "That's quite an outfit." It wasn't a compliment.

"Thank you," she said sweetly. "I rather like it myself." Actually, when they were dry, the roomy pink sweatpants were the most comfortable ones she owned, and comfort was a high priority, what with a cast the size of hers. Unfortunately, while dressing, she'd also been fighting with her mother, and consequently she'd pulled on the first sweatshirt that came to hand. It was teal colored, oversized and as comfortable as the pants, though it did clash slightly. And if the man had an argument with her orange leg warmers, that was his problem. The left one, stretched out and tucked into itself beyond her foot, had kept her toes warm and her cast dry. Her lone sneaker on the other foot, was pitifully wet.

So she didn't look like Jaclyn Smith advertising makeup. Deirdre didn't care. In the immediate future, she was going to be all alone on an island. No one would see her. No one would care what she wore. Practicality and comfort were the two considerations she'd made when deciding what to bring with her. The man with the dark, brooding eyes could thank his lucky stars he wouldn't have to see her beyond this day.

Muted pandemonium broke loose on the television screen as a player won a shiny red Mercedes. Looking up, Thomas grinned at the victory, but Deirdre merely lowered her head and pressed chilled fingers to the bridge of her nose. She hated game shows almost as much as she hated soap operas. On occasion when she passed through the lounge of the health club, the set would be tuned to one or the other. Invariably she'd speed on by.

Now she was speeding nowhere. That fact was even more grating than the sound of the show. Disgruntled, she shoved aside the wet strands of hair on her brow and focused on Thomas Nye.

Head tucked low once again, he was engrossed in his paperwork. He looked almost preppy, she reflected, appraising his corduroy pants, the shirt and sweater. A man of few words, and those spoken with a New York accent, he was apparently a transplant. Deirdre wondered about that. Was he antiestablishment? Antisocial? Or simply…shy? He seemed unable to meet her gaze for more than a minute, and though he was pleasant enough, he made no attempt at conversation. Nor had he introduced her to the man in the corner.

Just as well, she decided as she shifted her gaze. The man in the corner didn't appear to be anyone she'd care to meet. He was frowning toward the window now, his fist propped back against his cheek. The furrow between his brows was marked. His lips held a sullen slant. And if those signs of discontent weren't off-putting enough, the heavy shadow of a beard on his lower face gave him an even less inviting appearance.

Just then he looked her way. Their eyes met and held, until at last she turned her head. No, he wasn't anyone she'd care to meet, because he looked just as troubled as she was, and there was precious little room in her life for compassion at the moment.

At the moment, Neil Hersey was thinking similar thoughts. It had been a long time since he'd seen anyone as pathetic-looking as the woman across the room. Oh, yes, the weather had taken its toll, soaking her clothes and matting her short, brown hair in damp strands that grazed her eyelids. But it was more than that. The weather had nothing to do with the fact that she had one fat leg and an overall shapeless figure. Or that she was pale. Or that her crossness seemed to border on orneriness. He assumed Nye was shuttling her to one of the many islands in the Gulf of Maine. But he had woes enough to keep him occupied without bothering about someone else's.

His immediate woe was being landlocked. Time was passing. He wanted to be moving out. But Thomas Nye was calling the shots, a situation that only exacerbated Neil's dour mood.

He shifted restlessly and absently rubbed his hand over the rough rag wool of his sweater. Was that heartburn he felt? Maybe an incipient ulcer? He took a disgusted breath, shifted again and was about to glance at his watch, when he saw the woman do it.

"Mr. Nye?" she asked.

"Thomas," Nye answered without looking up.

"Thomas. How long will the crossing take?"

"Two hours, give or take some."

She studied her watch again, making the same disheartening calculations Neil did. "But if we're held up much longer, we won't make it before dark." It would be bad enough negotiating rugged terrain in daylight with her crutches, but at night? "That...could be difficult."

"Better difficult than deadly," Thomas replied gently. "As soon as the wind dies down, we'll go. We may have to wait till morning."

"Morning! But I don't have anywhere to stay," she protested.

Thomas tossed his head toward the ceiling. "I've got room."

She gave an exaggerated nod, which said *that* solved everything, when in fact it didn't. It wasn't what she wanted at all! She wanted to be on Victoria's island, comfortably settled in that spectacular master bedroom she'd heard so much about. She pictured it now— huge windows, an elegant brass bed, dust ruffles, quilt and pillows of a country-sophisticate motif. Silence. Solitude. Privacy. Oh, how she wanted that.

The awful fatigue she was fighting now she did not want. Or the ache in her leg that no amount of shifting could relieve. Or the fact that she was in a room with two strangers and she couldn't throw back her head and scream...

Neil had returned his attention to the window. What he saw there wasn't pleasing; the thought of spending the night in this tiny fisherman's house was even less so. *I've got room.* It was a generous enough offer, but hell, he didn't want to be here! He wanted to be on the island!

He was exhausted. The day's drive through the rain had been a tedious cap to six tedious weeks. He wanted to be alone. He wanted privacy. He wanted to stretch out on that king-size bed and know that his feet wouldn't hang over the edge. Lord only knew most everything else had gone wrong with his life lately.

"Does the boat have radar?" he asked on impulse.

"Yes."

"So we're not limited to daylight."

"No."

"Then there's still a chance of getting out today?"

"Of course there's a chance," Deirdre snapped, testy in her weariness. "There's always a chance."

Neil shot her a quelling look. "Then let's put it in terms of probability," he stated stubbornly, returning his attention to Thomas. "On a scale of one to ten, where would you put the chances of our making it out today?"

Deirdre scowled. "How can he possibly answer that?"

"He's a fisherman," Neil muttered tersely. "I'm asking for his professional estimate based on however many number of years he's worked on the sea."

"Three," Thomas said.

Deirdre's eyes were round with dismay. "On a scale of one to ten, we only get a *three?*"

Neil eyed her as though she were daft. "He's only been lob-stering for three years."

"Oh." She then focused on Thomas. "What *are* the chances?"

Thomas straightened a pile of papers and stood. "Right now I'd give it a two."

"A two," she wailed. "That's even worse!"

Neil glowered toward the window. Thomas stood. The Wheel of Fortune spun, gradually slowing, finally stopping on "bankrupt." The groans from the set reflected Deirdre's feelings exactly.

But she wouldn't give up. "How do you decide if we can leave?"

"The marine report."

"How often does that change?"

"Whenever the weather does."

The man in the corner snickered. Deirdre ignored him. "I mean, are there periodic updates you tune in to? How can you possibly tell, sitting here in the house, whether the wind is dying down on the water?"

Thomas was heading from the room. "I'll be back."

She looked at the man. "Where's he going?" He stared back mutely. "You're waiting to get out of here, too. Aren't you curious?"

Neil sighed. "He's getting the forecast."

"How can you tell?"

"Can't you hear the crackle of the radio?"

"I can't hear a thing over this inane show!" Awkwardly she pushed herself up, hopped to the television and turned the volume down, then hopped back. She was too tired to care if she looked like a waterlogged rabbit. Sinking into a corner of the sofa, she lifted her casted leg onto the cushions, laid her head back and closed her eyes.

Moments later Thomas returned. "Raise that to a seven. The wind's dying."

Neil and Deirdre both grew alert, but it was Neil who spoke. "Then we may make it?"

"I'll check the report in another half-hour." The lobsterman said no more, immersing himself back in his work.

The next half-hour seemed endless to Deirdre. Her mind replayed the events of the day, from her hospital discharge through the cab ride to her town house, then on to the unpleasant scene with her mother, who had been positively incensed that Deirdre would even think of leaving Providence. Deirdre would have liked to believe it was maternal concern for her health, but she knew otherwise. Her refusal to tell Maria where she was headed had resulted in even stronger reprisals, but Deirdre couldn't bear the thought that somehow her mother would get through to her on the island.

She needed this escape. She needed it badly. The way she felt, she doubted she'd get out of bed for days...when she finally reached the island.

Neil didn't weather the half-hour any better. Accustomed to being constantly on the move, he felt physically confined and mentally constrained. At times he thought he'd scream if something didn't happen. Everything grated—the lobsterman's nonchalance, the flicker of the television, the sight of the woman across the room, the sound of the rain. Too much of his life seemed dependent on external forces; he craved full control. Misery was private. He wanted to be alone.

At long last Thomas left the room again. Deirdre raised her head and held her breath. Neil waited tensely.

From the look on the fisherman's face when he returned, it seemed nothing had changed. Yet the first thing he did was flip off the television, then he gathered up his papers.

Aware that the man in the corner was holding himself straighter, Deirdre did the same. "Thomas?"

He said nothing, simply gestured broadly with his arms. Deirdre and Neil needed no more invitation. Within seconds, they were up and reaching for their jackets.

CHAPTER TWO

THE STORM MIGHT HAVE ABATED over the water, but Deirdre saw no letup on shore. The rain soaked her as she limped on her crutches to her car, which, at Thomas's direction, she moved to the deepest point in the driveway. Transferring her large duffle bag to the pickup was a minor ordeal, eased at the last minute by Thomas, who tossed her bag in, then returned to stowing boxes of fresh produce in the back of the truck. The other man was preoccupied, parking his own car, then loading his bag.

Gritting her teeth, she struggled into the cab of the truck. No sooner was she seated than the two men—the dark one, to her chagrin, had turned out to be every bit as large as the lobsterman—boxed her in, making the ensuing ride to the wharf damp and uncomfortable. By the time she was aboard Thomas's boat, propped on a wood bench in the enclosed pilothouse, she felt stiff and achy. Her sneaker was soggy. Her jacket and sweatpants were wet. She was chilled all over.

The nightmare continued, she mused, but at least its end was in sight. She'd be at Victoria's island, alone and in peace, by nightfall. It was this knowledge that kept her going.

The engine chugged to life and maintained an even growl as the boat left the wharf and headed seaward. Deirdre peered out the open back of the pilothouse for a time, watching Spruce Head recede and finally disappear in the mist. Burrowing deeper into her jacket, she faced forward then and determinedly focused on her destination. She pictured the island forested with pines, carpeted with moss, smelling of earth, sea and sky, kissed by the sun. She envisioned her own recovery there, the regaining of her strength, the rebirth of her spirit. And serenity. She conjured images of serenity.

Just as Neil did. Serenity...solitude... Soon, he told himself, soon. He'd wedged himself into a corner of the pilothouse, not so much to keep a distance from Nye's other passenger as to keep his body upright. It had been a long day, a long night before that. He'd grown accustomed to sleeplessness over the past weeks, but never had its effects hit him as they did now.

Though his fatigue was in large part physical, there was an emotional element as well. He was away from the office, relieved of his duties, distanced from his profession. This wasn't a vacation; it was a suspension. Brief, perhaps, but a letdown. And more than a little depressing.

A tiny voice inside accused him of running away; his abrupt departure from Hartford was sure to be seen by some as just that. Maybe he had run away. Maybe he was conceding defeat. Maybe…maybe… It was very depressing.

His pulse was steadily accelerating, as it always did when he pursued that particular line of thought. He wondered if he had high blood pressure yet. It wouldn't have surprised him, given the kind of nervous tension he'd been living with for days on end. He needed an outlet. Any outlet.

His gaze settled on the woman just down the bench. "Don't you think it's a little stupid going out in all this like that?" He jerked his chin toward the fat leg she'd painstakingly hauled up beside her on the hard bench.

Deirdre had been wondering apprehensively if the rhythmic plunge of the boat, noticeable now that they'd left the harbor behind, was going to get worse. She looked at him in disbelief. "Excuse me?"

"I said, don't you think it's a little stupid going out in all this like that?" He found perverse satisfaction in the verbatim repetition.

"That's what I thought you said, but I couldn't believe you'd be so rude." She had no patience. Not now. Not here. "Didn't your mother ever teach you manners?"

"Oh, yes. But she's not here right now, so I can say exactly what I want." Ah, the pleasure in blurting words out at will. He couldn't remember the last time he'd done it as freely. "You haven't answered my question."

"It's not worth answering." She turned her head away and looked at Thomas, who stood at the controls, holding the wheel steady. His body swayed easily with the movement of the boat. Deirdre wished she could go with the flow that way, but her own body seemed to buck the movement. She was glad she hadn't eaten recently.

In an attempt to divert her thoughts from various unpleasant possibilities, she homed in on the baseball hat Thomas had been wearing since they'd left the house. It had fared unbelievably well in the rain. "Are you a Yankees' fan, Thomas?" she called above the rumble of the motor.

Thomas didn't turn. "When they win."

"That's honest enough," she murmured under her breath, then raised her voice again. "You're originally from New York?"

"That's right."

"What part?"

"Queens."

"Do you still have family there?"

"Some."

"What were you doing before you became a lobsterman?"

A grumble came from the corner. "Leave the man alone. He's hardly encouraging conversation. Don't you think there's a message in that?"

Deirdre stared back at him. "He's a Maine fisherman. They're all tight-lipped."

"But he's not originally from Maine, which means that he *chooses* not to speak."

"I wish *you* would," she snapped. "I've never met anyone as disagreeable in my life." She swung back to the lobsterman. "How'd you get saddled with this one, Thomas? He's a peach."

Thomas didn't answer, but continued his study of the white-capped waves ahead.

Neil propped his elbow on the back of the bench, rested his cheek in his palm and closed his eyes.

Deirdre focused on a peeling panel of wood opposite her and prayed that her stomach would settle.

Time passed. The boat had the ocean to itself as it plowed steadily through the waves amid an eerie air of isolation. The smell of fish mingled with a decidedly musty odor, whether from wet clothing, wet skin or aged wood Deirdre didn't know, but it did nothing for the condition of her insides. She took to doing yoga breathing, clearing her mind, concentrating on relaxation. She wasn't terribly successful.

At length she spoke again, clearly addressing herself to Thomas. "Two hours, more or less, you said. Will it be more, in weather like this?" The rain hadn't let up and the sea was choppy, but, to her untrained eye, they were making progress.

"We're in luck. The wind's at our back."

She nodded, grateful for the small word of encouragement. Then she shifted, bending her good knee up and wrapping her arms around it.

"You look green," came an unbidden assessment from the corner.

She sighed. "Thank you."

"Are you seasick?"

"I'm fine."

"I think you're seasick."

Lips thinned, she swiveled around. "You'd like that, wouldn't you? You'd like to see me sick. What's the matter? Are *you* feeling queasy?"

"I'm a seasoned sailor."

"So am I," she lied, and turned away. Straightening her leg, she sat forward on the bench. Then, fingers clenched on its edge, she pushed herself up and hopped toward Thomas.

"How much longer?" she asked as softly as she could. She didn't want the man in the corner to hear the anxiety in her words. Unfortunately Thomas didn't hear the words at all. When he tipped his head toward her, she had to repeat herself.

"We're about halfway there," he replied eventually. On the one hand it was reassuring; halfway there was better than nothing. On the other hand, it was depressing; another full hour to endure.

"His island's near Matinicus, too?" The slight emphasis on the "his" told Thomas who she meant.

"There are several small islands in the area."

She moved closer and spoke more softly again. "Will you drop me first? I'm not sure I can take much more of this."

"I'm heading straight for Victoria's island."

She managed a wan smile and a grateful "Thank you" before

maneuvering back to her seat. She avoided looking at the man in the corner. He raised her hackles. She didn't need the added aggravation, when so much of the past week had been filled with it.

Neil was brooding, thinking of the last time he'd been on a boat. A seasoned sailor? He guessed it was true. Nancy had had a boat. She loved boats. Supposedly she'd loved him, too, but that had been when he'd had the world on a string. At the first sign of trouble she'd recoiled. Granted, her brother was on the board at Wittnauer-Douglass, so she'd been in an awkward position when Neil had been summarily dismissed. Still...love was love... Or was it?

He hadn't loved Nancy. He'd known it for months, and had felt guilty every time she'd said the words. Now he had a particularly sour taste in his mouth. Her words had been empty. She hadn't loved him—she'd loved what he was. She'd been enthralled by the image of a successful corporate attorney, the affluence and prestige. With all that now in doubt, she was playing it safe. And it was just as well, he knew, a blessing in disguise, perhaps. A fair-weather lover was the last thing he needed.

He looked over at the woman on the bench. She was another can of worms entirely. Small and shapeless, unpolished, unsociable, unfeminine—quite a switch from Nancy. "What did you do to your leg?" he heard himself ask.

Deirdre raised her head. "Are you talking to me?"

He glanced around the pilothouse. "I don't see anyone else with crutches around here. Did you break it?"

"Obviously."

"Not 'obviously.' You could have had corrective surgery for a congenital defect, or for a sports injury."

A sports injury. If only. There might have been dignity in that. But falling down a flight of stairs? "I broke it," she stated curtly.

"How?"

"It doesn't matter."

"When?"

Deirdre scowled. "It doesn't *matter*."

"My Lord, and you called *me* disagreeable!"

She sighed wearily. "I'm not in the mood for talking. That's all."

"You still look green." He gave a snide grin. "Stomach churning?"

"My stomach is fine!" she snapped. "And I'm not green...just pale. It's the kind of color you catch when you've been surrounded by hospital whites for days."

"You mean you were just released?" he asked with genuine surprise.

"This morning."

"And you're off racing through the rain to get to a remote island?" Surprise gave way to sarcasm once more.

"It's only a broken leg! The rest of me is working fine." Not quite true, but an understandable fib. "And, in case you're wondering, I didn't personally request the rain. It just came!"

"You were crazy to come out. Didn't your mother try to stop you?"

She heard the ridicule in his tone and was reminded of her earlier shot at him. Hers had been offered facetiously, as had his, yet he'd unwittingly hit a raw nerve. "She certainly did, but I'm an adult, so I don't have to listen to her!" She turned her head away, but it did no good.

"You don't look like an adult. You look like a pouting child."

Her eyes shot back to him reproachfully. "Better a pouting child than a scruffy pest! Look, why don't you mind your own business? You don't know me, and I don't know you, and before long, thank goodness, this ride will be over. You don't need to take out your bad mood on me. Just stay in your corner and brood to yourself, okay?"

"But I enjoy picking on you. You rise to the occasion."

That was the problem. She was letting him get to her. The way to deal with a man of his ilk was to ignore him, which she proceeded to do. Whether it worked or not she wasn't sure, because she suspected he had freely chosen not to speak further.

But he continued to look at her. She could feel his eyes boring into her back, and she steadfastly refused to turn. The man had gall; she had to hand it to him. He wasn't spineless, as Seth had been....

Seth. Sweet Seth. Parasitic Seth. He'd slipped into her world, taken advantage of her home, her job, her affections, and then turned tail and run when the family pressure had begun. Seth hadn't wanted ties. He hadn't wanted responsibility. And the last thing he'd wanted was a woman whose career demands and family responsibilities took precedence over his own needs.

The irony of it, Deirdre reflected, was that he'd had such little understanding of her. She'd never wanted Joyce Enterprises, and she'd told him so repeatedly. But he'd still felt threatened, so he'd left. In hindsight, she was better off without him.

She was drawn from her reverie when the man in the corner rose from the bench, crossed the pilothouse and positioned himself close by Thomas. He spoke in a low murmur, which, try as she might, Deirdre couldn't hear over the guttural drone of the engine.

"How much longer?" Neil asked.

Thomas glanced at one of his dials. "Half an hour."

"Where's she going?" He put a slight emphasis on the "she."

"Near Matinicus."

"Lots of islands, are there?"

"Some."

"Who gets dropped off first?"

"I'm heading straight for Victoria's island."

Neil considered that. "Look, it's okay with me if you drop her off first. She's really pretty pathetic."

Thomas's eyes remained on the sea. "I thought you didn't like her."

"I don't. She bugs the hell out of me. Then again—" he ran a hand across his aching neck "—just about anyone would bug the hell out of me right about now. She just happens to be here." He was feeling guilty, but was torn even about that. On the one hand, arguing with the woman was thoroughly satisfying. He needed to let off steam, and she was a perfect patsy. On the other hand, she was right. He'd been rude. It wasn't his normal way.

Head down, he started back toward his corner.

Deirdre, who'd been thinking just then about how badly she wanted, *needed* a bath, and what an unbelievable hassle it was going to be trying to keep her cast out of the water, stopped him mid-way. She was feeling particularly peevish. "If you think you can con Thomas into dropping you off first, don't hold your breath.

He's already set a course and it happens that *my* island's up there at the top of the list.''

"Shows how much *you* know," Neil mumbled under his breath. He passed her by, slid down into his corner of the bench, crossed his arms over his chest and stared straight ahead.

Deirdre passed his comment off as a simple case of sour grapes. He was an ill-humored man. Soon enough she'd be free of his company. Soon enough she'd be at the island.

"There it is," Thomas called over his shoulder a little while later. "Victoria's island."

Deirdre pushed herself to her good knee and peered through the front windshield. "I can't see a thing."

Neil, too, had risen. "No harm," he muttered.

"Do you see anything?"

"Sure. There's a dark bump out there."

"There's a world of dark bumps out there. How do you tell which one's a wave and which one's an island?"

"The island has trees."

The logic was irrefutable. "Swell," she said, sinking back into her seat. When they reached the island they'd reach the island. She'd have plenty of time to see it, time when she wouldn't be tired and uncomfortable and thoroughly out of sorts.

Neil stood by Thomas, watching the dark bump swell and rise and materialize into an honest-to-goodness land mass. It wasn't large, perhaps half a mile square, but it was surprisingly lush. Neither the rain, nor the clouds, nor the approach of dusk could disguise the deep green splendor of the pines. And the house was there, a rambling cape-style structure of weathered gray clapboard, nestling in a clearing overlooking the dock.

Deirdre was on her knee again. "That...is...beautiful," she breathed.

Neil, who was feeling rather smug at the perfection of his destination, darted her an indulgent glance. "I agree."

"For once. I was beginning to wonder if you had any taste at all."

His indulgence ended. "Oh, I've got taste, all right. Problem is that I haven't seen a thing today that even remotely appealed to it." His eyes didn't stray from her face, making his meaning clear.

It was an insult Deirdre simply couldn't let pass. "The feeling is mutual. In fact—"

"Excuse me," Thomas interrupted loudly, "I'll need everyone's help here. And it's still pouring, so we'd better work quickly." He was already cutting the engine and guiding the boat alongside the short wooden dock. "Neil, you go outside and throw the lines onto the dock, one at the bow, one at the stern. Then hop ashore and tie us up on those pilings. I'll pass supplies to you and Deirdre. Watch yourself on the dock, Deirdre. It'll be slippery."

Deirdre nodded and worked at the wet zipper of her parka, thinking what a waste it was to give a nice name like Neil to such an obnoxious man. But at least he was helping. She'd half expected him to insist on staying dry while Thomas got her set up on shore.

Neil zipped up his jacket and headed for the open pit of the boat's stern, thinking how ironic it was that a woman with as flowing a name as Deirdre should prove to be so thorny. But at least she'd agreed to help. That surprised him. Of course, Thomas hadn't exactly given her a choice.

"The line, Neil. We're here." Thomas's call ended all silent musings.

Head ducked against the rain, Neil raced to tie up the boat, bow and stern.

Biting her lip against a clumsiness foreign to her, Deirdre managed to lumber onto the dock with only a helping hand from Thomas. When she would have thanked him, he'd already turned away to begin off-loading. He handed things, first to her, then to Neil when he reached her side.

"I'll be back in a week with fresh supplies," instructed the lobsterman hurriedly. "These should be more than enough until then. Keys to the front door are in an envelope tucked in with the eggs. If you run into a problem, any kind of emergency, you can reach me on the ship-to-shore radio in the den. The directions are right beside it."

Deirdre nodded, but she was too busy concentrating on keeping her balance to answer. When her large duffel bag came over the side of the boat, she rearranged her crutches and somehow managed to hook the wide strap of the bag over her shoulder, then return the crutches to their prescribed position without falling.

Neil, busy piling boxes of supplies atop one another to keep them as dry as possible, looked up briefly when Thomas handed over his canvas cargo bag. He set it down on the dock, finished up with the supplies, put a box in one arm and the cargo bag's broad strap over his other shoulder, then turned back to thank Thomas.

The boat was already drifting away from the dock, which didn't surprise Neil. Thomas had said they'd work quickly. But there was something that did surprise him....

Deirdre, whose eyes had gone wide in alarm, cleared her throat. "Uh, Thomas?" When the boat slipped farther away, she tried again, louder this time. "Thomas?"

The engine coughed, then started.

This time it was Neil who yelled. "Nye! You've forgotten someone! Get back here!"

The boat backed around the tip of the dock, then turned seaward.

"Thomas!"

"Nye!"

"There's been a mistake!" Deirdre shrieked, shoving her dripping hair from her eyes, then pointing to Neil. "*He*'s still here!"

Neil rounded on her. His face was soaked, but his eyes were hard as steel. "Of course I'm still here! This is my friend's island!"

"It's *Victoria's* island, and Victoria is *my* friend."

"*My* friend, and she didn't mention you. She said I'd have the place all to myself!"

"Which was exactly what she told me!"

They glared at each other amid the pouring rain. "Victoria who?" Neil demanded.

"Victoria Lesser. Who's your Victoria?"

"The same."

"I don't believe you. Tell me where she lives."

"Manhattan. Park Avenue."

"She is Mrs. Arthur Lesser. Tell me about Arthur."

"He's dead. She's a widow, a wonderful...wacky..."

"Conniving..."

Scowling at each other amid encroaching darkness on that windswept dock in the rain, Deirdre and Neil reached the same conclusion at once.

"We've been had," he stated, then repeated in anger, "we've been had!"

"I don't believe it," Deirdre murmured, heart pounding as she looked out to sea. "Oh, damn," she breathed. "He's going!"

Simultaneously they began to yell.

"Thomas! Come back here!"

"Nye! Turn around!"

"Thomas! Don't do this to me, Thomas! Thomas!" But Thomas was well beyond earshot and moving steadily toward the mainland.

"That creep!" Neil bellowed. "He was in on it! Victoria must have known precisely what she was doing, and he went along with it!"

Deirdre didn't remember ever being as miserable in her life. All that she'd faced at home, all that she'd escaped was nothing compared to this having been manipulated. Her frustration was almost paralyzing. She took a ragged breath and tried to think clearly. "I've come all this way, gone through hell..." She brushed the rain from her cheek and looked at Neil. "You can't stay! That's all there is to it!"

Neil, who felt rain trickling down his neck, was livid. "What do you mean, I can't stay? I don't know what brought you here, but whatever it was, I need this island more, and I have no intention of sharing it with a sharp-tongued, physically disabled...urchin!"

She shook her head, sure she was imagining it all. "I don't have to take this," she spat. Turning, she set her crutches before her and started along the murky dock toward the even murkier path.

Neil was beside her. "You're right. You *don't* have to take it. I'll put through a call to Thomas and get him to come back tomorrow to pick you up."

Deirdre kept her eyes on the wet boarding, then the muddy dirt path. "I have no intention of being picked up, not until I'm good and ready to leave! You can put through that call to Thomas and have him pick *you* up!"

"No way! I came here for peace and quiet, and that's exactly what I'm going to get."

"You can get peace and quiet somewhere else. You sure can't get it with me around, and I sure can't get it with you around, and I don't know how you know Victoria, but she's been a friend of my family's for years and I'm sure she'll give me the right to this place—''

"*Right* to this place? Look at you! You can barely make it to the door!''

He wasn't far off the mark. The path was wet and slippery, slowing her progress considerably. It was sheer grit that kept her going. "I'll make it," she fumed, struggling to keep her footing on the slick incline. "And once I'm inside I'm not budging."

They reached the front steps. Deirdre hobbled up, then crossed the porch to the door. Neil, who'd taken the steps by twos, was standing there, swearing. "Tucked in beside the eggs..." He dropped his bag under the eaves, out of the rain, set down the box he'd carried and began to rummage through it. He swore again, then turned and retraced his steps at a run.

Weakly Deirdre leaned against the damp clapboard by the door. Pressing her forehead to the wood, she welcomed its chill against her surprisingly hot temple. The rest of her felt cold and clammy. She was shaking and perilously close to tears. How could the perfect solution have gone so wrong?

And there was nothing to be done about it, at least not until tomorrow. That was the worst of it.

Then again, perhaps it wasn't so bad. Once inside the house, she intended to go straight to bed. She didn't care if it was barely seven o'clock. She was beat and cold, perhaps feverish. Neil whoever-he-was could do whatever he wanted; she was going to sleep through the night. By the time she got up tomorrow, she'd be able to think clearly.

Neil dashed up the steps, his arms laden with boxes.

"I can't believe you did that," she cried. "You've got every last one of them piled up. It's a miracle you didn't drop them on the path, and then where would I be?''

He tossed his head back, getting his hair out of his eyes and the rain out of his hair. "Be grateful I did it myself. I could have asked you to help.''

She wasn't in the mood to be grateful. "The key. Can you find the key?''

He'd set the bundles down and was pushing their contents

around. "I'm looking. I'm looking." Moments later he fished out an envelope, opened it, removed the key and unlocked the door.

Deirdre, who feared that if she waited much longer she'd collapse on the spot, limped immediately inside. It was dark. She fumbled for a light switch and quickly flipped it on. In one sweeping glance she took in a large living room and an open kitchen off that. To the left was a short hall, to the right a longer one. Calculating that the hall to the right would lead to bedrooms, she single-mindedly headed that way.

There were three open doors. She passed the first, then the second, correctly surmising that they were the smaller guest bedrooms. The third... She flipped another light switch. Ah, she'd been right. It was much as she'd imagined it—a sight for sore eyes.

Swinging inside, she slammed the door shut with her crutch and made straight for the bed. She'd no sooner reached it than her knees buckled and she sank down, letting her crutches slip unheeded to the floor. Hanging her head, she took several deep, shaky breaths. Her limbs were quivering from weakness, exhaustion or chill, or all three. She was wet, and remedying that situation had to take first priority. Though the room was cold, she simply didn't have the wherewithal to confront that problem yet.

With unsteady fingers, she worked down the zipper of her jacket, struggled out of the soggy mass and dropped it on the rag rug by the side of the bed. She began to apologize silently to Victoria for making a mess, then caught herself. After what Victoria had done, she didn't owe her a thing!

She kicked off her sodden sneaker and tugged the wet leg warmer off her cast. The plaster was intact. Gingerly she touched the part that covered her foot. Damp? Or simply cold? Certainly hard enough. So far, so good.

Bending sharply from the waist, she unzipped her duffel bag and began pushing things around in search of her pajamas. Normally the neatest of packers, she'd been in the midst of the argument with her mother that morning when she'd thrown things into the bag. She'd been angry and tired. Fortunately everything she'd brought was squishable.

She'd finally located the pajamas, when the door to the bedroom flew open and Neil burst in. He'd already taken off his jacket, shoes and socks, but his jeans were soaked up to the thigh. Tossing his cargo bag onto the foot of the bed, he planted his hands on his hips.

"What are you doing in here? This is my room."

Deirdre clutched the pajamas to her chest, more startled than anything by his sudden appearance. "I didn't see your name on the door," she argued quietly.

"This is the largest bedroom." He pointed at the bed. "That is the largest bed." He jabbed his chest with his thumb. "And I happen to be the largest person in this house."

Deirdre let her hands, pajamas and all, fall to her lap. She adopted a blank expression, which wasn't hard, given her state of emotional overload. "So?"

"So...I want this room."

"But it's already taken."

"Then you can untake it. The two other rooms are perfectly lovely."

"I'm glad you feel that way. Choose whichever you want."

"I want this one."

For the first time since she'd entered the room, Deirdre really looked around. Nearly two complete walls were of thick, multi-paned glass, affording a view that would no doubt be spectacular in daylight. The large, brass-framed bed stood against a third wall; out of the fourth was cut the door, flanked by low, Colonial-style matching dressers, and, at one end, the pièce de résistance; a large raised hearth. Over it all was a warm glow cast by the bedside lamp.

Deirdre looked Neil straight in the eye. "So do I."

Neil, who'd never been in quite this situation before, was thrown off balance by her quiet determination. It had been different when she'd been yelling. This was, strangely, more threatening. Deirdre whoever-she-was was a woman who knew what she wanted. Unfortunately he wanted the same thng.

"Look," he began, carefully guarding his temper, "it doesn't make sense. I need this bed for its length alone. I'm six-three to your, what, five-one, five-two? I'll be physically uncomfortable in any of the other rooms. They all have twin beds."

"I'm five-three, but that's beside the point. I have a broken leg.

I need extra space, too...not to mention a bathtub. From what I've been told, the master bath is the only one with a tub. I can't take a shower. It'll be enough of a challenge taking a bath.''

"Try," Neil snapped.

"Excuse me?"

"I said, try."

"Try what?"

"To take a bath."

"And what is that supposed to mean?"

"What do you think it means?" he asked rhetorically. "You're filthy." He hadn't been able to resist. When he'd tried logic on her, she'd turned it around to suit herself. He didn't like that, particularly when he had no intention of giving in when it came to the master bedroom.

She looked down at her mud-spattered orange leg warmer and plucked at the odious wet wool. "Of course I'm filthy. It's muddy outside, and that boat was none too clean." She raised her head, eyes flashing. "But I don't have to apologize. Look at you. You're no prize, yourself!"

Neil didn't have to look at himself to know she was right. He'd worn his oldest, most comfortable jeans and heavy sweater, and if she could see the T-shirt under the sweater.... The stormy trip had taken its toll on him, too. "I don't give a damn how I look," he growled. "That was the whole purpose in coming here. For once in my life I'm going to do what I want, when I want, where I want. And that starts with this bed."

Jaw set, Deirdre reached for her crutches. "Over my dead body," she muttered, but much of the fight had gone out of her. Whatever energy she'd summoned to trade barbs with Neil had been drained. Draping the pajamas over her shoulder, she stood. "I have to use the bathroom. It's been a long day."

Neil watched her hobble into the bathroom and close the door. Again he found himself wishing she'd yell. When she spoke quietly, wearily, he actually felt sorry for her. She looked positively exhausted.

But damn it, so was he!

Taking his cargo bag from the foot of the bed, he put it where Deirdre had been sitting. He then lifted her soaked jacket by its collar, grabbed her duffel bag by its strap and carried them down the hall to the more feminine of the two guest bedrooms.

She'd get the hint. With luck, she'd be too tired to argue. Either that, or she'd come after him once she left the bathroom, and they could fight it out some more.

He sighed, closed his eyes and rubbed that throbbing spot on his forehead. Aspirin. He needed aspirin. No. He needed a drink. No. What he really needed was food. Breakfast had been a long time ago, and lunch had been a Whopper, eaten in sixty seconds flat at a Burger King on the turnpike.

Stopping briefly in the front hall to adjust the thermostat, he returned to the kitchen, where he'd left the boxes of food piled up. Plenty for two, he mused dryly. He should have been suspicious when Thomas had continued to hand out supplies. But it had been rainy and dim, and he hadn't thought. They'd been rushing. He'd simply assumed the girl would get back on the boat when the work was done.

He'd assumed wrong. Thrusting splayed fingers through his hair, he stared at the boxes, then set about unloading them. Soon he had a can of soup on to heat and was busy making a huge ham-and-cheese sandwich.

The kitchen was comfortable. Though small, it was modern, with all the amenities he enjoyed at home. He hadn't expected any less of Victoria. At least, not when it came to facilities. What he hadn't expected was that she'd foist company on him, not when he'd specifically said that he needed to be alone.

What in the devil had possessed her to pull a prank like this? But he knew. He knew. She'd been trying to fix him up for years.

Why now, Victoria? Why now, when my life is such a goddamned mess?

The house was quiet. He wondered about that as he finished eating and cleaned up. Surely Deirdre would be finished using the bathroom. He hadn't heard a bath running. Nor had he heard the dull thud of crutches in the hall.

Not liking the possible implications of the silence, he headed for the smaller bedroom where he'd left her things.

It was empty.

Nostrils flaring, he strode down the hall to the master bedroom.

"Damn it," he cursed, coming to a sudden halt on the threshold. She was in bed, albeit on the opposite side from his bag. She was in his bed!

His feet slapped the wood floor as he crossed the room and came to stand on the rug by that other side of the bed. "Hey, you! What do you think you're doing?"

She was little more than a series of small lumps under the quilt. None of the lumps moved. The bedding was pulled to her forehead. Only her hair showed, mousy brown against the pillow.

"You can't sleep here! I told you that!"

He waited. She gave a tiny moan and moved what he assumed to be her good leg.

"You'll have to get up, Deirdre," he growled. "I've moved your things to the other bedroom."

"I can't," came the weak and muffled reply. "I'm...too tired and...too...cold."

Neil glanced helplessly at the ceiling. *Why me? Why here and now?* He lowered his gaze to the huddle of lumps. "I can't sleep in any of the other beds. We've been through this before."

"Mmm."

"Then you'll move?"

There was a long pause. He wondered if she'd fallen asleep. At last, a barely audible sound came from beneath the covers.

"No."

He swore again and shoved another agitated hand through his hair as he stared at the bundle in the bed. He could move her. He could bodily pick her up and cart her to the next bedroom.

"Don't try to move me," the bundle warned. "I'll cry rape."

"There'll be no one to hear."

"I'll call Thomas. I'll make more noise than you've ever heard."

Rape. Of all the stupid threats. Or was it? There were just the two of them in the house. It would be her word against his, and "date rape" had become the in thing. If she was cruel enough to go through with it, she could really make a scene. And a scene of that type was the last thing he needed at this point in his life.

Furious and frustrated, he wheeled around and stormed from the room. When he reached the living room, he threw himself into the nearest chair and brooded. He threw every name in the book at

Victoria, threw many of the same names at Thomas, then at the woman lying in *his* bed. Unfortunately, all the name-calling in the world didn't change his immediate circumstances.

He was bone tired, yet there was enough adrenaline flowing through him to keep him awake for hours. Needing to do something, he bolted from the chair and put a match to the kindling that had so carefully been placed beneath logs in the fireplace. Within minutes, the fire was roaring. It was some comfort. Even greater comfort came from the bottle of Chivas Regal he fished from the bar. Several healthy swallows, and he was feeling better; several more, and his anger abated enough to permit him to think.

After two hours he was feeling far more mellow than he would have imagined. He wandered into the den off the shorter of the two halls and studied the directions taped beside the ship-to-shore radio. *Piece of cake.*

Unfortunately no one responded from Thomas's house.

Bastard.

Okay, Hersey. Maybe he's not back yet. After all, it was still raining, and the man was working in total darkness. No sweat. He'll be there tomorrow. And in the meantime...

Neil banked the fire, nonchalantly walked back to the master bedroom and began to strip. *Let her cry rape,* declared his muzzy brain.

Wearing nothing but his briefs—a concession that later he'd marvel he'd been sober enough to make—he turned off the light, climbed into his side of the bed and stretched out.

"Ah..." The bed was firm, the sheets fresh. He might have imagined himself in his own bed at home had it not been for the faint aroma of wood smoke that lent an outdoorsy flavor to the air. Rain beat steadily against the roof, but it, too, was pleasant, and beyond was a sweet, sweet silence.

He was on a remote island, away from the city and its hassles. Taking a deep breath, he smiled, then let his head fall sideways on the pillow and was soon sound asleep.

CHAPTER THREE

SEVERAL HOURS LATER Neil's sleep was disturbed. Brow puckering, he turned his head. The mattress shifted, but he hadn't been the one to move. He struggled to open an eye. The room was pitch-black.

When the mattress shifted again, he opened the other eye. Was it Nancy? No, Nancy never stayed the night, and he wasn't seeing Nancy anymore. Then...

It took him a minute to get his bearings, and by the time he did, a dull pounding had started at the back of his head. He rolled to his side, tucked his chin down and pulled his knees up. He'd fall back to sleep, he told himself. He'd keep his eyes closed, breathe deeply and steadily, and fall back to sleep.

A soft moan came from the far side of the bed, followed by another shift in the mattress.

Eyes flying open, Neil swore silently. Then, gritting his teeth, he moved nearer his edge of the bed and closed his eyes again.

For a time there was silence. He was nearly asleep, when another moan came. It was a closed-mouth moan, more of a grunt, and, as before, was followed by the rustle of bedding and the shimmy of the mattress.

His head throbbed. Cursing, he threw back the covers and stalked into the bathroom. The sudden light was glaring; he squinted against it as he shoved the medicine chest open. Insect repellent...Caladryl lotion...antihistamine...aspirin. Aspirin. He fought with the child-proof cap for a minute and was on the verge of breaking the bottle, when it finally opened. Shaking three tablets into his palm, he tossed them into his mouth, threw his head back and swallowed, then bent over and drank directly from the tap. Hitting the light switch with a blind palm, he returned to bed.

The aspirin had barely had time to take effect, when Deirdre moaned and turned again. Neil bolted upright in bed and scowled in her direction, then groped for the lamp. Its soft glow was revealing. She was still buried beneath the covers, but her side of the quilt was pulled up and around every which way. Even as he watched, she twisted, lay still for several seconds, then twisted again.

"Deirdre!" He grasped what he calculated to be a handful of her shoulder and shook her. "Wake up, damn it! I can't sleep with that tossing and turning."

There was movement, independent of his shaking, from the lumps beneath the quilt. One hand emerged, slim fingers clutching the quilt, lowering it until a pair of heavily shadowed and distinctly disoriented brown eyes met his.

"Hmm?"

"You'll have to settle down," he informed her gruffly. "It's bad enough that I have to share this bed, but I refuse to do it with a woman who can't lie still."

Her eyes had suddenly widened at the "share this bed" part; they fell briefly to the shadowed expanse of his naked chest, then flew back up. Slowly, slowly they fluttered shut.

"I'm sorry," she whispered with a sincerity that momentarily took the wind from his sails.

"Were you having a nightmare?"

"No. My leg kills."

He studied the thick wedge that had to be her cast. "Is there something you're supposed to do for it? Didn't the doctor give you any instructions? Shouldn't you elevate it or something?"

Deirdre felt groggy and exceedingly uncomfortable. "They kept it hitched up in the hospital—to minimize swelling—but I thought that was over."

"Great." Neil threw off the covers and headed for the door. "I'm stuck here with a dimwit whose leg may swell to twice its normal size." His voice was loud enough to carry clearly back to her from the hall. "And if that happens your circulation may be cut off by the cast, and if *that* happens, gangrene may set in. Terrific." He stomped back into the master bedroom, carrying two pillows under each arm, went straight to her side of the bed and unceremoniously hauled back the quilt.

"What are you doing?" she cried, blinking in confusion.

"Elevating your leg." He had two of the pillows on the bed and was trying to sort out the legs of her pajamas. "There's so much damned material here… Can you move your good leg? There, I've got it." With surprising gentleness, he raised her casted leg just enough to slip the pillows underneath.

"Gangrene won't set in," she argued meekly. "You don't know what you're talking about."

"At least I know enough to prop up your leg." With a flick of his wrist, he tossed the quilt back over her as he rounded the bed to reach his side. "That feels better, doesn't it?"

"It feels the same."

"Give it a minute or two. It'll feel better." He turned off the light and climbed back into bed, dropped his head to the pillow and massaged his temple. Seconds later he was up again, this time heading back to the bathroom. When he returned, he carried a glass of water and two pills. "Can you sit up?"

"Why?"

"Because I think you should take these."

The only light in the room was the sliver that spilled from the bathroom. The dimness made Deirdre feel at a marked disadvantage to the man who loomed above her. "What are they?"

"Aspirin."

He was so large…shadowed…ominous. He wasn't wearing much. What did he intend? "I don't take pills."

"These are harmless."

"If they're harmless, why should I bother to take them?"

"Because they may just help the ache in your leg, and if that happens you'll lie quietly, and then maybe I'll be able to sleep."

"You can always try another bedroom."

"No way, but that's beside the point. Right now we're discussing your taking two innocent aspirin."

"How do I know they're innocent? How do I know they're aspirin at all? I don't know you. Why should I trust anything you give me?"

Amazed that Deirdre whoever-she-was could be as perverse in the middle of the night as she was during the day, he gave an exasperated sigh. "Because, A, I took these pills from a bottle marked Aspirin, which I found in Victoria's medicine chest. B, I took three of them myself a little while ago, and I'm not up, down or dead yet. And C, I'm Victoria's friend, and that's about as good a character reference as you're going to get.'' He sucked in a breath. "Besides, it works both ways, you know.''

"What does?''

"Character references. I have to trust that you're clean—''

"What do you mean, clean?''

"That you don't have any perversions, or addictions, or contagious diseases…''

"Of course I don't!''

"How can I be sure?''

"Because I'm Victoria's friend—''

"And Victoria knowingly stuck us together, so we have to trust that neither of us is an unsavory character, because we both do trust Victoria. At least I do. Or did.'' He threw his clenched fist in the air. "I don't believe I'm standing here arguing. Do you, or do you not, want the damn aspirin?'' His fist dropped and opened, cradling the tablets.

"I want them.''

Neil let out an exaggerated breath. "Then we're back where we started. Can you sit up?'' He spoke the last very slowly, as though she might not understand him otherwise.

Deirdre was beyond taking offense. "If I can't, I have no business doing what I do,'' she muttered to herself, and began to elbow her way up. With her leg elevated, the maneuvering was difficult. Still, she was supposedly agile, an athlete, an expert at bending and twisting…

Neil didn't wait to watch her fall. He came down on a knee on the bed, curved his arm beneath her back and propped her up. "The pills are in my right hand. Can you reach them?''

His right hand was by her waist; his left held the glass. She took the tablets, pressed them into her mouth and washed them down with the water he offered.

Neither of them spoke.

Neil lowered her to the sheets, removed his knee from the bed and walked back to the bathroom. Quietly he set the glass by the sink, switched off the light and returned to bed.

Deirdre lay silent, unmoving, strangely peaceful. Her leg felt better; her entire body felt better. She closed her eyes, took a long, slow breath and drifted into a deep, healing sleep.

When she awoke it was daylight—overcast still, raining still, but daylight nonetheless. She lay quietly, gradually assimilating where she was and what she was doing there. As the facts crystallized, she realized that she wasn't alone in the bed. From its far side came a quiet breathing; she turned her head slowly, saw the large quilt-covered shape of Victoria's other friend, turned her head back. Then the crux of her dilemma hit her.

She'd fled Rhode Island, driven for hours in the pouring rain, been drenched, mud spattered, nearly seasick—all to be alone. But she wasn't. She was marooned on an island, some twenty miles from shore, with a grump of a man. Now what was she going to do?

Neil was asking himself the same question. He lay on his side with his eyes wide open, listening to the sounds of Deirdre's breathing, growing more annoyed by the minute. He did believe what he'd said the night before. If she was Victoria's friend—and she knew a convincing amount about Victoria—she couldn't be all bad. Still, she was disagreeable, and he wanted to be alone.

Pushing back the quilt, he swung his legs to the floor, then paused to give his head a chance to adjust to the shift in position. His head ached, though he was as ready to blame it on Deirdre as on the amount of Scotch he'd drunk the evening before.

"Don't you have something decent to wear?" came a perturbed voice from beneath the quilt.

His head shot around. Mistake. He put the heels of his hands on his temples and inch by inch faced forward. "There's nothing indecent about my skin," he gritted.

"Don't you have pajamas?"

"Like yours?"

"What's wrong with mine? They're perfectly good pajamas."

"They're men's pajamas." Even as he said it his arm tingled. It was his right arm, the one he'd used to prop her up. Sure, she'd been wearing men's pajamas, but beneath all the fabric was a slender back, a slim waist and the faintest curve of a hip.

"They're comfortable, and warm."

"I don't need warmth," he growled roughly.

"It's freezing in here. Isn't there any heat?"

"I like my bedroom cold."

"Great." It was an argument to be continued later. For the moment, there was something more pressing. Vividly she recalled the sight of his chest, the corded muscles, the dark swirls of hair. "It might have been considerate of you to put *something* on when you decided to crawl into bed with me."

"Be grateful for the consideration I did make. I usually sleep in the buff."

She clenched a fistful of quilt by her cheek. "So macho."

"What's the matter?" he shot back. "Can't handle it?"

"There's nothing to handle. Macho has never turned me on."

"Not enough woman for it?"

The low blow hit hard, causing her to lash out in self-defense. "Too much of a woman. I hate to disillusion you, but machismo is pretty shallow."

"Ah, the expert."

"No. Simply a modern woman."

Muttering a pithy curse, Neil pushed himself from bed. "Save it for Thomas when he comes back for you later. Right now, I need a shower."

She started to look up, but caught herself. "I need a bath."

"You had your chance last night and you blew it. Now it's my turn."

"Use one of the other bathrooms. They've got showers."

"I like this one."

"But it's the only one with a tub!"

"You can have it as soon as I'm done."

"What happened to chivalry?"

"Talk of chivalry from a modern woman?" he chided, and soundly closed the bathroom door behind him.

Deirdre did look up then. He'd had the last word...so he thought. Rolling to her side, she grabbed her crutches from the floor and hobbled from the bedroom. Off the short hall on the other side of the living room was a den, and in the den was the ship-to-shore radio.

She checked her watch. Ten-forty-five. *Ten-forty-five*? She couldn't believe she'd slept round the clock and then some! But she'd needed it. She'd been exhausted. And she'd slept soundly once she'd been settled with her leg propped up and aspirin dispersing through her system.

Ten-forty-five. Had she missed Thomas? Would he be home or out on the boat? It was rainy, true, but windy?

She studied the directions beside the radio and, after several unsuccessful attempts, managed to put through the call. A young man responded, clearly not the lob- sterman.

"It's urgent that I reach Thomas," she said.

"Is there an emergency?" the young man asked.

"Not exactly an emergency in the critical sense of the word, but—"

"Are you well?"

"Yes, I'm well—"

"And Mr. Hersey?"

Hersey. "Neil? He's well, too, but it really is important that I speak with Thomas."

"I'll have him call you as soon as he can."

She tightened her fingers on the coiled cord of the speaker. "When do you think that will be?"

"I don't know."

"Is he on the boat?"

"He's in Augusta on business."

"Oh. Is he due back today?"

"I believe so."

Frustration. She sighed. "Well, please give him the message."

After the young man assured her he would, Deirdre replaced the speaker and turned off the set. In Augusta on business. She wondered. Thomas would know precisely why she was calling; he'd known precisely what he was doing yesterday when he left both of his unsuspecting passengers on Victoria's island together.

She thought back to the things he'd said. He'd been smooth. She had to hand it to him. He'd been general enough, vague enough. He'd never lied, simply given clever, well-worded answers to her questions.

She wasn't at all sure she could trust him to call back.

Scowling, she turned at the sound of footsteps in the hall. So

Neil had finished his shower, had he? And what was he planning to do now? She listened. The footsteps receded, replaced by the sound of the refrigerator door opening, then closing. He was in the kitchen. Good. Now she'd take her bath, and she'd take her sweet time about it.

In truth, she couldn't have rushed if she'd wanted to. Maneuvering herself into the tub was every bit the hassle she'd expected. Particularly awkward—and annoying—was the fact that the tub was flush against one wall, and in order to drape her casted leg over its lip she had to put her back to the faucets. Her decision to climb in before she ran the water resulted in a considerable amount of contortion, not to mention the fact that when she tried to lie back, the spigot pressed into her head. She finally managed to wedge herself into a corner, which meant that she was lying almost diagonally in the tub.

It was better than nothing, or so she told herself when she gave up the idea of relaxing to concentrate on getting clean. That, too, was a trial. With both hands occupied soaping and scrubbing, she slid perilously low in the water. Just as well, she reasoned. Her hair needed washing as badly, if not more than the rest of her. How long had it been since she'd had a proper shampoo? A week?

"Yuk."

Tipping her head back, she immersed her hair, doused it with shampoo and scrubbed. Unfortunately she'd used too much shampoo. No amount of dipping her head in the water removed it completely, and by then the water was dirty. She was thoroughly disgusted. In the end she drained the tub, turned on fresh warm water, sharply arched her back to put her head in the stream and hoped for the best.

By the time she'd awkwardly made her way out of the tub, she was tense all over. So much for a refreshing bath, she mused. But at least she was clean. There was some satisfaction in that. There was also satisfaction in rubbing moisturizing lotion over her body, a daily ritual that had been temporarily abandoned during her stay in the hospital. The scent of it was faint but familiar. When she closed her eyes she could imagine that she was back home, in one piece, looking forward to the day.

She couldn't keep her eyes closed forever, though, and when she opened them, the truth hit. She was neither home, nor in one piece, nor looking forward to the day. Rather, she was in self-imposed exile on Victoria's island. Her left leg was in a heavy cast, her face was decidedly pale and she was pathetically weak. And she was not looking forward to the day, because *he* was here.

Angrily she tugged on her underwear, then the mint green warm-up suit she'd brought. It was loose, oversized and stylish, and the top matched the bottom. He couldn't complain about her clothes today.

Propping herself on the toilet seat, she worked a pair of white wool leg warmers over her cast, then her good leg, put a single white crew sock on the good foot, then a single white sneaker. She towel-dried her hair with as much energy as she could muster, then, leaning against the sink, brushed it until it shone.

She studied her face. A lost cause. Squeaky clean, but a lost cause nonetheless. It was pale, bland, childlike. She'd always looked younger than her years. When she'd been in her late teens and early twenties, she'd hated it. Now, with women her age doing their best to look younger, she had her moments of self-appreciation. This wasn't one of them. She looked awful.

A pouting child? Perhaps, but only because of *him*. With a deep breath, she turned from the mirror and began to neaten the bathroom. *Him.* What an unpleasant man, an unpleasant situation. And a remedy? There was none, until she reached Thomas, until she convinced him that, for her sanity alone, Neil Hersey should be removed from the island.

A few minutes later, she entered the kitchen to find the remnants of bacon smoke in the air, two dirty pans on the stove, the counter littered with open cartons of juice and milk, a bowl of eggs, a tub of margarine, an open package of English muffins and miscellaneous crumbs. Neil Hersey was nonchalantly finishing his breakfast.

"You're quite a cook," she remarked wryly. "Does your skill extend to cleaning up after yourself, or were you expecting the maid to come in and do it?"

Neil set down his fork, rocked back in his chair and studied her. "So that's why Victoria sent you along. I knew there had to be a reason."

Deirdre snickered. "If you think I'm going to touch this disaster area, you're crazy. You made the mess, you clean it up."

"And if I don't?"

"Then you'll have spoiled juice and milk, stale muffins and dirty dishes to use next time." She stared at the greasy pans. "What did you make, anyway?"

"Bacon and eggs. Sound tempting?"

Her mouth was watering. "It might if you didn't use so much fat. I'd think that at your age you'd be concerned about that, not to mention the cholesterol in however many eggs you ate."

"Four. I was hungry. Aren't you? You didn't have supper."

"I had other things on my mind last night." She sent him a look of mock apology and spoke in her sweetest tone. "I'm sorry. Were you waiting for me to join you for dinner?"

His lips twisted. "Not quite. I had better company than you could ever be."

"A bottle of Scotch?" At his raised brows, she elaborated. "It's sitting right there in the living room with a half-empty glass beside it. Now that was brilliant. Do you always drown your sorrows in booze?"

The front legs of his chair hit the floor with a thud. "I don't drink," he stated baldly.

"Then we must have a little gremlin here who just happened to get into the liquor cabinet."

Faint color rose on Neil's neck. "I had a couple of drinks last night, but I'm not a drinker." He scowled. "And what's it to you? I came here to do what I want, and if that means getting drunk every night, amen."

He was being defensive, and Deirdre found she liked that. Not just because she was momentarily on top. There was something else, something related to that hint of a blush on his neck. "You know, you're really not all that bad-looking." Her gaze fell to take in his large, maroon-and-white rugby shirt and slimmer fitting jeans. "Aside from a receding hairline and all that crap you've got on your face—"

Neil reacted instantly. His eyes narrowed and his jaw grew tight. "My hairline is not receding. It's the same one I've had for years,

only I don't choose to hide it like some men do. And as for 'all
that crap' on my face, they're whiskers, in case you didn't know.''

"You could have shaved."

"Why should I?"

"Because I'm here, for one thing."

"Through no choice of mine. This is my vacation you're intruding on, and the way I see it, you don't have any say as to what I
do or how I look. Got that?"

Deirdre stared mutely back at him.

"Got that?" he repeated.

"I'm not hard of hearing," she said quietly.

He rolled his eyes. "Thank goodness for that, at least."

"But you've got it wrong. You're the one who's intruding on
my time here, and I'll thank you to make yourself as invisible as
possible until Thomas comes to pick you up."

Neil stood then, drew himself up and slowly approached her.
"Make myself invisible, huh? Just how do you suggest I do that?"

He came closer and closer. Even barefoot he towered over her.
Deirdre tipped back her head, stubbornly maintaining eye contact,
refusing to be cowed. "You can clean up the kitchen when you're
done, for one thing."

"I would have done that, anyway...when I was done."

"For another, you can busy yourself exploring the island."

"In the rain?"

"For a third, you can take yourself and your things to one of
the other bedrooms."

His voice suddenly softened. "You didn't like my taking care
of you last night?"

His question hung in the air. It wasn't that the words were shocking, or even particularly suggestive, but something about his nearness made Deirdre's breath catch in her throat. Yes, he was large,
but that wasn't it. Yes, he looked roguish, but that wasn't it, either.
He looked...he looked...warm...gentle...deep?

Neil, too, was momentarily stunned. When he'd come up so
close, he hadn't quite expected—what? That she should smell so
fresh, so feminine? That the faint, nearly transparent smattering of
freckles on the bridge of her nose should intrigue him? That she
should have dusty brown eyes, the eyes of a woman?

Swallowing once, he stepped back and tore his gaze from hers. It landed on the littered counter. With but a moment's pause, he began to close containers and return them to the refrigerator. "How does your leg feel?"

"Okay," Deirdre answered cautiously.

"Any worse than yesterday?"

"No."

He nodded and continued with his work.

Deirdre took a breath, surprised to find herself slightly shaky. "I, uh, I tried to call Thomas. He wasn't in."

"I know."

So he'd tried, too. She should have figured as much. Hobbling on her crutches to the stool by the counter peninsula, she propped herself on its edge. "We have to find a solution."

"Right."

"Any thoughts on it?"

His head was in the refrigerator, but his words carried clearly. "You know them."

She certainly did. "Then we're stalemated."

"Looks that way."

"I guess the only thing to do is to dump the problem in Victoria's lap. She caused it. Let her find a solution."

The refrigerator door swung shut. Neil straightened and thrust a hand on his hip. "That's great. But if we can't reach Thomas, how in the hell are we going to reach Victoria?"

"We'll just have to keep trying."

"And in the meantime?"

She grinned. "We'll just have to keep fighting."

Neil stared at her. It was the first time he'd seen her crack a smile. Her teeth were small, white and even; her lips were soft, generous. "You like fighting."

"I never have before, but, yeah, I kinda like it." She tilted her head to the side, tipped her chin up in defiance. "It feels good."

"You are strange, lady," he muttered as he transferred the dirty pans to the sink with more force than necessary. "Strange."

"Any more so than you?"

"There's nothing strange about me."

"Are you kidding? I haven't been arguing in a vacuum, you

know. You even admitted that you enjoy picking on me. I dare you to tell me how that's any different from my saying I like fighting."

He sent a leisurely stream of liquid soap onto a sponge. "Give me a break, will you?"

"Give *me* a break, and hurry up, will you? I'm waiting to use the kitchen, or have you forgotten? It's been twenty-four hours since I've eaten—"

"And whose fault is that? If you'd stayed home where you belonged, you wouldn't have missed any meals."

"Maybe not, but if I'd stayed home, I'd have gone crazy!"

Neil stared at her over his shoulder; Deirdre stared back. The question was there; he was on the verge of asking it. She dared him to, knowing she'd take pleasure in refusing him.

In the end he didn't ask. He wasn't sure he wanted to know what she'd left that was so awful. He wasn't sure he wanted to think of someone else's problems. He wasn't sure he wanted to feel sympathy for this strange woman-child.

Perversely disappointed, Deirdre levered herself from the stool, fit her crutches under her arms and swung into the living room. Though it was the largest room in the house, it had a feel of coziness. Pine, dark stained and rich, dominated the decor—wall paneling; rafters and pillars; a large, low hub of a coffee table, and the surrounding, sturdy frames of a cushioned sofa and chairs. The center of one entire wall was bricked into a huge fireplace. Deirdre thought she'd very much like to see the fire lit.

Propping her hip against the side of one of the chairs, she gave the room a sweeping overview. No doubt about it, she mused sadly. The room, the house, the island—all had high potential for romance. Miles from nowhere...an isolated, insulated retreat...fire crackling mingled with the steady patter of rain. At the right time, with the right man, it would be wonderful. She could understand why so many of Victoria's friends had raved about the place.

"It's all yours," Neil said. Momentarily confused, Deirdre frowned at him. "The kitchen. I thought you were dying of hunger."

The kitchen. "I am."

"Then it's yours."

"Thank you."

He stepped back, allowing more than ample room for her to pass. "There's hot coffee in the pot. Help yourself."

"Thank you."

Just as she was moving by, he leaned forward. "I make it thick. Any objections?"

She paused, head down. "What do you think?"

"I think yes."

"You're right. I like mine thin."

"Add water."

"It tastes vile that way."

"Then make a fresh pot."

"I will." She looked up at him. His face was inches away. Dangerous. "If you don't mind..."

Taking the hint, he straightened. She swung past him and entered the kitchen, where she set about preparing a meal for the first time in a week.

It was a challenge. She began to remove things from the refrigerator, only to find that she couldn't possibly handle her crutches and much else at the same time. So she stood at the open refrigerator, balancing herself against the door, taking out one item, then another, lining each up on the counter. When she'd removed what she needed, she balanced herself against the counter and, one by one, moved each item in line toward the stove. A crutch fell. Painstakingly she worked her way down to pick it up, only to have it fall again when she raised her arm a second time.

For a woman who'd always prided herself on economy of movement, such a production was frustrating. She finally gave up on the crutches entirely, resorting alternately to leaning against counters and hopping. Each step of the preparation was an ordeal, made all the worse when she thought of how quickly and effortlessly she'd normally do it. By the time she'd finally poured the makings of a cheese omelet into the pan, she was close to tears.

Lounging comfortably on the sofa in the living room, Neil listened to her struggles. It served her right, he mused smugly. She should have stayed at home—wherever that was. Where was it? He wondered what would have driven her crazy had she not left, then he chided himself for wondering when he had worries aplenty of his own.

He thought of those worries and his mood darkened. Nothing had changed with his coming here; the situation would remain the same in Hartford regardless of how long he stayed away. He had to think. He had to analyze his career, his accomplishments and aspirations. He had to decide on a positive course of action.

So far he was without a clue.

The sound of shattering glass brought his head up. "What the hell..." He was on his feet and into the kitchen within seconds.

Deirdre was gripping the stove with one hand, her forehead with another. She was staring at the glass that lay broken in a puddle of orange juice on the floor. "What in the devil's the matter with you?" he yelled. "Can't you manage the simplest little thing?"

Tear-filled eyes flew to his. "No, I can't! And I'm not terribly thrilled about it!" Angrily she grabbed the sponge from the sink and knelt on her good knee.

"Let me do that," Neil growled, but she had a hand up, warding him off.

"No! I'll do it myself!" Piece by piece, she began gathering up the shards of broken glass.

He straightened slowly. She was stubborn. And independent. And slightly dumb. With her cast hooked precariously to the side, her balance was iffy at best. He imagined her losing it, falling forward, catching herself on a palm, which in turn would catch its share of glass slivers.

Grabbing several pieces of paper towel, he knelt, pushed her hands aside and set to work cleaning the mess. "There's no need to cry over spilled milk," he said gently.

"It's spilled orange juice, and I'm not crying." Using that same good leg, she raised herself. Her thigh muscles labored, and she cringed to think how out of shape she'd become in a mere week. "You don't have to do that."

"If I don't, you're apt to do even worse damage."

"I can take care of myself!" she vowed, then turned to the stove. The omelet was burning. "Damn!" Snatching up a spatula, she quickly folded the egg mixture in half and turned off the heat. "A crusty omelet. Just what I need!" Balling her hands against the edge of the stove, she threw her head back. "Damn it to hell. Why me?"

Neil dumped the sodden paper towels in the wastebasket and reached for fresh ones. "Swearing won't help."

"Wanna bet!" Her eyes flashed as she glared at him. "It makes me feel better, and since that's the case, I'll do it as much as I damn well please!"

He looked up from his mopping. "My, my, aren't we in a mood."

"Yes, we are, and you're not doing anything to help it."

"I'm cleaning up."

"You're making me feel like a helpless cripple. I told you I'd do it. I'm not totally incapacitated, damn it!"

He sighed. "Didn't anyone ever tell you that a lady shouldn't swear?"

Her lips twisted. "Oh-ho, yes. My mother, my father, my sister, my uncles—for years I've had to listen to complaints." She launched into a whiny mimic and tipped her head from one side to the other. "'Don't say that, Deirdre,' or 'Don't do that Deirdre,' or 'Deirdre, smile and be pleasant,' or 'Behave like a lady, Deirdre.'" Her voice returned to its normal pitch, but it held anger. "Well, if what I do isn't ladylike, that's tough!" She took a quick breath and added as an afterthought, "And if I want to swear, I'll do it!"

With that, she hopped to the counter stool and plopped down on it with her back to Neil.

Silently he finished cleaning the floor. He poured a fresh glass of juice, toasted the bread she'd taken out, lightly spread it with jam and set the glass and plate before her. "Do you want the eggs?" he asked softly.

She shook her head and sat for several minutes before slowly lifting one of the slices of toast and munching on it.

Neil, who was leaning against the counter with his ankles crossed and his arms folded over his chest, studied her defeated form. "Do you live with your family?"

She carefully chewed what was in her mouth, then swallowed. "Thank God, no."

"But you live nearby."

"A giant mistake. I should have moved away years ago. Even

California sounds too close. Alaska might be better—northern Alaska.''

''That bad, huh?''

''That bad.'' She took a long, slow drink of juice, concentrating on the cooling effect it had on her raspy throat. Maybe she was coming down with a cold. It wouldn't surprise her, given the soaking she'd taken the day before. Then again, maybe she'd picked up something at the hospital. That was more likely. Hospitals were chock-full of germs, and it would be just her luck to pick one up. Just her luck. ''Why are you being so nice?''

''Maybe I'm a nice guy at heart.''

She couldn't bear the thought of that, not when she was in such a foul mood herself. ''You're an ill-tempered, scruffy-faced man.''

Pushing himself from the counter, he muttered, ''If you say so,'' and returned to the living room, where he sat staring sullenly at the cold hearth while Deirdre finished the small breakfast he'd made for her. He heard her cleaning up, noted the absence of both audible mishaps and swearing and found himself speculating on the kind of person she was at heart. He knew about himself. He wasn't really ill-tempered, only a victim of circumstance. Was she the same?

He wondered how old she was.

By the time Deirdre finished in the kitchen, she was feeling a little better. Her body had responded to nourishment; despite her sulky refusal, she'd even eaten part of the omelet. It was more overcooked than burned and was barely lukewarm by the time she got to it, but it was protein. Her voice of reason said she needed that.

Turning toward the living room, she saw Neil sprawled in the chair. She didn't like him. More accurately, she didn't want him here. He was a witness to her clumsiness. That, on top of everything else, embarrassed her.

In the back of her mind was the niggling suspicion that at heart he might well be a nice guy. He'd helped her the night before. He'd helped her this morning. Still, he had his own problems; when they filled his mind, he was as moody, as curt, as churlish as she was. Was he as much of a misfit as she sometimes felt?

She wondered what he did for a living.

With a firm grip on her crutches, she made her way into the

living room, going first to the picture window, then retreating until she was propped against the sofa back. From this vantage point she could look at the world beyond the house. The island was gray and wet; its verdancy made a valiant attempt at livening the scene, but failed.

"Lousy day," Neil remarked.

"Mmm."

"Any plans?"

"Actually," she said with a grand intake of breath, "I was thinking of getting dressed and going to the theater."

He shook his head. "The show's sold out, standing room only. You'd never make it, one-legged."

"Thanks."

"Don't feel bad. The show isn't worth seeing."

"Not much is nowadays," she answered. If she was going to be sour, she mused, she might as well do it right. By nature she was an optimist, choosing to gloss over the negatives in life. But all along she'd known the negatives were there. For a change, she wanted to look at them and complain. It seemed to her she'd earned the right.

"I can't remember the last time I saw a good show, or, for that matter, a movie," she began with spirited venom. "Most of them stink. The stories are either so pat and contrived that you're bored to tears, or so bizarre that you can't figure out what's happening. The settings are phony, the music is blah and the acting is pathetic. Or maybe it's the casting that's pathetic. I mean, Travolta was wonderful in *Saturday Night Fever*. He took Barbarino one step further—just suave enough, just sweet enough, just sensitive enough and born to dance. But a newspaper reporter in *Perfect*? Oh, please. The one scene that might have been good was shot in the exercise class, but the camera lingered so long on Travolta's pelvis it was disgusting!"

Neil was staring at her, one finger resting against his lips. "Uh, I'm not really an expert on Travolta's pelvis, disgusting or otherwise."

"Have *you* seen anything good lately?"

"In the way of a pelvis?"

"In the way of a movie."

"I don't have time to go to the movies."

"Neither do I, but if there's something I want to see—a movie, an art exhibit, a concert—I make time. You never do that?"

"For basketball I do."

She wondered if he himself had ever played. He had both the height and the build. "What team?"

"The Celtics."

"You're from Boston?"

"No. But I got hooked when I went to school there. Now I just drive up whenever I can get my hands on tickets. I also make time for lectures."

"What kind of lectures?"

"Current affairs-type talks. You know, by politicians or business superstars—Kissinger, Iacocca."

Her eyes narrowed. "I'll bet you'd go to hear John Dean speak."

Neil shrugged. "I haven't. But I might. He was intimately involved in a fascinating period of our history."

"He was a criminal! He spent time in prison!"

"He paid the price."

"He named his price—books, a TV miniseries, the lecture circuit—doesn't it gall you to think that crime can be so profitable?"

Moments before, the conversation had been purely incidental; suddenly it hit home. "Yes," he said stiffly, "it galls me."

"Yet you'd pay money to go hear someone talk about his experiences on the wrong side of the law?"

Yes, he would have, and he'd have rationalized it by saying that the speaker was providing a greater service by telling all. Now, though, he thought of his experience at Wittnauer-Douglass and felt a rising anger. "You talk too much," he snapped.

Deirdre was momentarily taken aback. She'd expected him to argue, either for her or against her. But he was cutting the debate short. "What did I say?"

"Nothing," he mumbled, sitting farther back in his seat. "Nothing important."

"Mmm. As soon as the little lady hits a raw nerve, you put her down as 'nothing important.'"

"Not 'nothing important,' as in you. As in what you said."

"I don't see much difference. That's really macho of you. Macho, as in coward."

Neil surged from his chair and glared at her. "Ah, hell, give me a little peace, will ya? All I wanted to do was to sit here quietly, minding my own business."

"You were the one who talked first."

"That's right. I was trying to be civil."

"Obviously it didn't work."

"It would have if you hadn't been spoiling for a fight."

"Me spoiling for a fight? We were having a simple discussion about the ethics involved in giving financial support to convicted political criminals, when you went off the handle. I asked you a simple question. All you had to do was to give me a simple answer."

"But I don't have the answer!" he bellowed. A vein throbbed at his temple. "I don't have answers for lots of things lately, and it's driving me out of my mind!"

Lips pressed tightly together, he stared at her, then whirled around and stormed off toward the den.

CHAPTER FOUR

WITH NEIL'S EXIT, the room became suddenly quiet. Deirdre listened, knowing that he'd be trying to reach Thomas again. She prayed he'd get through, for his sake as well as hers. She and Neil were like oil and water; they didn't mix well.

Taking advantage of the fact that she had the living room to herself, she stretched out on the sofa, closed her eyes and pretended she was alone in the house. It was quiet, so quiet. Neither the gentle patter of rain nor the soft hum of heat blowing through the vents disturbed the peaceful aura. She imagined she'd made breakfast without a problem in the world, and that the day before she'd transferred everything from Thomas's boat without a hitch. In her dream world she hadn't needed help, because her broken leg was good as new.

But that was her dream world. In reality, she had needed help, and Neil Hersey had been there. She wondered what it would be like if he were a more even-tempered sort. He was good-looking; she gave that to him, albeit begrudgingly. He was strong; she recalled the arm that had supported her when he'd brought her aspirin, remembered the broad chest she'd leaned against. He was independent and capable, cooking for himself, cleaning up both his mess and hers without a fuss.

He had potential, all right. He also had his dark moments. At those times, given her own mood swings, she wanted to be as far from him as possible.

As she lay thinking, wondering, imagining, her eyelids slowly lowered, and without intending to, she dozed off. A full hour later she awoke with a start. She'd been dreaming. Of Neil. A lovely dream. An annoying dream. The fact that she'd slept at all annoyed her, because it pointed to a physical weakness she detested. She'd slept for fourteen hours the night before. Surely that had been enough. And to dream of *Neil*?

She'd been right in her early assessment of him; he was as troubled as she was. She found herself pondering the specifics of his problem, then pushed those ponderings from her mind. She had her own problems. She didn't need his.

What she needed, she decided, was a cup of coffee. After the breakfast fiasco, she hadn't had either the courage or the desire to tackle coffee grounds, baskets and filters. Now, though, the thought of drinking something hot and aromatic appealed to her.

Levering herself awkwardly to her feet, she went into the kitchen and shook the coffeepot. He'd said there was some left but that it was thick. She didn't like thick coffee. Still, it was a shame to throw it out.

Determinedly she lit the gas and set the coffee on to heat.

Meanwhile, Neil was in the den, staring out the window at the rain, trying to understand himself. Deirdre Joyce—the young man who'd answered at Thomas's house had supplied her last name—was a thorn in his side. He wanted to be alone, yet she was here. It was midafternoon. He still hadn't spoken with Thomas, which meant that Deirdre was going to be around for another night at least.

What annoyed him most were the fleeting images that played tauntingly in the corners of his mind. A smooth, lithe back...a slim waist...the suggestion of a curve at the hip...a fresh, sweet scent...hair the color of wheat, not mousy brown as he'd originally thought, but thick, shining wheat. Her face, too, haunted him. She had the prettiest light-brown eyes, a small, almost delicate nose, lips that held promise when she smiled.

Of course, she rarely smiled. She had problems. And the fact of the matter was that he really did want to be alone. So why was he thinking of her in a way that would suggest that he found her attractive?

From the door came the clearing of a throat. "Uh, excuse me?"

He turned his head. Damn, but the mint-green of her warm-up suit was cheerful. Of course, she still looked lumpy as hell. "Yes?"

"I heated up the last of the coffee, but it really is too strong for me. I thought you might like it.'' Securing her right crutch with the muscles of her upper arm, she held out the cup.

Neil grew instantly wary. It was the first attempt she'd made at being friendly. Coming after nonstop termagancy, there had to be a reason. She had to want something. ''Why?'' he asked bluntly.

''Why what?''

''Why did you heat it up?''

She frowned. ''I told you. I thought you might like it.''

''You haven't been terribly concerned with my likes before.''

''And I'm not now,'' she replied defensively. ''It just seemed a shame to throw it out.''

''Ah. You're making a fresh pot, so you heated the dregs for me.''

''I don't believe you,'' she breathed. She hadn't expected such instant enmity, and coming in the face of her attempted pleasantness, it set her off. ''You would have had me drink the dregs, but suddenly they're not good enough for you?''

''I didn't say they weren't good enough.'' His voice was smooth, with an undercurrent of steel. ''I reheat coffee all the time because it saves time, and yes, it is a shame to throw it out. What I'm wondering is why the gesture of goodwill from you. You must have something up your sleeve.''

''Boy,'' she remarked with a wry twist of her lips, ''have *you* been burned.''

His eyes darkened. ''And just what do you mean by that?''

''For a man to be as suspicious of a woman, he'd have to have been used by one, and used badly.''

Neil thought about that for a minute. Funny, it had never occurred to him before, but he had been used. Nancy had been crafty—subtle enough so the fact had registered only subliminally in his brain—but crafty nonetheless. Only now did he realize that often she'd done small things for him when she'd wanted something for herself. It fit in with the nature of her love, yet he hadn't seen it then. Just as he hadn't seen the potential for treachery at Wittnauer-Douglass.

''My history is none of your damned business,'' he ground out angrily.

''Fine,'' she spat. ''I just want you to know that it's taken a monumental effort on my part to get the dumb coffee in here without spilling it. And if you want to know the truth, my major motivation was to find out where you were so I'd know what room to avoid.'' She set the mug on a nearby bookshelf with a thud. ''You can have this or not. I don't care.'' She turned to leave, but not fast enough to hide the hint of hurt in her expression.

''Wait.''

She stopped, but didn't turn back. ''What for?'' she asked. ''So you can hurl more insults at me?''

He moved from the window. ''I didn't mean to do that. You're right. I've been burned. And it was unfair of me to take it out on you.''

''Seems to me you've been taking an awful lot out on me.''

''And vice versa,'' he said quietly, satisfied when she looked over her shoulder at him. ''You have to admit that you haven't been the most congenial of housemates yourself.''

''I've had…other things on my mind.''

He took a leisurely step closer. ''So have I. I've needed to let off steam. Yelling at you feels good. It may not be right, but it feels good.''

''Tell me about it,'' she muttered rhetorically, but he took her at face value.

''It seems that my entire life has been ruled by reason and restraint. I've never spouted off quite this way about things that are really pretty petty.''

She eyed him askance. ''Like my using the master bedroom?''

''Now that's not petty. That's a practical issue.''

''Then what about heat? The bedroom is freezing, while the rest of the house is toasty warm. You purposely kept the thermostat low in that room, didn't you?''

''I told you. I like a cool bedroom.''

''Well, I like a warm one, and don't tell me to use one of the other bedrooms, because I won't. You'll be leaving—''

''You'll be leaving.'' His voice had risen to match the vehemence of hers, but it suddenly dropped again. ''Only problem is that Thomas still isn't in, so it looks like it won't be today.''

''He's avoiding us.''

''That occurred to you, too, hmm?''

"Which means that we're stranded here." Glumly she looked around. "I mean, the house is wonderful. Look." She gestured toward one wall, then another. "Hundreds of books to choose from, a stereo, a VCR, a television—"

"The TV reception stinks. I tried it."

"No loss. I hate television."

"Like you hate movies?"

"I didn't say I hated movies, just that lately they've been awful. The same is true of television. If it isn't a corny sit-com, it's a blood-and-guts adventure show, or worse, a prime-time soap opera."

"Opinionated urchin, aren't you?"

Her eyes flashed and she gripped her crutches tighter. "Yes, I'm opinionated, and I'm in the mood to express every one of those opinions." Silently she dared him to stop her.

Neil had no intention of doing that. He was almost curious as to what she'd say next. Reaching for the mug she'd set down, he leaned against the bookshelf, close enough to catch the fresh scent that emanated from her. "Go on. I'm listening."

Deirdre, too, was aware of the closeness, aware of the breadth of his shoulders and the length of his legs, aware of the fact that he was more man than she'd been near for a very long time. Her cheeks began to feel warm, and there was a strange tickle in the pit of her stomach.

Confused, she glanced around, saw the long leather couch nearby, and inched back until she could sink into it. She raked her lip with her teeth, then looked up at him. "What was I saying?"

"You were giving me your opinion of the state of modern television."

"Oh." She took a breath and thought, finally saying, "I hate miniseries."

"Why?"

"They do awful things to the books they're adapted from."

"Not always."

"Often enough. And they're twice as long as they need to be. Take the opening part of each installment. They kill nearly fifteen minutes listing the cast, then reviewing what went before. I mean, the bulk of the viewers know what went before, and it's a waste of their time to rehash it. And as for the cast listings, the last thing those actors and actresses need is more adulation. Most of them are swellheaded as it is!'' She was warming to the subject, enjoying her own perversity. ''But the worst part of television has to be the news.''

''I like the news,'' Neil protested.

''I do, too, when it is news, but when stations have two hours to fill each night, a good half of what they deliver simply isn't news. At least, not what I'd consider to be news. And as for the weather report, by the time they've finished with their elaborate electronic maps and radar screens, I've tuned out, so I miss the very forecast I wanted to hear.''

''Maybe you ought to stick to newspapers.''

''I usually do.''

''What paper do you read?''

''The *Times*.''

''New York?'' He was wondering about her connection to Victoria. ''Then you live there?''

''No. I live in Providence.''

''Ah, Providence. Thriving little metropolis.''

''What's wrong with Providence?''

''Nothing that a massive earthquake wouldn't fix.'' It was an exaggeration that gave him pleasure.

She stared hard at him. ''You probably know nothing about Providence, much less Rhode Island, yet you'd stand there and condemn the entire area.''

''Oh, I know something about Providence. I represented a client there two years ago, in the middle of summer, and the air conditioning in his office didn't work. Since it was a skyscraper, we couldn't even open a window, so we went to what was supposed to be the in restaurant. The service was lousy, the food worse, and to top it all off, some bastard sideswiped my car in the parking lot, so I ended up paying for that, too, and *then* my client waited a full six months before settling my bill.''

Deirdre was curious. ''What kind of client?''

''I'm a lawyer.''

''A lawyer!'' She pushed herself to the edge of the seat. ''No wonder you're not averse to criminals on the lecture circuit. The proceeds could well be paying your fee!''

"I am not a criminal attorney,'' Neil stated. The crease between his brows grew pronounced. "I work with corporations."

"That's even worse! I hate corporations!''

"You hate most everything."

Deirdre's gaze remained locked with his for a moment. He seemed to be issuing a challenge, asking a question about her basic personality and daring her to tell the truth. "No,'' she said in a quieter tone. "I'm just airing certain pet peeves. I don't—I can't do it very often."

He, too, had quieted. "What do you do?''

"Hold it in."

"No. Work-wise. You do work, don't you? All modern women work."

Deirdre dipped one brow. "There's no need for sarcasm."

He made no apology. "You pride yourself on being a modern woman. So tell me. What do you do for a living?''

Slowly she gathered her crutches together. She couldn't tell him what she did; he'd have a field day with it. "That—" she rose "—is none of your business."

"Whoa. I told you what I do."

"And I told you where I live. So we're even." Leaning into the crutches, she headed for the door.

"But I want to know what kind of work you do."

"Tough."

"I'll bet you don't work,'' he taunted, staying close by her side. "I'll bet you're a very spoiled relative of one of Victoria's very well-to-do friends."

"Believe what you want."

"I'll bet you're here because you really wanted to be in Monte Carlo, but Daddy cut off your expense account. You're freeloading off Victoria for a while."

"Expense account?'' She paused midway through the living room and gave a brittle laugh. "Do fathers actually put their twenty-nine-year-old daughters on expense accounts?''

Neil's jaw dropped. "Twenty-nine. You're pulling my leg."

"I wouldn't pull your leg if it were attached to Mel Gibson!" she vowed, and continued on into the kitchen.

"Twenty-nine? I would have given you twenty-three, maybe twenty-four. But twenty-nine?" He stroked the stubble on his face and spoke pensively. "Old enough to have been married at least once." He started after her. "Tell me you're running away from a husband who beats you. Did he cause the broken leg?"

"No."

"But there is a husband?"

She sent him an impatient look. "You obviously don't know Victoria very well. She'd never have thrown us together if one of us were already married."

He did know Victoria, and Deirdre was right. "Okay. Have you ever been married?"

"No."

"Are you living with someone?" When she sent him a second, even more impatient look, he defended himself. "It's possible. I wouldn't put it past Victoria to try to get you to forget him if he were a creep.... Okay, okay. So you're not living with someone. You've just broken up with him, and you've come here to lick your wounds."

"Wrong again." Seth had left four months before, and there had been no wounds to lick. Propping her crutches in a corner, she hopped to the cupboard. She was determined to make herself a cup of coffee. "This is sounding like *Twenty Questions*, which reminds me of what I *really* hate, and it's game shows like the one Thomas was watching yesterday. I mean, I know why people watch them. They play along, getting a rush when they correctly guess an answer before the contestant does. But the contestants—jumping all over the place, clapping their hands with glee when they win, kissing an emcee they don't know from Adam..." She shook her head. "Sad. Very sad."

Neil was standing close, watching her spoon coffee into the basket. Her hands were slender, well formed, graceful. There was something about the way she tipped the spoon that was almost lyrical. His gaze crept up her arm, over one rather nondescript shoulder to a neck that was anything but nondescript. It, too, was graceful. Strange, he hadn't noticed before....

Momentarily suspending her work, Deirdre stared at him. Her eyes were wider than normal; her pulse had quickened. It occurred to her that she'd never seen so many textures on a man—from the thick gloss of his hair and the smooth slope of his nose to the furrowing of his brow and the bristle of his beard. She almost wanted to touch him…almost wanted to touch…

She tightened her fingers around the spoon. "Neil?"

He met her gaze, vaguely startled.

"I need room. I'm, uh, I'm not used to having someone around at home."

His frown deepened. "Uh, sure." He took a step back. "I think I'll…go take a walk or something."

Deirdre waited until he'd left, then slowly set back to work. *Take a walk. In the rain?* She listened, but there was no sound of the door opening and closing. So he was walking around the house. As good an activity as any to do on such a dismal day. She wondered when the rain would end. The island would be beautiful in sunshine. She'd love to go outside, find a high rock to sit on, and relax.

Surprisingly, when she thought of it, she wasn't all that tense, at least not in the way she'd been when she'd left Providence. In spite of the hassles of getting here, even in spite of the rain, the change of scenery was good for her. Of course, nothing had changed; Providence would be there when she returned. Her mother would be there, as would Sandra and the uncles. They'd be on her back again, unless she thought of some way to get them off.

She hadn't thought that far yet.

Carefully taking the coffee and a single crutch, she made her way into the den. She could put some weight on the cast without discomfort, which was a reassuring discovery. Carrying things such as coffee became a lot easier. Of course, it was a slow trip, and that still annoyed her, but it was better than being stuck in bed.

Leisurely sipping the coffee, she sat back on the leather sofa. Her duffel bag held several books, yarn and knitting needles, plus her cassette player and numerous tapes. None of these diversions appealed to her at the moment. She felt in limbo, as though she wouldn't completely settle down until Neil left.

But would he leave? Realistically? No. Not willingly. Not unless Victoria specifically instructed him to. Which she wouldn't.

Victoria had been clever. She'd known she was dealing with two stubborn people. She'd also known that once on the island, Neil and Deirdre would be virtually marooned. Thomas Nye was their only link with the mainland, and Thomas, while alert to any legitimate physical emergency, appeared to be turning a deaf ear to their strictly emotional pleas.

It was Neil and Deirdre versus the bad guys. An interesting prospect.

On impulse, she set down her cup and limped from the den. The house was quiet. She wondered what Neil was doing and decided that it was in her own best interest to find out. He hadn't returned to the living room while she'd been in the den, and he wasn't in the kitchen.

He was in the bedroom. The master bedroom. Deirdre stopped on the threshold and studied him. He lay on his back on the bed, one knee bent. His arm was thrown over his eyes.

Grateful she hadn't yet been detected, she was about to leave, when the whisper of a sound reached her ears. It was a little louder than normal breathing, a little softer than snoring. Neil was very definitely asleep.

Unable to help herself, she moved quietly forward until she stood by his side of the bed. His chest rose and fell in slow rhythm; his lips were faintly parted. As she watched, his fingers twitched, then stilled, and correspondingly something tugged at her heart.

He was human. When they'd been in the heat of battle, she might have tried to deny that fact, but seeing him now, defenseless in sleep, it struck her deeply. He was tired, perhaps emotionally as well as physically.

She found herself once again wondering what awful things he'd left behind. He was a lawyer; it was a good profession. Had something gone wrong with his career? Or perhaps his troubles related to his having been burned by a woman. Maybe he was suffering the effects of a bad divorce, perhaps worrying about children the marriage may have produced.

She actually knew very little about him. They'd been thrown together the moment she'd arrived at Spruce Head, and he'd simply provided a convenient punching bag on which to vent her frustrations. When she was arguing with him, she wasn't thinking of her leg, or aerobics, or Joyce Enterprises. Perhaps there was merit to his presence, after all.

He really wasn't so bad; at times she almost liked him. Moreover, at times she was physically drawn to him. She'd never before had her breath taken away by a man's nearness, but it had happened several times with Neil. For someone who'd always been relatively in control of her emotions, the experience was frightening. It was also exciting in a way....

Not trusting that Neil wouldn't awaken and lash out at her for disturbing him, she silently left the room and returned to the den. Her gaze fell on the ship-to-shore radio. She approached it, eyed the speaker, scanned the instructions for its use, then turned her back on both and sank down to the sofa. Adjusting one of the woven pillows beneath her head, she yawned and closed her eyes.

It was a lazy day. The sound of the rain was hypnotic, lulling, inducing the sweetest of lethargies. She wondered at her fatigue and knew that it was due only in part to her physical debilitation. The tension she'd been under in Providence was also to blame.

She needed the rest, she told herself. It was good for her. Wasn't that what a remote island was for? Soon enough she'd feel stronger, and then she'd read, knit, listen to music, even exercise. Soon enough the sun would come out, and she'd be able to avail herself of the island's fresh air.

But for now, doing nothing suited her just fine.

She was sleeping soundly when, some time later, Neil came to an abrupt halt at the door to the den. He was feeling groggy, having awoken only moments before. He wasn't used to sleeping during the day. He wasn't used to doing nothing. Oh, he'd brought along some books, and there were tapes here and a vast collection of old movies to watch, but he wasn't up to any of that just yet. If the weather were nice, he could spend time outdoors, but it wasn't, so he slept, instead.

Rationally he'd known that it was going to take him several days to unwind and that he badly needed the relaxation. He'd known that solutions to his problems weren't going to suddenly hit him in the face the moment he reached the island. Nevertheless, the problems were never far from consciousness.

Ironically Deirdre was his greatest diversion.

Deirdre. Looking down at her, he sucked in his upper lip, then slowly released it. Twenty-nine years old. He thought back to when he was that age. Four years out of law school, he'd been paying his dues as an associate in a large Hartford law firm. The hours had been long, the work boring. Frustrated by the hierarchy that relegated him to doing busywork for the partners, he'd set out on his own the following year. Though the hours had been equally long, the work had been far more rewarding.

Now, ten years later, he was approaching forty, sadly disillusioned. He knew where he'd been, saw his mistakes with vivid clarity...but he couldn't picture the future.

If Deirdre was disillusioned about something at the age of twenty-nine, where would she be when she reached his age? What did she want from life? For that matter, what had she had?

Lying there on her side, with her hands tucked between her thighs and her cheek fallen against the pillow, she was the image of innocence. She was also strangely sexy-looking.

He wondered how that could be, when there was nothing alluring about her in the traditional sense. She wore no make-up. Her hair was long in front, short at the sides and back, unsophisticated as hell. Her warm-up suit was a far cry from the clinging things he'd seen women wearing at the racquet club. The bulky fabric was bunched up in front, camouflaging whatever she had by the way of breasts, and yet...and yet...the material rested on a nicely rounded bottom—he could see that now—and she looked warm and vaguely cuddly. He almost envied her hands.

With a quick headshake, he walked over to the ship-to-shore radio, picked up the speaker, shifted it in his hand, frowned, then set it back down. Ah, hell, he told himself, Thomas wouldn't be there; he was conspiring with Victoria. Short of a legitimate physical emergency, he wouldn't be back soon. And that being the case, it behooved Neil to find a way to coexist in relative peace with Deirdre.

But what fun would that be?

Deirdre was, for him, a kind of punching bag. He felt better when he argued with her. She provided an outlet and a diversion. Perhaps he should just keep swinging.

Smiling, he sauntered into the living room. His gaze fell on the fireplace; the ashes from last night's fire lay cold. Taking several large logs from the nearby basket, he set them atop kindling on the grate and stuck a match. Within minutes the kindling caught, then the logs. Only when the fire was crackling heatedly did he settle back in a chair to watch it.

Strange, he mused, but he'd never come to the wilderness to relax before. He'd been to the beach—southern Connecticut, Cape Cod, Nantucket—and to the snow-covered mountains of Vermount. He'd been to the Caribbean and to Europe. But he'd never been this isolated from the rest of the world. He'd never been in the only house on an island, dependent solely on himself to see to his needs.

Nancy would die here. She'd want the option of eating out or calling room service. She'd want there to be people to meet for drinks. She'd want laundry service.

And Deirdre? Broken leg and all, she'd come looking for solitude. Perhaps stupidly, with that leg, but she'd come. Was she indeed a spoiled brat who had run away from all that had gone wrong in her life? Or was she truly self-sufficient? It remained to be seen whether she could make a bed....

"Nice fire."

He looked up. Deirdre was leaning against the wall by the hall, looking warm and still sleepy and mellow. He felt a lightening inside, then scowled perversely. "Where's the other crutch?"

Her eyes grew clearer. "In the kitchen."

"What's it doing there?"

She tipped her chin higher. "Holding up the counter."

"It's supposed to be under your arm. You're the one who needs holding up."

"I've found I can do just fine with one."

"If you put too much strain on the leg," he argued, "you'll slow the healing process."

"You sound like an expert."

"I broke my own leg once."

"How?"

"Skiing."

She rolled her eyes. "I should have guessed. I'll bet you sat around the ski lodge with your leg on a pedestal—the wounded hero basking in homage."

"Not quite. But what I did is beside the point. What you're doing is nuts. The doctor didn't okay it, did he?"

"*She* told me to use common sense. And what's it to you, anyway? You're not my keeper."

"No, but it'll be my job to do something if you fall and crack the cast, or worse, break the other leg."

She smiled smugly. "If anything happens to me, your problems will be solved. You'll get through to Thomas, zip, zip, and he'll be out to fetch me before you can blink an eye."

Neil knew she was right. He also knew that she had momentarily one-upped him. That called for a change of tactics. He took a deep breath, sat back in his chair and propped his bare feet on the coffee table. "But I don't want him to come out and fetch you. I've decided to keep you."

Her smile faded. "You've what?"

"I've decided to keep you."

"Given the fact that you don't *have* me, that's quite a decision."

He waved a hand. "Don't argue semantics. You know what I mean."

She nodded slowly. "You've decided to let me stay."

"That's right."

"And if I decide I want to leave?"

"Thomas won't give us the time of day, so it's a moot point."

"Precisely, which means that you're full of hot air, Neil Hersey. You can't decide to keep me, any more than I can decide to keep you, or either of us can decide to leave. We're stuck here together, which means—" Her mind was working along pleasurable lines. The grin she sent him had a cunning edge. "That you're stuck with me, bad temper and all." The way she saw it, he'd given her license to fire at will, not to mention without guilt. Battling with him could prove to be a most satisfying pastime.

"I think I can handle it," he said smugly.

"Good." Limping directly between Neil and the fire, she took the chair opposite his. "So," she said, sitting back, "did you have a good sleep?"

"You spied on me?"

"No. I walked into my bedroom and there you were. Snoring."

He refused to let her get to him. "Is that why you took your nap in the den?"

"You spied on me."

"No. I walked in there intending to call Thomas. Then I decided not to bother. So I came in here and built a fire. It is nice, isn't it?"

"Not bad." She levered herself from the chair and hopped into the kitchen. A bowl of fresh fruit sat on the counter; she reached for an orange, then hopped back to her seat.

"You're a wonderful hopper," Neil said. "Is it your specialty?"

She ignored him. "What this fire needs is a little zip." Tearing off a large wad of orange peel, she tossed it into the flame.

"Don't do that! It'll mess up my fire!"

"It adds a special scent. Just wait." She threw in another piece.

Neil stared into the flames. "I hate the smell of oranges. It reminds me of the packages of fruit my grandparents used to send up from Florida every winter. There was so much of it that my mother worried about it spoiling, so we were all but force-fed the stuff for a week." His voice had gentled, and his lips curved at the reminiscence. "Every year I got hives from eating so many oranges."

She pried off a section and held it ready at her mouth. "You said 'we.' Do you have brothers and sisters?" The orange section disappeared.

"One of each."

"Older or younger?"

"Both older."

"Are you close?"

"Now? Pretty close." He shifted lower in his seat, so that his head rested against its back, and crossed his ankles. "We went our separate ways for a while. John is a teacher in Minneapolis, and Sara works for the government in Washington. They're both married and have kids, and all our lives seemed so hectic that we really didn't push reunions."

"What changed that?" Deirdre asked.

"My mother's death. Something about mortality hit us in the

face—you know, life-is-so-short type of thing. That was almost seven years ago. We've been much closer since then.''

"Is your father still living?"

"Yes. He's retired."

"Does he live near you?"

"He still lives in the house where we grew up in Westchester. We keep telling him to move because it's large and empty but for him most of the time. He won't sell.'' Neil was grinning. "He travels. So help me, nine months out of twelve he's galavanting off somewhere. But he says he needs the house. He needs to know it's there for him to come home to. Personally—'' he lowered his voice ''—I think he just doesn't want to displace the couple who live above the garage. They've been overseeing the grounds for nearly twenty years. They oversee *him* when he's around, and he loves it.''

Absently Deirdre pressed another piece of fruit into her mouth. She chewed it, all the while looking at Neil. It was obvious that he felt affection for his family. "That's a lovely story. Your father sounds like a nice man.''

"He is."

She took a sudden breath. "So how did he get a son like you? By the way, aren't your feet freezing? I haven't seen you with socks on since we got here, but it's cold.''

He wiggled his toes. "I'm warm-blooded."

"You're foolhardy. You'll get splinters."

"Are you kidding? The floor's been sanded and waxed. Only the walls have splinters, and, thank you, I don't walk on walls.'' He swung his legs down and stood. "So you'll have to find something else to pick on me for.''

"I will," she promised. "I will." She watched him escape into the kitchen. "What are you doing?"

"Contemplating dinner."

"We haven't had lunch!"

"Breakfast was lunch." He flipped on a light in the darkening room. "Now it's dinnertime."

She glanced at her watch. It was well after six o'clock. She supposed she was hungry, though the thought of preparing another meal was enough to mute whatever hunger pangs she felt. So she remained where she was, looking at the fire, telling herself that she'd see to her own needs when Neil was done. She didn't want an audience for her clumsiness. Besides, between her hopping and Neil's size, they'd never be able to work in the kitchen at the same time.

She listened to the sounds of his preparations, wondering how he'd come to be so handy. Various possible explanations passed through her mind, but in the end the question remained. Then she heard the sizzle of meat and began to smell tantalizing aromas, and her admiration turned to annoyance. Why *was* he so good in the kitchen? Why wasn't he as clumsy as she? The men she'd known would have been hollering for something long before now—help in finding the butter or sharpening a knife or preparing vegetables for cooking. Why didn't he need her for something?

Pushing herself from the chair, she limped peevishly to the kitchen. What she saw stopped her cold on the threshold. Neil had set two places at the table and was in the process of lowering one brimming plate to each spot.

He looked up. "I was just about to call you." Her expression of shock was ample reward for his efforts, though his motives went deeper. If he helped Deirdre with things he knew she found difficult, he wouldn't feel so badly when he picked on her. Good deeds for not-so-good ones; it seemed a fair exchange. Not to mention the fact that keeping her off balance seemed of prime importance. "Steak, steamed broccoli, dinner rolls." He beamed at the plates. "Not bad, if I do say so myself."

"Not bad," she echoed distractedly. "You'd make someone a wonderful wife."

He ignored the barb and held out her chair. "Ms Joyce?"

At a loss for anything better to do, particularly when her mouth was watering, she came forward and let him seat her. She stared at the attractive plate for a minute, then looked up as he poured two glasses of wine. "Why?" she asked bluntly.

"Why wine? It's here for us to drink, and I thought it'd be a nice touch.

"Why me? I didn't ask you to make my dinner."

"Are you refusing it?"

She glanced longingly at her plate. Hospital food was nearly inedible; it had been days since she'd confronted anything tempting. "No. I'm hungry."

"So I figured."

"But you must have something up your sleeve."

He sat at his place, nonchalantly shook out his napkin and spread it on his lap. "Maybe I'm thinking of Victoria's kitchen. You broke a glass this morning. Another few, and we'll run low."

"It's not the glass, and you know it. What is it, Neil? I don't like it when you're nice."

He arched a brow as he cut into his steak. "Prefer the rough stuff, do you? A little pushing and shoving turns you on?" He put a piece of steak into his mouth, chewed it and closed his eyes. "Mmmm. Perfect." His eyes flew open in mock innocence. "I hope you like it rare."

"I like it medium."

"Then you can eat the edges and leave the middle." He gestured with his fork. "Go ahead. Eat. On second thought—" he set down the fork and reached for his wine "—a toast." When Deirdre continued to stare at him, he dipped his head, coaxing. "Come on. Raise your glass."

Slowly, warily, she lifted it.

He grinned. "To us." The clink of his glass against hers rang through the room.

CHAPTER FIVE

TO US. Deirdre thought about that through the evening as she sat pensively before the fire. She thought about it that night when she lay in bed, trying her best to ignore the presence of a large male body little more than an arm's length away. She thought about it when she awoke in the morning. By that time she was annoyed.

Victoria had fixed them up. Deirdre had always resented fix-ups, had always fervently avoided them. She'd never been so hard up for a man that she'd risk taking pot luck, and she wasn't now. Who was Neil Hersey, anyway? She asked herself that for the umpteenth time. After spending thirty-six hours with the man, she still didn't know. She did know that she'd been aware of him in some form or another for the majority of those thirty-six hours, and that her body was distinctly tense from that awareness.

She turned her head to study him. Sleeping, he was sprawled on his back with his head facing her. His hair was mussed; his beard sported an additional day's growth. Sooty eyelashes fanned above his cheekbones. Dark swirls of hair blanketed his chest to the point where the quilt took over.

One arm was entirely free of the covers. Her gaze traced its length, from a tightly muscled shoulder, over a leanly corded swell to his elbow, down a forearm that was spattered with hair, to a well-formed and thoroughly masculine hand. As though touched by that hand, she felt a quiver shoot through her.

Wrenching her head to the other side, she took a shallow breath, pushed herself up and dropped her legs over the side of the bed. For a minute she simply sat there with her head bowed, begrudging the fact that she found Neil attractive. She wanted to hate the sight of him after what he'd done to her dreams of solitude. But the sight of him turned her on.

She didn't want to be turned on.

Slowly she began to roll her head in a half circle, concentrating on relaxing the taut muscles of her neck. She extended the exercise to her shoulders, alternately rolling one, then the other. Clasping her hands at the back of her head, she stretched her torso, first to the left, then to the right. The music played in her mind, and she let herself move to its sound, only then realizing what she'd missed during the past week, finding true relaxation in imagining herself back at the health club, leading a class.

"What in the hell are you doing?" came a hoarse growl from behind her.

Startled from her reverie, she whirled around, then caught herself and tempered the movement. "Exercising."

"Is that necessary?"

"Yes. My body is tense."

"So is mine, and what you're doing isn't helping it." He'd awoken with the first of her exercises and watched her twist and stretch, watched the gentle shift in her absurdly large pajamas. And he'd begun to imagine things, which had quickly affected his own body. In other circumstances he'd have stormed from bed right then. As things stood—literally—he didn't have the guts.

"Then don't look," she said, turning her back on him and re-suming her exercises. It was spite that drove her on, but all petty thoughts vanished when a strong arm seized her waist and whipped her back on the bed. Before she knew what had happened, Neil had her pinned and was looming over her.

"I think we'd better get something straight," he warned in a throaty voice. "I'm a man, and I'm human. If you want to tempt me beyond my limits, you'd better be prepared to take the conse-quences."

Deirdre's trouble with breathing had nothing to do with exercis-ing. Neil's lunge had dislodged the quilt, leaving his entire upper body bare. The warmth of his chest reached out to her, sending rivulets of heat through her body, while the intensity of his gaze seared her further.

"I didn't know you were tempted," she said in a small voice. "I'm a bundle of lumps to you. That's all." She'd been a bundle of lumps to most men, lumps that were conditioned by steady ex-ercise, lumps that were anything but feminine. She'd always known she couldn't compete with the buxom beauties of the world, and she fully assumed Neil was used to buxom beauties. The way he'd looked at her that first day had left no doubt as to his opinion of her body. Then again, there had been other times when he'd looked at her...

"You are a bundle of lumps," he agreed, dropping his gaze to her pajama front. "That's what's so maddening. I keep wondering what's beneath all this cover." His eyes made a thorough survey of the fabric—she felt every touch point—before lazily meeting hers. "Maybe if I see, I won't be tempted. Maybe what we need here is full disclosure."

Deirdre made a reflexive attempt at drawing in her arms to cover herself, but he had them anchored beneath his and gave no quarter.

"Maybe," he went on, his voice a velvety rasp, "what I ought to do is to unbutton this thing and take a good look at all you're hiding."

"There's not much," she said quickly. Her eyes were round in a pleading that she miraculously managed to keep from her voice. "You'd be disappointed."

"But at least then I wouldn't have to wonder anymore, would I?"

Her heart was hammering, almost visibly so. She was frightened. Strangely and suddenly frightened. "Please. Don't."

"Don't wonder? Or don't look?"

"Either."

"But I can't help the first."

"It's not worth it. Take my word for it. I'm an athletic person. Not at all feminine."

Neil was staring at her in growing puzzlement. He heard the way her breath was coming in short bursts, saw the way her eyes held something akin to fear. He felt the urgency in his body recede, and slowly, gently he released her. Instantly, she turned away from him and sat up.

"I'd never force you," he murmured to her rigid back.

"I didn't say you would."

"You were talking, rationalizing as though you thought I would. I scared you."

She said nothing to that. How could she explain what she didn't understand herself: that her fear had been he'd find fault with her body? She didn't know why it should matter what he thought of her body....

"You didn't scare me."

"You're lying."

"Then that's another fault to add to the list." She fumbled for her crutches and managed to get herself to her feet. "I'm hungry," she grumbled, and started for the door.

"So am I," was his taunting retort.

"Tough!"

DEIRDRE MADE her own breakfast, grateful to find such easy fixings as yogurt and cottage cheese in the refrigerator. She waited in the den until she heard Neil in the kitchen, then retreated to the other end of the house for a bath.

At length she emerged, wearing the same bulky green top she'd worn during the drive up. This time she had gray sweatpants on, and though the outfit didn't clash, it was less shapely than yesterday's warm-up suit had been.

Reluctant to face Neil, she busied herself cleaning up the bedroom. Making a king-size bed by hobbling from one side to the other and back took time, but for once she welcomed the handicap. She went on to unpack her duffel bag. It wasn't that she hadn't planned on staying, simply that she hadn't had the strength to settle in until now. Yes, she did feel stronger, she realized, and found some satisfaction in that. She also found satisfaction in placing her books, cassette player and tapes atop the dresser. Neil had put his things on the other dresser; she was staking her own claim now.

Under the guise of housekeeping, she crossed to that other dresser and cursorily neatened Neil's things. He'd brought several books, a mix of fiction and nonfiction, all tied in some fashion to history. A glass case lay nearby, with the corner of a pair of horn-rimmed spectacles protruding. Horn-rimmed spectacles. She grinned.

Completing the gathering on the dresser was a scattered assembly of small change, a worn leather wallet and a key ring that held numerous keys in addition to those to his car. She wondered what the others unlocked, wondered where his office was and what it was like, wondered where he lived.

Moving quickly into the bathroom, she wiped down the sink and shower, then the mirror above the sink. She'd put her own few things in one side of the medicine chest. Curious, she slid open the other side. Its top shelf held a number of supplies she assumed were Victoria's. Far below, after several empty shelves, were more personal items—a comb, a brush, a tube of toothpaste and a tooth-brush.

Neil's things. He traveled light. There was no sign of a razor. He'd very obviously planned to be alone.

Strangely, she felt better. Knowing that Neil was as unprepared for the presence of a woman as she was for the presence of a man was reassuring. On the other hand, what would she have brought if she'd known she'd have company? Makeup? Aside from mascara, blusher and lip gloss, she rarely used it. A blow dryer? She rarely used one. Cologne? Hah!

And what would Neil have brought? She wondered.

Sliding the chest shut with a thud, she returned to the bedroom, where a sweeping glance told her there was little else to clean. She could always stretch out on the bed and read, or sit in the chaise by the window and knit. But that would be tantamount to hiding, and she refused to hide.

Discouraged, she looked toward the window. It was still raining. Gray, gloomy and forbidding. If things were different, she wouldn't have been stopped by the rain; she'd have bundled up and taken a walk. All too clearly, though, she recalled how treacherous it was maneuvering with crutches across the mud and rocks. She wasn't game to try it again soon.

Selecting a book from those she'd brought, she tucked it under her arm alongside the crutch, took a deep breath and headed for the living room. Neil was there, slouched on the sofa, lost in thought. He didn't look up until she'd settled herself in the chair, and then he sent her only the briefest of glances.

Determinedly she ignored him. She opened the book, a piece of contemporary women's fiction and began to read, patiently reread-ing the first page three times before she felt justified in moving on to the second. She was finally beginning to get involved in the story, when Neil materialized at her shoulder.

Setting the book down, she turned her head, not far enough to see him, just enough to let him know he had her attention. "Something wrong?" she asked in an even tone.

"Just wondering what you were reading," he said just as evenly.

Leaving a finger to mark her place, she closed the cover so he could see it.

"Any good?" he asked.

"I can't tell yet. I've just started."

"If it doesn't grab you within the first few pages, it won't."

"That's not necessarily true," she argued. "Some books take longer to get into."

He grunted and moved off. She heard a clatter, then another grunt, louder this time, and, following it, a curse that brought her head around fast. "Goddamn it. Can't you keep your crutches out of the way?" He had one hand on the corner of her chair, the other wrapped around his big toe.

"If you were wearing shoes, that wouldn't have happened!"

"I shouldn't have to wear shoes in my own home."

"This isn't your own home."

"Home away from home, then."

"Oh, please, Neil, what exactly would you have me do? Leave the crutches in the other room? You were the one who was after me to use them."

He didn't bother to answer. Setting his foot on the floor, he gingerly tested it. Then he straightened and limped across the room to stand at the window. He tucked his hands in the back pockets of his jeans, displacing the long jersey that would have otherwise covered his buttocks. The jersey itself was black and slim cut, fairly broadcasting the strength and breadth of his shoulders, the leanness of his hips. She wondered if he'd chosen to wear it on purpose.

Returning her eyes to her book, she read another two pages before being interrupted again.

"Crummy day" was the information relayed to her from the window.

She set the book down. "I know."

"That's two in a row."

"Three."

"Two full days that we've been here."

She conceded the point. "Fine. Two in a row." She picked up the book again. Several pages later, she raised her head to find Neil staring at her. "Is something wrong?"

"No."

"You look bored."

"I'm not used to inactivity."

"Don't you have anything to do?"

With a shrug he turned back to the window.

"What would you do at home on a rainy day?" she asked.

"Work."

"Even on a weekend?"

"Especially on a weekend. That's when I catch up on everything I've been too busy to do during the week." At least, it had been that way for years, he mused. Of course, when one was losing clients right and left, there was a definite slackening.

"You must have a successful practice," she remarked, then was taken aback when he sent her a glower. "I meant that as a compliment."

He bowed his head and rubbed the back of his neck. "I know. I'm sorry."

Deirdre glanced at her book, and realized she wasn't going to get much reading done with Neil standing there that way. She was grateful he hadn't made reference to what had happened earlier, and wondered if he was sorry for that, too. If so, she reflected, he might be in a conciliatory mood. It was as good a time as any to strike up a conversation.

"How do you know Victoria?" she asked in as casual a tone as she could muster.

"A mutual friend introduced us several years ago."

"Are you from the city?"

"Depends what city you mean."

For the sake of civility, she stifled her impatience. "New York."

"No." He was facing the window again, and for a minute she thought she'd have to prod, when he volunteered the information she'd been seeking. "Hartford."

A corner of her mouth curved up. She couldn't resist. "Ah, Hartford. Thriving little metropolis. I went to a concert there last year with friends. The seats were awful, the lead singer had a cold and I got a flat tire driving home.''

Slowly Neil turned. ''Okay. I deserved that.''

''Yes, you did. Be grateful I didn't condemn the entire city.''

He wasn't sure he'd have minded if she had. At the moment he felt the whole of Hartford was against him. ''My allegiance to the city isn't blind. I can see her faults.''

''Such as...?''

''Parochialism. Provinciality.''

''Hartford?''

''Yes, Hartford. Certain circles are pretty closed.''

''Isn't that true of any city?''

''I suppose.'' Casually he left the window and returned to the sofa. Deirdre took it as a sign of his willingness to talk.

''Have you lived there long?''

''Since I began practicing.''

''You mentioned going to school in Boston. Was that law school, or undergraduate?''

''Both.''

''So you went from Westchester to Boston to Hartford?''

He had taken on an expression of amused indulgence. ''I did a stint in San Diego between Boston and Hartford. In the Navy. JAG division.''

''Ah. Then you missed Vietnam.''

''Right.'' He had one brow arched, as though waiting for her to criticize the fact that he hadn't seen combat.

''I think that's fine,'' she said easily. ''You did something, which is more than a lot of men did.''

''My motive wasn't all that pure. I would have been drafted if I hadn't signed up.''

''You could have run to Canada.''

''No.''

The finality with which he said it spoke volumes. He felt he'd had a responsibility to his country. Deirdre respected that.

''How did you break your leg?'' he asked suddenly.

The look on her face turned sour. ''Don't ask.''

''I am.''

She met his gaze and debated silently for a minute. He'd opened up. Perhaps she should, too. Somehow it seemed childish to continue the evasion. She gave him a challenging stare. "I fell down a flight of stairs."

He held up a hand, warding off both her stare and its unspoken challenge. "That's okay. I'm not laughing."

Averting her gaze, she scowled at the floor. "You would if you knew the whole story."

"Try me. What happened?"

She'd set herself up for it, but strangely she wasn't sorry. It occurred to her that she wanted to tell the story. If he laughed, she'd have reason to yell at him. In some ways, arguing with him was safer than...than what had happened earlier.

Taking a breath, she faced him again. "I slipped on a magazine, caught my foot in the banister and broke my leg in three places."

He waited expectantly. "And...? There has to be a punch line. I'm not laughing yet."

"You asked what I did for a living." She took a breath. "I teach aerobic dance."

His eyes widened fractionally. "Ah. And now you can't work."

"That's the least of it! I've always been into exercise of one sort or another. I'm supposed to be ultracoordinated. Do you have any idea how humiliating it is to have done this slipping on a magazine?"

"Was the magazine worth it?" he asked, deadpan.

"That's not the point! The point is that I'm not supposed to fall down the stairs! And if I do, I'm supposed to do it gracefully, with only a black-and-blue mark or two to show for it." She glared at her leg. "Not a grotesque cast!"

"How does the leg feel, by the way?"

"Okay."

"The dampness doesn't bother it?"

"My thigh is more sore from lugging the cast around, and my armpits hurt from the crutches."

"That'll get better with time. How long will the cast be on?"

"Another five weeks."

"And after that you'll be good as new?"

Her anger was replaced by discouragement. "I wish I knew. The

doctor made no promises. Oh, I'll be able to walk. But teach?''
Her shrug was as eloquent as the worry in her eyes.

Neil surprised himself by feeling her pain. Wasn't it somewhat
akin to his own? After all, his own future was in limbo, too.

Leaning forward, he propped his elbows on his thighs. "You'll
be able to teach, Deirdre. One way or another you will, if you want
to badly enough.''

"I do! I have to work. I mean, it's not a question of money. It's
a question of emotional survival!''

That, too, he understood. "Your work means that much to you.''

It was a statement, not a question, and Deirdre chose to let it
rest. She wasn't ready to go into the issue of Joyce Enterprises,
which was so much more complex and personal. Besides, Neil was
a corporate attorney. He'd probably take *their* side.

"Well," she said at last, "I guess there's nothing I can do but
wait.''

"What will you do in the meantime?''

"Stay here for as long as I can.''

"There's nothing else to keep you busy in Providence while your
leg mends?''

"Nothing I care to do.''

Neil wondered at her mutinous tone, but didn't comment. "What
had you planned to do here? Besides read.''

Still scowling, she shrugged. "Relax. Knit. Listen to music.
Work up some routines. It may be a waste of time if it turns out I
can't teach, but I suppose I have to hope.''

"You could have done all that in Providence. I'd have thought
that with a broken leg and all, you'd be more comfortable there.
The drive up couldn't have been easy, and if Thomas had dumped
you on that dock alone, you'd have had a hell of a time getting
everything to the house.''

Her scowl deepened. "Thomas knew what he was doing. *You*
were here. Otherwise he'd probably have helped me himself.''

"Still, to rush up here the day you left the hospital... What was
the rush?''

"The telephone! My family! It was bad enough when I was in
the hospital. I had to get away!''

"All that, just because you were embarrassed?''

Deirdre knew that she'd be spilling the entire story in another minute. Who in the devil was Neil Hersey that he should be prying? She hadn't asked *him* why he'd been in such a foul mood from day one. "Let's just say that I have a difficult family," she concluded, and closed her mouth tightly. Between that and the look she gave him, there was no doubt that she was done talking.

Neil took the hint. Oh, he was still curious, but there was time. Time for...lots of things.

She opened her book again and picked up where she'd left off, but if her concentration had been tentative before, it was nonexistent now. She was thinking of that difficult family, wondering what was going to change during the time she was in Maine that would make things any better when she returned.

From the corner of her eye she saw Neil get up, walk aimlessly around the room, then sit down. When a minute later he bobbed up again, she sighed.

"Decide what you want to do, please. I can't read with an active yo-yo in the room."

He said nothing, but took off for the bedroom. Moments later he returned, threw himself full length on the sofa and opened a book of his own. He read the first page, turned noisily to the last, then began to flip through those in between.

"Are you going to read or look at the pictures?" Deirdre snapped.

His face was the picture of innocence when he looked up. "I'm trying to decide if it's worth reading."

She was trying to decide if he was purposely distracting her. "You brought it along, didn't you?"

"I was in a rush. I took whatever books I had around the house and threw them in the bag."

"Then you must have decided it was worth reading when you bought it. What's it about?" She wondered which he'd chosen.

"World War I. History fascinates me."

"I know."

His eyes narrowed. "How would you know?"

"Because I saw the books lying on your dresser, and every one of them dealt with history in some form. You know, you really should wear your glasses when you read. Otherwise you'll get eye strain.''

"I only wear them when I *have* eye strain, and since I haven't had much to look at for the past two days, my eyes are fine.'' He turned his head on the sofa arm to study her more fully. "You're pretty nosy. Did you look through my wallet, too?''

"Of course not! I was cleaning, not snooping. I've never liked living in a pigpen.''

"Could've fooled me, what with the way you've been dropping clothes around.''

"That was only the first night, and I was exhausted.'' She noticed a strange light in his eyes and suspected he was enjoying the sparring. It occurred to her that she was, too. "What's in your wallet, anyway? Something dark and sinister? Something I shouldn't see?''

He shrugged. "Nothing extraordinary.''

"Wads of money?''

"Not quite.''

"A membership card to a slinky men's club?''

"Not quite.''

"A picture of your sweetheart?''

"Not...quite.''

"Who is she, anyway—the one who burned you?''

The day before he wouldn't have wanted to talk about Nancy. Now, suddenly, it seemed less threatening. "She's someone I was seeing, whom I'm not seeing now.''

"Obviously,'' Deirdre drawled. "What happened?''

Neil pursed his lips and thought of the best way to answer. He finally settled on the most general explanation. "She decided I didn't have enough potential.''

"What was she looking for? An empire builder?''

"Probably.''

"You don't sound terribly upset that she's gone.''

"I'm getting over it,'' he said easily.

"Couldn't have been all that strong a relationship, then.''

"It wasn't.''

Deirdre settled her book against her stomach and tipped her head to the side. "Have you ever been married?''

"Where did that come from?"

"I'm curious. You asked me. Now I'm asking you."

"No. I've never been married."

"Why not?"

He arched a brow. "I never asked you that. It's impolite."

"It's impolite to ask a woman that, because traditionally she's the one who has to wait for the proposal. A man can do the proposing. Why haven't you?"

It occurred to Neil that there was something endearing about the way Deirdre's mind worked. It was quick, unpretentious, oddly refreshing. He smiled. "Would you believe me if I said I've been too busy?"

"No."

"It is true, in a way. I've spent the past fifteen years devoted to my career. She's a very demanding mistress."

"Then she's never had the right competition, which means that the old cliché is more the case. You haven't met the right woman yet."

He didn't need to ponder that to agree. "I have very special needs," he said, grinning. "Only a very special woman can satisfy them."

Deirdre could have sworn she saw mischief in his grin. She tried her best to sound scornful. "That I can believe. Any woman who'd put up with a face full of whiskers has to be special. Do you have any idea how...how grungy that looks?"

The insult fell flat. To her dismay, he simply grinned more broadly as he stroked his jaw. "It does look kinda grungy. Nice, huh?"

"Nice?"

"Yeah. I've never grown a beard in my life. From the time I was fifteen I shaved every blessed morning. And why? So I'd look clean. And neat. And acceptable. Well, hell, it's nice to look grungy for a change, and as for acceptability—" He searched for the words he wanted, finally thrust out his chin in defiance. "Screw it!"

Deirdre considered what he'd said. He didn't look unclean, or unneat, or unacceptable, but rather...dashing. Particularly with that look of triumph on his face. Helpless against it, she smiled. "That felt good, didn't it?"

"Sure did."

"You're much more controlled when you work."

"Always. There's a certain, uh, decorum demanded when you're dealing with corporate clients."

"Tell me about it," she drawled, bending her right leg up and hugging it to her chest.

Once before, he'd taken her up on the offer. This time he let it ride, because he didn't really want to talk about corporate clients. He wanted to talk about Deirdre Joyce.

"What about you, Deirdre? Why have you never married?"

"I've never been asked."

He laughed. "I should have expected you'd answer that way. But it's a cop-out, you know," he chided, then frowned and tucked in his chin. "Why are you looking at me that way?"

"Do you know that that's the first time I've heard you laugh, I mean, laugh, as in relaxed and content?"

His smile mellowed into something very gentle, and his eyes bound hers with sudden warmth. "Do you know that's the first time I've heard such a soft tone from you. Soft tone, as in amiable." As in womanly, he might have added, but he didn't. He'd let down enough defenses for one day.

For a minute Deirdre couldn't speak. Her total awareness centered on Neil and the way he was looking at her. He made her feel feminine in a way she'd never felt before.

Awkward, she dropped her gaze to her lap. "You're trying to butter me up, being nice and all. I think you're looking for someone to do the laundry."

Laundry was the last thing on his mind. "I don't think I've ever seen you blush before."

The blush deepened. She didn't look up. She didn't trust the little tricks her hormones were playing on her. She felt she was being toasted from the inside out. It was a new and unsettling sensation. Why *Neil*?

Lips turning down in a pout, she glared at him.

"Aw, come on," he teased. "I liked you the other way."

"Well, I didn't." It smacked of vulnerability, and Deirdre didn't like to think of herself as vulnerable. "I'm not the submissive type."

His laugh was gruffer this time. "I never thought you were. In fact, submissive is the last word I'd use to describe you. You prickle at the slightest thing. I'd almost think that *you*'d been burned."

The directness of her gaze held warning. "I have. I was used once, and I didn't like the feeling."

"No one does," he said softly. "What happened?"

She debated cutting off the discussion, but sensed he'd only raise it another time. So she crossed her right leg over her cast and slid lower in the chair in a pose meant to be nonchalant. "I let myself be a doormat for a fellow who had nothing better to do with his life at the time. The minute he sensed a demand on my part, he was gone."

"You demanded marriage?"

"Oh, no. It was nothing like that. Though I suppose he imagined that coming. My family would like to see me married. They don't think much of my…life-style."

"You're a swinger?"

She slanted him a disparaging glance. "Just the opposite. I avoid parties. I can't stand phony relationships. I hate pretense of any kind."

"What does pretense have to do with marriage?"

"If it's marriage for the sake of marriage alone, pretense is a given."

Neil couldn't argue with that. "Do you want to have children?"

"Someday. How about you?"

"Someday."

They looked at each other for a minute longer, then simultaneously returned to their books. Deirdre, for one, was surprised that she was talking about these things with Neil. She asked herself what it was about him that inspired her to speak, and finally concluded that it was the situation, more than the man, that had brought her out. Hadn't she come here to soul-search, to ponder the direction her life was taking?

Neil was brooding about his own life, his own direction, and for the first time that brooding was on a personal bent. Yes, he'd like to be married, but only to the right person. He was as averse to pretense as Deirdre was. Nancy—for that matter, most of the women he'd dated over the years—had epitomized pretense. One part of him very much wanted to put his law practice in its proper perspective, to focus, instead, on a relationship with a woman, a relationship that was intimate, emotionally as well as physically, and rewarding. And yes, he'd like to have children.

Absently he turned a page, then turned it back when he realized he hadn't read a word. He darted a glance at Deirdre and found her curled in the chair, engrossed in her book. She was honest; he admired her for that. She didn't have any more answers than he did, but at least she was honest.

Settling more comfortably on the sofa, Neil refocused on his book and disciplined himself to read. It came easier as the morning passed. The rain beat a steady accompaniment to the quiet activity, and he had to admit that it was almost peaceful.

Setting the book down at last, he stood. "I'm making sandwiches. Want one?"

Deirdre looked up. "What kind?"

His mouth turned down at the corner. "That's gratitude for you, when someone is offering to make you lunch."

"I can make my own," she pointed out, needing to remind him—and herself—that she wasn't helpless.

"Is that what you'd rather?"

"It depends on what kind of sandwiches you know how to make."

"I know how to make most anything. The question is what have we got to work with?" He crossed into the kitchen, opened the refrigerator and rummaged through the supplies. Straightening, he called over his shoulder, "You can have ham and cheese, bologna and cheese, grilled cheese, grilled cheese and tomato, grilled cheese and tuna, a BLT, egg salad, peanut butter and jelly, cream cheese and jelly—" he sucked in a badly needed breath "—or any of the above taken separately."

Any of the above sounded fine to Deirdre, who'd never been a picky eater. She tried not to grin. "That's quite a list. Could you run through it one more time?"

The refrigerator door swung shut and Neil entered her line of vision. His hands were hooked low on his hips and his stance was one of self-assurance. "You heard it the first time, Deirdre."

"But there are so many things to choose from…and it's a big decision." She pressed her lips together, feigning concentration. "A big decision…"

"Deirdre…"

"I'll have turkey with mustard."

"Turkey wasn't on the list."

"No? I thought for sure it was."

"We don't have any turkey."

"Why not? Thomas should have known to pick some up. Turkey's far better for you than ham or cheese or peanut butter."

Hands falling to his sides, Neil drew himself up, shoulders back. He spoke slowly and clearly. "Do you, or do you not, want a sandwich?"

"I do."

"What kind?"

"Grilled cheese and tuna."

He sighed. "Thank you." He'd no sooner returned to the refrigerator, when he heard her call.

"Can I have it on rye?"

"No, you cannot have it on rye," he called back through gritted teeth.

"How about a roll?"

"If a hamburg roll will do."

"It won't."

"Then it's white bread or nothing. Take it or leave it."

"I'll take it."

He waited a minute longer to see if she had anything else to add. When she remained silent, he tugged open the refrigerator and removed everything he'd need. He'd barely closed the door again, when Deirdre entered the kitchen.

"If you've changed your mind," he warned, "that's tough. Your order's already gone to the cook. It's too late to change."

She was settling herself on the counter stool. "Grilled cheese and tuna's fine." Folding her hands in her lap, she watched him set to work.

He opened a can of tuna, dumped its contents into a bowl and shot her a glance as he reached for the mayonnaise. A glob of the creamy white stuff went the way of the tuna. He was in the process of mixing it all together with a fork, when he darted her another glance. "Anything wrong?"

"No, no. Just watching. You don't mind, do you? I'm fascinated. You're very domestic for a man."

"Men have to eat."

"They usually take every shortcut in the book, but grilled cheese and tuna...I'm impressed."

"It's not terribly difficult," he scoffed.

"But it takes more time than peanut butter and jelly."

"Tastes better, too."

"I *love* peanut butter and jelly."

"Then why'd you ask for grilled cheese and tuna?"

She arched a brow, goading him on. "Maybe I wanted to see what you could do."

Neil, who'd been slathering tuna on slices of bread, stopped mid-stroke, put down the knife and slowly turned. "You mean you purposely picked what you thought was the hardest thing on the menu?"

Deirdre knew when to back off. "I was only teasing. I really do feel like having grilled cheese and tuna."

With deliberate steps, he closed the small distance between them. "I don't believe you. I think you did it on purpose, just like you asked for turkey when you knew damn well we didn't have it."

She would have backed up if there'd been anywhere to go, but the counter was already digging into her ribs. "Really, Neil." She held up a hand. "There's no need to get upset. Unless you're having ego problems with my being in the kitchen this way—"

The last word barely made it from her mouth, when Neil scooped her up from the stool, cast and all, and into his arms.

"What are you doing?" she cried.

He was striding through the living room. "Removing you from my presence. You wanted to get my goat. Well, you got it. Picking the most complicated sandwich. *Ego* problems." They were in the hall and moving steadily. "If you want to talk, you can do it to your heart's content in here." He entered the bedroom and went straight to the bed, his intent abundantly clear to Deirdre, who was clutching the crew neckline of his jersey.

"Don't drop me! My cast!"

Neil held her suspended for a minute, enjoying the fact of his advantage over her. Then, in a single heartbeat, his awareness changed. No longer was he thinking that she'd goaded him once too often. Rather, he was suddenly aware that her thigh was slender and strong beneath one of his hands, and that the fingertips of the other were pressed into an unexpectedly feminine breast. He was thinking that her eyes were luminous, her lips moist, her cheeks a newly acquired pale pink.

Deirdre, too, had caught her breath. She was looking up at Neil, realizing that his eyes, like her hair, weren't black at all, but a shade of charcoal brown, and that his mouth was strong, well formed and very male. She was realizing that he held her with ease, and that he smelled clean, and that the backs of her fingers were touching the hot, hair-shaded surface of his chest and he felt good.

Slowly he lowered her to the bed, but didn't retreat. Instead he planted his hands on either side of her. "I don't know what in the hell is going on here," he breathed thickly. "It must be cabin fever." His gaze fell from her eyes to her lips, declaring his intent even before he lowered his head.

CHAPTER SIX

HIS MOUTH TOUCHED hers lightly at first, brushing her lips, sampling their shape and texture. Then he intensified the kiss, deepening it by bold degrees until it had become something positively breathtaking.

Deirdre could barely think, much less respond. She'd known Neil was going to kiss her, but she'd never expected such force in the simple communion of mouths. He drank from her like a man who was dying of thirst, stumbling unexpectedly upon an oasis in the desert. From time to time his lips gentled to a whisper, touching hers almost timidly in reassurance that what he'd found wasn't a mirage.

His hands framed her face, moving her inches away when his mouth would have resisted even that much. "Kiss me, Deirdre," he breathed, studying her through lambent eyes.

His hoarse command was enough to free her from the spell she'd been under. When he brought her mouth back to his, her lips were parted, curious, eager, and she returned his kiss with growing fervor. She discovered the firmness of his lips, the evenness of his teeth, the texture of his tongue. She tasted his taste and breathed his breath, and every cell in her that was woman came alive.

"Deirdre," he whispered, once again inching her face from his. He pressed his warm forehead to hers and worked at catching his breath. "Why did you *do* that?"

Deirdre, who was having breathing difficulties of her own, struggled to understand. "What?"

"*Why did you do that?*"

"Do what?"

"Kiss me!"

The haze in her head began to clear, and she drew farther away. "You told me to kiss you."

His brows were drawn together, his features taut. "Not like that. I expected just a little kiss. Not...not that!"

He was angry. She couldn't believe it. "And who was kissing whom first like that?"

His breath came roughly, nostrils flaring. "You didn't have to do it back!" Shoving his large frame from the bed, he stormed from the room, leaving Deirdre unsure and bewildered and, very quickly, angry.

She sat up to glare in the direction he'd gone, then closed her eyes and tried to understand his reaction. Though she'd never, never kissed or been kissed that way, she wasn't so inexperienced that she couldn't see when a man was aroused. Neil Hersey had been aroused, and he'd resented it.

Which meant he didn't want involvement any more than she did.

Which meant they had a problem.

She'd enjoyed his kiss. More than that. It had taken her places she'd never been before. Kissing Neil had been like sampling a rich chocolate with a brandy center, sweet and dissolving—yet potent. He went straight to her head.

She touched her swollen lips, then her tingling chin. Even his beard had excited her, its roughness a contrast to the smoothness of his mouth. Yes, he was smooth. Smooth and virile and stimulating, damn him!

Dropping her chin to her chest, she took several long, steadying breaths. With the fresh intake of oxygen came the strength she needed. Yes, they were stuck under the same roof. They were even stuck, thanks to a matching stubbornness, in the same bed. She was simply going to have to remember that she had problems enough of her own, that *he* had problems enough of his own. And that he could be a very disagreeable man.

Unfortunately Neil chose that moment to return to the bedroom. He carried her crutches and wore an expression of uncertainty. After a moment's hesitation on the threshold, he started slowly toward the bed.

"Here," he said, quietly offering the crutches. "The sandwiches are under the broiler. They'll be ready in a minute."

Deirdre met his gaze, then averted her own, looking to the crutches. She reached for them, wrapped her hands around the rubber handles and studied them for a minute before raising her eyes again.

The corners of his mouth curved into the briefest, most tentative of smiles before he turned and left the room.

Leaning forward, Deirdre rested her head against the crutches. Oh, yes, Neil was a very disagreeable man. He also had his moments of sweetness and understanding, which, ironically, was going to make living with him that much more of a trial.

She sighed. It had to be done. Unless she was prepared to capitulate and leave the island by choice. Which she wasn't.

Struggling to her feet, she secured the crutches under her arms and, resigned, headed for the kitchen.

Lunch was a quiet, somewhat awkward affair. Neil avoided looking at Deirdre, which she had no way of knowing, since she avoided looking at him. She complimented him on the sandwiches. He thanked her. When they were done, he made a fresh pot of coffee— medium thick—and carried a cup to the living room for her. She thanked him. And all the while she was thinking of that kiss, as he was. All the while she was wondering where it might have led, as he was. All the while she was asking herself why, as was he.

Knowing she'd never be able to concentrate on her book, she brought her knitting bag from the bedroom, opened the instruction booklet and forced her attention to the directions.

Neil, who was in a chair drinking his second cup of coffee, was as averse to reading as she was, but could think of nothing else he wanted to do. "What are you making?" he asked in a bored tone.

She didn't look up. "A sweater."

"For you?"

"Hopefully." She reached for a neatly wound skein of yarn, freed its end and pulled out a considerable length. Casting on—that sounded simple enough.

Neil noted the thick lavender strand. "Nice color."

"Thank you." With the book open on her lap, she took one of the needles and lay the strand against it.

"That's a big needle."

She sighed. Concentration was difficult, knowing he was watching. "Big needle for a big sweater."

"For you?"

Her eyes met his. "It's going to be a bulky sweater."

"Ah. As in ski sweater?"

She pressed her lips together in angry restraint. "As in warm sweater, since it looks like I won't be skiing in the near future."

"Do you ski?"

"Yes."

"Are you good?"

She dropped the needle to her lap and stared at him. "I told you I was athletic. I exercise, play tennis, swim, ski... At least, I used to do all of those things. Neil, I can't concentrate if you keep talking."

"I thought knitting was an automatic thing."

"Not when you're learning how."

One side of his mouth twitched. "You haven't done it before?"

"No, I haven't."

"Was it the broken leg that inspired you?"

"I bought the yarn several months ago. This is the first chance I've had to work with it."

He nodded. She lifted the needle again, studied the book again, brought the yarn up and wound it properly for the first stitch. It took several attempts before she'd made the second, but once she'd caught on, she moved right ahead. Before long she had enough stitches cast on to experiment with the actual knitting.

When Neil finished his coffee, he returned the cup to the kitchen and started wandering around the house. At last, all else having failed to divert him, he picked up his book again.

By this time Deirdre was painstakingly working one knit stitch after another. The needles were awkward in her hands, and she continually dropped the yarn that was supposed to be wrapped around her forefinger. Periodically she glanced up to make sure Neil wasn't witnessing her clumsiness, and each time she was frowning when she returned to her work. Simply looking at him turned her inside out.

He was stretched full length on the couch...so long...so lean. The sleeves of his jersey were pushed back to reveal forearms matted with the same dark hair she'd felt on his chest. *Felt*. Soft, but strong and crinkly. The texture was permanently etched in her memory.

From his position on the sofa, Neil was also suffering distractions. His curiosity as to what Deirdre hid beneath her bulky sweatshirt had never been greater. He'd felt the edge of her breast. *Felt.* Strong and pert, but yielding beneath his fingertips. He'd carried her; she was light as thistledown and every bit as warm. He'd tasted her. That was his worst mistake, because there'd been a honeyed sweetness to her that he never would have imagined. Did the rest of his imaginings pale by comparison to the real thing?

From beneath half-lidded eyes he slanted her a look. Her hands gripped the needles, the forefinger of each extended. She was struggling, he saw, but even then the sweep of her fingers was graceful. Athletic? Perhaps. But if so, in a most healthy, most fitting, most feminine way.

Slapping the book shut, he sat bolt upright. Deirdre's questioning eyes shot to him.

"I can't read with that clicking," he grumbled. "Can't you be any quieter?"

"I'm having trouble as it is. Do you want miracles?"

"Not miracles. Just peace and quiet." Dropping the book on the sofa, he began to prowl the room.

"Book didn't grab you?"

"No." He ran a hand through his hair. "How about playing a game? Victoria has a bunch of them in the other room."

The knitting fell to Deirdre's lap. She wasn't sure she was up to playing games with Neil. "What did you have in mind?" she asked warily.

"I don't know. Maybe Monopoly?"

"I hate Monopoly. There's no skill involved."

"What about Trivial Pursuit?"

"I'm no good at history and geography. They make me lose."

"You make you lose," he argued. "The game doesn't do it."

"Whatever. The result's the same."

"Okay. Forget Trivial Pursuit. How about chess?"

"I don't know how."

"Checkers."

She scrunched up her nose in rejection.

"Forget a game," he mumbled.

"How about a movie?" she asked. It was a rainy day; the idea held merit. Her fingers were cramped, anyway.

"Okay."

"What do we have to choose from?"

In answer he started off toward the den. Deirdre levered herself up and followed, finding him bent over a low shelf in contemplation of the video tapes. She came closer, trying not to notice how snugly his jeans molded his buttocks, how they were slightly faded at the spot where he sat.

"*Magnum Force?*" he suggested.

"Too violent."

"*North by Northwest?*"

"Too intense." Leaning over beside him, she studied the lineup. "How about *Against All Odds*?"

"That's a romance."

"So?"

"Forget it."

"Then *The Sting*. Unromantic, but amusing."

"And boring. The best part's the music."

Her gaze moved across the cassettes, eyes suddenly widening. "*Body Heat.* That's a super movie. William Hurt, Kathleen Turner, intrigue and—"

"—Sex." Neil's head was turned, eyes boring into her. "I don't think we need that."

He was right, of course. She couldn't believe she'd been so impulsive as to suggest that particular movie.

"Ah." He drew one box out. "Here we go. *The Eye of the Needle.* Now that was a good flick."

It had action, intrigue, and yes, a bit of sex, but Deirdre felt she could take it. "Okay. Put it on." She set her crutches against the wall and hopped to the leather couch.

Removing the cassette from its box, Neil inserted it in the VCR, pressed several buttons, then took the remote control and sank onto the couch an arm's length from Deirdre. The first of the credits had begun to roll, when he snapped it off and jumped up.

"What's wrong?" she asked.

"We need popcorn. I saw some in the kitchen cabinet."

"But it takes time to make popcorn, and we're all set to watch."

"We've got time. Besides, it doesn't take more than a couple of minutes in the microwave." He rubbed his hands together. "With lots of nice melted butter poured on top—"

"Not butter! It's greasy, and awful for you."

"What's popcorn without butter?" he protested.

"Healthier."

"Then I'll put butter on mine. You can have yours without."

"Fine." She crossed her arms over her chest and sat back while he went to make the popcorn. Gradually her frown softened. It was rather nice being waited on, and Neil wasn't complaining. She supposed that if she'd had to be marooned with a man, she could have done worse. She *knew* she could have done worse. She could have been stuck with a real egomaniac. True, Neil had his moments. It occurred to her that while she'd given him a clue as to what caused her own mood swings, as yet she had no clue to his motivation. She'd have to work on that, she decided, merely for the sake of satisfying her curiosity. Nothing else.

Neil entered the room carrying popcorn still in its cooking bag. He resumed his seat, turned the movie back on and positioned the bag at a spot midway between them.

"Did you add butter?" she asked cautiously.

"No. You're right. I don't need it."

"Ah. Common sense prevails."

"Shh. I want to watch the movie."

She glanced at the screen. "I'm only disturbing the credits."

"You're disturbing me. Now keep still."

Deirdre kept still. She reached for a handful of popcorn and put one piece, then another in her mouth. The movie progressed. She tried to get into it but failed.

"It's not the same watching movies at home," she remarked. "A theater's dark. It's easier to forget your surroundings and become part of the story."

"Shh." Neil was having trouble of his own concentrating. It wasn't the movie, although as he'd seen it before, it held no mystery. What distracted him was Deirdre sitting so close. Only popcorn separated them. Once, when he reached into the bag, his hand met hers. They both retreated. And waited.

"You go first," he said.

She kept her eyes on the small screen. "No. That's okay. I'll wait."

"I've already had more. Go ahead."

"I don't need it. I'll get fat."

"You won't get fat." From what he'd seen, she wasn't a big eater; as for getting fat, from what he'd felt she was slender enough. Still, he couldn't resist a gibe. "On second thought, maybe you're right. You will get fat. You're smaller than I am, and I'm the one who's getting all the exercise around here. I'll wear it off easier."

He reached for the popcorn, but Deirdre already had her hand in the bag. She withdrew a full fist, sent him a smug grin and with deliberate nonchalance popped several pieces into her mouth.

Neil, who'd almost expected she'd do just that, wasn't sure whether to laugh or scream. Deirdre was impetuous in a way that was adorable, and adorable in a way that was bad for his heart. She had only to look at him with those luminous brown eyes and his pulse raced. He never should have kissed her. Damn it, he never should have kissed her!

But he had, and that fact didn't ease his watching of the rest of the movie. He was constantly aware of her—aware when she shifted on the couch, aware when she dropped her head back and watched the screen through half-closed eyes, aware when she began to massage her thigh absently.

"Leg hurt?" he asked.

She looked sharply his way, then shrugged and looked back at the screen.

"Want some aspirin?"

"No."

"Some Ben-Gay?"

"There is no Ben-Gay."

His lips twitched. "I'd run to the island drugstore for some if you'd let me rub it on."

She glared at the movie, but carried on the farce. "The island drugstore's out. I checked."

"Oh. Too bad."

Deirdre clamped her lips tightly, silently cursing Neil for his suggestion. *Let me rub it on.* Her insides tingled with a heat that, unfortunately, didn't do a whit to help her thigh.

Neil, too, cursed the suggestion, because his imagination had picked up from there, and he'd begun to think of rubbing far more than her thigh. He wondered whether her breasts would fit his hand, whether the skin of her belly would be soft....

He shifted away from her on the couch, and made no further comments, suggestive or otherwise. The movie was ruined for him. He was too distracted to follow the dialogue; the intrigue left him cold; the sex left him hot. The only thing that brought him any relief from the build-up of need in his body was the thought of Hartford, of work, of Wittnauer-Douglass. And because that upset him all the more, he was truly between a rock and a very hard place, where he remained throughout the evening.

He and Deirdre ate dinner together. They sat together before the fire. They pretended to read, but from the way Deirdre's eyes were more often on the flames than her book, he suspected that she was accomplishing as little as he was. He also suspected that her thoughts were running along similar lines, if the occasional nervous glances she cast him were any indication.

There was an element of fear in her. He'd seen it before; he could see it now. And it disturbed him. Was she afraid of sex? Was she afraid of feeling feminine and heated and out of control?

Even as he asked himself those questions, his body tightened. What in the hell was *he* afraid of? Certainly not sex. But there was something holding him back, even when every nerve in his body was driving him on.

He sat up by the fire long after Deirdre had taken refuge in bed. When at last he joined her, he was tired enough to fall asleep quickly. By the time the new day dawned, though, he was wondering whether he should relent and sleep in another room. Twice during the night he'd awoken to find their bodies touching—his outstretched arm draped over hers, the sole of her foot nestled against his calf.

What *was* it that made them gravitate toward each other? Each had come to Maine in search of solitude, so he'd have thought they'd have chosen to pass the time in opposite corners of the house. That hadn't been the case. Spitting and arguing—be it in the bedroom, the kitchen, the living room or den—they'd been together. And now...still...the bed.

He saw Deirdre look over her shoulder at him, then curl up more tightly on her side. Rolling to his back, he stared up at the ceiling, but the image there was of a disorderly mop of wheat-colored hair, soft brown eyes still misty with sleep, soft cheeks bearing a bed-warmed flush and lips that were slightly parted, unsure, questioning.

He had to get out. Though there was still the intermittent patter of rain and the air beyond the window was thick with mist, he had to get out. Without another glance at Deirdre, he flew from the bed, pulled on the dirty clothes he'd been planning to wash that day, laced on the sneakers that still bore a crust of mud from the day of his arrival on the island, threw his Windbreaker over his shoulders and fled the room, then the house.

Surrounded by the silence left in his wake, Deirdre slowly sat up. Being closed in had finally gotten to him, she mused. It had gotten to her, too. Or was it Neil who'd gotten to her? She'd never spent as uncomfortable an evening or night as those immediately past, her senses sharpened, sensitized, focused in on every nuance of Neil's physical presence. He breathed; she heard it. He turned; she felt it. Once, when she'd awoken in the middle of the night to find her hand tucked under his arm, she'd nearly jumped out of her skin, and not from fear of the dark.

Her body was a coiled spring, taut with frustration. She wanted to run six miles, but couldn't run at all. She wanted to swim seventy-two laps, but couldn't set foot in a pool, much less the ocean. She wanted to exercise until she was hot and tired and dripping with sweat, but...but... Damn it, yes, she could!

Shoving back the covers, she grabbed her crutches, took a tank top and exercise shorts from the dresser drawer and quickly pulled them on. She sat on the bed to put on her one sock and sneaker and both leg warmers, then pushed herself back up, tucked her cassette player and several tapes under one arm and her crutch under the other, and hobbled into one of the spare bedrooms. Within minutes the sounds of Barry Manilow filled the house.

Deirdre took a deep breath and smiled, then closed her eyes and began her familiar flexibility exercises. Her crutches lay on the spare bed; she discovered she could stand perfectly well without them. And the fact that various parts of the routine had to be altered in deference to her leg didn't bother her. She was moving.

In time with the music, she did body twists and side bends. She stretched the calf and ankle muscles of her right leg, and the inner thigh muscles of both legs. It felt good, so good to be feeling her body again. She took her time, relaxed, let the music take her where it would.

After several minutes, she moved into a warm-up, improvising as she went to accommodate her limited mobility. The music changed; the beat picked up, and she ventured into an actual dance routine. Though she couldn't dance in the true sense of the word, her movements were fluid and involved her entire upper torso as well as her good leg. By the time she'd slowed to do a cool-down routine, she'd broken into a healthy sweat and felt better than she had in days.

So immersed was she in the exercise that she didn't hear the open and closing of the front door. Neil, though, heard her music the minute he stepped into the house. He was incensed; it was loud and far heavier than the music he preferred. Without bothering to remove his wet jacket, he strode directly toward the sound, intent on informing Deirdre that as long as they were sharing the house, she had no right to be so thoughtless.

He came to an abrupt halt on the threshold of the spare bedroom, immobilized by the sight that met him. Eyes closed, seeming almost in a trance, Deirdre was moving in time to the music with a grace that was remarkable given her one casted leg. But it wasn't the movement that lodged his breath in his throat. It was her. Her body.

If he'd wondered what she'd been hiding beneath her oversized clothes, he didn't have to wonder any longer. She wore a skimpy tank top that revealed slender arms and well-toned shoulders. Her breasts pushed pertly at the thin fabric, their soft side swells clearly visible when she moved her arms. Her waist was small, snugly molded by the elasticized band of her shorts, and the shorts themselves were brief, offering an exaggerated view of silken thighs.

He gave a convulsive swallow when she bent over, his eyes glued to crescents of pale flesh. Then she straightened and stretched, arms high over her head, dipping low and slow from one side to the other. He swallowed again, transfixed by the firmness of her breasts, which rose with the movement.

Neil realized then that Deirdre's shapelessness had belonged solely to her bulky sweat clothes. Deirdre Joyce was shapely and lithe. With her hair damp around her face, her skin gleaming under a sheen of perspiration, with her arms flexing lyrically, her breasts bobbing, her hips rocking, she looked sultry, sexy and feminine.

He was in agony. His own body was taut, and his breath came raggedly. Turning, he all but ran down the hall, through the master bedroom, directly into the bathroom. He was tugging at his clothes, fumbling in his haste, knowing only that if he didn't hit a cold shower soon he'd explode.

His clothing littered the floor, but he was oblivious to the mess. Stepping into the shower, he turned on the cold tap full force, put his head directly beneath the spray, propped his fists against the tile wall and stood there, trembling, until the chill of the water had taken the edge of fever from his body. He thought of Hartford, of Wittnauer-Douglass, of his uncle who'd died the year before, of basketball—anything to get his mind off Deirdre. Only when he felt he'd gained a modicum of control did he adjust the water temperature to a more comfortable level for bathing.

Deirdre, who was totally unaware of the trial Neil had been through, finished her cool-down exercises and did several final stretches before allowing herself to relax in a nearby chair. Feeling tired but exhilarated, she left the music on; it was familiar, comfortable and reassuring.

At length she sat forward and reached for her crutches, knowing that if she didn't dry off and change clothes, her perspiration-dampened body would soon be chilled.

She turned off the music and listened. The house was still silent, which meant, she reasoned, that Neil was still outside, which meant, she reasoned further, that she could have the bathroom to herself without fear of intrusion. A warm bath sounded very, very appealing.

The smile she wore as she swung her way down the hall was self-congratulatory. She was proud of herself. She'd exercised, and in so doing had not only proved that she could do it, but had worked off the awful tension she'd awoken with that morning. So much for Neil Hersey and his virility, she mused. She could handle it.

Intending to fill the tub while she undressed, she passed straight through the master bedroom to the bathroom. The door was closed.

Without a thought, she shouldered it open and let the rhythm of her limp carry her several feet into the room. There she came to a jarring halt.

Neil stood at the sink. His head was bowed and he was bent slightly at the waist, his large hands curving around the edges of the porcelain fixture. He was stark naked.

The breath had left her lungs the instant she'd seen him, and Deirdre could do no more than stare, even when he slowly raised his head and looked at her. He had a more beautifully male body than she'd ever have dreamed. His back was broad and smooth, his flanks lean, his buttocks tight. Seen in profile, his abdomen was flat, his pelvic bones just visible beneath a casement of flesh, his sex heavy and distinct.

"Deirdre?" His voice was husky. Her eyes flew to his when, without apparent modesty, he straightened and turned to face her. Two slow steps brought him close enough to touch. He repeated her name, this time in a whisper.

She was rooted to the spot, barely able to breathe, much less speak. Her eyes were wide and riveted to his.

He brought up a hand to brush the dots of moisture from her nose, then let his thumb trail down her cheek, over her jaw to her neck and on to the quivering flesh that bordered the thin upper hem of her tank top. Her breath was suddenly coming in tiny spurts that grew even tinier when he slipped his hand beneath her shoulder strap and brushed the backs of his fingers lower, then lower. She bit her lip to stifle a cry when he touched the upper swell of her breast, and though she kept her eyes on his, she was aware of the gradual change in his lower body.

"I didn't know you looked like this," he said hoarsely. "You've kept it all hidden."

Deirdre didn't know what to say. She couldn't quite believe he was complimenting her, not when he was so superbly formed himself. Surely the other women who'd seen him this way had been far more desirable than she. And though she knew he was aroused, her insecurities crowded in on her.

The backs of his fingers were gently rubbing her, dipping ever deeper into her bra. "Take off your clothes," he urged in a rough murmur, eyes flaming with restrained heat. "Let me see you."

She shook her head.

"Why not?"

She swallowed hard and managed a shaky whisper. "I'm sweaty."

"Take a shower with me." His baby finger had reached the sensitive skin just above her nipple, coaxing.

Pressing her lips together to hold in a moan, she shook her head again. "I can't take a shower." Her voice was small, pleading.

"Then a bath. Let me bathe you."

She wasn't sure if it was the sensuality of his words, or the fact that his finger had just grazed the hard nub of her nipple, but her good knee buckled, and she would have fallen had not her crutches been under her arms. His finger moved again, then again, sending live currents through her body. This time she couldn't contain the soft moan that slipped from her throat.

"Feel good?" he whispered against her temple, his own breath coming quicker.

"I don't want it to," she cried.

"Neither do I, but it does, doesn't it?"

It felt heavenly—his touching her, his being so near, so naked. She wanted to be naked beside him, too, but she was frightened. He'd be disappointed. She was sure of it. She was an athlete, "boyish" by her family's definition, and that description had haunted her doggedly over the years. She wasn't soft and fragile and willowy.

And even if Neil wasn't disappointed looking at her, he'd be let down by what would come after that. She felt the ache, the emptiness crying out inside of her, and knew she'd want to make love. And then he'd be disappointed, and the illusion would be broken.

She hobbled back a step, dislodging his hand. "I have to go. I have to go, Neil." Without waiting for his reply, she turned and fled from the bathroom, taking refuge in the bedroom where she'd exercised, collapsing in the chair and cursing her failings. *So much for handling Neil's virility.* Hah!

She didn't know how long she sat there, but the sweat had long since dried from her skin and she was feeling chilled when Neil appeared at the door. He wore a fresh pair of jeans and a sweater, and was barefoot, as usual. She wished she could believe that things were back to normal between them, but she knew better.

Neil felt neither anger nor frustration as he looked at her, but rather a tenderness that stunned him. Padding slowly into the room, he took an afghan from the end of the bed, gently draped it over her shoulders, then came down on his haunches beside her chair. "What frightens you, Deirdre?" he asked in a tone that would have melted her if the sight of him hadn't already done so.

It was a minute before she could speak, and then only brokenly. "You. Me. I don't know."

"I'd never hurt you."

"I know."

"Then what is it? You respond to me. I can feel it in your body. Your breath catches, and you begin to tremble. Is that fear, too?"

"Not all of it."

"You do want me."

"Yes."

"Why don't you give in and let go? It'd be good between us."

She looked down at her hands, which were tightly entwined in her lap. "Maybe for me, but I'm not sure for you."

"Why don't you let me be the judge of that?"

"I'm an athlete, not soft and cuddly like some women."

"Just because you're athletic doesn't mean you're not soft and cuddly. Besides, if it was a cushiony round ball I wanted, I'd go to bed with a teddy bear."

As he'd intended, his comment brought a smile to her face. But it was a tentative smile, a nervous one. "Somehow I can't picture that."

"Neither can I, but, then, I can't picture myself being disappointed if you let me hold you...touch you...make love to you."

His words sent a ripple of excitement through her, and there was clear longing in her gaze as she surveyed his face. "I'm scared" was all she could manage to say.

Neil studied her a minute longer, then leaned forward and kissed her lightly. "I'd never hurt you. Just remember that." Standing, he left the room.

His words were in Deirdre's mind constantly as the day progressed. She believed that he'd meant what he'd said, but she knew that there were different kinds of hurt. Physical hurt was out of the question; Neil was far too gentle for that. But emotional hurt was something else. If their relationship should take the quantum leap that lovemaking would entail…and he should be let down…she'd be hurt. How it had happened, she didn't know, particularly since they'd spent most of their time together fighting, but Neil had come to mean something to her. She wasn't up to analyzing the exact nature of that something; all she knew was that she was terrified of endangering it.

If he'd thought long and hard, Neil couldn't have come up with a better way to goad Deirdre that day than by being kind, soft-spoken and agreeable. Without a word he prepared their meals. Without a word he did the laundry. He was indulgent when she tackled her knitting again, abiding the noise without complaint. He was perfectly amenable to watching her choice of movie on the VCR. He didn't start a single argument, but, then, neither did she. It was the quietest day they'd spent on the island.

Deirdre was as aware as he of that fact. She was also aware that, by denying her any cause to bicker, Neil was allowing her time to think about what he'd said and what she was going to do about it. If the issue had been entirely cerebral, she might have had a chance to resist him. But her senses refused to be reasoned with and were constantly attuned to his presence. That side of her she'd never paid much heed to was suddenly clamoring for attention. Though all was peaceful on the outside, inside she was a mass of cells crying for release from a tension that radiated through her body in ever-undulating waves.

By the time they'd finished dinner and had spent a quiet hour before the fire, she had her answer. Yes, she was frightened and very, very nervous, but she'd decided that if Neil approached her again, she wouldn't refuse him. The sensual side of her nature wouldn't allow her to deny herself.

Head bowed, she quietly got to her feet, secured her crutches under her arms and left the living room. Once in the bedroom, she slowly changed into her pajamas, then sat on the side of the bed and reviewed her decision. She was taking a chance, she knew. A big one. If things didn't go well, the atmosphere in the house would be worse than ever. Then again, maybe not. They might be able to settle into a platonic relationship for the rest of their time here. Then again, Neil might not even come to her....

Even as she pondered that possibility, she sensed his presence in the room. Her head swiveled toward the door, eyes following his silent approach. Every one of her insecurities found expression in her face. Her back was straight. Her hands clutched the rounded edge of the bed.

More than anything at that moment, Neil wanted to alleviate her fear. It tore at him, because he knew he was its cause, just as he knew that her fear was unfounded. If she worried that she wouldn't please him, she worried needlessly. Deirdre turned him on as no other woman had, turned him on physically and in a myriad of other ways he'd only begun to identify.

Hunkering down, he raised his eyes to hers. He wanted to ask, but couldn't find the words. One part of him was frightened, too—frightened of being turned down when the one thing he wanted, the one thing he needed just then, was to be accepted, to be welcomed. So his question was a wordless one, gently and soulfully phrased.

Deirdre's insides were trembling, but she wasn't so wrapped up in apprehension that she didn't hear his silent request. It was a plea that held its share of unsureness, and that fact, more than anything, gave her the courage she needed.

Of its own accord, her hand came up, touching his cheek, inching back until her fingers wove gently into his hair. Tentatively, nervously, she let her lips soften into the beginnings of a smile.

Neil had never seen anything as sweet. He felt relief, and a kind of victory. But more, a well of affection rose inside, spreading warmth through him. Whatever Deirdre's fears were, she was willing to trust him. That knowledge pleased him every bit as much as the prospect of what was to come.

Holding her gaze, he brought his hands up to frame her face. His thumbs stroked her lips for a minute before he came forward and replaced them with his mouth. His kiss was sure and strong, the sealing of a pact, but it was every bit as gentle in promise, and Deirdre was lost in it. It was almost a shock when he set her back and she remembered that there was more to lovemaking than kisses alone. Her expression reflected her qualms, and Neil was quick to reassure her.

"Don't be frightened," he whispered. "We'll take it slow." Sitting back on his haunches, he slid his hands to her neck, then lower to the first button of her pajamas, which he released. He moved on to the second button, working in such a way that some part of his hand constantly touched her flesh. For him, the touch point reflected sheer greed; for Deirdre it was a sensually electric connection that served as a counterpoint to her apprehension.

Only when the last of the buttons was released did Neil lower his gaze. With hands that trembled slightly, he drew back the voluminous pajama fabric, rolling it outward until her breasts were fully exposed. The sight of them, small and high, but well rounded, shook him deeply. He'd been right; imagination did pale against reality. Or maybe it was that he hadn't dared dream....

The cool air of the bedroom hit Deirdre simultaneously with trepidation, but when her arms would have moved inward, he gently held them still.

"You're beautiful, Deirdre," he breathed. "What could ever have made you think that you wouldn't be right for me?"

She didn't answer, because the light in his eyes was so special, so precious, that she was afraid of distracting him lest his fascination fade. So she watched, mesmerized, as he brought both hands to her breasts. Long fingers circled them, tracing only their contours before growing bolder. A soft sigh slipped through her lips when he began to knead her fullness, and the feeling was so right and so good that she momentarily forgot her fears.

When the pads of his fingers brushed her nipples, she stiffened her back, but it was a movement in response to the surge of heat, not a protest. She had to clutch his shoulders then, because he had leaned forward and opened his mouth over one tight nub, and the sensation was jolting her to her core.

His tongue dabbed the pebbled tip. His teeth toyed with it. And all the while his hand occupied her other breast, caressing it with such finesse that she bit her lip to keep from crying out.

At last, when she simply couldn't help herself, she began to whimper. "Neil...I don't think I can stand this...."

"If I can, you can," he rasped against her skin.

"I feel like I'm on fire...."

"You are."

"I can't sit still...."

"Sure you can. Let it build."

"It's been building for three days!"

"But it has to be slow, has to be right."

He drew back only long enough to whip the sweater over his head. Then he came up to sit beside her and take her in his arms. That first touch, flesh to flesh, was cataclysmic. Deirdre's entire body shook when her breasts made contact with his chest. Her arms went around him, holding him tightly, as though otherwise she'd simply shatter.

Neil's grip on her was no less definitive. His large body shuddered at the feel of her softness pressing into it. His breath came raggedly by her ear, while his hands hungrily charted every inch of her bare back, from her shoulders, over her ribs, to the dimpled hollows below her waist. Her pajama bottoms hung around her hips; he took advantage of their looseness to explore the creamy smoothness of her belly, the flare of her hips, the conditioned firmness of her bottom.

Deirdre, whose body all but hummed its pleasure, was finding a second heaven touching Neil. She loved the broad sweep of his back, the textured hollows of his collarbone, the sinewed swells of his chest. Slipping her hands between their bodies, she savored his front as she'd done his back. It was hairier, enticingly so, and his nipples were every bit as taut, if smaller, than hers were.

"What you do to me, Deirdre," he murmured dazedly, recapturing her face with his hands and taking her lips in a fevered kiss. "I think I agree with you. I'm not sure how much more I can stand, either."

She'd been right, he realized. Though they hadn't known it at the time, they'd endured three days of foreplay. From the very first there'd been curiosity. And it had grown more intense, despite every argument they'd had, despite every scathing comment they'd exchanged. Later he would wonder how much of the fighting had been caused by that basic attraction between them, but for now all he could think about was that their mutual desire was on the verge of culmination.

Coming up on one knee, he grasped her under the arms and raised her gently to the pillow. He eased the quilt from under her until she was lying on the bare sheet, then, unsnapping her pajama bottoms, he worked them down her legs and over her cast, finally dropping them to the floor.

Deirdre experienced a resurgence of anxiety when he sat back and looked at her, but his gaze was filled with such reverence that those fears receded once again. The hand he skimmed up her leg was worshipful, and when he reached the nest of pale hair at the juncture of her thighs, he touched her with care that bordered on awe.

She felt totally exposed, yet treasured. Looking at Neil, seeing the way his large frame quivered with restrained desire, she marveled that fate had brought him to her.

"Neil...please..." she begged in a shaky whisper. "I want you."

He needed no more urging. Sitting back, he unsnapped his jeans and thrust them down his legs along with his briefs. Within seconds he was sliding over her, finding a place for himself between her thighs, threading his fingers through hers and anchoring them by her shoulders.

Bearing his weight on his elbows, he rubbed his hot body back and forth over hers. He made no attempt to penetrate her, simply sought the pleasure of his new level of touching. But the pleasure was galvanic, causing them both to breathe quickly and unevenly.

Deirdre had never before known such anticipation. She wasn't thinking about her fears, wasn't thinking about what would happen if Neil didn't find her lovemaking adequate. She was only thinking of the burning deep within her, knowing that she needed his possession now.

Eyes closed, she arched upward, hips straining toward his in a silent plea that dashed the last of his resistance. Nudging her legs farther apart, he positioned himself, then tightened his fingers around hers.

"Look at me, Deirdre," he whispered. "Look at me, babe."

Her eyes opened, then grew wider when, ever so slowly, he entered her. She felt him clearly, sliding deeper and deeper; it was as though each individual cell inside her responded to his presence, transmitting one heady message after another to her brain. By the time he filled her completely, she knew that she'd never, never be the same again.

Neil closed his eyes and let out a long and tremulous sigh. Satisfaction was so clearly etched on his features that Deirdre would have breathed a sigh of relief, too, had she been able to. But he'd begun to move inside her, and breathing became increasingly difficult. All she could do was to give herself up to the spiral of passion he created.

The heat built steadily. Neil set a pace that maximized her pleasure, knowing precisely when to slow, precisely when to speed up. She moved to his rhythm, following his lead with a flair of her own that drove him on and up.

Then, when the fire within her became too hot for containment, she arched her back a final time, caught a sudden deep breath and dissolved into a seemingly endless series of spasms. Somewhere in the middle, Neil joined her, holding himself at the very entrance of her womb while his body pulsed and quivered.

It was a long time before either of them could speak, a long time during which the only sounds in the room were the harsh gasping for air and the softer, more gentle patter of the rain. Only when they'd begun to breath more normally did Neil slide to the side, but he brought her with him, settling them face to face on the pillow.

"Well," he asked softly, "what do you think?"

For an instant, Deirdre's old fears crowded in on her. "What do *you* think?" she whispered.

"I think," he said slowly, reining in a smug smile, "that for a lady with a sharp tongue and a questionable disposition, you're one hell of a lover."

CHAPTER SEVEN

RELIEF WASHED OVER HER, this time thoroughly wiping away whatever lingering doubts she'd had. A smile lit her face, unwaveringly, even as she raised her voice in mock protest.

"Sharp tongue? Questionable disposition? It was all because of you, Neil Hersey. You were the one who wasn't supposed to be here!"

Neil was undaunted. His own euphoria was too great. "And if I hadn't been," he ventured naughtily, "just think of all we'd have missed."

Deirdre had no suitable answer for that, so she simply continued to smile, and he was content to bask in her sunshine. After a time, he tenderly brushed a damp wisp of hair from her cheek.

"You're looking happy."

"I am…happy…satisfied…relieved."

"Was it that awful—the thought of our making love?" he chided.

"Oh, no, Neil," she answered quickly. "It was exciting. But you knew I was frightened."

"I'm still not sure why. It couldn't have been the athletic thing alone. Did it have something to do with the fellow who burned you once?"

She thought about that. "Indirectly, I suppose." Her gaze dropped. "Things were okay between us…sexually. It's just that when he got the urge to leave, he up and left, like there really wasn't anything worth sticking around for. On a subconscious level, I may have taken it more personally than I should have." She lapsed into silence as she considered why that had been. Her fingers moved lightly over the hair on Neil's chest in a reminder of what had just passed between them, and it gave her the courage to go on.

"I think it relates more to my family than Seth. I've always been the black sheep, the one who didn't fit in. My mother is the epitome of good manners, good looks and feminine poise. My sister takes after her. I've always been different, and they've made no secret of their opinion of me."

He cupped her throat in the vee of his hand, while his thumb drew circles on her collarbone. "They don't think you're feminine enough?"

"No."

His laugh was a cocky one. "Shows how much they know."

She rewarded him with a shy smile. "You're talking sex, which is only one part of it, but you're good for my ego, anyway."

"And you're good for mine. I don't think I've ever had a woman want me as much as you did just now. I know damn well that sex was the last thing on your mind when you got here, and that makes your desire so precious. I'd like to think it wasn't just any man who could turn you on like that."

"It wasn't!" she exclaimed, then lowered her voice. "There's only been one man, and that was Seth. I'm not very experienced."

"Experienced women are a dime a dozen. You're worth far more."

"I've never been driven by sexual need. I've never seen myself as a sexual being."

"We're all sexual beings."

"To one degree or another, but those degrees can vary widely." She moved her thigh between his, finding pleasure in the textural contrast of their bodies. "I guess what I'm saying is that I've always assumed myself to be at the lower end of the scale."

"Do you still?" he asked softly.

The look she gave him was every bit as soft. "With you? No."

He ran his hand down her spine, covered her bottom and pressed her hips intimately close. "That's good," he said, and sucked in a loud breath. "Because I think I'm needing you again."

Deirdre couldn't have been more delighted. Not only was he proving once again that her fears had been unfounded, but he was mirroring the state of her own reawakening desire. She followed the progress of her hand as it inched its way down his chest. "I think the needing is mutual."

"Any regrets?" he asked thickly.

"Only that I can't wrap both legs around you."

"It is a challenge with your cast. I didn't hurt you before, did I?"

She was fascinated by the whorl of hair around his navel. "Did I sound like I was in pain?" she asked distractedly.

"Dire pain."

"It had nothing to do with my leg." Her hand crept lower, tangling in the dark curls above his sex.

"Deirdre?" He was having trouble breathing again.

She was too engrossed in her exploration to take pity on him. "You have a beautiful body," she whispered. Her fingers grazed his tumescence. "I didn't have time to touch you before."

"Oh, God," he breathed when she took him fully into her grasp. His hand tightened on her shoulder, and he pressed his lips to her forehead. "Oh…"

"Do you like that?" she asked, cautiously stroking him.

"Oh, yes…harder…you can do it harder." His body was straining for her touch; when she strengthened it, he gave a moan of ecstasy. "Almost heaven—that's what it is."

"Almost?"

He opened his eyes and gazed at her then. "True heaven is when I'm inside." Inserting his leg between hers, he brought her thigh even higher. "You're hot and moist and tight, so tight. The way I slip in—" he put action to words "—shows how perfectly you…ummmmmm…how perfectly you were made…for me."

It was Deirdre's turn to gasp, then moan. He was lodged deeply within her, while his hand was caressing the rest of her with consummate expertise. When he withdrew, then surged back, she thought she'd explode.

The explosion wasn't long in coming. His mouth covered hers and he filled her with his tongue, as his manhood already filled her. One bold thrust echoed the other in a rhythm that repeated itself until all rhythm was suspended in a climactic surge.

This time when they tumbled back from that pyrotechnic plane, they had neither the strength nor the need to talk. Fitting Deirdre snugly into the curve of his body, Neil held her until her breathing was long and even. Soon after, he, too, was asleep.

THE NEXT DAY was the most glorious one Deirdre had ever known. She awoke in Neil's arms with a smile on her face, and if the smile ever faded, it was never for long. He instructed her to stay in bed while he showered, then he returned and carried her in for a bath. By the time he'd washed her to his satisfaction, they were both in need of satisfaction of another sort. So he carried her back to bed, where he proceeded to adore every bare inch of her body.

He taught her things about herself she'd never known, banishing any modesty she might have had and reaping the benefits. With deft fingers, an agile tongue and pulsing sex, he brought her to climax after climax, until she pleaded for mercy.

"A sex fiend!" she cried. "I'm stranded on an island with a sex fiend!"

"Look who's talking!" was all he had to say. Not only had she been as hungry as he, but she'd taken every one of the liberties with his body that he had with hers.

They didn't bother to get dressed that day. It seemed a waste of time and effort. The weather was as ominous as the thought of putting clothing between them. When they left the bedroom, they shared Deirdre's pajamas—the top was hers, the bottom his. He teased her, claiming that she'd brought along men's pajamas with precisely that goal in mind, but he wasn't about to complain when he knew all he had to do—whether in the kitchen, the living room or the den—was to raise her top, lower his bottom, and enter her with a fluid thrust.

Deirdre let his presence fill her, both body and mind. She knew they were living a dream, that reality lurked just beyond, waiting to pounce. But she refused to be distracted by other, more somber thoughts when she was feeling so complete. Neil accepted her. He'd seen her at her worst, yet he accepted her. His attraction to her wasn't based on who she was, what she did for a living, or what she wore; he liked her as the person she was.

Neil was similarly content. The realization that he was avoiding reality did nothing to temper his feelings about Deirdre. He refused to dwell on the fact that she didn't know about the downturn his life in Hartford had taken, because it didn't seem to matter. She was happy; he'd made her happy. She didn't care about his financial prospects or his reputation. She was satisfied to accept him as he was.

And so they didn't think about the future. One day melded into the next, each filled with relaxation, leisure activity, lovemaking. Deirdre finished one book and started a second. She got the hang of knitting well enough to begin work on the actual sweater, and made commendable headway on it. She exercised each day but made no attempt to devise new routines, loath to do something that might start her brooding on whether she'd be able to teach again.

Neil did his share of reading. He continued to take responsibility for most of the household chores, and it was his pleasure to do so. From time to time Deirdre tried to help, but he saw the frustration she suffered with her cast, and it was enough to tell him that he wasn't being used.

The bickering they'd done during those first three days was, for all intents and purposes, over. This was not to say that they agreed on everything, but compromise became the mode. Neil accepted the loud beat of Deirdre's music, while she accepted the drone of his radio-transmitted Celtics games. She subjected herself to a clobbering at Trivial Pursuit, while he endured the gyrations in *Saturday Night Fever*.

One night, when he was feeling particularly buoyant, he took a Havana cigar from his bag, lit it and sat back on the sofa in bliss. Deirdre, who'd watched in horror his elaborate ceremony of nipping off the end of the cigar, then moistening the tip, simply sat with one finger unobtrusively blocking her nose. It was an example of how far they'd come; as disgusting as she found the smell, she wasn't about to dampen his obvious pleasure.

He'd been smoking for several minutes before he cast her a glance and saw her pose. "Uh-oh. Bad?"

She shrugged. "Are't dose tings illegal in dis country?" she asked, careful to breathe through her mouth.

"It's illegal to import them. But if a foreigner brings them in for his own personal use and shares them with his friends, it's okay."

"Is dat how you got it?"

"I have a client from Jordan who has business interests here. He gave me a box several months ago." Neil eyed the long cigar with reverence. "I'm not usually a smoker, but I have to admit that if you want to smoke a cigar, this is the way to go."

"Da Mercedes of cigars?"

"Yup." Eyes slitted in pleasure, he put the cigar to his mouth, drew on it, then blew out a narrow stream of thick smoke. "Should I put it out?"

"Dot on my accou't. But do't ask me to kiss you later, commie breath."

His lips quirked at the corners. Leaning forward, he carefully placed the cigar in an ashtray, then stood and advanced on her.

She held up a hand. "Do't come closer. I dow what you're goi'g to do."

He propped his hands on the arm of her chair and bent so that his face was inches from hers. He was grinning. "I'll kiss you if I want to, and you'll like it, commie breath and all."

"Deil, I'm warding you—"

Her warning was cut short by his mouth, which took hers in a way that was at once familiar and new. After the initial capture, his lips softened and grew persuasive, coaxing hers into a response she was helpless to withhold.

When at last he ended the kiss, he murmured softly, "You can breathe now."

Deirdre's eyes were closed, and the hand that had protected her nose had long since abandoned that post and moved from the rich texture of his beard up into his thick, brown hair. "How can I do that...when you take my breath away...." When she pulled him back to her, he was more than willing to accede to her demands.

As time passed the cigar burned itself out, but neither of them noticed.

EARLY IN THE MORNING of their one-week anniversary on the island, Thomas called them from shore. Neil was the one to talk to him, but Deirdre, standing by, heard every word.

"How're you folks making out?"

Neil grinned, but made sure his voice was suitably sober. "Okay."

"I got your messages, but I've been away most of the week. I figured that you'd keep trying if there was any kind of emergency."

"He feels guilty," Deirdre whispered mischievously. "Serves him right."

Neil collared her with a playful arm as he spoke grimly back into the receiver. "We'll live."

"Deirdre's doing all right with that leg of hers?"

Neil hesitated before answering. Meanwhile, he toyed gently with Deirdre's earlobe. "The house has taken a beating. She's not very good with her crutches."

Deirdre kicked at his shin with her cast. He side-stepped her deftly.

"Oh," Thomas said. "Well, that's Victoria's problem. Are you two getting along?"

"Getting along?" Deirdre whispered. She slid her hand over Neil's ribs and tucked her fingers in the waistband of his jeans.

Neil cleared his throat and pulled a straight face. "We're still alive."

"You'll drive him crazy," she whispered. "He's dying of curiosity."

"Let him die," Neil whispered back, eyes dancing.

During the brief interlude, Thomas had apparently decided that what was happening between Neil and Deirdre was Victoria's problem, too. "Well," came his staticky voice, "I just wanted to let you know that you've got a store of fresh supplies on the dock."

"On the dock?" Neil looked at his watch. It was barely nine. "You must have been up before dawn."

"I left them last night."

"Coward."

"What's that?" came the static. "I didn't get that last word?"

Deirdre snickered noisily. Neil clamped a hand on her mouth. "I said, thank you," he yelled more loudly than necessary into the handset.

"Oh. Okay. I'll be out next week to pick you up, then. If there's any change in plans, give me a call."

For the first time, Neil's hesitation was legitimate. Looking down, he saw that Deirdre's too, was suddenly more serious. His fingers grew tighter on the handset.

"Will do" was all he said before switching off the instrument and replacing it on its stand. He stood silent for a minute with his arm still around Deirdre. Then, with a squeeze of her shoulder, he took a fast breath. "Hey, do you see what I see?"

She was ready for a diversion. Any diversion. Thomas's last comment had been a depressant. "I don't know. What do you see?"

He raised his eyes to the window. "The sun. Well, maybe not the sun itself, but it's brighter out there than it's been in a week, and it hasn't rained since yesterday, which means that the paths will have begun to dry out, which means that I can get the things in from the dock pretty quick, which means—" he gave her shoulder another squeeze "—that we can take a walk."

Deirdre followed his gaze, then looked back up at him. "I'd like that," she said softly. "I'd like it a lot."

THE BREAK IN THE WEATHER offered new realms of adventure for them. As though determined to restake its claim after a long absence, the sun grew stronger from one day to the next. The air remained cool, and Deirdre's mobility was limited by her crutches, but she and Neil managed to explore most of the small island. When they weren't wandering in one direction or another, they were perched atop high boulders overlooking the sea. They watched the sun rise one morning, watched the sun set one evening, and in between they agreed that neither of them had ever visited as serene a place.

Unfortunately, with greater frequency as the days passed, their serenity was disturbed by the memory of Thomas's parting words. He'd be by to pick them up at the end of a week, and that week seemed far too short. Deirdre began to brood more and more about Providence, Neil about Hartford, and though the making up was always breathtaking, they began to bicker again.

Finally, three days before they were to leave, things came to a head. They'd finished dinner and were seated side by side in the den, ostensibly watching *Raiders of the Lost Ark*, but in truth paying it little heed. With an abruptness that mirrored his mood, Neil switched off the set.

Deirdre shot him a scowl. She'd been thinking about leaving the island, and the prospect left her cold. "What did you do that for?"

"You're picking your fingernail again. The sound drives me

crazy!'' What really drove him crazy was the thought of returning to Hartford, but Deirdre's nail picking was as good a scapegoat as any.

''But I wanted to watch the movie.''

''How can you watch the movie when you're totally engrossed in your nail?''

''Maybe if you weren't rubbing that damned beard of yours, I'd be able to concentrate.''

His eyes darkened. ''You haven't complained about my beard for days.'' In fact, she'd complimented him on it. It was filling in well, she'd said, and looked good. He'd agreed with her assessment. ''And maybe I'm rubbing it to drown out the sound of your picking! Why do you *do* that?''

''It's a nervous habit, Neil. I can't help it.''

''So why are you nervous? I thought you were supposed to be calm and relaxed.''

''I am!'' she cried, then, hearing herself, dropped both her gaze and her voice. ''I'm not.''

Silence hung in the air between them. When Deirdre looked up at last, she found Neil studying her with a pained expression on his face.

''We have to talk,'' he said quietly.

''I know.''

''Thomas will be here soon.''

''I know.''

''You'll go back to Providence. I'll go back to Hartford.''

''I *know*.''

''So what are we going to do about it?''

She shrugged, then slanted him a pleading glance. ''Tell him we're staying for another week?'' Even more frightening to her than the prospect of returning to Providence was the prospect of leaving Neil.

He snorted and pushed himself from the sofa, pacing to the far side of the room before turning on his heel. ''I can't do that, Deirdre. Much as I wish it, I can't.''

''Then what do you suggest?''

He stood with one hand on his hip, the other rubbing the back of his neck. His gaze was unfocused, alternately shifting from the wall to the floor and back. "I don't know, damn it. I've been trying to think of solutions—No, that's wrong. I've avoided thinking about going back since I arrived, and as a result, I have no solutions. Then there's *this* complication."

Deirdre didn't like the sound of his voice. "What complication?"

He looked her in the eye. "Us."

It was like a blow to her stomach. Though she knew he was right, she couldn't bear to think of what they'd shared in negative terms. "Look," she argued, holding up a hand in immediate self-defense. "*We* don't have to be a complication. You can go your way, I can go mine. *Fini.*"

"Is that how you want it?"

"No."

"How do you want it?"

"I don't know," she cried in frustration. "You're not the only one who's avoided thinking about going back. I haven't found any more solutions than you have."

"But we do agree that we want to keep on seeing each other."

"Yes!"

His shoulders sagged in defeat. "Then it is a complication, Deirdre. On top of everything else, what we have is very definitely a complication." He turned to stare out the window.

Deirdre, in turn, stared at him. "Okay, Neil," she began softly. "You're right. We have to talk. About everything." When he didn't move, she continued. "When we first came here, you were as bad-tempered as I was. I know my reasons, but I've never really known yours. At first I didn't want to know, because I have enough problems of my own. Then, when things got...better between us, I didn't want to ask for fear of upsetting the apple cart." She was sitting forward on the couch, a hand spread palm down on each thigh. "But I'm asking now. If we're going to figure anything out, I have to know. What happened, Neil? What happened in Hartford that brought you up here in such a temper? Why did you need to escape?"

Neil dropped his chin to his chest, her questions echoing in his brain. The moment of truth had come. He gnawed on the inside of his cheek, as though even doing something so pointless would be an excuse for not answering. But it wasn't. Deirdre was curious, and intelligent. As much as he wished he didn't have to tell her, she more than anyone deserved to know.

He turned to face her but made no move to close the distance between them. "I have," he said with a resigned sigh, "a major problem back home. It involves one of my principal clients—strike that, one of my prinicipal *ex*-clients, a very large corporation based in Hartford." He hesitated.

"Go on," she urged softly. "I'm with you."

"I've been chief counsel for the corporation for three years, and during that time I've come to be increasingly familiar with various aspects of the business. Last summer, quite inadvertently, I stumbled onto a corruption scheme involving the president of the corporation."

Deirdre held her breath and watched him with growing apprehension. She refused to believe that he'd knowingly condone corruption, yet, as corporate counsel, his job was to side with his client.

"No," he said, reading her fear, "I didn't demand a cut—"

"I never thought you would! But you must have been put in an awful position."

He was relieved by her obvious sincerity, but in some ways that made his task all the more difficult. He would have liked to be able to tell her that his practice was successful and growing even more so. He would have liked to have shone in her eyes. But the facts were against him.

Deirdre didn't deserve this. Hell, *he* didn't deserve it!

"Awful is putting it mildly," he declared. "I could have chosen to look the other way, but it went against every principle I'd ever held. So I took the matter before the board of directors. That was when things fell apart."

"What do you mean?"

"They were involved! All of them! They knew exactly what was going on, and their only regret was that I'd found out!"

Deirdre felt her anger rising on his behalf. "What did you do?"

"I resigned. I had no other choice. There was no way I'd sit back and watch them pad their own pockets at the expense of not only their stockholders but their employees. Their employees! The last people who could afford to be gypped!"

"But I don't understand, Neil. If you resigned, isn't it all over? You may have lost one client, but you have others, don't you?"

"Oh, yes," he ground out with more than a little sarcasm. "But those others have dwindled with a suddenness that can't possibly be coincidental." His jaw was tight. "It seems that Wittnauer-Douglass wasn't satisfied simply with my resignation. The executive board wanted to make sure I wouldn't do anything to rock a very lucrative boat."

She was appalled. "They blackballed you."

"Worse. They passed word around that I'd been the mastermind behind the corruption scheme. According to the chairman of the board—and I got this from a reliable source—if I hadn't left, they'd have leveled charges against me."

"But they can't say that!"

"They can say anything they damn well please!"

"Then they can't *do* it!"

"I'm not so sure. There's a helluva lot of murky paperwork in the archives of any large corporation. That paperwork can be easily doctored if the right people give the go-ahead."

"But why would the board at Wittnauer-Douglass want to even mention corruption? Wouldn't it spoil their own scheme?"

"Not by a long shot. They simply reorganize, shift outlets, juggle a few more documents. When you've got power, you've got power. It's as simple as that."

"And you can't fight them." It was a statement, a straight follow-up to Neil's. Unfortunately it touched a nerve in him that was all too raw.

"What in the hell can I do?" he exploded, every muscle in his body rigid. "They've spread word so far and so fast that it's become virtually impossible for me to practice law in Hartford! The major corporations won't touch me. The medium-sized ones are leery. And it's gone way beyond my profession. Nancy—the woman I was seeing—quickly opted out, which was okay, because it was only a matter of time before we'd have split, anyway. But before I knew what had happened, I'd been replaced as chairman of the hospital fund-raising drive. That did hurt. Word is that I'm a crook, and even if some people believe in my innocence, there are still appearances to uphold. Hell, I can't even find a squash partner these days. I've become a regular pariah!''

"They can't do that!''

"They've done it," he lashed back. His anger was compounding itself, taking on even greater force than it had held in Hartford, mainly because he detested having to dump this on Deirdre. "I've worked my tail off to build a successful practice, and they've swept it away without a care in the world. And do you know what the worst part is?'' He was livid now, furious with himself. "I didn't see it coming! I was naive...stupid!''

Deirdre was on her feet, limping toward him. "It wasn't your fault—''

He interrupted, barely hearing her argument over the internal din of his self-reproach. "How could I have possibly spent so much time working with those people and not have seen them for what they are? I'm too trusting! I've always been too trusting! Good guys finish last, isn't that what they say? Well, it's true!''

She took his arm. "But trusting is a good way to be, Neil,'' she argued with quiet force. "The alternative is to be an eternal skeptic, or worse, paranoid, and you couldn't live that way.''

"My friends. They even got to my *friends*.''

"A real friend wouldn't be gotten to.''

"Then I've been a poor judge of character on that score, too.''

"You're being too harsh on yourself—''

"And it's about time! Someone should have kicked me in the pants years ago. Maybe if they had, I wouldn't have been such a damned optimist. Maybe I would have seen all this coming. Maybe I wouldn't be in such a completely untenable position now.''

"You can find new clients,'' she ventured cautiously.

"Not the kind I want. My expertise is in dealing with large corporations, and those won't come near me now.''

"Maybe not in Hartford—''

"Which means relocating. Damn it, I don't want to relocate. At least, not for that reason.''

"But things aren't hopeless, Neil. You have a profession that you're skilled in—''

"And look where it's gotten me,'' he seethed. "I have a great office, two capable associates and a steadily diminishing clientele.

I have a condominium, which the people I once called friends won't deign to visit. I have a record for charity work that's come to a dead halt. I have squash gear and no partner.''

Deirdre dropped her hand from his stiff arm. ''You also think you have a monopoly on self-pity. Well, you don't, Neil. You're not the only one who has problems. You're not the only one who's frustrated.''

''Frustrated?'' He raked rigid fingers through his hair. ''Now *that's* the understatement of the year. And while we're at it, you can add guilt to the list of my transgressions. I came up here and took every one of those frustrations out on you!''

''But you weren't the only one to do it! I used you for that too, Neil, so I'm as guilty as you are.''

''Yeah.'' His voice was calm now. ''Only difference is that your problem has a solution in sight. Once the cast is off—''

''It's not only my leg,'' Deirdre snapped, turning away from him. ''I wouldn't have been in such a lousy mood if it was simply a question of my leg. There's a whole other story to my life, and if you think that in its own way my situation isn't as frustrating as yours, you can add egotistical to that list you're drawing up.''

There was silence behind her. For the first time since he'd begun his tirade, Neil's thoughts took a tangent. *A whole other story to my life,* she'd said. He was suddenly more nervous than he'd been angry moments before, inexplicably fearful that his world was about to collapse completely.

''What is it—that other story?''

Head down, she hobbled over to rest her hip against the desk. A dry laugh slipped from her throat. ''It's ironic. There you are, without a corporation to represent. Here I am, with a corporation I don't want.''

''What are you talking about?''

Slowly she raised her head. Almost reluctantly she replied, ''Joyce Enterprises. Have you ever heard of it?''

''I've heard of it. It's based in...'' The light dawned. ''Providence. You're that Joyce? It's yours?''

''Actually, my family's. My father died six months ago, and my sister took over the helm.''

Neil frowned. "I didn't make the connection...I never...it doesn't fit."

"With who I am?" She smiled sadly. "You're right. It doesn't fit. I don't fit, and that's the problem. My parents always intended that the business stay in the family. Sandra—my sister—just can't handle it. I have two uncles who are involved, but they're as ill-equipped to run things as my mother is."

Neil had come to stand before her. "So they want you in."

"Right."

"But you don't want in."

"Right again. I tried it once and hated it. I'm just not the type to dress up all day and entertain, which is largely what the head of a business like that has to do. I don't take to diplomatic small talk, and I don't take to being a pretty little thing on display."

"That I can believe," he quipped.

Deirdre responded to his teasing with a scowl. "I wish my family could believe it, but they won't. They keep insisting that I'm their only hope, and maybe I would be able to handle the management end of the business, but the political end would drive me up a tree! For six months now they've been after me, and while I was busy doing my own thing I had an excuse. At least, it was one I could grasp at. I've always known that sooner or later, as I got older, I'd slow down, but I thought I had time to find a substitute. Now I don't. Suddenly I can't do my own thing, and they've started hounding me to do theirs. Even before I left the hospital they were on me." She paused for a breath, then continued.

"They think I'm selfish, and maybe I am, because I want to be happy, and I know I won't be if I'm forced to be involved in the business. It's really a joke—their pushing me this way. I've always been odd in their minds. I'm a failure. They look down their noses at the work I do. And even beyond that, I don't have a husband, or children, which compounds my sin. What good am I? Nothing I do is right, so they say. Yet they stand over me and insist that I help run Joyce." She rubbed a throbbing spot on her forehead, then looked up at Neil.

"The family needs me. The business needs me. Can I stand by and let it all go down the tubes? Because it will, Neil. I keep telling them to bring in outside help, but they refuse, and if they continue to do that, the whole thing is doomed. Oh, it may take a while. The corporation is like a huge piece of machinery. It's showing signs of wear and tear right now, but the gears are still turning. When it comes time to oil them, though, and there's no one capable of doing the job, things will slow down, then eventually grind to a halt.''

She gave a quick, little headshake, more of a shiver. ''Talk of guilt, I've got it in spades. I have a *responsibility*, my mother keeps reminding me. And that's the worst part, because as much as I can't bear the thought of having anything to do with the business, I do feel the responsibility. I deny it to them. I've denied it to myself. But it's there.'' She looked down at her fingers and repeated more softly, ''It's there.''

Neil wrapped his hand around her neck and kneaded it gently. ''We're a fine twosome, you and I. Between us, we've got a pack of ills and no medicine.''

She gave a meek laugh. ''Maybe the island drugstore has something?''

He sighed. ''The island drugstore filled the prescription for two souls who needed a break, but I'm afraid it doesn't have anything for curing the ills back home.''

''So,'' she breathed, discouraged. ''We're back where we started. What are we going to do?''

He looked at her intently, then dipped his head and took her lips with a sweetness that wrenched at her heart. ''We are going to spend the next three days enjoying each other. That is, if you don't mind dallying with a man who has a very dubious future…''

It was at that moment, with Neil standing close, looking at her as though her answer were more important to him than anything else in the world, that Deirdre knew she loved him.

She smiled softly. ''If you don't mind dallying with a woman who would rather spend the rest of her life on this island than go back to the mainland and face up to her responsibilities…''

His answer was a broad smile and another kiss, this one deeper and more soul reaching than anything that had come before. It was followed by a third, then a fourth, and before long, neither Neil nor Deirdre could think of the future.

THEIR FINAL DAYS on the island were spent much as the preceding ones had been, though now there was direction to their thoughts, rather than a random moodiness. For his part, Neil was relieved to have told Deirdre everything, even if the telling hadn't solved a thing. She'd accepted his quandary without criticism, and her affection—yes, he was sure it was that—for him seemed, if anything, to have deepened.

For her part, Deirdre was relieved to have shared her burden with an understanding soul. Neil hadn't jumped on her for her failings; if anything, his affection—yes she was sure it was that—for her seemed stronger than ever.

If that affection took on a frantic quality at times, each attributed it to the fact that the clock was running out.

Thomas had arranged to pick them up at eight o'clock in the morning on that last day. So the night before they found themselves cleaning the house, making sure that everything was as it had been when they'd arrived two weeks before. Tension suddenly surrounded them, reducing them to nearly the same testy state they'd been in when they'd arrived.

Neil did a final round of laundry, inadvertently tossing Deirdre's teal green sweatshirt into the wash with the towels, half of which were an electric blue not far different from her sweatshirt, half of which were pure white. When the white towels emerged with a distinct green tinge, he swore loudly.

"Goddamn it! I thought you'd packed this thing already!"

"I haven't packed anything yet." She'd been putting that particular chore off for as long as possible. Now, studying the once-white towels, she scowled. "Didn't you see the sweatshirt when you put the towels in?"

"How could I see it in with these blue ones?"

"The sweatshirt's green!"

"That's close enough."

"You must be color-blind."

"I am not color-blind."

They were glaring at each other over the washing machine. Deirdre was the first to look away. "Okay," she said, sighing. "We can put the white towels through again, this time with bleach."

"The little tag says not to use bleach."

Fiery eyes met his. "I've used bleach on towels before, and it does the trick. If you don't want to take the risk, you find a solution." Turning, she swung back to her cleaning of the refrigerator, leaving Neil to grudgingly add bleach to a second load.

Not long after, intent on doing the packing she'd put off, Deirdre was headed for the bedroom, when her crutch caught on the edge of the area rug in the living room. She stumbled and fell, crying out in annoyance as well as surprise.

"Who put that stupid rug there?" she screamed.

Neil was quickly by her side, his voice tense. "That 'stupid' rug has been in exactly the same spot since we got here. Weren't you watching where you were going?"

"It's the damned rubber tips on these crutches!" She kicked at them with her good foot. "They catch on everything!"

Rescuing the crutches, he put an arm across her back and helped her up. "They haven't bothered you before. Are you okay?"

"I'm fine," she snarled, rubbing her hip.

"Then you're lucky. Damn it, Deirdre, are you trying to kill yourself? Why don't you watch where you're going next time?"

"Watch where I'm going? I was watching!"

"Then you were going too fast!"

"I wasn't going any faster than I ever go!"

"Which is too fast!"

Deirdre, who had returned the crutches to their rightful place, backed away from him, incensed. "I don't need advice from you! I've taken care of myself for years, and I'll do it again! Just because you've helped me out this week doesn't give you the right to order me around. If you really wanted to help me, you'd offer to take that damned corporation off my back!"

"If you really wanted to help *me*, you'd *give* me the damned corporation!" he roared back.

For long minutes they stood glaring at each other. Both pairs of eyes flashed; both pairs of nostrils flared. Gradually both chests stopped heaving, and their anger dissipated.

"It's yours," Deirdre said quietly, her eyes glued to his.

"I'll take it," he countered, but his voice, too, was quiet.

"It's a bizarre idea."

"Totally off the wall."

"But it could offer an out for both of us."

"That's right."

They stood where they were for another long minute. Then, resting a hand lightly on her back, Neil urged her toward the sofa. When they were both seated, he crossed one leg over his knee, propped his elbow on the arm of the sofa and chafed his lower lip with his thumb.

"I've done a lot of thinking since we talked the other night," he began, hesitating at first, then gaining momentum. "I've been over and over the problem, trying to decide what I want to do. There are times when I get angry, when the only thing that makes any sense to me is revenge. Then the anger fades, and I realize how absurd that is. It's also self-defeating, when what I really want to do is to practice law." He paused, lowered his hand to his lap and looked at her. "You have a corporation that you don't want. I could make good use of it."

Nervously she searched his features. "For revenge?"

"No. Maybe it'd be a sort of reprisal, but that wouldn't be my main objective. I need something, Deirdre. It kills me to have to say that, especially to you. It's hard for a man—for anyone, I suppose—to admit that he's short on options. But I'm trying to face facts, and the sole fact in this case is that Hartford is no longer a viable place for me to work."

"You said you didn't want to relocate."

"I said I didn't want to relocate because of Wittnauer-Douglass. Maybe it's convoluted logic, but I'm beginning to think that Joyce Enterprises would have attracted me regardless of the problems in Hartford. No matter what you see happening now within the company, Joyce has a solid reputation. I wouldn't be afraid to put my stock in it. And it may be the highest form of conceit, but I do think that I have something to offer. I'm a good lawyer. I'm intimately familiar with the workings of large corporations. I may not be an entrepreneur, but I know people who are. And I know of a headhunter who could help me find the best ones to work with.

"Unfortunately—" he took a breath and his eyes widened as he broached the next problem "—that would mean bringing in an outsider. From what you say, your family has been against that from the start, which raises the even more immediate issue of whether or not they'd even accept me.''

Deirdre tipped up her chin in a gesture of defiance. "I hold an equal amount of stock to my mother and sister. If you were to enter the corporation alongside me, they wouldn't dare fight."

"But you don't want to enter the corporation. Wasn't that the point?"

"Yes, but if we were..." She faltered, struggling to find the least presumptive words. "If we were together.... I mean, if I made it clear that we were...involved..."

"That we were a steady couple, as in lovers?"

"Yes."

He gave his head a quick shake. "Not good enough. It'll have to be marriage."

"Marriage?" She'd wanted to think that they'd be tied somehow, but marriage was the ultimate in ties. "Isn't that a little radical?"

Neil shrugged, but nonchalance was the last thing he felt. He'd been searching for a way to bind Deirdre to him. He loved her. Somewhere along the line that realization had dawned, and it had fit him so comfortably that he hadn't thought of questioning it. He couldn't say the words yet; he felt too vulnerable. Marriage might be sudden, but it served his purposes well. "Radical only in that we've known each other for such a short time. We get along, don't we?"

"We fight constantly!" she argued, playing the devil's advocate. If she knew that Neil loved her she wouldn't have had an argument in the world. But he hadn't said those words, and she didn't have the courage to lay herself bare by saying them herself, so she felt obligated to resist.

"Not constantly. Only when we're frustrated by problems that seem beyond our control. We've had our smooth times, haven't we?"

"Yes," she admitted, albeit reluctantly.

"And if this whole plan solves our problems, we won't have cause to fight, will we?"

"Every married couple fights."

"Then we wouldn't be any different. Look at it objectively, Deir-

dre. We have similar values and interests. We've already proved
that we can live with each other. If we survived these past two
weeks, being together twenty-four hours a day, we've got one foot
up on many other couples who marry.''

She didn't want to look at it objectively. Love wasn't objective.
''But we've known each other in such a limited sphere. This isn't
the real world. It's possible that we could return to Providence and
find that we *hate* each other.''

''That's your insecurity talking.''

''Okay, maybe it is. I don't think I'm cut out to be a corporate
wife any more than I'm cut out to head that corporation.'' She
waved a hand back and forth. ''I'm not the prissy little hostess. I'm
not the adorable little lady who always wears and says the right
things.''

''I'm not complaining about who you are. And I wouldn't ask
you to do anything you're uncomfortable with. If we entertain—
and I assume there'd be some of that—you'd look as beautiful as
any woman in the room. And rather than having you cook we could
take people out or have something catered.''

''In my modest town house?'' she squeaked.

''In the house I'd buy for us.'' He sat forward, determination
strong in the gaze he sent her. ''I'm not a gigolo, Deirdre. I
wouldn't go into this if I felt I was getting a free ride. You may
not know it yet, but I do have my pride. If we agree to go ahead
with this scheme, I'll work my tail off in the business. I'll be the
one to support us, and that means providing the kind of home for
you that I think you deserve. I guess I'm old-fashioned in that
way.''

''Does that mean I can't work or do whatever else I want?''

''You can do anything you want. I'm not *that* old-fashioned. And
if you think I'm bothered by the thought of your teaching aerobics,
think again. I adore your athletic body. Don't you know that by
now?''

She simply slanted him a wry glance.

''Exercise is the way to go nowadays,'' he continued. ''I'll be
proud to have a wife who keeps her body toned.''

''If I can,'' she muttered. ''Whether I teach or not is still a big
question.''

"You'll teach. I told you that. When the cast comes off, you'll have physical therapy or whatever else it takes to get that leg working right."

"But...even if that happens, many of my classes are evening ones. How will you feel when you come home to an empty house after a hard day's work and there isn't even a hot meal ready?"

"I can cook. You know that. I'll be proud of you, Deirdre. My wife will be doing something that's constructive, something she enjoys." He paused for a breath, sobering. "And while we're talking of pride, if you agree to marry me, I'll insist on a prenuptial agreement."

Deirdre couldn't conceal a quick flare of hurt. "I don't want your money!"

"You've got it backside-to. It's you I want to protect. If you agree to marry me, I'll draw up a paper stating that your holdings in Joyce Enterprises—and anything else you now have to your name—will remain solely yours. If you should decide, at any point, that you want out of the marriage, you'll have everything you had when you entered into it. And if, at any point, you decide that I'm a detriment to Joyce Enterprises, you'll have the full right to can me."

She couldn't imagine that ever happening. For that matter, she couldn't imagine ever wanting out of a marriage to Neil. Unless he wanted it. "But what about your interests? They won't be protected if you sign a document like that. You thought you'd been naive regarding Wittnauer-Douglass. Isn't your plan now equally shortsighted?"

"I'd rather think of it as a challenge, one I'm approaching with my eyes wide open. I think I can make a go of running Joyce Enterprises, and if I do that, you won't have any cause to let me go. Like I said before, I'm not looking for a handout. I'm prepared to do the job. Yes, you'd be doing me a favor by giving me the chance, but I'd be doing you every bit as big a favor by relieving you of a responsibility you don't want."

He took her hand and studied the shape of her slender fingers. "You'd have a husband, which would please your family. And don't you think it's about time, anyway? I know it is for me. I'm not getting any younger. I'm more than ready to settle down."

But love? What about love? Deirdre pleaded silently. "Somehow it seems very...calculated."

"Sometimes the best things are."

"You don't have to marry me. We could still work all of this out."

"I'm sure we could, but marriage will be expedient when it comes to your family. They don't have to know about any agreement we sign. As far as they're concerned, what is yours is mine. I'll be a member of your family. The 'family business' will stay intact." He curved his fingers around hers and lowered his voice. "And I *want* to marry you. I wouldn't be suggesting it if that weren't the case."

But why do you want to marry me? she ached to ask, but didn't. He could give her the answer she craved, which would thrill her, or he could repeat the practical reasons he'd listed earlier, which would distress her. Rather than take the risk, she simply accepted his statement without prodding.

"Will you marry me, Deirdre?" he asked softly.

She met his gaze, knowing that love shone in her own with a strength she was helpless to dim. Silently she nodded, and closed her fingers around his.

CHAPTER EIGHT

As HE'D PROMISED, Thomas was at the dock bright and early the next morning to pick them up. His curiosity was evident in the surreptitious glances he cast toward Deirdre, then Neil, at well-spaced intervals. They simply smiled at each other, feeling smug, but more than that, pleased with what lay ahead. If they'd dreaded the day they'd have to leave their island refuge, the knowledge that they were going to be together reduced that dread to a small twinge of sentimentality as the island faded behind them.

Neil had wanted to drive Deirdre back to Providence, but she insisted, with reason, he finally agreed, that it made no sense for her to leave her car in Maine when she'd want to use it at home. So he followed her on the highway, making sure she stopped periodically to stretch, then later, eat lunch.

It was mid-afternoon when they pulled up at Deirdre's mother's house. They'd discussed that, too, agreeing that the sooner they broke the news of their impending marriage to Maria Joyce the better. And, anticipating that the woman might give Deirdre a hard time, given her history of doing just that, Neil was vehement that he be present.

Maria was in the library when Deirdre called out from the front door. She came quickly, exclaiming loudly even before she entered the hall, "Deirdre! It's about time! I've been worried sick about where you were and how you were making out. If I hadn't thought to call Victoria—" She stopped short when she caught sight of her daughter, leaning on her crutches, beside a tall, bearded man in jeans. "Good Lord," she whispered, staring at the pair, "what have you brought home this time?"

Deirdre felt a movement by her elbow and knew that Neil was trying not to laugh. For that matter, so was she. In her eyes, Neil looked positively gorgeous, but she knew that her mother was wondering what the cat had dragged in.

"Mother, I'd like you to meet Neil Hersey. Neil, Maria Joyce."

Neil stepped forward and extended a firm hand, which Maria had no choice but to meet. "It's my pleasure, Mrs. Joyce. Deirdre has told me a lot about you."

Maria didn't take the time to wonder about the nature of that telling. She was too concerned about retrieving her hand from what was a far-too-confident grip. She nodded at Neil, but her focus was quickly on Deirdre.

"Victoria finally admitted that you'd gone to Maine. I can't believe you did that, Deirdre. The place is totally isolated, and in your condition—"

"My condition is fine. And Neil was there with me." Before her mother could pounce on that, she rushed on. "Neil is a friend of Victoria's, too. Now he's a friend of mine. Furthermore—" she looked at Neil "—we're going to be married. We wanted you to be the first to know." She took perverse delight in her mother's stunned expression.

For a minute the older woman was speechless. Then, pressing a hand to her heart, she revived.

"You can't be serious."

"We are. Very."

"Deirdre, you don't know this man!" She gave Neil a once-over that was disapproving at best.

"You'd be surprised, mother. Two weeks on an island, with no one else around—you can get to know a man pretty well."

Neil rolled his eyes at her smug tone and quickly sought to make amends to Maria. "What Deirdre means is that we had a chance to talk more than many people do in months. We shared responsibility for the house and everything to do with our daily lives. We feel that our marriage would be a good one."

Maria, who'd been eyeing him warily during his brief speech, closed her fingers around the single strand of pearls she was wearing with her very proper silk dress. "I think I need a drink," she said, and turned toward the living room.

Deirdre took off after her, with Neil following in her wake. "It's the middle of the afternoon! You don't need a drink in the middle of the afternoon!''

"Oh, yes, I do," came Maria's voice. She was already at the elegant cherrywood bar, fishing ice from a bucket. "When a woman hears that, after years of nagging, her daughter has decided on the spur of the moment to get married—and to a man she thinks she knows, but can't possibly, since she met him a mere two weeks ago—she needs a drink, *regardless* of the time of day!''

Deirdre took a deep breath and sent Neil a helpless glance before lowering herself to a nearby ottoman. "I think you ought to listen to the rest of what I have to tell you before you pass judgment. You may say something you'll later regret.''

"I doubt that," Maria stated. She'd poured a healthy dose of bourbon into the glass and was standing stiffly by the bar. "I don't know where I failed with you, Deirdre, but I very definitely have failed. I've tried to instill in you certain values, and you've rejected every one of them. I tried to raise a lady, but you insist on running around in leotards—''

"Not leotards, mother. A tank top and running shorts. Leotards cut off my circulation.''

She waved that aside. "Whatever. The point's the same. I tried to raise you with a sense of family, but you've insisted in going your own way. I've tried to make you see that you have an obligation to the business, but you won't hear of that. And now, when you've got nothing better to do with your time, instead of giving us a hand, you run off, meet up with a passing...hippie, and decide to marry him.''

Neil, who'd been standing quietly at Deirdre's shoulder, felt that he'd heard enough. He didn't mind the insults to him, but they were a smaller part of insults to Deirdre, and he wouldn't have that. "I don't think you understand the situation, Mrs. Joyce," he said with such authority that Maria was forced to listen. "I am not a hippie, nor am I passing. If you've formed an opinion of me based on the way I look, I think you should remember that I've just come from a two-week vacation. The bulk of my life is spent in tailored suits, suits that would hold their own—'' he looked at the bench before the grand piano "—with that Dunhill tapestry." He shifted his gaze to the small painting to the left of the bar. "Or that Modigliani.'' He dropped his eyes to the marble coffee table by Deirdre's knees. "Or that Baccarat vase.''

Deirdre looked up at him. "I'm impressed,'' she mouthed.

He nudged her hip with his knee, shushing her with a frown.

Maria arched a well-shaped brow, but she wasn't about to be fully appeased. "The slickest of con men pick up a wealth of knowledge about fine accessories, Mr. Hersey. What is it you do for a living?''

"I'm a lawyer. I head my own firm in Hartford, specializing in corporate work. I can give you a full list of my credits, starting with law review at Harvard, but I don't think that's necessary. Suffice it to say that in recent years I've done work for Jennings and Lange, KronTech, and the Holder Foundation, as well as the Faulkner Company here in Providence.'' He was confident that the corporations he'd named would give him solid recommendations. He was equally confident that Maria Joyce had heard of them. She would have also heard of Wittnauer-Douglass. There was always the possibility that if the woman ran a check on him, she'd come across that problem, but it was a risk he'd have to take. And besides, by the time she learned anything, his marriage to Deirdre would be a fait accompli.

Maria dipped her head in reluctant acknowledgment of his credentials. "All right. I'll admit that my judgment may have been premature, but the fact remains that this marriage is very sudden. When was it going to take place?''

Deirdre opened her mouth, but Neil spoke first. "As soon as the law will allow. I believe there's a three-day waiting period once the license has been taken out and the blood tests done. I know a judge here in Providence who might cut even that down.''

Maria studied her bourbon, pressing her lips together as she ingested that information. "Is there a rush?'' She sent Deirdre a meaningful glance. "I know that there are home tests on the market that can give instant results—''

"I am not pregnant, mother,'' Deirdre interrupted. "And even if I were, I'd have thought you'd be pleased. You've been harping on having grandchildren since I was old enough to vote.''

"Every woman wants grandchildren,'' Maria countered in self-defense.

"So you've said many times. And here's your chance. I don't know why you're complaining. Even if I *were* pregnant, Neil and I will be married before anyone is the wiser. At most, the baby would be born two weeks early, so to speak, which no one would think twice about. You wouldn't have any cause for embarrassment."

Maria scowled at her daughter. "All right," she said crossly. "Forget a pregnancy." Her annoyance broadened to include Neil. "You'll get married and take off for Hartford, leaving Joyce Enterprises in the lurch yet again. Honestly, Deirdre, is that fair?"

Neil answered. "We won't be living in Hartford. We'll be living here."

Maria arched a skeptical brow. "You'd walk away from that successful law practice?"

"I can practice law anywhere," he returned, tamping down a moment's discomfort. "Providence is as good a place as any."

"The fact is, Mother," Deirdre spoke up, "that we are going to bail you out, after all. Neil has agreed to help me with Joyce Enterprises."

For the second time in a very short period, Maria Joyce was speechless. She looked from Deirdre to Neil and back, then raised her glass and took a bolstering drink. By the time she'd lowered the glass, she'd regained a small measure of her composure, though not enough to keep the glass from shaking in her hand. She set it carefully on the bar.

"That," she began slowly, "is an unexpected turn."

"So is our wedding," Deirdre pointed out, "but it all makes sense. You've been after me for years to help with the business. I've been convinced that I'm not right for the job, but I'm equally convinced that Neil is." And she was. She had no doubts but that Neil could handle Joyce Enterprises. "You've wanted to keep things in the family. Neil will be in the family. What more could Dad have asked for than a son-in-law who could take over where his daughters left off?"

"But he's a lawyer," Maria argued, though more meekly this time. "He's not trained in this type of work."

"Neither am I—nor Sandra, for that matter."

Neil joined in. "I've worked closely with large corporations like

Joyce for years, so I'm starting with a definite advantage. And I've had the benefit of seeing how other corporations function, which means that I can take the best of the systems and strategies I've seen and implement them at Joyce.'' He paused. ''I think it could work out well for all of us, Mrs. Joyce. I assure you that I wouldn't be putting my career on the line if I didn't feel that the odds were in my favor.''

Maria appeared to have run out of arguments. She raised both brows and nervously fingered her pearls. ''I...it looks like you've thought things out.''

''We have,'' Deirdre said.

The older woman shook her head, for the first time seeming almost confused. ''I don't know, Deirdre. It's so sudden.... I was hoping that when my daughters got married they'd have big weddings, with lots of flowers and music and people.''

Deirdre's shoulders rose with the deep breath she took. ''I've never wanted that, Mother. I'll be perfectly happy with something small and private.''

Maria looked at them both. ''You will be happy? This is what you truly want?'' They knew she wasn't referring to the wedding, but to the marriage itself.

Neil's hand met Deirdre's at her shoulder. ''It is,'' Deirdre said softly.

Neil echoed the sentiment. ''We'll be happy, Mrs. Joyce. You can take my word for it.''

FEELING AS THOUGH they'd overcome their first hurdle, they left Maria, stopped for their marriage license and blood tests, then went to Deirdre's town house. Though Neil agreed that it was on the small side, he was charmed with the way she'd decorated it. Whereas old-world elegance had been the word at her mother's house, here everything was light and airy. The furniture was modern, low and cushiony. One room opened into another with barely a break. There were no Dunhill tapestries, no Modiglianis, no pieces of Baccarat crystal, but a small and carefully chosen selection of work by local artists and artisans.

''I feel very much at home here,'' Neil said to Deirdre as they lay in bed that night.

Chin propped on his chest, she smiled at him. "I'm glad."

"It's pretty and bright, uncluttered and unpretentious. Like you."

She tugged at his beard. "I think you want something. What is it?"

He smiled back and wrapped an arm around her waist. "Just that when we find the right home, you do it like this. I don't want to live in a museum or…or in a shrine to a decorator."

Deirdre narrowed her eyes. "Is that what your place is like?"

"A shrine to a decorator? Yes, it is, and I never thought twice about it until now, but I don't want that, Deirdre. There's a sophistication in the simplicity here. That's what I want. Okay?"

"Okay."

"No argument?"

"No argument."

"Good."

THEY HEADED for Hartford the next day. Neil had a long list of things to take care of, the most pressing and difficult of which was informing his associates that he'd be leaving. Both men were talented lawyers, but being young they hadn't yet developed reputations that would attract new business. Neil gave them the choice of joining other firms or taking over his practice themselves. When they opted for the latter, he assured them that he'd do everything he could to help them out, which included drawing up a letter to send his clients, telling them of the change and assuring them that they'd be in good hands if they remained with the firm.

The second order of business was putting his condominium on the market. The real estate agent, who had a list of people waiting for openings in that particular building, was delighted.

"Are you sure you want to sell it?" Deirdre asked timidly.

"Why not? I won't be living here."

"But if you find that you don't like Providence…or that things don't go well…"

He took her firmly by the shoulders. "I will like Providence, and things will go well. I'm making a commitment, Deirdre. There's no point in doing it halfway."

She didn't argue further, particularly since his confidence buoyed her. So they returned to Providence and went house hunting. Once again luck was on their side. They found a charming colonial on the outskirts of the city, not far from Deirdre's mother's house ironically, but in a younger neighborhood. The property encompassed three acres of land, with a wealth of trees and lush shrubbery, and though the house needed work, the previous owners had vacated several weeks before, and the work could begin immediately.

Three days after they arrived back from Maine, Deirdre and Neil were married in the church Deirdre had attended as a child. Her mother had made the arrangements—Deirdre felt it was as good a consolation prize as any—and there were more people, more flowers, more food than Deirdre might have chosen herself. But she was too happy that day to mind anything.

Neil looked breathtaking in his dark suit, white shirt, striped tie and cordovans. He'd had his beard professionally trimmed, along with his hair, and she decided that he looked far more like a successful businessman than a conservative corporate lawyer.

Deirdre, who'd had a walking cast put on to replace the original, wore a long white dress, the simplicity of which was a perfect foil for her natural good looks. She'd applied a minimum of makeup— touches each of blusher, mascara, eyeliner and shadow—and though never one to lean heavily toward jewelry, she'd taken pride in wearing the pearl earrings and matching necklace that her father had given her for her twenty-first birthday.

The ceremony was short and sweet, and Deirdre was all smiles as she circulated through the luncheon reception on the arm of her new husband. He'd given her a stunning gold wedding band, as simple as her gown, with a tracing of diamond chips forming a central circle, but she would have been happy with something from the five-and-dime, as long as it told her they were married. Though he still hadn't said the words, she was sure she'd seen love in his eyes throughout that day, and it was the proverbial frosting on the cake.

THE NEXT FEW WEEKS were hectic ones. Neil threw himself fully into Joyce Enterprises, determined to familiarize himself with every aspect of the business. Sandra readily accepted him; not only was she relieved to have the brunt of the load taken from her shoulders, but Deirdre suspected that she was enthralled by Neil. And rightly so. He exuded confidence and was charming not only to Sandra, but to the uncles, as well. If he came home exhausted at night, Deirdre was more than willing to understand. She was also more than willing to make a challenge out of reviving him, which she did with notable success.

He kept her abreast with what was happening at work, sharing his observations, discussing his plans. And he was even eager to hear about the progress at the house, the redecorating of which she was orchestrating with an enthusiasm that surprised her. She'd never seen herself as a decorator. When she'd moved into her town house she'd simply papered and carpeted to suit herself. Knowing that Neil approved of her taste was a major stimulant—that and knowing the house she now decorated was for the two of them.

By the time they moved in three weeks after the wedding, Deirdre was reeling with confidence. A week later her cast came off, and if that confidence faltered when she experienced a fair amount of pain, Neil was the one to offer encouragement. He personally helped her with the exercises the doctor had outlined, and when those exercise sessions ended more often than not in lovemaking, Deirdre wasn't about to complain. In lieu of verbally professing their love for each other, this physical bonding was crucial to her.

Deirdre put off returning to work, knowing that her leg wasn't ready. Strangely, she didn't miss it as much as she'd thought she would, but, then, between setting up the house and joining Neil for those social engagements he'd warned her would be inevitable, she had little time to miss much of anything.

Strangely, she didn't mind the social engagements, either. But, then, she was with Neil. He never failed to compliment her on the way she looked; as a result, she found that dressing up wasn't as odious as it had been in the past. Moreover, he was the perfect host, drawing her into conversations with their guests such that she experienced far less pain on that score than she'd anticipated.

Neil was exceedingly satisfied with the way things had worked out. Deirdre was as wonderful a wife as she'd been a lover, and as they'd left most of the bickering behind in Maine, he found her to be a thoroughly amiable companion. The only thing that bothered him from time to time was his awareness of the agreement they'd struck. He wanted to think that they were together out of love, not simply taking advantage of a mutually beneficial arrangement. Since the latter was what had brought about this marriage, he went through passing periods of doubt regarding Deirdre's feelings for him.

He had no such self-doubt when it came to Joyce Enterprises. The work was interesting and challenging, and he seemed to have a natural affinity for it. As he'd intended, he brought in a highly experienced executive from a Midwest corporation. Together they mapped out a strategy for keeping Joyce Enterprises not only running smoothly but growing, as well. Between them, they provided the vision that had been lacking since Deirdre's father's death.

Deirdre was thrilled. Her faith in Neil had been justified.

Maria Joyce was likewise pleased, though she made sure Deirdre knew of the risks involved. "I checked up on Neil," she informed her daughter when the two were having lunch at a downtown restaurant one day. "Neither of you was fully honest with me about his past."

Deirdre, who'd been savoring her victory, paused. "We were honest."

"You didn't tell me about Wittnauer-Douglass."

"There wasn't anything to tell. He had a bad experience with one client and was forced to terminate that particular relationship, but it was an isolated incident. He did the same kind of quality work for Wittnauer-Douglass that he did for the rest of his clients."

"According to my friend Bess Hamilton, whose husband is on the board at Wittnauer-Douglass, Neil took part in some unethical dealings."

Deirdre's anger was quick to rise. "If Bess Hamilton's husband was on the board, *he* was involved in the unethical dealings. Neil resigned because he wouldn't have anything to do with it!"

"That wasn't what Bess said."

"And who do you choose to believe, your friend or your son-in-law?"

Maria's gaze didn't waver. "I don't have much choice, do I? Neil is firmly entrenched in the running of our business—"

"And he's doing an excellent job. You can't deny it."

"But I have to wonder what his motives are. From what Bess said, he was washed out in Hartford."

"He wasn't *washed out*. His two associates are doing fantastically well with the business he left them, and if it hadn't been for his own urgings, those clients would have left in a minute and gone elsewhere. They had faith in Neil, which is why they followed his recommendation and stayed with the firm."

Maria wasn't about to be fully convinced. "Still, he got a good thing going for him when he married you. It was a shrewd move."

"What are you trying to say, Mother?" Deirdre asked through gritted teeth.

"Just that I think you ought to be careful. I think we all ought to be careful. He may be trying to take over Joyce Enterprises and sweep it away from us."

"Neil wouldn't do that."

"How do you know?"

"Because I'm *married* to him. Because I *know* him."

"You love him, and love sometimes clouds people's judgment."

"Not in this case. I trust him." She also knew of the papers she'd signed before she and Neil had been married, but she didn't feel that was any of her mother's business. "And I'd think that if you can't find it in yourself to trust him, as well, the least you can do is appreciate him. He's taken a load off all our backs, and what he's doing with Joyce Enterprises would have made Dad proud."

Maria had nothing to say on that score, so she changed the subject. Her words, however, lingered for a long time in Deirdre's mind.

Deirdre had meant what she'd said—that she trusted Neil. There were times, though, when she wondered about the energy he was pouring into the business. Rarely did a night pass when he didn't bring a project of some form home from the office with him. The enthusiasm he had for his work seemed boundless....

Perhaps, Deirdre mused, she was simply jealous. She recalled the days they'd spent in Maine, and there were times when she wished for them again. Neil had been totally devoted to her there; here she had to share him with a very demanding job. She recalled his saying that he'd never married before because the law was such a demanding mistress. At the time she'd argued that the right woman had simply never come along.

Now she wondered if *she* was the right woman, and let her insecurities suggest that she might not be. Yes, Neil was warm and affectionate. Yes, he put aside his work when she came to talk with him. Yes, he was patient with her frustration when her leg seemed to take inordinately long in healing.

But he went off to work quite happily each morning. And he never said that he loved her.

Then again, she realized, maybe her unease was reflective of nothing more than the changes her life had undergone in a few short months. The work on the house was now finished. It was furnished to their mutual satisfaction in the style of understated sophistication that Deirdre had never before thought of as a style; it was merely the way she wanted to live. She wasn't one to spend hours simply looking at the finished product or wandering from one room to another, and the demands Neil made on her for evening engagements weren't enough to occupy her time.

As time passed she grew restless.

She started going to the health club. Though she probably could have taught, she didn't want to. She felt tired. Her leg, though better, still bothered her. She began to wonder whether her compulsion to teach had been directly tied to her need to escape Joyce Enterprises. Since that need was no longer there the compulsion had faded.

She sat at home for long hours, missing Neil, wondering what to do with herself. She lunched with friends, but that brought no lasting relief from her malaise. She took part in the planning of a ten-kilometer charity run, but that occupied far too little of her time.

Finally, on impulse one day, she flew down to meet Victoria for lunch. They hadn't seen each other since the wedding, which Victoria had proudly and delightedly attended, and Deirdre was counting on her friend to bolster her morale.

"How long have you know Neil?" Deirdre asked, broaching the topic as soon as the waiter had left with their order.

"Three years," Victoria answered, cocking her head to the side. "Why do you ask?"

"Did you know him well during that time?"

"We didn't see each other often, but if I were to judge from the quality of the time we spent together, I'd say we were close." She pursed her lips. "Something's up, Dee. Spill it."

Deirdre shrugged, absently playing with the moisture on the outside of her water glass. "I don't know. It's just that everything between us happened so fast. I sometimes wonder if we rushed things."

"You have doubts about Neil?"

"No. Well, maybe once in a while. My mother said something a few weeks ago that bothered me, something about Neil—"

"Your mother," Victoria scoffed. "Your mother is a good friend of mine, but that doesn't mean I can't see her faults. She's one of those people who are never satisfied. You take her too seriously, Dee. I've told you that before."

"I know. But I can't help hearing her little 'words of wisdom.'"

"You may have to hear them. You don't have to heed them."

"But it's like they niggle in the back of my mind and they refuse to go away." She raised beseeching eyes to her friend. "Victoria, do you think Neil is ambitious?"

"I should hope so. No one is successful if he isn't ambitious."

"Ruthlessly so? Would you call Neil ruthlessly ambitious?"

Victoria didn't have to think about that. "No. Unequivocally. Neil is not a ruthless person. If anything, the opposite is true. If he had a little more of the bastard in him, he might not have had that problem with Wittnauer-Douglass."

"If he hadn't had that," Deirdre pointed out with a lopsided grin, "he'd never have run off to Maine and I'd never have met him, so I can't be sorry about Wittnauer-Douglass." Her grin faded. "It's just that my mother learned about all that, and she suggested that Neil might be out for himself when it comes to Joyce Enterprises."

"Is that what you think?"

"No. At least, I want to think that it isn't so. But he's taken to his work with such...such *glee*, and there are times when I wish he showered more of that glee on me."

"You can't have it both ways, Dee. If he's to turn Joyce Enterprises around, he's going to have to put in the hours. Take my word for it, though. Neil Hersey has nothing but the most upstanding intentions when it comes to your business. I don't think there's a selfish bone in that man's body. Did he ever tell you what he did for my niece?''

Deirdre frowned. "No. He never mentioned your niece."

"He wouldn't. That's his way."

"Well? What did he do?"

"A while ago, my niece got involved in a criminal matter. The girl was only nineteen at the time, and her mother—my sister—was frantic. They live in a small town in western Connecticut and aren't very well off, and they didn't know where to turn for help. I called Neil, knowing that criminal law wasn't his specialty but hoping that he'd be able to refer us to a capable person. Not only did he do that, but he personally involved himself in the case, and then, when the other lawyer would have given him a referral fee, he insisted that the man deduct it from the fee he charged my sister—a fee, mind you, that was on the low side, anyway, considering that my niece got away with nothing but probation. Now—'' she tipped up her chin "—if Neil were only out for himself, would he have done all that for my niece?"

Deirdre felt a rush of pride in her husband. "No. And I know that he's always done charity work. It's just that the situation with us is so different. There's so much at stake for him now."

"I doubt he'd consider anything more important than your love."

Deirdre held her breath.

"Dee? You do love him, don't you?"

"Oh, yes!"

"But...?"

"I'm not sure he loves me."

"Are you kidding?"

Deirdre responded defensively. "No, I'm not kidding. He's never told me he loved me. Our marriage was...was...expedient, and that was his own word."

Victoria pressed a calming hand on her arm. "Look, sweetheart, I know enough about each of your situations to realize that your getting married solved certain problems for you both. But I saw Neil at your wedding, and if that man wasn't in love, I'll turn in my matchmaker badge.'' She paused. ''What does he say when you tell him that you love him?''

Deirdre didn't have to answer. Guilt was written all over her face.

''My Lord, Dee. Why not? You're no wilting pansy!''

''But I don't want to pressure him. Worse, I don't want to say it and not have him say it back. And anyway, when he's home there's so much else we talk about, and then we don't want to talk at all....''

Victoria shot her a knowing grin. ''That's more like it.'' She raised her eyes when the waiter approached with their plates, and waited until he'd deposited the meal and gone. ''So, Neil is very busy with work, and you're feeling lonesome.''

''Yes.''

''Have you told him that?''

''No.''

Victoria cast pleading eyes toward the ornate ceiling high overhead. ''I know I shouldn't ask this, but why not?''

''Because in the first place, I don't want to sound like a complainer. When we first got to Maine, that was all I did—bitch at him, and everything else in sight. Then our relationship gelled, and I stopped griping. I liked myself a lot more then. I don't want to go back to that other way.'' She paused for an exaggerated breath. ''And in the second place, there's nothing he can do about it.''

''He can reassure you, maybe help find something to keep you busy.''

Deirdre shook her head sadly. ''I don't know, Victoria. I look at you and I'm envious. When you finish one thing you start another. I used to have a million and one things to do with my day, but now I can't seem to find anything that tempts me.''

''You want to be with Neil. Everything else is...blah. So why don't you work part-time at the office?''

''That'd be tantamount to surrender. I swore I'd never work there.''

''And you're so rigid that you can't reconsider, particularly knowing that working there now would be out of choice, rather than need?''

Deirdre didn't respond immediately; she sat absently nudging her cold salmon with a fork. "Put that way, I sound pretty childish."

"If the shoe fits…"

"I don't know, Victoria. I'm not sure that's what I want, either."

"Do me a favor, Dee, and talk with Neil? He's a patient man. Really, he is. And he's resourceful. Most important, he's your husband. He wants you to be happy." She speared a firm green bean and held it over her plate. "Will you?"

"I'll try."

"Don't try. *Do* it!"

DEIRDRE WOULD HAVE done it that night, had Neil not offered her a solution before she'd been able to utter a word. He'd come home particularly tired, and they were relaxing in the living room, sharing a glass of wine.

"I need your help, Deirdre," he announced in a businesslike tone.

"There's a problem at the office?"

He nodded. "In personnel. Art Brickner, our man there, is giving us flack about hiring people to fill in certain gaps. He wanted to bring people up from the ranks, and I agree with him in theory, except that in several of these cases there simply is no one to bring up from the ranks. Most of his resistance is to new blood, and I fall prominently in that category. Art was one of your father's original men."

"I know… But how can I help?"

"Work with him. Ease him through the transition. He's a good man—"

"He's stodgy."

Neil chuckled. "Yes, he's stodgy, but his instincts are good, and your presence in his office might just remind him that, contrary to what he fears, all is not going down the tubes at Joyce Enterprises."

"Oh, Neil…what do I know about personnel?"

"You have common sense, and a feel for the company. Art will take care of the mechanics, while you handle the, uh, the spiritual end. What do you think?"

"I think," she said, studying the features she adored so much, "that you look exhausted. You're working too hard, Neil."

Loosening his necktie, he sank deeper into the sofa. "You're right. But it has to be done." His eyes narrowed. "You look exhausted, too. Was it running down to New York to have lunch with Victoria?"

"Uh-uh. I'm tired from having too much time on my hands."

"Then helping Art could be just the thing."

"Neil—"

"You wouldn't have to work full-time, only twenty hours a week or so."

"But I—"

"You could wear whatever you wanted, since you wouldn't be in the limelight."

"But what—"

"I'd even pay you." He grinned broadly. "How does that sound?"

She sighed, stared at him in exasperation for a minute, then took his silent offer and settled under the arm he held out. "When you smile at me like that, Neil Hersey, I'm a goner. But you know that, don't you, which is why you do it! I'm a sucker. That's all. A real sucker."

"Then you will work?"

"Yes, I will work."

"And you'll tell me if it turns out to be too much?"

"It won't turn out to be too much. I'm young. I'm full of energy. I'm brimming with enthusiasm...."

BUT IT DID TURN OUT to be too much—or rather, it put a strain on Deirdre that she hadn't expected. She worked from nine to two every day, and was positively drained. After a week of mornings when she couldn't seem to get going, she began coming in at ten. Even then she was dragging by the time Neil arrived home at night.

Witnessing her struggle, Neil grew more and more tense. He waited for her to come to him, to broach the subject, but she didn't. Finally, after two weeks of helplessness, he took matters into his own hands.

Arriving home early from work, he found Deirdre curled beneath an afghan on their king-size bed, sound asleep. He sat on the bed beside her, leaned down and kissed her cheek.

Her lashes fluttered, then rose. "Neil!" she whispered, pushing herself up. "I'm sorry. I never dreamed you'd be home this early!"

He pulled a bouquet of flowers—actually, three roses and an assortment of greens—from behind him. "For you."

Groggy still, she looked from him to the roses and back, smiling at last. "They're lovely. Any special occasion?"

"Mmm-hmm. Today's the day we admit that you're pregnant."

Deirdre's smile vanished, as did what little color had been on her cheeks. She lay back on the bed, closed her eyes and spoke in a very small voice. "How did you guess?"

Neil was stricken by the unhappiness he saw on Deirdre's face. He'd assumed that she'd been afraid to tell him—though he didn't know why—but apparently there was more than fear involved. He answered her quietly. "We've been married for nearly three months, and during that time you haven't had a single period."

"I'm an athlete," she pointed out. "That can do strange things to a woman's system."

"You're constantly tired. Even the slightest activity exhausts you."

"It's everything that's happened in the past few months. I'm on emotional overload."

"And the greater fullness of your breasts?" he asked, his voice deep and low. "And the slight thickening of your waist? Things that nobody else sees, I do. Come on, Deirdre. Let's face the facts. You're pregnant. Is it so awful?"

She focused tired eyes on him. "I feel so lousy right now that, yes, it's awful."

"Then you agree that it's true?"

"It's true."

"But you haven't been to a doctor."

"No."

"Why, Deirdre? Don't you want to have a baby?"

"I do!" she cried, then lowered her voice. "It's just that, on top of everything else, it's so sudden...."

"We weren't using any birth control. You had to know there was a possibility this would happen."

"How did you know I wasn't using birth control?" she countered, being contrary.

"Deirdre, I was with you constantly. I would have known."

"Not if I'd had an IUD."

"But you didn't have one, and you're pregnant now!"

"Thanks to you. If you knew I wasn't using anything, why didn't *you* use something?"

"Deirdre, I do not pack prophylactics as a matter of habit. The last thing I expected when I went up to Maine was that I'd be with a woman."

"So neither of us was prepared, and both of us knew it, and we did nothing, and look what happened."

"I don't think it's such a horrible situation, Deirdre."

"You don't?"

"Of course not."

"You don't feel that it's just another burden on your shoulders?"

"Have I ever talked of burdens?"

"No. But they're there."

"This one's a nice one. I told you I wanted children."

"'Someday,' you said."

"Then 'someday' is now. And the more I think about it, the happier I am." Scooping her up, he tucked her against him. "I know you're not feeling great, Deirdre, but once you see a doctor and he gives you vitamins, and once you pass the initial few months, you'll feel better."

To Deirdre's dismay, she began to cry. Her fingers closed around the lapel of his suit jacket, and she buried her face in his shirt.

"I'll be…be fat."

"You'll be beautiful."

"You'll…you'll be stuck with me."

"I'm not complaining."

"You're being so…kind."

"You're being such a ninny." He hugged her, trying his best to absorb whatever pain she was feeling. He knew she'd been through a lot, and that having a baby at a later time would probably have been better for her, but he wasn't sorry. It bound her all the closer to him.

Weeping softly, Deirdre was thinking similar thoughts. Oh, yes, she wanted the baby, but because it was Neil's, more than for any other reason. When she thought of it, having his baby made the tie between them even more permanent than marriage. It was both a reassuring and a frightening thought, because if something went wrong and Neil decided he'd had enough, a wholly innocent child would be affected.

The scent of roses by her nose interrupted her sniffles. She opened her eyes and saw Neil touch each bloom.

"One for you, one for me, one for baby. A nice bunch, don't you think?"

His sweetness brought a helpless smile to Deirdre's wet face. "A very nice bunch."

Later, she told herself, she'd watch for the thorns. For now, she was too tired to do anything but relax in Neil's arms.

CHAPTER NINE

ONCE DEIRDRE accepted the fact of her pregnancy, she was better able to cope. She saw a doctor and began a regimen of vitamins that compensated for what the baby demanded of her body. She continued working with Art Brickner, adjusting her hours to accommodate her need for sleep.

Neil seemed legitimately pleased about the baby, and that relieved her most of all. In turn, she made up her mind to do everything in her power to make their marriage work.

When she was at the office, she dressed accordingly, intent on making Neil proud. When she was at home she planned their meals and coordinated the various cleaning efforts so that the house was always immaculate should Neil decide to bring people home at the last minute. At Neil's insistence, though, they'd hired a maid to help. She resumed her visits to the health club—the doctor had okayed that—and though she didn't teach, she took part in classes. She swam. She diligently kept herself in shape—as much as a woman with a slowly growing belly could.

And she never argued with Neil. She didn't complain when he was delayed for several hours at the office and dinner was held up. She didn't say a word when he had to go away on a business trip. She didn't nag him to take time off from work to play tennis with her. She graciously attended cocktail parties and dinners, and when she and Neil were finally alone at night, she did her very best to satisfy him, both physically and emotionally.

But because she refused to give him any cause for displeasure, the frustration that had built within her had nowhere to go. She wished he didn't work so hard, but she didn't say so. She yearned for time alone with him—even their weekends revolved around business demands—but she didn't say so. She ached, positively ached to hear him say that he loved her, but she didn't say so, and he didn't tell her what she wanted to hear. She felt as if she were walking a tightrope.

The tightrope began to fray when her mother dropped in one morning. Deirdre was getting ready to leave for work.

"Have you heard his latest scheme?" Maria asked with an arrogance Deirdre found all too familiar. They were standing in the front hall; Deirdre knew enough not to invite her mother to sit, or she'd be in for an even longer siege.

"That depends on which scheme it is," Deirdre countered with confidence. "Neil's had a lot of them lately, and they're all very promising."

"This one isn't."

"Which one?"

"He's bidding on a government contract for the electronics division."

Deirdre had known that. "Is there a problem?" she asked blandly.

"We've never bid for government contracts. We've always devoted ourselves to the private sector."

"That doesn't mean we can't change now, if doing so will be good for the company."

"But will it? That's the question. Is Neil bidding for that contract because it will be good for the company or for him?"

"Aren't they one and the same?" Deirdre asked, ignoring her mother's barely veiled reference to the earlier accusation she'd made.

"Not by a long shot. You may not know it, but one of the other bidders is Wittnauer-Douglass."

Deirdre hadn't known it. She ignored the frisson of anxiety that shivered through her. "I'm sure there are many other bidders—"

"None Neil holds a grudge against."

"Neil doesn't hold a grudge against Wittnauer-Douglass," Deirdre insisted. "What happened there is done. He is very successful in what he's doing now. I think you're way off base."

"You've thought that from the start, when I told you to be careful, but this is the evidence I need."

"Evidence? What evidence?"

"Your husband is involving Joyce Enterprises in something solely for the sake of avenging himself. He would never be bidding for a government contract if it weren't for that. Think about it. Isn't it awfully suspicious that the first time we do anything of this sort, a major competitor is the very one Neil has a gripe against?''

Deirdre set her purse down on the table. "Do you know the details, Mother? Who submitted a bid first, Wittnauer-Douglass or Joyce Enterprises?''

Maria fumbled with the collar of her sable coat. "I don't know that. How could I possibly know that!''

"If it's evidence you're looking for, that'd be a place to start. If Neil submitted his bid first, without ever knowing that Wittnauer-Douglass would be a competitor, his innocence would be obvious.''

"The rest of the evidence is against him.''

Deirdre was losing her patience. "What evidence?''

"Deirdre,'' her mother said, sighing. "Think. Neil met you at a time when he needed a change of location and occupation.''

"He did not need—''

"He latched onto what you had to offer, married you as quickly as possible and set about implementing his plans.''

"The plans he implemented were for the resurgence of Joyce Enterprises, and he's done a remarkable job! He's done us a favor!''

"He's done himself a favor. Look at it objectively. He's at the helm of a successful corporation. He's become so well respected in the community that the two of you are in demand at all the parties that matter—''

"If you had any sense of appreciation, Mother, you'd spend your time tallying all he's done for *you*. He's married the more undesirable of your two daughters and is about to give you a grandchild. He's taken responsibility for the family business—and even gotten *me* involved in it. What more do you want?''

"I want Joyce Enterprises to remain in the black.''

"And you think that bidding on a government contract will prevent that?'' Deirdre asked in disbelief. "He's just bidding.''

"If he wants that contract badly enough, he'll bid low enough to undercut Wittnauer-Douglass, and if he does that, he could jeopardize our financial status.''

"And if he does that,'' Deirdre pointed out angrily, "he'll be jeopardizing the very position he's built for himself. It doesn't make sense, Mother. You're being illogical.''

"It's a risk—his bidding for that contract."

"There's always a risk if the prize is worth anything. If Neil only stuck with what was safe, the business would be at a standstill."

"He's being rash. I think you should talk with him."

Deirdre had had enough. "I don't have to listen to this." She snatched up her purse, took her coat from the nearby chair and headed for the door. "You can stay if you like. I have to get to work."

Deirdre might have been fine had the conversation she'd had with her mother been the only one of its kind. But several days later, Art Brickner raised the issue, complaining that Neil had spoken with him about hiring an enlarged cadre of workers if the government contract came through. Art questioned both the logistics and the wisdom of what Neil proposed, and all Deirdre could do was to support Neil and insist that his plan was sound.

Several days after that, she was approached by one of the long-standing vice presidents of the company, who, too, had doubts as to the direction in which Joyce was headed. Again Deirdre expressed her support for Neil, sensing that what she was hearing was simply a resistance to change, but she grew increasingly uncomfortable.

She didn't tell Neil about any of the three discussions. She didn't want to anger him by suggesting that she had doubts, when, in fact, she had no qualms about the viability of winning and working through a government contract. What bothered her was the possibility that his motives weren't entirely pure, that, as her mother had suggested, he was being driven by a desire for revenge. She tried to ignore such thoughts, but they wouldn't leave her.

At the root of the matter were the doubts she had regarding their relationship. Oh, they were close. They said all the right things, did all the right things. To the outside world—and to themselves, on one level—they were a loving couple. If she recalled the original reasons for their marriage, though, as she did with increasing frequency, she couldn't help but question what it was that drove Neil. His questionable motives bothered her far more than the prospect of any contract, government or otherwise.

So she walked the tightrope. On one end was what she wanted; on the other what she thought Neil wanted. The rope frayed. It finally snapped when he arrived home unexpectedly one afternoon. She was instantly pleased, delighted by the thought of spending stolen time with him. The sight of him—ruggedly handsome, with his beard offsetting his more formal suit—never failed to excite her, as did the inevitable kiss with which he greeted her.

Threading his arm through hers, he led her into the den. When he held her back, though, the look of tension on his face told her something was amiss.

"I need a favor, Deirdre. I have to run to Washington for a meeting tonight. Do you think you could handle the dinner party on your own?"

They'd long ago invited three couples to join them at a restaurant in town. Deirdre knew the couples. They weren't her favorite people.

Her face fell. "Oh, Neil...do you have to go?"

"I do. It's important." He felt like a heel, but there was no way around it.

"But so sudden. You were planning to go down for the presentation tomorrow morning, anyway. Can't you have this meeting then?"

"Not if I want the presentation to be the best it can be."

"It will be. You've been working on it for weeks."

"I want that contract," he stated, then coaxed her more gently. "Come on. You can handle things at the restaurant."

"You know how I hate dinners like that."

"I know that you manage them beautifully." She'd proved it in the past weeks, and he'd been proud of her.

"With you by my side. But you won't be, which makes the whole thing that much more distasteful."

"I'm asking for your help. I can't be two places at once."

Annoyances, past and present, rose within her. She left his side, grabbed a throw pillow from the sofa and began to fluff it with a vengeance. "And you choose to be in Washington. If you wanted to be here, you could send someone else to Washington. Why can't Ben go?" Ben Tillotson was the executive Neil had brought in from the midwest.

"Ben's daughter is visiting from Seattle. He feels badly enough that he has to leave her tomorrow."

"Well, what about me? You have to leave me tomorrow, too."
She dropped the first pillow and started on another.

"It's my responsibility before it's Ben's."

"Then if Ben can't make it, why don't you let Thor go?" Thor
VanNess headed the electronics division. In Deirdre's mind, he'd
be the perfect one to attend the meeting.

"Thor is fantastic at what he does, but he is not a diplomat, and
the meeting tonight is going to involve a fair share of diplomacy."

"And you're the only diplomat at Joyce?"

Her sarcasm was a sharp prod, poking holes in Neil's patience.
"Deirdre," he said, sighing, "you're making too much out of a
single meeting. If you want, I can have my secretary call and cancel
the dinner party, but I'd hoped that wouldn't be necessary. Believe
me, I've looked for other outs. I've tried to think of someone else
who can get the job done tonight in Washington, but there is no
one else. It's *my responsibility*."

She tossed the second pillow on the sofa and leaned forward to
straighten a small watercolor that hung on the wall. "Then you
take too much on your own shoulders. I was under the assumption
that delegation was critical to the smooth functioning of a corporation this size." She lowered her voice in an attempt to curb her
temper. Yes, she was making too much out of a single meeting,
but it had become a matter of principle. She faced him head-on.
"Send someone else. Anyone else."

"I can't, Deirdre. It's as simple as that."

"No, it's not," she declared, unable to hold it in any longer.
"It's not simple at all. You put your work before every other thing
in our lives, which shows where *your* priorities lie."

Neil bowed his head and rubbed the back of his neck. "You're
being unfair," he said quietly.

"Unfair? Or selfish? Well, maybe it's about time!" She stalked
to the large ship's clock that hung on another wall, took a tool from
its side, opened it and angrily began to wind it.

"Take it easy, babe. You're making a mountain out of—"

"I am not!"

"You're getting upset." His gaze fell to the tiny swell just visible in profile beneath her oversized sweater. "It's not good for
you *or* the baby."

She turned to glare at him. "That's where you're wrong. It's the *best* thing for me, and therefore for the baby, because I can't pretend anymore. I'm being torn apart inside.''

Neil stiffened. "What are you talking about?''

"I can't stand this, Neil. I've tried to be the perfect wife for you. I've done all the things I swore I'd never do, and I've done them without argument because I wanted to please you. I wanted to make this marriage work.''

"I thought it was working. Do you mean to tell me you were faking it all?''

She scrunched up her face in frustration. "I wasn't faking it. On one level the marriage does work. But there has to be more. There has to be total communication. You discuss the business with me, but I don't know what you're really thinking or feeling. There are times when I feel totally left out of what's happening.''

"You could ask more.''

"You could offer more.''

"Damn it, Deirdre, how do I know what you want if you don't ask?''

"Don't you know me well enough to know what I want without my having to ask?''

"No!'' he exploded, angry now himself. "I thought you wanted me to make a go of your damned business, but it looks like I was wrong. I've been busting my ass in the office racking my brain, dipping into resources I didn't know I had, looking for one way, then another to make Joyce Enterprises stronger.''

For an instant she was taken back. "I thought you enjoyed the work.''

"I do enjoy the work, but that's because I've been successful. I've felt good knowing that I was carrying out my part of the bargain, knowing that I had the business moving again. Every bit of my satisfaction relates directly or indirectly to you.''

Deirdre eyed him skeptically. "Are you sure? Isn't there a little satisfaction that relates solely to you?''

"I suppose,'' he answered, rubbing his bearded cheek. "If I stand back and look at what I've been able to do in a few short months, yes, I'm proud of myself. I'm a lawyer by training, not a businessman, yet I've taken on entrepreneurial tasks that two, four, six years ago I'd never have dared tackle.''

"But you have now. Why?''

Neil was still for a moment, his tone almost puzzled when he spoke. "It was part of the agreement we made."

"No. Go back further." Her hand tightened around the clock tool. "Why did we make that agreement?"

"Because you needed me and I needed you."

"That's right. And I guess it's one of the things that's been eating at me. You needed a means of reestablishing yourself after what happened in Hartford. You came in here, took over the reins, and you've done more with this company than anyone else—including my father—has done in years. You've done everything I expected, and more. Why, Neil? Why so much?"

"That's an absurd question," he snapped. "If there are things to be done, I believe in doing them. Yes, I could have stopped thinking a while ago, and Joyce Enterprises still would have been in far better shape than it had been. But I've seen potential in the company. I'm trying to realize it."

Replacing the clock tool, Deirdre moved to a plant hanging by the window and began to pick dried leaves from it. "Or are you trying to prove to Wittnauer-Douglass that you can beat them at their own game?"

"What?" He tipped his head and narrowed one eye. "What are you talking about?"

"This government contract. You've told me all about your end of it, and I've been in favor of it. What you didn't tell me was that Wittnauer-Douglass is bidding for the same contract." She crushed the dried leaves in her hand. "My *mother* had to tell me that, and at the same time she leveled a pretty harsh accusation."

"Your mother's leveled accusations before, and they've proved unfounded." He was staring hard at Deirdre. When she reached toward the plant again, he bellowed, "Leave the damn plant alone, Deirdre. I want your full attention right now."

Slowly she turned to face him, but she didn't say a word, because his expression was suddenly one of fury, reminiscent of their first days in Maine, but worse.

His lips were thinned; tension radiated from the bridge of his nose. "You think that I'm going for this contract to get even with Wittnauer-Douglass!" he spat, his eyes widening. "You actually think that I'm out for revenge, that everything I've done since we've been married has been with this in mind! I don't believe you, Deirdre! Where have you *been* all these weeks?''

She grew defensive. ''I didn't say I thought that. I said my mother thought that.''

''But you're raising it with me now, which means that you have your own doubts.''

''Yes, I have my doubts! I've stood behind you one hundred percent, defending you before my mother, before Art Brickner, before others of my father's people who've approached me with questions. I've been as strong an advocate as I can possibly be, but after a while all I can think of is that our marriage was *expedient*.'' She covered her face with one rigid hand and spoke into her palm. ''I hate that word. God, do I hate that word.''

''Then why do you use it?'' he yelled back.

She dropped her hand. ''Because *you* used it, and it's stuck in my mind like glue, and I try to shake it off, but it won't let go! We married for the wrong reasons, Neil, and it's about time we faced it. I can't go on this way. It's driving me nuts!''

Neil thrust a hand through his hair. ''Driving *you* nuts! Do you think it's any different for me? I've tried my best to make things work, and I thought they were working. Now I find out that every one of my efforts has been in vain. I thought you trusted me, but maybe all you wanted was someone to bail you out. Now that I've done that, I'm expendable. Is that it?''

''No! I never said that!''

''Then what are you saying? What in the hell do you want?''

She was shaking—in anger, in frustration, in heartache. Clenching her fists by her sides, she cried, ''I want it *all*! I don't want an expedient marriage! I never did! I want *love*, Neil! Damn it, *I want the real thing*!''

Neil was far from steady himself. Equal parts of tension, fear and anguish thrummed through his body, clouding his mind, robbing him of the thoughts, much less the words to fight her. Feeling more impotent than he'd ever felt in his life, he turned and stormed from the room.

Deirdre wrapped her arms around her middle and tried to control the wild hammering of her heart. She heard the front door slam, then, moments later, the angry rev of the LeBaron. It had long since faded into silence before she began to move in small, dazed steps, working her way slowly toward her favorite room, the loft above the garage.

Late-afternoon sun filtered in across the polished wood floor, splashing on bare stucco walls with a cheeriness that eluded her at the moment. Her cassette player and a pile of tapes lay in one corner. She'd often used the room for exercise, though what she'd really hoped was that one day it would be a playroom for their children.

Now all that seemed in doubt.

Carefully easing herself down onto the cushioned sill of the arched window, she tucked her knees up, pressed her forehead to them and began to cry.

Neil didn't love her. If he had, he'd have said so. She'd given him the opening; she'd told him what she wanted. And he'd left her. He didn't love her.

And their future? A big, fat question mark. In some respects they were back where they'd started when they'd first arrived on Victoria's island.

What had she wanted, really wanted then? Love. She hadn't realized it at the time, but in the weeks since, she realized that everything else would have fallen into place if she'd found love. She could teach, or not. She could work at Joyce Enterprises, or not. The one thing that held meaning was love.

NEIL DROVE AROUND for hours. He stopped at a pay phone to call the office, but he had no desire to show up there. He had no desire to go to Washington. He had no desire to bid for, much less win, that government contract he'd sought. He had no desire to do anything…but return to Deirdre.

That was the one thing that became eminently clear with the miles he put on his odometer. Deirdre was all that mattered in his life.

He relived their meeting in Maine, their arguments, their eventual coming to terms with each other. He reviewed the months they'd been married and all that had happened, both personally and professionally, during that time. But mostly he replayed the scene he'd had with Deirdre that day. He heard her words, pondered them, analyzed them.

And it occurred to him that he was possibly on the verge of making the biggest mistake of his life.

Stopping the car in the middle of the street, he ignored the honking of horns, made a U-turn and mentally mapped the fastest route back to the house. When he arrived, it was nearly ten o'clock. The house was every bit as dark as the night was, and for a minute he feared he was too late. Then his headlights illumined Deirdre's car, parked as unobtrusively as she'd left it beneath the huge maple tree. Pulling up behind it, he jumped from his own and ran inside.

"Deirdre?" he called, flipping lights on in each of the ground floor rooms. "Deirdre!" There was no anger in his voice, simply worry. With the irrational fear of a man in love, he conjured up every one of the dreadful things that might have happened to her during his absence. She was upset. She was pregnant. Oh, God...

Taking the stairs two at a time, he searched their bedroom, then the others. Only when there was still no sign of her did he stop to think. Then, praying that he'd find her there, he headed for the loft.

"Deirdre?" Fearfully he said her name as he switched on the light, then caught his breath when he saw her curled on the window seat, her head having fallen against the windowpane. In the seconds it took him to cross to her, he added even more dreadful things to his list of fears.

Lowering himself by her side, he brushed her cheek with his thumb. Dried tears streaked her skin, but her color was good and she was warm.

"Deirdre?" His voice was soft and shaky. "Wake up, sweetheart. There's something I have to tell you." He smoothed the hair from her forehead, leaned forward to kiss her wheat-hued crown, framed her face with both hands. "Deirdre?"

She took in a hiccuping breath and, frowning, raised heavy lids. Disoriented, she stared at him for a minute, then her eyes opened fully and she pushed herself up against the window frame. "You're back," she whispered.

He smiled gently. "Yes."

"What...what happened to Washington?"

"It's not important."

"But the contract—"

"Isn't important."

"But you wanted it—"

"Not as much as I want you." When her eyes filled with confusion and disbelief, he explained. "I've driven around for hours thinking about things, and when I went back over what you said earlier, I realized that I may have got things wrong. I was so convinced that you wanted out of the marriage, that you'd gotten tired of me and it, that I took your words one way, when they could have been taken another." His hands were cupping her head, thumbs stroking the short, smooth strands of hair behind her ears. "I may be wrong again, but I think it's worth the risk."

He took a deep breath. Once there might have been pride involved, but he'd gone well beyond that. Still, he was nervous. His words came out in a rush. "I love you, Deirdre. *That* was why I wanted to marry you in the first place. Anything else that came along with the marriage was nice, but purely secondary. Maybe I've had my guard up, because I never knew for sure why, deep down inside, you agreed to marry me. And I was afraid to ask outright, because I didn't want to know...if you'd married me simply because of our bargain. But what you said earlier set me to thinking. What you said, and the anguish in it, would make sense if you love me and fear that I don't love you back." His eyes grew moist, and his voice shook again. "Do you, Deirdre? Do you love me?"

Tears welled on her lower lids, and her chin quivered. "Very much," she whispered, which was all she could manage because emotion clogged her throat, making further sound impossible.

Neil closed his eyes in relief and hauled her against him. "Oh, Deirdre," he rasped, "we've been so foolish." His arms wound fully around her; hers had found their way beneath his jacket and held him every bit as tightly. "So foolish," he whispered against her hair. "We never said the words. The only words that mattered, and we never said them."

Deirdre's heart was near to bursting. "I love you...love you so much," she whispered brokenly, and raised her eyes to his. "We had so much going for us, and we nearly blew it."

A shudder passed through him. He took her mouth in a fierce kiss, gentling only when he reminded himself that she wasn't going to leave. "When I think of everything else I've had in my life, things I've risked, things I've lost, they seem so unimportant now.

You're what matters. This is where you belong, in my arms. And I belong in yours.''

"I know," she said, and buried her face against his neck. The scent of him was familiar and dear; it was an aphrodisiac in times of passion, a soothing balm in times of emotional need. She breathed deeply of it, and her face blossomed into a smile. Then the smile faded, replaced by a look of horror. "Neil!" She pushed back from his arms. "The dinner party! They'll have gone to the restaurant and we've stood them up!"

He chuckled. "Not to worry. I called my secretary and had her cancel on our behalf. We'll make it another time. Together."

Deirdre wrinkled her nose. "I don't like the Emerys. He is an arrogant bore, and she has bad breath." Neil laughed aloud, but she hadn't finished. "And Donald Lutz is always checking out the room, on the lookout for someone important to greet, while that wife of his can't take her hand off the chunky emerald ring she wears. And as for the Spellmans, they're—"

Neil put a hand over her mouth, but he was grinning. "They're important clients. Once in a while we have to sacrifice our own personal preferences for the sake of the corporation."

"Speaking of which…" She mumbled into his hand, then spoke more clearly, if softly when he removed it. "I don't distrust you, Neil. Everything you've done at Joyce has been good. And I *am* in favor of the government project if it comes through."

"I didn't do it because of Wittnauer-Douglass, Deirdre. I didn't even know they were bidding for the same project."

"That was what I suggested to my mother," Deirdre said, feeling faintly smug. "She's a troublemaker. Do you know that? The woman is a born troublemaker! I never realized it, because I always assumed that she was right and that everything was my fault, but she's been dead wrong about us from the start. Victoria had her pegged. My mother is one of those people who are never satisfied. It may be a little late, but I actually feel sorry for my father. No wonder he poured so much of his time and energy into the business. He was running away from her!''

Hearing her evaluation of her parents' relationship gave Deirdre a moment's pause. Her confidence wavered. "Were you doing that, Neil? Were you running away from me, spending every minute thinking about the business?''

"A good many of those minutes you thought I was thinking about the business, I was thinking about you," he said with a crooked smile. Then the smile vanished. "I wanted to please you. I felt that if I couldn't win your heart, I'd at least win your respect."

"You've had that from the start. And I admire—no, I stand in awe of—what you've done with the business." She sharpened her gaze on him. "But I meant what I said about delegating authority. I want more of your time, Neil! I want to do things with you. I want to go out to romantic little lunches every so often, or play tennis, or take off for the weekend and go...wherever!"

His eyes twinkled. "I think I can manage that."

"And I want to go to Washington with you tomorrow."

"No."

"Why not?"

"Because I'm not going."

She stared at him for a minute. "You're not?"

"No. Ben can handle it."

"But you're the best one for the job! You know it, and I know it."

"But there is a question of conflict of interest."

"I don't believe that! I was angry, or I'd never have even suggested it!"

"Now you're being diplomatic," he teased.

"I am not!"

He grew serious. "I thought a lot about that situation, too, while I was out driving. No, I didn't originally know that we'd be competing against Wittnauer-Douglass for that contract, but I have to admit that when I found out, there was intense satisfaction in it. I mean, we may not get the contract. The bids are sealed, and I have no way of knowing who bid what. The contract may go to Wittnauer-Douglass, or it may go to one of the other bidders. But I did get an inordinate amount of pleasure knowing that Joyce is right up there in the Wittnauer-Douglass league."

"There's nothing wrong with that—"

"But the point is that I have already avenged myself."

"Yes, but through honest hard work and talent. Not just anyone could have done what you've done, Neil. Joyce Enterprises was marking time. You have it moving forward. If you won't take the credit, then I'll take it for you!"

Her pride in him gave him a thrill. "You will, will you?"

"Uh-huh." She thought for a minute. "But what about practicing law. That was what you really wanted to do. Don't you miss it?"

"I've been practicing law at Joyce, but with lots of other things thrown in. I do think it's time Ben and I switch places, though. I want to maintain a position of power, because I've enjoyed having a say in what we do when, but I don't need a fancy title, and I *don't* need the full burden of responsibility I've been carrying." He paused. "But what about you? You haven't been teaching, and that was what you really wanted to do. Don't you miss it?"

"No," she said firmly, then grew pensive. "Maybe I've outgrown it. Maybe the need just isn't there anymore. It filled a void in my life, but the void is gone. Being a helpmate to you is far more satisfying than teaching ever was."

He hugged her. "The things you mentioned before—things we could do together—I want to do them, too, Deirdre. We never did take a honeymoon."

"We had that before we were married."

"But I want another one. A *real* one. You know, a luxurious cottage someplace warm, champagne at sunset, hours lying on the beach in the sun, maid service and laundry service and room service."

Deirdre slanted him a mischievous grin. "What happened to the man who could do it all himself?"

"He wants to be able to concentrate solely on his wife. Is that a crime?"

"You're the lawyer. You tell me."

He never did. Rather, he kissed her with such sweet conviction that she didn't care if they broke every law in the book.

HEAT LIGHTNING
Anne Stuart

CHAPTER ONE

THE MAN WAS PURE TROUBLE. It didn't take much to see that, and Jassy Turner was a little more observant than most. It came from having to keep an eye out for details, for the little things that could turn triumph to disaster, turn a happy family evening into a screaming tangle, turn a successful fund-raising event into a debacle.

She'd worked hard that hot August day to make sure everything was just right at Belle Rive. The wide, manicured lawns leading down to the river were covered with brightly colored fair booths, with immaculately dressed men in their pale linen suits, with women in their floating summer tea dresses. The children tumbled around at their feet, grubby, noisy, bringing their own vitality to the stifling atmosphere. If it had been up to Jassy, the annual hospital fete, the fund-raising event that had been the Turners' pet project since the beginning of time, would have been for children only. Except that children couldn't dig deep into their pockets to keep the tiny little hospital going.

So while the lawns were covered with pony rides and games and even a carousel trucked in from Sarasota, the wide veranda was covered with long, linen-covered tables, and her mother, Claire, presided at the huge silver teapot, the trembling in her hands stilled by a discreet, purely medicinal, shot of vodka.

She'd known these people all her life, Jassy thought, moving through the crowd to the edge of the veranda, resting her hands on the wide stone railing. She'd never been away for longer than a few months, and she knew what every single one of them was thinking as the stranger made his way through the crowds, moving directly toward the veranda.

"My God, Jassy, who is that?" Mary-Louise Albertson hissed in her ear, her eyes bright with appreciation.

Jassy couldn't pretend to misunderstand. The noise from the children below covered up the sudden quiet on the veranda, but the forty or so people enjoying Miz Claire's tea managed an impressive buzz of conversation. And Jassy knew perfectly well at least half of them were discussing the sudden appearance of the stranger.

"I don't know," she replied, wishing she could turn away, unable to move. She brushed her hands down the length of her pale peach dress, and found they were cool and sweaty on this stifling hot day.

"He sure is a hell of a lot more man than I've seen around here in a long time," Mary-Louise said with a sigh. "The men around here were born wearing suits, I swear. I don't think I've seen that much chest since I saw a Patrick Swayze movie last year. The man is absolutely sinful, he's so good-looking."

"Patrick Swayze?" Jassy murmured.

"Him, too," Mary-Louise allowed. "But he's not here. The man who's heading directly toward us is in the flesh, and what wonderful flesh it is. My heavens, is that an earring he's wearing?"

"It is. I think you'd better forget him, Mary-Louise. Your mama won't allow you to keep company with a man wearing an earring," Jassy said with her first touch of humor.

"My mama wouldn't allow me to keep company with a man who wears shabby jeans, an old work shirt unbuttoned to the waist, and hair hanging down to his collar. However, my mama didn't raise no dumb chickies. What she doesn't know won't hurt her. I'm certainly not planning on making her privy to all my peccadillos."

Jassy felt a real pang of dismay. "Mary-Louise, your divorce isn't even final yet...."

"I'm only going to play with him, Jassy. I'm not going to marry him. I've just got to figure out how I'm going to plan my attack." She drifted away, deep in thought. Jassy didn't even turn to watch her go.

He was halfway there now, and he'd stopped to talk to a little boy who was sobbing loud enough to be heard over the general din. At his feet was a smashed ice-cream cone, and the dark-haired child was crying with an enthusiasm found only in the young.

A moment later, after a short, earnest conversation with the stranger, the tears had miraculously stopped. In the next, a replacement ice-cream cone found its way into little Tommy Lee Philips's grubby fist. His mother was there, casting a wary eye at the stranger, and Jassy watched as he charmed the mother as effortlessly as he charmed the child.

Trouble, she thought again, acknowledging the little burning feeling in the pit of her stomach. And he's heading this way.

He wasn't particularly aware of her watching him. He had to know that almost everyone was watching his approach, either openly or covertly, and one pair of eyes wasn't going to mean any more than another.

Mary-Louise was right: he *was* more man than they'd seen in a long time. She was surrounded by southern gentlemen, all tall and immaculate in their white linen suits, Princeton basketball players and gentlemen farmers, her own brother, Harrison, included. The man coming up the lawn was cut from a different cloth.

He was tall, but not as tall as the men surrounding her, probably not much more than six feet. He wore scuffed leather boots, dusty, ripped jeans, and a work shirt open to his waist, exposing a great deal of bronzed, glistening chest. The men around her didn't sweat. Probably because they didn't do enough hard work to sweat, she thought with a trace of humor.

He was wearing dark glasses in the bright midafternoon sun, and they obscured half his face. His dark-blond hair was shoved back, and there really was a gold hoop in his left ear. A small one, but there nonetheless, and she could just imagine Harrison's contempt when the man finally had the nerve to reach them.

Except the man didn't seem to be lacking in nerve. His advance was steady, determined, his walk an inexplicable part of his presence. It wasn't a swagger—he was too sure of himself to need to swagger. It wasn't a stroll—he had too much intensity to stroll. It was a combination of both, a purposeful stride that allowed time for distractions like crying children, but moved inexorably onward.

He glanced her way when he reached the bottom step of the veranda. The polite murmur of the well-bred group crowded onto the wide stone terrace abated only slightly, and yet Jassy knew that every eye, every ear of the upper crust of Turner's Landing was concentrating on the rough stranger's presence.

Even behind the sunglasses the heat of his gaze was able to touch her. As it touched all the women present, impartial, seductive, an instinctive flirtation that meant absolutely nothing. If Mary-Louise wanted him she'd probably have no trouble getting him. But not for long.

"Jassy?" Her mother's cool, calm voice held not the slightest bit of slur. Thank heaven for small favors. Claire didn't usually do well on days like these.

Jassy forced herself to turn away from the stranger, moving to her mother's side with unhurried grace. "Do you want me to take over for you, Mama?"

"I do not. I'm doing just fine. I want you to tell me who that man is, and what he's doing here."

Even her mother's somewhat bleary eyesight was clear enough to detect trouble when it walked up her front lawn. "I don't know, Mama," she said. "Maybe he just heard about the tea?"

"Dressed like that?" Her mother sniffed with disapproval. "Things may have changed, but we don't have to get slack, dear. I refuse to pour tea for a man who's not wearing a tie."

"He's not wearing much of a shirt, either," Jassy murmured. "As a matter of fact, I don't think he's here for the fete, or the tea."

"Then what's he here for?" Her mother's voice was querulous, and Mary-Louise's mother cast a disapproving glance in their direction.

"I don't know. Mama, lower your voice. Mrs. Stevenson is watching us."

"Old biddy," Claire said. "She hoped I'd be indisposed this afternoon so she could play the grande dame. As long as I'm on this earth I'll be the one to pour at the hospital fete. Do you hear me, Jassy?"

"I hear you, Mama," Jassy said wearily. "So does everyone else." In point of fact, no one else was paying any attention to Claire and her daughter. That usual source of gossip was small potatoes compared to the man who'd mounted the wide stone steps and was moving without haste toward the group of people in the center.

Jassy edged away, toward the upcoming confrontation. She didn't know what she was expecting, or how she thought she might be able to stop it, but she knew she had to try.

She expected the stranger wouldn't be quite so devastating up close. She'd been wrong. The closer he got, the more overwhelming he seemed. He was a few feet away from her when he stopped, directly in front of her older brother, Harrison, lord of the manor, de facto king of Turner's Landing.

No one made any more polite pretense of conversation. The citizens of Turner's Landing were well-bred, but some things were even too much for their ingrained manners. The distant noise of shrieking children provided only a backdrop for the silence that enveloped Harrison Turner and the stranger.

Harrison, immaculate and polite as always, turned to the stranger, an uneasy expression in his brown eyes. "Can I help you?"

The stranger smiled. He had a wide, mobile mouth beneath the sunglasses, and the smile should have been charming, infectious. Indeed, the men surrounding Harrison managed uncertain smiles themselves. Jassy wasn't in the mood to smile. She stood there, behind Harrison, ready to do battle to protect her brother, if need be. He might not realize the stranger was trouble, yet. But she did.

"I'm Caleb Spenser," he said, his voice a smooth, easy drawl, roughened just slightly from cigarettes, like liquid honey laced with whiskey. "I've just bought the place down the road and I thought I'd stop by and make your acquaintance. Perhaps I picked an awkward time."

Jassy could see Harrison's broad shoulders relax. "Now's a fine time," he said, his voice a hearty boom that signaled a return to a semblance of normalcy. "We're having a fund-raiser for our little hospital, and we're counting on all the local landowners to do their share. I'm Harrison Turner, by the way, and these are some of my friends and neighbors." He introduced the small group of men surrounding him, deliberately omitting Jassy at his shoulder.

Caleb Spenser's smile didn't change. Harrison seemed to take it at face value, an affable expression of goodwill. Jassy wasn't so sure. "I'll be more than happy to do my share," he said in that deep voice of his that sent flutters down half the female backbones on the veranda. Even hers, Jassy had to admit.

"Whereabouts did you buy?" Harrison inquired, still sounding like the gentleman farmer talking to poor white trash. "I hadn't heard that any land was on the market." His condescending tone suggested that if he had, he would have been certain to have bought it himself, or at least made sure that whoever did purchase it passed his strict standards.

"An old place down by the swamp," the man said. "Used to be a bordello, I hear."

Harrison's slightly rosy complexion paled. "The Moon Palace? You bought the Moon Palace? What in hell for?"

Caleb Spenser shrugged. "I kind of liked it. Besides, it's what I do. I buy run-down places, fix them up and sell them."

"You won't find any buyers for the Moon Palace," Harrison said flatly. "This happens to be the one town in the whole damned state of Florida that hasn't been affected by the real estate boom. If you think you're gonna turn around and make a killing with some developer, you better think again, son. We're a tight-knit place, and we like things as they are."

"I bet you do," Caleb murmured. "But things don't stay the same. I expect you've lived long enough to discover that." He pushed his sunglasses up to his forehead, and Jassy took a deep, involuntary breath, one loud enough to get his attention.

He had the most extraordinary eyes. They were a light, translucent, almost silvery gray, with just a touch of blue in them, like the shimmer of color on a frosty morning. They held just as much warmth. In the tanned planes of his face they made his smile seem the cynical thing that it was. If anyone had any doubt that Caleb Spenser was a man to contend with, all they had to do was look into those clear, cool eyes and they'd know better. Trouble, Jassy thought, as his eyes met hers beyond Harrison's shoulder. Real trouble.

"Do I know you?" Harrison demanded, unaware of the byplay going on behind him. "You look real familiar."

Jassy felt herself dismissed, as once more those mesmerizing eyes met her brother's, and Caleb Spenser's smile was not a pleasant sight. He looked like a shark at feeding time. "I've never been in Turner's Landing before," he said, not answering the question.

"But I'm sure I've seen you before."

Caleb Spenser shrugged. "Now that you mention it, you look familiar to me. I used to know someone who looked a lot like you. But his name was Billy Ray Smith, not Harrison Turner."

For a moment Jassy thought her brother was going to throw up. He looked at that cool, smiling intruder with a pale, sickly expression, and Jassy's worst fears were confirmed. She still didn't know how, or why. She only knew what.

"Sorry," Harrison managed, his voice strained. "I'm not in the habit of using aliases."

"I wouldn't have thought so, a fine gentleman like yourself," Spenser said easily, and most people would have thought he'd dropped the notion. Jassy knew otherwise. "Would you mind if I looked around, met a few people? I'm planning on being in these parts for a while, and I'd like to find out what kind of people I'll be dealing with."

Jassy couldn't stand it anymore. Her brother still looked tense and sick beside her as she stepped into the group. "You're not from around here, Mr. Spenser?" she inquired, pulling out all her charm.

"I'm from just about everyplace but here, Miss...?"

"This is my baby sister, Jacinthe," Harrison said, suddenly protective.

Spenser nodded, getting the message. "As I was saying, I'm from about everyplace but the gulf coast of Florida. I've spent a lot of time in Louisiana, in Georgia, Tennessee, South Carolina. What time I've spent in Florida was mainly on the East Coast. Near a little town called St. Florence."

Once again she felt Harrison's turmoil, and she knew the obscure name of that town wasn't an accident.

"Well," she said brightly, "we're glad you're here now. We're very proud of our little town. Turner's Landing is one of the few undeveloped, unspoiled little towns in this part of Florida. I think you'll enjoy your stay here."

"Oh, I expect to, Miss Turner," he said. "I surely do." If the man had had a hat he would have tipped it. Instead he sort of nodded his head and drifted away, politely enough, but then he was gone. Jassy didn't move, watching as he drifted over toward the group of women by the railing who'd been watching him avidly, Mary-Louise included. Even from a distance she could see them preen and pout prettily.

She didn't blame them. She, who was usually immune to that

type of flirtation, that type of man, had felt the intense charm he seemed to turn off and on automatically. She wouldn't be surprised to see Mary-Louise biting his ankles in another minute.

But then he was gone, leaving the women staring after him, hungry looks on their faces. She watched as he worked the crowd, moving from group to group with that same inexorable charm. Harrison stood beside her, watching in the same silence as the men around them turned to a polite discussion of the weather. Caleb Spenser was too close to be discussed, as everyone was longing to.

Claire even poured him a cup of tea. But then, Claire had never been much of a judge of character, starting with Jassy's father. She seemed to have forgotten her disapproval of his casual attire, and her face looked positively youthful as she looked up at Spenser from her thronelike position behind the huge silver teapot. Jassy could feel Harrison's outrage, and she turned, half expecting him to join Spenser and Claire. Half expecting him to pick the stranger up by the scruff of his neck and throw him off the terrace.

But Harrison had never been one to deal with things directly. Instead he turned on his heel, disappearing into the house without a word.

Jassy was torn. On the one hand, she wanted to go after her brother, to demand to know what was going on. It was more than clear to her that he'd known Caleb Spenser at some time in the past, and that association wasn't the slightest bit pleasant. He just as obviously didn't want people knowing about it.

But it wasn't an accident that Spenser had showed up there in a crowd of friends and family. And he'd known who he'd find when he reached the veranda—he'd headed straight toward Harrison. It wasn't an accident that he'd bought the old Moon Palace. The tumbledown building lay on a knoll by the edge of a swamp, and it had been vacant for the better part of twenty years. He'd have no use for it in a conventional sense. Even fixed up and spruced up, he'd be hard put to find buyers. It was too damp, too remote, and as Harrison had told him, Turner's Landing was on the back end of beyond. The place was unspoiled and undeveloped, not because of any great nobility on the landowners' parts, but because no one had offered enough money. No one had even been interested.

Jassy glanced behind her, at the closed screen door where Harrison had disappeared. His wife, Lila, for once was unaware of her husband's absence, as she did her social duties and kept up a conversation with the dragonlike Mrs. Stevenson. No one seemed to have noticed he was gone, and she was torn by her need to go after him, to confront him. And to stay and guard the terrace.

Harrison could wait. She wasn't going to abandon the battlefield until the enemy had left. And that's who Caleb Spenser was, for sure. The enemy.

She felt a sudden prickling at the back of her neck. She turned, and found he was standing in front of her, too close, crowding her. She could smell his skin, smell the dust and sweat and heat of him, and she wanted to step back, away. She held her ground.

"Mr. Spenser," she said politely.

"Just Spenser," he said. "Unlike most people around here, I'm not the Mister type."

"And what type are you?"

"Why don't you find out?" he said, soft enough so that even the ruthlessly eavesdropping Mary-Louise missed it.

She was used to this, Jassy reminded herself. She was used to macho men who had to flirt with anything in skirts in order to assert their masculinity. It was just that Caleb Spenser was much better at it than most.

"Are you flirting with me, Mr. Spenser?" she inquired coolly. "Because if you are, I may as well tell you you're wasting your time. You may have all the other women eating out of your hand, but I'm a lost cause. Anyone around here can tell you that. I don't flirt, and I don't respond to men like you."

"Men like me, Miz Turner? And just how do you define a man like me?"

"Trouble," she said flatly, without thinking.

He laughed then, throwing back his head, and his teeth were very white, very large in his wide mouth. Like a shark, she thought again. "You've got more brains than most of the people around here," he said.

"Remember that, Mr. Spenser. You aren't going to be able to charm me into thinking you're harmless."

"Oh, I wouldn't ever want you to think I'm harmless," he said softly. "That's half the fun."

"Mr. Spenser..."

"Spenser," he corrected softly. And then he was gone. Moving down the front steps and across the lawn with a graceful stride that wasn't the slightest bit leisurely. She watched him go, and she shivered in the humid August heat, suddenly chilled.

"Well, what did he say to you?" Mary-Louise demanded. "You were both looking pretty intense. I wouldn't have thought he'd be your kind of man."

"He's not," Jassy said absently. He was out of sight now, and it was hard to believe he'd ever been there, unsettling everyone. But he had.

"That's good. I told you, I saw him first."

"Actually," Jassy pointed out with a strained return to impartial good humor, "I noticed him first. But you've known me for almost all my thirty-one years, Mary-Louise. Do you think he's my type?"

Mary-Louise laughed. "Point well taken. What do you suppose he's doing here?"

"Didn't you hear? He bought the Moon Palace. He's planning to renovate it."

"For heaven's sake, why?"

"Maybe he's planning to run it."

Mary-Louise laughed. "Honey, that man doesn't look like a pro-curer. Besides, I don't think this depressed area can support a high-tone bordello. Not unless he was going to work it himself. I think he just might be worth paying for."

"Mary-Louise!" Jassy sounded just as scandalized as Mary-Louise wanted her to. "You're incorrigible."

"It's true," Mary-Louise said.

"What's true?"

"That I'm incorrigible. And that he'd be worth paying."

"Behave yourself," Jassy said. "I'm going in to check on Harrison. I don't want you climbing on the table and doing a striptease over the punch bowl while I'm gone."

"There'd be no point in it," Mary-Louise said cheerfully. "Mr. Spenser's already left." She glanced after him, sighing exaggeratedly. "What's wrong with Harrison, anyway? He was looking sick as a dog."

"He has a touch of the stomach flu," Jassy, who never lied, said smoothly. "I told him he should take it easy, but you know Harrison. A firm believer in his social duties."

"A firm believer in parties," Mary-Louise said with a note in her voice Jassy couldn't quite decipher. "Give him a kiss for me. I'll go rescue poor little Lila from my mother."

"She'd appreciate it. My sister-in-law has never known how to stand up to anyone, and your mother even puts the fear of God in me."

"And you're so tough," Mary-Louise said with light mockery.

"Yes, I'm so tough," Jassy murmured to herself as she headed through the French doors.

The house was still and quiet, slightly cooler than the thick heat on the terrace. They were due for a whopper of a thunderstorm. Overdue, in fact.

She found Harrison in the study, sitting behind his desk, a half-empty glass of very dark whiskey in his hand. He didn't bother to look up when she entered—he'd know she'd be the only one who'd dare come after him.

She wasn't one for drinking, but somehow the circumstances seemed to call for it. She poured herself a half an inch of bourbon in a glass, filled the rest with water, and moved to the chair beside the desk.

"Cheers," she said, holding her glass aloft.

Harrison glared at her morosely. "I'm in a mess of trouble, Jassy." It was an uncharacteristic admission. Usually Harrison would choke before admitting a weakness. The situation must be even worse than she thought.

"No," she said, taking a delicate sip and shuddering. "We're a family. If one of us is in trouble we all are. You want to tell me about it?"

Harrison glanced at her. He was a very handsome man—in truth, much better looking than the insolent stranger who'd invaded their afternoon tea party. His charm was also legion—the paternalistic variety that made most women trust him.

He shook his head. "I've got to think about it for a while. Come up with a plan. In the meantime, what you don't know won't hurt you."

"Harrison..."

"It's not women's business," Harrison said firmly. "You let me take care of it and don't worry your pretty little head about a thing."

It was moments like these that made Jassy long to pour her drink into his lap. She'd fought his condescension for years, and had finally given up, learning she could get her own way, run things pretty much as she liked, as long as her brother thought he was in charge. He wasn't very cheerful right now, but it would take more than the appearance of a dangerous stranger to make him take action.

It would be up to her in the long run. And if he wouldn't tell her why Caleb Spenser was here, there was only one way to find out. She'd ask Spenser herself.

She smiled at Harrison, resisting the impulse to pat his hand, just as she'd resisted the impulse to dump her drink. "All right, Harrison. You know best."

And Harrison, self-absorbed as always, believed her.

CHAPTER TWO

JACINTHE AMALIA CLAIRE TURNER was a thirty-one-year-old spinster of this parish. Or so she liked to think of herself. Devoted to good works and her family, she worked tirelessly on whatever seemed to call for her efficient good humor. She was on the hospital fund-raising board, as all Turners were, she tutored high school students, she drove the ambulance for the local rescue squad, organized the church auctions, worked on the volunteer fire department, and single-handedly ran the battered women's shelter in town. In her spare time she ran the huge, rambling house called Belle Rive, and her motley family besides.

She fully expected to get married eventually. She'd had more than her share of beaux—handsome, gentlemanly men who knew how to treat a lady. Kindly, friendly, moderately liberated men she'd known since childhood, and even though most of them had married and were busy raising families, there were still at least three suitable prospects waiting in the wings. The forerunner was Jim Roberts, the local veterinarian, a man too well-bred to ever make demands or to push her.

She was planning to wait, however. Lila and Harrison had been trying desperately for children for the three years they'd been married. They didn't need the added stress of a full-scale wedding and a possibly ensuing pregnancy. Jassy still had a few years leeway. As soon as Lila conceived she'd consider getting married. In the meantime, there was no hurry.

Harrison and Lila didn't need the added stress of Caleb Spenser's arrival in town, either, but it was several days before Jassy had time to deal with it. The cleanup from the fair was a major undertaking, one which she oversaw and pitched in with her usual calm energy. Then Lila needed someone to drive her down to Clearwater for the next round of tests, someone to hold her hand while she cried all

the way home, someone to listen while she poured out her insecurities and fears. Lila had always been a clinging, frail girl, and
she was terrified that Harrison would leave her when she couldn't
provide him with a child. Harrison and his family had done everything to reassure her, but she still bordered on panic.

Then Claire went into a slump, refusing to leave her room, refusing to eat, refusing to do anything but sit in front of the television and sip delicately at her medicinal bottle. It took all Jassy's
patience and determination to coax her back into civilization once
more, and then there was a crisis down at the Women's Center.
Tommy Lee Philips's father had once more taken his fists to
Tommy's pretty mother, and the two of them had fled to the shelter
for the third time that year. Jassy had the depressing feeling that it
wouldn't be the last, but she was sympathetic, supportive and non-
judgmental. Faith Philips wouldn't leave Leroy and break the cycle
of battering until she was ready to, and haranguing, lecturing and
sermonizing wouldn't do any good but make her feel more miserable.

In the end, four days had passed before Jassy could put her hastily formed plan to work. During those four days, wherever she
went, people talked about Spenser. About the huge order he'd
placed at the lumber yard. About his charm with the ladies. About
his secretive ways. And about the eventual fate of the Moon Palace.

She didn't bother telling anyone where she was going that steaming hot Thursday afternoon. For one thing, people seldom asked,
unless they needed her for something, and she deliberately picked
a time when everyone was well taken care of. Claire had gone out
for a bridge game with Harriet Stevenson and her cronies, fortifying
herself beforehand. Harrison was at work in the library, dealing
with estate matters, and Lila, glutton for punishment that she was,
had gone to visit a friend's new baby. She'd be in for a storm of
weeping when she returned, and Jassy would need to be there to
provide a shoulder. But in the meantime she had a few hours to
herself, a few hours to see what she could learn about the stranger
in their midst.

She took the old Jeep rather than her serviceable Ford. The roads
leading to and from the old bordello were muddy and rutted, and
four-wheel drive would come in handy. Besides, she didn't want

to appear to be too much of a lady bountiful when she paid her social visit.

She put the basket on the seat beside her in the Jeep, then glanced down at her clothes, for the first time wondering whether she should have put a little more care into what she was wearing. It was too hot to wrap up, much as a small, insecure part of her wanted to. The oversize white shirt was buttoned up higher than the sultry weather required, the ankle-length cotton skirt was loose enough to let the air circulate. She probably should have worn boots rather than sandals. Water moccasins were known to frequent the swamps around Turner's Landing. One might have paid Spenser a visit.

It would probably be for the best if one had curled right up next to him. Harrison had been secretive, on edge, since the man's arrival, and the entire household mirrored his moods. Claire's recent bout stemmed directly from Harrison's snappiness, and Lila's crying jags seemed more frequent.

But she couldn't really wish ill on a stranger. Even if that stranger probably wished the Turners, Harrison in particular, a great deal of ill, she didn't want him dead. She just wanted him gone, out of their safe, comfortable life.

He wasn't going to budge, however, without a push. And while she didn't consider herself a pushy person, she did pride herself on being able to get people to do what she wanted with a minimum of fuss.

She didn't expect it to be easy. She didn't expect it to be fast. But she expected to win in the end, simply because she always did. And the well-being of her family mattered too much to her to even contemplate losing.

The Moon Palace was set a good five miles out of the small town of Turner's Landing, on the edge of Beeman Swamp. During the twenties, thirties and forties the randy young bucks of Turner's Landing had beaten a path to the door, learning the first lessons in the art of love. But the fifties had been a slowdown, and by the late sixties the place had closed down and been abandoned to the encroaching wilderness. Most people forgot it existed—the road led to nowhere but the Moon Palace, and the place was damp, mosquito-ridden and decaying. If people were looking for housing, they

did better with one of the anonymous little boxes Harrison had built
on a tract of land on the west side of town.

She pulled the Jeep to a stop beside an ancient, beat-up old
pickup truck, turning off the engine. The place was still, silent, only
the sound of a faint, lazy breeze riffling through the trees breaking
the stillness. No sounds of saws or hammers, no sign of anyone
working on the place.

It was a large, rambling building, conscientiously antebellum.
She'd explored it when she was younger, with Mary-Louise trailing
along behind her, and the two of them had giggled and made wild,
anatomically inaccurate guesses as to what had gone on in those
decaying bedrooms with the red flocked wallpaper stained with
damp. The old house still had a sort of sexual mystery about it,
with the huge live oaks looming over the front, dripping Spanish
moss halfway down to the overgrown grounds. Jassy could tell
herself the couplings that went on behind those doors were sad,
financially inspired ones. But in truth, she could still feel some of
the lazy, erotic energy of the place.

Reaching up, she made sure her thick brown hair was tucked
securely back. Hair like hers was a trial and a blessing. It was much
too thick and curly, and the humidity of late August made it an
impossible mass to control. She had no choice but to pin it back,
off her neck, if she wanted to survive the heat. She'd cut it short
once, and ended up looking like a clown. Nowadays she just let it
grow, pinning it back and ignoring the wisps of hair that escaped
to curl around her face.

Grabbing her basket, she slid from the Jeep and approached the
front door. It stood open, letting in mosquitoes and whatever critters
felt the urge to frequent the Moon Palace, and Jassy hesitated before
knocking on the peeling doorjamb.

Not a sound. The house was dank and dark inside, and she hesitated, too well-bred to simply walk into a stranger's house without
an invitation. She checked her hair again, a nervous gesture she
wasn't usually prone to make, and called out.

"Mr. Spenser?"

She heard a noise then, a rough scrabbling sound, and a dog
appeared in the hallway. At least, she assumed it was a dog. He
was absolutely huge, a motley shade of black and brown, and his

ancestry was as mysterious as the old house. She could see New-
foundland in his size and the shape of his head, retriever in his coat
and heaven knows what else in his sway back and short legs.

He opened his mouth, displaying an impressive set of canine
teeth, and whoofed lightly. And then he padded forward, butting
his huge head under her hand.

Jassy squatted down, scratching him lightly. "What a big, silly
dog you are," she murmured affectionately. She loved animals, but
Harrison was allergic to them, and she'd never owned a pet larger
than a goldfish. "You're not much of a watchdog, I'll say that for
you."

"He's not supposed to be." He was there, watching her, his eyes
shadowed in the dark hall. "I can take care of my own."

Jassy looked up, swallowed convulsively, and rose. He was shirt-
less today in the still, moist air, and he hadn't bothered to shave.
He should have looked derelict. Instead he simply looked...
dangerous.

She picked up her basket and advanced, a determined, unwavering smile on her face. "I'm the local representative of the welcoming committee, Mr. Spenser. As your nearest neighbors we
thought we ought to welcome you to Turner's Landing."

He didn't move, just let his eyes drift down over her body.
"Who's we? Don't tell me your brother's decided I'll be an asset
to the community?"

She considered lying, then thought better of it. She made it a
habit not to lie—it was too easy to get caught. Besides, she had
the unnerving feeling that this was a man who could see through
lies. Who could see through almost any kind of falsehood.

"Actually he doesn't know I'm here," she said cheerfully. "But
he knows I usually make an effort to welcome any newcomer, and
if he didn't feel you were welcome I'm sure he would have said
something. Do you think he doesn't want you here, Mr. Spenser?"

"Just Spenser," he said. "What's in your basket?"

She gripped it in both hands. "Answer my question and I'll
answer yours."

His smile was slight, enough to make her wish she'd worn a

turtleneck shirt in this vast, humid heat. "Games, Miss Turner? I think you'll find I'm not a good man to play games with."

"I don't tend to play games with men."

"Don't you? They can be fun. As long as you're prepared to face the consequences."

He was too much for her. She could feel the sweat forming at the small of her back, between her breasts, and she shifted the weight in her basket. "Red beans and rice," she said, answering his question. "Two loaves of fresh bread, a dozen chocolate chip cookies and a bottle of Miss Sadie's elderberry wine."

He reached over and lifted the red-checked cloth covering her offering. "Who's Miss Sadie?"

"Our cook, housekeeper, savior of our souls, warden. We wouldn't survive without her. Most of this is compliments of Miss Sadie."

"Give Miss Sadie my thanks. What isn't her doing?"

Trust him to pick up on that tiny slip. Once more she considered lying, and then thought better of it. Why should she lie? "The cookies, of course. Miss Sadie never could make enough to keep me happy, so I learned to cook early on."

"You have a sweet tooth, Miss Turner?"

"Please, you make me sound like some ancient southern belle. My name is Jassy." She kept her voice light, casual, trying to keep her mind from the opulent, decaying bedrooms upstairs and what she used to imagine went on in them.

"Jassy," he said, and she wished he hadn't. He took the basket from her hands and she stepped back, a little too quickly, then cursed her nervousness. "This is quite a friendly little town. More so than I would have imagined."

"We don't get too many strangers around here."

"So I gather. I would have thought that would make you more skittish."

He'd chosen that word deliberately. For one of the first times in her life she was feeling skittish, and the knowledge that he'd recognized that fact, commented on it, lashed her pride back into existence.

She straightened her back, pushing a hand through her escaping hair. "We have nothing to fear from strangers, Mr. Spenser."

His smile was small, secretive and unsettling, but he made no comment. "Would you like a tour of the place?" he said instead.

What she wanted was to get as far away from there as she could, as fast as she could go. But she'd come for a reason, and she wasn't about to leave empty-handed. "If I'm not interrupting your work," she said politely.

He shook his head. "Things are still in the planning stage. I haven't quite decided what I'm going to do with all this." He held out his arm for her, but she stayed back, finding there were limits, after all, to her pride and bravery.

"You lead the way," she said with only a tiny bit of breathlessness in her voice. "I'm afraid of snakes."

"The snakes are in the basement, Jassy," he said. "I wasn't planning on taking you down there." But he moved ahead anyway, and she followed him, watching the smooth strength in his tanned, bare back.

He must have started in the kitchen. This room, at least, was bare of rubbish and filth. The windows let in the greeny gray light reflecting off the swamp, but those windows were spotless, as was the sturdy oak table in the middle of the room, the old iron sink, the cracked linoleum floor with its cabbage rose pattern just discernible. He set the basket down on one narrow wooden counter, and Jassy noticed the other offerings.

There were pickles and jams, cakes and cookies, homemade wine and fine whiskey. She imagined the old-fashioned refrigerator that was humming busily was probably chock full of casserole dishes, all designed to feed the stranger. "I guess I wasn't the first to bring you a welcoming package," she said, moving past him to pick up a familiar-looking pickle jar. Mary-Louise prided herself on her spicy relish, doling it out like a miser at Christmas. She'd brought him three bottles of the precious stuff. Jassy could just guess what else she'd welcomed him with.

"Not the first," Spenser agreed. "But certainly the most interesting."

She turned to look at him, her earlier nervousness vanishing. "Why do you say that?"

"Oh, I've heard all about Miss Jassy Turner. The hardworking Jassy with her good deeds and her clean living. As far as I can tell, just about everyone who's come to visit has tried to warn me off you.''

"I can't imagine why.''

"Can't you?'' He shrugged. "It's fairly obvious to me. The gentlemen who've come to visit, to check out the place and to bring me whiskey, have felt protective. They don't want the stranger to mess with their local saint. The women don't want the competition.''

"Full of yourself, aren't you, Mr. Spenser?'' she said coolly.

"Just realistic. This is too hard a life to let yourself be blinded by sentiment or the proper thing to think and say. But you wouldn't know about that, would you? I bet you spend all your time being proper.''

"I didn't come here to discuss my behavior.'' Her voice was sharp as she leaned against the counter, keeping her gaze in the vicinity of his stubbled chin. His shirtlessness bothered her. His entire body bothered her.

"Then why did you come here, Jassy?'' He moved closer, his voice dropping a notch. "Did you want to check out the new talent like your friend Mary-Louise?''

Jassy didn't flinch. "Not exactly.''

"Then why the Lady Bountiful act?''

"I want to know why my brother is frightened of you.''

She'd taken him by surprise. There was a hot, damp breeze coming in through the window, and it stirred the tendrils of hair that escaped her hairpins. It ruffled the hem of her skirt, it danced through his slicked-back blond hair. It slithered around them, between them, through them, as they faced each other in silence.

And then he shuttered those extraordinary light eyes of his, and withdrew. "Ask him,'' he said, and she knew the subject was closed.

"I'll do that,'' she said. She glanced around her. "How about that tour?''

If she still surprised him he didn't let it show. He simply smiled, reaching out his long arms, and for one startled moment she thought he was going to pull her against his tanned, strong body. She didn't move, mesmerized, as he pulled open the refrigerator and grabbed two long-necked beer bottles. She'd been right—the old wire shelves were loaded down with casseroles. Including one of Mary-Louise's.

He shut the door again, opened both bottles and handed her one. "I didn't say I wanted a beer," she pointed out.

"I didn't ask." He tipped a goodly part of the bottle down his throat, and she watched him swallow, watched as drops of condensation from the dark brown bottle dripped onto his chest.

She took a hasty gulp of her own beer, letting the cool, peaty taste of it slide down her throat. It was a dark beer, stronger than the pale yellow stuff she was used to. She liked it.

He didn't try to take her arm again. He led the way, letting her pick her path through the rubble, the piled lumber, the barrels of trash and the broken floorboards. The red-flocked wallpaper was mildewed, stained, peeling off the walls on its own accord. The wide, curving stairs were missing banister rails, and one of the steps had a gaping hole in it leading down to the basement. And the snakes.

She followed him, quietly enough, as he led her through the empty bedrooms. One room was used to store furniture, an old Victorian bed frame, several marble dressers, an old chifforobe. The rooms had been swept free of rubbish, rat droppings and broken glass, but none of them were occupied.

"Where do you sleep?" she inquired artlessly as they reached the head of the stairs again.

He stopped a few steps down, so that his face was level with hers. He was too close, but this time she wasn't going to step back like a nervous ninny. "I didn't know you were interested." He'd finished his beer, leaving the empty bottle on the top stair. Hers was still half-full, and she had no intention of drinking any more. He addled her enough.

"I'm not..." she began, but he didn't let her finish.

"I guess you're not the clean-living saint everyone thinks you are. You're just as curious about forbidden fruit as the rest of them." He took the bottle from her hand, setting it down beside his, and she knew he was going to kiss her. The second time in her life she'd seen the man, and he was going to kiss her. And God, she wanted him to. She wanted to taste the beer and cigarettes on his mouth, she wanted to feel that naked, warm chest against hers.

She jerked away, nervously, before he'd even touched her. "I'd better be going," she said, moving past him with sudden clumsiness, kicking the two bottles so that they rolled and tumbled down the long flight of stairs, her own spraying beer all over the place. "I...I'm sorry," she said, rushing past him, half-expecting him to reach out and stop her.

He didn't. He simply stood near the top of the stairs and watched her run, a small, enigmatic smile on his face.

"You come back now, y'hear," he said, his voice mocking the typical southern farewell.

"Not if I can help it," she muttered under her breath, practically sprinting for the front door.

This time she didn't look for snakes as she ran across the overgrown patch of ground to the Jeep. It wasn't that she expected him to come after her. He hadn't put out a hand to stop her when she'd run like a frightened rabbit—he'd hardly be likely to come running after her into the murky afternoon heat.

She had to get out of there, before her brains melted into a little pool of sweat. The sheer sensuality of his presence, his subtle and not so subtle come-ons to her didn't have a thing to do with Jassy Turner. They probably didn't have much to do with whatever lay between him and Harrison. He flirted automatically, with whatever female was present. He probably would have been more than happy to take her to bed if she'd been willing, and it would have meant nothing more than the icy cold beer he'd just drunk. A pleasant way to satisfy a physical need and then forget about it.

He was the type of man she always steered clear of. The kind who let frustration reach their fists, and used those fists on whoever was too weak to hit back. She'd seen men like him every day, trying to get their battered wives back home to cook and clean and lie still for them. She never could understand why those women had gone in the first place.

Now she could.

She couldn't let him get to her like that. For all the danger he represented, the fact that she was just another in a long line of females was actually an advantage. He didn't see her as the enemy.

He was still her best chance of finding out what Harrison was so frightened of.

She'd just need to be better prepared. Not go traipsing over to a place like the Moon Palace alone on a steamy afternoon. She should recognize dangers when she saw them. A place like the old bordello, reeking of ancient sex. A man like Caleb Spenser, exuding his own powerful attractions. Next time she saw him it had better be on her own turf, with her defenses tight around her. Because the next time she might not get out in time.

CHAPTER THREE

CALEB SPENSER leaned against the open doorway, watching as his visitor disappeared down the twisty road leading away from the old bordello. A huge, shaggy head poked its way beneath his hand, and he stroked it with absent fingers. "What do you think of her, Dog?" he asked. "Not much like her brother, is she? Or am I wrong?"

Dog grinned his huge, doggy grin, panting in the humid heat, then flopped down at Spenser's feet, covering the toes of his scuffed boots and blocking the entranceway. "You're not sure, are you?" Spenser said. "Well, neither am I. On the one hand, she might be just what she seems. A slightly nervous, slightly scattered lady who's out to protect her family from marauding strangers.

"On the other hand, she might know perfectly well why I'm here. She must be...let's see, late twenties? Early thirties? We'll compromise at thirty. That would have made her seventeen when it happened. Would the old man have told her? Probably not. You know these old suthun gennulmun, Dog. They don't confide in their womenfolk unless they have to.

"Junior's another matter, though. He's a sniveling coward. Just the sort to turn to his little sister and see whether she could bail him out of his troubles. Of course, he'd already gotten his Daddy to do just that, so there'd be no need to confide in little Jassy." He pushed away from the door, heading back into the house and picking up the fallen beer bottles. The smell of spilled beer didn't make much of a dent in the thick odor of mildew, rotting vegetation and general decay, and her horrified expression as they tumbled down the stairs had been worth it. He could almost believe her, except that he didn't believe anyone was that sweet and innocent anymore.

Dog got up and lumbered after him. "Yes, I know. Maybe I'm too hard on her. Maybe not. I expect she's really just like her friends. Like that hot-blooded creature who came out yesterday, loaded with pickle relish and chicken casseroles and come-hither glances.''

Dog groaned, his paws tapping noisily on the old wood floors as they headed back out to the kitchen. ''You don't need to tell me,'' Spenser said, setting the bottles down in the sink. ''I was crazy to turn down all that ripe female flesh. Clearly the woman wasn't expecting it. But you know, when you get to my advanced age you get a little tired of being expected to provide stud service for any randy female who has an itch to scratch.'' He leaned back against the counter, surveying Mary-Louise's hot pickle relish, and he shook his head. ''But you know, Dog, for Jassy Turner I might be willing to make an exception.''

Dog woofed softly, shaking his big head toward his food dish in a meaningful gesture. ''The thing I like best about you, Dog,'' Spenser said, opening the refrigerator door and staring inside, ''is your conversational abilities. You don't always try to bore me with your problems, you're just content to hear mine. I appreciate that, Dog. As a matter of fact, to show how much I appreciate it, I'm going to give you a treat. I'm not really in the mood for Mary-Louise Whatever-her-name-is's chicken casserole.'' He pulled it from the fridge. ''It's your treat.'' And he set it down on the cracked linoleum with a thump.

Dog padded over to it, sniffing for a moment, and Spenser had the notion that Dog didn't care for Mary-Louise and her come-hither glances any more than he did. But food was food, and Dog had never been big on moral gestures.

''I wouldn't have minded Mary-Louise,'' Spenser continued, pulling out another beer, ''if she hadn't found it necessary to cut out the competition first. I mean, the lady had curves in all the right places, a talented-looking mouth, and a man's got needs, right?''

Dog kept eating.

''But I didn't like her. I didn't like the way she had to tell me all about how boring and sexless Miss Jassy Turner was, or how sought-after Miss Mary-Louise was, and what a great favor she was doing me. If she was that sought-after, why was she sniffing around after me?''

Dog lifted his head, granted Spenser a quizzical expression, and then adjourned to his water dish. ''Yeah, I know,'' Spenser said, levering himself up on the counter. "I have this knack. Women fall at my feet. It's come in handy over the years, you got to admit that. There were times when the two of us would have gone hungry if it hadn't been for sympathetic women and my pretty face. But things are better now. We don't have to worry about where the next meal comes from. And I don't have to take everything that's offered. I can pick and choose."

Dog went over and scratched at the kitchen door. Spenser had replaced the hinges yesterday, so that it no longer opened at the merest nudge, and Dog looked up with an aggrieved expression on his face. "All right, all right," Spenser said, getting down off the counter and opening the door. Dog bounded out with his usual enthusiasm, heading straight for his favorite live oak. Spenser leaned in the doorway, watching him. "I don't have time for recreation, anyway. I'm here for a reason, a very definite reason, and I'd do a hell of a lot better if I concentrated on it. Jassy Turner's a sister to that reason, which is why I'm going to concentrate on her. See whether that skittish look she gets in her eyes comes from fear or wanting. Or maybe both. See how she looks with that hair hanging down her back. See how she looks beneath those baggy clothes."

Dog finished his business and started back up the porch steps at a measured pace. "Yeah, I know," Spenser said. "I'm a class-A bastard. My daddy told me that from just about the day I was born, and I'm doing my level best to live up to it. I'm not going to let sentiment get in the way of what I've got planned for Harrison Turner. And I expect Jassy Turner will help me get what I want. Whether she's as straightforward and innocent as she seems, or just another version of Mary-Louise Whatsername. And it won't matter," he continued, shutting the door behind Dog, "if she is innocent. This life eats that kind of innocence alive. After I get through with her she'll learn not to be so trusting. I'll be doing her a favor, Dog."

Dog simply looked at him with an expression Spenser knew too well. "Maybe not," he said, draining his beer. "But whether I leave her alone or not, she's going to get hurt when her precious brother comes crashing down. If I know Harrison, he'll drag her with him." He reached into his back pocket for a battered pack of cigarettes. He didn't smoke much nowadays, but there were times when nothing else would do. "You know what I'm in the mood for tonight, Dog? Not casseroles or pickle relish or homemade wine or ancient bourbon. I think I'm gonna have me a meal of Miss Jassy Turner's chocolate chip cookies."

Dog whoofed with approval, butting his head against Spenser's leg. "Okay, Dog," he said. "Some for you, too."

"WHERE THE HELL have you been?" Harrison was standing in the middle of the hallway, fuming, his tie pulled loose, his white linen suit rumpled, his dark hair awry.

Jassy had had the entire trip back in which to calm herself and put things into perspective. The rush of hot wind through her hair as she drove too fast back to Belle Rive had loosened the pins, and once she was well away from the Moon Palace and its new owner she'd undone another couple of buttons on her white shirt. By the time she'd parked the Jeep and mounted the front steps to the house she felt a lot more in control of both herself and the situation. She wasn't about to let Harrison in one of his moods rile her again.

"Out," she said briefly. "What's up?"

"Mother came home early from her bridge party. Claimed she was under the weather, but you and I know perfectly well that that witch, Harriet Stevenson, was probably serving sherry just to see how Mother could hold it. And Lila's been up in her room, crying loud enough to be heard all over the damn house, and Miss Sadie's saying she doesn't know what to cook for dinner, since Claire and Lila informed her they wouldn't be eating and you didn't see fit to tell her where you were going or when you'd be back, and I haven't been able to concentrate for a moment, what with all this fuss, and…" He suddenly let out a loud, incredulous sneeze, followed by another equally explosive one.

At least it silenced his tirade. Jassy immediately put first things first. "Have you been up to see Lila?"

"She refuses to talk to me. I told her she shouldn't go see Lorelei and the new baby, but would she listen? No siree. And she's been after me to have some more tests done, but that's ridiculous, since the doctors have said I'm perfectly fine, and the fault's got to be with her."

"Not fault, Harrison," Jassy reminded him gently.

"Well, I'm getting damn sick of it. If she'd just..." He sneezed again, violently. "If she'd just..." Another sneeze. "If she'd..."

Jassy put a hand on his arm. "Why don't you go up and see her? Don't lecture her, don't argue with her, just hold her. She needs that sometimes."

Harrison sneezed, looking aggrieved. "Have you been around animals, Jassy?"

She could think of one particular swamp rat she'd been far too close to, but she doubted whether Caleb Spenser could set off one of Harrison's allergic attacks, no matter how much Harrison disliked the man. And then she remembered the dog.

"Harrison, go see Lila, and I'll deal with Claire." She started toward the front stairs, twice as broad as the curving, damaged ones at the Moon Palace. This time, however, the man she was talking with reached out and grabbed her arm, not gently.

"Lila and Claire can wait," Harrison said, mopping his nose with a linen handkerchief. "You still haven't told me where you were."

"Do I need to report my activities to you, Harrison?" she asked quietly.

He looked intensely frustrated, that frustration complicated by still another bout of sneezing. "I worry about you, Jassy. I'm your older brother and responsible for you. This town isn't as safe and innocent as it appears. There are riffraff lurking about, and I wouldn't be doing my duty as head of the family if I didn't see to your well-being."

Jassy always hated it when Harrison tried to be paternal. He wasn't cut out for it, and she'd bailed him out of trouble too many times to play the subservient younger sister. However, she'd also learned over the years that life went on a lot more easily if she played the game. "I do appreciate it, Harrison. I am capable of seeing to my own well-being, but it's nice to know others care about me." She cast a meaningful glance down at her arm. There were times when Harrison didn't know his own strength, but she didn't want to offend him by pointing out that he was probably leaving bruises.

He released her. "I know you pride yourself on your self-sufficiency, Jassy, but you don't always know what's best for you. There are times when you simply must be guided by those older and wiser.''

Jassy controlled her instinctive snort, still hoping she'd be able to get away without having to tell him where she'd been. ''Yes, brother,'' she said mildly, starting to move past him, but his voice forestalled her.

''You still haven't told me, Jassy,'' he said, and his voice was low and strangely ominous. ''Where were you?''

She couldn't lie. Indeed, there was no need to. She turned back with a limpid smile. ''Visiting our new neighbor and taking him some of Miss Sadie's red beans and rice. Just one in a long line, I'm afraid. Most of the citizens of Turner's Landing seem to have made their way out to the Moon Palace in the last few days, if his larder is any way to judge it. I can't decide whether everyone's curious about the old bordello or the new owner. Probably a little bit of both.''

She'd never seen such a lack of expression on her brother's face. He simply stared at her, blankly, his brown eyes distant, his face completely unreadable.

''I don't want you going out there again,'' he said, his voice flat and expressionless.

''I don't imagine I'll have any need to. I've brought him a basket of food, which, I might add, I told him was from all of us, and I welcomed him to the neighborhood.''

''You told him *I* welcomed him to the neighborhood?''

''Well, I admit he found that a little difficult to believe,'' Jassy said.

''And did he say why?'' There was no missing the underlying intensity beneath Harrison's oddly blank expression.

''No.''

''Did you ask? Foolish of me, of course you did. And he refused to tell you?''

Jassy nodded. ''He told me if I wanted to know why you were…didn't want him around, then I'd better ask you myself. So I'm asking you. Again. What has he got against you?''

That unnerving lack of expression vanished, leaving her brother looking like the old Harrison. Slightly shifty, infinitely charming, looking for the easy way out. "It's ancient history, Jassy. Something I'd almost forgotten, but apparently he hasn't. Don't worry about it. He'll make up his mind what he wants from me sooner or later, and we'll come to an agreement. He's just trying to extort money from us."

"How can he do that unless you've got something to hide?" she asked shrewdly.

"Everyone's got something to hide. Particularly Mr. Spenser. It all depends on just how desperately one wants to cover up, and how much one is willing to pay in order to do so. I haven't made up my mind how high I'll go, and he obviously hasn't made up his mind exactly what he wants."

"You'll pay him off?"

"In one way or another." He sneezed again, looking fretful. "You go and see Lila while I go pour myself a bourbon. This has been a hell of a day."

For me, too, Jassy wanted to say, but she bit her tongue. She'd gotten off lightly—Harrison was capable of making a major fuss if he set his mind to it, and while she didn't like to cave in, she found it much easier to get her own way if she went around it sideways, instead of confronting things headfirst. Some people might call if manipulation. She preferred to think of it as self-defense.

"All right," she said evenly. "Come up when you can." She climbed the stairs, resisting the impulse to rub her arm where his steely fingers had dug into the flesh, resisting the impulse to glance behind her. She knew he was standing there, watching her. And for the first time in her life, she had absolutely no idea what her usually transparent brother was thinking.

THE HEAT CONTINUED into the next day, with no relief in sight from the crippling humidity. Jassy pushed her hair off her neck, wishing the women's shelter could afford an air conditioner that worked. The one she had stuck in the window made a humming noise, and it sounded as if it was doing its job, but the air in the small, drab office was only marginally cooler than the blistering moist heat outside. On top of that, the damned machine ate electricity for breakfast, all without providing a lick of coolness.

However, it was even worse when she turned it off. The office became an oven, a hot box that turned her into a pool of sweat, made her stick to everything, including the old metal desk someone had donated.

She was going to have to go to Harrison for money to pay the electric bill. Maybe even see if he could make an additional donation, enough to get a new air conditioner. Or at least see if some life could be pumped into this tired old one. This might be the hottest August on record, but September tended to be almost as bad. She couldn't make it through another two or three months of living in a steam bath.

She hated having to ask Harrison, but donations had been down lately, due, no doubt, to the miserable economy and the generally depressed region. There were times when she almost hoped the developers would finally discover Turner's Landing, bringing in jobs and money and color and excitement.

She'd lose the peace and quiet she loved, she'd lose the clear waters and untouched swamplands. She'd lose the one parcel of Florida that hadn't been turned into a tourists' playground. But while a part of her loved Turner's Landing, its peace and solitude, another part recognized the fact that she'd lived there all her life. And she needed something more.

It was hard to weigh people's livelihoods against something as ephemeral as a piece of untouched swamp. She spent every day dealing with the fallout of poverty and hopelessness. How could she turn her back on a chance for renewed prosperity for the people she'd known all her life?

Fortunately it wasn't up to her to make the decision. She didn't own anything but a small patch of swampland with a tumbledown cabin, and no one was going to turn that section of soggy wilderness into a golf course.

No one had made any offers for any part of Turner's Landing, not since the big boom in the seventies when her father, the Colonel, had sent those land-hungry developers about their business. She'd always been deeply grateful he'd resisted temptation. She wasn't as certain Harrison was equally happy with that decision.

She might have a hard time getting money out of him. She'd already spent her monthly allotment on groceries for several families, and a bus ticket out of town for another. There was just so far her money could stretch, and Harrison had proved intractable when she'd tried for an increase.

Damn all southern men, her father included. He'd left her money, of course. He'd just left it entirely in Harrison's control, so that she had to go to him like a beggar looking for handouts.

It was good for her soul, she reminded herself. She spent a great deal of her time looking for handouts from the local citizenry, for the women's shelter, for the volunteer fire department and rescue squad, for the church. Pride was a waste of time.

Unfortunately, Harrison had never shown much sympathy for the women's shelter. He felt a Turner should concentrate on more lady-like activities, such as the hospital, and not the trash who beat each other with regularity. He probably felt the women deserved it, even if he never dared voice such an opinion within Jassy's hearing.

Well, she'd get the money out of him, and more besides. She hadn't gotten very far in this life by accepting defeat before she'd even tried.

She was accepting defeat for this office, however, she thought, pushing back from the desk and switching off her ancient electric typewriter. It was too hot and humid to concentrate. She'd take her paperwork back out to Belle Rive and try to accomplish something in the air-conditioned coolness of her bedroom. If anyone in Turner's Landing needed help they'd know where to find her.

She turned off the air conditioner, listening to it sputter and sigh to a damp stop. If Harrison proved intractable she could always sell something. Or hit up Claire.

The house was still and quiet when she returned home, parking her car in the shade of a live oak. Not that she would have expected otherwise—Harrison and Lila had gone to Clearwater for the week-end, and Claire was usually resting at that hour. She'd have the place pretty much to herself.

She heard the sound of voices from the front veranda as she started up the stairs. Claire's voice, sounding younger than it had in years, light with laughter. And Lila's, equally happy.

Jassy took an immediate turn, heading for the veranda. Some-thing wonderful must have happened, for the two unhappy women of Belle Rive to sound so lively. Maybe Lila had finally conceived. Maybe there'd been a sudden windfall. Maybe...

Maybe Caleb Spenser had come to visit, she realized as she stopped still in the doorway, looking at the tableau set out in front of her. Claire was sitting at the table, her graying hair neatly coiffed, clasping a tall glass of iced tea, and smiling at their visitor with a complete lack of judgment. Lila was stretched out on the chaise, her long, quite spectacular legs displayed attractively, though Spenser was either too polite or too Machiavellian to notice. Probably the latter. The three of them looked dangerously cozy, and Jassy's sense of foreboding couldn't have been stronger.

"There you are, darling!" Claire greeted her, her eyes for once bright and lively. "We were afraid you were going to be chained to that old desk all day long."

"Then I would have missed this little tea party," she said, stepping out into the dappled sunlight, putting a nervous hand to her hair. The other women were dressed in flowing summer dresses, flowery, feminine. She was still dressed in her work clothes—wrinkled khaki pants and a wilted oversize shirt. She felt rumpled and grubby, and the fact that Caleb Spenser was seeing her in such a state didn't help matters.

"Ring for Miss Sadie," Lila said lazily. "She'll bring you a glass of tea."

Jassy wanted to rush upstairs, jump into the shower and throw on one of her own flowered summer dresses. But by then Spenser would be gone. Or if he hadn't, it would give him more time alone with the vulnerable members of her family, and she wasn't about to let that happen.

"Sounds wonderful," she said firmly, taking the seat between Spenser and Claire. "I'm parched."

"Take mine," Spenser said, his tone polite, only Jassy hearing the insinuation beneath the light words. "I've barely touched it."

It was a challenge, and she knew it. "Do you have a cold, Mr. Spenser?" she inquired, delaying.

"Nothing infectious," he said, his light eyes meeting hers. *I dare you,* they said.

She took the glass, feeling the cool sweat of it in her hot hands. "I'm very resistant anyway," she said, taking a deep swallow.

"I imagine you are," he murmured, watching her.

Suddenly she was reckless. The glass was so cool, and she was so damned hot. Her shirt was unfastened halfway down, exposing the upper part of her chest. She took the cold, damp glass and pressed it against her throat, slid it down between her breasts, closing her eyes as the delicious coolness washed over her. And then she opened her eyes again, to meet his. And she was hot all over again.

"Wasn't it nice of Mr. Spenser to visit us?" Claire cooed. "And Lila and I were feeling so bored, what with Harrison tearing off on some scheme."

"Very nice," Jassy murmured, staring at her hands.

"I had to come and thank you all for the basket of goodies," Spenser said. "I particularly liked the chocolate chip cookies."

She looked up then, straight into his challenging eyes. And then her backbone stiffened, and she pulled her generations of Turner sangfroid back around her. "I'm glad you came," she said. "I've been wanting to talk to you."

He smiled, that damnable, sexy smile that had half of Turner's Landing swooning, her mother and sister-in-law included. "Talk away," he offered. "I'll be glad to listen."

She was immune, she reminded herself. "We can talk in the library."

"We need privacy, Miss Jassy?"

"Not privacy, Mr. Spenser. It's a business proposition. Business bores Mother and Lila."

"It certainly does," Lila said lazily. "You two go off and talk your business, but you come back out here when you're done. It's too hot a day to do anything but sit around and drink iced tea."

"My pleasure, Miss Lila," Spenser said, rising.

Why did he seem so tall? Harrison was taller, broader, physically more intimidating. So why did Spenser seem to invade her space, overwhelm her being?

She led the way, telling herself he wasn't watching her hips in the baggy khakis, telling herself that even if he was, it didn't matter. She waited until he followed her into the library, Harrison's domain, and then she shut the door behind them, wondering how she was going to broach this.

She needn't have worried. Spenser's grin was quizzical. "So how much are you offering me to get out of town?"

CHAPTER FOUR

ONE THING SHE had to learn about Caleb Spenser, Jassy thought. To expect the unexpected. She did her best not to let her surprise show, moving past him into the room to gain herself some time.

"How much would it take?" she countered coolly.

"More than you have, sugar," he said lazily, sauntering over toward Harrison's broad walnut desk. It was covered with its customary neat little piles of paper, and with no shame whatsoever Spenser began glancing through them.

"How do you know?" She moved to stop him, then thought better of it. What would Harrison have to hide?

Spenser looked up, clearly having decided the desk held no secrets, and he smiled. "I know everything I need to know about the Turners. Particularly about their financial situation. I know, for instance, that you pump all your money into your various good works. I know that Harrison controls everyone's money, and you're all fools enough to trust him."

"Harrison's very good with investments."

"If you say so. Investing is like gambling, and I expect Harrison doesn't know diddly squat about either. He's the type who never knows when to fold or when to raise, and he'll always call at the wrong time."

"Harrison doesn't gamble," she said stiffly.

Spenser raised an eyebrow. "Is that so? You could have fooled me."

"And how do you happen to know so much about our financial situation?" she pushed on. "It's not any of your business."

"Now that's a moot point. I know everything I want to know. As a matter of fact, I was thinking of making a little donation to your pet project."

"Which one? I have a lot of charities."

"The women's shelter. It looks like that could use a little ready cash."

"Guilty conscience, Mr. Spenser?"

He looked startled for a moment, as he understood her meaning. And then he grinned. "No, honey. I don't have to beat women to get them to do what I want."

Jassy swallowed. Her reaction, and her pride. "We'd be more than happy to accept any donation you might care to make. I hadn't realized you were so wealthy."

"I'm not. I'm just a working man, wanting to do my best to make this life a little better for those less fortunate."

"Very pious."

"Yes, ma'am."

"But you clearly don't need work."

"What makes you think that?"

"Well, you've got the Moon Palace to keep you busy, and you have enough extra cash for charitable donations."

"I'm always interested in work. Did you have anything particular in mind, Miss Jassy? You want me to be your hired man?"

Why did everything he said sound like a come-on? At least today he was clothed, all that tanned, muscled flesh covered up by a fresh white shirt and linen pants. No tie or jacket, of course, and that gold hoop in his ear was ridiculous. How could anyone be taken seriously when they wore an earring?

Except that she needed to take him seriously, very seriously indeed. He was a dangerous man, and the worst mistake she could make would be to underestimate his danger.

"Just a little renovation job," she said, moving over to the window and looking out on the veranda. Claire and Lila were still sitting there, looking uncustomarily peaceful. "I have a piece of land and a cabin out in Rayder Swamp. It's not much, just one room and a veranda. I was thinking I'd like to see if it can't be fixed up, or at least kept from falling into the swamp."

"I didn't know you owned any land."

"Why should you? As a matter of fact, it was left to me by an old friend. He used to live there, up until he had to go into a nursing home five years back. When he died he left it to me. I don't usually get out there, and it seemed to be in pretty rough shape, but I thought it would be nice to have a place to escape to.''

He moved closer, with that insinuating grace of his. ''Now what would you need to escape from, Miss Jassy?''

Since the only response she could think of was, *you,* she kept her mouth shut. He moved closer still, coming up behind her as she stared out the window. She could feel the heat from his body on this hot, humid day, feel the faint stirring in her hair as he spoke. ''And you'd like me to come out and have a look at it?''

She swallowed, reaching out to touch her tightly pinned hair. ''If you're interested.'' She didn't dare turn around. He was standing too close. If she turned, she'd be in his arms.

''Oh, I'm interested. I surely am. Just so long as you're not planning to take an ax to me and feed my remains to the gators.'' He'd stepped back, and she used that extra space to turn around and face him.

''You certainly have a lurid imagination, Mr. Spenser. Is that more of your guilty conscience?''

''We never established that I had any guilty conscience in the first place, sugar. When do you want to go out to the swamp?''

''As soon as you're able.'' She had no idea where Harrison had gone or how long he'd be away, but the sooner she got Caleb involved in renovating the old cabin, the better. Rayder Swamp was on the other side of Turner's Landing, and the cabin was well in there. He'd be gone from morning till night, if he decided to take the job, and the longer he was away from the little town the better.

She had no idea how she was going to pay for it. Rowdy's inheritance hadn't included much more than that piece of swamp and the cabin that sat on it, and Harrison watched her expenditures like a hawk, demanding accountings for anything above and beyond her childish allowance.

But she'd get it, someway or another. If worse came to worst she could leave Turner's Landing and get a job. Heaven knows, she'd been tempted often enough. Break the apron strings, leave Claire and Harrison and all the people who seemed to need so much from her and make her own life.

So far she hadn't been able to do it. Every time her family pushed her too far, seemed to be draining her dry, someone else would come to her, and she'd know she couldn't abandon them. She couldn't abandon Claire to Harrison's tender mercies, she couldn't abandon Harrison to the house and Miss Sadie and his own reckless temper. Most of all, she wasn't sure she wanted to leave. This was home, and her brief sojourns in other places had left her restless and longing to come back.

She still had some jewelry she could sell. Some stocks that she could insist Harrison liquidate. She had resources, as hard as it seemed to find them.

"What about tonight?" Spenser said.

"Tonight?"

"What better time to check out the swamp than by moonlight? We can watch the swamp gasses."

"How enchanting," she said coolly. "But there won't be a moon tonight. And the moment the sun goes down the mosquitoes start playing for keeps. What about tomorrow morning?"

"Afraid you're going to get caught in the dark with me, Miss Jassy?"

"I'm not afraid of anything about you," she said flatly.

"You lie, Miss Jassy. Didn't your mama teach you to tell the truth?"

"You've met my mother, Mr. Spenser. You just spent the last half hour or so trying to charm her. Surely you must have guessed that she taught me to tell the truth when the circumstances merited it."

She wanted to slap him. Her palm itched with the need to do just that, she who never hit anyone in her life.

It was his smile that did it to her. She wouldn't have minded a big, smug grin. She wouldn't have minded a small, nasty little smirk. His smile was neither. It never reached his eyes, it simply curled the corners of his wide, mobile mouth and said, *I dare you.*

He was smiling at her now, that cool, double-dare smile, and she wanted to smack him as hard as she could. "Tomorrow morning, Mr. Spenser. I'll come by and fetch you."

"I don't think you want to do that, Jassy. I sleep naked and I don't have an alarm clock. You might just show up at the wrong time." He moved toward the door. "I'll come by and get you."

"I don't think that would be a wise idea."

"Harrison's out of town till Monday, Jassy. He won't be here to threaten me with a shotgun."

Her eyes widened. "How did you know that?"

"That he'd threaten me with a shotgun?"

"I think we all know that, even if no one happens to know why," she said irritably.

"I know why."

"And you're not going to tell me, right?" He nodded his assent. "I mean how did you know Harrison was out of town till Monday?"

He opened the door, glancing back at her with that cool smile. "I could tell you I have mysterious, arcane sources. I've already told you that your family holds no secrets from me. But the answer is a lot more prosaic—Lila told me."

"It figures. That woman's tongue is hinged in the middle. It's a good thing Harrison doesn't trust any woman, or the family secrets would be public knowledge."

"Now that's real interesting, Jassy," Spenser said, pausing in the doorway. "What family secrets are you talking about? And does that mean your brother doesn't even trust you?"

"I'll see you tomorrow morning, Mr. Spenser," she said, smiling her own secret smile as she refused to answer him.

He closed the door behind him. She turned back to the window, watching him as he stepped out onto the veranda. He was different around her mother and Lila. There was no underlying threat in his manner, no hint of a ruthless sensuality bubbling beneath the surface. She could only see his back, but she watched the women's reactions to him. Lila's shy, flattered smile. Her mother's faded glow. And she wondered if she had the same besotted expression on her own face when she looked at him.

Reaching up, she touched her skin. She knew her features so well, knew what he'd be assessing every time he looked at her. They were regular, even, unremarkable. Hazel eyes that sometimes looked green. An average nose. Regular cheekbones, a wide mouth and a chin that somehow made her look vulnerable on odd occasions. He probably saw that chin and figured she was a chump.

But she wasn't. If Harrison wouldn't cooperate she was going to have to take matters into her own hands. She wasn't going to take an ax to Caleb and feed him to the gators. But she had every intention of keeping him so busy out on Rayder Swamp that her brother would forget his existence. At least long enough for her to find out what the hell was going on.

She waited until he left. Waited until he walked across the broad lawn, circling the house to the side driveway, where she could just see his battered old pickup truck. Waited until she heard the noisy rumble of its engine, and then he was gone. And then, and not until then, did she release her pent-up breath.

SHE'S A HELL OF A WOMAN, Spenser thought as he drove down the twisting, overgrown road to the Moon Palace. And part of what made her so delicious was the fact that she didn't realize it. She kept that tangled hair of hers pinned tightly back, but it kept trying to escape. She probably kept all her passions locked up just as tight. Were they trying to escape, too?

He'd thought about going after the wife. She was vulnerable, easy pickings, and a man was bound to be more territorial about a wife than a sister. But Lila Turner wasn't really to his taste. She was a little too skinny, a little too frilly, a little too wounded. She had that look in her pale blue eyes, like life had dealt her a hard blow. Hell, she didn't know the half of it.

Anyone married to Harrison Turner had more than their share of trouble. She just might not know it yet. And it wasn't up to him to set her straight. Or to add to her worries. Things were going to be tough enough for her when he got through with the Turners.

He'd even considered using Mrs. Turner, the Colonel's widow. But one look at the flushed cheeks, overbright eyes and slight tremor in her hands, and he knew she was already paying the price for her husband and son. Besides, he'd been around enough drunks in his life to feel both irritation and pity. Since he didn't have to live with her, he could let the pity rule.

That left sassy Miss Jassy. With her loose-fitting clothes and her tight-fitting smile, she was just the woman to provide him with the means to an end. The end of Harrison Turner's life of leisure. And he had every intention of enjoying that journey.

She thought she could outsmart him. She didn't realize she was dealing with someone who'd learned the hard way. Being the son of a preacher man should have taught him something, but then, she hadn't known his father. Buck knew early on that there was hell and damnation in his only son, and he did his best to beat it out of him. The only thing he managed was to beat more rage into his already angry son.

Prison hadn't helped much, either. Doing three years for killing a rich college boy wasn't conducive to a rosy view of life. When he got out he'd found he'd turned downright mean on occasion. And there were times when he wondered whether he'd ever come back.

He'd spent close to ten years looking for Harrison Turner. Now that he'd found him, he wasn't going to let him go, not for all the tears of all the sisters and wives and mothers. And if those sisters and wives and mothers got hurt along the way, that was just too damned bad.

At least Jassy Turner struck him as someone who could take care of herself. She was also the one most determined to protect her brother and the status quo. It stood to reason she'd be the way to get to Harrison. He found himself wondering whether there really was a sleeping tiger beneath her cool, patrician face and clear, steady gaze. He intended to use their trip to the swamp to find out.

Dog was lying on the front stoop when he drove in, a disgruntled expression in his canine face. Spenser could see why. Mary-Louise Albertson's Mustang convertible was parked haphazardly in the thickening shadows. Dog had the good taste not to like the lady. Spenser didn't care much for her, either, but she certainly was persistent. Maybe she had her own hidden agenda that went beyond a hunger for a new male body. Maybe he'd wait to see what she had to say before chucking her out.

She was sitting on the stairs, waiting for him. She was wearing one of those frilly summer dresses, but hers was strapless, and her abundant breasts spilled over the top of it. Her blond hair was awry, her feet were bare, and her solid gold bangle bracelets clinked as she raised the bottle to her lips. He recognized the brand of bourbon from where he stood. He recognized that it was half-gone.

"Well, there you are, sugar," she purred. "I was wondering

where you were. And you look mighty fine. I didn't know you could clean up so nice."

She was drunk, all right. But she wasn't as drunk as she was pretending, a fact that interested Spenser a lot more than her cleavage. She was here for a reason, and he was more than willing to play along.

"I was off visiting your best friend," he said, taking the bottle from her and tipping some down his throat. A better brand that he usually drank, but then, he didn't have the sophisticated palate that came along with old southern money.

"Jassy? Why would you want to visit her for? She's not your type."

"Why not? I like to think of all women as my type." He leaned against the wall, watching her out of hooded eyes.

"Not Jassy. She's too straitlaced for a wild one like you. Who'd know that better than me? She's what you'd call a semi-virgin. Tried sex once and didn't care for it. You need a real woman. Like me."

"What makes you think she tried sex once?"

"Spenser, honey, I'm her best friend. I know all about the night she spent with Jimmy Pageant, and I know what she's thought about every man who's sniffed around her ever since. She's not interested."

"What does she think about me?" he asked lazily.

Mary-Louise pouted. "You're not seriously thinking about sleeping with her? It would be a waste of time. Even if you managed to get her into bed she'd be no fun at all. You need someone with experience. Enthusiasm. Imagination." She leaned forward, her breasts plumping out of the top of the dress. "Leave Jassy to her charities and her good deeds. Leave her to the indigent mothers whose husbands beat them up every Friday, leave her to church auctions and family teas. Take me."

"Take you where, Mary-Louise?"

She brightened, some of the phony drunkenness vanishing. "Well, now that you mention it, New Orleans would be nice this time of year. Or even up north, away from this stinking humidity. I don't know how people can bear living in it. Let's go away,

Spenser. Somewhere far away from here and the boring people who live here.''

He took another slug of the bourbon, then set it back on the stair beside her. "Did Harrison put you up to this?''

She stared at him, too bad an actress to fake it. "What the hell kind of question is that?'' she demanded in a screechy voice.

"You're sleeping with him, aren't you? Isn't that part of why Lila's looking so downright miserable? He must have sent you down here to see whether you could lure me out of town. How did he think that would solve anything? Sooner or later I'd come back, after I'd enjoyed your luscious body, and then he'd have to deal with me. That's the problem with Harrison—he never did think very far ahead. He should have known I'd come after him, sooner or later. That I'd find him, track him down, no matter where he chose to hide.''

"I don't know what you're talking about,'' Mary-Louise said with a trace of desperation in her voice. She rose on unsteady feet, leaning toward him. "I just thought you and I might have something special together.''

"There's nothing special about what you have in mind, Mary-Louise. Enjoyable, certainly, but it's been going on in this house since it was built.''

It took her a second. "Are you calling me a whore?'' she demanded with lofty dignity.

"Yes, ma'am. You're ready to use your body to do what Harrison tells you to do. Where I come from that's called whoring.''

"Well,'' she said, putting all her huffiness in that one word. She brushed past him, heading toward the front door in her bare feet. Dog moved out of the way, growling low, and if the front door weren't being planed and sanded on a couple of sawhorses she would have slammed it. She stopped, turning around with an accusing glare, and he braced himself for a noble speech.

"You're wrong about one thing, Spenser,'' she said. "It wasn't just because Harrison told me to.''

He listened to the sound of her Mustang as it roared to life, glancing down at the whiskey bottle on the step. He'd hate like hell to have to do the gentlemanly thing and drive her home, but he wasn't going to send a drunk out on the road. He took another tentative slug, noticing for the first time that it was almost half water. She'd been no drunker than Claire Turner on a pilfered glass of sherry.

Even in her temper she was driving a straight line as she tore down the road. He reached down and scratched Dog's huge head. "I'm a fool and a half, aren't I, Dog? She's a good-looking woman, not too skinny, and she was more than willing. Why the hell didn't I take what was offered? That bed is mighty big, and it's been too damned long. Hell, I could have closed my eyes and pretended she was Jassy Turner."

Dog drooled, sinking his head down on his paws. "Yeah, I know," Spenser said. "Why settle for imitation when I can have the real thing? But the real thing is going to be a peck of trouble. I'd do much better to concentrate on the wife and forget about the sister. I don't really want the wife."

Dog woofed softly in the gathering dusk. "Still," Spenser said, "there's no reason why I can't enjoy myself while I take care of Harrison. And there's no reason why I have to make it easy. Maybe once I get Miss Jassy to let her hair down I won't be that interested."

Dog gave him a look of canine incredulity. "All right, maybe she'd be the most fascinating woman since Mata Hari. That, or Saint Joan. Either way, it doesn't matter. I'm going to screw her brother, and if I get the chance to screw her in the process then that's just gravy. And don't look at me like that. You're too soft-hearted. She's a Turner. She doesn't deserve any sympathy."

Dog rose, haughty and disapproving, and lumbered toward the back of the house, his huge shoulders and haunches expressing his disdain, his long, looping tail not even wagging. "Stupid dog," Spenser muttered to himself, sinking onto the stairs and taking another slug of the watered-down whiskey. "What does he expect me to be? A decent human being? It's too damned late for that."

And from somewhere in the kitchen he heard a low, mournful howl.

CHAPTER FIVE

MOST OF THE Turners loved Belle Rive with a deep, possessive passion. Jassy could never see why. It wasn't as if it were the family mansion, lived in for generations. Her father, the Colonel, had bought it from a horse breeder who'd dabbled a bit too improvidently before the Second World War. After generations of genteel poverty the Turners were back on their feet again, thanks to the Colonel's acute business sense and astounding good luck. Jassy couldn't remember when things hadn't been as comfortable, but her mother could, and every now and then she could see a worried expression in Claire's faded blue eyes as she looked around her precious elegance.

For Jassy, the house was a little too stiff. A little too conscientiously gracious, with its chintz-covered furniture, its expensive antiques, most of which actually did belong to the Turners of old. The carefully manicured grounds were soothing to the eyes and pleasing to walk through, but a part of her preferred the wildness of the surrounding swamps.

She'd tried to make inroads on her room but she hadn't gotten very far. At least she'd been able to replace the pale peach walls with a stark white, and throw out the chintz priscillas with their matching draped dressing table. The huge tester bed was comfortable enough, though when she was young she would have sold her soul for a bunk bed. And she banished the rest of the overstuffed furniture, including the de rigueur chaise, to the attics, stripped the rugs off the cypress floors, and found some measure of peace in the uncluttered stillness of the room.

The bathroom she shared with Lila was pink. Pink shower curtain, pink lace curtains, pink wall-to-wall carpeting, even a pink toilet seat. She bore it with good grace. As long as she had her retreat, she could stand anything.

Her room, however, wasn't inviolate. The French doors led out to a communal veranda, Lila could and did wander through the bathroom into her room anytime she pleased, and everyone knew where to find her. If the cabin out in Rayder Swamp could be made habitable she'd be out of reach, with no one to answer to but herself.

She didn't fool herself into thinking she was some sort of martyr. There were a number of very good reasons why she seemed to have taken on the well-being of everyone she'd ever met.

For one thing, she was good at it. Good at organizing, at soothing, at coming up with creative alternatives and facing up to an intractable bureaucracy. She could make things happen when they needed to. And they often needed to.

For another, she had the time. She had no regular job, no husband, no children, no lover. No excuses, if someone needed her.

And the most telling reason of all. She liked it. She liked to feel needed. She liked to accomplish things, to solve problems, to take care of the wounded and sorrowing. Even if her own life was emotionally arid, she could bring a little rain to the parched souls of others.

But it had been a long time since she'd been able to say no. A long time since she'd been able to curl up in a little ball and think only of herself. To read a favorite book, wrapped in a comforter. To drink herb tea and watch old movies on television, to wax her legs and pluck her eyebrows. She needed a retreat, and Rowdy's old cabin would provide just that, as long as she wasn't overly frightened of snakes and gators and mosquitoes. And, having lived near the Gulf coast of Florida all her life, she wasn't.

Tonight wasn't bad, though, she thought, wandering barefoot through the perfect rooms of Belle Rive. Lila had gone out with a couple of girlfriends to see the new Kevin Costner movie, Claire had retired early as usual, and Miss Sadie and her husband were tucked up safe in their quarters. She had no one to make demands—she could wander through the place as she pleased, sipping on Harrison's very best cream sherry and thinking about winter.

She had real doubts as to whether that season would ever come. The humidity was so thick around Turner's Landing that it was hard to breathe, and even the night didn't bring much respite. Tonight for example, she thought, stepping out on the deserted veranda that overlooked the broad front lawn, the temperature couldn't have dropped more than five degrees, and the hot wind riffling through her hair only made her feel restless. Oddly anxious. Longing for something she couldn't even begin to name.

She leaned her arms on the railing, staring out over the empty lawn. For a moment she could almost imagine Caleb Spenser, moving toward the house through the crowds of people, inexorable, determined, handsome as sin and twice as mean. She'd known he was trouble the moment she saw him. Now she knew he was more than that. He was disaster, pure and simple. He threatened everything she held dear, she knew that with instincts as sure as death and taxes. He didn't threaten only Harrison. He was a danger to all of them.

So why did she keep thinking about his bare chest? His mouth? His long, hard-looking hands? His mesmerizing eyes?

She shook her head, slapping at the hungry mosquito feeding on her upper arm. She was tired, that was it. She'd been doing too much for too many people, and it had made her foolish, vulnerable, prey to fancies that had nothing to do with what she really wanted or needed in this lifetime. She would have been much better off joining Lila for the Kevin Costner movie. Except that Caleb Spenser would even put Kevin Costner to shame.

And she was going to be spending hours with him tomorrow. It took at least half an hour to drive as close to the cabin as they could. That meant half an hour shut up in the front seat of his pickup. Talking about the weather, probably. And half an hour back. Alone. With him.

She took another sip of her sherry, shaking her wet tangle of hair back away from her face. She'd taken a shower, hoping to wash away some of the fretful malaise that was dogging her. It hadn't done any good. The heat, the sultriness of the night air only added to the inexplicable sense of longing. But she refused to recognize what she was longing for.

She glanced up at the house. Claire's light was on. She usually fell asleep with all the lights blazing, her reading glasses slipping down her nose, an unread book propped against her chest. Jassy always checked her.

The doctors kept prescribing sedatives, sleeping pills, tranquilizers. She kept dosing herself with secreted bottles of vodka. Jassy was half-afraid she'd wake up some morning and find her mother dead from some lethal, accidental combination.

So every night she checked, unable to sleep unless she were certain her mother was safe. Harrison told her she worried too much, that she was imagining a problem where none existed. That Claire's mostly discreet tippling was harmless. She only wished she could be convinced.

Lightning speared across the sky, a jagged streak of white slicing the roiling purple. The thunder was distant, far too distant to be anything more than nature's cruel taunt. Just more heat lightning, flash and fire, signifying nothing. She would have given ten years off her life for a cool, cleansing downpour.

She turned and headed back inside, rubbing her arms briskly, almost imagining a chill where none existed. She needed her sleep. Tomorrow was going to tax all her emotional and mental reserves. Caleb Spenser was no boy. He was all male, all threat, all overpowering presence. She would need her wits about her if she was going to win. And she had no intention of losing. The stakes were simply too high.

Her room was just as hot and sticky as the rest of the house, but it felt cooler, with its uncluttered walls and bare floors, when she entered after turning Claire's light off. Stripping off her clothes, she pulled on a skimpy silk chemise and climbed up onto the high bed, grimacing in the darkness. She would have slept nude were it not for Lila's habit of walking in unannounced. Jassy wasn't particularly modest, but she hated the idea of being vulnerable. At least the whisper-thin silk felt almost as light as nothing at all.

She lay back against the feather pillows, staring at the canopy over her head. Some night she'd like to sleep out under the stars. Drag her mattress out onto the veranda, let the warm breezes blow over her, even let the mosquitoes feed on her. Sometime, before she grew too old to care, she was going to do that. And let the warm night air caress her.

She turned over on her stomach, punching the pillow, snorting at her own fanciful notions. What in heaven's name had gotten into her recently? Must be an early mid-life crisis. Didn't women go through traumas when they reached thirty? Must be hormones.

But she knew it wasn't. She closed her eyes, trying to shut out all conscious thought, trying to see nothing but cold water and rain clouds. But she knew what had gotten her into such a turmoil.

Caleb Spenser.

"DARLING," Lila said artlessly as she poured herself a cup of coffee, "you look like you have the world's worst hangover."

Claire dropped her cup with a loud clatter, splashing coffee on the white tablecloth. It was after nine the next morning, and for once the three Turner women were together at the breakfast table.

Jassy and Lila tactfully ignored her. "It's no wonder," Jassy said, aware of her mother's barely concealed sigh of relief as she realized Lila was talking to her daughter. "I don't know that I slept more than three hours last night. If this weather doesn't break soon I think I'll go mad."

"That lightning," Lila said. "I see it flash outside, and I think it's got to mean something, and it doesn't. Just heat lightning, promising relief, giving nothing. I wish I'd gone with Harrison after all."

"Exactly where did Harrison go?" Jassy asked, slathering butter on one of Miss Sadie's fresh biscuits. "I thought you two were going to Clearwater to visit the Stillmans."

"Something came up at the last minute," Lila said, that worried expression back in her fine blue eyes.

"Like what?" Jassy persisted.

"Oh, you know your brother. He never likes to bother me with the details of his business. He says I haven't got the head for it, and you know, he's right. It was something more important, whatever it was. I think he's gone over to St. Florence on the East Coast. I can't imagine why—I don't know of a thing that ever came out of St. Florence."

Except Caleb Spenser, Jassy thought. It was no surprise. Harrison had been too riled by Spenser's appearance to be able to concentrate on anything else. She knew perfectly well his abrupt disappearance had something to do with the stranger in their midst. She just didn't know what.

"Harrison had a friend who lived just outside of St. Florence." Claire spoke up in her absent voice. "A nice young boy he went to Princeton with. Sherman, his name was. Sherman Delano."

"Maybe he went to visit him," Jassy suggested, reaching for another biscuit when she knew perfectly well she should reach for the grapefruit instead. Lila, who beat and coerced her lithe body into shape, frowned at her disapprovingly. Jassy reached for the butter.

"I doubt that," Claire said, leaning back in her chair. As usual she'd barely touched a bite of food. "He was murdered."

"Murdered?" Lila echoed, immediately fascinated. "You're kidding!"

"It's perfectly true. Someone stabbed him in a gambling game. They caught the man. Or boy, I think it was. I don't know whether he was executed or just put away for life."

"How awful for his parents," Jassy said.

"Whose parents? Sherman's or the killer's?" Lila asked with an uncharacteristic tartness.

"Both, I suspect. Did Harrison know both of them, Mama?"

"I couldn't say. I do know that Harrison was quite upset at the time. Of course, this was quite a while ago. Maybe ten, fifteen years ago." Claire took a discreet sip of her coffee. "I hadn't thought of Sherman in such a long time."

"Why would Harrison suddenly remember him?" Jassy swallowed the biscuit, controlling her urge to reach for another.

"What makes you think he has? After all, St. Florence isn't that small a town. There must be other things there. Besides, Sherman lived outside the town, and I think his parents moved away after he was killed. Still, I imagine it must be hard for Harrison. He's bound to think of Sherman while he's there."

"What did you say his name was again, Mama?" Jassy asked innocently, pouring herself an unwanted cup of coffee so that she wouldn't have to meet anyone's eyes.

"Sherman Delano. Some distant relative of the northern Delanos, I suppose, though I never asked."

"Maybe he was related to the northern Shermans," Jassy suggested with a touch of mischief.

"I doubt that," Claire said haughtily. "That wouldn't have gone over too well in the south, and Florida is, after all, a southern state.''

"Yes, ma'am," Jassy said meekly, meeting Lila's amused gaze.

"So what are your plans for the day, Jassy?" Lila asked, tactfully changing the subject. Claire had come from old Georgia stock, and for her the Civil War was only a few generations old.

"I'm taking Caleb Spenser out to Rowdy's cabin."

Her words couldn't have had a greater effect if she'd dropped a water balloon on the damask-covered tablecloth. "I beg your pardon?" Claire said.

"You're *what?*" Lila shrieked at the same time.

Jassy sipped at her cold coffee, trying to look innocent. "Whatever's wrong with that? You know I've been wanting to fix up the place. Caleb's a carpenter. I need some carpentry work done. It all seems perfectly logical to me."

"Caleb?" Lila echoed. "I thought he wanted to be called Spenser."

"So he said. I, however, plan to call him Caleb. It has a nice, biblical ring to it. Maybe it'll remind him of his Christian duty."

"That man's a pagan if ever I've seen one," Claire said with a discreet snort.

"I didn't think he was just a carpenter," Lila said. "I got the impression he was more of a contractor and developer. I mean, just any carpenter couldn't come in and buy the Moon Palace, no matter how tumbledown it was."

"They couldn't have been asking that much."

"Seventy-five thousand, Eldon Reynolds told me yesterday. And he paid it. In cash."

Suddenly Jassy began to feel queasy. The butter and cold black coffee weren't sitting too well on a stomach that had already survived a restless night of intermittent sleep. "Cash?" she echoed.

"I wouldn't have believed it, but Eldon's sister works for Junior MacCoy in his real estate office, and she saw it. A whole mess of hundred-dollar bills, she told him. Gives a person thought, doesn't it? Do you suppose it's...drug money?" Her eyes were huge at the very idea.

"I suppose it's possible. Somehow he doesn't seem that type. Don't drug dealers drive better cars?" Jassy said, still troubled.

"And wear better clothes," Lila agreed. "And they don't look so...healthy." She let out a lascivious sigh. "That boy looks extremely healthy."

"The two of you are being absurd," Claire said in her most reproving voice. "The man isn't a drug dealer, he's simply a hardworking businessman. Though why someone who has seventy-five thousand dollars in cash to toss around would be interested in a little pick-up carpentry work on that tumbledown cabin in the swamp is beyond me."

"Beyond me, too," Jassy murmured. "Maybe I should call and tell him I've changed my mind."

"Has he got a telephone?"

"I don't think so."

"That settles that. Besides, I think that was his disreputable pickup truck that just drove up our driveway. You're too late."

Jassy sighed. "I guess it's out of my hands, then. If he's willing to take the job then why should I argue?" She pushed back from the table, wishing she felt as confident as she sounded.

"You gonna invite him in for coffee?" Lila asked, putting an anxious hand to her perfect coif of stylish blond hair. "I'm not in any shape to receive callers."

Jassy knew perfectly well that Lila's vanity was automatic. Unlike most of the young women in Turner's Landing, her reaction to Caleb Spenser was instinctive and impersonal. She flirted with everyone, it was part of her charm, but it had nothing to do with her emotions. She was deeply, truly in love with Harrison, and all the handsome outlaws riding into town wouldn't make a lick of difference.

"I thought we'd take right off. I had Miss Sadie pack us a picnic basket if we get hungry. It's a bit of a hike out there."

"You're going like that?" Lila shrieked.

Jassy looked down at her clothes. She'd gone through seven changes of clothing, and when, not if, Lila made herself at home in Jassy's room she'd discover the other six choices lying discarded on the bed. She'd finally settled on the least conspicuous outfit she could find—an old faded pair of jeans, scuffed boots, an oversize white shirt in deference to the heat, with a thin silk camisole underneath. She'd braided and pinned her hair back, and she looked practical, no-nonsense, down to earth. As far removed from the fluttering debs of Turner's Landing as could be found.

"Yes, I'm going like this. Did you think I was going to wear a tea dress and heels to a swamp?"

"What about a little makeup, dear?" Claire murmured. "And couldn't you do something with your hair?"

"It's hot. It's more than hot, it's an oven around here, and Rayder Swamp will be a steam bath. Makeup would melt right off my face, and my hair's already a mass of frizz. I'm going out for business, Mama, not seduction."

"A girl should always keep her future in mind," Claire murmured absently.

"Claire!" Lila said, astonished. "You're not thinking that Jassy should keep company with Mr. Spenser? He's not really our kind."

Nothing was more calculated to make Jassy's hackles rise than her family's instinctive snobbery. Setting her hands on the table, she leaned toward Lila. "Well, honey," she said flatly, "neither am I." And she turned and headed for the door.

Caleb was there, a shameless eavesdropper, a faint smile curving his mouth. "Morning, ladies," he said.

Lila blushed a deep, unflattering red, one that mottled her fine chest and clashed with her peach robe. "Good morning, Mr. Spenser," she said, struggling for her usual ladylike demeanor. "Beastly hot day, isn't it?"

"Hell on wheels, Miz Lila," Spenser said. "You ready to romp in the swamp, Jassy?"

This time it was Lila's turn to drop her coffee cup in shock. Jassy, however, was more than ready for him. Since the moment she saw him lounging in the doorway like a lean and hungry tomcat waiting to pounce on a fat, juicy little mouse, her resolve and her backbone had stiffened. "I believe this was more in the line of a job interview, Mr. Spenser."

"It's whatever you want to make it, Miz Turner." He mocked her use of "mister."

She had to learn not to underestimate him. Lila's artless disclosure of just how much ready cash he had on hand had set Jassy's few preconceived notions about the man into an uproar. Obviously he didn't need the job of fixing up Rowdy's cabin. Just as obviously, he was prepared to take it. Or at least prepared to accompany her out there to check it out. And she knew damned well it wasn't because he needed the work.

So why was it? What went on behind those clear, unnerving gray eyes, that wicked smile, that lounging, graceful posture? And did she have any reason to be as frightened as Harrison so clearly was?

"I'm ready to go. Unless you'd like some coffee first?" She gestured toward the table.

"No, ma'am. I've been up since five this morning. I've had more than my share of caffeine. At least for now. Nice seeing you ladies," he said to the two Turner matrons.

"And you, Mr. Spenser," Claire replied with her customary graciousness. And Jassy wondered how far into the day Claire would make it without resorting to her medicinal bottle.

He trailed behind her as she headed back toward the hallway, not too close, but she was acutely aware of him. He caught up with her by the door, and there was just a hint of mockery in his drawling voice.

"That was real nice, the way you took up for me back there," he said.

"What do you mean by that?"

"You know perfectly well what I mean by that, don't pretend otherwise. I didn't think you were the kind to play games like your sister-in-law and your friends."

"Well, you're wrong. I've been taught the same games as everyone. I may like to handle things a little more directly, but I'm just as capable of avoiding what I want to avoid as anyone else."

"Yes, ma'am," Caleb murmured. "So am I."

"There's a hamper over there. I thought we might like a thermos of coffee and some sandwiches. It's a long ride out to Rayder Swamp and back."

"Does that mean we might not get back before nightfall?"

"Not a chance," she said flatly.

"I just thought I'd ask. I didn't want to get my hopes up." She hated that smile of his, that damnable, double-dare grin. At that moment there wasn't anything she wouldn't do to wipe it off his handsome face.

"Tell me something, Mr. Spenser."

"Sure thing, Miz Turner," he said.

Here goes, she thought, holding her breath, knowing the danger she was stepping into. Or at least guessing at it. "Did you happen to know a boy named Sherman Delano?"

He didn't move for a moment, and his clear, winter-colored eyes were blank. "What makes you ask me that?" He finally spoke, his voice even. Deceptively so.

"He lived around St. Florence. You mentioned you'd spent some time in that area, and I wondered if you'd ever met him." She tried to look as innocent as possible, but underneath her calm exterior her heart was beating way too fast. She'd stepped into currents she hadn't expected.

"I met him," Caleb said flatly. "Are we going out to Rayder Swamp or are we going to spend all morning jawing?"

She wanted to push, just a little bit further. She prided herself on being fearless, able to face down just about anything. She could stand up to abusive husbands, three-alarm fires, the horrifying results of a car accident and her family, all without flinching.

But something told her that there were times when it was much better to just drop something, then pick it up at a more opportune time. Now was definitely not the time to quiz Caleb Spenser about a murdered young man.

"We're going to Rayder Swamp," she said. "That is, if you're still interested."

This time she was almost happy to see his mocking smile break the eerie stillness of his face. "Believe me, ma'am," he said, opening the door to the pickup for her, "I'm extremely interested. You might almost say obsessed."

And Jassy, in the smothering heat of the late-morning sun, felt a little chill race across her skin.

CHAPTER SIX

CALEB KEPT HIS eyes on the road, humming lightly beneath his breath as they bounced and jounced over the rutted surface that led to Rayder Swamp. The Everglades were much farther south than this particular stretch of the Gulf Coast, but one couldn't tell that by the swamps that were in abundance around Turner's Landing. That might account for the surprisingly undeveloped state of the area. That, or someone might have made a big mistake. One they hadn't lived to regret.

Jassy Turner was curled up on her side of the bench seat, clinging to the door handle, and he couldn't be sure whether she was holding on because of the rough ride, or to be ready to jump if he scared her. It would be easy enough to find out. She was one tough lady, despite the occasionally vulnerable look in her warm hazel eyes, and he imagined there were few things on this earth that frightened her. He also knew perfectly well that he was one of the chosen few.

He'd thought about that when he was driving over to the Turner's antebellum mansion. He wasn't given to much brooding about women, and there was certainly more than enough distraction around Turner's Landing that he didn't have to concentrate on anyone as problematic as Jacinthe Turner. But he was having a hard time getting her out of his mind. It might have been the fact that she was so intimately related to the object of his vengeance. Or it might have been the fact that she stood up to him, when he clearly made her intensely uneasy.

Or maybe it was simply that he was a sucker for greeny brown eyes, and a soft mouth, and the kind of body he suspected lurked beneath her deliberately baggy clothes.

It didn't really matter, since anything he did to involve her would rebound on Harrison, making revenge all that sweeter. If he brought down Harrison's baby sister along with the man himself, it would only add to Harrison's crushing burden of guilt. Not that the man had seemed in the slightest bit afflicted by regrets over the past. But no one could watch their safe little life destroyed without remorse.

It would make everything that much more devastating to leave Harrison with a publicly drunken mother, a cuckolding wife, a broken-hearted sister, bankruptcy and a jail term. He could hardly ask for a more complete revenge, though he liked to call it justice.

And he could break Jassy's heart; he knew he could. For all her matter-of-fact manner, her cool gaze and touch-me-not attitude, he suspected that she could break as easily as a china figurine. When touched by the right man.

"So why do you want to fix up an old cabin?" He broke the silence, and she jumped, nervously, clutching the door handle before forcing herself to release it. "Why don't you just sell it?"

"Because it's mine."

"Do you hold on to everything you own, Jassy? I'd think you'd start to run out of space."

"I hold on to what's important. Don't you?"

"No."

She looked up at him, startled, and he could see her shoulders relax slightly beneath the oversize shirt. "What do you mean?"

"I mean I don't hold on to anything. I travel light. I go from job to job. I buy places, fix them up, and sell them as soon as someone makes an offer. I rarely get to finish the job before someone wants to come in and do it their way. And they're willing to pay me good money for that privilege."

"Doesn't it give you a sense of unfinished business? A lack of completion?"

"Honey, I live and breathe unfinished business. I got used to leaving things hanging years ago. Nowadays I concentrate on tying up the loose ends that matter, and let the rest go to hell."

"Is my brother one of the loose ends that matter?"

"Ask him."

She let out a little sigh of exasperation, and he waited for another question, but she surprised him by dropping it. "So if you don't hold on to things that matter, where did your dog come from?"

Caleb stretched, rolling down the window even farther to let the thick, damp air billow through. "He showed up at a construction site one day, a frayed rope wrapped around his neck. He looked hungry, so I fed him. He's been following me ever since." He didn't bother mentioning the marks of abuse on the dog, the fear in Dog's huge black eyes, the time it had taken to coax a snapping, edgy, overgrown puppy into the relatively peaceful oaf that lounged around the Moon Palace nowadays.

"What's his name?"

"Dog." He drummed his fingers on the steering wheel. "I figured I didn't have any right to name him. If I named him I own him, and I don't figure on being that beholden to any living creature. But we get along well enough, and he listens to me complain. Dog and this old truck are about the only constants in my life."

She glanced at the bleached, cracked dashboard, the broken speedometer, the overflowing ashtray and the toolbox at her feet. "I bet you've got a sports car stashed away someplace. If you could afford to pay cash for the Moon Palace you can afford a better vehicle than this."

"Someone told you about that, did they? I should have known— this town is small enough that only the important secrets are kept. I do appreciate your taking the time to ask about me, though. Did you find out anything exciting?"

"Not what I wanted to know. So *do* you?"

"Do I what?"

"Have a Corvette stashed someplace like Tampa or St. Pete?"

"Think you're pretty smart, don't you? As a matter of fact, I used to own a Mercedes. I sold it when I discovered it wasn't really my style. This truck is all the transportation I want or need. Don't let her shabby looks fool you. Beneath that rusty hood is the sweetest V-8 engine this side of Daytona. She can go from zero to sixty in a matter of seconds, and the air conditioner, when I choose to use it, works great."

She looked over at him. He could see a faint sheen of perspiration on her upper lip, and just above the top button of her shirt. "Then why don't you choose to use it?"

"Maybe I like to see you sweat."

She reached over and shoved the button marked Air with a defiant glare, retreating back to her corner. He pushed it off. She reached for it again, and he caught her wrist in a grip that was just hard enough for her to realize he was serious. Not enough to hurt her.

She backed off, and he released her. "Typical," she said.

"Typical what? I don't like back-seat drivers messing with my instrumentation."

"You're a bully, just like the kind of men I hear about at the women's shelter. You're a typical male using brute force to get what you want. You're not above hurting someone if they get in your way."

He waited until his first anger had abated. "You're right," he said flatly. "I don't mind hurting someone if they get in my way. And I'll use force to get what I want. But unlike your pet charity, I don't use my fists on helpless women when I've had too much to drink or I'm in a bad mood, or for any other reason. I don't beat on women. There's a difference, subtle, I grant you, but there's a difference."

"Not as far as I'm concerned," she said, her face stubborn beneath the thick tangle of dark hair.

"Then maybe I'm just going to have to educate you about those differences," he drawled.

He got the reaction he wanted. She was almost too easy, sometimes, the way she'd react to the things he said and did. Except that she immediately erected her defenses, and that shocked expression vanished from her hazel eyes, leaving her stern and determined. "We'll see about that," she said.

"Uh-huh."

The shabby cab of the old pickup lapsed into silence, and Caleb considered flicking on the radio. He would have, if he'd known what would be most likely to irritate her, but chances are she'd like the same kind of music he did. Besides, he liked listening to her breathe.

The old narrow road grew steadily worse, bumpier, more overgrown, until it ended in a vast slime-covered expanse of water. He could probably drive through it, but he was too fond of his truck to risk it. He stopped the truck and turned off the engine.

"Where do we go from here?"

Jassy was already out of the truck. "We're lucky it's been so dry. Normally we'd have to use Rowdy's old boat, but right now we can make it on foot."

"I take it the cabin's smack dab in the center of the swamp?" Caleb was resigned, reaching for his tools.

"Hardly. I doubt we could reach the center of the swamp, even with a boat, it's so overgrown. It's just a little ways in—far enough to keep out visitors, close enough to be reachable."

"You want to keep out visitors? I thought you were out to save the world." He slammed the door shut behind him and immediately slapped away a hungry mosquito.

"You can't save the world all the time," she said without looking back, taking off on a narrow path of dry land. "Even a saint like me needs time off."

He paused for a moment, watching her move farther into the swamp. A saint wouldn't have such an unconsciously seductive grace about her. A saint wouldn't have the very definite effect she had on him. It was a good thing she wasn't a saint. He'd have a hard time keeping his hands off her if she was. And he had no intention of behaving himself. She was just too damned enticing, whether she knew it or not.

The hike to the cabin was a lengthy one. The ground was wet and soft beneath his boots, and he could tell that its sojourn out of water had been brief. One good rainstorm and it would be flooded once more. They climbed over downed cypress trunks, mangrove roots, pushed Spanish moss out of their hair as they moved doggedly farther into the murky depths of Rayder Swamp. The sun didn't penetrate very far into the overhung green depths. The humidity, so omnipresent around Turner's Landing, was even thicker here, so he could practically see the oozing green of the air around him. He unbuttoned a couple of buttons on his chambray work shirt, and wondered how Miss Jassy Turner was surviving under that tent of a shirt.

His first glance at Rowdy's cabin was a daunting one. A ramshackle little building, it was half sunk in the mud. The tar-paper siding was ripped and peeling, the roof looked about to collapse, and the windows were cracked with some of them missing altogether. Jassy turned when she reached the sagging little porch that ran the length of it, looking at him with such innocent pride that he almost grabbed her there and then. She reminded him of Dog when that canine had managed some particularly impressive feat. Proud and anxious at the same time. Clearly she loved her tar-paper shack. And just as clearly, to his professional eyes, there was no saving it.

"I know it's falling apart," she said, letting her hand touch the railing in an unconscious caress. "And I don't have a whole lot of money to put into it. I just don't want it to get into any greater disrepair. If you could see what it would take to shore it up for a while, keep it from falling into the swamp until I can fix it up right."

It was already falling into the swamp. It wouldn't take much more than a strong wind to finish the job. That, or a push from him.

But for some reason he wasn't ready to douse that light shining in Jassy's eyes. For the first time she was looking at him without wariness, her delight and anxiety over her tumbledown piece of real estate wiping out all other considerations.

He needed to make use of that temporary trust. Right now she'd forgotten he was the enemy, and that she'd gotten him out there for nefarious purposes of her own. It hadn't taken much to guess those purposes—she obviously hoped she could keep him out of Turner's Landing and Harrison Turner's way while he worked on this place, giving her enough time to find out what was going on.

Since she was part and parcel of what was going on, he'd been perfectly willing to comply. Any time spent with her, away from Harrison Turner, was not necessarily time wasted. There were several means to his particular ends, and Jassy Turner was one of the most attractive ones.

But he could see without coming closer that Rowdy's cabin wasn't going to provide him with much of an excuse to work on her. He was going to have to take full advantage of today, and trust in Jassy's coming up with another excuse when this one fell through. Knowing her determination to take care of her worthless older brother, he had no doubt whatsoever that she'd manage to do just that.

She set the picnic basket on the porch and busied herself with the fancy lock. "You know, half the windows are broken on the place," he drawled, stepping onto the narrow porch with her and feeling the old rotten boards sag beneath his feet. "If someone wanted to get in they wouldn't bother with the locked door."

She pushed the door open, propping it a bit as it sagged on a broken hinge. "It's the principle of the thing. There are people around here who know that if someone bothers to lock a place, it belongs to them. If I didn't lock it, they'd consider it public domain." She disappeared into the darkness, and he followed her, gingerly, uncertain whether he was going to go crashing through the floorboards into the swampy muck below.

After the green murky light of the swamp, the shadowed interior of Rowdy's cabin wasn't much darker. It was a tiny place, not more than eight by ten feet, and sparsely furnished. An old table, a stool and a sagging cot comprised most of the furnishings, along with an old bureau stacked with rusting tin cans. An old wood cookstove stood in the corner, equally rusty, its stovepipe dismantled.

Caleb glanced around him. "So what do you use this place for? Meetings with your lovers?" He was teasing her, but she took the question with her usual seriousness.

"I don't have lovers," she said. "And if I did, I'd hardly bring them to a place that only had a cot, would I?"

He strolled over to the cot and sat down on it. It had less give than the aging floorboards. "It can be managed," he drawled.

"I'm sure it can," she said tartly. "Are you hungry?"

He looked up at her. "Uh-hunh." He smiled a lazy smile, wondering what it was going to take to get her on that narrow cot, lying beneath him. Whether that was what she'd had in mind all along. All she had to do was move a tiny bit closer and he'd catch her hand, pull her down to meet his hungry mouth, and...

"I'll get the food," she said breathlessly, whirling away before he could move. And he watched her go, telling himself the regret he was feeling wasn't as strong as acid. Telling himself his time would come. And so would she.

She sat on the floor, well out of reach, as they finished the coffee and half a dozen honey-laced biscuits. She still had every button but one done up on her shirt, and he wondered what she was wearing underneath. He wondered whether he was going to find out.

Finally he pushed himself off the cot, grimacing as he felt the sponginess of the floorboards beneath his booted feet. "I'd better check this place out," he said. "Take a few measurements. I wouldn't be real hopeful if I were you."

She looked up at him like a wounded fawn, and for some reason he felt more guilty about her ridiculous cabin than about what he had planned for her brother. "What do you mean?"

"It's falling apart. I think it might have been left too long to save it."

"But surely…"

"I can't tell until I check it out," he forestalled her pleading, trying to ignore the vulnerable eyes. "It'll take me about an hour to make sure. Do you want to stay put or come back and get me?"

"It'd take me longer than that to go anywhere. I've brought a book." She held up a paperback, and he noticed with real amusement that it was a florid-covered romance. Miss Jassy had more vulnerabilities than she realized.

But he decided not to tease her. He simply nodded, heading out to the porch where he'd left his tools, and began taking stock of the tumbledown cabin.

FOR A MOMENT Jassy didn't move from her spot on the cabin floor. She could see him from where she was, watch him as he stripped off his shirt in the hot, humid air, reaching for his tape measure with unconscious grace. For a moment she simply stared, bemused at the honey-colored tan that covered his body, the wiry muscles. She'd kept her eyes away from his body the time she'd visited him, made uneasy by all that bare flesh. For the moment she could look her fill, without him being aware of it.

She'd seen naked chests before. There was no reason for her particular fascination with this one naked chest. Except that she wasn't usually alone with them.

And having seen so many, she could tell that Caleb Spenser had a particularly nice one. A flat stomach, not too much hair, and the understated muscles that didn't bulge and lump all over the place, but nevertheless were more than sufficient for getting the job done. She wondered what his skin would feel like. Warm, smooth, hot?

He turned sideways, and for the first time she saw the scar. It wasn't that large, and it was no wonder she'd missed it before in her determined effort to keep her gaze at shoulder level or above. It was a nasty slash of whiteness in the bronzed skin, just beneath his ribs, and she knew with unquestioning instincts that it came from a knife.

She closed her eyes, but the vision remained. She'd thought watching him would have blunted some of her fascination. It only fed it. Moving away from temptation, she climbed onto the cot, still warm where he'd lounged. She picked up the book, determined to concentrate on boardroom and bedroom politics and ignore the sounds of him moving around outside. She could hear the lazy buzzing of a bee, far enough away that she didn't need to worry. The quiet sound of the water moving slowly around their tiny spit of land. The soughing sigh of the wind through the cypress trees overhead. She closed her eyes, for one short moment, and she was asleep.

When she opened her eyes the cabin was dark. And then she realized that the murky light from the front door was blocked by the man sitting on the cot beside her, his face shadowed in the darkness.

"What time is it?" she asked, her voice rusty from sleep.

"A little after three. You looked so peaceful lying there—I didn't have the heart to wake you."

She hadn't thought he had a heart at all, but she didn't say it aloud. "I didn't sleep well last night," she murmured instead.

"Didn't you? I never have any trouble sleeping."

"The result of a clean conscience, no doubt," Jassy said tartly, struggling to sit up.

"No doubt," he said, not moving, simply watching her, holding himself as still as an alligator waiting for its prey to make a foolish move.

Jassy felt sudden coolness against her skin, and she looked down to see that her shirt was unbuttoned, exposing the maroon silk camisole she'd worn beneath it. She yanked the open edges of her shirt together, telling herself that the shaking in her hands came from rage that he would touch her while she slept.

She didn't even need to accuse him. He simply shrugged. "You looked so hot, buttoned up like a nun. I thought you'd sleep better if you had a little ventilation."

"You're lucky I didn't wake up and start screaming."

"No one would have heard you." His voice was very gentle, but it in no way blunted the effect his words had on her. She told herself they were a threat, of the most basic sort. But he made no move to touch her.

Instead he rose, moving away from her, tucking his hands into the pockets of his tight jeans. He'd put his shirt back on, but he hadn't bothered to button it or tuck it in, and the effect was still completely disturbing. "This place is hopeless," he said, a deliberate change of subject. "But I suspect you already knew that."

Her fears forgotten, Jassy leaped off the cot and followed him. "I didn't suspect any such thing. And nothing's hopeless. Surely there's something we can do. Shore up the place, put a few new beams in..."

He stepped out onto the porch, and she followed him, using all her self-control not to catch his arm and plead with him. Touching him would not be a good idea. Not at all.

"Let me give you a little lesson in construction, Jassy. This place is built on cypress pilings sunk into the muck. Those pilings have lasted a long time, but they're rotten through and through. Normally the next step would be to jack up the house and put new pilings in. But in this swampy area there's nothing to rest the jacks on, and if there were, the rotten timber in the house would crumble from the weight. All this place needs is one good blow and it'll tumble back into the swamp."

"But..."

"All you can do," he continued ruthlessly, "is to tear it down and build something completely new."

For a moment she didn't say a word. "I can't afford to do that."

"I know."

The Turners didn't seem to have any secrets from him, financial or otherwise, and lying wouldn't get her anywhere.

"So that's that," she said tonelessly.

"If I were you, I wouldn't even come out here again. The place is downright dangerous. The roof won't stand a good soaking rain, and if the water level rises the whole thing might collapse." He picked up his toolbox.

"Thanks for your concern. If you send a bill for your time out here..."

"Consultations are free," he said, and there was a trace of irritation in his usually slow, deep voice. "Would you stop looking like I kicked your dog? I'm sorry this place is in such a state, but there's not a damned thing I can do about it. You'd be better off putting the money into a bus ticket and getting the hell out of town."

She looked at him with astonishment, but he already seemed to be regretting his hasty words. "Why should I get out of town?" she asked in a calm enough voice.

"Forget I said it."

"I don't forget things. Why should I leave town?"

"You might be happier if you did." He moved closer to her, and she could feel the heat from him in the hot afternoon air. Overhead she could hear the distant rumble of thunder. Another false promise from the sky, and she'd had too many false promises.

He looked down at her, his light eyes no longer cool and calculating, but suddenly hot. He put his hands on her, resting on her shoulders, and they were strong, heavy, and she knew they were going to pull her close, closer, until she rested against his chest and her mouth met his. And she'd go, willingly, open her mouth to his willingly, and they'd go back into that room and see whether the cot was really too small.

She had to stop it, while she still could. She squirmed, and his fingers tightened, just briefly, before releasing her. At the same time he released his pent-up breath. "Let's get out of here," he said in a neutral voice, as if the momentary flash of something between them had never existed. "Maybe for once that thunder means business."

But she didn't trust him. If he changed his mind, reached for her again, she wouldn't back away. Her only defense was words. "It's not going to rain," she said, picking up the picnic basket and locking the door behind them. She could feel his eyes on her, watching, waiting, and she said the only thing she could think of to throw him off.

"Where did you get that scar?"

He was silent, and she turned to look at him, uncertain whether he had heard. "Which scar?" he asked finally, and if she'd thought she'd thrown him off balance she could see she'd underestimated him.

"The one under your ribs. It looks like it came from a knife."

"Very observant, Miss Jassy. I didn't know you were watching so closely."

Her turn to flush. "I just happened to notice it."

"Sure," he said. "And you're right. It's from a knife. A couple more inches and I wouldn't be here right now."

"Lucky for me," she said dourly. "How'd you get it?"

"You are nosy today, aren't you?" he murmured. "You aren't going to be happy with the answer."

"I assume it was in some fight."

"You assume correctly. I got it when I was in the state penitentiary."

She swallowed, the thick, hot air choking her. "What were you in jail for?" she asked, then wished she hadn't.

Caleb Spenser smiled. "Why, for murdering your brother's friend, Sherman Delano. Didn't you guess?"

CHAPTER SEVEN

IT DIDN'T MAKE for a comfortable ride back toward Turner's Landing. For once in her life Jassy was simply too shocked to ask questions. The more she turned it over in her brain the more she knew she shouldn't have been so surprised. There was something going on—something that involved her brother, Caleb Spenser and a long-ago murder. She just hadn't guessed how bad it was.

Neither of them said a word until they had driven out of the roughest part of the swamp. There was a great deal of difference in their moods. While Jassy struggled with the shocking information he'd so casually imparted, he seemed more concerned with the state of the roads. He was humming something lightly, under his breath, and his expression was deliberately bland and guileless. He'd set out to shock her on purpose, she knew that full well.

Finally she couldn't stand the silence any longer, that damnable humming that was making her want to commit murder herself. "Mother said the man who killed Delano was executed."

At least he stopped humming. He glanced over at her, an amused expression on his face. "Honey, your mama doesn't know diddly. I got seven years for manslaughter, and I served three of them, with time off because I was such a good boy."

"You needn't seem so lighthearted about it. Murder's a serious business."

"I've lived with it for a long time, Jassy. It no longer has the power to surprise me."

She glanced at him, caught by something in his voice. "Surprise you? You were surprised that you killed a man?"

"You could say so."

"Does Harrison know you killed Sherman Delano? Of course he must. That's why he's so frightened of you, he knows you're a killer."

"Now, Jassy, do I look like a cold-blooded killer to you?" he said, the epitome of reason. Except that she wasn't buying it.

"You look like you're capable of anything you set your mind to." She shivered in the thick, humid air, remembering that she'd almost kissed him, minutes ago. Realizing that she still wanted to. "Does Harrison have anything to do with...with..."

"With the killing? Why don't you ask him?"

"I'm asking you."

"And I'm not answering." He pulled onto the paved highway, stepping down on the accelerator, and Jassy realized he hadn't exaggerated the old truck's potential. It shot forward with the smoothness of a brand-new sports car, and instinctively she reached for the door handle. "I have to stop by my place before I drop you off. I need to see whether the lumber company has finally made the delivery they've been promising. If they haven't, I need to go kick some butt after I leave you home."

"My brother has part ownership in the lumber company," she said, then could have kicked herself. "And I'd prefer to go straight home."

"I'm sure you would. But I'm the driver, and I'm going by way of the Moon Palace. If you've got a problem you can walk."

"I guess they didn't teach you manners in prison," she said, half-shocked at her boldness.

He grinned then, amused rather than irritated. "Well, if they tried, it's worn off by now. I got out more than ten years ago."

"But Mama said Sherman was only killed ten years ago."

"Honey, your mama is a lush. Everyone knows that, no matter how hard you all try to cover up for her. You'd best not take her word for anything. Sherman Delano died on November 23, 1979. Southern justice moved swiftly, for once, and I was neatly convicted and serving time within six months."

"Harrison was in school up north back then," Jassy said slowly. "He couldn't have been anywhere around when Delano was killed."

"Thanksgiving break," was all Caleb said.

"Are you telling me my brother had something to do with it?" she asked sharply.

"Ask him."

"Stop saying that, damn you. You can't just drop hints and then clam up like some sphinx."

"Honey," he said, pulling to a stop in front of the decaying old building. "I can do anything I damn please."

Dog bounded out of the front door, a huge, quivering mass of canine delight. Caleb was already out of the truck, rubbing Dog's head with his large strong hands and crooning to him before heading on into the house. Dog looked over at her, still sitting in the truck, then turned to look back at his master disappearing through the front door. He let out a mournful little whimper, torn between two human delights, and Jassy took pity on him, climbing down from the rusty old pickup and approaching him.

Dog whoofed in joy, prancing over to her and slobbering all over her hands, batting his huge head against her hip before rolling over on his back to have his shaggy tummy scratched. She squatted down beside him. "You're ridiculous, Dog, you know that? I think you need a name, though, and an owner who's going to take more responsibility."

"I take enough," Caleb said from above her.

She leaped up, startled, but he was so close she rammed into him. He put out his hands to steady her, and she looked at them, at him, and the breath left her body. She didn't move, and neither did he, and this time he was going to kiss her, and if he didn't, she was going to kiss him. It didn't matter, as long as his mouth was on hers and his body was touching hers and his arms were...

"Whoof." Dog jumped up, placing his huge paws on Caleb's chest and slurping him happily, knocking him back away from Jassy before it could happen.

Jassy didn't wait for regret, or another chance. She ran back to the truck, jumping onto the seat, and fastening the frayed seat belt around her like a chastity belt.

"I'm going to turn you into alligator food," Caleb informed Dog, scratching his head. "I thought you were more sophisticated than that." He climbed back into the truck, swinging his long legs in first, and glanced over her way.

"Did the lumber get delivered?" she asked in an effort to forestall conversation about anything more intimate.

"No. Got any suggestions?"

"Can you work on this place if they won't deliver?"

"Yes and no. I can have the lumber trucked in from outside, which I certainly will. It'll mean a couple of days' delay, but I'm sure I can find ways to keep me busy while I'm waiting."

Jassy swallowed. "I'll have a word with Ed down at the yard. I'm sure your lumber will be delivered by tomorrow."

"I should have come to you first."

"I understand threats better."

"I'm not threatening you."

"Aren't you? It seems to me that you're threatening my brother, for whatever misguided reason, and anything or anyone that threatens my brother threatens me."

"Such family loyalty." The shadows were getting longer on the old narrow road, and the constant rumble of thunder only added to her sudden sense of unease.

"Most people can understand family loyalty," she said stiffly.

"Not me. I got away from my family as soon as I was old enough to run, and I haven't been back. Not that there's anyone to go back to now. But I learned early on you look out for yourself and yourself alone. Your family will stab you in the back if it suits them."

"Your family, maybe. Not mine."

"You really don't think Harrison would throw you to the wolves to save his own worthless hide?"

"Of course not," she said, shocked.

Caleb laughed, but there was no humor in the sound. "I wish you didn't have to find out otherwise. But I expect you will. As long as I'm here."

"Then why don't you leave?"

"Not a chance. I've got unfinished business to take care of. As soon as that's done, I'll be gone."

"I can't wait," she said stiffly.

He didn't bother replying. The wind had picked up, thrashing the trees about overhead, and the rumble of thunder was growing louder. Jassy cranked down the window, peering out, when suddenly Caleb's hand reached out and caught her forearm, yanking her away.

"What...?" she started to protest.

"Get down on the floor," he ordered her.

"Are you out of your mind? Why should I...?"

"Don't argue with me, just get down. We've got trouble." He shoved her, hard enough so that she had no choice but to duck down, and she did so, muttering imprecations about abusive men.

And then the truck came to an abrupt halt, and Caleb's hand came down on her head, keeping her down as he leaned out his window.

"Can I do anything for you boys?" he asked, slow and affable, the tension in the hand on Jassy's head at odds with the ease in his voice.

"That depends." It was a voice Jassy didn't recognize, and she knew everyone who lived within twenty miles of Turner's Landing. "We're looking for a troublemaker, name of Caleb Spenser. Ever heard tell of him?"

"Maybe," Caleb drawled. "What do you want with him?"

"Why, we thought we might learn him a lesson or two. Such as not to cause trouble for peaceful, law-abiding folks. Such as, maybe he'd better git back to where he come from, if he wants to stay in one piece." She heard another noise, an ominous sound somewhere between a slap and a thud. The kind of sound a board would make if it were being slapped against a waiting hand.

"Maybe Caleb Spenser doesn't take to learning too well," Caleb said. The engine was still running in the truck, and Jassy crouched there, wondering why in heaven's name he didn't just drive through them.

"Then maybe we're going to have to be real thorough in teaching him," another stranger's voice spoke.

"Tell you what, boys," Caleb said easily. "You want to have a go at me, and it doesn't look like I'm going to have much to say about it. So why don't you let me pull the truck off the road and we'll see about it."

"He's gonna drive away, Jesse," the first stranger warned. "Don't let 'im."

"Don't be a fool, Willard. That truck can't get around this here tree. Not until we decide to move it. As a matter of fact, I kind of like that truck. She's sort of beat-up, but that's a sweet-purring engine."

"Leave the truck alone," Caleb said flatly. "And you'll have an easier time with me."

"Hell, we don't want an easier time with you. There are three of us, and only one of you. And I want to know why you're so durn protective of that truck."

It happened so fast she barely realized what was going on. The passenger door was slung open, and meaty hands reached in, hauling her out into the gathering dusk. Hurtful hands, and she fought instinctively, biting down hard on the nearest wrist.

One of them howled with rage, shoving her away from him and backhanding her across the face. "Damned bitch bit me," he moaned. "I guess I'm gonna have to learn her a lesson, too...."

The sound of a gunshot brought them to a curious standstill. Jassy looked up from her position on the hard ground, aching all over, staring at Caleb in shock. He stood in the open doorway of the truck, a very large, very nasty-looking gun in his capable-looking hands. "Now, I'm not a believer in violence," he said amiably, "but I think I've had plenty of provocation. Why don't you just run along now, while I'm still in the mood to let you go? Not you, there...." The gun pointed at the man who'd hit Jassy. "You stay put. Your friends can find you later."

The other two jumped into the old pickup parked on the other side of the fallen tree blocking the old road, and a moment later they roared off into the gathering darkness, leaving their comrade behind.

Caleb jumped down from the truck, the gun held loosely in his hand, and he strode over to Jassy. "You all right?" he asked, running a critical eye over her.

She managed to climb to her feet, brushing the dirt from her clothes. Her face throbbed, her heart was pounding, and her hands were cold and damp and shaking. She wanted to cry, she wanted to scream. Instead she nodded. "I'm fine."

He smiled at her then, a look of particular sweetness with none of his dare-you quality, and she had the sudden thought that he knew everything that had gone through her head, up to and including bursting into tears. "Good girl," he said. "Now you just stay out of the way while I let Willard try to teach me that lesson he was talking about."

"You're pretty tough when you're the one with the gun," Willard sneered. He was a huge, hulking brute, several inches taller than Caleb and outweighing him by a considerable amount of poundage, at least half of which was muscle. Jassy knew for certain she'd never seen him or his friends around Turner's Landing before.

"The gun bother you, Willard?" Caleb said gently. "Then I'll ask Miss Turner to hold it for me. That way if by any remote chance you happen to best me, she can still blow your ugly face off if you come anywhere near her."

"Miss Turner?" Willard echoed, suddenly looking uneasy.

"The name ring a bell, Willard?" Caleb asked. "Maybe whoever hired you happens to have the same one. How's he going to like hearing that you slapped his sister? I don't think he's going to be pleased."

"I don't know what you're talking about," Willard said sullenly, watching out of beady little eyes as Caleb placed the gun in Jassy's unwilling hands. The metal was warm from Caleb's grip and from its recent firing. Jassy knew about guns, knew and hated them. But she also had no great confidence in Caleb's ability to best someone who was bigger and probably meaner than he was. She set the firing mechanism, holding the gun in capable, steady hands.

"You know, Willard," Caleb said in a low, almost seductive voice, "it strikes me that I'm not the only one who needs to be taught a lesson. I think you need to learn not to hit women, not unless they're tough enough to take you on. Now, Miss Turner's plenty tough, and if it came to a battle of wills she'd win, hands down. But she's just not as big as you are, and not as strong, and I don't believe she's into physical violence." The two of them were circling around each other like wary dogs. "However," Caleb added with his dare-you smile, "I am."

With a roar Willard charged at him, and Jassy let cowardice overcome her, shutting her eyes for a moment, unable to watch Caleb being pounded to a pulp. And then she opened them, to see Willard lying flat on his back like a landed fish, gasping and groaning in agony, struggling and failing to get to his feet.

Caleb stood over him, an enigmatic expression on his face. "Not so tough, are you, Willard?" he said in a soft voice, one that barely carried to Jassy's ears. "This one's for the lady." And to Jassy's horror he brought his boot down on Willard's right hand, hard.

Willard's shriek of pain echoed through the night, but Caleb had already turned away, taking the gun out of Jassy's limp hands. "Shall we go?" he asked in a pleasant voice.

She looked up at him, shell-shocked. The violence of the last few minutes hung in the air like a sour perfume, and now that she no longer held the gun she found she was shaking. "What did you do to him?"

If he noticed her reaction he didn't mention it, simply putting an impersonal hand under her arm and escorting her to the old truck. "Broke his hand," he said. "Stay in the truck while I move that old tree out of the way."

"You can't just leave him there...."

"His friends haven't gone far. They'll be back to get him."

"But..."

"It'll give him time to meditate on the error of his ways. Unless you'd rather have me shoot him and be done with it?"

"No!" she shrieked, and then realized he didn't mean it. She leaned back against the bench seat of the truck, shivering. "Just take me home."

The tree they'd dragged across the road was an old oak, fallen years ago but still heavy. Caleb pulled it out of the way with seemingly little effort, not even glancing at the man writhing on the ground as he headed back for the truck. There wasn't a mark on Caleb, Jassy thought, touching her own cheek with a rueful hand.

"We should go to the police," she said, forcing her weakness away.

"Why?"

"Because those men were lying in wait for you. They were planning to beat you up. You need to report it, have them arrested for assault...."

"I think after what I did to Willard the shoe might be on the other foot. After all, they didn't manage to touch me. Willard's not in very good shape." He started the truck, flicking on the lights against the gathering gloom and driving very carefully around Willard's writhing body.

"Someone hired those men...."

"I don't think you want that someone found," he pointed out. "It doesn't take much to guess who has it in for me. I thought your family loyalty came above all things."

"I'm willing to bet you have a lot more enemies than my brother," she said with a certain amount of shrewdness. "And even if he did hire them, he shouldn't have. Taking care of my brother includes stopping him from doing jackass things."

They were coming to the fork in the road. Belle Rive was to the left, the tiny town of Turner's Landing, complete with sheriff's office, was to the right. He slowed the truck on the deserted road. "Take your pick," he said, as if her decision meant absolutely nothing to him.

Perhaps it didn't. "Take me home," she said finally. "I'll call Clayton Sykes from there."

He nodded, turning left, and they drove on in silence for a while, the rush of hot moist air blowing through the windows, soothing Jassy's bruised cheek. He'd hit her on the right side of her face—if there was any mark she kept it averted from Caleb's too observant eyes.

"We've got one little problem," he said as they started up the long, curving driveway that led to the front entrance of Belle Rive.

"What's that?"

"A convicted felon doesn't have the right to own a handgun. Particularly a concealed, loaded one in a vehicle."

She looked at him. "Gun? I didn't see anyone with a gun there."

He smiled at her, and then his eyes narrowed, and he pulled the truck to a stop halfway up the driveway, with the lights of the big house visible in the distance, and she knew he'd seen her face.

He reached out to touch her cheekbone, very lightly, but she flinched anyway. "I should have killed him," he said in a flat, emotionless voice, and once more she believed him.

She tried to pull away, but his other hand reached up and caught her neck, gently, his thumb tracing gentle patterns on her exposed throat, while he pushed the tumbled hair away from her bruised face. "You're going to have a mark there tomorrow," he said. "You'd better lie down with an ice pack the moment you get inside."

"After I call the sheriff." Her voice came out strangled. She wanted to tell him to take his hands off her, but if he did she thought she'd die. He was looking at her out of those clear, light eyes, and he was close, much too close.

"What are you going to tell your family?"

"The truth."

"Even Harrison?"

"Particularly Harrison. I still refuse to believe he's responsible for those men, but just in case he is, he needs to see what a stupid move like that can bring about."

Caleb's smile was wry, self-deprecating. "I don't think he's going to learn his lesson, Jassy." His fingers were lightly stroking her face, whisper soft against her hairline, soothing her, as his thumb danced across her sensitive throat.

She pulled all her resolution around her. "I think you'd better drive me home," she whispered, wetting her lips in sudden nervousness.

"I know I'd better," he said. "There's just a little something I have to do first. I've been putting it off for too long." And his mouth dropped down on hers, cutting off the light.

She'd expected something more forceful. Strength and violence, demanding a response. She could have fought that. Instead his lips feathered across hers, a gentle wooing, clinging for a moment, traveling on, across her cheekbone to brush gently against her abraded cheek before returning to her lips.

She'd drawn in her breath at the first touch of his mouth, steeling herself to fight him, but there was no defiance in her. He nibbled at her mouth, softly, teasingly, coaxing her lips apart in a lazy seduction that had her moaning deep in the back of her throat, half longing for the fierce demand she'd been prepared to resist.

He knew women too well. He pulled away, leaving her dazed, aching, longing for more, and his old smile was back in place. He didn't say a word as he started up the truck again, pulling up to the front of the house and leaving the engine in neutral. His voice was neutral, too.

"You want me to come in with you?" he asked. "Looks like Harrison's come home."

He'd noticed Harrison's late model Buick before Jassy had.

"Maybe I'd better deal with this on my own," she said, her voice husky.

"Suit yourself. You know I'd prefer to come in."

"Please…"

He nodded. "If you call the sheriff…"

"*When* I call the sheriff," she corrected him.

"Tell him I'll be at home if he has any questions."

"I'll do that." She opened the door, sliding out before he could touch her again. She had no idea whether he'd planned to, and no idea how she'd react if he did. She was better off not knowing. "Those men won't be waiting for you, will they?" she asked, suddenly worried.

"I doubt it. Willard's going to need to see a doctor real bad, and the other two were cowards. They weren't told to kill me, otherwise they would have had guns of their own. I expect I'll be just fine. Don't worry about me, Jassy. I always come out okay."

"I'm not worried," she denied. "I just don't want my brother brought up on charges of murder."

Caleb's laugh was chilling in the hot evening air. "I don't think that's going to be up to you, sugar." And before she could say anything more, he drove away, speeding down the driveway with all the power his deceptively ancient truck could offer.

CHAPTER EIGHT

"WHAT IN GOD'S NAME happened to you?" Lila was standing in the hallway. Her face was blotchy and red from tears, but for once Jassy couldn't summon forth her usual concern.

"I got hit," she said flatly. "I gather Harrison's back?"

"I can't believe it!" Lila said in a carrying voice. "That man actually hit you? Harrison's going to kill him."

"Who am I going to kill?" Harrison appeared in the doorway, dwarfing the generous proportions. He had a drink in his hand, and a sullen, belligerent expression on his handsome face.

"Look at your sister," Lila said shrilly.

"I'm looking." He set the drink down. "We're calling Clayton Sykes. That boy's butt is going to be in a sling before he knows what's happening. He's gonna go back to jail so fast he won't know what's happening to him. Unless the people of Turner's Landing find out what he did to you and get to him first."

Jassy took all this in quite calmly. "I was just about to call Clayton," she agreed. "Though why the two of you idiots think it was Caleb Spenser is beyond me. I got mauled by one of the gorillas who was after Caleb. The man defended my honor."

"Spenser doesn't know what the word means."

"Maybe not. But he doesn't stand around and let women get hit without doing something about it."

"Who hit you, Jassy? And where's Spenser now?" Lila asked, coming toward her and putting her arms around her, her own troubles temporarily forgotten.

"We were coming back from the swamp when three good old boys stopped the truck. They'd dragged a tree trunk across the road and were waiting in ambush. Caleb made me hide on the floor while he tried to deal with them, but they found me." She shrugged.

"One of them hit me. Caleb scared the other two off and beat the hell out of the one who'd touched me."

"Whereabouts did this happen?" Harrison was looking remote, and if she didn't know better she would have thought he was half-drunk.

"Right before the old Wilson place." Too late she realized just what she was saying.

"That's on the road from the Moon Palace. I thought you said you were coming from the swamp," Harrison said.

"We stopped at the Moon Palace on the way back. Caleb had to check on a few things."

"I'll just bet he did. You don't have a lick of sense, do you, Jassy? Women like you are easy prey for a con man like Spenser. All he has to do is crook his finger and you're flat on your back for him...."

"Harrison!" Lila said, shocked.

"I never thought to see the day that my own little sister was a disloyal tramp! The man's trash, a worthless, no-good jailbird who's come here to cause trouble, and you lift your skirts like you're not better than you should be. It's a good thing Papa isn't alive to see this day, it's a good thing Mama's indisposed...."

"Mama isn't indisposed, she's drunk," Jassy said tartly, having had enough of this. "And it's none of your damned business, but I didn't sleep with Caleb Spenser. He was going to do some work for me on Rowdy's cabin, and we were checking it out. He was a perfect gentleman at all times." Or almost, she thought, remembering the heated expression in his clear, light eyes.

"That's another thing. Why the hell did you hire him to work for you, when there are any number of unemployed carpenters hanging around the general store in town, just begging for work?"

"Because I wanted to find out what the hell is going on between the two of you. You won't tell me a damned thing, I thought maybe I could get it out of him."

Harrison was suddenly very still. "And did he tell you?"

"Not a blessed thing."

There was no missing the faint sheen of relief in Harrison's dark eyes. "What about the cabin? Is he going to work for you? Try and resurrect that old relic?"

Harrison had done nothing but lie to her. For the first time in her life she had no compunction about lying right back to him. "We're still in the negotiation stage."

"Damn it, Jassy, I want that man out of this county!"

"You can't make him leave. And siccing out-of-town thugs on him doesn't help matters."

"What are you saying, Jassy?" Lila demanded. "You couldn't think Harrison had anything to do with those men."

"Couldn't I? Where else would they come from?"

If Harrison was responsible he was more than adept at hiding it. "A man like Spenser would have hundreds of enemies. I'm not the only one he has it in for."

"You're the only one around here."

"I wouldn't count on that, little sister. I don't think you're any too safe from him, either."

That hit a nerve, one she couldn't quite disguise. She didn't trust her brother, but she sure as hell didn't trust Caleb Spenser, either. She had no idea what he wanted in Turner's Landing, either from her brother or from her, but she had no doubts whatsoever that he'd ride right over her if she got in his way.

"I'm not worried about him," she said coolly. "Right now all I want is a telephone. I've got to call Clayton and see if he can find out where those men went. They shouldn't be too hard to find. The one named Willard needed a doctor."

"Don't bother Clayton with that nonsense, Jassy," Harrison said, picking his drink up again. "He won't be able to find them. You know Clayton—he couldn't find his own backside. Those men will be out of the county by now. They were probably just troublemakers from wherever Spenser came from, out for a little revenge. I doubt anyone's going to hear from them again."

"I'm still going to report them."

"Why don't you let Spenser take care of that?"

"He doesn't care whether they're reported or not."

"Then why should you?" Harrison asked in a reasonable tone. "I think what you need is a nice stiff drink, an ice pack for your face and a good night's sleep. We don't need to get involved in that man's business. He's nothing but trash, and the sooner he's gone, the better."

"The drink and the ice pack sound fine. But I'm calling Clayton."

"Suit yourself. But don't drag me into it. I'm not interested in Mr. Spenser's troubles," Harrison said.

"You're not interested when a man hits your sister?" she countered.

He glanced toward her bruised cheek, then shifted away uneasily. "It wouldn't have happened if I'd been around. I would have put my foot down and refused to allow you to go out with that man this morning."

"Harrison, I'm thirty-one years old. I'll go where and with whom I please."

"Not while you're living under my protection." He drained his glass, and there was no mistaking the belligerence in his stance.

"I'm going upstairs," Lila said faintly, an unwilling witness to the sibling argument. "I've got a headache."

"You do that, my dear," Harrison said, and Jassy remembered Lila's pale, tear-streaked face when she'd first arrived home. She must have interrupted them in the midst of some battle, only to provide her own fuel to the fire.

"I'll come up with you and make sure you're settled."

Lila's blue eyes took on an odd, startled expression. One that almost looked like fear, though Jassy knew perfectly well that Lila had no cause to fear her brother. "Thank you," she said, in a small, quiet voice, starting upstairs.

"Wait a minute, Harrison," Jassy said as her brother moved past her.

"What now?" His tone was aggrieved.

"What's wrong with Lila?"

"What's always wrong with Lila?" he countered, as his wife disappeared on the upper landing. "She's fussing about children again. She's badgering me to take those stupid tests. There's nothing wrong with me, and she knows it. She's just clutching at straws."

"Can't you humor her?"

"Hell, no! You don't understand what it means to be a man, Jassy. We have pride. We have dignity. We don't want our intimate functions messed with by some damned quack."

"But your wife can go through all sorts of painful tests...."

"She's the one who's so all-fired set on having babies," he said in a sulky tone.

Jassy just stared at him. At the handsome, sullen face, the belligerent set to his broad shoulders, and she wondered if, after thirty-one years, she really knew him at all. "I'm calling Clayton," she said.

"Give him my best." Harrison started up the stairs, but her voice called after him.

"Just one thing, brother mine. How did you know Caleb Spenser had spent time in jail?"

Harrison turned and looked at her, the contempt on his face plain. "How did you, Jassy?" And without another word he continued up the stairs.

THERE WAS NO SIGN of Willard or his friends when Caleb drove back down the old road to the bordello, but then, he hadn't expected there to be. They were long gone, at least for now. He had little doubt either, they or a reasonable facsimile, would be showing up later. Harrison wasn't going to give up on him, any more than he was going to let Harrison slip away from the justice he so richly deserved.

It was fully dark by the time he pulled up outside the old house, and Dog was waiting for him, howling plaintively, a reproachful expression in his huge dark eyes.

"Yeah, I know, you didn't want me leaving you," Caleb said, cuffing him playfully as he strode through the darkness to the house. "But I need you to play watchdog, you know that. No one in their right mind will mess with my things if you're around, for all that Jassy Turner thinks you're just a sweet, overgrown puppy."

Dog woofed cheerfully, as if in agreement. "Yeah, I can't say much for her judgment. She can't see the wolf in you, and she probably thinks I'm not nearly as dangerous as people think. She's wrong in both cases, dead wrong."

Dog looked aggrieved, his nails clacking on the worn wooden floor as he followed Caleb into the sparse kitchen. "I know. You wouldn't hurt her. You've fallen for her, you big stupid canine, and if it came to choosing between her and me you'd probably forget all I've ever done for you and pick her. She has that ability. A talent for making people forget what they should be remembering. Things like anger, justice, revenge. It sure would be nice just to wrap her around me and forget about why I'm here. But I can't do that. And don't you expect me to, either.''

Dog wandered over to his empty dish and sank down with a disapproving sigh. ''I know you think I ought to let her be. Hell, you probably think I ought to forget about the whole damned thing. But I can't. Not after three years of my life were ripped away by that sniveling coward and his old man. Not after spending the next ten years trying to track him down. I just can't let go of it. Even if I wanted to. And I don't. You hear me, Dog? I don't want to let go.'' He opened the refrigerator, pulled out a beer for himself and a pot of leftover stew for Dog. He dumped it down on the linoleum, but Dog only looked up at him out of reproachful eyes.

''Don't look at me that way. I'm not listening to you.'' He opened the beer, tilting back a goodly swallow down his throat, then running the cold bottle against his forehead. ''You know what I need, Dog? I need a woman. Maybe that'll take my mind off Jassy Turner. Maybe I'll just go look up Miss Mary-Louise Albertson. She's certainly been more than willing.''

Dog growled, low in his throat.

''I didn't say I was going to bring her back here. I just thought maybe I could take the edge off my mood. A couple of hours between the sheets with Mary-Louise might make me see things a little more clearly. Even if I'd rather be between the sheets with Jassy.''

Dog let out a little bark of enthusiastic agreement. ''Pervert,'' Caleb said cheerfully. ''Don't think you're going to get to watch. When I bring Jassy back here we're not going to want any distractions. You're going to stay outside and guard the place.''

Dog sighed, nibbling at the congealed beef stew. ''*If* I bring her back here. I'd be much better off leaving Jassy Turner strictly alone. She's the most distracting woman I've met in a long time.'' He strode past Dog's disapproving figure, into the back room that served as his headquarters, bedroom, office, what have you. He laughed at the thought of what prim and proper Miss Jassy Turner would say if she saw where he slept.

The old billiard table was one of the few sturdy pieces of furniture left in the old place. He'd considered sleeping in one of those oversize, red-flocked bedrooms upstairs, but while the wooden frames of the old beds were still in worthwhile shape, the springs and mattresses had rusted and sagged their way into oblivion, and he sure as hell wasn't going to spread his sleeping bag on the floor. One of the first things he'd done after he'd bought the place was head down to Clearwater and bring back a queen-size mattress to throw on top of it. Pool tables were made of slate, and this one was as heavy as hell. He liked a hard bed, and the pool table gave him that. He just wondered how Miss Jassy would feel stretched across it, looking up at him.

He climbed up on it, leaning back, his half-empty beer in one hand as he unbuttoned his shirt to the warm night breezes blowing through the house. The thunder had died away long ago, the promise of a cooling rain unfulfilled. He could feel the tension thrumming through him, frustration, edginess, all boiling away in the pit of his stomach. He wasn't going after Mary-Louise—at least not now. He wasn't in the mood for dealing with all the little games you had to play to get someone into bed.

Something had to happen, and happen soon, before he exploded. The confrontation tonight with Willard had only heightened his tension, set his nerve endings on edge, so that he wanted to smash his fist into someone's face.

It had to rain. Or Harrison had to make one false move. He couldn't get him yet, and indeed, he didn't want to. He wanted the man to sweat. To suffer. To know that retribution was waiting for him, ready to pounce when he least expected it. To know that his comfortable little life was going to dissolve into ruin, and there was nothing he could do to stop it.

He heard one distant rumble of thunder, and he drained his beer, dropping it over the side of the bed and letting it clank   to the bare wood floors. Closing his eyes, he thought of all the people who'd made love under the shabby roof of the old place. He tried to think of Mary-Louise and the smug promise in her ripe mouth. But instead, all he could think of was Jassy Turner, of the trembling softness of her lips beneath his, the way she tried to look so cold and starched up, and the way her breasts looked beneath that thin silk camisole. He groaned out loud in the dimly-lit room, and Dog replied from the kitchen with a commiserating whine.

"Life's a bitch, Dog," Caleb muttered. "I just wish to hell I knew of a way to get my cake and eat it, too. I want Harrison Turner strung up and I want Jassy Turner spread out, and I don't think I'm gonna manage both. But I'll tell you one thing, you mangy, flea-ridden critter. I sure as hell am going to try."

And Dog, wagging his ponderous tail in agreement, sank onto the floor beneath the billiard table, feeling more secure in that moment than Caleb had ever felt in his entire life.

IT WASN'T ANY HOTTER in the stifling office at the women's center than it had been two days earlier, it just felt that way. The air conditioner was groaning like an arthritic old lady climbing stairs, the plastic chair was sticking to Jassy's thighs through the loose cotton skirt and her state of mind was a match for the day.

Clayton Sykes had been everything that Harrison had warned her. Supremely uninterested, unwilling to take a statement, condescending and smugly superior, he'd suggested that she was exaggerating the whole incident. No one else in town had noticed three strangers, and in a place as small as Turner's Landing, someone would have said something. If Caleb Spenser had anything to complain about, maybe he'd better be the one to file the complaint. Otherwise, Miss Jassy ought to pour herself a stiff drink and get a good night's sleep.

Jassy had slammed down the phone on him. She was getting tired of men telling her she should have a stiff drink. If that was the way men had always treated her mama when she was younger then it was no wonder that Claire was in her current state.

Damn Caleb Spenser. She'd worked so hard at making excuses for her mother, refusing to see what Claire had become. With a couple of blunt sentences Caleb had ripped that comfortable veil away, and she saw her mother as she really was.

Worry about Claire hadn't improved her state of mind that day. Nor did the sight of her bruised cheekbone. She'd pulled her hair loosely around her face, trying to cover some of the telltale mark, but when Lizzie Grady and Faith Philips came by midday they'd taken one look at her poor excuse at subterfuge and given her commiserating looks.

They hadn't said anything, and Jassy hadn't bothered coming up with excuses, such as running into a door. Both women knew far too well what kind of mark a man's fist left on a woman's face, and they thought they recognized another victim.

Her only success that day had been in dealing with Ed down at the lumberyard. She'd explained to him in short, succinct sentences that he'd best get Spenser's load of lumber delivered to him that morning, or the uncomfortable situation out at the Moon Palace was bound to get a great deal more uncomfortable. Ed had always been a reasonable man, and he was fonder of Jassy than her brother, and to her surprise he'd agreed without more than a token protest. He'd never cared for the way Harrison tried to run the town, and the Turner investment in Ed's lumberyard wasn't as high as it was in some of the other town industries.

But the rest of the day had gone from bad to worse, until the air conditioner had finally let out a long, gasping wheeze and settled into an ominous silence. Jassy had stared up at it in dismay, her lower lip quivering at this final insult of fate, when she realized that someone was lounging in the open door. The person she most and least wanted to see.

"You look like you're in a rare mood," Caleb drawled. "Things not going too well?"

"You could say so." She put her hands in her lap. She wanted to push her hair out of her face, she wanted to cover the mark on her cheek, she wanted to wet her lips and pull her loose shirt around her. She forced herself to sit utterly, completely still.

Caleb pushed away from the door frame. "I wanted to thank you for talking to the folks down at the lumberyard. My delivery was on my doorstep at eight-thirty this morning."

"That didn't take long." She'd talked to Ed at just after eight. He must have gone right out and made the arrangements.

"Dog scared the hell out of them, though, showing up like they did. I guess I'm going to have to have a telephone put in, much as I hate the damned things." He pushed his dark blond hair away from his face, and his gold hoop glinted in the afternoon light. "Dog doesn't like unannounced visitors."

"Don't be ridiculous. Dog is nothing more than a gentle old pussycat."

"That's when he likes someone. You have his seal of approval, for some reason." He shut the door behind him, and the place suddenly seemed ten times smaller and a hundred times hotter. "So what did the sheriff say when you called him?"

He didn't ask whether she'd bothered calling. At least he knew her well enough to realize she'd follow through with what she said she'd do. "He told me not to worry my pretty little head about it," she said, her voice rich with disgust.

He didn't look surprised. "I told you it was a waste of time. What did he say after you told him where to stick it?"

"I didn't. I just hung up on him."

"I guess you save the bulk of your hostility for me."

"I don't feel hostile toward you," she said hotly, lifting her head.

His eyes focused on her cheekbone, narrowed, and she could feel the warmth of his gaze. "Maybe I should have killed him," Caleb said softly.

"Clayton?" Jassy asked, momentarily confused.

"Willard. Does it hurt much?"

She shook her head, giving up any attempt at camouflage. "As a matter of fact, it has its advantages. The women around here don't seem to think I'm that much of an elitist do-gooder with a man's bruise on my face. At least now they figure I know what I'm talking about."

He smiled briefly, that brief upturning of his mouth signifying his disagreement. "You don't know anything about the kind of lives most people live," he said. "You've been protected all your life."

She wished she could dispute him, but she knew it was true. She'd been wrapped in cotton wool from the day she was born, and if she weren't so determined she'd be just as helpless and dependent as Lila and Claire were.

But she was determined, and she wasn't going to spend her life locked in the safety of Belle Rive. Away from men like Caleb Spenser. "Was there anything else, Mr. Spenser?" she asked coolly, deciding to put this conversation on a more businesslike note.

He grinned, leaning back in his chair and stretching his long legs out in front of him. "As a matter of fact, there were several things. We haven't finished discussing the condition of the place out in Rayder Swamp."

That jarred her out of her self-possession. "I thought you said it was hopeless."

"Not necessarily. There are a couple of things I could try. If you're willing."

"I'd need an estimate. I told you, I'm not sure how much money…"

"It'll depend on whether it works. If it doesn't, there'll be no charge. If it does, I'll charge you what's fair."

"And I'm supposed to trust you?" she asked.

"Yes, ma'am. You're supposed to trust me." He leaned forward, across the desk, and she wanted to reach out and touch his hands, feel the strength in them, the rough, hardworking texture of his skin.

She nodded, not committing herself. She'd be a fool and a half to trust him in any way. And yet she knew she did, on some basic level that she didn't even understand. "All right," she said. "Do what you can. What else?"

"What else what?"

"What else did you want to see me about?"

He glanced around him. "It doesn't look like you're so damned busy that you can't spare a few minutes in socializing. The wife-beating business must be a little slow these days."

"It's no joking matter."

"Honey, life's a joking matter. If you take it too seriously you'll wind up dead or drunk or crazy."

There was no way she could refute it. "What do you want from me?" she asked in a low voice.

He just looked at her for a moment, and she could see into his mind so clearly that it shocked her. And then he smiled. "We'll get to that part later," he said mildly. "In the meantime, I want an invitation to dinner."

"I beg your pardon?"

"I want you to ask me up to the big house for dinner. Your brother's been slinking around like a polecat with a guilty conscience. Don't you think it would be better if he just faced me like a man?''

"Not with women present," she muttered.

"I'm not going to lay a finger on him." He gave her what he obviously thought was his most disarming smile. She didn't believe him for a minute. "Maybe he'll find that I'm not the threat he imagines me to be."

"And maybe all hell will break loose."

"Maybe," he allowed. "But if it does, it's bound to happen sooner or later. You want to put it off, dreading it? Or do you want to see what happens when you push things?"

She had to be crazy. But the tension in the house kept escalating, until there were times when she thought she might scream. Caleb was right, all hell might break out. But she'd had enough of heat lightning. It was time to risk a real storm, one that would wipe away the tension and shadows and half-truths. It was time for rain.

CHAPTER NINE

"SO WHAT MADE YOU invite Mr. Spenser for dinner?" Lila stood in the open bedroom door, her blue eyes surveying Jassy with critical approval. "I thought you considered him to be dangerous."

"I do." She poked herself with the mascara she used to darken her naturally thick eyelashes, cursed, and wiped away the excess. "I figured it would be better to keep an eye on him. Besides, Harrison isn't accomplishing anything by trying to avoid him. The sooner he faces up to Caleb, the sooner we'll get past the feeling we're walking on eggs."

Lila looked doubtful. "I'm not certain Harrison is ready to face him. Don't you think it might have been better if you'd asked him before inviting Mr. Spenser into the family home?"

"You mean because he's not 'our kind'?"

"I never should have said that," Lila said.

"You're right." Jassy sat back and surveyed her appearance with uneasy satisfaction. She'd loosened the thick cloud of hair, fastening it at the back of her neck with an antique silver barrette, and she'd even gone to the trouble of putting on makeup. Clothing now lay strewn all across her bed, a fact that hadn't escaped Lila's too-observant eyes, and her final choice, a plain beige linen sheath, had to be the worst one. She'd rejected a Belle France dress that made her look like a virginal schoolgirl, another navy outfit that made her look like a spinster. Everything else was too small, too big, too short or too long. She'd finally thrown in the towel and picked her most innocuous dress. She'd just as soon fade into the woodwork when Caleb Spenser turned those mesmerizing eyes her way.

Not that he'd be looking at her. She had every certainty that he'd be concentrating on Harrison, and not Harrison's little sister. Which was just as well. He wouldn't expect her to be much protection. It was always better to be underestimated.

"Not that it isn't true," Lila persevered, coming into the room and dropping onto the littered bed. She was dressed in something flowery and frilly, her attributes displayed by the low-cut neckline, her long, silk-covered legs stretched out. "He isn't our kind, and you know it. Call me a snob if you like, but I've learned that it's better if like marries like. Even if there are problems, disagreements, at least you have a shared heritage, background..."

Jassy swiveled around to stare at Lila. "Are you and Harrison having problems?"

Lila flushed. "Of course not. You know I absolutely worship your brother. The only problem in our relationship is my barrenness. I'm just grateful he's so patient with me. It's no wonder that sometimes he gets a little...upset. After all, I have been obsessing about it, and a man like Harrison needs distractions after the problems of the day, not new problems."

"Upset?" Jassy repeated softly.

Lila jumped up from the bed, busying herself sorting through the discarded clothes. "I can't imagine why you've chosen to wear that old thing. Half these clothes look better on you. Not that I approve of Mr. Spenser, but if you've decided you're attracted to him you ought to at least make an effort. The makeup's good, but you could use more eye shadow. I have a delicious shade of nile green that would really bring out the color of your eyes, and it looks terrible with my blue eyes. And you could let me do something with your hair, instead of just bundling it back there. After all, you are a lady, whether you accept that fact or not, and Mr. Spenser ought to be reminded of that fact and not think you're just a social chippie like..."

"Like who?" Jassy asked, having listened to Lila's nervous babbling with an uneasy fascination.

"Like your friend Mary-Louise," Lila said defiantly.

"Mary-Louise's great-grandfather was a general of the Confederacy," Jassy pointed out, wondering where in heaven's name all this sudden antipathy came from. As far as she knew, Lila and Mary-Louise had always been cordial, if not terribly close.

"Well, there's trash somewhere in her bloodlines," Lila said flatly, dropping the folded clothes back onto the bed with a complete disregard for her careful neatness. "Her mother ought to keep a better eye on her if she doesn't want the family name dragged in the mud.''

"Mary-Louise is thirty-two years old. That's a little long in the tooth for her mother to be keeping watch over her. And she's no longer a Stevenson, so Blanche doesn't need to worry about the family name. Not that there'd be any controlling Mary-Louise. She's always done exactly as she's wanted to do, and the devil with everyone else. That's one of the things I've most admired about her.''

"Admired about her?'' Lila shrieked. "Her blatant disregard of honor and decency and other people's feelings?''

"No,'' Jassy said, rising. "But her refusal to kowtow to foolish opinions when something really matters.'' She crossed the room to Lila, putting her hands on her shoulders. "What's got you so upset, Lila? I know it can't be Mary-Louise, or Caleb Spenser for that matter. Why are you so wound up?'' The thin shoulders beneath Jassy's hands felt like iron from the tension thrumming through her body.

Lila shook her head, managing a totally unconvincing smile. "Nothing,'' she said. "I'm just a little high-strung nowadays. This damnable weather.'' She glared out the French doors to the darkening night beyond. "If only it would rain.''

"The same problems will be here, whether it rains or not,'' Jassy pointed out.

Lila squirmed away from Jassy's touch. "Yes, but I might be able to deal with them a little more rationally. We'd better get downstairs, don't you think? We don't want Harrison and Spenser meeting up without a referee, do we? They may end up killing each other.''

Jassy closed her eyes for a moment, remembering Caleb's merciless expression. If he killed one man, he could surely kill another. If only she knew why he'd want to. What he had against her brother. Maybe Harrison testified against him. No, that was unlikely. She would have heard about it.

Far more likely that he could have testified in Caleb's favor, and had simply taken off. Hadn't Caleb said something about knowing Harrison under another name? And why had he waited ten years to confront Harrison? Unless it had taken him that long to find him.

If only one of those damned men would simply answer a straight question! If she didn't start getting some answers soon she was going to have to take matters into her own hands. Trials were a matter of public record. She could go over to St. Florence and check old newspapers from thirteen years ago. She could hire a private detective, if there was any way she could come up with some ready cash. But she wasn't going to sit around any longer and be patted on the head and told to be a good girl and not ask questions.

"We'd better get downstairs," she agreed, pausing a moment to glance at her reflection in the mirror. She looked as though she had no curves at all in that beige dress. No color, either; nothing but legs that were too long and hair that was too frizzy. "You keep Harrison in line, I'll control Caleb."

Lila shook her head. "If only it were that simple." And she left the room before Jassy could ask her to explain.

Obviously she meant Jassy controlling Caleb. Though she couldn't rid herself of the feeling that there was something going on between Harrison and Lila. Lila's struggles to conceive were bad enough, but there was something else happening, something dark and troublesome, something that might or might not have to do with Caleb Spenser's precipitate arrival in Turner's Landing.

If Lila resented Caleb's presence at Belle Rive, you certainly couldn't tell it to look at her, Jassy thought critically a few moments later when she walked into the living room. Caleb had already arrived, and he was seated next to Lila on the sofa, flirting with her quite blatantly, and Lila was flirting back, her soft voice trilling with laughter, and her big blue eyes batting at him fatuously.

For a moment Jassy paused in the doorway, taking in the scene. Caleb had dressed for the occasion, wearing a freshly ironed striped shirt, the sleeves rolled up to reveal his strong forearms, his dark blond hair slicked back away from his face, the gold hoop in his ear glinting in the light. He looked like a pirate, Jassy thought. A dangerous marauder, out to pillage the countryside. And there was no one to stop him. Certainly not the two gullible women in her family.

Claire was sitting in the chair next to Caleb, a tall glass of iced, amber-colored liquid in her pale hand. Jassy frowned at it, wondering if she dared to say anything, when the happy trio finally noticed her arrival.

"Jassy," Claire said with uncustomary brightness, "we wondered what was keeping you. Would you like a glass of iced tea, or something stronger?"

Iced tea, she thought, relaxing a bit as Caleb rose to his feet with an insolent grace that took most of the politeness out of the gesture. At least Claire wasn't drinking tonight. And curse Caleb for making her see exactly what she didn't want to see. How far her mother's drinking had gone.

"Tea would be fine," she murmured. "Sorry I'm late."

"It was worth the wait," Caleb said with mocking gallantry that she didn't believe for a moment. "You look very...dignified."

She had to bite back her instinctive, shocking retort. Instead she gave him a sickly sweet smile. "Compliments *do* go to my head," she murmured, moving to the heavy silver tray of drinks and pouring herself a tall glass of tea. Given the circumstances she would have been much happier with a whiskey and water, but she decided the least she could do was join Claire in abstinence. Besides, she'd need all her wits about her to chart their way through the dangerous waters that surrounded them that night. "I can't imagine what's keeping Harrison. He knows we serve dinner at seven, and he's usually home well before then."

"Maybe he heard he had guests," Caleb murmured.

Jassy sat down across the room from the three of them, crossing her legs and swinging one foot gently. "Perhaps. My brother's not a coward, Mr. Spenser."

Caleb sat down again, closer to Lila this time. Lila didn't move away. "I never said he was," he said, in the tone of voice that conveyed quite clearly that Harrison's cowardice was a given.

"Jassy, darling, you're sounding awfully cantankerous," Claire said in a reproving tone of voice.

"It's this weather," Caleb drawled. "Miz Lila and I were just discussing how this heat and humidity can make one want to commit murder."

She looked him in the eyes, and her message was clear. Of all people, he should know what it was like to commit murder. He smiled then, just a faint quirk of his mouth that deepened the groove in his cheek as he acknowledged her silent message and she felt herself relax. After all, how bad could things get? Caleb Spenser was a reasonable man. Her brother was civilized. They weren't going to kill each other.

If she expected the evening to be awkward she hadn't counted on one very salient point. The other three members of their mismatched dinner party were adept at acceptable social behavior. Claire could keep any conversation going, and put anyone at ease, as long as she herself was in a comparatively sober state. It didn't take much to charm Lila out of her snobbish misgivings, and she flirted as naturally as she breathed. It had been too long since she'd been given a chance to exert her inborn feminine wiles, and she was having a glorious time of it, batting her eyes at Caleb and giggling at each one of his sallies.

As for Caleb, he was a past master at manipulation. As before, he had both women eating out of his hand, forgetting their initial mistrust. His charm was as natural as Lila's, though he put it to more constructive use.

The only one spared was Jassy. She sat across from them, nursing her iced tea, watching him wrap the two other Turner women around his little finger, and she wondered why he didn't bother with her. Why he'd simply glance over at her now and then, an odd expression in his eyes, before turning back to her mother and sister-in-law. Did he think she was already so completely smitten that he didn't have to bother? Or conversely, did he consider her such a tough nut to crack that he couldn't waste his time?

Except there was something faintly conspiratorial in the covert looks he'd cast her every now and then. As if he knew perfectly well that she saw through his charming act, and even preferred that she did. As if the two of them shared a secret, one that might make the others appear foolish, but never cruelly so.

It was an unsettling, intimate feeling, one she was powerless to break. And she wondered whether she'd been right in the first place. That he'd simply known that he had her, come hell or high water, and could concentrate his energies on the unknown quantities.

"I think we'd best go in to dinner," Claire finally announced. "I don't know where Harrison is, but we can't wait any longer or

Miss Sadie will put us all on bread and water. I'm sure he'll turn up sooner or later.''

Caleb rose swiftly, offering Claire his arm with all the flourish of a southern gentleman of old. "Does he do this often?" he murmured, and Claire didn't even notice that the question was none of his business.

"Oh, Harrison is always busy. We learn to work around his schedule. Sometimes he doesn't get home till midnight...."

The sound of mingled laughter drifted in from the front hall, and Jassy felt the adrenaline shoot through her. She couldn't just wait for the confrontation—the long delay in Harrison's appearance had strung her nerves so tightly they felt as if they might snap.

"Here he is now," she said brightly. "You go on in to dinner and I'll let him know we have a guest."

Caleb reached out a restraining hand, a frown on his face, but she skirted him effortlessly, ignoring him. She practically raced to the front hall, half-afraid he'd try to stop her, but when she glanced behind her she saw the three of them had gone in to dinner.

Harrison wasn't alone. Mary-Louise was with him, laughing, her full-lipped mouth curved in delicious humor. "We wondered what was keeping you," Jassy said, pausing in the doorway.

Harrison looked up. He had his arm around Mary-Louise's shoulders, and he looked more relaxed than he had in weeks. He frowned at her implied question, but before he could say anything, Mary-Louise spoke up.

"Your brother was kind enough to give me a hand with my finances," she said smoothly. "You know what a cotton-headed creature I am. The divorce settlement makes no sense to me whatsoever, and Harrison spent several hours explaining it all to me. Then of course the dear man insisted I come to dinner, so here we are."

"Here you are," Jassy echoed dully. Mary-Louise had a financial mind of steel. She knew down to the penny the details of her divorce settlement, and had fought for them more intently than her barracuda of a lawyer.

She was also one of the most fastidious of women. She seldom had a hair out of place, a shiny nose, a smudge of lipstick around her full mouth.

Her hair was perfect, her nose freshly powdered, her lipstick new and creamy. And her blouse was buttoned wrong.

Suddenly it all made sense. Lila's antipathy and barely controlled hysteria. Jassy looked at the two of them, and contempt filled her.

She smiled grimly, not showing a sign of it. "We are always glad to see you, Mary-Louise. As a matter of fact, we have another guest tonight and we've just gone in to dinner. I'll have Miss Sadie set another place. Come along." She turned back to the dining room.

"Who's here?" Harrison demanded, following behind her.

"A surprise," Jassy said, not pausing.

The only problem with leading those two in, she thought, was that she couldn't appreciate the full effect of Harrison's expression when he saw Caleb Spenser sitting at his table with his mother and wife. She could only see Caleb's expression, distant, unreadable, a faint smile of satisfaction on his mouth as Harrison stopped abruptly behind her.

She took the seat next to him, glancing up at her brother. Harrison was statue-still in the doorway, all color drained from his face, his brown eyes bulging faintly. By his side, Mary-Louise looked more troubled than she had any right to be.

The silence was thick and angry as the undercurrents of emotion swept through them. Lila's cheerful flirtatiousness had died an abrupt death when Mary-Louise sauntered into the room. The hatred that flowed between the two men was as tangible and as raw as the swamp, though a lot swifter moving. Jassy herself was feeling ready to scream, and more than anything she wanted to break the mood, to make some smart comment about one big happy family.

Fortunately Claire's years of breeding came through before Jassy could precipitate a showdown between any of the warring groups of people. "There you are, Harrison. We waited as long as we could, but you know how evil-tempered Miss Sadie gets. And Mary-Louise, how lovely to see you, dear. Take the seat beside me, and Harrison will set a new place. I gather the two of you must have met Mr. Spenser. I thought it would be nice to invite him to dinner. I have no reliance on any bachelor being able to provide himself with a decent meal. I'm sure the ladies of this town have done their best, but it's nice to eat with other people, use fine china, drink wine.'' The last sounded wistful, but Claire sailed on, blithely ignoring the tension in the room. ''Maybe you could open the French doors while you're at it, Harrison. It's beastly hot, as always. Harrison?''

Harrison hadn't moved, and for a moment Jassy wondered whether he'd do what he obviously wanted. Lunge across the damask- and china-covered table and go for Caleb's throat.

In truth, she wouldn't have blamed him. Caleb had that damnable, taunting smile on his face as he looked at Harrison, the others around them, including Jassy, forgotten. She held her breath, waiting, and then swallowed her sigh of relief as Harrison moved toward the window to do his mother's bidding.

The remaining place at the table was directly opposite Spenser. Harrison sat down, looking across at his nemesis, and for the moment his expression was completely unreadable. ''Spenser,'' he said in a dull monotone, by way of a greeting.

Caleb's smile didn't change. ''Harrison,'' he replied, just as circumspect, and Jassy was reminded of two wary dogs, circling each other, hackles rising, waiting for the other one to attack.

''So tell me, Mr. Spenser,'' Claire said, still firmly in charge of the social amenities, ''how's the work going on the old Moon Palace?''

''Just fine, Miz Turner. Now that my lumber order has been delivered I should be able to make some progress.''

''You had trouble getting your deliveries?'' Harrison asked in a silken voice.

''Until Jassy kindly helped out. All she had to do was make a phone call and the lumber arrived.''

Harrison didn't even bother to look at her, but Jassy could feel his anger nonetheless, and knew he'd be dealing with her later. When his main object was out of the way. ''Seems like a mighty big job for one man,'' he said, leaning back in his chair, seemingly at ease. Except that Jassy could see the faint quiver in the slightly pouchy skin beneath his left eye, and she knew that relaxation was all sham. ''And I still can't imagine why you'd want to do it. The Moon Palace is at the end of a dirt road—I can't imagine why anyone would want to live there.''

"Some people prefer seclusion," Caleb drawled, taking a sip of wine. "And I'm not doing it alone. My crew is arriving tonight."

Harrison paled slightly, and he picked up his heavy silver fork, tapping it against the thick damask cloth. "Crew?" he echoed. "How many men?"

"Just two at this point. The rest of my men are busy on a job up in Mobile. They'll come down here later to finish up."

"I didn't realize you were such an entrepreneur, Mr. Spenser," Lila said with a toss of her head. The flirtation was back, this time with a harder edge, and she shot a defiant glance at her husband.

Harrison was too absorbed to notice, though Jassy had the feeling that Lila would be called to account later, just as she would be.

Caleb smiled at her, and Jassy noticed with sudden irritation that there was a different quality to the smile he gave her sister-in-law. As if he realized, beneath her silliness and vanity and snobbery, that she was sweeter and more vulnerable than the lot of them. "I've had a certain amount of success, Miz Lila," he said. "I pick places no one's interested in, and hire people no one's interested in. The combination is good for everyone—any success is unexpected."

"What do you mean, people no one's interested in?" Mary-Louise spoke up, and Harrison cast her a quelling frown.

The feral edge was back in Caleb's smile, and Jassy didn't know whether she was pleased or not. "All my workers are ex-convicts, Mrs. Albertson. Forgotten men and women who just need a second chance."

"You're bringing jailbirds to town?" Claire demanded faintly, disapproval wiping out some of her calm demeanor.

"They're all fully rehabilitated," he said. "Bo and Ray wouldn't hurt a fly. Unless that fly were causing an undue amount of trouble. I imagine you heard about the little mess Jassy and I got into last night."

All eyes turned to Jassy, to the bruise on her cheek she'd tried to cover with makeup, and she squirmed.

"We heard," Harrison drawled. "I just figured you must have done it yourself. With a mouth like that girl has on her it's amazing she hasn't been smacked before."

"Harrison!" Claire said, shocked.

Jassy didn't say a word, too busy observing the others. The dangerous way Caleb's eyes narrowed. The pale chalkiness of Lila's complexion. And the covert smugness in Mary-Louise's big blue eyes.

Caleb leaned back, a slight, contemptuous smile on his face, as something passed between the two men that neither of them understood. "I don't hurt women, Harrison," he said. "I save my violence for those who deserve it."

The look the two men shared was steady, implacable and chilling, and the silence that filled the room was broken only by the distant sound of thunder. And then Caleb broke the moment deliberately, leaving Harrison with no choice but to stare down at his plate.

"Anyway, Miz Turner," he said, turning to Claire, "I wouldn't worry about having ex-cons around. Why, I've been here a week and I haven't caused a lick of trouble. Have I?"

And there was no answering his innocent, engaging smile.

CHAPTER TEN

JASSY HAD HAD MORE palatable meals in her lifetime. As it was, she was barely able to choke down any of Miss Sadie's succulent roast chicken with oranges, and the flaky biscuits went untouched.

She didn't know what twisted her stomach the most. The sight of Mary-Louise, her bright eyes avid and completely guiltless as she surveyed the people who had been a second family to her. Or Lila's miserable expression and arch attempts at flirtation.

Maybe it was Harrison's barely repressed violence. Or the slightly glassy expression in Claire's eyes after she returned from an overlong trip to the bathroom that had to have included a detour by way of the vodka bottle. Maybe it was a combination of all those things.

But deep inside she knew better. She'd been through any number of meals with Claire getting quietly drunk, Harrison sulking and Lila overbright and miserable.

No, it was the presence of Caleb Spenser that was turning her life upside down along with her stomach. Of all the people at the formal dinner table, he was the only one who ate with unconcealed gusto, clearly enjoying the food and everyone's discomfort. Jassy could watch her fill, for the simple reason that Caleb had obviously forgotten she was there. She'd always suspected she was a means to an end, and tonight he was proving it. He was watching everyone but her. Subtly, but definitely, those clear, light eyes of his took in every nuance at the table. Except her reaction.

She told herself it was a great relief. She was a strong woman, one who could stand up to other women's abusive husbands, recalcitrant bureaucrats, Harrison when he sulked, and even hungry alligators when they wandered out of the shallow river onto the broad front lawn of Belle Rive. But she couldn't stand up to Caleb Spenser when he turned those cool, light eyes on her, put his hard,

strong hands on her body. For some reason she was far more vulnerable to Caleb than she had been to any man in her entire life.
She felt much safer when he was distracted.

Claire reached for the little silver bell on the table, missed it, and
reached again. "The ladies will retire," she announced with great
solemnity.

Lila and Mary-Louise glared at each other across the table. The
thought of being trapped in a room with those two snarling cats,
while Claire probably sank into a discreet stupor, was more than
Jassy was willing to accept. "Don't be gothic, Mama," she said
flatly. "I'm not going anywhere."

"Suit yourself," Harrison snapped, pushing back from the table.
"But Spenser and I have business to discuss. And we don't need
your help, little sister."

She turned questioning eyes to Caleb, but he didn't even glance
her way, all his attention on Harrison. There was a combative light
in his eyes, one that sent chills down Jassy's spine.

"It's past time," he said in his slow, deep voice, rising with
insolent grace and following Harrison out of the room.

"They're going to kill each other," Jassy said flatly.

Mary-Louise shrugged. "Don't be ridiculous, Jassy. Why should
they?"

"Didn't Harrison tell you?" Lila broke in, her voice icy with
rage.

Mary-Louise's smug smile would have enraged a saint. Lila
wasn't a saint. "Harrison doesn't do much talking."

The word Lila used was one that Jassy would have thought her
demure sister-in-law didn't even know. Clearly the pampered Claire
had never heard it, for she simply blinked, looking confused.
"Come along, Jassy," she said. "The gentlemen have business to
discuss."

Jassy rose promptly enough. Instead of following the quarrel-
some women, however, she went after Caleb, trailing at his heels
just like his disreputable dog, moving into the library behind the
two men.

Harrison caught her arm, spun her around, and marched her right
out again, his fingers digging in tightly. "This is none of your
damned business, Jassy," he announced.

She cast a beseeching glance at Caleb, but he didn't even look in her direction, his eyes cold and focused on Harrison's back with something that couldn't be mistaken for anything other than hatred. And then the door was shut in her face, and locked, securely.

She waited a moment, wondering if she were going to hear the sounds of a scuffle. As far as she knew, Harrison didn't have any guns in the room, but that didn't mean they couldn't find other, more creative ways of killing each other. Putting her ear against the heavy cypress door, she listened. All she could hear was the muffled sound of conversation.

She considered banging on the door, kicking and fussing. Emotionally it was what she wanted to do; rationally she knew better. Besides, the night wasn't as stifling as it had been, and it had looked as if the French doors to the veranda were open. If she scooted around outside she could manage to hear most of their conversation, and if worse came to worst, she could leap through the door and fling herself between them. She certainly wasn't going to let her brother kill Caleb, much as he obviously wanted to. And she wasn't going to let Caleb commit another murder.

Lila was stalking up the stairs, her back straight with anger and hurt, when Jassy raced through the hallway. She could hear the soft murmur of voices in the drawing room, Mary-Louise and Claire probably discussing the church auction or something equally innocuous. Jassy slipped out onto the veranda, feeling the soft night air close down around her.

Some of the humidity of the day had dissipated, some but not all. The sky was dark, clouds scudding past the quarter moon in angry swirls. If only those clouds meant rain. But Jassy knew better than to count on false promises.

The doors to the office were open to the night air. She moved stealthily along the terrace, concentrating on the polite murmur of voices, as phrases and sentences reached her.

"...can't prove anything," Harrison was saying. "You couldn't...too much time..."

"...not enough money. I want more." Caleb sounded cold, implacable, not an ounce of his lazy charm in evidence.

"What? I can be reasonable. If it's not money you want, Spenser, what is it?"

"Revenge."

"I can't give you that."

"The hell you can't," Caleb shot back, his voice cold and savage. "I'm going to take everything you ever cared about."

"Can't we be reasonable about this? It all happened so long ago. We were both kids. Times change, we get older, we learn from our mistakes...."

"I'm taking you down, Turner. I'm taking your wife, your sister, your money and your reputation. And there's not a damned thing you can do to stop me. All the good old boys you can dig up can't lay a finger on me. You're going to have to watch me pick things off, one by one, until you're left with nothing."

"I'll see you dead first."

"You can try," Caleb said. "I have an advantage over you, Harrison. I spent three years in prison for murder. That's hard time, and I learned a lot more than you ever picked up at Princeton. I intend to put that expensive education to good use when it comes to you and your family. You're going to be sorry you were ever born."

"I can come up with fifty thousand dollars...."

"Chicken feed," Caleb scoffed.

"You don't want my wife." Harrison's voice was high-pitched with blustery bravado, and if it weren't for his words Jassy would have exploded with the need to protect and nurture him. "She's no good in bed, anyway, and she whines. If you're looking for entertainment you'd be better off with Mary-Louise. She's very inventive. Or my sister. I've seen you look at her, Spenser. She's not going to stand by while you bring me down. If you want a chance at her you're going to have to think twice about some crazy scheme for revenge."

"I don't give a damn about your sister," Caleb said flatly, and Jassy believed him. "She's a means to an end, Turner, and you're that end. I'm going to have you by the short hairs, and you're going to be screaming for mercy."

There was a long silence. "When?" Harrison asked hoarsely.

Jassy didn't have to see Caleb's smile to know what it looked like, wreathing his cold, handsome face with its double-dare mockery. "When you least expect it," he said.

The wind picked up, swirling the hot, damp air along the veranda, and the live oaks on the front lawn creaked noisily. A night bird swooped close, making a raucous noise, startling Jassy, and by the time she turned back the room was silent. She craned her neck forward, peering into the library, wondering whether she'd see one of the men stretched out on the floor, the other with his hands around his neck, when she felt his presence behind her.

"Learn anything interesting?"

She refused to move quickly. She could feel the flush mount her face, and hoped that if she climbed down from her precarious perch slowly enough it might fade before she had to face him. Not that it mattered. Even if the color had faded from her face when Caleb saw her, he'd still know it had been there. He knew far too much.

The veranda was dark except for the yellowish light coming from the French doors. The shadows danced fitfully around them both, but she could see the glitter of his pale eyes, the glint of the gold hoop in his ear. He looked like a pagan tonight, she thought. Savage, vengeful, totally without conscience or heart. He'd proved that tonight in his conversation. So why wasn't she running from him like he was the devil?

She brushed imaginary dirt off her hands, then ran them down her rumpled linen sheath. "Nothing I didn't already know," she said. "Harrison has some connection with Sherman Delano's death. You're here to exploit that connection, and you don't give a damn who you hurt in the bargain. Me included."

That cold, dangerous expression lifted for a moment, as a trace of distant humor lit his eyes, curved the hard edges of his mouth. "Now how could I possibly hurt you, Jassy?" he said. "You wouldn't let me get close enough to do you any harm. You have to care about someone to let them hurt you. And you sure as hell don't care about me, do you, sugar?"

She didn't say a word. There was no way she could refute him, short of making a declaration she wasn't ready to make. Something she wasn't ready or willing to face, and the longer she put it off, the better chance she had of avoiding it entirely.

"You don't let anyone care about you," she said finally.

It wiped the humor off his dark, saturnine face. For a moment he simply looked at her blankly, startled out of his usual cool self-possession. "Well, I wouldn't want to start with you, honey. I'd tear you into little pieces without even trying."

"I'm tougher than I look."

"I know that. But I'm a hell of a lot meaner than I look."

"I don't think so."

She could see the perceptible relaxing of his shoulders. "Honey, you're an innocent. Haven't you learned that the world is full of nasty people?"

"Yes. I'm just not convinced you're one of them."

He shut his eyes for a moment, a parody of amused exasperation. "Honey, I'm the baddest of the bad. A convicted murderer, and one of the meanest SOBs you'd ever hope to meet. I came to Turner's Landing with the express purpose of destroying your brother, and quite possibly your whole family besides, and you just overheard me tell your brother that you don't mean diddly squat to me. So how can you stand there and tell me there's salvation for me?"

"I didn't say there was salvation. I just don't think you're as evil as you want people to believe."

"I'm going to destroy your brother. If I'm in the mood for it, I'll take you down, too."

"And I won't have any say in the matter?"

"You'll be begging for it." There was no sensual threat in his voice. He sounded bleak.

But it was that bleakness that gave Jassy hope. If he were as cold and vicious as he pretended to be then he wouldn't have any scruples about destroying them all. And clearly he had scruples aplenty. For the first time in hours she smiled, her mouth curving upward in a gentler version of Caleb's mocking challenge. "Maybe," she said. "Or maybe it'll be you doing the begging."

She took him by surprise. The starkness washed out of his face as he laughed, a brief, startled sound of pure amusement. "Mermaids shouldn't swim with sharks," he said.

"I'm not..." She didn't have time to finish the sentence. He'd dragged her into his arms, holding her tightly against his hard body, and one hand caught her chin, holding her face still.

"I'm a dangerous man, Jassy," he muttered. "Haven't you realized that by now? I'm a danger to all you love and care about, and I wish to God you weren't here. Why don't you pack up and leave? Go down to Miami, fly up north, just go away for a while. When you come back it'll all be over and you can pick up the pieces. You're good at that, aren't you? Picking up the pieces of people's broken lives.''

"Will there be anything left to mend?''

"Not of Harrison.''

"Caleb...''

"Don't reason with me. Don't beg me, don't plead, don't bribe, and for God's sake, don't treat me like I have a conscience. I don't.''

He was so close. His body was rock hard, and hot against hers. She could smell the warmth of his skin, the whiskey he'd had before dinner, the night air surrounding them. "Of course you do,'' she said.

"I guess I'm going to have to prove it.'' He pushed her back against the stucco wall of the house and his mouth covered hers with savage insistence. There was no tenderness in the hard mouth on hers, no seduction, no wooing, no sweet promise. It was demand, pure and simple, mixed with threat, and he allowed her no room to respond. She could simply hold still for the erotic assault of his kiss, his mouth wet and hungry on hers, his body already hard against hers.

She put her hands against his chest, pushing against him, but he was too strong. He was out to frighten her, part of her understood that, and she knew she should struggle. But if she struggled, he'd move away, and she knew if he did she'd die. Her arms slid around his waist, clinging tightly, and she shut her eyes, giving herself up to the overwhelming power of his kiss.

He moved his head a few inches away, staring down at her in confusion as his breath came rapidly. "You're supposed to fight,'' he said in a rough voice. "You're supposed to scream and slap me.''

She managed a smile. "I try very hard not to do what I'm supposed to do,'' she said, her voice equally shaky. "Why don't you kiss me again? This time a little softer. Maybe give me a chance to kiss you back.''

He didn't move. She could see that telltale light of amusement break through his dark expression. "I'm trying to scare you."

"You aren't succeeding."

"I can see that." He released her, and it took all her considerable willpower not to cling. "You're a hell of a woman, Jassy. You deserve a good man to love you. Not a few hot sticky hours in bed with a no-good like me."

"I beg your pardon?" She leaned back against the stucco wall, welcoming the cool roughness, feeling a little faint at the image his words had produced.

He reached out and touched her flushed face, trailing his fingers down her neck, the front of her linen dress, the swell of her breast in a caress that was calculatedly erotic. She jerked away in sudden nervousness, and that mocking smile was back in full force, in no way belied by the dark desire in his eyes.

"Do I shock you, lady? You're used to your polite, starched gentlemen, taking you to fancy teas, holding doors for you. I bet you've never heard a harsh word in your life. I'm kinda direct, myself. Downright crude, sometimes. I want you, Miss Jassy. I want you real bad. But I want your brother even more. Now clearly he doesn't give a rat's behind whether I take you or not. If he thought it would save him he'd hand you over without a second thought. So I can't get to him through you. Anything we do together under the sheets will be simply for mutual pleasure. It won't stop me from going after him, you need to know that from the outset." He stepped back, his large body no longer intimidating her smaller one. "So what's the answer, Miss Jassy?"

She felt shaken, deep inside, but she managed to lift her head, to meet his dark, hot gaze fearlessly. "What's the question?"

He took her hand in his large one. His skin was rough, callused from hard work, his fingers long and deft, curling around her small, softer one. He put her palm against his chest, where his shirt was open to the night air, and his skin was hot, hair roughened, faintly damp. She could feel the slow, steady beat of his heart through her own skin, and the sensation was intimate, erotic, disturbing. "If you don't know, Jassy," he said softly, "then we shouldn't even be having this conversation."

She took a deep breath, feeling it shake and tremble down her throat. "We probably shouldn't be," she whispered, her voice not strong enough for anything louder.

He smiled then, and moved her hand down, across his bare chest, past the buttons of the shirt, to the solid leather and brass of his belt. Her eyes looked into his, shocked, startled, as he moved her hand lower, to cover the thick, pulsing heat of him.

The veranda door slammed open, bouncing against the side of the house. "Jassy?" Harrison demanded. "Are you still out there?"

She tried to yank her hand away, but he held her still, his grip tight and inexorable. They were in the shadows, Harrison couldn't possibly see them, but she still felt suffused with embarrassment. "Answer him," Caleb said in a quiet voice. "Answer him, or he'll come and find you."

Somewhere she managed to find her voice. "I...I'll be right in."

Harrison stepped out on the porch, his large figure dwarfing the light. "Are you alone out there?"

She could feel the rough texture of the denim beneath her fingers. The metal of the zipper, the hot, turgid size of him. She could feel the blood pulsing through him, hot. For her.

"Answer him, Jassy," Caleb whispered, his voice low and insinuating. "The truth, or a lie. It's up to you."

She'd kept her hand flat in his grip. Now she let her fingertips move, tracing the length of him, and she saw his response in his flared nostrils, the darkening of his eyes, the sudden intake of breath.

"I'm alone," she called. "I'll be there in a minute."

Harrison didn't move from his spot in the doorway, waiting for her. Caleb's fingers covered hers, pressing her harder against him. "I bet you're a real hellcat when you're aroused," he whispered. "You just haven't met anyone who's man enough to rouse you."

Jassy stared at him. She felt wild, reckless, a gypsy stranger who'd taken over her prim body. And then common sense reasserted itself, and she yanked her hand away as if she were burned. She could feel shocked color flood her face, and she knew if she didn't get away, and fast, she might be totally southern belle enough to faint at the man's feet.

She ran across the slate terrace, not daring to look back, running as if all hell was at her heels. She knew Caleb would wait there in the shadows, not ready for his revenge. Not yet. He didn't make a sound, but she thought she could hear the soft note of his mocking laughter follow her as she caught up with her brother at the terrace door.

"What were you doing?" Harrison demanded grumpily.

It was too dark to see the flush of color on her face, the suspicious brightness in her eyes. Besides, Harrison was scarcely the most observant of men where his baby sister was concerned.

"Just having a breath of air."

"This air's too thick to breathe."

She was acutely aware of the man in the shadows, watching, listening. "Let's go in...."

"Not yet. I want to talk to you, Jassy, and I don't want anyone overhearing us." He put his hand on her arm, and for some reason it felt heavier, crueler than Caleb's imprisoning grip.

"I don't want to discuss it, Harrison. It's between you and Lila...."

"I'm not talking about that," he said impatiently. "I want to talk to you about Spenser."

She tried to yank away. "I'd really rather talk inside."

"Mary-Louise is inside, and you know as well as I do that she can't keep her mouth shut. She maneuvered this little scene tonight, just to see what would happen."

"If you feel that way about her, then why...?"

"I told you, I don't want to discuss it. It's none of your business."

"You've already told me that what's between you and Caleb Spenser is none of my business, either." It took all her concentration to keep from glancing over to the shadows, where Caleb was watching.

"That was before you chose to involve yourself. I know you, Jassy. I've known you all your life. I can't say I approve of your taste in men, but I know better than to interfere." His voice was expansive, indulgent, at odds with the restraining hand on her forearm.

She stared up at him. "What are you talking about?" She didn't want to hear what she knew was coming. And she most particularly didn't want Caleb to hear.

"If you want Caleb Spenser I won't interfere."

He laughed, that grating, unbelievable laugh, and she could hear the desperation, the real fear beneath it. "You're an adult, he's an adult," he continued. "What you two do together hasn't got a thing to do with me. I'm giving you my blessing."

"You mean you're telling me it's okay to sleep with him? The man you've been treating like he's your mortal enemy?"

"I'm telling you to do whatever you like. If you're as attracted to him as you appear to be, then maybe it could be used to the family's advantage. Don't look at me like I'm expecting you to whore yourself. You're obviously infatuated with the man. I'm just saying you could serve the family and your own biological needs at the same time."

She wanted to throw up. The knowledge that Caleb was hearing Harrison's cold-blooded proposal made it even worse. "My love life has nothing to do with what the family does or doesn't need," she managed to say in a deceptively calm voice.

Harrison, self-absorbed as always, released her arm and patted her cheek. "Of course, Jassy. I just thought I'd mention it. Are you coming in?"

Clearly the subject had been dismissed. "Not quite yet," she said evenly. "I still need a little fresh air."

"Don't take too long. Mary-Louise was saying she hadn't seen enough of you recently."

She waited until he stepped back into the house. Wrapping her arms around her, she shivered in the humid air, wondering how she was going to face Caleb.

She needn't have worried. When she reached the stretch of terrace in the shadows outside the library, Caleb had vanished.

She could only wonder if he'd left before or after her brother encouraged her to sleep with him.

CHAPTER ELEVEN ·

CALEB DROVE HOME SLOWLY, letting the old truck with its deceptively powerful engine make its way down the gravel roads to the Moon Palace at a leisurely pace. He was feeling restless, edgy, like the wind rushing through the live oaks overhead. He could hear the distant rumble of thunder over the quiet sound of the radio, and he shifted in the seat. People around Turner's Landing seemed to think that once it rained, people's tensions would ease.

Personally he didn't think it would be that simple. The rain wouldn't make any difference in his plans for revenge. The rain wouldn't make him less angry, less determined. Or less horny, for that matter.

Of course, there were any number of ways he could handle the last problem, beginning with Mary-Louise Albertson. Despite, or maybe because of her relationship with the very married Harrison Turner, she was obviously more than available. He could have offered to drive her home. He could drive back into town and wait outside her mother's house.

There were other women around who'd made sure he'd feel welcome. He'd been flattered by their offers, but not interested. He was interested tonight.

But he didn't want a bored housewife, a randy young professional, a lusty divorcée or a precocious teenager.

He wanted Jassy Turner.

He still didn't know why. Why an ordinary attraction would become an obsession, one that threatened to rival his desperate need for revenge. Sometimes at night he woke up in a sweat, thinking he was back in prison, thinking Harrison was smug, laughing at him, triumphant once more.

But nowadays, just as often, he'd wake up thinking about Jassy, hard and aching for her. And he'd lived long enough, had enough women to know that a substitute wasn't going to work. It might take the edge off his need, but it wouldn't obliterate it. It would take Jassy herself to ease him.

That was one reason he'd walked away tonight, after he'd heard her brother's charming suggestion. Not that he expected her to act on it. She was going through a period of intense disillusionment where her darling brother was concerned. As the man said, she ain't seen nothing yet.

But she was too damned distracting. If he'd pushed it, taken her back home with him, or even simply pulled her into the woods and stripped that stupid brown dress off her, he'd forget all about Harrison, at least for a while. And he couldn't afford to do that.

If he had any sense at all he'd play it safe and forget about Jassy Turner. There were other ways he could get to Harrison, more effective ways. He should concentrate on them, on Harrison's wife and mistress, both of whom were more vulnerable than Jassy and infinitely tougher. He couldn't break their hearts. He could smash Jassy's.

Of course if he were showing sense, interested in playing it safe, he wouldn't be in Turner's Landing, stirring up a can of worms. He'd be somewhere else, making good money, the past behind him.

But he couldn't put the past behind him until he'd dealt with it. Dealt with Harrison Turner. And if he couldn't talk Jassy into leaving, he was going to have to deal with her, too. One way or another.

The Moon Palace was dark and still when he drove in. Dog was standing in front of a parked van, a disgruntled expression on his face. Caleb parked the truck, sliding out of the front seat and approaching the van warily.

The window rolled down. "Can you call this damned dog off?" Bo demanded. "Stupid mutt can't remember a friend for more than a week."

"Serves you two right for bringing the new van," Caleb said, signaling Dog to relax. "Besides, we've had a little trouble."

"Trouble?" Ray echoed, climbing out of the van and giving both Dog and his owner a doubtful glance. "Is that why we're here?"

"Among other things. Maybe I just got lonesome," Caleb drawled.

Dog was busy slobbering over Bo's hamlike hand. "So now

we're friends, you damned dog,'' Bo said grumpily, scratching Dog's huge head. ''Can't you keep your master better company so he doesn't drag us out here into the back of beyond?''

''I figured you guys were having it too soft up in Atlanta,'' Caleb said. ''Besides, I'm pulling the whole crew down here once I get a little personal matter settled.''

Bo glanced over at the Moon Palace. He was a huge man, with shaggy blond hair and eyebrows, massive shoulders and the gentle spirit of a lamb. He didn't like to talk about the reasons for his six-year prison term, but one night, after a bottle of Jack Daniel's, he'd told Caleb about the man who'd molested his little brothers and gotten off with a suspended sentence. The man who wouldn't be hurting any more children.

Ray was smaller, more wiry, more sly. He'd been a car thief, probably still would be if he hadn't met Caleb inside. Caleb had no illusions about him. Their friendship kept them together, and kept Ray on the straight and narrow. If something happened to Caleb, Ray would be back on the streets in no time.

There were others, all ex-cons, who depended on him in one way or another. If something happened, if this mess with Harrison Turner backfired, it wouldn't be just his life down the toilet.

But he couldn't give it up. Not yet. Not now. Not until he'd extracted at least a measure of revenge.

''This place is going to need all of us,'' Bo said in his slow, deep voice that made people foolishly assume he wasn't as bright as he was. ''Why the hell did you pick such a spot?''

''Personal reasons. You'll meet them later. Besides, it's in a lot better shape than it looks.''

''It better be,'' Ray said. ''I don't fancy spending the next year in the boonies.''

''Did you bring any beer?'' Caleb started toward the house, Dog bounding along like an innocent puppy, batting his head against Bo's big hand.

''Is the Pope catholic?'' Ray countered.

''This damned dog,'' Bo grumbled cheerfully. ''You wouldn't believe that ten minutes ago he was ready to tear out my throat if I stepped out of the van.''

''I believe it. Dog doesn't accept anyone totally, except for me.

And maybe...'' He shut up, too late, not wanting to explain Jassy Turner to his friends. At least, not until they'd gone through a six-pack or more.

Despite Bo's slow-moving demeanor he was right on top of things. ''Maybe who?''

Caleb smiled wryly. ''All in good time, my friend. She's one of the reasons you're here.''

''She?'' Ray echoed. ''Since when did you start changing plans for any 'she'? I thought you were Spenser the untouchable.''

''Still am.''

Bo's snort of disbelief made Dog whoof sharply. ''I've known you for eleven years, man. You can't con me. Something's got your tail in a twitter, and it ain't Harrison Turner. You've lived with that for a long time, made your plans clear years ago. So what's messed things up?''

He should have known he couldn't pull anything over on men who knew him better than he knew himself. ''His sister,'' he said glumly.

''Oh, hell,'' Bo said with heartfelt sympathy.

''You got it right the first time,'' Spenser said. ''Oh, hell indeed.''

JASSY SHIFTED, burying her head beneath the thin pillow and moaning. Something was pounding, clanging, inside her head, rattling her teeth, trying to drag her from sleep with angry claws, and she struggled, desperate for a few more minutes, a few more hours. If she had to wake, why did it have to be in the midst of the most erotic dream she'd had in memory?

She burrowed deeper into the lumpy mattress, but there was no respite. No bringing back the delicious feeling of his hands on her body, no bringing back the taste of his mouth. Flopping over onto her back, she opened her eyes and stared up at the water-stained ceiling, and she slowly remembered why she wasn't in her own bed, and why she was so desperately tired. And tried to forget who was with her in her dream.

She sat up, the concave cot sagging beneath her. She was in the back room of the women's shelter, trying to catch a few minutes' sleep before driving back to Belle Rive. Pushing her tangled hair out of her face, she frowned, trying to place the banging, clanging sound that was coming from her office.

It might very well be Leroy Philips. When Faith had first called the emergency number Jassy had had a hard time recognizing her voice through the muffled tears. Her first sight of Faith's swollen, bruised face and mouth had explained that. She and little Tommy Lee had huddled in the secure back rooms of the shelter while Jassy had made hot chocolate and coffee, soothed and comforted and made absolutely no suggestions. She'd learned long ago that you couldn't tell a woman to leave. She had to make that decision on her own.

This was Faith and Tommy's fifth visit to the shelter in the past year. It was all Jassy could do to control her whoop of joy when Faith announced it was her last. She and Tommy were heading north, to her aunt's house in Boston, and she was never going to hold still for Leroy's brutal fists again.

Jassy let her make all the plans. Faith needed to learn she could rely on herself, not on someone else to rescue her. It was her need to be rescued that had made her turn to a handsome bully like Leroy Philips when she was sixteen. She was a smart, attractive woman who could take care of herself and her son just fine, if she only realized it. She was finally beginning to.

They shopped for new clothes from the closets full of donations in the shelter. Jassy wrote Faith a glowing recommendation for her considerable clerical skills while Tommy slept the sleep of exhaustion in the back room. And at quarter of six in the morning she emptied out the emergency fund, drove them to Clearwater for the bus, and saw the two of them off on their new life.

They were going to make it, she told herself as she drove back. She'd seen enough to know which ones would make the break, which ones would succeed. Faith would make it, through her brains and talent and determination. Not to mention her considerable love for her son. She'd put up with the abuse when it had only affected her. When it started spilling over onto Tommy she'd finally had enough.

Jassy had been too tired to make it out to the house. She'd gone back to lock up the shelter, then decided to try to catch just a few moments' sleep before driving back. She peered at her digital watch, the cheap model that had replaced the Rolex her daddy had given her on her eighteenth birthday. She'd sold that and plowed the funds into the shelter, and she doubted if Harrison had ever forgiven her. It was quarter past ten, and whoever was pounding in her front office sounded more determined than enraged. It couldn't be Leroy.

The man in her office didn't hear her when she opened the door. It was no wonder. The tall, shaggy giant had her recalcitrant air conditioner torn apart, pieces all over a greasy scrap of cloth, while he hammered away at a small metal piece, whistling underneath his breath.

She cleared her throat, but he didn't hear. She slammed the door behind her, and he jumped up, banging his head on the overhanging air conditioner and cursing fluently.

"I didn't know anyone was here," he said, looking sheepish, and some of Jassy's initial panic faded.

"How did you get in? For that matter, who are you and what are you doing here?" She moved into the room, shutting off the shelter from his curious eyes, and she felt a little more self-assured. This large stranger didn't have a lick of meanness in his face.

"That's a lot of questions," he said, looking her up and down in frank curiosity. "I'm fixing your air conditioner. My name's Bo, and I'm a friend of Caleb Spenser. He sent me here, along with a donation." He nodded toward the desk, and Jassy could see a green check lying there. She let out a tiny sigh of relief. She'd had to float a check from the shelter account to cover the rest of Tommy and Faith's bus fare, and she had strong doubts about Harrison's willingness to cover it. At least a token contribution might help.

"That still doesn't explain how you got in."

"The door just opened."

"It was locked."

"Not to me," Bo said sweetly, and Jassy didn't bother arguing. She went over to the desk for lack of something better to do and picked up the check.

She dropped it as if it burned her fingers. "Is this real?" she gasped.

Bo looked up. "I didn't look real close. Why wouldn't it be?"

"It's for so much!"

Bo shrugged. "You do good work around here. Besides, Caleb's got money to spare. He lives pretty sparsely."

She picked the check up again with trembling hands, folding it in half and putting it into her pocket carefully. "You said you're a friend of his?"

"I've known him for a long time. I work for him."

"Oh," Jassy said blankly.

"That's right, I'm an ex-con," Bo said cheerfully. "And you must be Harrison Turner's sister."

"What do you know about Harrison?"

"Just what I hear from Caleb."

"And what's that?"

"Ask..."

"Don't tell me," she interrupted him. "Ask Caleb, right?"

"Or your brother."

"The next person who says that to me is going to wish he hadn't," Jassy said between clenched teeth. "Are you going to be able to fix the air conditioner?"

"Probably. She's all gunked up with oil, but she's still basically sound. If I can't, Caleb told me to go out and buy you a new one."

"Just like that?"

"Just like that."

"Sounds like the man has a guilty conscience."

Bo looked at her in confusion for a moment, then he laughed. "You mean you think he hits women? Not likely. Caleb can be downright nasty on occasion, but he doesn't take it out on anyone or anything that can't handle it. I guess you don't know him very well, ma'am."

"I guess not. Are you going to help him with the Moon Palace?"

Bo nodded. "Me and Ray drove down from Atlanta last night. I guess one motel's as good as another, and I sort of like that old place. Don't know how Caleb thinks he can turn a profit from it, but if anybody can, he's the one. He's got a magic touch with things like that."

"You're staying at the motel? I would have thought he'd want you out at the Palace."

"Caleb likes his solitude, and it's not really set up for more than one person. Besides, it doesn't take long to drive. Is there any reason why we should be out there?'' he asked with sudden shrewdness.

"Ask Caleb," she said sweetly. "Or ask my brother. See if you get any further than I did."

Bo laughed. "I'll do that, ma'am."

In the end it was absurdly easy, so easy that she wondered why she'd never attempted it before. While Bo worked on the air conditioner, Jassy took a cup of instant coffee into the back room and went to work on the telephone. Within half an hour she'd managed to get a helpful clerk at the *St. Florence Register* to read her the account of Sherman Delano's murder some thirteen years ago in that small coastal town.

A drifter named Caleb Spenser, age twenty-one, was arrested for the murder of a local citizen, Sherman Delano of Wayfield Drive. Apparently they'd been involved in a high-stakes gambling game, one man accused the other of cheating, and Spenser pulled a knife. There was a witness, one Billy Ray Smith, and it was an open-and-shut case. They ended up plea bargaining, and the case never even went to trial.

The clerk had promised to send copies of all the pertinent newspaper articles. Jassy thanked her profusely, knowing that she'd already heard enough. It all jibed with the little Caleb had told her. What the newspaper articles didn't explain was her brother's connection.

"Find out anything interesting?"

Jassy looked up, startled, at the sound of Caleb's voice. She hadn't heard him come in, hadn't bothered to lock the secure back door into the dormitory-style room. "What are you doing here, Caleb?" she asked evenly, controlling her urge to leap off the sagging cot where she was sitting, cross-legged, a pad of paper in her lap.

"I thought I'd come to see how Bo was doing. He's got the air conditioner fixed." The room was dimly lit. It was an overcast, muggy day, and the light filtering in through curtained windows was diffuse, shadowy. Caleb was leaning against the open door, his chambray work shirt open halfway down his chest, his gold hoop glittering against the darker gold of his long hair. "You didn't answer my question."

"I don't remember what it was."

His faint smile told her he recognized a lie when he heard it. "I asked if you learned anything interesting. I figure you were checking up on me."

"Isn't that egocentric of you? Maybe I have other concerns."

He shook his head, moving into the room. "Maybe you do. But right now the risk I pose to your family's got you in a swivet. Not to mention the risk I pose to you, personally."

"I wasn't aware you were any particular risk to me."

Dare you, his smile said. He moved closer, glancing down at her scribbled notes, verifying his suspicions. "Did you ask about your brother?"

She didn't bother denying it. "I didn't ask anyone questions. I just had someone read me the newspaper articles concerning Sherman Delano's death."

"Learn anything new?"

"Not really."

Caleb nodded, more to himself, and then dropped onto the cot beside her. She pulled her legs away from him, but he merely smiled at her skittishness. "You look worn-out, lady," he murmured. "What have you been doing all night?"

"Helping someone."

"Who?"

"None of your business."

"Honey, this is a small town, and even a newcomer hears everything sooner or later. There's no such thing as professional discretion around here."

She knew he was right. "Faith and Tommy Lee Philips," she said. "I've lost count of how many times they've come to the shelter in the past year. Leroy's getting meaner and meaner, and he was no sweetheart to begin with. Thank God she finally decided she'd had enough. I put the two of them on a bus for…for parts north," she amended hastily. "She looked like she'd been hit by a Mack truck."

"Someone needs to have a conversation with Leroy," Caleb said in a diffident tone of voice.

Jassy wasn't fooled for a minute. "Please don't," she begged. "More violence won't help matters. Faith and Tommy Lee are safe, and there's no one for him to turn his fists on. He'll have to find some other way to beat out his frustrations, and I'd rather they weren't on you.''

"Why?''

"For one thing, he's about half a foot taller than you are and maybe fifty pounds heavier. Bo out there might stand a chance against him, you wouldn't.''

Caleb smiled, not bothering to deny it. "So you don't want me turned into hamburger? Why not? It would put me out of commission for a while, keep me away from your precious brother.''

"Violence never solves anything,'' she stated flatly, knowing she sounded priggish, believing it anyway.

"Now there you're wrong,'' Caleb said, leaning against the white-painted walls. "Violence, directed at someone who sure as hell deserves it and is man enough to take it, can solve a whole lot of problems.''

"I don't think I'm going to be trying it.''

He turned his head to look at her. "Admit it, Miss Jassy. Wouldn't you just love to haul off and slap me sometimes? Wipe that grin off my face?''

Her hand was already itching, she didn't bother to deny it. "That's different.''

"No,'' he said, "it's not. It's a matter of degree. And I know perfectly well that no matter how mad you get, no matter how tempted, you'd never hit anything smaller or weaker than you are.''

"Of course not,'' she said indignantly.

"The same holds true for me. Remember that.''

She looked at him out of steady eyes. "There's more than one kind of violence. What you're planning to do to my brother is going to hurt Lila, hurt my mother, hurt me. We're all smaller and weaker than you are.''

"I wouldn't count on it,'' he muttered under his breath. "The three of you are a hell of a lot tougher than you think.''

"Maybe I am, but…''

He shook his head. "You're the most vulnerable. You think you have to take care of everyone else, particularly your family, when if you just let them be you'd find they were perfectly capable of handling their own problems. I'm not so sure you are.''

"You don't think I'm capable of handling my problems?" She was incensed.

But Caleb refused to be drawn. He shook his head. "I'm your biggest problem, Jassy. Think you can handle me?"

"With one hand tied behind my back." It was a mistake the moment she said it. His light eyes suddenly darkened with intent, and she knew he could lean across that concave cot, cover her smaller body with his, and show her just how incapable she was of handling him. And as inevitable as that moment was, she wasn't certain she was ready to deal with it right now.

The banging from the front room grew suddenly louder, and that slumberous, intent expression vanished from Caleb's face, to be replaced with a wary one. "That's not Bo," he said. "I sent him out for coffee."

She was about to protest the ramifications of that when the door slammed open again, a huge figure filling it. Larger than the hulking Bo, and far more dangerous.

"Bitch," Leroy Philips spat, his furious dark eyes focusing on Jassy and ignoring the man beside her. "What the hell have you done with my wife?"

CHAPTER TWELVE

CALEB BEGAN TO UNCURL himself from the cot with slow, dangerous deliberation. Jassy moved faster, jumping up and moving toward Leroy with a heedless unconcern for her own safety. Caleb grabbed for her, but he was too late, and he watched with mingled horror and pride as she confronted the vicious-looking man in the doorway, not a trace of fear in her slim, straight body.

"She's gone, Leroy," she said flatly. "She took Tommy Lee and went west, and she's never coming back."

The word Leroy roared was almost unintelligible, except that Caleb had experience with words like that. His meaty fist slammed out, almost connecting with Jassy's fragile jaw, but this time Caleb was lightning fast, shoving her out of the way and catching Leroy's blow on his shoulder.

It was a solid one, and the thought of all that force slamming into Jassy wiped out whatever compunctions Caleb had. He stood his ground, facing the furious man, his fists ready.

"Who the hell are you?" Leroy bellowed.

"Someone who's going to teach you a lesson, Leroy," he said in a low, mean voice. "One you're not likely to soon forget."

Leroy looked down at him, and spat. "You and who else?" he demanded. And then he charged, like a maddened bull.

In the distance Caleb heard Jassy scream, "No!" He paid her no mind. He waited till the last minute, then moved in, under Leroy's furious bulk, hitting him hard in his soft gut. Leroy doubled over, and Caleb slammed his fist down on the back of his neck, hard. Leroy went down fast, and his eyes glazed over for a moment, but Caleb wasn't fooled. Someone as mad as Leroy didn't fold that easily.

Reaching down, he grabbed a handful of Leroy's greasy hair and hauled his head up. "You don't hit women," he said between gritted teeth. "You hear, boy? You don't hit kids, either, or kick dogs, or pull the wings off butterflies. If you want to hit someone, try to hit me."

With a roar Leroy surged upward, batting Caleb backward as if he were nothing more than a rag doll. His fist connected with Caleb's mouth, and he went soaring through the air, landing on one of the narrow beds and collapsing it with his weight. "You got it, boy," he said, advancing on Caleb as he lay in a tangle against one broken cot. "I'm gonna teach you a lesson you ain't never gonna forget."

Caleb heard Jassy's scream of horror when she saw the knife glinting in Leroy's meaty fist, and he felt his own frisson of panic sweep over him. Not because he had any doubts as to his ability to deal with Leroy's little pigsticker. But because he was afraid Jassy would do something foolish like try to protect him.

Sure enough, she was getting ready to move when Caleb leaped to his feet. The thought of her putting her body between the two of them, being on the receiving end of Leroy's knife, wiped out any trace of conscious thought. Rage swept over him, a killing rage, and he flew at Leroy with a guttural cry.

The last thing he noticed was the expression of primal fear on Leroy's thick, stupid face as he leaped at him. And then it was over, too quickly. The knife went skittering across the old pine floor, and Leroy was down, unconscious, blood pouring from his broken nose.

Caleb leaned down to check his pulse. It was slow, steady, like an ox. He hadn't killed the man, he'd simply put him out of action for a while. He considered breaking a few bones, just to ensure that Leroy stayed out of the way for a while longer, and then he looked up at Jassy and thought better of the notion.

She was staring at him in utter, complete horror, her face white, her soft mouth crumpled with fear. She'd been pampered and protected all her life, he knew that. For all her concern about battered women, she'd never seen violence up close, nasty and bloody and dangerous. Even the night when Harrison's good old boys had jumped him had been fogged in shadows.

He rose, still breathing deeply from his exertions. His back ached where it had slammed against the broken cot, his shirt was torn half off, and he was angry, sweaty and ready for a confrontation. She was looking at him out of frightened eyes as if he was a devil straight out of hell, and it riled him, pure and simple.

He stepped over Leroy's body, crossed the room to stand in front of her. Without even thinking about it he put his hand behind Jassy's neck, underneath her thick fall of hair, and pulled her up to him, setting his bruised mouth on hers with a hot, hungry kiss.

She tried to push against him for a moment, but he ignored her struggles, and after only a moment they weren't struggles at all. She put her arms around his waist, beneath the ripped shirt, and opened her mouth for him. She didn't bother trying to kiss him back. He wasn't in the mood to be kissed. He was in the mood to claim, and that's what he did, kissing her with a hard, possessive fury that swept over his entire body and then began to cover hers. He felt her shake in his arms, felt the edgy, tremulous beginnings of surrender; it was all he could do to rip himself away.

But that was exactly what he did, pulling himself out of her arms as his body screamed in protest. She had blood on her mouth, his blood, and her eyes were wide, dark, shocky.

That kiss hadn't slowed his breathing any, but now was hardly the time or place to make love to her, much as he wanted to. He wasn't going to have her on a narrow cot with an unconscious bully lying on the floor and Bo ready to walk in at any moment. When he took her to bed he was going to have plenty of time to do it right.

He took a deep, shaky breath. "I'll have Bo get rid of this garbage," he said in a deceptively even voice. "You better go home."

She looked dazed, confused, staring at him as if she'd seen a ghost. "Go home?" she echoed.

"Unless you want to come home with me?"

Slowly his question penetrated her confusion, and she shook her head. He reached out, and she tried to flinch away. He cursed, caught her shoulder, and with his other hand touched her mouth, bringing his blood away on his hand. "Go home," he said again. "When you want me you know where to find me."

There was no question as to his meaning, to either of them. She squirmed away, and he released her this time, walking away from her. He knew her eyes were following him, but he didn't look back. If he looked back, he might not leave her.

Bo was coming in the front door, two cups of coffee in his hands. "Job for you in there," Caleb said laconically. "See that he gets the message."

Bo let out a long, low whistle as he surveyed Caleb's bruised mouth. "Is there anything left for me to clean up, boss?"

"Enough. See that Jassy gets home."

"Shouldn't that be your job?"

"It should," Caleb agreed. "But it's not." And he slammed the door behind him as he headed out into the thick, humid heat of the late morning.

THERE WAS BLOOD on her mouth. His blood. Jassy stared in the mirror, remembering that he'd wiped some of it off. Some remained on her swollen lower lip. He'd marked her, and she thought of fox hunting, how the novice would be marked with the blood of the first kill. Stained by some rite of passage.

She took a washcloth and began to scrub her face, trying to scrub away the blood. But she couldn't wash away the feel of him, his mouth on hers, angry, possessive, his hard, hot body pressed against her, the strength and power in his hands. Hands that hadn't hurt her. Wouldn't hurt her. But hands that had almost killed a man. Hands that had killed a man in years past.

Leaning down, she splashed cold water on her face, again and again. She must be out of her mind. Try as she might, she couldn't wipe the memory from her. The sheer possession on his face when he'd risen from the man on the floor and looked at her. It had been primitive, sexual, and if he'd wanted she would have stripped off her clothes and lain with him on the bare wood floor. She would have done anything he wanted.

It was disgusting, she told herself, splashing more water on her face. Vile and base and degrading and absolutely awful. She was a civilized woman, from generations of civilized women, and her reaction to his savagery had been primal, basic and…and…

She could still feel it, thrumming through her body. The longing for him, a longing that was physical and something more, something even more disturbing. It was a need for him that had grown to unmanageable proportions, one of mind and soul as well as body, and she didn't know how much longer she could fight it. To give in to it would mean her destruction. To fight it was tearing her apart.

The only way she could keep her sanity was to ask his help. He didn't really want her, she was sure of that. He'd flirted with her as he'd flirted with every female, impartially, as naturally as breathing. If his attention had focused on her at all, then it was only as a temporary distraction. No one mattered to him, only whatever lay between him and Harrison. And she wasn't going to be a victim of that tangled history.

She could ask him. Beneath his cynical exterior there was some kernel of decency, she knew that. The shockingly large donation was a sign of it, the repaired air conditioner, his enraged, oddly gallant defense of her were all further proof. If she went to him, asked him to leave her alone, he would.

She shivered, looking at her reflection in the mirror again. Beneath the drops of water her face was pale, her eyes large and haunted, the feel of his mouth still lingering on hers. He'd agree, he'd have to. And Jassy didn't know if that mercy she counted on would be her salvation.

Or her despair.

"DAMNED WOMAN," Caleb said, draining his glass of whiskey.

"Haven't you had enough?" Ray inquired lazily, snagging the bottle from his hand and pouring himself a generous portion. Bo shook his head when he offered it to him, content with beer, as the three men sat in the kitchen of the old bordello.

"I know when I've had enough," Caleb snarled. "I don't need you to tell me."

"No, I suppose you don't," Ray said cheerfully enough. "What are you going to do about her?"

"Not a damned thing. You sure you took care of Leroy, Bo?"

Bo nodded. "I told you before, Caleb, he's resting peacefully in the county jail. A man on parole isn't allowed to carry a gun, and he was found smelling like a brewery with a pistol tucked in his pants pocket. I don't think they're gonna let him out for a good long time."

"Lucky for him," Caleb said in a sour voice. "I still wish I'd broken his arm."

"You break too many arms, Caleb. You can't save the world."

Caleb laughed without humor. "That's what I told Jassy."

"Maybe you two have something in common."

"Don't count on it. She looked at me like I was a monster from outer space after I gallantly defended her honor."

"You mean after you squashed Leroy like a June bug?" Bo countered. "So she's not used to the rough side of life. She's tough enough, she'll survive."

"She's not as tough as she looks."

"She's tougher," Bo asserted.

"You've seen her for maybe ten minutes. I've been around her for a hell of a lot longer. What makes you an expert?"

"Maybe because my glands aren't involved," Bo said.

Caleb's response was brief and obscene and he poured himself his third drink. Thunder rumbled overhead, a long, low grumble in the evening air, but he ignored it.

"At least we'll get some rain," Ray said from his spot in the corner of the old kitchen. "This place is like a sweat box."

"Don't count on it. That's heat lightning. There hasn't been a decent rain in months, the way I hear it. Not that anyone's worried about it—there's enough water in this damned swamphole to keep things going for twenty years."

"Place could do with a real thunder-boomer," Bo said. "It might clear the air."

"Nothing'll clear the air," Caleb said morosely. "The sooner I get things taken care of and we get the hell out of here, the better we'll be."

"What things taken care of, boss?" Bo asked. "The renovations on this old place? Or your business with Harrison Turner?"

"I'm sorry as hell I ever told you about Turner," Caleb muttered.

"Why?" Ray asked lazily. "You afraid we're gonna horn in on your fun? You should know we'll let you fight your own battles, until you call on us. We're here if you need us, but we're not going to interfere."

Caleb tipped back in the chair, running a hand through his hair.

"I know. This place is driving me nuts. This place, and the people in it."

"Which people?" Bo asked with just a trace of too much innocence.

Caleb glared at him. "Don't go jumping to conclusions. The only person I'm concerned with is Harrison Turner."

"Uh-huh," Bo agreed, and Caleb knew him well enough to recognize that he hadn't fooled him for a minute. "You want us to bed down out here tonight?"

"There's no need. Leroy's out of action, and Harrison's not about to make his move. You might as well have a decent bed. I don't think Dog's managed to dispose of all the rats in this place yet, and I know how you two feel about rats."

Ray shuddered. "I'll take the motel. Besides, there's a waitress at the local tavern with the cutest little…"

"You're gonna get in trouble one of these days," Bo rumbled.

"And you're gonna die a saint," Ray said.

"Hey, I'm saving myself for true love," Bo said placidly. "That doesn't mean I won't drink with you."

"Thank heaven for small favors. But keep your eyes off the waitress. I saw her first."

Caleb stood in the doorway, watching them drive away, and that restless edge was still there. "Maybe I should have gone with them, Dog," he said to his companion. "Maybe Ray's waitress was just what I needed."

Dog whoofed with canine contempt. "No, you're right," Caleb said, turning back into the house, shutting the new screen door against the teeming mosquitoes. "Ray's waitress wouldn't do me any good. I know what I want, and if it's eating a hole in my gut I can damned well ignore it. She's not what I need."

Dog sank his huge body down where he stood, lying crossways across the hallway and panting lightly. Caleb looked at him in disgust for a moment, then stepped over him. "I'm taking a shower," he told him. "A cold shower. Why don't you make yourself scarce? Go outside and guard the place. Catch a few rats. Make yourself useful."

Dog lumbered to his paws, giving Caleb a hurt, soulful look before he padded out the door, pushing the screen with his huge head. Caleb watched him go, feeling ridiculously guilty. He was getting in rough shape, when he started worrying about a dog's feelings. Maybe he better stop pussyfooting around, finish up with Harrison Turner, and get the hell out of there.

The shower didn't do much toward improving his mood, or lessening the tension that crept along his muscles. He pulled on a clean pair of jeans, zipped but didn't bother to snap them, and was reaching for a T-shirt when he heard the car drive in.

He held himself very still, waiting for the sound of Dog as he terrorized whoever dared show up at that hour, unannounced. There wasn't a sound. Which meant only one person could have driven down the long, winding road to the Moon Palace.

He dropped the shirt back on the chair and headed toward the front door, watching, unseen behind the screen, as Jassy Turner made her way across the scarred and weedy path to the front door, while Dog did his best to overwhelm her with love and approval.

He almost called Dog off. He was big enough to knock her over, but Jassy seemed capable of dealing with his slobbering affection, and Caleb simply watched.

He wondered what that thick, curly mane of dark hair would look like if she loosened it. It was already curling around her face, ignoring her efforts to control it, and he found himself smiling faintly in the darkness, wondering if the rest of her body was the same. Fighting when she tried to repress its natural urges.

She was wearing a baggy shirt and skirt, as usual, and he couldn't begin to guess what kind of body she had underneath. He didn't really care. Plump or skinny, he wanted her, wanted her so badly he ached with it. She could be flat-chested or voluptuous, soft or muscled. None of it mattered. She'd managed to become an obsession, one he didn't want, didn't need, but one that haunted him when he least expected it.

She had a determined expression on her face, only softened for a moment as she rubbed Dog's huge head. She wasn't coming out to the Moon Palace at a quarter to ten at night for a social call, he thought. Or for a roll in the hay. She was coming with a purpose, and he probably wasn't going to like it. And he probably wasn't going to pay a lick of attention to it, either.

He pushed the screen door open, startling her. She looked up at him, for a moment completely vulnerable, and if he'd been a few inches closer and Dog hadn't been in the way he would have grabbed her then and there.

But as quickly as that look had passed over her features it was gone again, and her brown eyes were cool, determined, her soft mouth set in her face.

He realized then that he thought she was beautiful. He knew she wasn't—her mouth was too wide, her nose a little too short, her chin too vulnerable, her forehead too broad. None of that mattered. Her face mesmerized him, even set in its current, stern expression.

"Little late for a social call," he said, leaning against the open doorway.

"This isn't a social call," she said, concentrating on his shoulder.

"Did you come for sex?"

That jerked her head up, wiping that detached expression from her face, replacing it with rage and shock. "I did not! Is that all you ever think about?"

"Whenever you're around," he muttered beneath his breath, opening the door further, still not moving. "So why did you come?"

"I need to talk to you."

"We talk too much."

"May I come in?"

"I'm not stopping you." He still didn't move. She'd have to brush past him to step inside the dimly lit house, and he wanted that. He wanted the feel of her body, her clothes, brushing against him. He wanted her to know the feel, the warmth, of him.

She pulled her skirts close against her as she stepped inside, but the faint, flowery fragrance of her perfume danced around him. "Stay," he ordered Dog, slamming the screen in his face. Dog made a low, aggrieved sound, and then sank onto the front doorstep, ready to guard his master's privacy.

"We can talk in the kitchen," Caleb said behind her as she paused in the hallway, "or my bedroom. It's up to you."

"The kitchen," she said flatly, and Caleb forced himself to release some of his pent-up breath. He wasn't going to make it through the night, he knew that with sudden clarity. If he didn't put his hands on her he was going to die. Pure and simple.

By the time he reached the kitchen she'd already seated herself on the stool that Ray had recently vacated. She looked prim and proper, that big shirt done up almost to her throat, her legs tucked under her, close together, her knees touching. She was wearing sandals again, ignoring the danger of swamp creatures. She had wonderful toes.

"Beer or whiskey?" he asked.

"This isn't a social call, Mr. Spenser."

He poured her a whiskey. "We dispensed with Mr. Spenser a long time ago, Jassy. Drink up."

She wouldn't have, except she was nervous, her eyes shifting everywhere but at him, her hands needing something to do. He'd poured the whiskey neat, and she coughed slightly, frowning at the glass.

He took the chair opposite her, turning it around and straddling it. He liked looking up at her. He knew the change in position bothered her, and he liked bothering her.

"You can imagine why I'm here," she began in a voice unlike her own, high-pitched, nervous, as her hand fiddled with the top button of her shirt. He only hoped she'd fiddle enough to unfasten it.

"No, I can't," he drawled. "Unless you're making a personal visit to thank me for the donation to the women's shelter."

That threw her off for a moment, and real warmth lit her brown eyes. "That was so generous of you," she said. "Are you certain you can afford it? We surely do need it, but..."

"I can afford it," he said flatly. "If that's not why you came out here, why don't you get it over with?"

She hesitated, her eyes skittering over him once more. "Do you suppose you could put on a shirt?"

He'd had enough. "What the hell do you have against a man's body? I'd like to know what's riled you so. I just took a shower, I know for sure I don't smell. So what's got you in such a taking?"

She shut her eyes for a moment, steeling herself. "I want you to leave me alone."

He just looked at her. "That's not what your brother wants."

"You heard that, did you? I thought you might have. That's not the way Harrison usually is. You've pushed him, frightened him. Otherwise he never would have suggested such a thing."

"Hell, I thought it was the smartest thing I ever heard him say," Caleb drawled.

She came off her stool, fast, leaning over the table that stood between them. "It's not. You don't want me, Caleb, not really. You want to use me to get to Harrison. I know you're not really a mean person. You don't want to hurt anyone. I don't think you even want to hurt me. Please, Caleb," she said, her eyes huge and beseeching, her mouth soft and vulnerable.

He didn't move. "Please, what?"

"Let me go. You're only going to break my heart, and I don't need that. I don't want a man like you. I want someone who respects me, who's tender, sweet and gentle. Someone who'll consider my needs, my feelings, before his own. Someone who…"

"You want a gentleman," he said savagely, rising and kicking his chair out of the way. "You want a sweet, pale-skinned, soft-handed little gentleman to do your bidding and never say a harsh word to you. Well, honey, I'm not a gentleman. I'm not going to be what you think you want. But I sure as hell am going to be what you need."

"Caleb…" She was off the stool, backing away from him, but he wasn't going to let her go. He'd waited long enough, and so had she, whether she recognized that fact or not.

"Your friend said you're a semi-virgin," he said, advancing on her, smooth and steady, his intentions clear. "That you tried sex and didn't like it. You just didn't try it with the right man, sugar."

Her back was up against the door. He saw a flash of real fear in her dark eyes, and he stopped, every nerve in his body on fire. "Caleb," she said, her voice low and husky, "what if I say no?"

His need for her was so intense he thought he might explode from it. He'd never wanted a woman so much in his entire life, even after he'd spent three years locked away from them. He didn't smile. "Then I'll let you go," he said. "This time. And the next. And each time. Until you say yes."

He watched as a little shiver washed over her body, and her eyes were wide, full of sexual awareness. "How about maybe?" she whispered.

"Maybe's good enough." And he crossed the distance between them, knocking the table out of the way, and put his hands on her.

CHAPTER THIRTEEN

JASSY COULD FEEL the hardness of the door behind her back, the strength of his hard hands on her shoulders. He was close, too close, the smooth-skinned chest tantalizingly near to her mouth, and she was afraid. Afraid of him, of what he wanted of her. Afraid he'd be disappointed. Afraid she'd be disappointed. Afraid of staying with him. Afraid of running.

She forced herself to look up into his eyes, those clear, light eyes that saw too much. He could see through her right now, her indecision, her longing, her fears. Even fully dressed, she was more naked with him than she'd ever been in her life.

"Made up your mind yet?" His voice was soft, low, insinuating, and the gold hoop glinted in the shadow light.

She searched for her voice, but it had vanished. She swallowed, wondering if she dared change her mind. Wondering whether there really would be another chance.

She was going to be just as frightened, later. He was a frightening man. Or maybe it was the intensity of her confused feelings that frightened her. That turned her safe, reliable world on end, upsetting everything she thought she could trust and believe in.

"No," she said in a whisper.

"No?" he echoed, his mouth brushing her ear, his voice only a breath of sound, as soft as her strangled answer. "No, you don't want this? Or no, you're not sure?" His teeth caught her earlobe, gently, a tiny little pressure that sent shivers through her body.

She couldn't answer, couldn't bring herself to form the words, particularly since she didn't know what those words were. She let out a deep, shaken breath, one of surrender, and his hard hands slid down her arms, pulling her against him.

His skin was hot, blazing hot, burning her fingertips as she pressed against him. His mouth was hot, hot and wet as it closed over hers, and the fierce hunger of his kiss filled some deep, long-hidden need she never knew existed.

He put his hands on either side of her face, pushing her against the door, his hips holding her, his hands holding her, as he kissed her, long and hard and deep, allowing no shyness, no hesitation, no second thoughts. Tendrils of panic danced through her brain, entwined with a desire that was rapidly wiping out all conscious thought. She could feel his arousal against her stomach, and she wanted it, wanted him, so completely that everything else was receding. Common sense, family loyalty, age-old fears. When he pulled his mouth away from hers he was breathing deeply, and his eyes glittered in the shadowy kitchen. He tasted like whiskey, and love.

"Last chance," he said in a whisper. "No more maybes. Run now, little girl."

She didn't move. She couldn't move. Trapped between his strong body and the closed door, she couldn't have walked away if her life depended on it. She knew with sudden clarity that he'd let her. All she had to do was push, gently, against his chest, and he'd move away. And he was lying about it being her last chance. At no point was he going to force her to do anything she didn't want to do. He was going to seduce her into it, and if she had any sense at all she'd get out, now, before she lost her mind and her soul.

But she had no sense. She closed her eyes for a moment, unable to meet his too-knowing gaze. "No more maybes," she agreed. "But Caleb...be gentle with me." Silence, and she opened her eyes again.

"Honey, you don't need another night of sex that you can pretend didn't happen. When I get through with you you're going to know you've been taken care of. Well and thoroughly." His long fingers stroked the side of her neck, and she lifted her head to stare at him. "Think you can handle that?"

No, the last remnants of fear and sanity cried out. "Yes," she said, her voice shaky and uncertain.

There was no mocking quality to his smile, no double-dare-you grin. Just the light of pure satisfaction, tinged with an anticipation that both scared and aroused her.

A moment later she was in his arms, scooped up effortlessly and held high against his hard, hot chest as he kicked the door open behind her. The room was dark, but in the center she could see a pool table, covered with a mattress.

He dropped her onto the hard surface, and she stared around her wildly. "You're not going to make love to me on a pool table," she said flatly.

"Honey, it's that or the floor. Take your pick." He didn't wait for her answer, following her down on the mattress, covering her with his strong, hard body.

She expected it fast. She expected it rough. When he reached between their bodies for the buttons of her shirt he ripped it open, buttons flying everywhere. But when his hands touched her they were gentle, unfastening the front hook of her bra with deliberation, touching her skin with the rough texture of his work-hardened fingers like an artist discovering the beauty inside a blank canvas, an unworked lump of clay. He covered her bare breasts with his hands, and she arched upward, a wordless little sound escaping her lips as his thumbs brushed the rapidly hardening peaks into exquisite sensibility.

"You know how much I want you?" he whispered in her ear, his voice soft and mesmerizing as his hand swept down to the waistband of her skirt, yanking it open. "Every night I lie in this bed and think about you. About sweet little Miss Jassy, with her baggy clothes and her shy eyes, and I get so hard I think I'm going to explode. And the damnable thing is, no one else will do. Your buddy Mary-Louise would have been on her back in a flash if I'd let her. There are any number of bored women in Turner's Landing who'd be real happy to lay down for me. But I haven't wanted them. I've wanted you. And in the past week I've built up a powerful hunger."

He pulled the skirt down her legs and tossed it over the side of the pool table, leaving her wearing nothing but a modest pair of white cotton bikinis and her opened shirt and bra. He put his hand between her legs, against the soft white cotton, caressing her, and she jerked, startled, automatically raising her hips for him without realizing why.

Her body had taken over. Any protective instincts had vanished, overwhelmed by her need for this man, this moment. She made no protest when he pulled the rest of her clothes from her, so that she lay naked and vulnerable beneath him. She made no protest when he took her hand and placed it against the straining zipper of his faded jeans. Instead, her fingers caressed him, with a boldness that should have shocked her, but somehow felt right.

"That's it, sugar," he murmured, low in his throat. "You've been making me crazy ever since I saw you, all starched up and pretty at that stupid garden party. Let me see you sweat, lady. Let me hear you cry for me." His mouth covered hers, his tongue thrusting inside, and she kissed him back, completely, holding nothing in reserve, as he covered her body with his, the rough denim against the heat and dampness of her flesh.

She bucked against him, needing him, wanting him, wanting him inside her. He broke the kiss, staring down at her, and his light eyes were wild, glittering in the darkness as he watched her. Wild, possessive, determined. "You still want to run away?" His voice was husky.

"I don't know," she said, her voice equally raw.

"You're about to find out." He rolled off her, and with a deft movement stripped off his jeans, leaving him hot and naked and more aroused than any man she'd ever seen in her life.

Now was the time for panic. Now was the time to run away, let self-preservation and common sense reassert themselves. She tried to summon up even a trace of sanity, and then he touched her, his hand between her legs, stroking her, readying her, and all she could do was bite back the cries of complete surrender as she arched up to meet his hand, opening to him, her head flung back against the pillow as sensations began to shimmer through her body, shimmer and slide and soar and crash and she was sobbing his name, weeping, as her body convulsed against him.

He didn't give her time to recover, or even catch her breath. Before the last shock wave had died away he was over her, pulling her legs around his hips, pressing against her as she still trembled with response. "The running's over, lady," he said. And he sank into her, heavy and hard and deep, filling her with his massive strength, stretching her until she thought she couldn't handle any more, and then showing her that she could. She clutched his shoulders, slippery with sweat, and he pulled her legs around him, locking them behind his hips, as he pushed into her, slamming her against the mattress, and his mouth claimed hers, his tongue moving in the same demanding rhythm as his body, as he filled her, again and again and again.

Darkness swirled around her, thick and rich and dizzying, as she reached for that place she'd just been. He took her hands from his shoulders and shoved them down on the mattress, covering them with his larger, harder ones, his fingers entwined with hers, his body entwined with hers, as they rode the whirlwind that threatened to destroy them.

He lifted his head, and for a brief moment she opened her eyes in the darkness to see the expression of sheer wonder cross his face. And then her own body convulsed, shattered beneath him, dissolved into a million particles of sensation, until there was nothing left but the core of her, panting, sweating, barely breathing, as he lay on top of her, his heavy body pinning her down against the pool table, his arms cradling her head.

It was a long time before some form of sanity returned. She could feel him shudder against her, as he struggled to regulate his breathing. He was crushing her, but for some reason she didn't mind. A strange, delicious lassitude had warmed her body, accompanied by a sense of absolute wonder. This was what she'd been missing. She slid her arms around his waist, holding him for a moment, and her mouth opened against his sweat-slick shoulder, kissing him, tasting him, in a lazy aftermath of sensual delight.

"Don't do that," he said gruffly, rolling off her with a suddenness that left her feeling bereft. And then his words penetrated, and some of that rosy glow began to fade in the face of such blatant rejection. She sat up, reaching blindly for her discarded clothes, wanting to run, when his strong arm snaked around her, pulling her back down against him, curling into the side of his body.

"Don't do that," he whispered again, his mouth brushing hers, "or I won't answer for the consequences."

He was burning hot, and she was cold, so cold. She let him move her closer, pressed up against his body on the hard mattress, and she felt shaken, disoriented. "Consequences?" she echoed in a whisper.

"You're not ready for them," he murmured, stroking her hair

away from her face and pressing it against his damp shoulder. "Even if I am."

She tilted her head to look up at him. "You are?"

"You forget—I've been wanting you for too long. It's going to take a hell of a lot to make up for weeks of abstinence."

She shouldn't feel safe in his arms, not when he frightened her. She shouldn't feel secure, when he was the one man most likely to shatter the tenuous security of her life. She shouldn't be feeling the slow, burning tendrils of arousal blazing in her belly again, not after she had just experienced the most physically satisfying moment of her life. But she felt all those things, sensible or not.

She slid her hands down his chest, over his flat belly until she reached his unwavering arousal. He groaned, deep in his throat, and she found she could smile.

"I've been wanting you all my life," she said, ignoring the foolishness of such a rash statement. "It's going to take a hell of a lot to make up for a lifetime of abstinence."

He smiled then. A smile of pure, sensual joy, that lightened his dark face and chased away the shadows. Before she realized what he intended he'd flipped over on his back, taking her with him, so that she was straddling his hard body. "Sugar," he said, "I'm the man to do it." And taking her hips in his big, rough hands, he lifted her up and over him, pulling her down onto him, filling her.

For a moment she was motionless with shock. And then the sensations began to shimmer outward, as he arched up into her, and she put her hands on his shoulders, leaning forward to brace herself, her thick curly hair falling around them like a curtain, as he thrust into her.

She thought she was doing this for him. She'd misjudged her capacities. One moment she was concentrating on his almost agonized expression as he surged up into her, the next she'd shattered once again, lost in the darkness of the sultry night, found in the haven of his strong body.

She wasn't even aware of collapsing on top of him. Nor did she notice when he put her aside with surprising tenderness, tucking her once more against the shelter of his big body. She was dazed, shell-shocked, beyond coherent thought or speech. She opened her eyes for a moment, and it was dark all around. In the distance she could hear the rumble of thunder, and against the wall she could see the reflected crackle of the heat lightning. And then she slept.

CALEB WONDERED if it was going to storm. Part of him felt as if the promise of heat lightning had already been fulfilled. The fine edge of tension that had clawed at the back of his neck, prickled his spine, burned in his belly had, for the moment, abated.

He knew why, and he knew it wouldn't last. Much as he wanted to, he couldn't spend the rest of his life making love to Jassy Turner. Sooner or later he was going to have to climb down off this makeshift bed and get on with his life, his quest. And once he did that, it would signal the end to his involvement with Jassy.

She wasn't worth changing more than a decade's worth of plans. She wasn't worth forgetting that a part of his life had been thrown away, and the rest of it changed forever, because of a spoiled rich boy and his powerful father. She wasn't worth it. But damn, he was tempted.

She looked young and vulnerable, curled up against him in sleep, her tangled, curly hair twined around both of them. He knew it was no illusion. She *was* young and vulnerable, despite her thirty-one years. He doubted he'd ever been that innocent, that trusting. He certainly never would be again.

The sullen daylight was spearing into the room, a murky green light that presaged another muggy day. She was going to wake up soon, and he knew what would happen next. She'd blink, confused and disorientated for a moment. Then her hazel eyes would focus, on the room, on the bed, on him, and horror and regret would wash over her. Her creamy skin would turn pink with embarrassment, and she'd struggle to sit up. She'd probably attempt a casual conversation, and she'd give it up, running away from her night of indiscriminate sex with the poor trash who was out to destroy her brother.

He could let her go, secure in the knowledge that she'd never show up at his place again, looking for something she didn't know she wanted or needed. He'd be able to concentrate on Harrison, get on with the reason he came here, without the distraction of Jassy Turner.

Or he could pull her back down on the bed, stop her nervous

babbling with his mouth, and kiss her into temporary acquiescence. Until the next time she came to her senses.

She stirred, tucking her hand under her chin, and he knew he didn't have much time to make up his mind. And then suddenly his time was up, as her eyes flew open, meeting his.

He was lying on his side, watching her, a light sheet pulled up around them. He held very still as her eyes widened in remembered astonishment, and he waited for the panic, the embarrassment, the rejection.

It started in her eyes, warming with memory, and traveled to her mouth, curving in a lazy, happy smile, reaching her arms, as they slid around him. She wiggled her body closer across the hard mattress, burying her face against his chest, pressing her cool body up against his, and she let out a sigh of complete trust and satisfaction.

He wrapped his arms around her instinctively, as his mind tried to deal with the shock. He wasn't used to being mistaken, particularly about women. But then, he already knew this wasn't just any woman. Jassy Turner had the potential of being his total downfall if he didn't watch it, all the more so because she was so obviously unaware of it. He had defenses against women who had designs on him. He had no defenses at all against trust.

He felt her lips against his throat, and he wanted to take those lips, that mouth of hers, and show her what mouths could do. His body was hard with wanting her, something she couldn't escape noticing, but he wasn't going to have her. The dark of night, when hormones and tensions ran high, was one thing. The hot, murky light of day was another.

She had an expression of such warmth and happiness on her face that he felt gut-punched. No one had ever smiled at him like that in his entire life. And then to top it off she kissed him, her mouth soft and damp and delightful.

He had to kiss her back. If he didn't he'd die. Pushing her back on the mattress, he cradled her head with his arms and kissed her, with all the passion and desperation that were at war in his body. When he lifted his head to look down at her, her smile had faded somewhat.

"Why did that taste like goodbye?" she asked softly.

He kept underestimating her. Pulling out of her arms, he sat up, swinging his legs over the side of the bed and reaching for his jeans. "You want some coffee?" he asked, not replying to her astute question.

Silence, but he couldn't turn and look at her. He had to give her time to pull her own defenses back around her. He owed her pride at least. "Sure," she said finally, her voice flat, devoid of emotion. "And then I'd better get home."

"Yeah," he said, zipping his jeans with difficulty as he kept his back to her. "Big brother's gonna be out for blood."

"Harrison doesn't interfere with my private life," she said. "Last night didn't have anything to do with him." There was a pause. "Did it?" Her voice cracked, almost imperceptibly, and never, in a life of feeling like a worthless heel, had Caleb Spenser ever felt worse.

But he didn't answer. Didn't reassure her, just walked to the door without looking back. "There's a bathroom and shower off to the left. I've only got one set of towels—you'll have to make do."

"Did it?" she persisted, her voice calmer.

He turned then, expecting despair or hatred. She was sitting in the bed, the sheet pulled up around her, a cloud of tangled brown curls rippling down her back. Her face was calm, and he knew she wasn't going to throw a fit. Only the darkness of her eyes reflected any of the pain she was feeling.

"You figure it out," he said flatly.

The string of names he called himself was long and inventive, obscene and colorful, as he heard her move around in the other room, the noise of the newly installed shower running full blast. He made a pot of the strongest coffee he could, his mind preoccupied. It was after seven—Ray and Bo would be showing up in a little while for work. He'd prefer it if they didn't see Jassy. It was the only thing he could do to protect her. All the other pain was a necessary part of his plan. Wasn't it? Damn it, wasn't it?

He didn't hear her come up behind him. "Coffee ready yet?" she asked in a calm voice.

He turned to look at her. Her hair was damp, fastened behind her head with a strip of material. She'd tied the shirt around her waist—he must have torn the buttons off last night, and her feet were bare. She looked calm, accepting, as if the night he'd passed between her long, lithe legs had never existed. Except for the fact that her eyes were red from weeping, no one would ever have guessed that he'd done his best to break her heart.

He poured her a mug, and his fingers brushed hers as she took it. She jerked, startled, and the coffee slopped over both their hands, burning them, splashing down on the stained floor between their bare feet.

"Sorry," she said briefly, moving away to the stool where she'd sat last night. "I'll be out of here in a moment. I can't move without caffeine."

He didn't believe her. She was still holding out a ray of hope, and he needed to smash that hope, quickly, before it grew to unmanageable proportions. For both of them.

"I didn't kill Sherman Delano," he said.

She'd arranged herself on the stool like a demure schoolgirl, her long skirt tucked over her legs, her ripped blouse pulled together. She looked up at him, suddenly wary. "I wondered about that," she said finally. "I don't think you're a killer."

"Now that's where you're wrong. I didn't kill Sherman Delano, even though I was framed and spent three years of my life in prison for a crime I didn't commit. But I have every intention of killing the man who did it. After I make him suffer."

The wariness was full-fledged panic. "Don't say it," she begged.

"Your brother," Caleb said, his voice flat, emotionless. "Harrison Turner killed Sherman Delano, and then he and your daddy made me take the fall for it. And I'm going to kill him."

CHAPTER FOURTEEN

CALEB WAITED for her reaction. He knew exactly what it would be. Shock, disbelief, rage. That innocent, hurt expression in her huge eyes would turn to anger, and she'd leave, calling him every name in the book, up to and including murderer.

He waited, and once more she was the one to shock him. "You're wrong," she said flatly. "I believe you when you said you didn't do it. But you're mistaken about my brother. I've known him all my life. He couldn't kill someone and then make someone else pay for it...." Her voice trailed off as her eyes clouded, and he could imagine the unwelcome memories that were forcing their way into her consciousness.

"Oh, yeah?" he drawled, leaning back against the counter and warming his hands around the mug of coffee. It was a hot, muggy day, like every day had been since he'd come to this benighted section of Florida, but he felt cold, chilled to the bone. "You mean he never made you take the rap for something he did?"

He struck home, as he expected. She flushed. "Silly things," she said. "Childish things. A broken window. A scraped fender. A few hundred dollars..." Her voice trailed off with the damning indictment.

He took a sip of coffee, giving her time to deal with it. "I'm not talking about conjecture, Jassy," he said, keeping his voice cold and uninvolved, even as his eyes took in the shocked misery in her eyes. "I'm talking about an eyewitness."

"They might have lied...."

"Me, Jassy. I'm talking about me. In the wrong place at the wrong time, as usual. I was just a kid, too wild for my own good and with half the brains I thought I had. I was doing some work for a small-time crook in Jacksonville, and I was running the high-stakes poker game where Sherman Delano brought his college buddy. They were drinking too much, they both got belligerent, and one of them was cheating. I couldn't tell which, and I didn't care. I kicked them both out of the game, but they weren't about to listen to some white trash kid who was younger than them to begin with. They kept quarreling, and the next thing I knew Delano was on the floor with a knife in his throat.''

Jassy swallowed nervously. "It must have been self-defense...."

"The knife belonged to your brother. Delano was unarmed."

"But..."

"Unfortunately everyone else had cleared out when they realized trouble was brewing. The three of us were the only ones in the room. Your brother very calmly offered me a thousand dollars if I just got the hell out of there and never said anything to anybody. Since that was exactly what I was intending to do, it seemed reasonable enough to me. So he reached down and took the money from Delano's body." He shuddered slightly at the memory, a memory that had haunted him for years.

"But why didn't you go to the police?"

"The poker game was illegal, and I'd been on my own since I was fifteen, long enough to learn that the police were the last people you could trust. I didn't want to have anything to do with the whole stinking mess, I just wanted to get the hell away from there. I didn't get very far.

"Your brother waited until I left and then he called the cops. By that time the murder weapon had disappeared, so there was no problem with fingerprints. Your brother never even had to testify, so I never found out his real name. My court-appointed public defender talked me into plea-bargaining, and it seemed the smartest thing to do, considering that Florida was implementing the death penalty. So I did my time, and there wasn't a minute, a second of those three years that I didn't think about what I was going to do to that rich, spoiled kid and his daddy when I found them."

"His daddy?"

"Who do you think masterminded the whole thing?" Caleb said. "Harrison couldn't even do that much for himself. He called his daddy, and his daddy came running to bail him out. I saw him, just once, when I was going in for sentencing. A fine, upstanding southern gentleman, with his starched collar and his soft manicured hands. He looked right through me, like I wasn't even there, and kept on talking to your brother. That was when I decided I was going to kill him first.''

"You were too late," she said, her voice dull and lifeless. "He died three years ago.''

"I know. I can only hope it was slow and painful." Caleb was cold, savage, implacable.

"Cancer usually is," she said flatly. "So what happens when you kill Harrison? You got off lightly the first time, whether you did it or not. If it's premeditated you're far more likely to get the death penalty.''

"It'll be self-defense.''

"I beg your pardon?''

"I'm going to push him so hard he has to turn and fight. He'll make the first move.''

"You don't know Harrison as well as I do. He's a physical coward. He'll send someone after you, rather than face you himself.''

"He's tried that already and he didn't get very far. I'm not weak like Harrison. I'm patient. I've waited thirteen years. I can wait a few days, a few weeks longer.''

She hadn't touched the coffee she'd professed to need, but he could see her hands were trembling as she held on to the mug. "So was I part of your master plan? If so, you miscalculated. Harrison wouldn't care if you slept with me—he wouldn't care if you'd slept with Lila even. He'd use anything to keep you away from him. But then, you knew that, didn't you? You overheard him suggesting I offer you a virgin sacrifice.''

"Not quite virgin," he drawled, watching the flush mount her unnaturally pale cheeks.

"So I imagine my abasement was the only way you could get back at my father from beyond the grave.''

It was like a punch in the gut, one he refused to react to. "Abasement?" he drawled. "Now I don't know if I would have put it quite that way. You didn't look abased as you writhed on top of me last night. But maybe I was misunderstanding your reactions. Maybe that was disgust that made you make those hot, hungry little sounds when I filled you. Maybe it was degradation that made you dig your nails into my back when you came. Maybe it was…"

"Maybe it was this morning, when you made me feel cheap and unwanted and in the way," she said, the color in her cheeks even brighter. "Maybe it was the way you made me fall in love with you, come to need you so much that I forgot about sanity, reality, family loyalty."

"Love?" he mocked. "Don't be a fool! What the hell does love have to do with one helluva good roll in the hay? And what do you know about it?"

"What do you know about love?" she countered, her voice raw with emotion.

"Enough to know it doesn't exist," he said flatly.

She shook her head, and her thick mane of hair loosened around her face. "Then you're the one who's the fool," she said, her voice as calm as his.

They both heard the noise of the vehicle as it drove up to the house. For a moment neither of them moved, listening to the sound of male voices, the slam of a car door. Caleb leaned back against the counter, forcing the noticeable tension from the set of his shoulders. There was no way he could rid himself of the intensity eating at his gut, but he didn't need to advertise it.

"Maybe it's your brother, come to defend your honor," he said in a lazy drawl.

But she was beyond rising to his bait. Her face was pale, troubled, ignoring his taunt. "Something's not right," she said.

"You just discover that?"

She ignored him. "Why is it so quiet? Where is…?"

At that moment Bo and Ray came into the kitchen, their huge, boisterous presence drowning out her words. "Hey, old man, you sleep late or something?" Ray demanded, not noticing the other occupant of the room. "You should have come to the bar with us last night. The women were hot and hungry. Not that Bo took advantage of the situation, but I sure as hell made up for him. You should have joined us."

"I don't think he needed to," Bo said quietly, looking at Jassy.

Ray turned to stare at him, and Caleb saw the calculating expression in the smaller man's eyes. Ray had always fancied himself a ladies' man, and any female was considered worthy prey. In the past Caleb had never objected—he wasn't the kind of man who put claims on the women he'd slept with. He wasn't going to put any claims on Jassy Turner, either. He was simply going to break Ray's teeth if he so much as touched her.

"Guess we should have knocked," Ray said. "You want us to make ourselves scarce?"

"No need," Caleb said, wishing them on the other side of the world. "Jassy was just getting ready to leave."

This time she didn't react, that troubled expression still in her eyes. "Caleb, where's Dog?"

Bo looked up from his shy perusal of the floor. "I was just about to ask the same thing. Where's the Hound from Hell? He usually keeps us penned in the truck until you call him off. You been giving him tranquilizers or something?"

"Hell," Caleb said, quiet and controlled. And he took off out the hallway at a dead run.

JASSY WAS THE ONE who found him. He was lying down by the stream, his eyes glazed and glassy, his huge, shaggy sides barely moving even as he struggled for breath. She screamed for Caleb, sinking beside the animal with a complete disregard for her own safety.

Bo was there first. "Don't touch him, Miss Turner. When a dog's hurt he'll turn on his best friend, and this one's always had an uncertain temperament."

Jassy ignored the warning, putting her hands on Dog's big head. For a moment he tried to lift it, and he focused on her, just barely managing a panting, doggy smile, before he sank back again, all his energy concentrated on breathing.

She put her body over him, listening for a heartbeat, hugging him in a useless effort to warm his ominously cool body. "Get Caleb," she said over her shoulder. "We've got to get him to a vet."

A moment later Caleb was on his knees in the muck beside her, his strong hands gentle as they pried Dog's clenched jaws apart. "Has he been shot?"

She sat up, tears blurring her vision. "Not that I can tell. I think—'' Her voice broke, but she forced herself to say it, ''I think he's been poisoned.''

Caleb's light eyes were blank as they looked into hers. Both of them knew perfectly well who would have poisoned Dog—there was no need to say a word.

''Go start the van,'' Caleb said over his shoulder. ''I'll carry Dog.''

''Need any help?'' Bo offered. ''He's sure a handful.''

''He'd still bite your hand off,'' Caleb said, scooping up the massive weight with seeming effortlessness. Only Jassy was close enough to see the strain in his muscle, feel the tension rippling through him. She trailed along after him to the van, preparing to climb in after them when Caleb managed to get Dog's limp body into the back, when his words forestalled her.

''Where do you think you're going?'' he demanded. ''Hasn't your family done enough? We don't need you.''

''The hell you don't, turkey! Dog won't let anyone else near him, and he's too damned big for you to keep hold of all by yourself. And none of you know where the vet is. So shut your mouth and let me in.''

She expected more of an argument. She never thought she'd see the light of grudging respect that might, in other circumstances, have held a trace of amusement. ''Then don't waste your time talking,'' he said. ''I don't know how much time he's got left.''

The drive to the Roberts Veterinary Hospital was grim, fast and silent, broken only by Dog's labored breathing. Caleb didn't say a word, his face blank, emotionless, chilling. Even when Dog made a sudden, heartrending yelp of pain he didn't react, but Jassy watched his big hand clench in Dog's shaggy fur, almost involuntarily.

Jim Roberts was standing beside his truck, about to go out on his morning rounds, when they skidded into the yard. He started toward them, his earnest young face creased with concern, when he caught sight of Caleb Spenser struggling with his heavy burden.

''We think he's been poisoned,'' Jassy said, scrambling out after them. ''We don't know how long ago—it may have happened last night. His breathing is steady but weak, so we brought him straight in....'' Her voice trailed off as Jim made no move to come forward.

Normally she would have expected all speed and efficiency from him, leading the way into the examining room and setting right to work. But he didn't move.

"I'm sorry," he said, his voice guilty and miserable.

Caleb stood still, shifting his heavy burden in his arms, and his face was cold. He glanced at Jassy. "He's not going to help us. Where's the nearest vet?"

"Don't be ridiculous," she snapped. "Of course he's going to help us. He's not going to ignore an animal in pain...." She looked back at Jim. She'd known him since grade school, a decent, bright, well-meaning boy. He still hadn't moved.

"Jassy, I can't!" he said, his voice pleading for understanding. "Your daddy got me into Cornell, he paid my way, damn it! I can't go against your family. Don't ask it of me."

Caleb had turned, heading for the van, his face grim and murderous. She reached out, grabbed his arm and held. "Wait right here," she said.

Releasing him, she crossed the dusty yard, ignoring the swelter of heat as it pressed down around her, ignoring her own mud-stained, ripped clothing. Reaching out, she took the lapels of Jim Roberts's jumpsuit in her strong hands and yanked, hauling his face down even with hers. "You're going to open up your examining room," she said fiercely, "and you're going to save that dog's life, and you're going to do it right quick. I don't give a damn how much my father did for you—you don't owe him your honor and decency. And if you're worried about loyalty, remember that I'm the colonel's child just as much as Harrison is. If you don't get your butt in gear I'm going to report you to the state veterinary board, or whoever it is who grants licenses, and you're going to be answering a lot of uncomfortable questions. You hear me, Jim Roberts?" She was shouting in his face, rage and frustration exploding out of her as she'd never allowed it to before. Jim was staring at her in absolute shock, and she jerked him one more time, just for good measure.

Then he nodded. "Bring him right in," he said, detaching himself from Jassy's fierce grip and heading for the infirmary.

Caleb hesitated, not moving. Jassy turned on him, still brimming with fury. "Get the hell in there. You can't afford to be picky. The nearest vet is a good forty miles away, and he's a drunk. Jim may be a wimp but he's a damned good doctor.''

Caleb didn't wait any longer. Jim had already opened the doors, and Dog's huge weight couldn't have been an easy load. He walked past Jassy, carrying him effortlessly, not bothering to look back at her.

Jassy watched them disappear into the examining room, and the sheer force of will vanished, leaving her trembling with reaction. She wanted to burst into tears, but that was hardly feasible, not with Ray and Bo staring at her with unabashed fascination. "You okay?" Bo asked, moving toward her.

"Sure," she said, her eyes bright with unshed tears. "I just need some coffee. I forgot to drink mine."

"I got a thermos in the van," Ray offered, his earlier leer forgotten. "I imagine we've got a bit of a wait."

He'd understated the matter. The three of them camped out in the waiting room, sharing the too-sweet coffee, barely talking, as the minutes, then hours, went by. There was no sign of Caleb, no sign of Jim or Dog. All they could do was sit and wait.

At one point Jassy tried to start a conversation, her years with Claire reminding her to practice her social graces, but neither men were in the mood to talk. Nor, for that matter, was she. She simply asked the question that mattered most. "What will happen if Dog doesn't recover?"

Ray stretched back and lit a cigarette in defiance of the No Smoking notice posted on the faux-paneled walls. "Now that all depends. Caleb might not make a fuss at all. He's always said that dog is a pain in the butt, and he's never been one for responsibilities and commitments. Dog was about all the commitment he cared to make, and I imagine he'd be just as happy to be free of it."

"If you believe that you're an idiot," Bo said flatly. "You shouldn't take Caleb at face value. He and Dog have been together a long time. I wouldn't like to be the man who poisoned him if he doesn't recover."

Jassy stretched her legs out in front of her. She'd managed to slip on her sandals before she'd run out to look for Dog, but tramping through the marshy land around the Moon Palace had liberally splattered her legs with mud. She wanted a hot bath, she wanted a drink, she wanted peace of mind. She'd get the first two. The last was a luxury she doubted she'd enjoy again for a long, long time.

"I've done everything I can do." Jim Roberts was standing in the doorway, exhaustion on his face. His jumpsuit was stained with blood, and he was alone.

"Is he dead?" Bo asked bluntly.

"Not yet. He's a tough old mutt, he might still make it. He's a fighter, but he was out there a long time before anyone found him. My guess is he...ate something tainted around midnight. That gave the stuff a hell of a long time to work in his system, and it's anybody's guess how bad the damage is."

Jassy closed her eyes in silent pain. While she and Caleb had been lying on the pool table, Dog had been alone and in pain. If Caleb didn't hate her before, he certainly did by now.

"I'm just going to have to keep a watch and see. The next few hours will make the difference. You might as well go home." Jim couldn't quite meet Jassy's eyes, and she knew the guilt he was feeling. Guilt, he more than deserved.

"Where's Caleb?" Bo demanded, lumbering to his feet.

Jassy expected Jim to say he was staying by Dog's side until the crisis passed. But Jim nodded his head in the direction of the yard. "He said he'd wait for you in the van. You want me to give you a ride home, Jassy?"

For a moment she considered it. Caleb probably didn't want to see her, and she wasn't positive she was in the mood to face his despair and anger. But she'd never been a coward in her life, and now wasn't the time to start. "Caleb can give me a ride home. I imagine you don't feel like facing Harrison right now." She kept the contempt out of her voice with an effort. In the end he had done everything he could to save Dog. It was up to fate to see whether it had been enough.

"That's a fact. Besides, I ought to stay here until my assistant shows up."

"Don't worry, little lady," Ray said, taking her arm. "I'll protect you from Caleb's temper."

"I wouldn't do that if I were you," Bo said mildly as they headed out into the blistering heat.

"Do what?"

"Put your hands on Caleb's lady."

"He's never been possessive before," Ray said in a defensive voice.

"There's a first time for everything."

Ray glanced toward the van. "Spoilsport," he said in an aggrieved tone, releasing her arm.

Caleb was sitting in the driver's seat, staring straight ahead, his hands draped loosely, casually over the steering wheel. He glanced up as they climbed into the van, his expression impassive. "We'd better get a move on," he said, his slow, deep voice devoid of feeling. "We've already wasted half the day."

Jassy stared at him. She'd had no choice but to climb into the front seat beside him—Bo and Ray had scrambled for the back. There was no sign whatsoever that Dog's eventual fate mattered to him, he merely looked impatient. "Would you mind dropping me off at Belle Rive on your way?"

"What about your car?" he asked with excruciating politeness.

"I can pick it up later."

"I'm not sure that's a good idea."

"Tough," she said, hoping to jar a reaction from him. It failed. He simply shrugged, started the van, and took off down the road, at a far more sedate pace then their headlong dash for help.

He stopped at the end of Belle Rive's long, curving driveway. "You'll forgive us if we don't drive you up to the front door," he said with exaggerated courtesy. "We're already behind on our work."

She sat there and stared at him for a moment, searching for signs of pain, of sorrow, of remorse, of caring in his bronzed, distant face. Not a trace. He wasn't even human, except that she knew differently. Every square inch of her body knew differently.

"You don't fool me," she said, reaching for the door handle.

"I hadn't intended to," he murmured in a bored voice. "You might be better off picking up your car before dark. We'll be off at a work site until then."

"But how will you get word about Dog?"

He shrugged again. "I'll find out sooner or later. Either he'll live or he'll die. There's nothing I can do about it, so I may as well get on with things. There's no room in this life for sentiment."

"Where will you be working? I can come out with word…"

"Goodbye, Jassy," he said, his tone of voice final.

She wasn't sure what she wanted to do. Scream at him. Cry. Or haul off and hit him. She sat there, motionless, silent, as she considered the possibilities, then decided against doing anything at all.

The two men were watching and listening with far too much interest. And if she hit him she was afraid of the consequences. Not that he'd hit her back. She had not the slightest trace of doubt that that was the last thing he'd do.

But that he'd kiss her. And that would do far more damage.

"Later, Caleb," she said firmly. And without another word she slid out of the van, slamming the door behind her.

CHAPTER FIFTEEN

BELLE RIVE was still and silent when Jassy let herself in the front door. The huge old grandfather clock in the front hall was just chiming the hour. Eleven o'clock. Jassy blinked at it in disbelief. It seemed days since they'd raced to the animal hospital, hours and hours and hours that they waited for word. She couldn't believe it was still before noon.

It explained why the house was empty, which suited Jassy just fine. She wasn't in the mood for a confrontation with Harrison, not yet. Not till she had time to absorb all the shocking things Caleb had said, not until she could decide what might have a kernel of truth to it. Not that she thought Caleb was lying to her. Whatever his faults, and they were legion, she didn't think he was a liar.

But he had to be mistaken. There had to be a reasonable explanation for the things he said. And the fact that Dog was struggling for life at Jim Roberts's place was a coincidence. He was obviously poisoned, but it had to be something like tainted meat, a wild mushroom, even a snake bite. No one could have deliberately set out to hurt a helpless animal.

Not that Dog was necessarily helpless. He was a big, oofy baby, but she could take other people's word for it that he could turn chillingly fierce when his loved ones were affected. If someone wanted to sabotage the Moon Palace, if someone wanted to sneak up on Caleb without warning him, then disposing of his guard dog was an effective first strike.

No, her mind screamed. It had to be a coincidence. She couldn't have spent all her life believing in her family, only to find her life of security was built on a foundation of lies. There had to be a reasonable explanation...there had to be.

She was heading up the stairs when she heard the insistent buzz of the telephone. She considered ignoring it. At that hour Claire would be sleeping off the effects of the previous evening, her shades drawn, her telephone extension turned off. Harrison would be in town, Lila had one of her never-ending doctor's appointments in her quest for pregnancy, and even Miss Sadie would be doing the morning shopping.

She could wait for the answering machine, but it might be Jim. Without another moment's hesitation she raced across the floor, grabbing the phone just as the answering machine clicked in.

"Mrs. Turner?" the voice at the other end was feminine, efficient, and Jassy didn't bother correcting her. "This is Dr. Bertram's office. The doctor asked me to call you and tell you there's really no need to repeat your husband's fertility test. His vasectomy was judged to be one hundred percent successful when it was performed five years ago. Unless he's interested in reversing the process there's no point in retesting."

"Five years ago?" Jassy said weakly. Harrison and Lila had been married for three years, had ostensibly been trying to get pregnant for the last two.

"Your husband made it clear that reversal was not something that he would consider. Has he changed his mind?"

Jassy sank onto the satin-covered chair by the phone. "I...I don't think so," she said numbly.

"Well," the woman said briskly, "if there's any way we can be of service please don't hesitate to call."

Jassy heard the platitude numbly. She made the only logical response. "Have a good day," she murmured in a faint voice, putting the receiver down.

Lies. Lies, and more lies. She'd spent hours holding Lila's hand while Lila wept over the bitterness of a fate that had made her barren with no discernible cause. And all the time there had been a very obvious cause. Harrison's selfishness, and Harrison's lies.

He'd never liked children, she'd always known that. And he'd never liked to share the center of attention. He was used to being cosseted and petted by the doting women of his family, his idiot sister included. The colonel had bailed him out of more trouble than Jassy could even begin to know about, and he'd always winked and smiled and said boys will be boys.

If Harrison could lie about something as elemental as this, if he could stand by and watch Lila go through a battery of painful, useless tests, if he could be sympathetic and patient, all the time knowing what was behind it and never say a word, then he was capable of anything. Possibly including murdering another boy in a blind rage and then letting someone else take the blame for it.

"You look like you've seen a ghost." Claire stood silhouetted in the garden doorway, the bright sunlight behind her.

Jassy swallowed her panicked shriek of surprise. "I didn't think you'd be up."

Claire stepped into the hallway, where Jassy could get a good look at her. Her silvery hair was neatly coiffed, there was a faint, healthy glow of color on her papery cheeks, and her eyes were clear. "I slept well for a change," she said with a careless shrug. "I thought I might do a bit on the garden. The men do their best, but they don't really understand roses."

"No, they don't," Jassy said lamely, knowing no such thing. One thing was clear; for once her mother had foregone her nightly tippling. Maybe in the face of family disaster there was a ray of hope after all. "Do you know where Harrison and Lila are?"

"Lila's at the doctor's again. She's been after Harrison to go in for more tests, but he's refusing. I understand his point. After all, he's been proven to be healthy. The problem is obviously with Lila, and she just can't admit it. The sooner she does, the sooner they can decide about adoption. Not that Harrison would ever agree," she said with a sigh. "He's a great believer in bloodlines. Personally I think our bloodlines could do with a fresh transfusion. But you know you can't reason with your brother."

"No," Jassy said flatly.

"I would like grandchildren," Claire went on in her mild voice. "If Harrison and Lila aren't able to provide me with any, you might consider paying attention to your own biological clock. You have any number of suitable beaux. Don't you think you might consider making your choice?"

Jassy closed her eyes for a moment, picturing a most unsuitable beau, someone wild and dangerous who'd already gone out of his way to reject her that morning. "I'm afraid I already have. For what good it will do me."

Claire looked at her, not saying a word, and Jassy had the odd notion that perhaps her mother knew her better than she'd ever imagined. "Things have a habit of working out for the best," she murmured, stripping off her gardening gloves and laying them on a side table.

"I don't know about that. I think disaster has a habit of crashing down." She stared out into the blazing sunlight, wishing it matched her gloomy mood.

"Perhaps," Claire agreed. "But it doesn't do any good to sit and wait for it. Will you join me in a glass of iced tea?"

For a moment Jassy didn't answer, distracted by the sudden memory of Caleb's hands on her body. Then she shook herself, forcibly banishing the rush of emotion. "After I change out of these muddy clothes." She started for the stairs, then paused. "Aren't you going to ask me where I was last night?"

"I have a fairly good idea."

"I'm in love with him," she said, shocking herself with the bald statement, hoping to shock her mother.

Claire simply smiled. "I know."

The front door swung open, and Jassy jumped nervously, wishing she'd had time to make it upstairs, to figure out how she was going to deal with the unwelcome information that had just come her way, when Lila and Harrison walked in the door. Lila was laughing, and her slender arm was tucked in Harrison's elegantly suited one. He was looking indulgent, handsome, even downright noble. And for the first time in her life Jassy hated her brother.

She didn't move, and for a moment they didn't see her, paused halfway up the winding stairs. Claire greeted them with calm affection. "What are you two so cheerful about?" she asked.

"We've decided to go on a cruise," Lila said. "Just go off for a couple of weeks and forget about babies and money and worries. Who knows, I might even come back pregnant."

Harrison patted her hand affectionately, and Jassy wanted to scream. Instead she gripped the smooth cypress stair rail, and the slight movement caught their attention. "When are you going?" she forced herself to ask.

"Day after tomorrow," Harrison replied, his eyes narrowing as he saw far too much in her rigid stance. "As soon as they can make the arrangements. I figured it might be good for both of us to get away from here."

Get away from Caleb Spenser's revenge, more likely, she thought. Or maybe provide himself with an alibi while another set of hired thugs tried to drive him away. "Sounds good to me," she said evenly. She started back up the stairs, paused, and turned around. "Oh, Harrison?"

"Yes, Jassy?"

"I had a long talk with the nurse at Dr. Bertram's office," she said in her sweetest, most innocent voice. "They thought you ought to come in for a recheck."

It wasn't Harrison's expression that frightened her. It was the absolute lack of it, as Lila let out a whoop of excitement, that sent a sudden tendril of dread down her spine. His handsome mouth curved in a polite smile, as his eyes were blank and chilly. "I appreciate that, Jassy," he said, his voice smooth and mellifluous. And suddenly Jassy was more frightened than she'd ever been around Caleb Spenser.

She dismissed the notion as absurd. Tossing her head, she gave him an equally phony smile. "Just thought I'd mention it," she said. "I'm going for a shower and a nap. I'll talk to you later."

"Yes," said Harrison grimly, ignoring the happy chattering of his wife and mother, "you will."

THE MOON PALACE was dark and deserted when Caleb drove up that evening. He'd ignored Bo's and Ray's offers of companionship, their invitations to come drinking, to play poker, to shoot the breeze and wait for word of Dog. He didn't need their heavy-handed sympathy. Hell, Dog was only a dog. A worthless mutt who'd lived off his generosity for a long time. The two of them rubbed along pretty well together, but that didn't mean he was going to go into some kind of decline if he didn't make it. Dogs didn't live as long as humans did. If you had a dog, you were bound to watch him die. He'd learned that as a kid, when the worthless crossbreed he'd bought for a dollar at the county fair had been killed. Dollar had been the first living creature he'd loved who'd loved him back unconditionally. When his father had shot him he'd learned about unconditional hatred.

He never should have fed Dog in the first place. Taken him in, fixed up his sores and bruises, taken him to a vet. Hell, there were always strays—he couldn't save the world. He told Jassy Turner that, when he should have been reminding himself.

He cursed then as he stepped into the empty house, suddenly remembering the hurt in her wide hazel eyes. He'd always been partial to blue eyes and blond hair. He'd never realized how beguiling, how downright hypnotizing that greeny brown shade could be. He had the uneasy feeling that he'd never like blue eyes again.

More sentimental crap, he told himself briskly, heading for the kitchen and a long-necked bottle of beer. He didn't need Jassy Turner, he didn't need Dog, he didn't need anybody. All he needed was a cold beer, and lukewarm shower, and something to eat, and he'd be as happy as a clam.

The shower didn't do much to ease his aching muscles. He'd spent too many days on his butt and not enough working. He'd worked today, worked so hard he'd hoped to blot everything out of his mind. Unfortunately things didn't work that way. But tomorrow he'd do it again. And again. Work his tail off, while he finished up with Harrison Turner. And then get the hell out of this steamy, godforsaken town and into a place with air-conditioning or at least a breeze.

He heard the distant rumble of thunder as he peered into his refrigerator, and he cast a sour look out into the gathering gloom. "You don't fool me," he said out loud. "Just more of a tease. Heat lightning, and nothing but." The contents of his refrigerator weren't encouraging. Dried-up cheese, moldy bread, several ancient casseroles. He slammed it again.

"The cupboard's bare," he said out loud, not thinking. "Sorry, Dog, you'll have to..." The words trailed off as he realized he was alone in the kitchen. Alone, as he'd always been.

He leaned his hands on the counter, and dropped his head down, staring at the cracked linoleum on the floor, staring as it fuzzed and faded, as inexplicable drops of wetness landed on his bare feet. He stood without moving for a long, long time, his muscles clenched with the need not to feel.

He almost didn't hear her come in. He didn't hear her car, or the front door open. He just knew. He looked up, and saw her, standing silhouetted in the doorway.

It was too dark to see her face, but her body was tense, wary, and he knew what she'd come to tell him. "He's dead," Caleb said flatly, no emotion in his voice whatsoever. He managed to sound bored by the whole thing, something he told himself he could be proud of.

She shook her head. "Jim says he's going to be fine. We can pick him up tomorrow morning."

For a moment Caleb didn't move. He tried a careless shrug, but it didn't work. Suddenly he felt like a ten-year-old kid again, tears streaming down his dirt-streaked face as he knelt in a dusty road and howled out his rage over the cruel injustices of life.

"Damn," he said, and his voice broke. "Damn."

In a moment she was there beside him, her arms wrapped around his waist, tight, her face pressed against his back. She held him, and for the first time since he was that ten-year-old kid he let the rage and grief out, shaking with it, as she held on for dear life.

When the first storm of emotion passed he turned in her arms, seeking her mouth blindly as he pulled her tight against him. She went willingly, and her own face was wet with tears. And suddenly he had to have her, now, immediately, not to blot out his feelings, but to celebrate them, feel them, feel them all.

He lifted her, moving her backward to the solid oak table, shoving the dishes off it onto the floor and pushing her back. He yanked at her clothes, and she helped him, ripping off her loose T-shirt as he stripped off her panties beneath the full skirt. By the time he unfastened his jeans he was fully aroused and ready for her, beyond ready. Pulling her legs around his hips, he sank into her wet, sleek warmth, feeling her shudder with pleasure as her hands reached up and caught his arms as he braced himself on the table. Her fingers dug into his skin as her eyes closed, and he watched her face as he drove into her, hard, watched the pleasure ripple through her skin, until her huge hazel eyes opened with a kind of shocked surprise, and she made a funny little catching sound in the back of her throat that could have been his name, and then he felt the unmistakable convulsions around him, convulsions his own body answered, as he pulsed and exploded within her.

It was all he could do to keep standing at the edge of the table. His body was trembling, his muscles weak, and he felt like crawling on top of the heavy maple and sinking onto her. But she was trembling, too, her eyes open now with shock and maybe self-consciousness, and he didn't want her to be self-conscious. He wanted to make love to her in every place, every way, until she forgot to be embarrassed and shy.

Carefully he pulled away, catching her hands as she tried to pull her skirt down. "Don't be ridiculous," he said in a husky voice, as he unfastened the side button with slightly trembling fingers. She let him, too bemused to stop him, as he stripped the rest of her clothes off, then stepped out of the jeans that had been shoved halfway down his legs, kicking them across the kitchen floor.

He reached down for her, lifting her into his arms, and she was shivering in the steamy heat of the kitchen. Outside heat lightning snaked across the landscape, followed by a distant rumble of thunder, and he held her close against him, letting his heat sink into her. He carried her into the bedroom without a word, putting her down on the mattress and following her down, drawing her into his arms and telling himself she needed reassurance, comfort. Knowing he needed them just as much.

Slowly her shivering stopped. She reached up to touch his face, her fingers smoothing the dampness away, and she managed a tentative smile. "It's all right to feel things, you know," she said, her voice not much more than a whisper. "It's all right to hurt."

He wanted to deny it, but it would have been a waste of time. He rolled onto his back, taking her with him, tucking her head against his shoulder. She sighed, as the last bit of tension left her body, and she was warm and pliant against him, completely trusting. "I don't want to," he said, his voice rusty in the shadowy room.

"I know."

He considered that. "You shouldn't be here," he said finally, keeping his arm around her, keeping her tucked at his side. Not that she was making any effort to leave.

"Why not?"

"Because I'm trash. I may not be a murderer, but there's not much else I haven't done, or wouldn't do. I was born bad—my daddy told me that from as early as I can remember, and I did my best to live up to it.''

"Nice father," Jassy said. "What made him such an authority?"

"Hell, my daddy knew everything about right and wrong. He was a preacher man, an old-fashioned, Bible-thumping, scripture-quoting, devil-wrestling man of God. He knew a spawn of the devil when he saw one."

"If he was your father then you must have been his spawn."

"Exactly," Caleb said, exhaling, forcing some of the tension from his body. "My daddy warned me I was born to raise hell, and he did his best to beat repentance into me. It took me a while to realize he was trying to beat repentance into himself, and I was just a convenient outlet. He was shot by a jealous parishioner who found him in his wife's bed, and I took off. But I've got his gift. A sweet-talking ladies' man, just like my old man, and worth about as much."

"Caleb…"

"Don't try to convince me of my essential goodness, Jassy," he said, shoving a hand through his hair as he stared up at the old tin ceiling. "Don't try to tell me my father was full of crap. I know that. And I know I'm just as bad. I don't have any illusions about this life or myself."

"Then maybe you need some." She sat up, her thick, curly hair hanging around her, for once completely unselfconscious about her nude body. "You're a good man, Caleb Spenser. You hate to admit it, but no matter how hard you try to be a no-good waster you end up doing the right thing."

"You think coming here to kill your brother out of revenge is the right thing? You think going after you as part of my grand scheme, no matter how much it hurt you, was the right thing?"

She didn't move, as her body seemed to absorb the blow, considering whether it was fatal or not. And then she lifted her head. "You went to bed with me last night as a way to get back at my brother?" She sounded frankly skeptical.

He considered lying. In the long run it might be the kindest thing to do for her, but right then he wasn't feeling kind and self-sacrificing. Right then he needed her, needed her too badly to be noble. "No. I took you to bed because I couldn't stand to be without you for another moment."

She smiled then, a sweet upturning of her mouth, and without thinking he pulled her down to him, tasting that mouth, feeling it soften against his while his body hardened against hers. When she pulled back a moment she reached out and pushed his long, damp hair away from his face. "You're not going to kill my brother," she said, her voice soft and certain. "You're not going to break my heart, either. There's a lot more possibilities in this life than you're even considering. There are happy endings."

"Not for me."

"Sorry," she said firmly. "But I don't intend to settle for less. And it's come to the point where my happy ending is dependent on yours. So you're going to have to accept it."

"You can't go around saving lost souls," he said.

"I can if I love them enough."

"You don't love me. We have good sex together. Hell, we have terrific sex together. The best. But that's not love."

Nothing was going to dent her certainly. He could probably shove her off the makeshift bed and she'd simply climb back on. "The best?" she asked, looking pleased. "I didn't have much to compare it to but it certainly was astonishing to me. I figured maybe that was the way it was supposed to be."

He didn't know whether to shake her or kiss her. To laugh or to cry. "It's supposed to be that way," he said, "but it seldom is. Life would be a lot less complicated if it were. Fewer divorces."

"Fewer divorces? Is that a proposal?"

"Jassy," he said with a warning sigh.

"Never mind, Caleb. I don't want to argue with you. There are a lot of better things we can do."

He looked at her warily. He didn't know when an uptight, semi-virgin suddenly became such a threat to his plans and his well-being. If he'd had any notion she was going to turn his life upside down he would have kept his distance. If he could have. "Like what?" he said.

She levered forward, her hair hanging around them, her lips brushing his, as her small, perfect breasts brushed his chest. "Use your imagination," she whispered. "We've got all night."

"Shameless," he murmured against her mouth, as he reached for her. "Completely, wonderfully shameless." He cupped her face, pushing her back for a moment, denying himself the distraction of her increasingly inventive mouth. "And what happens in the morning?"

"I turn back into a pumpkin," she said. "And you turn back into a rat."

He didn't move. "God help me," he murmured. And he kissed her, hard, and there were no more words.

CHAPTER SIXTEEN

"I NEED TO GO HOME," Jassy murmured, her face buried against Caleb's shoulder.

"Um-hmm," he agreed, not moving.

It was morning. How early, Jassy had no idea. All she knew was she didn't want to move. She wanted to spend the rest of her life wrapped around Caleb Spenser. If she got up and went home she'd have to face Harrison.

She couldn't pretend as if nothing had happened. She needed to hear Harrison's side of the story—she owed him that at least. It would most likely be a pack of self-serving lies, ones he probably didn't realize weren't the truth. That was the way people's minds worked. Few people did wicked things and reveled in their evil. They somehow worked out a justification for it all, to a point where they no longer realized they'd done anything wrong. She'd known Harrison all her life, had helped bail him out of trouble since she was old enough to lie for him. She could practically write the scenario herself.

"I don't want to talk to Harrison," she said out loud. Caleb's muscles tensed beneath her, but his hand didn't stop stroking her arm.

"Then don't. What do you expect to accomplish? Do you expect to find out the truth?"

"I don't think my brother knows what the truth is anymore. But I need to tell him why I'm leaving."

This time the stroking of her arm halted. "Leaving?" he echoed, his voice flat. "Where are you going?"

She sat up then, and he made no move to stop her. His face was remote again, unreadable in the early-morning light. "With you?"

He didn't say a word. It took all her self-control to be patient, to wait for him to say something. She wanted to scream at him, to beat on him with her fists, but she waited.

Slowly he shook his head. "It won't work."

"Why not?"

"There's too much between us. Don't look like I kicked your dog, Jassy, you know I'm right. It doesn't matter how good we are together. The fact remains that I spent three years in prison for a crime I didn't commit, and I was put there by your brother's lies. It doesn't matter how much I care about you. I'm still going to destroy your brother."

"And then you'll go back to jail, maybe to the electric chair. They kill people for premeditated murder in this state, Caleb. And you've certainly made it clear to any number of witnesses that you're out for Harrison's blood."

"I have no intention of killing your brother," he said wearily. "Much as the thought gives me a certain satisfaction. There's more than one way to destroy someone. You can take their money, their reputation, their family from them, so that they have nothing left. Then they might as well be dead, and maybe they'll take care of it themselves. Either way, I'll have my revenge."

"And revenge is more important than me?" She knew she shouldn't ask him. She was forcing him to choose, and she wasn't going to be able to live with that choice.

"Yes," he said flatly, and she couldn't be certain if there was doubt in his clear, light eyes or whether she was just clinging to a vain thread of hope.

But she couldn't beg. Couldn't weep and plead, bargain or argue. She climbed off the high bed, for once unselfconscious in her nudity. "Then there's nothing more I can do," she said. She walked into the kitchen, picking up her scattered clothes from the floor and pulling them over her. At least this time he hadn't torn them off her, she thought, fastening the button of her loose skirt. When she walked back into the bedroom he hadn't moved. He lay on the mattress, the white sheet pulled up to his hips, his face as cool and calm as the day was hot and windy.

She waited for him to ask her not to leave, to reach out his strong, tanned hand for hers, and she would have climbed right back up on that absurd bed with him. But he didn't. He didn't say a word, just continued to watch her out of distant, hungry eyes.

"How long do you think this is going to take?" she asked.

She'd managed to startle him. "How long is what going to take?"

"Your grand scheme of revenge. How long will it take you to ruin my brother?"

She'd asked the question in a calm enough voice, and he answered her in the same way, sitting up in the bed and watching her. "He's already managed to bring himself to the brink of financial ruin, with his gambling and his other women. One stiff breeze and it'll topple like a house of cards."

"All the family money is tied up together, including mother's and mine. Does that mean that we're going to be paupers as well?"

"Yes."

She nodded, refusing to flinch at the brutal news. After all, that wasn't his fault, it was Harrison's, and theirs, for trusting him. "What about the rest? What about his friends? What about his family?"

"His friends will drop him when they learn he's lost his money, his home, through dishonest dealings. It's too late to prove anything that happened thirteen years ago, but I have friends in the press who just love to muckrake, and they don't need a whole lot of concrete evidence if they're convinced of the facts."

"And his family?"

"His wife has been turning a blind eye to his extracurricular activities. She won't be able to do that once it's published. And Claire's more interested in the bottle than she is in Harrison."

"So that leaves me."

"That leaves you," he agreed. "The loyal, self-sacrificing sister, who does everything for everybody. Are you going to stand by him, hold his hand as he faces ruin?"

She moved to the edge of the bed, close enough for him to touch if he reached out his hand. Close enough to reach him if he gave her any sign. "Do I have anyplace else to go?" she asked quietly.

He closed his eyes for a moment, as pain washed over his face. "What do you want from me, Jassy? I can't be the kind of man you deserve. I can't give you what you need."

"You already have."

"We're not talking about sex, damn it, we're talking about life!"

"You are my life," she said desperately. "You're the air that I breath, the blood in my veins. I existed before you, existed on a diet of good works and doing for others. You showed me what it was like to be alive. You gave me a taste of a feast, and I don't want to go back to the way it was before. Weak tea and cucumber sandwiches and bridge parties, and people with ice water in their veins. I want to live, Caleb. I want to live with you."

She didn't wait for his answer. She was too afraid of what it might be. She turned and ran.

She'd managed to stop crying by the time she turned into the long, winding driveway to Belle Rive. The dashboard clock read a surprising 11:15. The day was dark, overcast and stiflingly warm at that hour in the morning, and the breeze that riffled through the live oaks was a hot, angry one. A storm wind, she thought as she parked the car haphazardly. Maybe a hell of a storm, to blow away all the misery and lies that festered in Turner's Landing.

She heard the sound of voices as she let herself in the front door, and she paused there, silent, still. Harrison was home in the middle of the day, not that unlikely an occurrence, but still something she hadn't counted on. For a moment she was tempted to sneak upstairs, lock her bedroom door until she was ready for the confrontation she knew was inevitable. She could hear Claire's plaintive tones, that faint whine in her voice that was tinged with a slur, and a sudden foreboding filled her. Ignoring her original intention, she turned and walked into the living room, in time to see Harrison handing Claire a tall glass of clear iced liquid. One that certainly wasn't ice water.

"Isn't it a little early for vodka?" she asked abruptly.

Claire jumped, startled, a guilty expression on her pale face. "Jassy, you frightened me," she said, placing a trembling hand against her narrow chest.

"Did I?" Jassy walked into the room, past her brother. "You don't need a drink at this hour."

"How dare you talk to me like that?" Claire said in a weak attempt at bravado. "And you know perfectly well I don't drink

anything more than a little light wine. That's ice water…Jassy!''
she shrieked as Jassy took the glass out of her hand and took a
swallow.

The vodka hit her like a taste of liquid fire. He hadn't even
bothered to water it down, and the two ice cubes were more for
decoration. Jassy looked down at the glass, wanting to hurl it
through the French doors in sudden rage. Except that her rage and
hurt were for Caleb, not her mother.

She set the glass back down on the table beside her mother with
a quiet little click, as she pulled her emotions back tightly around
her. ''I can't stop you from drinking,'' she said quietly. ''It's your
life, and your body. But you ought to think twice before you let
Harrison bring you down.''

She walked from the room, not bothering to look at her, her
contempt and dislike too overwhelming.

He caught up with her at the top of the stairs, and his hands were
hard, painful on her arm. Why hadn't she noticed what a bully he
was before, she wondered, tugging uselessly at her arm.

''What the hell did you mean by that crack?'' he demanded, and
she could see the slight bulge of vein at his temple, the fury in his
eyes. ''Mama's drinking problem isn't my fault.''

''She's been sober the past few days. You were the one handing
her a tall glass of vodka, Harrison.''

''You're a fine one to pass judgment. Where the hell were you
all night? You come home looking like a slut, smelling of sex, and
you dare to act like I'm the bad guy.''

The pain in her arm was intense, shockingly so. For a moment
she wondered whether he might actually break her arm. ''I was
sleeping with Caleb Spenser. That's what you told me to do, isn't
it? Aren't I the obedient little sister, always ready to do my best
for you?''

He shook her, hard, and she half expected to hear the bone crack.
''What's he been saying to you? It's all lies, you know that. Who
are you going to believe, a convicted murderer or your own
brother?''

''I don't know who to believe anymore,'' she said coolly, trying
to ignore the faintness that was closing in around her. She stopped
trying to pull free, hoping he'd loosen his vicious grip. ''And you

forget, I've talked to more people than Caleb. What about Dr. Bertram's office?''

He looked dark, wary and very dangerous. "What about Dr. Bertram's office?'' he asked in a cold, evil voice.

"You had a vasectomy five years ago, a little fact that you failed to mention to your wife as she's gone through extensive fertility testing. There's no problem with Lila's fertility. Just in her choice of husbands.''

They both heard the gasp of horror. Lila was standing in her doorway, her face pale, eyes red and swollen from earlier tears.

It happened so fast Jassy couldn't be clear. Harrison uttered a filthy word beneath his breath, and finally released her arm. Released it as he shoved her, as hard as he could, toward the deadly marble floor at the bottom of the long flight of winding stairs.

Someone screamed, Jassy, or Lila, or maybe Claire, who'd come out into the hallway during the last few moments. The world tilted as Jassy fell, floating, dizzy, flying through the air toward certain death.

She slammed up against the railing and it took a few breathless, hysterical moments to realize that she'd managed to grab the banister and break her fall. Struggling for breath, she looked up to the top of the stairs, to see Harrison backhand Lila across the face. And watched, as Lila took it with nothing more than a resigned whimper.

The bedroom door slammed behind them, and through her struggles for breath Jassy could hear the sound of Lila's quiet weeping. A moment later Claire was standing over her, her hands gently removing Jassy's death clutch on the banister. "You shouldn't have riled him,'' she said quietly. "You've always underestimated Harrison. He's got a streak of meanness that shouldn't be tampered with.'' She surveyed her daughter critically. "You're all right, aren't you?''

Jassy stood up, her knees trembling, her hands shaking. "In one piece.'' Both women heard a thud, and Jassy started up the stairs purposefully, when Claire caught her arm, holding her back.

"Don't do it,'' she said quietly. "You'll only make it worse.''

"I'm not going to sit by and let my own brother beat his wife,'' she said savagely.

"She's used to it. If you interfere she won't thank you. She knows best how to calm him down."

"You can't be defending him...."

"I'm not. I just know the best way out of these things," Claire said quietly. "The less fuss you make, the sooner these things blow over. Harrison's a good husband in other ways, a good son. These little incidences don't happen that often."

"Little incidences?" Suddenly Jassy wanted to throw up. There was quiet from the room upstairs, just the muffled sound of voices as the violence passed. "Go back to your vodka, Mother," she said coldly. "I'm getting out of here." She pushed past her, starting back down the stairs.

"Where are you going?"

For a moment she thought of the Moon Palace, of Caleb Spenser's bleak face and beautiful body, then dismissed that notion as effectively as he'd dismissed her. "I'm not sure. Just away from here."

SHE WASN'T USED TO running away. She wasn't used to backing down from abusive husbands or sticky situations. But that hot August day things suddenly became too much for her. She ran, driving her little Ford Escort as fast as she could, away from Turner's Landing. Away from love, and betrayal, and pain that she simply wasn't ready to face, ran until the gray, stormy day turned into darkness, and she found herself at the edge of the swamp road.

She'd stopped at the women's shelter long enough to take a shower and grab a change of clothing from the neat closet full of donations. She took a couple of moth-eaten blankets, a lumpy pillow and a little bit of food, and then struck out for Rowdy's cabin. The darkness of the afternoon sent little tendrils of unease through her, and the intermittent streaks of lightning made her jump, but she forced herself to ignore them. The storm was nothing but a lie, an empty promise of rain that would never come. The rumble of thunder was another lie, and she'd had enough of lies.

The path through the swamp was trampled down, more than she'd remembered, and she wondered if hunters had been out there, using Rowdy's makeshift cabin. For a moment she was tempted to turn back. She wasn't in the mood to face interlopers at this point, or to stake her claim to a shack that was falling into the swamp. And then she stiffened her back. She'd accepted defeat too many times in one day. She wasn't giving up the last thing that mattered to her.

The air was thick with humidity and a dark, shadowy mist was rising from the swamp. The rumble of thunder had become a steady companion by the time she reached the clearing at the edge of the water, and it took her a moment to focus, another to believe what she was seeing.

The fresh lumber was piled beside the cabin, and the smell of freshly sawn pine mingled with the scent of damp vegetation. The roof was already replaced, the door rehung, the rotten boards on the porch now white and shiny new. The building still sagged precariously, but some of the thick posts that lay in the pile of lumber must be intended for shoring it up. He was going to save it for her, even when he'd told her it was a lost cause.

She wanted to cry, but she'd cried too much that day, and there were no more tears left. Besides, she was no longer sure what her tears would be for. There was no reason for him to work on her hopeless cabin. Except that he cared for her, much as he tried to deny it.

She was tired, so tired, that she just tossed her bedding onto the rickety old cot and collapsed on top of it, ignoring the food she'd brought, ignoring the gathering storm outside. With the new roof and door she'd be safe if miracles still occurred and they actually got some rain. She didn't need to worry.

She had no idea what time it was. She hadn't bothered to bring matches or a flashlight, and the darkness was growing thick and heavy around her. She hadn't had much sleep in the last forty-eight hours, and she was so tired she thought she could sleep forever. Her last thought, as she closed her eyes and let exhaustion take over, was that it was far too dark for five o'clock in the afternoon.

SHE DREAMED of violence. Of blood and death and anger, of rage so deep that the world shook and roared. When she opened her eyes finally she discovered it was no dream. All hell had broken loose.

The rain had come, finally. And not just rain. A violent, soaking downpour that was pounding against the new roof, soaking through the thin pine walls, puddling on the floor as it seeped underneath the door. The lightning was coming at regular, breathless intervals, barely moments apart, lighting up the blackness with eerie brightness. Jassy scuttled back on the cot, fighting the panic that beat down around her, as she listened to the storm scream in fury.

She'd never felt so alone in all her life. A few miles away her mother would be quietly drinking herself into a stupor, or maybe she'd already passed out. Harrison and Lila were probably in the honeymoon stage that inevitably followed an episode of violence. He'd promise all sorts of things, and she'd believe him, because she wanted to so desperately.

As for Caleb, he'd dismissed her from his mind. He was probably sitting in the kitchen of the Moon Palace, drinking beer and planning his vengeance. If he thought of her at all it might be with regret that it was the wrong time and place. But he'd shrug and accept it. And then forget it, as he concentrated on what was important to him.

God, what a pitiful mess she was, she thought. Sitting huddled in a decrepit shack, feeling sorry for herself. She needed to get off that cot and figure out how she was going to get out of the situation she'd gotten herself into. And then she'd figure out how she was going to fix everything else. She wasn't one to accept defeat easily. She was tired and emotional now, but it wouldn't last. If she couldn't have Caleb Spenser, she could at least see what she could do about the rest of her family.

No, damn it. Maybe she'd better see what she could do about her own life, and let the rest of her family figure out their own problems. She couldn't fix everything, hadn't Caleb told her that time and time again? Right now she wasn't even sure she could fix the unpleasant situation she was currently in.

The water was ankle deep on the cabin floor when she climbed off the cot. The door was stuck, and she struggled with it for a moment, only to have it jerked out of her hands by the furious wind. It slammed against the side of the cabin, and splintered, half of it hanging on the newly replaced hinges, the other half floating into the swamp.

Jassy backed into the cabin in panic at the fury of the storm. As she watched, a huge live oak toppled over with a great rending sound, missing the roof of the cabin by no more than a few feet. This was no ordinary storm raging. This was something of biblical proportions, and Jassy was trapped, with no ark in sight.

Her shoes were floating away in the murky light, and she dived for them, slipping and falling on her knees in the water. There were creatures around her, frightened inhabitants of the swamp struggling to find safety in a storm that had uprooted their lives along with the tree, and Jassy scrambled to her feet in panic, remembering the alligators, the cottonmouths that usually kept away from their natural enemy, man.

She had two choices. She could stay huddled in the flooded cabin and hope the storm would pass. Or she could strike out in the darkness, trying to find the path that would now be several inches deep in water, and hope she didn't stumble deeper into the swamp.

She didn't like either choice. At that moment something slithered by her leg in the deepening water, and she screamed, jumping onto the rickety table and pulling her legs under her.

The table wasn't made for a hundred-plus pounds of frightened female. It creaked and shifted beneath her, and she knew it was going to collapse without much help from her. She moaned, a frightened little sound, but the noise of the wind swept the noise away. She sat there on the table, huddled in the darkness, and wondered what in God's name was going to happen to her.

She heard the curses first. Rich, inventive profanity over the howl of the wind as his shadow filled the broken doorway. A flashlight swept the room, finally landing on her as she crouched on the table, and his cursing increased.

"What the hell are you doing out here?" Caleb shouted furiously, wading through the water that was now calf deep. "Don't you listen to the radio? Don't you pay any attention to the weather? For God's sake, you've lived here all your life, don't you know there are hurricanes this time of year?" He took her shoulders in his hands, and she knew he wanted to shake some sense into her. Instead he pulled her into his arms, and she could feel the faint tremor in his iron-hard muscles, and knew that imperceptible weakness came from relief.

She buried her face in his neck, against the cool wetness of his rain poncho, and clung tightly, so tightly she thought she'd never let go. He held her just as fiercely as another tree thundered down into the swamp nearby.

"We've got to get the hell out of here," he said thickly. "This cabin isn't going to last much longer in this kind of wind."

"But the work you've done..."

"I told you it would be a waste of time." He held her away for a moment, and the movement made the precarious table collapse underneath her, sending her tumbling into the water. He caught her, of course, swearing again. "You don't have any shoes?"

"They floated away."

"Then I'll have to carry you."

"Caleb..."

"Don't argue with me, Jassy. We don't have time." He bent down in the water. "Climb on my back."

She didn't say a word. She climbed on, wishing she hadn't eaten cheesecake last week, wishing, if she were going to die, that at least she'd die in bed with Caleb. He started out into the rain. "Keep your head down," he shouted, and the wind took his voice and hurled it into the darkness. "And say your prayers."

And he started out into the raging hell of the hurricane.

CHAPTER SEVENTEEN

JASSY COULDN'T SEE, couldn't hear, couldn't breathe in the raging turmoil of the storm. She buried her face against Caleb's back and held on, shuddering as the thunder and lightning crashed around them. He moved steadily, surely, his body buffeted by the fierce winds but seemingly untroubled by her weight as the rain poured down over their heads.

Over the shriek of the winds she heard a loud, rending sound, and she lifted her head, jerking around and almost throwing Caleb off balance. Through the sheets of rain she could see the collapsed shell of the cabin as it floated on the rising waters of the flood.

"Hold still!" he shouted, though she could only guess what he was saying through the noise of the storm. She put her head down, clinging tighter, and wept as the only thing that had ever been hers and hers alone was washed away.

It took centuries to cross the water-filled pathway back to the cars. She was convinced he must have set out in the wrong direction, that they were heading out into the middle of the swamp and certain death, and she was unsure whether she minded or not. As long as she was wrapped tightly around him, the insanity of nature couldn't frighten her.

And then he stopped, sliding her down onto solid ground, and she staggered, falling against the solid wet metal of his pickup. Yanking the door open, he pushed her inside, then waded around to the driver's side.

For a moment the comparative silence was deafening. Even with the roar of the wind outside the truck, the grinding energy of the engine as he turned the key, his muttered, continuous cursing under his breath, it felt suddenly peaceful. She leaned back, closing her eyes, and let out a long, shaky breath of relief.

"You'd better hold on," he muttered. "This isn't going to be an easy ride."

That was, if anything, an understatement. She barely had time to appreciate the consummate, desperate skill in his driving as he dodged floating tree trunks, debris, even the corpse of a dead deer, as he raced through the rapidly deepening flood waters. The truck was built high, the water only coming partway up the wheels, but Jassy knew that area far too well. With the steady, deadly downpour, the waters could rise rapidly, as riverbanks overflowed and saturated land could no longer absorb the rainfall.

"Where are we going?" she shouted over the noise of the storm.

"My place," he muttered, not taking the time to even glance in her direction as he concentrated on the dangerous driving.

"But it's near the swamp. It'll be flooded…and it's old. It might not withstand these winds…."

"I wouldn't have bought it if it weren't as solid as a rock," Caleb shot back. "And it's set higher than it looks. Higher than Belle Rive, for that matter. You'll be safe enough there."

"My mother," Jassy said. "I've got to make sure she and Lila are all right. When I left…"

"Harrison will take care of them."

"Harrison will take care of himself," she said bitterly. "If you won't take me there I'll walk."

"You mean you'll swim," he said bitterly, jerking the wheel of the truck to avoid a thick tree limb. The turnoff to the Moon Palace loomed up, and he slowed the truck. Then he cursed, stomped his foot on the accelerator, and shot past it. "You're a pain in the butt, you know that," he muttered. "I'm not in the lifesaving business. Your mother and sister-in-law can fend for themselves."

"Then why are you driving me to Belle Rive?"

"To get rid of you?" he suggested.

She pushed her sopping hair out of her face, wiping away some of the moisture. "Nope."

"Don't start with me, Jassy. This isn't the time or place to argue."

"I'm not arguing. I'm—" Her calm voice deteriorated into a panicked shriek as Caleb slammed on the brakes, throwing them both hard against the dashboard. One of the huge live oaks had

come down across what Jassy could only assume was the driveway
to Belle Rive. The rain was too heavy to be certain, but she thought
she could see the pale bulk of the house in the distance.

Without hesitation she opened the truck door, ready to jump out,
when Caleb hauled her back in. "You'll never make it," he said.
"Stay put and let me go."

"Not on your life. It's my family, my responsibility, not yours,"
she shouted back, struggling.

She hadn't realized how strong he was, or how he'd held back
when he'd touched her before. He wasn't holding back this time.
There was no way she could break free of his grip, no way he
couldn't overpower her.

"Your family can take care of itself," he said. "You don't need
to risk your life for them."

She became very still. "You're right," she said in her calmest
possible voice. "They're probably safe and sound in town somewhere."

Under normal circumstances he wouldn't have been fooled. But
with the violence of the storm raging around them, he took her
word and released her, putting the truck in reverse.

She was out in the rain before he'd even let up on the clutch.
She heard his shout of rage follow her into the stormy night, and
then nothing but the solid noise of the storm as she fought her way
toward the house.

The house was pitch-dark when she staggered in the front door.
"Lila!" she screamed. "Mother! Is anyone here?" Silence answered her, and she wondered if she'd been a crazy fool to risk her
own life for a family that was more than capable of taking care of
themselves. She called out again, prepared to head to the highest
part of the house and wait out the storm, when she heard a noise.
It sounded like a cat, a weak, mewling sound, coming from the
living room. Except there were no cats at Belle Rive. Harrison
wouldn't allow it.

She moved slowly across the marble floor, ignoring the puddles
her soaking clothes were making, ignoring the thin layer of water
that was seeping in from the terrace. The living room was full of
dark, huddled shapes, until the lightning flashed once more, and
she could see someone curled up in a corner.

It was Lila.

Jassy rushed to her side, stubbing her bare feet on the overturned furniture, and sank onto the floor beside her sister-in-law. "Lila, are you all right?" she asked urgently. She reached to put protective arms around her, but Lila flinched away in terror, letting out that strange, miserable little cry. "Where's Claire, Lila?" she forced herself to ask calmly.

Through the almost constant flashes of lightning Jassy could see Lila fight to control herself. "I don't...know," she said finally, her voice muffled. "In her room..."

"We've got to get you out of here," Jassy said briskly. "It's flooding, and I don't know how strong the foundations are of this old place. Let me help you out to the car and then I'll go back for mother. There are some trees down, but if I drive across the lawn we should be able to make it."

"Harrison..."

"Is he here?"

"I don't know," Lila moaned.

"We won't worry about him. Harrison can take care of himself." She put her arms around Lila, feeling her shiver. "Stand up, Lila. We need to get you out of here." Slowly, carefully, she pulled her to her feet, and the lightning flashed again, illuminating her face.

Jassy sucked in her breath in shock, but the sound of the storm covered the noise. Lila staggered, then righted herself, wrapping an arm around her waist, and it took all of Jassy's concentration to ignore the rage that swept over her. Lila had been beaten, so badly she could scarcely see, scarcely stand, and there was no question at all as to who had done it.

They moved through the hallway toward the front door when a tall male figure loomed out of the shadows. Lila screamed then, a sound of such heartrending panic that Jassy almost screamed, too. And then the lightning flashed again, and she knew it was Caleb.

"Take her to the truck," he said tersely, making no move to touch her, understanding far too much without even being able to see. "Where's your mother?"

"Passed out upstairs, I think," Jassy said.

"I'll get her. What about Harrison?" Caleb said.

"I don't know."

"No," Lila said in a panic. "I can't go. He'll kill me. Don't, Jassy, please…"

Her babbling pleas made no sense at all. Jassy uttered soothing noises as she led her toward the storm. "Don't worry, Lila. Everything will be all right. You'll see. Just come with me. Caleb's truck is out there, and it's warm and dry and safe. We'll get out of here, and you'll be fine, just fine."

For a moment the fear left Lila. She stood still in the open doorway of the old house, silhouetted against the lightning-filled sky. "Don't you realize, Jassy," she said, "that it will never be all right again?"

Jassy cast a glance over her shoulder, but Caleb was already sprinting up the wide, curving stairs toward Claire's bedroom. She didn't bother wondering how he knew his way around the place—it was one of those things Caleb would know. She had to simply trust that he'd be able to find Claire in the darkness and get her out of there safely. Someone had to get Lila to the truck, and she wasn't in any shape to tolerate the help of a man.

The water was ankle deep by the time she got Lila safely stowed. They'd slipped, climbing over the massive trunk of the fallen oak tree, and the Spanish moss had tangled in their legs. "Stay put," Jassy shouted through the rain. "We'll be back in a moment."

"Harrison," Lila moaned, and Jassy wasn't sure whether she was afraid they wouldn't find him. Or afraid they would.

"Stay put," she said again, striking off back toward the house.

The sky was a little lighter as she looked toward the huge old house, illuminated against the angry sky, and she wondered whether the merciful eye of the storm might be approaching, allowing them enough time to get to safety before the next torrent hit. But there seemed no letup to the buckets of rain, and she realized with sudden horror that the brightness around Belle Rive was no longer the streaks of lightning but the bright glow of a burning building.

She started running. She stepped on something sharp and painful, fell face first into the rising waters, and then rose and ran again, ignoring the pain, ignoring everything in her desperation to reach the house, and Caleb, before the entire place went up in flames. The front door was open, and the glow of the fire spread out in a deceptively welcoming light. She raced through, shrieking his name, and then skidded to a halt in the water-filled front hallway as she looked up in horror.

Claire was standing there, her gray hair long and straggly, her robe pulled loosely around her weaving body. She was holding on to the banister, a dazed expression on her face, barely conscious of the confrontation a few feet away. Harrison and Caleb.

"For God's sake," Caleb said, his body rigid, "let me get your mother out of here. What's between us can wait."

He was backed against the wall at the top of the stairs, not moving. Things were no longer dark, they were illuminated by the blaze and crackle of the rapidly spreading fire, and even the downpour overhead seemed to have no effect on it.

Harrison stood silhouetted against that blaze, and his very calm was the most horrifying of all. He was perfectly dressed, even to the linen suit, his hair neat, his white suit spotless, his manicured hand holding the hunting knife as if it were a Cross pen.

"You've destroyed me," Harrison said in a calm, eerie voice. "You've wrecked my reputation, my business prospects, you've taken my wife from me. All because I saw you kill Sherman Delano."

Jassy didn't move, confusion sweeping over her. She believed Caleb; deep in her heart she'd never had any doubt. But how could Harrison stand there and lie?

"You know I didn't kill him, Harrison," Caleb said gently. "You know I haven't gone near your wife...."

"She told me!" Harrison's voice rose in a little scream. "I beat the truth out of her, until she couldn't lie anymore. She told me about all the times she slept with you. How she spent last night in your bed, making love, laughing at me."

Jassy moved forward, opening her mouth to protest, but a small, imperceptible movement of Caleb's hand waved her to silence. She hadn't even realized he knew she was there, but he was aware of everything. Including the acrid smoke and stench of the fire as it billowed through the hallway toward them.

"It's not your wife I've been sleeping with, Harrison," Caleb said. "It's your sister."

"That tramp. I'll deal with her after I'm finished with you. You've all betrayed me. I won't let you do it. I won't let you take everything away from me. It's mine, all of this, it's mine, and you can't touch it." He sounded like a spoiled child, an angry little boy who didn't want to share his toys.

"Fine. We'll go away. Let me help your mother...." He reached toward Claire's woozy figure, and Harrison slashed out with the knife.

"Leave my mother alone. She'd rather be dead than accept help from murdering trash like you." He moved a little closer, and Jassy saw with sudden horror that there was blood on the wicked-looking blade. He must have caught Caleb with that last flashing attack. "I'm going to kill you. I'm going to cut your heart out, and leave you here to the fire, and no one will ever know. Jassy won't say anything. She's loyal, beneath all her willfulness. And Claire wouldn't testify against me. After all, I'm just righting a wrong. You should have paid with your life for Sherman's death, you and I both know it."

"Harrison, you killed Sherman," Caleb said flatly. "You and I both know it."

"No!" he screamed in rage. "You did, you did, you did, you did, you...!"

Claire had lifted her head and staggered toward them in sudden, brief consciousness. Harrison reached out and slammed her out of the way, giving Caleb his chance. Caleb dived at him, ignoring the knife, and for a moment Jassy couldn't watch as the life-or-death battle raged above her.

A column of smoke billowed out, obscuring them. And then she heard the still, horrifying cry, as a body crashed through the cypress railing and tumbled down to the marble floor below.

Jassy didn't move. She could see her brother's white-suited body spread-eagled on the floor, and she knew without a doubt that he was dead. That he might have been dead before he fell, with that vicious-looking knife stuck in his chest.

Caleb emerged from the fire, Claire's comatose body held in his arms. He paused at the bottom of the stairs, to look at Harrison, to look at Jassy, and once more there was no expression in his light eyes. No grief, no regret, no triumph. Just a bleak emptiness.

CALEB DROVE with single-minded concentration, ignoring the three women squeezed into the front seat of his pickup. Harrison Turner's women. Belonging to the man he'd just killed.

His hand clenched around the steering wheel as he avoided a fallen tree trunk, and he barely noticed the pain. He'd never killed a man before. He'd thought about it, long and hard. In particular about killing that man. He didn't know when he'd finally given up the idea, when he'd let go of the need for vengeance in place of justice. For what good it had done him. In the end Harrison had won. Harrison had given him no choice at all, and with that act he'd sealed his own fate. He'd become what Harrison had made him.

The light that was Belle Rive was only a faint glow in the stormy, sullen sky. No one looked back as he'd driven away, no one had asked any questions. The questions would come later, from people like Clayton Sykes and the law-abiding citizens of the town. And the answers would come from the women in the truck.

He slammed on the brakes, cursing. "We can't make it into town," he announced to no one in particular. Harrison's wife was staring out the window, in some distant world, his mother was passed out. Only Jassy was listening.

"Why not?" She sounded unnaturally calm, polite, and he wanted to curse again.

"See for yourself. The road's flooded. We'll have to wait for the police to come to us."

If he'd hoped to startle some sort of reaction out of her, he failed. "They'll find us," she said evenly.

He half wished he were wrong about the Moon Palace. That it had collapsed in the storm like the flimsy little shack where he'd found Jassy hiding out. But it stood in a shallow pool of water, straight and tall and oddly welcoming.

"What the hell happened?" Bo waded out to the truck, opening the door as Lila tumbled out into his arms. She let out a panicked shriek, one Bo seemed to take in his stride. Somehow he was able to calm her, shepherding her into the old bordello with his usual gentleness as Jassy followed after them.

Claire was a dead weight. Her eyes had been open, though, and clear as she watched the struggle at the top of the landing. She'd provide a creditable enough witness if it came to that. He had no intention of letting it come to that.

He carried her into the house, settling her in the spare room where Ray and Bo had set up cots. The beds were unmade but warm and dry, and he doubted Claire was in any condition to be fussy. She was snoring slightly as he covered her up, and he wondered whether she might black out everything that happened. He could hardly count on it.

Jassy was standing in the door, watching him. The place was lit with a combination of candlelight and kerosene lanterns, and she looked like a drowned rat with her clothes plastered against her, her hair long and wet against her body. She'd never looked so desirable.

"She should sleep it off," he said.

"Yes," Jassy said, her voice cool.

"How's Lila?"

"Bo's taking care of her. She'll survive, I'd say. She's pretty shaken up, bruised and battered, but I don't think any bones are broken."

"What makes you so sure?"

"I'm used to seeing women who've been beaten by their husbands, remember? I know what broken bones look like."

"I guess you do." He started to move past her, but she didn't get out of his way.

"Where are you going?"

He grinned then, a sour, humorless smile. "Think I'm going to run away? The way I see it I've got two choices. I can get the hell out of here and start a new life someplace. I figure there's a good chance I could make it. The truck can go almost anyplace, and the police are going to have their hands full with the hurricane. They won't even know anything happened out at Belle Rive until I'm long gone. I don't have a telephone here, so you can't call them, and I've got the only vehicle that stands a chance of getting through high water."

"What's your other choice?" She sounded no more than casually interested.

"Wait for that sheriff of yours. Sykes, wasn't that his name? The one who lived in your brother's back pocket. I figure I stand a real good chance of getting lynched, if I'm lucky.''

"Doesn't sound like much of a choice. You're going to run.''

"Not likely,'' he said in a savage undertone. "I've had enough of running. I'm staying put. Don't you worry about me tarnishing the family reputation. You'll still be lily-white. I wouldn't expect anyone to believe me anyway, so why waste my breath? It all boils down to the fact that I came here for Harrison Turner, goaded him until he was beyond rational thought and ended up killing him. Those are the facts, and anything else is just extraneous.''

"Extraneous,'' she echoed. "Like the fact that I love you?''

"Don't!'' His voice was raw, anguished. "Don't even think it. I killed your brother, Jassy. He was right, I'm nothing but murdering trash, and if you ever let me put my hands on you again you'd end up despising yourself. Didn't you listen to him? He never admitted it. His last words were accusing me of killing Delano. How can you be foolish enough to believe me?''

"Because I *know* you. I know you're not a murderer, and never were. And Harrison was. I don't think he was lying at the end, I think he no longer knew the truth. He'd spent so many years covering up and rearranging the past to his own satisfaction that he no longer knew what was real.''

"Jassy, it's hopeless. Let it go.''

She didn't move. "All right,'' she said. "If you do.''

"Do what?''

"Leave. Get out of here. You won't get a fair deal from Clayton, I know that as well as you do. Harrison had everyone fooled into thinking he was a hell of a nice guy, and they're going to think you're a cold-blooded killer. It won't matter if you tell them about Sherman Delano, it won't matter if they see Lila's face. They'll believe what they want to believe, and you won't stand a chance against them.''

"Sorry,'' Caleb said. "I'm sick of running. I've been running since I was fifteen, and I'm not running anymore.''

"Caleb...''

"I hate to interrupt anything.'' Ray appeared in the hallway beyond them. "But why are the police here?''

Caleb suddenly became utterly still. "That settles that," he said. "I guess there must be more than one way from town."

"The high road through Whitler," Jassy said. "I should have remembered. Caleb, please..."

"You heard the man, Jassy. It's too late. For both of us."

CHAPTER EIGHTEEN

"NOW WE CAN DO this the easy way or the hard way," Clayton Sykes said as he heaved his impressive bulk onto the kitchen stool. "I ought to take the bunch of you down to headquarters for your statements, but we got a bit of a problem with the roads. Not to mention that this damned hurricane doesn't seem to want to give up, and I've got other problems besides the Turners to deal with. So we're gonna try it this way, nice and easy, and if you give me any trouble we'll go into town come hell or high water, and it looks like we're having a taste of both outside. You ready to take down their statements, Orville?"

"Yes, sir." Orville, the lanky, red-faced deputy who trailed in Clayton's shadow had to content himself with leaning against the counter, steno pad propped on the new Formica.

"So who wants to go first? You think you're feeling up to it, Miz Claire?"

Claire nodded weakly. She'd been pumped full of coffee, and she'd managed to put her long gray hair in a semblance of order and straighten her old robe. Even so, for the first time in Jassy's memory she looked her age, and then some. "Certainly, Clayton…"

"I'll go first," Caleb said, his voice low, deep, authoritative.

Clayton didn't like anyone else sounding authoritative. "I'm the one who's gonna say who's going first," he said flatly. "You take your time, Miz Claire. I don't want to make this any harder on you than it is already. Maybe Miz Lila…"

"No," said Bo, not the slightest bit intimidated. "She's lying down, and she doesn't need to be bothered by a lot of upsetting questions."

"Who the hell are you, boy, to talk that way to me?" Clayton demanded. "You another one of Spenser's ex-cons?"

"You still can't talk to her," he said stubbornly,.

"Well, hell," Clayton snarled. "You all want to tell me when you're ready and I'll be glad to accommodate you...."

"I told you, Sheriff—" Caleb began, but Jassy interrupted, slipping past him and perching on the stool opposite Sykes before he could stop her.

"Ladies first," she said, trying to control the hammering in her heart. She saw Caleb subside, leaning against the doorway with that same shuttered expression on his face. She knew what he wanted—the one thing she couldn't give him. He wanted to be punished, and she figured he'd been punished enough.

"So what the hell happened, Jassy?" Clayton was demanding. "Belle Rive's an inferno—not even forty days and nights of flood could stop it. And where the hell is Harrison?"

"Inside," she said flatly. "He's dead, Clayton. I don't really know how to explain it. He...he's had some business losses lately."

"Hell, it's worse than that. He was facing bankruptcy. Criminal charges, too, for embezzlement. I'd been doing my best for him, but I was on my way out to arrest him when the storm hit. I'm real sorry, Jassy, but the money's gone."

She nodded. "He was a little crazy, Clayton. Caleb had driven me out there to see whether they needed help. He was helping Mother down the stairs when Harrison came at him with a knife. The house was already on fire, and he slipped and fell over the banister, landing on his knife."

Clayton just looked at her as silence filled the crowded kitchen, broken only by the steady drone of the rain against the windows. "That's the poorest excuse for a reasonable story that I've ever heard, Jassy," he said finally. "So damned poor, as a matter of fact, that I'm almost tempted to believe you."

"It's true, Clayton." Claire spoke up, her voice surprisingly clear. "I was a witness, as Jassy was. Harrison wasn't quite... rational. The floor was wet with rain, smoke was pouring out, and he fell."

"What do you say to that, Spenser?" Clayton barked at him.

Jassy held her breath. Throughout her brief testimony he'd said nothing, his face distant and unreadable, the gold hoop in his ear winking in the kerosene light. She was suddenly, terribly afraid he'd do something stupid like tell the truth. But after a moment he simply nodded. "I wouldn't contradict two ladies, Sheriff."

"No," Clayton said wearily. "Neither would I." He heaved his bulk off the stool. "Which I suppose means you're free to go. Which I suggest you do. As far away from here and as fast as the storm will let you. No later than tomorrow. You hear, boy?"

Caleb looked at him. "I hear."

"Miz Claire, why don't we drive you and Miz Lila into town? There are any number of people who'd be happy to take you in while you get things settled."

"No, thank you, Clayton," Claire said with dignity. "If Mr. Spenser doesn't mind, I think we'll just wait out the storm here."

"Stay as long as you like, Miz Turner," Caleb said. "I won't be back. The place is yours if you'd like."

"I couldn't possibly…"

"Go ahead, lady," Ray said. "He doesn't need it. We'll fix up the place for you, make it real homelike. Won't we, Caleb?"

Caleb nodded, his face remote, already miles away. And then he pushed away from the counter, following Sykes and his deputy out into the hallway without a backward glance.

"He couldn't mean it," Claire was saying with a fluttering nervousness.

"He means it," Jassy said abruptly. "You and Lila should be very comfortable here once it's finished."

"What do you mean, 'you and Lila'? Where will you be?"

Ray smiled, and his dark, ferretlike face brightened. "You better hurry," he offered.

"You're not leaving?" Claire demanded in a shriek. "Jassy, you can't abandon us. Not now! We need you. Our lives are in ruin. How can we…?"

Jassy leaned over and kissed Claire's withered cheek. "You'll have to do it by yourself, Mother," she said gently. "I'm gone."

The rain had slowed in the past few minutes, down to a quiet drizzling, and the heavy winds had let up. The lightning had passed, along with the thunder, and in the distance she could see a faint glow. This time it wasn't Belle Rive. It was the astonishing approach of sunrise. Another day. A new life. An end to the old one.

Dog was already in the truck, his tongue lolling out as he greeted her happily. "You don't look any the worse for wear," she said, climbing in beside him. "Do you suppose he's in the market for another stray? Or do you think he'll kick me out?"

Dog tried to crawl onto her lap, an impossible feat for an almost-Newfoundland-size dog. She shoved him onto the floor with gentle hands, rubbing his huge head. "You'll have to bite him if he tries it," she told him. "I'm not sure if I've got any fight left in me."

"CAN'T TALK YOU into staying?" Ray asked, watching Caleb as he threw his clothes into a duffel bag.

"What's the use? You heard the man. I'm not welcome around here anymore. Which suits me fine—I've had enough of backwater Florida towns."

"Where are you going?"

"I don't know yet. I'll send word. Don't worry—you'll get your weekly paychecks."

"Don't insult me. I've never worried about getting paid with you, boss. I just don't like to see you heading out like this."

Caleb paused for a moment, feeling the heaviness press around his chest. His heart, as much as he hated to admit it. "It's for the best. You and Bo look after the women, Ray. Make sure they're okay, that they have what they need."

"I think Bo'll do just fine with his broken bird. He'll have her eating out of his hand in no time. And the old lady's tougher than she looks. She'll be okay."

"And Jassy," Caleb forced himself to say.

Ray grinned at him. "You want me to take care of her, boss? I'd be more than happy to, but I kind of thought..."

"Keep your hands off her," he growled, "or I'll cut your heart out. She deserves something better than you or me and, damn it, she's going to get it." He slung the duffel over his shoulder and started for the door. "I'll be in touch."

He kept his head down as he made his way across the soggy ground. He didn't notice her until he opened the driver's door and tossed the duffel bag behind the seat. He stood there in the light drizzle, staring at her.

"What the hell do you think you're doing?" he asked in a roughened voice.

"Coming with you."

He looked at the two of them. Dog, with his huge, doggy grin on his face. And Jassy, her long, thick hair curling wildly around her face as it dried, the same hopeful, determined look on her beautiful face.

"I killed your brother," he said flatly.

"Not in cold blood."

"There was too much smoke. It was dark. You couldn't see clearly."

"I *know,*" she said. "I didn't have to see. You can haul me out of the truck but I'll just follow you. I'll turn up on your doorstep when you least expect it, I'll haunt you. You might as well accept it, Caleb. I'm your destiny. You're never going to get rid of me."

For all her bravado she was frightened. He could see it in the faint tremor of her lush red lips, in the shadow behind her eyes. She'd been crying, and he'd made her cry too much in the last twenty-four hours. He couldn't stand to make her cry again.

It was that fear that decided it for him. That melted his heart, destroyed his resolve and defeated him. He climbed into the truck beside her, slid his hand beneath her wet tangle of hair and pulled her against him, settling his mouth on hers.

When they finally moved apart the sun had broken through the twilight of early morning. "You'll regret this every day of your life," he said, his voice husky. "But I can't give you up."

"Why?"

He never thought he'd say it. In the end, it was inevitable, and simple, and right. "Because I love you."

Her smile was brighter than the sun. "Then there'll never be anything to regret."

She threaded her arm through his, leaning against him as he started the truck, and he found, to his absolute amazement, that he believed her.

The morning was cool and silent, the oppressive heat vanished in the face of the violent, cleansing storm. He could hear the distant sound of birds singing, and suddenly life seemed new, and full of hope, as together they drove off into the glorious colors of the sunrise. The storm was over. A new day had begun.

FATHER: UNKNOWN
Tara Taylor Quinn

CHAPTER ONE

"YOUR NAME IS ANNA."

Anna. She wasn't sure she liked the name. Certainly didn't feel any affinity to it, any sense of ownership. Her heart started to pound.

"No one seems to know who you are," the doctor said almost conversationally. "You didn't have ID on you when they brought you in, just a locket around your neck engraved with that name. We were hoping you could tell us more."

Terror threatening to consume her, she shook her head. "Where am I?" Even her voice was unfamiliar, husky.

She tried not to flinch as he lifted her eyelids and shone his light into her eyes. "You're on the fifth floor of Madison General Hospital in New York City. I'm Dr. Gordon, a neurologist and your attending physician." The tall, thin white-coated man spoke as if reassuring a child.

New York.

"What day is it?"

"Tuesday. The first of July."

July. Summer.

"How long have I been here?"

"Since late yesterday afternoon."

She digested that piece of information slowly, but the cotton wool surrounding her mind remained alarmingly intact. Time meant nothing to her, either, it seemed. "What's wrong with me? Why don't I remember anything?" she cried.

"You took quite a bump on the head, and though the tests show no real damage, temporary memory loss isn't that unusual in this type of situation. If you'll just relax, things will probably start coming back to you almost immediately. In a few days you should be just fine," the doctor said with a smile, although he was watching her intently. "The baby doesn't seem to have suffered at all."

"Baby?" she whispered. *What baby? Where?* She looked around her at the sterile empty room. "I have a baby?"

"You're eight weeks pregnant, Anna," he said, feeling her pulse. His watchful eyes continued to study her.

Anna. Pregnant. Pregnant Anna.

"None of this sounds familiar?" the doctor asked kindly.

She shook her head, and her fear increased when she saw the disappointment cross his face. Both he and the nurse who'd been in her room when she awoke had been kind to her. She clung to that kindness as Dr. Gordon's words failed to jar any memory from her at all.

"Well, just to be certain that there wasn't more damage than at first appeared, I'm going to write an order for more tests this afternoon. But don't worry, Anna, traumatic memory loss isn't uncommon. Chances are your memory will return shortly."

And what if it doesn't?

Dr. Gordon continued to explain her condition, speaking of a subway crash she had no recollection of, the trauma to her brain, the news bulletins being issued statewide in an attempt to reach anyone who knew her. But his words were like background noise, an irritation, nearly drowned out by the voice in her head aimlessly repeating the only words that meant anything to her—and yet meant, frighteningly, nothing at all. *Anna. Pregnant.*

She didn't feel like an Anna. She ran her hand along the flatness of her belly beneath the stark white hospital sheet. And she certainly didn't feel pregnant.

A baby. Surely the doctor was wrong. She'd remember something as important as a baby growing inside of her. She'd remember the man who'd helped put it there. Wouldn't she? Her chest constricted, making it difficult to breathe.

"Am I crazy, Doctor?"

"No! Of course not." He patted her foot beneath the covers. "The mind has its own ways of dealing with shock. Yours is merely doing its job, protecting you to get you through a hellish ordeal. You were one of the lucky ones, coming out of the crash virtually unscathed."

Anna nodded.

"Do you have any more questions?"

Of course she did. A million of them. But only one that mattered. And apparently one he couldn't answer. *Who* am *I?*

She shook her head again, harder. And then wished she hadn't as a wave of dizziness washed over her. She did have another question. *What's going to happen to me?* But she didn't ask it. She couldn't. Not yet. She was too afraid of the answer.

"We'll talk later," the doctor said, smiling down at her. "Right now you just need to rest—and eat. You're far too thin."

Was she? Tears flooded Anna's eyes as she realized the doctor knew her body better than she did. Did she have freckles? Birthmarks he knew about and she didn't? Scars she wouldn't know the history of? What color were her eyes? Was there anyone she knew on the subway with her?

"Do you have a mirror?" she asked, hoping he couldn't hear the panic in her voice. How did you live in a stranger's body, in a stranger's mind?

"I'll have a nurse bring one in." Dr. Gordon turned away, almost as if he was finding this incredibly horrible situation as difficult as she was. "You probably have your own obstetrician, but I'm going to send Dr. Amy Litton in to see you later today to talk to you about vitamins and prenatal care. She was called in yesterday when your condition was first discovered. In the meantime try to rest, Anna. There'll be plenty of time for questions tomorrow."

Tomorrow. Anna lay completely still after the doctor left, her heart pounding as his last word brought on another attack of sheer terror. Tomorrow. How could she face tomorrow when she didn't even recognize today?

Dear God. What's to become of me? Slowly, concentrating, absorbing every sensation, she pulled her hands up the sides of her body and out from under the sheet she'd found tucked around her when she'd first awoken. Her skin was soft, her breasts firm, full. But she was bony, just like the doctor had said. Hadn't she had enough money to eat properly? And what about the baby? If there really was one, had she been taking care of it?

She reached for her hair with trembling fingers. A band at the back of her neck held it in place. So it was long. Long enough for a ponytail. Her fingers explored slowly. The strands weren't silky smooth as she somehow knew they usually were; she needed to wash it. Grabbing her ponytail, she pulled her hair around where she could see it. Blond.

She didn't know what she'd been expecting, but she didn't feel like a blonde any more than she felt like an Anna. Or an expectant mother.

Ceasing her exploration, Anna raised her fist to her mouth, stifling a sob, trying to remember something—anything. And drew a complete blank. What about her baby's father? Had he been on the subway with her? Was he lying in this very hospital, unidentified, as she was? Was he hurt? Or worse? Nausea assailed her.

What if her memory didn't come back as the doctor believed? How was she going to survive? How was she ever going to take care of herself when she didn't even know who she was? When she didn't know what she could do. If she was trained for anything. Where she came from. If she had anyone...or not.

She's pregnant. She has no memory. What's she going to do next? Anna suddenly stepped outside the situation, giving her problems to another woman, an imaginary unthreatening character over whom she had complete control. Something that felt strangely natural. All she had to do was decide what the woman was going to do next.

She's going to handle it. That's what. Somehow.

Deserting the imaginary woman, Anna slid her arms back beneath the sheet and closed her eyes. Her head hurt. A concussion, the doctor had said. A subway crash. She was lucky. Lucky. Trapped in a stranger's body, she didn't feel lucky at all.

WEEKDAY-EVENING newscaster Jason Whitaker choked on his coffee, barely setting the cup down before grabbing the remote control on the table beside him and jamming his thumb down on the rewind button. He'd been watching a clip that was scheduled for the six-o'clock news, reviewing the copy that went along with it. Thirty-seven people injured, two dead, one woman suffering from amnesia. And suddenly Anna's face had been there, transposing itself over the sketch of the woman he was going to be talking about.

Leaning forward in the chair in his dressing room, he watched the screen intently. It couldn't be... He'd just had one too many late nights. He should have gone straight home after the eleven-o'clock show last night, instead of stopping at the piano bar around the corner. He should have gone to bed at a decent hour for once, gotten some sleep—except that he'd known he wouldn't sleep. He'd have lain there in the bed he'd once shared with Anna, albeit in another city, and tear himself up wondering who she was lying with these days. Which was why he'd gone to the bar, instead.

The VCR clicked and Jason jabbed the start button. He was so tired he was seeing Anna everywhere. Even in the poor amnesiac from yesterday's subway crash. The woman shared her first name. Period. He'd better get a grip. Quickly. He hadn't seen Anna in months. It was time to be over her. To move on. To find a woman who wanted him. To find one *he* wanted.

He sat through the first part of the clip again, this time hardly registering the impossibly twisted subway train, the flattened steel of the maintenance vehicle it had collided with, the battered and broken wall that had ended the train's uncontrolled flight. Frightened people poured out of doors that had had to be forced open, some dragging bodies, others trampling over them. Emergency vehicles, police authorities, medical personnel scrambled on the screen. Tearful faces telling of panic, of despair, filled the background.

And then there she was again. Jason froze the frame. The vacant look in her eyes slammed into him, knocking the breath out of his lungs. He shook his head, trying to clear his vision, but she was still there. Not exactly as he remembered her, and yet there was no doubt that the Anna he was supposed to be reporting on was none other than the woman he'd left behind in California three months before—the woman who'd refused his offer of marriage. What was she doing in New York?

His blood pumped feverishly. Had she realized she couldn't live without him, after all? Had she come to her senses? Was she here to beg him to take her back?

The images from the clip suddenly crystallized. The tragic subway crash, the injured, the amnesia victim no one had claimed, the plea for anyone who knew the woman to contact Dr. Thomas Gordon at Madison General.

Oh, my God. The crash. Anna had been in the crash.

Blood running cold, he reached for the phone, dialing the number on the monitor in front of him.

"Dr. Thomas Gordon please." His words were clipped, and the pencil he'd picked up tapped furiously on the table.

"Who's calling, please?"

"Jason Whitaker, Channel Sixteen News." He used his position unabashedly. Anna had obviously suffered some kind of head injury. He had to know how bad it was. What else she'd suffered.

"One moment, sir."

The wait was endless. Jason was tempted to drop the phone and head immediately for Madison General. But with the Friday-afternoon New York City traffic, his chance of getting his answers any more quickly that way were nil.

"This is Tom Gordon."

"Jason Whitaker, Channel Sixteen News, Dr. Gordon. What can you tell me about your amnesia victim?"

"We sent a report to—"

"What's her current condition?" he said, cutting the doctor off. He knew about the report. He'd read and reread it. It didn't tell him what he needed to know.

"Relatively unchanged." The doctor sounded hesitant, and Jason couldn't really blame the man for taking him for an overzealous reporter looking for a scoop.

Throwing the pencil down on the table, taking a deep breath, he stared again at the monitor. "I think I may know her, Doc."

"You think you may? You aren't sure?"

"All right," Jason sighed, still not believing what his eyes insisted was true. "I do know her. Her name's Anna Hayden."

"You know her family? Where she comes from? Where she lives?" Suddenly the doctor was interviewing *him.*

"I know her family, where she comes from. I'm not sure where she's living," Jason said, still studying the vacant eyes of the pencil drawing on the television screen, the blurry photo beside it of the same woman, pale and sleeping. "I haven't seen or heard from her since I moved here three months ago."

"So she's not from New York?" the doctor asked, as if that explained something.

Jason shook his head, thinking of the little beach house Anna had shared with her sisters, those long-ago nights he and she had spent making love under the stars, the sound of the surf drowning out their cries....

"Mr. Whitaker?" The doctor's voice brought him firmly back to the present.

"She was born and raised in Oxnard, California, just north of LA. How bad is she, Doctor?"

"She's a very lucky lady, actually. A concussion, some minor contusions. Nothing that won't quickly heal. If she has someplace to go, I'll probably release her tomorrow."

Thank God. Jason expelled his breath, the knot in his stomach loosening a little.

"And her memory loss?"

"How well do you know Anna, Mr. Whitaker?"

Not nearly as well as I thought. "Very," he said. "And, please, call me Jason."

"Is there someone we can contact? Any family?"

"She has a sister. And parents, though I'm not even sure they're in the States," Jason said, suddenly afraid again. "Why? What's wrong with her, Doc?"

"I'm sorry, but I can only disclose the particulars of her case to a family member."

Frustrated, frightened and strangely hopeful as he considered Anna's presence in New York, Jason dropped the receiver back into the cradle after giving the doctor the information he needed. All he could do now was wait. And pray that Abby would call him.

He'd give her ten minutes, and then he was going to the hospital to get his information from Anna herself if he had to. He'd been in love with her for more than two years. He had a right to know whatever the doctor wasn't telling him.

And if she was alone in New York, she was going to need a friend.

ABIGALE HAYDEN gave a start, her gaze racing to the phone hanging on the wall in the kitchen of her beach cottage, daring to hope, even after two months of silence, that the caller would be Anna.

Hope dropped like lead in her stomach when the caller turned out to be male. How could Anna bear not to call? She had to be suffering the same agony at their separation that Abby was.

"Is this Abby Hayden?"

"Yes." Impatiently Abby waited for the telephone solicitor to recite his spiel so she could tell him she wasn't interested.

"I'm Dr. Thomas Gordon, a neurologist at Madison General Hospital in New York."

No, God. Please. No. She'd only assumed Anna had gone to New York. She could be wrong. She had to be wrong.

"Ms. Hayden? Are you there?"

"Yes."

"I have your sister, Anna, here, Ms. Hayden. She was on the subway that derailed…"

No! She couldn't lose Anna, too. She just couldn't. She still couldn't believe Audrey was gone, still had days when she just plain couldn't cope. If she lost Anna…

"…only minor bruises and contusions—"

"She's okay?" Abby interrupted frantically as the doctor's words started to register again. *God, please. Just let her be okay.*

"All things considered, she's a very lucky woman."

Abby's stomach clenched even more. "All things considered?" she asked, not liking the hesitancy she heard in the doctor's voice.

"Other than the memory loss I just told you about."

"Memory loss." Abby forced herself to pay attention. The doctor must think her an idiot.

"I'm afraid her amnesia is total at this point, Ms. Hayden. She didn't even know her own name."

"It's Anna." Abby blurted inanely, trying to absorb all the ramifications of the doctor's news through a fog of numbness. Anna couldn't remember her? Couldn't remember *them?* Frightened, Abby had never felt so adrift in her life.

The doctor told her more about Anna's condition; the slight concussion she'd suffered, her overall good health, her confusion. He told her about the engraved locket she'd been wearing that had been the only clue to her name.

"We all three have them," Abby said, ridiculously comforted by the fact that Anna was still wearing hers.

"Three?" Dr. Gordon asked.

"My two sisters and I," Abby said with barely a pause. "Is Anna going to be all right, Doctor? Will her memory return?" It had to return. Abby would sit with Anna every day, work with her around the clock, fill in every memory of every moment they'd ever lived if that was what it took to get her back.

"I expect it to return any time now, or at least portions of it, with the remainder following in bits and pieces. The blow she sustained wasn't particularly severe. I don't foresee any permanent damage."

"Thank God." Abby sank to the floor.

"I'd actually expected her to begin remembering already," the doctor continued, that hesitancy in his voice again. "The fact that she hasn't leads me to wonder if we're dealing with more than just shock here."

"Like what?" The fear was back stronger than ever.

"Ms. Hayden, has your sister suffered any emotional trauma lately? Anything from which she might want to escape?"

Abby almost laughed, except that she suspected the doctor would hear the hysteria in her voice. "Our sister, Audrey, died a little over a year ago."

"I'm sorry."

Abby blinked back tears when she heard the sincerity in Dr. Gordon's voice. "Me, too." She paused, took a deep breath, pushed away memories of that horrible day. "Anna handled it all pretty well, considering," she said. And then had to be honest. "Though Jason would probably know that better than I. He's probably the one you should be talking to."

"Jason Whitaker?"

"You know him?" Abby's heart rate sped up. Had she been right, then? Was Jason there with Anna now? Had the two of them managed to undo the damage Abby had done?

"I haven't actually met him. He called in answer to a story we'd put out asking for information."

"Did he say if he'd seen her recently?" Abby held her breath.

"To the contrary—he hadn't even known she was in New York. Said he hadn't heard from her in more than three months."

Oh, God.

"Do you have any idea what she's doing in New York?" the doctor asked gently. "Does she have a home here?"

Tears sprang to Abby's eyes once again, and again she forced them back. "I don't know." It was one of the hardest things she'd ever had to admit. "She called a meeting in my father's office about two months ago to tell us—my parents and me—that she was going away for a year. She said she had to prove to herself that she could get by without us to lean on. She wouldn't tell us where she was headed, and she said she wouldn't be phoning us. She made us promise we wouldn't follow or try to find her."

"And you haven't heard from her since?"

Not in fifty-nine hellish days. "No."

"Do you know if she went alone?"

"No. But I'd hoped she went to Jason."

"Apparently not."

"So what's she doing in New York?" Abby cried, more to herself than to Anna's doctor.

"That seems to be one of many things locked away in your sister's mind at the moment."

"There's more?" Abby asked.

"Anna's about eight weeks pregnant."

The fog swirled around Abby, cloaking her, making it nearly impossible for her to form coherent thoughts. Anna, pregnant? And Abby hadn't known? Hadn't felt…something? There had to be a mistake.

"How?" she asked, slowly getting to her feet.

The doctor coughed. "In the usual way, I suppose."

"Who's the father?"

"I was hoping you could shed some light on that."

Abby shook her head. She could think of no one. Only Jason. It had always been only Jason. And if he hadn't seen Anna…

"…so, I'd like to fax you some information on amnesia, various theories and treatments, if you have someplace you can receive a fax…"

Abby tuned in again in time to rattle off the fax number at the shop. And to inform the doctor, when he asked, that her parents were vacationing abroad, but that she'd leave word immediately for them to call her. Not that she expected much support from them once they learned Anna wasn't in any real danger.

"What happens next?" Abby asked, already looking through a drawer in the kitchen for the number of their travel agent.

"That, in part, depends on Anna. And on you, too." He paused, took a breath. "My recommendation is that you tell Anna nothing, let her remember on her own—particularly because we don't know what aspects of her life she might be trying to escape. But I want you to read the information I'm sending before you make any decisions."

Abby nodded, still looking for the number. "Is Jason with her?" she asked.

"Not yet," Dr. Gordon said. "I wasn't at liberty to apprise him of Anna's particulars without first checking with her family. Especially in a case like this when Anna can't possibly vouch for him herself."

"I'd trust Jason Whitaker with my life, Doctor," Abby answered immediately, almost defensively. "And Anna's, too." He'd been their strength after Audrey died—and so much more. He'd taught them to laugh again.

"Would you like me to call him?" the doctor asked.

"No." Abby stopped rummaging through the drawer. "I'll do it myself." The phone call wouldn't be easy, but she owed it to Jason. She owed him something else, as well, and knew, suddenly, that she'd just been handed a way to right the terrible wrong she'd done Anna and Jason. If she was strong enough.

"Dr. Gordon?" she said quickly, before she lost her courage.

"Yes?"

"As long as Jason's there and I'm not, and assuming he's willing, he's in charge." If Abby hadn't interfered, the right would have been his, anyway. He'd have been Anna's husband by now.

"You're sure?"

She'd never been less sure of anything in her life. "Any choices that have to be made come from him," she said firmly. And then, more for herself than for the doctor, she added, "I'll abide by whatever decisions he makes." With her eyes squeezed tight against escaping tears, she prayed to God that Jason would include her every step of the way.

Though, with her history of unanswered prayers, that didn't seem likely.

NINE AND A HALF MINUTES after he'd hung up from Dr. Gordon, Jason's telephone rang.

He grabbed the receiver. "Abby?"

"Jason?" Anna's sister was distraught, as he'd known she'd be. The amazing thing was she'd called him.

"I can't believe this is happening," she said, hardly a trace of the old Abby in her subdued tone. "Dr. Gordon says you haven't seen her?"

"Only on a piece of footage. I was waiting to hear from you," Jason said, trying to gauge her mood—their relationship. "What else did Dr. Gordon say?"

"He said Anna's fine other than the amnesia," she told him. "He needs to know if there are any emotional traumas she might be trying to block." Abby paused. "I told him you would probably know that better than I."

He could hear the hurt in her tone, mingling with her worry. Not that he blamed her. He'd accused her of some pretty nasty things before leaving California. And she *did* have a tendency to control things, always thinking she knew best for everybody, but it hadn't really been her fault that Anna had chosen to stay with her only living triplet, instead of moving across the country with him.

"Did you tell him about Audrey?" Jason asked gently. He loved Abby like a sister. He was sorry he'd hurt her, sorry, too, that Anna's love for him had hurt her.

"Briefly." She paused, then said in a rush, "But then I discovered that I really don't know how Anna dealt with all that. I mean, she never talked to me about it very much." Another pause. "Which is why I told Dr. Gordon he was probably better off speaking with you." Her last words, an admission that had to have cost her plenty, were almost a whisper.

"She never talked to me much about it, either, Abby," he said, feeling compelled to ease her obvious suffering. "You know Anna, she's always been the type who keeps her pain to herself."

A heavy silence hung on the line. Jason would have moved

mountains to turn back time, to erase that last scene with Abby. He'd missed her. He'd missed them all.

"Will you talk to him, Jason? Please?" she finally asked.

"Sure. Of course. You know I will."

Another silence and then, tentatively, "So she hasn't been with you these past two months?" It sounded as if she was fighting the tears another person would have cried. Which was so like Abby. Always intent on remaining in control.

"I wish," he said. And then the significance of her question hit him. "You don't know where she's been? She's been away from home for two months?"

"I hoped she was with you." Abby lost her battle with the tears.

"I haven't heard from her since I left California. What's going on, Abby?"

"I don't know," she whispered, sniffing. He could picture her standing in the kitchen of the beach house, scrubbing at her nose with a tissue, her long blond hair falling around her shoulders. "She called a meeting with me and the folks just a few weeks after you left, said she was going away for a year—had to know whether or not she could make it on her own." Abby paused, taking a deep breath, and then continued, "She made us promise not to follow her or contact her until the year was up, at which time she promised to come home—at least for a visit."

His own disappointment was crushing. She'd been gone for two months. She hadn't just left home, just arrived in New York. She'd had two months to contact him. And she hadn't.

"What did I do, Jason? Why won't she talk to me anymore?" Abby cried.

"I don't think it's just you, Abby," he said, glancing again at the vacant stare on the sketch still frozen on his television monitor. "Audrey's death brought home to Anna that the three of you were three separate beings, not one whole as she'd always thought. Maybe she just needs to find out who her part of the threesome really is."

He hoped so. God he hoped so. Because until Anna truly believed she could survive apart from her identical sisters, she'd never be able to live her own life, to love.

"Maybe." Abby didn't sound convinced. And Jason had to admit that his reasoning was probably just wishful thinking.

"How soon are you flying out?" Jason asked, a little surprised she wasn't already on her way. Abby had pulled her sisters through every crisis in their lives.

"I'm going to reserve a flight for tomorrow, but I'll wait to hear from you before I buy the ticket. I won't come if Anna doesn't want me there."

Shocked, Jason said, "It sounds to me like she's not going to know what she wants." What the hell was going on?

"You'll call me as soon as you see her? As soon as you talk to Dr. Gordon?"

"Of course."

"Jason?" her voice was tentative again, but warmer. "You really haven't seen her since you left here?" she asked. "Not even once?"

"No."

"Oh."

"I'll call you later," he said, anxious to get to the hospital, to find out just what he was dealing with.

"Jason?" She hesitated. "I, uh, told Dr. Gordon that you're in charge." Another hesitation when Jason had no idea what to say. "For as long as you want to be," she finished.

Jason had waited too long for Abby to abdicate a single decision in Anna's life to quarrel over the fact that she was doing so three months too late. "Fine."

"You'll be there for her, won't you, Jason? No matter what you find?"

Her query was odd enough to send a fresh wave of apprehension through him. Was Anna's amnesia more serious than he thought? Was it permanent?

"As long as she needs me," he said, wondering if she ever really had. The Hayden sisters had grown up in their own little cocoon, buffered from the world by the unusual bond they shared, a bond made stronger by having been born to two people who were wonderful providers but terrible parents. He'd been a fool to think he could ever penetrate that cocoon, be a part of their world. But then, when it came to relationships, he'd always been something of a fool.

CHAPTER TWO

ANNA WANTED OUT. It was bad enough being mentally trapped, but to be stuck in a hospital room, too, was driving her insane. After another nap, a huge lunch and a visit from Dr. Litton, she was ready to get on with things. Whatever they were.

As she lay in bed, her restlessness grew. She needed to take a long walk, to smell the breeze. To do something.

But fear kept her paralyzed. What would she do? Where would she go? What clothes was she going to wear to get there? She could hardly wander around New York City dressed in a hospital gown. Her nurse had told her not to worry, that the city was assuming full liability; she'd have money for new clothes, might even end up a rich woman when all was said and done. Her nurse didn't seem to understand that money was the least of Anna's worries at the moment.

She'd had the second set of tests Dr. Gordon ordered, but she hadn't seen him again since she'd awoken that morning. Was it a bad sign that so many hours had passed and she still hadn't remembered a single thing? She was trying to relax like he'd said, but was beginning to suspect it was time to panic.

What happened to people like her? Were they institutionalized? Locked away until their only reality was the walls around them? If so, she'd rather have died in the subway crash.

Her gaze darted desperately about the small room—and alighted on the pamphlets Dr. Litton had left for her to read. The authorities couldn't put her away. At least not anytime soon. She was going to have a baby.

Picking up one of the pamphlets, Anna's panic eased just a bit. She liked Dr. Litton. Whether or not she ever remembered seeing another obstetrician, she wanted Dr. Litton to help her bring this baby into the world.

Baby. She was going to have a baby. Sometime around the middle of January.

As crazy as it seemed, Anna was glad.

DR. GORDON HAD a gentle bearing that bespoke calm, as well as confidence. Jason liked the middle-aged man immediately. Sitting in the doctor's office at Madison General, he listened intently while Dr. Gordon described Anna's condition.

"Her amnesia is a direct result of a blow to the lower left portion of her cranium. As the brain doesn't appear to be anything more than superficially bruised, I must wonder if perhaps her subconscious has used the impact as an opportunity to escape something that came before the crash," he said, joining Jason on the couch opposite his desk.

"You mean, something she saw just before the accident, something like that?" Jason asked.

"Possibly." The doctor's clasped hands lay across his stomach. "But I would expect the memory loss to cover just those few minutes if that were the case."

"Are you saying there's more to her condition than just the crash?"

"I believe she might be suffering from a post-traumatic stress form of amnesia, sometimes called hysterical amnesia."

Jason's blood ran cold. Was the doctor trying to tell him Anna's condition was permanent? That she was mentally ill?

"Which means what?" he asked. They'd handle it. Whatever it was, they'd handle it together. His right leg started to move up and down rapidly, the motion barely discernible, keeping time with his thoughts.

"Simply that she was suffering from an emotional crisis that was more than she believed she could bear. When she hit her head, lost consciousness, her subconscious grabbed the opportunity to escape."

"Permanently?"

"Most likely not," Dr. Gordon said. "When her subconscious believes she can handle whatever it is she's trying to escape from, her memory will return. Though probably not all at once."

Jason stared silently at the doctor, trying desperately to grasp the big picture. He had so many questions vying for attention, he couldn't settle on a single one of them.

"This reaction is really quite healthy in one sense," Dr. Gordon said, as if he knew Jason needed a little time to arrange his thoughts. "Rather than having a breakdown or falling prey to various other stress-induced mental and physical disorders, Anna is simply taking a vacation, gaining herself a little time to shore up the defenses necessary to handle whatever it is that's bothering her."

Jason's heart faltered as he realized the extent of the pain Anna must have been in to react like this. "How long do you think it's going to take?"

Shrugging, Dr. Gordon sat forward, steepling his fingers in front of him. "That's entirely up to Anna." He looked directly at Jason, his expression serious. "Her sister tells me you might be able to shed some light on whatever it is Anna's running from."

"Abby told you about Audrey?"

"Only that she died last year."

"Did she tell you the three of them were identical triplets?"

"No!" The doctor frowned. "But that explains a lot. The premature death of a sibling—only twenty-seven, Abby told me—is hard enough to cope with, but the loss of an identical sibling..."

Jason thought of that time, the horror. Hell, he'd been practically living at the beach house, ready to ask Anna to marry him, when their world had exploded around them.

"Audrey didn't just die, Doctor, she was murdered," he said, his throat dry. An entire year had passed—and the pain was still as fresh as if the murder had happened yesterday.

The doctor moved to the seat behind his desk, grabbing a pad of paper. "What happened?"

Jason shrugged. "No one knows for sure. After months of investigation the police determined that the whole thing was the result of an attempted assault that Audrey resisted."

"You say that as if you don't agree." Dr. Gordon looked up.

"I have no reason to doubt them, except that Audrey wasn't the type to resist...anything. She was the baby of the threesome and always seemed to take the easiest route."

"Did Anna accept the police explanation?"

Again Jason shrugged. "Let's just say she never expressed any disagreement with it. But then Anna has always kept her thoughts to herself. Comes from being the middle triplet I guess." His leg continued to vibrate, marking time.

"What about the girls' parents? Abby said this afternoon that they're in Italy. Do they travel a lot or were they around at the time of Audrey's murder?"

"They were around, as much as they ever are. The Haydens love their daughters, but they make much better entrepreneurs than they do—or ever did—parents." Jason thought of the handsome older couple, of how little he knew them, considering all the time he'd spent at their daughters' beach house the past couple of years. "The triplets weren't planned," he told the doctor. "I've pretty much figured out that practically from the stage they were in diapers, Abby stepped in to fill the void their parents' frequent absences left in the girls' lives. She's always watched out for them, made their business her business, bossed them around." He studied the diamond pattern in Dr. Gordon's tie. "But she's also, in all the years I've known them, put their needs before her own."

Dr. Gordon stopped writing and laid down his pen. "And yet Abby tells me that she hasn't seen or heard from her sister in over two months. From what you describe, this in itself is highly unusual."

"It is. I can hardly believe it." Standing, Jason paced slowly around the couch. "In all the time I've known Anna, she's never made a move without discussing it with Abby first." He shook his head. "I actually thought Anna's leaving was a good sign when Abby told me about it," he admitted. "I hoped it meant that Anna was finally beginning to believe she's a person in her own right, not just a third of a whole."

"Seems logical." The doctor nodded. "Or at least that Anna was ready to find out one way or the other. According to her sister, Anna said she was leaving to prove to herself that she could handle life on her own—apart from her family."

Jason stopped pacing and placed his hands on the back of the couch. "Do you think this could be what's behind her amnesia? Is she maybe allowing herself a respite from the compulsion to return to California, time to find out who she is apart from Abby?"

"I suppose it's possible," Dr. Gordon said, frowning again. "She might even have been at war with herself—unable to make it on her own, unable to cope with *not* being able to make it alone."

"You don't sound convinced."

The doctor fixed Jason with an intent look and asked, "Just what is your relationship with Anna?"

Jason resumed his pacing. With the past three months uppermost in his mind—that last terrible scene with Anna still haunting him—he wasn't sure how to answer.

"We're friends," he said finally, stopping once again behind the couch and clutching the frame.

"You said when you called earlier that you haven't seen her since you left California, that you didn't know she was in New York?" Dr. Gordon continued to probe.

"That's correct," Jason admitted.

"Did her sister say anything to you about anyone else in Anna's life? Someone she may have been seeing? Either before she left home or just after?"

Jason shook his head. "No one's heard from her in two months. Why?" he asked, although judging by the concern in the doctor's face, he was pretty sure he didn't want to know. Had Anna said someone's name in her sleep? Someone none of them knew?

"She's pregnant."

Jason's knuckles turned white as he gripped the back of the couch. He'd heard wrong. He thought the doctor had said Anna was pregnant.

"Under the circumstances I can't help but wonder..." Dr. Gordon's words were muted by the roaring in Jason's ears. "...perhaps Anna's pregnancy is what she's hiding from. At no more than two months, she can't have known very long herself..."

Two months pregnant. God. No.

"...entirely possible she's not ready to handle the circumstances behind the child's conception."

Conception. I haven't slept with her in over three months. Oh, God. No!

"You think she was raped?" Jason's voice was a rasp. *Please, God, not my precious Anna. Anything but that.*

"It's possible." Dr. Gordon shrugged. "But I don't think so.

The amnesia appears to have affected only the personal portion of her memory, not the memory that controls basic needs. If she'd been raped, I would expect to see signs of fear for her physical self, even if she didn't understand why she felt those fears.''

The back of Jason's neck ached. "So, what..." his words trailed away. He couldn't believe it. Anna was pregnant. With another man's child. The world had tilted on its axis and he had a feeling it wasn't ever going to right itself again.

Dr. Gordon stood up, coming around to lean one hip on the corner of his desk. "It's my belief that Anna's amnesia is emotionally based," he said. "That she's running from something. Perhaps she doesn't want the baby." He lifted a hand and let it drop back to, his thigh. "Maybe the father is married, or maybe it's someone her family wouldn't approve of, or even someone who didn't want her."

None of which applied to Jason. He continued to grip the back of the couch, using it to hold himself upright. He thought he was going to puke. If, by some miracle, Anna's baby had been his, she'd have known she could come to him. She *would* have come to him simply because she would never have kept something like this from him.

The phone rang and Dr. Gordon excused himself, turning his back as he picked up the receiver and spoke quietly.

Jason continued to stand, still as a statue, his thoughts torturing him. Anna's family, her sister, would have been supportive if Anna was pregnant with his child. He'd been a part of them for so long he'd forgotten they weren't actually his family—until the day Anna had told him she wouldn't marry him, wouldn't move to New York with him. The day Anna had chosen Abby. Two days later Jason had hunted Abby down, hurling all his anguish, his pain at her.

But even that had been more like a brother furious with his sister than anything else.

Left to his thoughts as the doctor continued his low-voiced conversation, Jason faced the truth. Anna was no more than two months pregnant. He hadn't slept with her in more than three. Anna had been with someone else. Her baby wasn't his.

So what was wrong with the bastard? Why wasn't he here now, claiming her, claiming his child? Was he someone who, as Dr.

Gordon suggested, would shock her family? Family was the one thing that mattered most to Anna—or at least Abby was. Anna truly didn't believe she could exist without Abby. He'd learned that the hard way. Had this other guy, too? Had Anna loved him and then sent him out of her life?

"Sorry about that," Dr. Gordon said, hanging up the phone. "My wife's pregnant with our first child at forty-one, and she's a nervous wreck." He shook his head. "We were all set to adopt, and my wife suddenly turns up pregnant. After more than ten years of trying."

Jason appreciated the doctor's attempt to lighten the moment, but he could barely manage a smile. He needed to throw something.

"You know, there's a remote possibility that Anna knew she was pregnant before she left home," Dr. Gordon said.

Jason remained silent, a raised eyebrow the only acknowledgment that he'd heard the other man.

"She could have left home to have the child in secret," the doctor continued. "She may have been planning to give the baby up for adoption without anyone ever knowing she'd had it. Hence her request for a year with no contact."

She'd left home only four weeks after he'd last seen her. Could the baby possibly be his, after all? Jason wondered. Had she taken their breakup to mean he wouldn't expect to know if he'd fathered a child? The thought wasn't pleasant.

"You said she's two months along. Could she be more? Say thirteen, fourteen weeks?"

Dr. Gordon shook his head. "I seriously doubt it. Judging by the baby's measurements from yesterday's ultrasound, eight weeks is just about max. Could be closer, in fact, to six or seven."

"But you just said she may have known about the pregnancy before she left."

The doctor shrugged. "With early detection, women can sometimes know within days after conception," he said. "Then again, she may have known only that she'd had unprotected intercourse at her fertile time."

In that instant the vulnerable part of Jason that had somehow survived his childhood died. While he'd been making himself crazy with wanting Anna, she'd been making a baby with someone else.

Hell, maybe there'd been someone else all along. Maybe that was why she wouldn't marry him. Maybe the unusual bond between Anna and Abby wasn't the problem at all—but rather, an excuse.

No. That didn't ring true. He knew that Anna would never have made love with another man while still sleeping with him. He knew, too, that her bond with Abby *had* been the biggest rift between them. Still, Jason couldn't escape one undeniable fact. Anna was pregnant and he wasn't the father.

She must have fallen head over heels in love with someone the second he left town. And if that was the case, he really had no one to blame but himself. He'd given her an ultimatum. And then he'd walked out on her.

Which was just what he wanted to do again.

Dr. Gordon's name suddenly came over the loudspeaker. "I'm going to have to go," he said. "If you don't mind, I'd like you to wait to visit Anna until I can go with you," he added, putting Anna's file back together.

Jason nodded, grateful for the reprieve.

"Can you meet me here this evening, say, around eight?"

Eight o'clock was right between shows. He could make it back. But he knew he'd have been there even if it wasn't convenient. "You think she might remember something when she sees me?" he asked, following the doctor out into the hall.

"It's possible," Tom Gordon said. "I think we need to be prepared for that eventuality. See you at eight," he called as he rounded the corner and was gone from sight.

Jason strode from the chilly hospital into the warm July sun, as if by leaving the building he could leave behind everything that waited for him there. Except that Anna was still in his heart, and he had to take that with him.

ABBY WAITED for his call. She had errands to run, some fabric to pick up for the shop, an order to deliver to the new kids' shop out by Beverly Center, but it all had to wait. When Jason heard what Dr. Gordon had to tell him, he was going to need to talk. Abby would have told him herself except she hadn't had that much courage. Hadn't been able to bring herself to hurt him again.

They hadn't parted well. And because of that last horrible scene, they'd both been awkward on the phone earlier. But he was family. By virtue of his love for her sister, his unending support to all of them when Audrey was killed the year before, he was family. Besides, as much as she hated the things he'd said to her that last day, the brutal accusations, she was grateful to him, too. If not for him, she probably never would have seen that she was ruining her sister's life with her controlling ways. When her sister had come to her telling her she was leaving, she'd have talked her into staying. Because she'd have been so sure that staying would have been best for Anna.

She wasn't sure about anything anymore. Except that Jason would call. Because of the baby. And she owed it to him to be there when he did. He was going to be devastated.

He'd been on her conscience for three long months. She'd never seen anyone as hurt, as bitter, as he'd been the day he'd stormed into the back of the shop. And he'd been right to accuse her of creating a rift between Anna and him.

She'd ruined his life. And probably Anna's, too. She'd never seen two people more in love, more suited to each other than Anna and Jason. And she'd been too selfish to free her only living triplet from *their* bond, to let Anna share an even closer bond with the man she loved. She'd been too blissfully blind to see that she had the power to hold Anna—or to let her go. She'd been so sure she and Anna were meant to live out their lives together, neither one making a decision without the other—almost as if she, Abby, had one part of their brain and Anna another. Audrey had had the third.

It had always been that way. The three of them together, through thick and thin, grades and boyfriends, lost friends and forgotten birthdays. No one had ever told them it would ever be any different. They were a package deal, their fate sealed in their mother's womb.

The phone rang, and Abby jumped, knocking over a stool as she grabbed for the telephone hanging on the wall.

It was Jason. And doing worse than she'd feared.

"You've heard," Abby said. She was having trouble comprehending that Anna was pregnant without her knowing, without her sharing in Anna's elation, her excitement, her fears. Jason had to be feeling ten times worse.

"Who is he?"

Tears sprang to her eyes at the raw emotion in his voice. "I don't know. I was praying it was you."

"No chance."

"Oh, God."

Silence fell heavily on the line. Abby felt as if she was coming unglued. She could hardly concentrate, couldn't make sense out of the past six hours at all. Her sister had been a victim in a serious accident, had amnesia and was pregnant, and she'd known nothing about any of it. Shouldn't she have sensed Anna's need? *Shouldn't Anna have reached out to her?*

"Have you seen her?" she asked, unable to stand the silence any longer.

"No." The single syllable was racked with pain.

Abby was almost afraid to ask. "Are you going to see her?" Anna would be all right if Jason was there. She didn't know why she was so sure of that, but she was.

"Of course," he said, and Abby heaved a sigh of relief. "Dr. Gordon was called away in the middle of our meeting," Jason continued, "but he asked me to wait to see her until he can go with me."

He didn't sound like he objected to the delay all that much. "Does he expect something to happen when she sees you?"

"I don't think he knows what to expect," Jason said on a sigh. "This is Anna's show all the way."

"She loved you, Jason, with all her heart," Abby felt compelled to tell him.

"Right." His sarcastic tone cracked across the wire.

"Those weeks after you left were awful." Abby insisted. "I've never seen Anna like that, not even after Audrey died."

"Yeah, well, apparently she recovered."

Abby had to find a way to make this all better. There was no one in the world she loved more than Anna—but Jason came in a close second. She'd always wanted a big brother, had often fantasized as a child about having someone older and stronger to look after them.

"Maybe he was just a one-night stand," Abby said in a rush. "You know, someone she turned to in a fit of loneliness, pretending he was you."

"Maybe."

He wasn't buying it and she couldn't blame him. But neither could she imagine, in any way, shape or form, that Anna had fallen in love with another man. Her sister was too besotted with Jason even to look at anyone else. Anna was the most steadfast person she'd ever known, and she'd given her heart completely to one man. She just wasn't the type to give it to another, not if she lived to be a hundred and never saw Jason again in her life. That was Anna. Though even Abby hadn't understood the depth of Anna's commitment—not until she'd seen what having to choose between conflicting commitments had done to her sister.

"What are you going to tell her?" Abby asked. She was almost afraid to hear the answer. Would Anna hate her when she heard about the part Abby had played in her life? If Anna had no memory of her love for her sister, Abby could well believe it.

"I don't know, yet," Jason said. "I suspect that's one of the things Dr. Gordon will go over before we see her."

He sounded tired and Abby's guilt grew.

"Call me, okay?"

"Yeah. You coming out?" he asked.

Abby shook her head, her tears finally brimming and falling down her face. "I don't know," she said. She wanted to—more than anything. But only if Anna and Jason both wanted her there. "I'll wait and see what happens tonight."

And she would. Wait right by the phone. She simply didn't know what else to do. Her entire life had consisted of taking care of her sisters, getting them out of scraps, Audrey mostly, guiding them, loving them when their parents weren't around to do it. But Audrey was dead. And Anna no longer remembered her. So what was left?

CHAPTER THREE

HE DID THE NEWS BROADCAST. He even gave the report on Anna. For all he knew, the father of her child was in the city somewhere, willing to claim her. Jason almost hoped another man *would* come forward—then he, Jason, would be free to walk away. But somehow, as he took a cab back to the hospital shortly before eight, he had a feeling that no matter what transpired, he wasn't going to be free from Anna Hayden for a very long time. Possibly never.

And in the meantime no one had reported her missing. She was all alone—and pregnant—in a strange city, thousands of miles from home. He couldn't walk away. He couldn't leave her lying there. But neither could he help wishing that the child she was carrying was his, that by some fluke her baby could really have been conceived fourteen weeks ago, instead of eight. That he actually had a right to be the one to care for her, to claim her.

The sick feeling increased as soon as he walked in the door of Dr. Gordon's office. There was nothing wrong with the room. Standard desk littered with charts, bland blue couch and matching armchairs, carpet, diplomas on the wall, and books. Lots of books. But Jason hated the room; he hated being there.

Hanging up the phone as Jason walked in, Dr. Gordon frowned. "That was the police," he said. "No one's come forward, yet."

Jason nodded, truly undecided whether this was good news or bad.

"Do you think she'll know me?" Jason asked the question that was uppermost in his mind. This wasn't how he'd pictured his reunion with Anna. In every single one of his fantasies, she not only knew who he was, but insisted she couldn't live without him.

The doctor leaned his hip on the corner of his desk. "It's possible she'll recognize you," he said. "But don't be surprised if she doesn't."

"Is she, you know, normal? Other than her memory, that is?" he asked quickly.

"Her intelligence hasn't been affected, if that's what you've been imagining," Dr. Gordon said, smiling. "Information is stored in many different areas of the brain. General learned information is separate from personal or emotional memories, for example. Apparently the only area in Anna's brain that's been affected is this last one," he said. "Which is, again, why I feel certain that she's suffering from hysterical amnesia."

At least somewhat relieved by the doctor's words, Jason asked, "So do we tell her who I am?"

The doctor gave Jason an assessing stare. "How recent is your personal history with her?"

"I'm that obvious?" Jason asked. It was impossible to feel embarrassed with this man.

"Not really," the doctor said. "But her pregnancy hit you hard."

Jason nodded. "I asked her to marry me a little over three months ago," he admitted. "She refused."

Dr. Gordon watched him for another moment and then got up to go sit behind his desk. "I'm sure there's more there, but I've heard enough to know that if she doesn't recognize you, we're going to have to proceed with caution." He pulled some printed material from a folder on top of his desk and handed it to Jason.

"I ran this off for you earlier," he said. "You're going to find that amnesia isn't treated like other mental illnesses. Some doctors are skeptical about its even being a valid diagnosis."

"They'd think Anna's faking it?" Jason asked.

The doctor shrugged.

"Do you think she is?"

"I'm certain she's not," Dr. Gordon said, leaning back in his chair. "But as you read, you'll find that even among the medical professionals who do recognize amnesia as a legitimate condition, there's a vast difference in beliefs when it comes to treatment."

Jason looked down at the pages the doctor had given him, and then back at Dr. Gordon. The man had instilled trust from the moment Jason had met him.

"Go on," he said.

"All right, I will give you my recommendations, but with the understanding that after you've done some reading, you call in other opinions if you feel the need.''

"I'll fax the stuff to Abby tonight."

The doctor shook his head. "No need," he said. "I've already done it. I spoke to her again a little over an hour ago."

"And?"

"She agrees, though not enthusiastically, with my recommendation, but will abide by whatever you and Anna decide."

She'd said the same to Jason earlier, but until that minute he hadn't really believed she'd follow through on it. Abdicating decision making was so un-Abby-like Jason felt his world tilt just a little bit more. Maybe this was all just one hell of an alcohol-induced nightmare.

But he knew it wasn't. Anna lay in a hospital bed just floors away from him, their love not even a memory.

Jason set the papers down beside him. "So what do you recommend?"

"Assuming she doesn't recognize you, I'd say as little as possible. Because as certain as I am that this is temporary, I have to warn you that if you try to force Anna to listen to what her mind's not ready to deal with, you could very well send her into a permanent state of memory loss. If we knew for certain what she's trying to escape, we could just avoid those areas, but since we don't, the less said the better."

Recognizing the sense in the doctor's words, Jason nodded, but he didn't like what he was hearing. How could he see Anna, possibly spend time with her and act as though he hadn't spent the best two years of his life with her? "Can I tell her I know her at all?" he asked.

"Certainly," Dr. Gordon replied, steepling his fingers under his chin as he watched Jason. "Tell her you're an old friend of the family. Tell her she *has* family. Even tell her that, according to her sister, she's in New York on a sort of year's sabbatical from her life. She should know that she demanded her family leave her alone for a year. Anything to give her confidence in her own mental strength.

"What I wouldn't do," he continued, "is tell her anything emotionally threatening. I wouldn't tell her that she's one of a set of triplets, for instance, which means that it might very well be best to keep Anna and Abby apart for the time being. You said they're identical?''

"Completely," Jason said, nodding. Though *he'd* never had trouble telling them apart. By the time he'd met her sisters, he'd already been half in love with Anna. Their resemblance to each other had taken some getting used to, though; three gorgeous, blond-haired, brown-eyed beauties. But he'd never confused them. They were such different people, in spite of their physical sameness.

"Which means it would be impossible to keep Anna's multiple-birth status a secret if the two women met, and since being one of triplets is one of the things we suspect she's running from…''

Jason nodded, following the doctor's train of thought as the older man's words trailed off.

"I also wouldn't mention Audrey's murder or your own recent breakup," Dr. Gordon continued. "All these things combined are very likely a large part of what's paralyzing her.''

"But there could be more," Jason said, thinking about what the doctor had already told him. "Something that happened in the past two months that we know nothing about. Something to do with the baby.''

What hurt most of all was knowing Anna had been in New York, in trouble, and she hadn't called him. That, more than anything else, killed the hope he'd been harboring that she would one day come back to him.

"I suspect that Anna's suffering from not one huge trauma, but rather a combination of traumas—put together, they became too much for her. I'd say most definitely something in the past two months has contributed to her current condition.''

Jason nodded numbly as he accepted the need to ride this thing out. To let Anna remember her life in her own time. "How soon can she leave here?" he asked.

"Tomorrow if she has a place to go. Physically there's no reason for her to stay in the hospital.''

"She has a place." It didn't matter how stupid he knew it was, he couldn't have walked away from Anna if his life had depended on it.

Dr. Gordon stood up, accepting Jason's claim without further question, as if he'd been expecting the response. "Are you ready to see her?"

As ready as he was going to get, Jason thought. But still... "There's no chance she's three months pregnant?" He felt compelled to try one more time.

Dr. Gordon shrugged, heading for the door. "Anything is possible," he said—but he didn't sound like he believed it. "Anna's underweight, which could make her baby small."

The doctor stopped, looking at Jason, one male to another. "You want my professional opinion?"

Jason looked away from the pity reflected in the other man's eyes. He was done fooling himself with false hopes, with dreams.

"Of course."

"She's eight weeks along."

Filled with apprehension, his stomach tied in knots, he followed the doctor from the room. After three months of being haunted by images of this moment, none of which were even remotely accurate, he was finally about to see the woman he loved again.

STROLLING DOWN the hallway for what seemed like the hundredth time, Anna studied everything around her. Surely something would spark a memory. A color, an emblem, a hairdo. Something must be familiar to her.

But nothing was. Except for the nurse who'd been caring for her most of the day. Anna smiled as the woman hurried past. Eileen. One of the three people Anna knew by name in the whole world. The other two were the doctors who'd visited her that day. Ready to climb the walls, instead of walking calmly beside them, she returned to her room and slipped back into bed, deciding it was more comfortable than the chair by the window. She knew, because she'd spent more time than she cared to think about in the chair that afternoon staring out into the summer sunshine, hoping to see someone or something she recognized, and then she'd remember.

There was no reason for her to remain in the hospital taking up a bed someone else might need. Physically she felt fine. Amazingly unaffected by the crash, considering the fact that she was two months pregnant.

But if she left the hospital, where would she go? How would she get there? What would she do once she arrived? Where would she get the money to survive? Especially if the city hadn't settled with the accident victims yet?

She started to shake when she came up with no answers. Because she had to do something. She could hardly raise her baby in a hospital room.

Nervously she reached for the chain around her neck, pulling the locket out from beneath her hospital gown. She'd kept the locket on all day because it had her name on the inside, but she didn't like wearing it. Though it appeared to be good quality gold, it had a very odd shape. Reaching up, she unclasped the chain, pulling it from around her neck, and suddenly felt better than she had in hours. Freer. She could no more explain the odd sensation than she could say who'd fathered her child, but she decided to leave the chain off.

She lay back against the mound of pillows, the locket clutched in her fist. She was going to have to find someplace safe to keep it. As much as she didn't want to wear it, she couldn't bear the thought of losing it.

Men's voices could be heard just down the hall, and Anna sat up straighter in anticipation. *Dr. Gordon.* When you only knew three people in the world, it was an event to see one of them. And if anyone could make this feeling of panic go away, Dr. Gordon could.

They came into the room together, Dr. Gordon and an incredibly handsome man. He was tall, well over six feet, with thick blond hair and blue, blue eyes. She could tell because they were trained right on her. As Dr. Gordon came forward, the stranger's eyes never left Anna, never even glanced around the room. A part of her was aware that she should be uncomfortable, maybe even offended by that piercing stare, but instead, all she wanted to do was stare right back. Her heart sped up in excitement.

"Anna, I've brought someone to meet you," Dr. Gordon said, ushering the stranger forward. "This is Jason Whitaker, a longtime friend of your family."

Her heart continued its rapid beat, but now it was in fear. *She didn't recognize him at all.* Her gaze flew to Dr. Gordon as her mind tumbled over itself, searching frantically for something that just wasn't there. Even faced with proof of her former existence, she couldn't recall any of it. Was this it, then? Was she trapped in this terrifying void forever?

"Hello, Anna." Her head jerked toward the stranger as he spoke. He had a wonderful voice. Just not one she'd ever heard before.

"Hello." She tried to act normally, but she could hear the panic in her voice.

"Anna—" Dr. Gordon started.

"It's okay, Anna," the man called Jason Whitaker interrupted. "Just try to relax."

And strangely, although he didn't sound the least bit relaxed himself, his words had some effect. The bands around her chest loosened enough for her to speak.

"But I don't know you," she said, staring at him, at his face, at his broad-shouldered physique. She'd never seen the man before in her life.

Her words hit him hard. Not only did he flinch, but she saw the quick flash of anguish in his eyes before he quickly recovered. "It's okay, honey," he said. "Dr. Gordon warned us this might happen."

He smiled at her and there was no doubt that that, at least, was genuine.

Suddenly the ramifications of the man's presence hit her and she sat straight up. "Us?" she asked. Dr. Gordon had introduced him as a friend of the family. Which meant she *had* a family. She clutched that one small piece of information for all she was worth.

"Who am I? Where are they?" she cried, looking around.

Jason glanced at the doctor and Anna's gaze followed. Filled with a sense of foreboding, she watched as the men came forward and flanked her bed. Jason reached for her hand, but pulled back before he made contact. She couldn't believe how much she'd wanted him to touch her.

"What is it? What's wrong?" she asked. Was her family dead? Had they been in the crash with her?

"You have a sister and parents living in Oxnard, California," Dr. Gordon finally said slowly.

A sister. Parents. The relief was so great it left her light-headed. She wasn't alone.

"Do they know...about me?" she asked. Were they on their way to see her? Take her home?

The doctor nodded. "Your sister does," he said. "Your parents are traveling in Europe and your sister's still trying to reach them."

A sister. Anna smiled. She was really glad to have a sister, someone she assumed would know her like no one else in the world could. Someone she could trust.

"What's her name?" she asked, looking from one man to the other.

"Abby." Jason's voice was odd, but Anna was too overwhelmed to do more than notice.

"Abby," she said, testing the name, liking it. The usual lack of familiarity didn't scare her as much now.

"Is she coming here to get me?" she asked, somehow knowing that if this Abby were there, everything else would be okay.

"That's up to you, Anna," Dr. Gordon told her, his face, as usual, a study in kindness.

Anna frowned. "Of course I want her here." Her sister would be able to fill in all the gaps in her life, wouldn't she? Abby could simply tell her everything she couldn't remember, until her mind was as full as if she'd never lost her memory.

Abby would know who'd fathered her child.

The two men looked at each other, and watching the silent exchange, Anna could see exactly when Jason Whitaker abdicated to Dr. Gordon, leaving the doctor to explain whatever they were hiding from her. What was going on here?

And then it hit her. Horrifyingly, embarrassingly. Was Jason Whitaker the father of her child? Was that why he was here?

"Did I sleep with you two months ago?" Anna blurted, in spite of the blush she could feel creeping up her throat and face. She was beyond manners. If Dr. Gordon and Jason knew something about her, she had to know, too.

Still suffering from acute embarrassment, still hardly comprehending what it might mean to have Jason Whitaker so intimately entangled in her life, crushing disappointment tore through her as he shook his head.

"I haven't seen you since I moved to New York three months

ago,'' he said. He sounded sad, and she hated that he must pity her.

"I didn't even know you were in New York." He twisted the knife further.

Anna nodded. Her limited experience left her no clue what to say. How to handle such awkwardness was beyond her.

"You're in New York on a self-imposed sabbatical, Anna." Dr. Gordon freed her from the horrible moment.

"According to your sister," he continued, "you left home two months ago saying that you wanted to have a year apart from your family, that you needed to prove you could make it on your own. You demanded your family promise not to contact you for any reason during that year."

"Two months ago?" Anna asked. Right about the time she got pregnant—or right before.

Both men nodded. "No one's heard from you since," Jason said.

"Did you tell my sister, uh, Abby, about my baby?" Her eyes were pinned firmly on the doctor as she asked the question. She couldn't even look at Jason Whitaker.

The doctor nodded again. "I did."

"Does she know who the father is?" Anna whispered. She had to know whose baby was growing inside her. She had to see the man, find out what part he was going to play in her life, in his child's life.

Tears flooded her eyes when the doctor shook his head. She was falling apart and she couldn't help it. A victim of the confusing and volatile emotions swarming around inside her, she had no memory of how to cope with them. She was losing it.

The touch of Jason Whitaker's hand distracted her. "We wouldn't tell you, Anna, even if we knew," he said, his gaze full of something warm and powerful that she didn't understand, but that made her want to trust him.

"Do *you* know?" she asked, tears running slowly down her face. The irony of her situation hadn't escaped her. She'd left home to find herself and, instead, had lost all recollection of herself completely.

"No."

"I've told both Jason and Abby that I believe it would be harmful to fill you in on your past, Anna.'' Dr. Gordon broke the silence that had fallen. ''Your mind is hiding from something, and until your subconscious feels you're ready to cope with it, any attempt to force you to shoulder it could result in permanent memory loss.''

''Oh.'' She wiped her tears with her free hand. Her head was hurting again.

''Amnesia is a gray area, Anna. Each case is different. And while some doctors would probably tell you that to be informed of your past might be for the best, I believe such a move is potentially dangerous.''

''Dangerous,'' she repeated, and felt Jason squeeze her hand more tightly.

Dr. Gordon nodded and continued to gaze kindly down at her. ''But I also believe, as do the associates I've conferred with, that when you're ready, you'll remember everything.''

''But how long will that take?'' she cried. Couldn't they understand she didn't have the time to just sit around and wait? She had to get on with her life—whatever it was.

The doctor shrugged. ''That's entirely up to you, Anna.''

''And what if I say I want to be told, anyway? In spite of the risk?''

''Then we'll tell you,'' Jason said immediately. ''But according to Dr. Gordon, even if the information doesn't cause permanent memory loss, you won't know later if you're remembering things because you truly recall them, or only because you're remembering what we've told you.''

''Keep in mind,'' Dr. Gordon added, ''that neither your family nor Jason know anything about the occurrences of the past two months of your life.''

Anna's gaze moved sharply between the two men, although she continued to cling to Jason's hand. ''You think what my mind can't cope with is something that happened since I left home?''

''Possibly,'' the doctor answered. ''It's more likely a combination of things.''

Anna thought she'd experienced every kind of fear imaginable over the past hours, but nothing compared to the dread freezing her now as she contemplated doing anything that could impair her complete recovery. Nor was she honestly sure she wanted to know—at least not yet—what possible horrors had led her to this place, this time. And perhaps this pregnancy?

Pulling her hand from Jason's, she asked the doctor, "Do you think I was raped?"

She almost started to cry again, with relief this time, when he shook his head. "Apart from the bruises you suffered in the crash, there's no physical or psychological evidence of abuse," he said. "No old contusions, no neurotic fears when people get close to you, touch you."

"But if I don't remember anything, why would I act afraid?"

"You don't remember experiences, Anna, but fear for your physical safety is a conditioned response. In cases like yours, that's usually not something the patient loses."

"Okay." She needed to believe the doctor, to trust him, to trust someone. "Say we do it your way—no one tells me anything. What happens next?"

His brows raised, the doctor looked at Jason, who nodded. "Your sister has put Jason in charge of that," Dr. Gordon said. "And I'll be back to see you in the morning. If you're satisfied with what Jason has to offer, I'll release you then."

"Thank you," Anna murmured, watching as the doctor turned and left the room. She continued to stare at the empty doorway until she'd worked up the courage to look at the man still looming over one side of the bed.

He wasn't watching the door. He was staring straight at her, and the longing she thought she glimpsed in his eyes before he quickly shadowed them made her feel incredibly sad, though she had no idea why.

"You're sure you're just a friend of the family?" she whispered, frustrated to the point of despair that she couldn't remember, that she had nothing to call upon to tell her the reason for his lost look—or her reaction to it.

"Positive," he said.

"And you really didn't sleep with me two months ago?"

He shook his head. "I wish I could tell you I had, Anna," he said with such finality she knew he spoke the truth.

Knew, too, inexplicably, that she wished his answer was different.

CHAPTER FOUR

"YOU WANT ME to come live with you?" Though Jason still stood beside her bed, Anna couldn't look at him, couldn't meet his eyes. Not because she was embarrassed by what he had in mind. She'd be an idiot to think that this gorgeous man could possibly have any sexual interest in a pregnant, currently demented family friend. He was taking pity on her, nothing more. No, what embarrassed her was her own reaction to his offer.

She *wanted* to go with him. She suddenly felt exposed, naked, vulnerable. She, who hated being a burden, who went out of her way not to bother anyone, wanted to saddle this man with an unexpected and very troubled houseguest.

"Oh!" she said suddenly, frantically retracing the pattern of her thoughts.

"What?" Jason leaned down. "What is it? Does your head hurt?" His worried gaze traveled over her. "Or...?"

"No! I..." How could she explain without sounding completely stupid? But looking into his eyes, how could she not? "I just had a thought, that's all. I knew something about myself. Really knew."

"You remembered something?"

She shrugged. Thinking back, she couldn't be sure how solid the feeling had been, was afraid to analyze it, afraid to dig too deeply, afraid she'd lose that little glimpse that was all she knew about herself. She was also afraid to test his reaction to her discovery. How well did he know her? Well enough to know she *hadn't* been overly concerned with being a bother in her other life? That these feelings were new, brought on by this horrendous situation? Not a part of her lost self at all?

"Whatever it was, it's gone," she said disappointedly, already convinced that her great self-discovery had been no discovery at all, but merely a reaction to her current circumstances. How could she possibly know whether or not she'd been a burden in someone's life when she didn't even know if she'd *been* in someone's life?

"It's okay, Anna." Jason sounded encouraging. "It's still a good sign. The doctor said things will probably come back only a little at a time."

She nodded, but it wasn't okay at all. He was suddenly too large, cramping her with his size, his broad determined shoulders blocking the door from her view, his optimism hanging over the room, pressing down on her, until her chest felt so tight it hurt to breathe. It took everything she had just to hold herself together. Optimism was beyond her.

Was this how it was to be? Was she to go through life looking for things that didn't exist, reading more into every situation because she so desperately wanted more to be there?

"My place is in Chelsea. It's fairly large for being in the city," Jason continued as though the last moments had never happened. "There's a loft bedroom, and a bedroom downstairs, as well."

Anna's gaze followed his back as he moved to the window and gazed out into the night. There must be a woman someplace who wouldn't like a stranger moving into his home. No one as charming, as handsome as he was, would be living his life alone.

"You're welcome to stay as long as you like," he added.

He was being so nice. And without a dime to her name at the moment or anything else, for that matter, she had almost no immediate options. Still, she wasn't sure she could take him up on his offer, mostly because she wanted to so badly.

"You live alone?"

His shoulders stiffened, not markedly, but knowing nothing about him, about herself, her senses were acute to every nuance in her small world.

"Yes," he said, his voice as captivating as ever, no sign of the tension she'd witnessed—or thought she'd witnessed. "But you'll be perfectly safe. Your sister can vouch for me."

Funny, she'd never even considered her safety, although she supposed she should have. She was contemplating putting herself into this man's hands. Did she trust him so instinctively? Or had she just lost her common sense, along with her memories?

And what about her sister? Wouldn't *she* take her in? Would it really hurt to go back home to heal?

"Tell me something about Abby," Anna pleaded. "Anything." She'd agreed not to probe, but the blankness was more frightening than she could stand.

Jason spun around. "You've changed your mind, then? You want to go against the doctor's advice?" There was no condemnation in his voice, but there was urgency.

Anna shook her head. "I just need something a little more tangible than a name. Something to hold on to." She felt ridiculous pouring her guts out to a perfect stranger, and yet she couldn't stop herself. Because he was easy to talk to, or because she was just so damn needy, she didn't know.

Shoving his hands into his pockets, he watched her silently. Anna could almost see the thoughts running through his mind, see him discarding one after another. She waited for him to find something he could share until she was ready to scream. Every thought he was discarding was something she desperately wanted to know.

"Is she close to me in age?" she finally blurted. Or was this phantom sister a mere baby? Someone too far removed from her in years to be truly close.

He deliberated for a couple of seconds. "Yes."

"Older or younger?"

Another hesitation. And then, "Older."

Anna laid her head back against the raised mattress behind her. She was glad she had an older sister. The thought was comforting.

"Do you really believe that whatever I'm running from—" she flipped her hand up toward her recalcitrant brain "—is back in California? That to go back, to possibly force memories I'm apparently not ready to face, could do permanent damage?"

"I do."

And he knew things she didn't know. Suddenly the thought of California frightened her—and yet, at the same time, called out to her.

"Would you like to speak to Abby?" Jason asked, indicating the phone on the nightstand beside her bed. "We can call her."

Turning, Anna glanced at the phone. Willing it to tell her what she should do.

"Is she home?" she whispered. Never had she been so tempted—at least, she didn't think she had. Just to hear her sister would be bliss. To have a voice on the other end of the line belong to her. Still, she couldn't forget the sabbatical she'd apparently taken from her family. Couldn't help but wonder why.

"She's home," Jason said, maintaining his position by the window. "Waiting to hear how you are."

Anna wondered what he thought she ought to do, but was reluctant to ask. He was leaving this completely up to her. Just as he should. So, had she and Abby had a fight? Was there a rift in their family? Had she, Anna, caused it? She didn't feel like the kind of person who would throw a tantrum or leave town in a huff, but then, she could hardly claim to know herself.

"She's waiting for me to call?" she asked.

"Or me."

Anna studied his face, looking for a sign, anything that would help her. His expression remained blank. Kind, but impassive.

"Do you think there was a valid reason for my going away?" How could she possibly know what to do when she had nothing to base a decision on?

"You weren't irresponsible, Anna," he said slowly, as though choosing his words carefully. "I fully believe that you thought things through and felt you had to leave."

"Do you know the reason?" She was being unfair, asking him for information that, were he to give it, could very well harm her permanently, but she couldn't help herself.

"Do you really want me to answer that?"

Yes. No! She wanted to get well.

"I'm not asking you to tell me the reason, Jason," she said, her voice stronger than it had been all day. "But give me a break here. I have no idea whether I'm apt to dream things up or to see clearly. Was my reasoning generally sound, or was it cockeyed?"

"Your reasoning was always sound."

His words were reassuring, but it was the steady look in his eyes, the way he spoke to her without words, that calmed the panic rising inside her.

She nodded, holding that gaze for another couple of seconds.

"Then I'm just going to have to trust myself, huh?" she finally said, trying for a grin and missing. "Until I know why I demanded no contact with my family, I'm going to abide by my wishes."

Jason nodded, saying nothing, but Anna could tell he was pleased. Satisfied she'd crossed one small hurdle successfully, she turned her thoughts to more immediate decisions. Like where did she go when the doctor released her tomorrow? With nothing to her name, not even a shirt on her back, her options were nil.

"I must have a place somewhere." She hadn't meant to voice the thought.

"If you do, we'll find it," Jason said. "I have most mornings free, and a bit of investigative skill left over from my reporter days. Finding your place'll be a piece of cake."

"And a job. Surely I was working."

"As soon as we find out where you were living, we'll be able to ask your landlord where you work. Or your neighbors. You may even have a check stub lying around somewhere."

There was that damned optimism again. But this time she welcomed it. She needed his encouragement. And he said he had investigative skills, too.

"What do you do?" she asked, suddenly realizing how little she knew about him.

He blinked, opened his mouth to speak and then closed it again. "I'm a newscaster," he finally said, still holding guard at the window.

"I knew that, didn't I?"

He nodded. And it hit her then how hard this had to be for him. How awkward and uncomfortable she must be making him feel. To be looking at a friend and yet speaking with a stranger. A stranger he was determined to help whether she agreed to his plan or not. And he was acting as though there was nothing to it, as if she hadn't already taken up more of his time than she had any right to, as if he, a busy newscaster, didn't have a million other things he could be doing. Would rather be doing. She made up her mind then and there to make this whole ordeal as easy on her benefactor as she could.

"This is really what you want—for me to come home with you?"

He crossed his arms over his chest. "Yes."

"And you honestly don't mind me camping out at your place until I find my own?"

"Nope." He stood still as a statue, waiting.

She wanted to ask once more if he was sure she wasn't going to be any trouble, but she didn't. Of course she was going to be trouble. She was going to be a complete nuisance for a day or two. She'd just have to make sure that it *was* only a day or two. Forty-eight hours to find her life. It would have to be enough.

"Then, thank you. I accept."

Jason glanced at his watch. "Okay, then, I've got to go," he said, moving toward the door almost as if, now that he had her acquiescence, he suddenly couldn't get away fast enough. "I'm on the air in half an hour. But I'll be back around ten in the morning."

Struck with sudden irrational fear as he departed, Anna lay perfectly still and closed her eyes. She might not remember anything, but at least she knew who she was now. And she wasn't all alone. She opened her eyes to stare at the telephone. She could always call the sister she'd left behind if she had to.

"Anna?" Jason's blond head appeared again around her open door.

With her stomach flip-flopping at the sound of his voice after she'd thought him gone, she met his gaze.

He pulled a card out of his jacket pocket and walked over to drop it on the nightstand. "That's my number," he said, backing slowly toward the door again. "If you need anything, call." A couple of more steps and he'd be history. "Anytime. I'm a light sleeper."

Her throat felt thick. "Thanks," she said, trying to smile without letting the tears fall.

Now he was at the door, standing there poised to leave, and yet, still there. She withstood his perusal, holding his gaze.

"It's good to see you again," he said finally. And then he was gone.

Her taut body relaxed back against the mattress, a tiny smile contrasting with the tears that dripped down her face as she reached for the television remote control. She just had to wait thirty minutes and he'd be there on her screen.

HE MADE IT to the station in time to change into his jacket. Barely. And he made it through the show, as well. Though not with his usual style. The natural repartee for which he'd become known wasn't flowing, his mind not on what he was saying but on the woman lying alone and frightened in a hospital bed across town.

"You feeling okay?" his co-anchor, Sunny Lawson, asked as soon as the On the Air light clicked off.

"Fine," he lied. He didn't need her attentions tonight.

She pouted her lovely lips at his curtness, her flirtatiousness as natural as her beauty. "What's wrong?"

"Nothing." Clearing his papers, Jason stood up, hoping to leave the set without hurting Sunny's feelings. She'd been a good friend during the months he'd been in town. He just wasn't fit company tonight.

Walking beside him, her heels clicking on the cement floor in front of their set, she suggested, "How 'bout a drink?" She linked her arm through his. "You can tell me all about it."

The offer was nothing new. He and Sunny often had a bite between shows or a drink afterward. "Not tonight," he said impatiently, realizing he should have suggested a rain check.

"Jason?" She stopped, hauling him to a standstill beside her. "You mad at me or the world in general?" she asked, frowning.

He opened his mouth to tell her about Anna. But the words didn't come. He didn't want to talk about Anna. Not yet. Not while he still felt so raw.

Leaning over, he planted a friendly kiss on Sunny's full lips. "I'm not angry. Just tired," he said, feeling a twinge of guilt as he kissed her again just to shut her up.

His guilt increased as the kiss worked. She smiled at him. "You should have left when I did last night, instead of staying for one more," she said.

"I know," he acknowledged. "Which is why I'm leaving tonight. Right now."

"Well, get some sleep, friend," she said, chuckling. "Your disposition could use some improvement."

"I'll be asleep the second I get home," he assured her, leaving her at her dressing-room door, feelings intact.

HE CALLED ABBY the second he got in. It was after midnight in New York, but only nine-thirty at the beach house in California.

"How is she?" Abby said in lieu of hello.

"Fine." He shrugged out of his sport coat and tossed it on the back of a kitchen chair. "Good. Really," he added as Abby's silence hung on the line. "Considering."

"You've seen her?"

Abby was crying and trying to hide it. He ached for her. For all of them.

"Yeah. She looked good, Ab, really."

"She looked the same?" Abby asked.

"Her hair was pulled back in a ponytail, but she was as beautiful as ever." Which was an understatement. To his starved eyes she'd been a vision, stealing the breath from his lungs.

"So what'd she say? Was—" Abby took a shaky breath "—was she crying?" Then Abby lost her own battle with tears completely.

Jason swallowed, hating the helplessness he felt, his inability to make everything right for them. "She cried a little." He rubbed the back of his neck. "She's confused, Ab, frightened," he admitted. "But she's strong, too. In a way I've never really seen before." He took a breath and plunged ahead. "She's coming home with me tomorrow. She's going to stay at my place until we can find out where she lives, where she works."

Abby digested that in silence, and Jason knew she was drawing the right conclusions—just as he'd meant her to. Anna had decided not to go home.

"I didn't think she'd stay in New York."

"I know." Jason hadn't been sure, either, that Anna would be strong enough to fight the temptation to run to Abby. Whether she remembered home or not, some habits were just too ingrained to break. He'd seen Anna looking at the telephone, had felt her teetering with indecision. But she'd refused to call. That was when he'd known he was in for the long haul.

Silence once again stood between Abby and him. Silent accusation, silent concession, silent relief.

"You told her about me?" Abby finally asked.

"Of course." It bothered him she even had to ask, that things had become so strained between them she'd wonder such a thing. "Although Dr. Gordon advised against telling her you're triplets."

"I know." She sighed. "And as much as I hate it, I think he's right."

"I think so, too, Ab," he told her. "And who knows, it might only be for a few days. The doctor said her memory could start coming back anytime." He didn't tell Abby about the brief flash Anna had had earlier that evening; he didn't want to get her hopes up, having her waiting for breakthroughs by the hour. Especially since this one had gone as quickly as it had come.

"I got hold of Mom and Dad." The words were too casual. "They're in France now."

"And?"

"They were horrified of course, but calmed right down when I told them you were with her."

"Are they coming home?"

"Not just yet." The words were almost defensive. "They're thinking about investing in some perfume company, already have meetings scheduled for next week," she explained in a rush. "I told them there wasn't any real danger. And it's not like we can see her."

No. But they could have come home for Abby's sake. Their eldest daughter was all alone, confused, hurting.

"Did you tell them about the pregnancy?"

"No."

Some things never changed. The elder Haydens sailed through life focused only on themselves and left Abby to bear the burdens.

"Anna was thrilled to know she had a sister," he said when Abby was silent for too long. "And though she'd already made the decision to abide by Dr. Gordon's advice, you should have heard her pumping me for information about you."

Abby chuckled through her tears. "She was always the smartest one of us."

From his tenth-floor window Jason looked out over the flickering lights of New York, wondering if one of the lights was Anna's, if she was sleeping. "Don't sell yourself short, Abby," he said. "You did a damn fine job holding the three of you together all these years." There. It was three months overdue, but it needed to be said.

"Yeah, right," she snorted. "Damn fine. That's why we're all living happily ever after."

The bitterness in her voice worried him. "You can't control fate, Ab," he told her sternly.

"That's not what you said three months ago," she reminded him. "I remember quite clearly you telling me I control everything."

He hadn't put it so nicely. "I'm sorry, Abby."

"I know," she said, her voice softer, more like the Abby he knew. "Me, too."

There was more Jason needed to say, but he'd be damned if he could come up with any words. Glib, smooth-tongued, always-know-what-to-say Whitaker was fresh out.

"The doctor said Anna came in with no ID on her except her locket," Abby said, rescuing him.

"Apparently her purse and whatever else she had with her was either destroyed in the crash or stolen during the mayhem that followed."

"That means she won't have her health-insurance card."

Right. Good. Something practical to think about. Jason grabbed a pencil, repeating the information Abby was reading to him from the health-insurance policy the triplets had through their shop.

"She's probably not going to need this," he said, the phone held to his ear with his shoulder as he wrote. "The city's liability insurance will cover her medical expenses—and probably a lot more. The accident was so clearly the fault of a system's engineer—he was in the wrong place at the wrong time—that there's already talk of settlements."

And then another thought struck him. "What about her pregnancy?" he asked. He was doing his damnedest not to think about that part of Anna's life at all. But she'd need to know. "Will the shop's insurance cover that?"

"Yes." And that quickly, the tension was back. "So...how are you doing?" Abby's voice was soft.

"Fine," Jason lied. His insides felt ripped apart, but that was his own business.

"You'll keep in touch?"

"Of course." He should really turn on some lights. Except that he preferred the darkness.

"Jason?"

"Yeah?"

"Thanks."

Grunting a reply, he rang off, stripped to his briefs and dropped to the hardwood floor, doing as many pushups as his tired body would allow. Forty-nine. Fifty. Getting involved with Anna again was sheer stupidity. One hundred. It was nothing short of lunacy. One hundred fifty. It was masochism. Two hundred. Suicide.

But he'd loved her once. Had actually, for the first time in his life, believed himself loved. And love meant you cared even when it hurt. It meant putting someone else's needs above your own. It meant loyalty and reliability. It meant all the things he'd always wanted but never known. It meant everything that was most important to him.

Rolling over, he lifted his legs an inch off the ground and crunched forward, pressing his lower back into the floor. One, two, three...fifty-one, fifty-two, fifty-three... Though he wouldn't have thought it possible, he'd underestimated how much he'd missed her. He'd also thought he'd suffered as hellishly as any one person could and still function, until she'd turned those big brown eyes on him—and hadn't known him from Adam.

One hundred twenty-one, one hundred twenty-two. She didn't know she'd sent him out of her life.

Jason spent the next hour moving his things to the downstairs bedroom. Whether she remembered growing up by the ocean or not, Anna would crave the openness of the loft just as he did, and he wanted her as comfortable as he could make her. Besides, he'd sleep better knowing she couldn't slip out without him knowing. His bedroom door was right at the bottom of the stairs.

Not that he thought for a second that Anna would run out on him. Or that she wouldn't be leaving just as soon as she was able. But old habits died hard. He couldn't stop people from leaving him. It was a fact of life—at least of *his* life. But he was damn well going to watch them go. He'd learned a long time ago that goodbye didn't hurt quite so badly when he knew it was coming.

It was when he cleared the last load of his clothes out of the closet that he saw the box he'd known was waiting there. Still taped up from the move from California, the small cardboard carton had one word scrawled across the top in black magic marker. *Anna.* Jason ripped it open.

He'd found a few of her things at his condo when he'd packed up so hurriedly to leave for New York. He hadn't been in any kind of mood to return them to her, to see her again. But he hadn't been able to toss them away, either. So like a fool, he'd thrown them in a box and carted them across the country with him.

A couple of pairs of silky bikini underwear. His body hardened immediately as he pictured her roaming around his condo back in California in them—and nothing else. Making them both breakfast or a midnight snack. Always fresh from lovemaking.

A long black spaghetti-strap nightgown he'd bought for her, but she'd never worn. Not because she hadn't liked it, but because once he got her to his place, he never gave her time to put it on.

And a couple of the loose-fitting, earth-toned dresses she wore almost every day of her life. Garments that would have looked drab on most women, but flowed lovingly around Anna's curves, giving her an air of womanly grace.

Jason smiled, remembering the first time he'd seen Anna standing on the street outside her shop in Oxnard, the wind whipping a dress just like one of these up around her hips while she'd laughingly tried to preserve some dignity. He hadn't had a hope in hell of escaping her allure. He'd been turned on then, as he pretended not to notice her gorgeous thighs, and ever since. Of course later, when he'd known she wore nothing under her dresses but silky bikini briefs, the damn garments had driven him crazy.

He was going to have to iron at least one of them. Three months in a box hadn't done them any favors. Both dresses had tints of mauve in them as did most of Anna's things. She'd told him once that she loved the shade because of its softness, its ability to meld with other colors without causing a stir. Only Jason had seen the fire hidden in her favorite hue.

After ironing and then showering, he finally lay down in his newly made bed sometime around three. And although he'd been up more than fifteen hours and was both mentally and physically exhausted, he still didn't sleep. In less than eight hours Anna was going to be here. In his home. With him. Just where he'd refused to allow himself to picture her for three torturous months.

And then she'd be leaving. Because while he'd been spending his nights trying not to remember her in his bed, she'd been in bed with someone else.

He'd deal with it. Anna wasn't his anymore. It was over. She'd told him so more than three months ago. He was a little slow, but he was getting it. Finally. She was just an old friend in need. He could handle this. No problem.

No problem to give her this chance to find out for herself who she really was. Anna Hayden. One person. Not Audrey, Anna and Abby.

All of this would be worth the effort if Anna discovered she could be Anna alone, not Anna, one-third of a whole—working a job she didn't love for a sister she did. Living a life that was content, but couldn't include the frightening, exhilarating experience of being completely, totally, in love. Couldn't include commitment to anyone but the other two-thirds. Anna, one-third of a whole, believing in her sister's opinion as much or more than she believed in her own. Believing that her strength and Abby's was to be found only in their togetherness.

Anna, one-third of a whole, and never really happy.

CHAPTER FIVE

SHE WAS GOING TO BE horribly embarrassed. She'd called the nurse, a new one since yesterday, and that harried woman had assured Anna that she'd see about getting her something to wear. But it was almost ten o'clock. Jason Whitaker was due to arrive momentarily, and Anna still had nothing on but a very short, very thin hospital gown with a slit all the way down the back. And her hair was still dirty. The hospital had been without hot water for most of the morning.

She considered calling the nurse one more time, but hated to be a bother. The woman was obviously busy taking care of people who really needed her. Sick people who were suffering. People who couldn't care for themselves. Anna felt like a fraud for even considering taking up the woman's time.

Of course the alternatives weren't much better. Either leave the hospital wrapped in a robe, assuming they'd let her borrow one, or ask Jason to go out and buy her some clothes with money she didn't have, and then come back and get her.

Or she could ask the doctor to delay her release for one more day, call her sister and have Abby wire her some money. Better yet, have Abby send her a plane ticket home.

Home. She closed her eyes, willing something, anything, to appear in the blankness—a picture, a feeling. A memory. But try as she might, she couldn't raise a single image of the place where she'd grown up, or the people she'd known. Knew only that she didn't want to go there now. Not until she remembered why she'd left.

What she wanted to do was see Jason Whitaker. She wanted him to help her find her life. She wanted to get to know him again, this family friend who'd come to rescue her. Though she'd awoken this morning with the now familiar emptiness, the horror of living with a mind that had let her down, she'd also felt a flicker of anticipation. Simply because she was going to see Jason Whitaker again.

And therein lay her biggest fear of all.

Because she was scared to death he wasn't going to come get her. Surely, with time to consider the commitment he'd made, he'd change his mind. Any sensible person would. She could hardly blame him for not wanting to saddle himself with a crazy woman who also happened to be homeless, temporarily penniless, pregnant and who had absolutely no recollection of the father of her baby.

Jason had no way of knowing that his presence was the only thing that had made her feel safe since she'd opened her eyes the day before to a waking nightmare. That she was holding on to his offer to help her with every fiber of her being. That he made her believe she really could get her life back together, that somehow she'd find a way to be a mother to the child she knew she carried, but had yet to feel.

He owed her nothing. She hadn't even done him the courtesy of remembering him. Had no idea how close a family friend he was. He'd be a fool to come back. And if he didn't...

She'd been fighting her fears all morning, trying to concentrate on the mundane tasks necessary to prepare herself to go out in public, tracking down a toothbrush, washing her face, contemplating her nonexistent wardrobe. But as ten o'clock drew nearer, she could no longer keep her panic at bay.

He wasn't going to come. How could she possibly expect him to come? The walls started to close in on her. She was going to have to go back to California—without any idea what kind of a minefield she'd be walking into. Or maybe, worse yet, everyone would keep her reason for leaving a secret forever, treat her like some kind of invalid. What if they coddled her so much she'd never again have a life of her own, never be able to take care of herself, let alone be a good mother to her baby? She'd rather die first.

"Hey, sunshine, you ready to blow this joint?" Jason's cheerful voice put an end to her frantic soul searching.

Tongue-tied, Anna stared at him as he came through her door. He'd come back. And this morning, in form-fitting faded jeans and a polo shirt, he looked so classically gorgeously male he took her breath away.

When she didn't speak, he frowned, coming closer. "What's wrong?" he asked. He set a bag she hadn't even noticed he'd been carrying on the end of her bed.

"Nothing," she said, hot color spreading up her neck. How could she possibly ask this man to go buy her some underwear? She pulled the sheet up to her chin. "I, uh, have a small problem."

"Something we can fix, I hope?"

His warm blue eyes met her gaze directly, full of friendliness—and something more. Something she couldn't define or understand.

She couldn't do it. She just couldn't ask him for panties.

He picked up the paper bag he'd dropped on the end of the bed and tossed it onto her lap. "Tell you what," he said, backing toward the door. "I'll go get some coffee from the machine I saw down the hall while you get ready, and then we'll talk. Okay?"

He smiled, sending shivers all the way down to her toes, and she merely nodded. If there weren't clothes in this bag, she was going to crawl under the covers and never come out. And if there were, then he was the most amazing... He was a good friend. That was what he was. All he could ever be. Period. And she needed to get that straight right now. No matter how attractive she may find him, no matter how thoughtful and warm and kind, no matter how attached to him she was growing already, she was pregnant with another man's baby.

As soon as he was out the door, she ripped into the bag. Clothes. Thank God! Pulling them out of the bag as she climbed from the bed, she hurried into the bathroom. She was at least going to have the armor of decent covering the next time she came face-to-face with Jason Whitaker.

She liked his taste in clothes. The dress was loose and flowing, and the soft cotton felt good against her skin. As did the silky panties she found folded up inside the dress.

Blushing from head to toe, she slipped them on beneath the dress, chastising herself for thinking of the man who'd brought them as she slid them up her thighs. She might as well commit herself to the loony bin if she was going to start having romantic thoughts about her benefactor. Not only would it be sheer stupidity to think that Jason could ever be attracted to her, lunacy to read anything personal into his friendly gestures, it was also impossible to involve herself with anyone at this point in her life.

Somewhere in the world there lived a man with whom she'd quite recently been intimate. A man she hoped to God she loved, since she had his baby growing in her womb. A man who, if she saw him, may just attract her more than Jason Whitaker did. It was this crazy situation, that was all. Jason was the knight saving the damsel in distress. And he was the only attractive man she could ever remember seeing. Her strong reaction to him was because of the situation. It had to be.

And then it hit her. There'd been no tags on the clothes she was wearing. The underwear, in fact, while fresh and clean, was faded. She couldn't help wondering whom they belonged to or how well Jason knew the woman. And couldn't seem to help the sick jealousy that attacked her as she answered her own question.

Swearing at herself, she yanked the band from her hair, resecuring the ponytail with more force than necessary. One thing she knew for sure, she needed to find her own place—damn quickly. Had to get out into the world, meet so many people that rather than being the sole individual in her life, Jason Whitaker was merely one of a crowd. A huge crowd.

She was starting to obsess about him and was at least rational enough to recognize the very real danger in allowing herself to need him too much. He was making it so easy for her to rely on him for everything. But he was going to be gone from her life in just a day or two, back to his own life, his own woman, and she had to be able to stand by herself when he left. For her baby's sake and for her own. She couldn't afford another problem.

Her resolution to get away from him lasted right up until he came walking back into her room five minutes later. He smiled at her. And all she could do was smile back.

"You look good. Just like your old self."

His words gave her pause. It was so hard for her to accept that while she was getting to know a stranger, he was seeing an old friend. "I like the dress," she said. "Thanks."

He opened his mouth, closed it then opened it again to say simply, "You're welcome."

Anna had a burning urge to know what he'd almost said, but she didn't ask. She also didn't ask whose dress she was wearing. She wasn't ready to hear about another woman in his life.

"You ready to go?" he asked, looking the room over as if she might be forgetting something, as if she had something of her own to take with her. She followed his gaze around the stark room, struck again by the total emptiness that was her life.

"I don't know what I'm supposed to do about the bill," she admitted, something else that had been on her mind that morning. "I don't even know if I have health insurance."

"You do." Jason handed her a slip of paper. "That'll see you through until you can get a new card, but you won't need it today," he said. "The city is covering all your medical expenses. There'll probably be a settlement shortly, as well."

Anna stared at his forceful handwriting, wondering how many other things he knew about her that she didn't. She hated the way her condition made her so helplessly vulnerable, hated Jason seeing her like this. She swore to herself that she wouldn't rest until she'd taken back control of her life—and that once she had, she'd never let it go again. The insurance card was a good start. She no longer had to worry about financing her pregnancy. Now she just had to figure out how she supported herself.

"What kind of settlement?" she asked, sitting down in the wheelchair she had to be wheeled out of the hospital in.

Jason shrugged. "I don't know yet, but the city has already admitted liability. It's just up to their lawyers to determine amounts."

She turned to look at him as he pushed her from the room. "Do I need a lawyer?"

"I don't think so, honey. Only if you're not satisfied with whatever amount they offer."

"It was an accident, Jason," she said, crossing her arms over her chest. "They don't owe me anything."

"*They* seem to think they owe you something," he said, stopping at the nurses' station. "So I'd take what they offer—just to see you through until you're back on your feet."

Understanding that she would be less of a burden to him with money of her own, Anna just nodded and proceeded to sign the papers the nurse handed her. The sooner she was back in her own place the better. She had to believe that.

JASON THOUGHT it best to put off their investigating until the next day. "You're probably going to tire a little more easily than you're used to," he'd said.

And because she'd read his words to mean that he had something else to do, she'd agreed with him. But after a brief shopping trip for some toiletries, another dress, purchased with money he'd lent her, and moving her few things into the beautiful loft bedroom in his apartment, she wished she hadn't agreed so readily. He wasn't going anywhere. And surely a possible bout of fatigue, heck, even passing out at his feet, was better than sitting intimately on his couch in the quiet of his apartment. She had nothing to say, no repertoire of small talk, of reminisces to draw upon. And the way he was looking at her, his eyes brimming with things she couldn't decipher, was making it hard for her to remember the reasons she couldn't allow him to mean anything to her.

"How well do I know you?" she asked suddenly. He had all the advantages and she had none. Had she been fond of him before? Was that why she was so instantly drawn to someone who, for all intents and purposes, was a complete stranger?

He shrugged, looking away. "I've known your family for several years."

"Well? Or just acquaintances?"

"Well."

"Did we see each other often?" she asked. She couldn't see how, if they were at all close, she hadn't been head over heels in love with him.

"We saw each other fairly often," he finally said.

"Why?" She couldn't have been in love with him. Loving Jason wasn't something she would ever forget. Not in a million years, or after a million bumps to her head. But even more, being her lover wasn't something he'd keep quiet about. Especially not now—not with her pregnant.

"You have a nice family, Anna. I enjoyed being with you all."

"Were you a friend of my parents?"

His right heel started to bounce, almost imperceptibly, his leg up and down. "Not until you introduced me to them."

"*I* introduced you?"

His leg was still. "You and Abby."

"Do you have a nice family, too?" Her bluntness made her uncomfortable, but the void where there should have been memories drove her on.

He shrugged. "They're nice people. I just don't see them much."

"They live faraway?"

His leg started to move again. "No."

She was treading on sensitive territory, and yet she wasn't getting any signals from him to stop. "Did you have a falling-out with them?"

He stretched his arm along the back of the couch, the tips of his fingers almost touching her shoulder. "My parents divorced when I was five," he said. "I grew up spending three days a week at one house and four at the other."

"Almost like a visitor," she said, frowning. "That must have been hard. Did you have a room in each house? Where'd you keep your toys?" She couldn't imagine anyone agreeing to raise a child that way.

He smiled sadly and she had a feeling she was seeing a part of Jason not many people saw, and wondered if he was telling her things he'd told her before. Or if, perhaps, the fact that he was to all intents and purposes a stranger to her made it easier for him to speak of things he usually kept to himself.

"For a while I had a room in both places," he said. "Until my father moved closer to work and my mother remarried."

"What a tough way to grow up." She wondered if she'd ever met his parents. And if she had, if she'd been able to be civil to them. "I can't believe the courts allowed it."

"It was pretty unheard-of back then," he said. "It's not so unusual now. That way the child is still raised by both parents, has the benefit of a close relationship with both parents." His leg continued to bounce.

"Was that how it was with you?" she asked, filled with a need to understand everything she could about him.

"My father had his career." He shrugged. "Mom, her husband and new baby daughter. I always knew they cared—I just wasn't their first priority." He said the words easily, but Anna didn't believe for a second that his feelings were that uncomplicated.

And as he talked to her, as she caught a glimpse of the sensitive boy he'd been—sensitive to hurt, but sensitive to his parents' needs, as well—Anna wondered again why she hadn't been in love with him.

Had she already been in love with someone else? Someone who affected her even more deeply than he did?

"Were you ever in love?" she blurted. *Was I?*

He stiffened. "I thought I was."

It had to be difficult for him, hearing her ask things she should already know, but as long as he was willing to answer, she had to ask. And he'd just cleared up one mystery. There'd never been anything more than friendship between them because he'd been involved with someone else.

"What happened?" She curled her legs up beneath her.

"She chose someone else." And he was still hurting.

Anna couldn't imagine any woman turning Jason Whitaker away. Quite the opposite, in fact. She'd been picturing a string of broken hearts leading straight to his door. Maybe her own included. Maybe she'd loved him—and he'd loved someone else.

"I'm sorry."

He glanced over at her, a sardonic grin on his lips. "Don't be," he said. "It doesn't matter anymore." But somehow she knew it did.

"Did I know her?"

"Yes."

Anna wondered if she'd ever been as jealous of this unknown woman as she was of the woman whose dress she now wore. "Did I like her?"

He looked at her, his assessing gaze making her uncomfortable. "You never told me you didn't."

His fingers moved absently along the back of the couch, and Anna could feel every imaginary brush through the thin material of her dress, aware of him in a way that could only embarrass him, stir his pity. She was crazy. And pregnant. And the man was probably still in love with someone else.

"How long ago was this?" she asked.

"A few months." He looked away and then back again, his leg still. "Just before I came out to New York."

This woman was in California, then, Anna thought, worried by her sudden sense of relief. But worried even more by how deeply she felt the pain he was denying. In any way that mattered, she'd just met this man. "She was a fool," she said aloud.

He shrugged. "It's history."

She wasn't sure she believed him.

IT WAS A RELIEF to leave for work. Though he felt guilty about leaving Anna alone sooner than he had to, Jason gave himself enough time to walk part of the way to the station that balmy New York evening, catching a cab at Madison Square. People had been complaining about the summer humidity, but having grown up on the coast, Jason found New York's humidity no problem. And as much as he missed the ocean, he loved New York. He loved the rush, the life that surged around him every time he stepped outside his door. Everywhere were people with goals to achieve, important things to do, destinations to reach. He needed to get caught up again in the activity, the enthusiasm, remember who he was, the person he'd become since leaving California. He also needed to lose some of the tension that was building to an exploding point within him.

He needed a break from Anna.

She'd been in his home one afternoon and he was falling in love with her all over again. She was another man's woman now. A woman who was sitting in his apartment in the dress he'd stripped off her the last time she'd worn it, and she was carrying another man's child.

He'd had to leave before the anger building inside him spewed out and scalded them both. How could she have allowed another man to touch her, to know her, to leave his seed in her? And why wasn't she different because of it? Why was she still, even minus her memory, so much the Anna he'd known and loved more than anyone else, ever?

He'd have given his life for the woman. And she was giving life to another man's baby.

While he, like some kind of sick fool, still burned with desire for her. Her scent, her soft husky voice, the way she glided when she moved—all had driven him to the point of insanity that afternoon.

He understood how her separation from Abby had been more

than Anna could bear. Understood that she badly needed this chance to emerge from the cocoon of her family to become a separate and complete individual. Accepted the fact that her mind was ensuring she got that chance.

But as the afternoon dragged on, even stronger than his need to take her to bed, stronger than his anger, was the hurt he'd thought he'd buried forever, rising closer and closer to the surface. He was having a hard time accepting, forgiving, that she'd forgotten *him.*

"Sleep improved your tongue, but it didn't seem to do much for your disposition," Sunny said as they left the set after the six-o'clock news.

She hadn't appreciated his curt acquiescence when she'd asked him out to dinner. But at least he'd been at his best on the air. His thoughts had flowed as freely as the cue cards, allowing him to add his own slant to the news he imparted the way his loyal viewers had come to expect. And if his grand performance had had anything to do with the fact that he knew Anna was watching him, he damn sure didn't want to know about it.

"Let me make a phone call and we can go to dinner," he said, tossing his station jacket on a chair just inside the door of his dressing room. "But I'm buying."

For once she didn't argue with him.

Sunny drove a fire-engine red Mercedes convertible, and Jason envied her only for having a garage close enough to home to drive her car to work almost daily. The Jaguar he'd brought with him from California was every bit the vehicle her Mercedes was, but it was a twenty-minute cab ride away, parked in a garage that cost him nearly as much as his apartment did each month.

Still, he appreciated a powerful car, and Sunny was a good driver. Settling back in the passenger seat, he enjoyed the view, the warm breeze in his hair, as she maneuvered through midtown Manhattan toward the seafood restaurant she currently favored on the Upper East Side. Anna had already eaten, she'd assured him when he'd called her from his dressing room. She'd found the stash of TV dinners in his freezer and had eaten one while watching his show. She was understandably exhausted and was planning to shower and be in bed by nine o'clock. He was planning not to think about her in that spaghetti-strap nightgown.

"So what's got you so uptight?" Sunny asked as soon as they had their predinner drinks in front of them.

"You remember that amnesia victim?" he asked her, studying the ice in his glass. It was going to take a lot more than a glass of scotch to put him to sleep tonight.

"The one from the subway crash? Anna, didn't they say?"

"Anna Hayden," he said. "I knew her in California."

"And?" she said when he paused. She'd stopped swishing her straw in her drink and was staring at him. Sunny wasn't going to like what he had to tell her.

"She's staying at my place for a few days."

"Why?" The softly spoken word hung between them.

He could tell her that Anna had no place else to go, that she knew no one else in the city. "Because I asked her to."

"Why?" she asked again. She'd made no secret of the fact that she'd been hoping for more between them than friendship. But he'd been honest, too. He wasn't ready for the kind of relationship Sunny wanted.

He took a sip of his drink, sending his co-anchor a warning look over his glass.

"I wanted to," he finally answered. It was the only part of the truth she'd care about.

She nudged her drink away. "How well did you know her in California?"

"Well."

Breaking eye contact with him for the first time since the conversation began, Sunny said, "Oh."

Jason sipped his drink, waiting. Knowing Sunny, she wasn't going to give up that easily. He'd known when he invited Anna home that Sunny wasn't going to like it. His relationship with her had started out as a publicity stunt. She was to be full of light sexual innuendoes and lots of personal approval as they worked together on the air, the idea being that if she approved of Channel Sixteen's new co-anchor, so would her loyal viewers. And if viewers tuned in to see a little chemistry between Sunny Lawson and her new co-anchor, so much the better.

In silence they ate their meal, lobster for Jason, crab salad for Sunny. He'd have enjoyed the food a lot more if it wasn't sharing space with the rock in his gut. His relationship with Sunny was important to him, in more ways than one. Just not the way she wanted most.

When Jason had first come to town, not knowing a soul, he'd been only too willing to spend a lot of time with Sunny, to be seen about town with her, appear in all the right places with her on his arm—all in the name of business. She was a beautiful woman, and with her sharp mind, good company, too. But as they'd gradually grown more comfortable together, their relationship had become more than business. After three months of sharing dinners with her, working with her, drinking with her, Sunny had become a good friend.

She wanted to be his lover.

But as beautiful as Sunny was, as tempting as he found her, Jason did not intend to take her to bed. Sunny wasn't looking for a no-strings-attached affair, and he wasn't sure he'd ever want more than that with a woman again.

There was his job to consider as well. He cared about his job. A lot. And he had to work with Sunny. Though he'd given the show a much needed ratings boost, Channel Sixteen News had been hers long before he'd come along.

She waited until he'd pushed his plate away. "When's she leaving?" she asked.

"I don't know."

He couldn't give her any more than that.

"Are you sleeping with her?"

"No."

"Do you intend to?"

It was on the tip of his tongue to tell Sunny that whether or not he slept with Anna was none of her business. But because she was a friend, because it was the truth, he answered her. "No."

Her shoulders relaxed. "Does she know that yet?" she asked in the voice that had made her famous.

"She's pregnant, Sunny." And then, when he saw the horror in her eyes, "The baby's not mine."

"Oh," she said. "Good."

Picking up her abandoned fork, she attacked her half-eaten salad with gusto and he waited while she ate, well aware of how beautiful she was, of the male eyes watching her appreciatively, of the envy surrounding him in the elite little restaurant. Well aware, too, that Sunny was his for the taking. He wondered if he'd eventually give in and take her to his bed without love. Good sex could go a long way toward covering up what wasn't there.

"You ready?" he asked as soon as she finally laid down her fork.

"Yes," she said, standing and waiting while he settled the check.

Any other time she'd have argued over whose turn it was to pay; tonight, she was claiming the right to have him buy her dinner. Jason didn't miss the message she was sending him. He was hers and she wasn't giving him up.

He could have told her she didn't have a damn thing to worry about where Anna was concerned. His housemate already had a man in her life. And she'd probably be running back to him just as soon as she remembered who he was.

CHAPTER SIX

ABBY AWOKE with a start. Cold sweat trickled down her back and she sat up, looking around her small bedroom in the back of the beach house. Something was wrong. Engulfed in fear, she slid soundlessly from the bed, eyes glued on the open door in front of her. Her own safety didn't matter, not until she assured herself that her sisters weren't hurt. She hadn't heard anything, but she never ignored her instincts. She'd awoken for a reason.

Slipping out her door and into the room immediately to her right, she saw the empty bed. Audrey's bed.

As reality crashed in, a cold calm settled around Abby's heart. Out of a lifetime of habit, she checked the rest of the cottage. But when she found it empty, as empty as her life, she lay slowly down on the kitchen floor, welcoming the coolness of the tile against her cheek, aware only then of the tears running down her face.

God, she hurt. Was going crazy with the pain. Not because she wasn't strong enough to shoulder it. She'd been feeling for three all her life. Whenever her sisters were in need, she knew. When one suffered, they all three suffered. They'd felt each other's thoughts—seemed to share a single soul. Just as they'd all shared a remarkable comfort in each other. The most agonizing heartache became less unbearable simply because it was shared.

But not anymore. Abby was alone now. And this solitary pain was much harder to bear than any she'd known before. Why was she still sensing things that no longer existed? Feeling bonds that had long been broken?

She ached so badly she wished she'd just die and be done with it. And no one knew she felt this way. Which was the worst part of all. For the first time in her life, no one knew.

ANNA FLEW out of bed before she was fully awake, running down the loft stairs with only one thought in mind. To get help. She had to get help.

Jason caught her by the shoulders just outside his bedroom door.

"Anna! What's wrong?"

"Let me go!" She fought his hold. She had to get help.

He held her captive. "What is it, honey? What's happened?"

She heard the concern in his voice, but she couldn't take time to explain. "I've got to get help!" she cried, still struggling to break away from him.

"Why? Are you in pain?" He pulled her closer, turning her face up to his.

His blue eyes bore into hers, full of worry—and something more. Something that reached down to soothe away the panic that had spread through her while she slept. She stared back at him, speechless, wondering how she could possibly explain her frantic urgency when she didn't understand it herself.

"Anna?" He continued to watch her.

She shook her head. Was she losing her mind?

"I…" She looked away, embarrassed, afraid. Confused.

"What frightened you, honey?" His voice was soft, understanding—and yet so very masculine.

"I… It was just…" What? How could she tell him without sounding crazy?

"Were you sleeping?" he asked, leading her over to the couch.

She nodded.

He sat down beside her, still holding on to one of her hands as he reached up to brush the hair from her face. It was a damp tangled mess.

"You just had a nightmare," he said gently. "Dr. Gordon warned us this might happen."

Still silent, she nodded again. Let him think that was all it was. Let her try and believe it.

"Were you dreaming about the crash?" he asked.

"Yes." She forced the word and barely got a whisper. That was how her dream had started, anyway. But there'd been more. Something that when she'd awoken hadn't vanished with the dream. Someone calling out to her, frantically, painfully, needing her so desperately she still felt the echo of it singeing her nerves.

Jason pulled her into his arms. "You're shivering," he said. "Are you cold?"

Shaking her head, she burrowed her face against him, realizing his chest was bare only when her cheek pressed against the warmth of his skin. *Please, God. Make me not be crazy,* she prayed, too weak to pull away from Jason even though she knew that snuggling against him wasn't right.

He settled back into the couch, cradling her. "Talk to me, Anna."

She wanted to. God knew she wanted to share everything with this man. These past few days, she'd been traveling the streets of New York with him on a so far fruitless search for her identity. Living with him, watching him on the news, hearing on the television show what he'd neglected to tell her himself—that his partner considered him the day's best catch—had so intensified her inappropriate attraction to Jason that being with him had, in some ways, become pure hell.

And in other ways, it seemed so natural. Jason knew her even if she didn't know herself. He knew what foods she liked best, what colors. He knew when she was bothered, when something amused her. Through him, she was gaining back bits of herself.

"Did I used to talk to you?" she asked now, allowing herself just a few seconds of touching him, of taking advantage of the strength he was so willing to share with her. Then she'd move, put the length of the couch between them, just as their lives pushed them apart in every other way.

"More than you talked to most people, I guess," he said. He'd considered her question carefully.

Anna was glad she didn't have to look at him. "Was I a pest?"

"Hell no!" His response was immediate, the first personal response he'd given her without first carefully choosing his words. "It used to drive me crazy the way you'd keep things to yourself," he continued. "If anything, I wished you'd open up more."

"I didn't talk much, huh?" Anna smiled. "Somehow that doesn't surprise me." In fact, this discovery felt gloriously right, familiar. Finally. Something felt familiar.

Jason tightened his hold on her. "You talked, Anna. Just not always about the things that mattered."

And what might those things have been? Maybe if she'd talked more, her mind wouldn't have needed to run and hide.

"Were we close, Jason?" She wanted to think that, though they hadn't been lovers, at least they'd been friends. Good friends. The kind of friend you could run to when the world was too much to bear.

Jason didn't answer. She'd whispered the words, so perhaps he hadn't heard.

As she lay there, her mind taunted her, playing absurd guessing games with his possible thoughts. How did you tactfully tell someone she wasn't your favorite person? Especially when that person was sitting half on top of you, helpless with need. How could he say that she'd been a difficult person to like? That while she was nice enough now, she'd been a pain in the ass in her other life? Or worse, how did he tell her that he'd tried his best to steer clear of her because of the embarrassing unrequited crush she'd made so obvious?

"Not as close as we are now," he answered after such a long time had passed she'd been certain her question had gone unnoticed.

Listening to his heart beat, she thought about his answer. *Not as close as we are now.* She wanted to ask him to explain, but was afraid to push him too far. She was afraid of his answer. Was something the matter with her that made it hard for people to get close to her? Had she been the type of person that someone good and decent like Jason wouldn't want to be close to?

The damn black hole that was her mind tormented her with its silence, frustrating her, angering her. What the hell had happened to her? What had driven her to running away from herself?

"Is that why I didn't contact you when I came to New York?" The warmth of his arms gave her the courage to ask.

"There was no reason you should have," he said, his voice even, as though he was reporting the news. "You didn't even know where I lived."

She continued to lie pressed against him, the darkness loosening her tongue. "Did I know you'd moved to New York?"

"You knew I was going to."

"You didn't tell me goodbye when you left?"

"No."

So they must not have been all that close. "Did you tell my sister goodbye?"

"Yes," he said, still reporting impassively. "I saw her before I left. You'd gone down to San Diego. She said she'd say goodbye for me."

Which made perfect sense.

The warmth of Jason's hands radiated through the thin silk of her gown, and as she relaxed, Anna was suddenly too aware of them clasped just beneath her right breast. He was wearing nothing but a pair of thin cotton shorts, hastily donned, if the undone drawstring at the waistband was any indication.

And as she studied that waistband in the shadows, Anna noticed something else, something that sent her heart slamming against her ribs. He was aroused.

Her throat felt dry; her nipples tightened. She could move just a little bit lower and his hands would slide over her aching breast. Just a little bit lower...

"Do you have any idea who the father of my baby is?" Her words crashed into the intimate silence that had fallen around them. She had to keep her mind on what mattered, or she was going to make a terrible mistake. One she wouldn't be able to live with when she regained her memory—and her life.

"None." The word was clipped, his hold on her loosening.

"Are you just saying that, or do you really not know?"

He sat up on the edge of the couch, setting her away from him, leaning forward with his hands clasped between his knees. "I had no idea you were seeing anyone."

"But—"

"It's late, Anna," he interrupted. "No more questions tonight, okay?"

"Just one more, Jason, please." She had to know. Especially after the way she'd just reacted to him, she had to know.

"What?" He turned to look at her, frowning, his eyes shuttered in the shadows.

"Was I the type to sleep around?"

He jumped up from the couch. "What kind of question is that?"

"Please, Jason," she begged, burying her pride to find the truth that was haunting her, the truth she feared almost as much as she feared never finding it. "Was I the type to sleep around?"

He stared at her silently, a shadow in the dark. But his silence drove her on, her stomach knotting. Was it possible that *she* hadn't known who'd fathered her baby? Even before she'd lost her memory?

"I have to know."

His shoulders relaxed, but the frown remained. "I wouldn't have thought so."

"You don't know for sure?"

"No. I don't know for sure."

IF THEY DIDN'T FIND her place soon, he was going to have to tell her who he was. Traipsing around Manhattan on foot in the hopes she'd notice something she'd missed from the cab had done nothing but tire her—and stretch his endurance so dangerously thin he was actually considering trying a little psychology of his own. He'd been tempted from the first moment he'd walked into her hospital room, when she looked at him with the eyes of a stranger. Tempted to lay her down in his bed, strip away her clothes and talk to her with his body as he'd done so often in the past. He just couldn't believe that once he'd made love to her she wouldn't remember him, wouldn't remember the love they'd shared.

"God, I hate that place," she said, her voice tired, worn. They were midtown, not far from the station, but several blocks from Central Park where he'd had the cab drop them off.

Feeling guilty for pushing her too far too fast in his own selfish need to get her out of his apartment before he did something he'd regret, it was a full moment before Jason saw what she was talking about.

Central Deli and Restaurant.

But she loved deli food. And Central was the best. On East Thirty-fourth Street it was a bit of a jog from the station, but the restaurant was good enough to be one of Sunny's current favorites. So why would Anna hate it?

How did she know she hated it? Jason stopped in his tracks, the flow of Manhattan pedestrian traffic bumping into him, and Anna, too, as he pulled her to a halt beside him.

"You remembered something," he said.

Shock crossed her face, followed almost immediately by a smile that took his breath away. "Yeah," she said, grinning. "I guess I did."

The crowd moved around them, too intent on business to be slowed down by a couple of idiots grinning at each other on the sidewalk. "So why do you hate Central?" Jason asked.

"I haven't a clue." She laughed out loud at the absurdity of the situation.

Jason grinned, taking her hand as they finally had to give in and join the Friday after-work throng. He hadn't realized until that moment how worried he'd been that the doctor had been wrong, that Anna's memory loss was permanent, that maybe there *had* been some brain damage.

"Do you think I lived around here?" she asked him as they reached the end of the block.

"It's possible. We can check the phone book, call places nearby."

"I'll make a list tonight while you're at work."

Galvanized by Anna's small victory, Jason insisted on walking around the block three more times, making sure she didn't miss even a speck of gravel on the sidewalk. She'd been there before. Anything could spark a memory, lead them to her life, get her out of his.

And suddenly he wasn't sure he should push her. She'd remembered something. That was enough for one day. Telling her he had to get to work, he dropped her off at the apartment and took a cab to the station. And immediately called Abby.

HE AND ANNA spent the next morning sitting on his couch, the list of phone numbers she'd made the night before on the coffee table in front of them, taking turns with his mobile phone—but every call they made was another dead end. No landlord in the immediate vicinity of Central Deli had ever heard of Anna Hayden, no one had had a tenant missing for the past several days, not one they were aware of, anyway. No one recognized her description.

But Anna wouldn't be daunted. "I remembered that place, Jason," she said late that morning. "I *did* have a life here and I'm going to find it."

Jason couldn't help but admire her persistence, her surge of confidence springing from one small victory.

"Then get back on that phone, woman."

She picked the phone up and started to dial, but stopped. "You telling me what to do?" she asked, her eyes glinting with laughter.

"Not if you don't want me to." She never had liked to be ordered about; gently directed by Abby always, but never ordered.

"Good, 'cause I make my own decisions," she announced, dialing the next number on their list.

They were the sweetest words Jason had ever heard her utter.

THEY FINALLY HIT pay dirt midway through the afternoon. Jason had run through his introduction by rote, already hearing the negative response on the other end of the line before realizing he hadn't received one. The brisk woman wouldn't confirm that Anna was one of her tenants, said she managed so many buildings she couldn't keep track of who lived in them, but she agreed to look at her records.

She called back five minutes later, telling them to meet her at a brownstone in Gramercy, not too far from Central Deli.

A SATURDAY-AFTERNOON lull hung over the city, streets filled with more shopping bags than briefcases, but the traffic was steady, cabs honking, cars zipping in and out of spaces they should never have tried to inch through. And suddenly Anna wanted to stay right there, enjoying the sun on her skin, and watch the people, wonder where they were going and why. Anything but walk the two more blocks to the life that was waiting for her.

She wasn't going to be able to stand it if this was another dead end. If the apartment wasn't hers. And she was scared to death about what might happen if it *was*. Would she remember it? Remember everything? Was she ready to face whatever she'd run away from?

Did she want to go back?

Living with Jason was the only life she knew. And after just a few days, it was a life she was happy with.

So what if it wasn't real?

And what if she discovered her old life and still didn't remember it? If the apartment was hers and none of it was familiar? Could she carry on without any memories? Did she have any choice?

Butterflies swarmed her stomach as she and Jason approached the building. They'd covered the last few blocks silently, and Anna couldn't help wondering what he was thinking. Was he thanking his lucky stars that he was about to be rid of her?

She had to admit that as much as she liked living with him, as secure, as welcome, as he'd made her feel, she hated having to rely on him. Hated him knowing she had to rely on him. Hated being nothing more than a charity case.

She climbed the steps to the brownstone, praying the apartment they'd come to see was hers.

But what was she going to do when Jason left her there all alone?

CHAPTER SEVEN

ANNA HATED the apartment. Brown vinyl furniture, scarred tables, not even a view out the one tiny window. The only redeeming things about the place were its tidiness and gleaming wooden floor.

"I don't recognize any of it," she said, feeling like a trespasser in a stranger's home—a stranger's life. But Mrs. Walters had recognized Anna, had shown them Anna's name on the mailbox just before she'd given them the key to the apartment. She'd left before Anna could ask the woman any questions but not before making it clear that Anna could stay only as long as she wasn't a bother to anyone—they weren't in the health-care business—and as long as Anna paid her rent.

"Relax, Anna," Jason said. He was standing by the nook that served as a kitchen, watching her. "You rented it furnished and you've only lived here a couple of months."

Relax. She'd just been made to feel like some kind of freak by her landlady, she didn't recognize a single stick of furniture, didn't like it either. Somehow she didn't think this was a relaxing situation. Damn him and his optimism, anyway. What did he know about losing all knowledge of everything you'd been, everything you'd ever hoped or dreamed to be? What did he know about letting yourself down so badly?

Crossing to the far corner of the apartment, Anna flung open the closet door, revealing a sparse row of uncomfortable-looking cotton shorts and shirts. She hated the clothing more than she hated the furniture. "Did these come with the place, too?" she asked, doing her best to stave off an attack of panic with a show of anger.

It was bad enough that nothing was familiar, but she didn't even like the stuff she was seeing. What if she didn't like the woman she'd been any better?

Jason crossed the room, dismissing the clothes with barely a glance as he took her by the shoulders. "You must have wanted a change when you came to New York," he said, holding her gaze with his own. "You never wore shorts."

She wasn't ready to be mollified. Not even by him. "It's not a good change."

"So don't wear them," he said, rubbing her shoulders. "But stop being so hard on yourself."

More than his words, the look in his eyes spoke to her, telling her he believed in her, that he knew she'd make it through this awful time.

But how could she believe in herself when her loss of memory was proof of her inability to handle her life?

"It's been almost a week, Jason. Don't you think I should be getting somewhere by now?"

"Dr. Gordon said it could take a while. You remembered the deli. That's a start."

And with that she would have to be satisfied. Except she didn't feel satisfied at all. Looking around, she tried to see the room from another perspective, as if this were all happening to someone else. How should a woman in her situation react? What should she do? What was the answer?

She just didn't know.

A perfunctory search of the apartment turned up a checkbook with a balance that would see her through several months; there were lots of Saltine crackers stashed in a drawer of the end table by the pullout couch, in the bathroom cupboard, in the single kitchen cupboard with a couple of cans of soup to go with them. The only other personal items were a laptop computer Jason said she'd used to keep her personal finance records, and a beautiful music box shaped like a castle. Jason listened to the tune, rewound it and listened again. He seemed more than casually interested in the box, almost as if surprised to see it there; but when she asked him about it, he merely shrugged and said she'd received the box from a friend.

And—in a table drawer—a personal address book. Shaking, afraid to open it, she stared at the flowered cover.

Eyes closed, she held the book to her breast. Between its covers lay details of her life, people she'd known. And suddenly she couldn't open the book quickly enough. Scanning the pages so urgently she almost tore them, her gaze flitted from one entry to the next, until she reached the last page.

"Nothing," she said as the book fell from her fingers. "I don't recognize a single name, not a place, not a number. I don't even recognize the handwriting." Her eyes burned with tears, her heart with failure.

"I've never seen this before," Jason said. She heard him pick up the book, riffle through the pages, and just didn't care. She was a great big nothing. The father of her baby could be listed there, and she wouldn't even know it.

"They're all from back home," Jason said, having reached the last page of the book.

"You know them?"

"Every one of them."

"We were that close that you knew everyone I knew?"

Setting the book on the end table, Jason pivoted away from her. "We ran in the same circles, shared a lot of mutual friends," he said. "This book looks new, as if you copied those numbers all at the same time."

She'd noticed that, too. Every entry was in the same ink, the handwriting neat.

"And I never met a person, made a phone call, wrote down an address since coming to New York?" she asked. She couldn't help the bitterness she heard in her voice. It was as if she didn't even exist anymore.

"You had a planner you kept things in," Jason said as if just now remembering. "Everything from business cards to appointments. You carried it in your purse."

"Which was lost in the crash." She was not having a good day.

After knocking fruitlessly on the doors of her immediate neighbors—they were either not at home or said she'd kept so much to herself they knew nothing about her—Anna and Jason stood awkwardly in her apartment again, surrounded by furniture neither of them recognized. And then there was nothing else to do but say goodbye. Jason invited her to spend one last night at his place, but precisely because she was tempted, she declined his offer. It was Saturday night, and he was sure to have his pick of beautiful women with whom to spend it. His beautiful co-anchor, Sunny Lawson, for one. The woman had undoubtedly been more than patient.

Jason accepted her refusal easily, almost insultingly easily, but Anna couldn't blame him. Instead, she chastised herself for being hurt, made certain he saw none of her uncertainty as she waved to him at the door and kept herself well hidden as she watched him all the way down the block through her one small window.

Then, desultorily, she made another search of her apartment, acquainting herself with where she kept the silverware and napkins, what kind of makeup she used, her few pieces of jewelry. She added her locket, which she'd been keeping in the inside pocket of her new purse, to the box containing her other jewelry. And then pulled it right back out again, dropping it into an envelope before placing it back inside her purse.

Dr. Gordon had warned her about depression, so she continued to poke into drawers, touching her things, trying to get a sense of the woman she'd been, pretending that she cared. But she still felt as though she were trespassing in a stranger's life, one she couldn't identify with, one she wasn't sure she even wanted to know.

First thing tomorrow she was going shopping for some more dresses. Right after she packed up every last pair of shorts for the Salvation Army.

Finding the key to her mailbox in a corner of the kitchen drawer, Anna went down to check her mail, retrieving only a couple of bills and some solicitations. She returned the wave of a small dark-haired woman coming out of a door down the hall from her before locking herself back inside her apartment, making sure to secure all three locks as Jason had instructed.

The entire episode ate up fifteen minutes of an evening that stretched beyond eternity. With the walls of the small apartment closing in on her, increasing the agitation that already drove her day in and day out, she sank onto the couch, telling herself to relax, to hold on, to be patient and let her mind heal itself. Yet the future loomed ahead of her, a dark specter in the night, frightening her with its blankness. What was she going to do with the rest of her life? What was she going to do tonight, and tomorrow, and the day after that?

She had no idea where she'd worked, if she'd worked, but judging by the size of her checking account, work wasn't going to be of pressing concern anytime soon—she was going to be receiving a settlement from the city, as well. Besides, it wasn't as if she'd be much use to anyone at the moment, not having the slightest idea what she could do or memory of any training she'd had. And there was always the chance that her employer would view her exactly as her landlady had, a burden to be pitied. Nothing more.

For now, work was out.

Her stomach tightened, the horrible fear looming darkly over her again, consuming her. What was she going to do if she never remembered? And what was going to happen if she did? What horrible things would be there waiting? Would she still not be able to handle them? Would she flip out? Have a breakdown? Go mad?

She thought about calling Abby. About California. About going home. At least there she'd have someone to talk to. Someone to take care of her. Someone to commit her if she went over the edge.

And she thought about Jason. His tall athletic body. The way his eyes always made her feel warm, special. His laugh. His charm. His arousal the other night.... And she thought about Sunny Davis in his apartment, maybe that very moment.

She thought about the child she carried, the conception that had vanished from her memory as if it had never been. The man whose baby she carried. Then she started to cry. Was he out there somewhere thinking she'd deserted him? Or had he deserted her? Would he think her a weak fool for having a mind that checked out as it pleased?

Did *she* think herself a fool?

Anna stopped crying. Stood. Paced her small living room. And faced the truth. She did think herself a fool. And worse. She hated herself for refusing to deal with her life and escaping into this...emptiness. Hated the weakness, the cowardice surrounding her condition. But worst of all, she hated herself for wishing she could run back to Jason, bury herself in his arms and never remember at all.

HE BOUGHT HER groceries, called her four times a day, asked her to breakfast, to lunch, and beat the hell out of a racquetball while convincing himself that he was just being a friend, that he wasn't getting involved. That he'd be able to walk away.

He always had, hadn't he? Every time his mother called, he was there for her, no strings attached. No expectations. No recriminations when his birthday rolled around, Christmas, sometimes even a year or two with no word from her. Helping was what a man did. What a man *should* do.

"Jason?" He'd known it was Anna on the phone even before he answered it Tuesday morning. She was the only one who would dare call him before noon. In recent months, as his nights stretched till dawn, he hadn't been awake much before then.

"I found a file box in the back of the closet," she said. She was sounding stronger each day, taking control of her life. He admired the hell out of her. "There's this pay stub, just like you said there might be, from a place called Old World Alterations. It's in Little Italy."

Grabbing his keys off the coffee table, Jason said, "I'm on my way."

THE PLACE WAS a modern day sweatshop. Standing with Anna on the sidewalk outside the building that gray New York day, Jason stared with horror at all the women crammed into the small space, some sitting at sewing machines, others in hard-backed chairs, stitching by hand. No one spoke. No one smiled. But their fingers flew, racing to finish one job only to start another.

Sick to his stomach at the thought of Anna sitting in there like that, working as though she was a slave, Jason turned away. He'd seen enough. If Anna had worked there, she would no longer. He'd pay her damn rent if he had to. She wasn't going back in there.

Except she was. She reached for the door handle.

"Anna."

She dropped her hand and turned, surprised, almost as if she'd forgotten him.

"Do you remember being here?" he asked her.

She shook head distractedly.

"Do you know if I can sew?" she asked him.

The way she said it was so odd he had to ask, "Why?"

"I feel like I can sew," she said slowly.

She was remembering. "You can."

Someone bumped into her and she stepped back along the wall of the building. "Am I any good?"

"Very." She'd made money—a lot of it—sewing up Abby's designs for a line of children's wear that sold in exclusive shops all over Southern California.

Frowning, she looked at the women. "I don't think I like it," she said, sounding perplexed.

A sigh eased through Jason, releasing a spring of hope. He'd always suspected that sewing wasn't what Anna wanted to do, rather, what she did for Abby. But she'd never before admitted as much—even when he'd confronted her about it before leaving for New York. Perhaps, just perhaps, her memory loss was doing something for her he never could, getting her to know herself.

"Let's go in," Anna said. Her mind was obviously made up. She was going to follow up on this lead. Jason went with her inside.

"Anna!" The accented male voice came from someplace in the rear of the shop. "You've come back to us!"

Anna froze inside the door, immediately wary, though she had no idea why. The man sounded friendly enough. He'd been sitting at a desk and now he jumped up and came forward, weaving his thin body between the sewing machines.

Several women looked over at her behind his back, smiling tentatively, but then bowed their heads and resumed their work before she could return their smiles.

"I can't believe you've come back to us," the man said. Ignoring Jason, he reached for Anna's hand, kissing it before pulling her forward.

Anna wanted to slap him. In fact, the urge was so strong she had to move away.

She tried to concentrate on what he'd just said. He couldn't believe she'd come back. As though he hadn't been expecting to see her again. "I don't work here anymore?" she asked.

"Of course you work." He winked at her. "I give you lots of work!"

Jason stepped forward so that he stood between Anna and the man.

"You know about the subway crash," he said, his usual charm nonexistent. Anna had never seen him like this before.

"Oh!" The man hit his palm to his forehead. "It was you!" He looked at Anna. "The Anna they say was hurt. She was you?"

Anna nodded.

"And you still don't remember?"

Anna shook her head before realizing she was under no obligation to tell this man anything.

"My poor Anna," he said. "Come here and let your Roger make it all better." He tried to pull her into his arms, but Anna held back.

"My Roger?" she asked, managing little more than a whisper. Jason was frozen beside her.

"Of course you don't remember, but not to worry. I will remember for both of us." He grabbed Anna again, holding her close as he whispered, "What we had was good, no?"

Nausea overwhelmed her. It was all Anna could do not to be sick all over the man's dirty white shirt.

"You were so good, my little Anna." He kissed his fingertips.

Had she actually slept with this creep?

Oh, God. Was it his baby she carried?

With a quick look at Jason's horrified face, she dashed for the bathroom, getting there just in time to lose her breakfast. Hunched over the toilet, she heaved until she thought her ribs were going to break, but nothing could take away the sick feeling washing over her.

How could she go out there? Jason had heard the man. He'd obviously reached the same conclusion she had. And was disgusted. How could she ever face him again? How could she ever face herself?

Finally she rose, wetting a piece of paper towel under the sink and holding it against her burning face. If this was the life she'd left behind, she'd rather die than go back to it.

"Anna?" Jason's voice came through the door.

"Anna?" Roger's suggestive calling of her name nearly sent her back to the toilet.

"Ohhh, go away," she cried softly to herself, and opened the door.

"You're still sick from your crash?" Roger asked, not quite as enthusiastic once he got a look at her pale face.

All Anna could see was Jason, standing in front of the other man, his eyes searching her face intently. "You okay?"

She shook her head, silently begging him to get her out of there, to make the nightmare go away.

The phone rang and one of the women answered it, calling Roger to talk to someone named Baker.

"I'll be right back," he said to Anna as he walked off.

"Pssst."

Anna looked at Jason. Had he said something?

"Pssst."

A woman over by the door was trying to get her attention. Jason motioned Anna ahead, and they eased their way to the front of the shop.

"You no work here no more," the woman whispered in fractured English. She stared at the pair of men's slacks she was hemming by hand, her fingers never missing a stitch as they flew along the dark material.

Anna didn't respond, afraid to draw attention to the fact that the woman was speaking. But she nodded, hoping the woman would understand that she was listening.

"Quit, six, eight weeks ago. Very sudden. No one say why."

Exchanging a glance with Jason, Anna nodded again.

"Boss, he like you. Not like he like good worker." She lifted the pants to her mouth, cut the thread with her teeth and looked out the window.

The conversation was over.

Roger could still be heard in the back of the shop, speaking rapidly in a foreign language, glancing out every now and then, making certain Anna was still there. Jason grabbed Anna by the arm and pulled her out the door of the shop into the gloomy morning. She hurried silently beside him as he led her down the street, eager to put as much distance as she could between her and the disgusting slimy man whose touch had made her want to curl up and die. The man who could very well be the father of her baby.

JASON DIDN'T SLOW down. Not even after they'd traveled enough blocks and made enough turns to have lost the bastard should he *have* followed them. He continued to walk simply because he didn't know what else to do. He had to think, to make sense out of the past half hour, consider the woman he'd known and loved for more than two years and somehow find the truth.

"Am I carrying his child?" Anna's cry was so distraught passersby on the sidewalk stopped and stared.

"No!" Jason said, pulling her against him, sheltering her from a young man who was sending her furtive looks over his shoulder.

"How do you know?" she asked more softly. He could hear tears in her voice. Tears and something else—a distress so deep he knew she'd never recover if her fear turned into truth.

"I know you." But did he? "You'd never have gone for a man like that, Anna. Never."

The Anna he'd known wouldn't have. But the Anna he'd known would never have slept with another man only six weeks after leaving his bed. Or left Abby, either.

CHAPTER EIGHT

NEITHER OF THEM had an appetite for lunch and, at Anna's suggestion, headed back to her apartment. She had to search it again, tear it apart, look through everything she could find for something that would prove Roger was not the father of her child. Jason helped her look, but found nothing.

She had books—lots of those—blank computer disks, they even found the name of the obstetrician she'd made her first appointment with, one she missed the day after the subway crashed.

Getting out the phone directory, Jason started calling alteration shops in the area. None of them had employed or ever heard of Anna Hayden. Anna contacted the phone company, the electric company, asking for the job information recorded on her billing records. Old World Alterations.

"The first person someone calls after changing jobs usually isn't a utility company," Jason pointed out when she hung up the phone for the second time.

Anna felt like crying. She could feel the tears welling behind her lids and forced them away. On top of everything else, she wasn't going to cry on him. Jason hated tears.

Her head shot up, her heart beating against her ribs as she stared at him.

"What?" he asked.

She shook her head, flooded with confusing emotions, glee, fear, a sense of helpless foreboding left from the morning's ordeal—and hope. Grabbing her shoulders, Jason pulled her closer, holding her gaze. "What, Anna? You look like you've seen a ghost."

Her tears won the battle, trickling down her cheeks, but she smiled up at him, grateful beyond anything she'd ever known to have this one precious memory. This connection. To him.

"You hate tears," she said.

She laughed at the astonished look in his eyes. The delight. And was puzzled by the shadows that immediately followed. "You remember me?" he asked, letting her go.

She shook her head, still smiling in spite of his puzzling behavior. "Just that you hate tears." She really had known him before. Not that she'd ever doubted his word, but it was just so damn good to know something simply because she knew, not because she'd been told.

He nodded. "You're right. I do. Or I did. Until a friend pointed out how ridiculous I was to feel threatened by a simple expression of emotion." He continued to study her, his hands in the pockets of his chinos.

"Why would I know such a thing?"

"We went to see *While You Were Sleeping.* Your sister balled like a baby and I got on her case for it."

"*While You Were Sleeping?* Is that a movie?"

He nodded, still watching her.

"Why'd it make her cry?"

"Because all the woman in the movie wanted was to be part of a family and yet, in spite of her efforts, she was always on the outside looking in."

Sounded to Anna like something that might have touched Jason, as well, knowing what she did about his lonely childhood.

"So who had the guts to tell you how ridiculous it was to feel threatened by tears?"

"You did." He turned away from her. "In Abby's defense."

For the first time in days he was measuring his words again. There was more to that story. He just wasn't telling her. But at the moment she was so giddy with her proof of his place in her life she couldn't worry about the secrets lurking just beyond her grasp.

She remembered knowing Jason.

HER NEWFOUND REMEMBRANCE, minute as it was, had a disturbing repercussion. Sitting on her couch, munching an early dinner, Anna watched Jason on the six-o'clock news that evening. She took pride in how he looked in his navy jacket with the station's emblem above the pocket; only Jason's broad shoulders could look that good. She loved the way his eyes crinkled when he smiled, approved of his witty repartee and generally felt privileged for knowing personally one of the city's most sought-after bachelors. And was shocked at the proprietary nature of her feelings.

When Sunny Lawson laid her perfectly manicured fingers on his forearm, Anna wanted to claw her eyes out. Afraid of the vehemence of the feeling, of what it meant, she forced herself to think about all the reasons Jason needed a woman like Sunny in his life, why, as a friend, she, Anna, had to hope they'd be very happy together. Why she had no business feeling jealous over a man she wasn't free to have. Even if she wasn't living in this half world of no memories, she had no right to Jason. She was bound to another man—and to the child she'd created with him.

Making herself watch Jason and Sunny together, Anna tried not to care. But no matter the logic of her reasoning, she couldn't stop her chest from tightening, her skin chilling, the butterflies invading her stomach.

And the more she panicked, the more panicked she grew. Was she so unstable that she was going to fall apart at everything? The woman she was now had only known Jason a matter of days. She couldn't possibly care for him so much that merely seeing another woman touch him was ripping her heart out.

But Jason was all she had. The only person she knew. It was natural for her to feel a bit possessive, she thought, trying to reassure herself. She just had to make certain she didn't get carried away with her possessiveness.

Jason had other friends. He played racquetball. One time when she'd been at his place, he'd received a phone call from a buddy of his in California. She wasn't the only person in his life by a long shot—wasn't even the most important person in his life.

Suddenly, out of nowhere, Anna was struck with the need to talk to Abby. Jason wasn't the only person in her life, either. He wasn't even the only one who cared. She knew Abby had been keeping in close contact with Jason. He'd told her so.

Picking up the phone with shaking fingers, Anna realized she didn't even know Abby's number. She refused to be daunted, dialing the operator, instead, requesting the area code for Oxnard, California, dialing long-distance information, only half-aware that she knew exactly how to do so. Yes, there was a listing for Abigale

Hayden. Anna scribbled while an automated voice intoned the number.

She dialed the number quickly, giving herself no time to change her mind. She'd only talk for a couple of minutes. She just had to connect with someone who knew her, who hopefully loved her, unconditionally, as family was meant to. Someone who would still love her if Roger was the father of her baby. Someone who would love her even if she found herself hopelessly, dangerously attracted to another man. Someone who knew Jason.

But before the phone rang even once, Anna hung up, remembering Dr. Gordon's warning not to contact her family. And even more, his admonition to learn to trust herself. She'd had a real live memory that day. She couldn't give up now, couldn't let herself down. As the doctor had reminded her more than once, she'd requested a year away from her family for a reason. And that reason might very well be connected to the vacation her mind had taken.

She had to learn to trust herself. Regain some faith in herself. And that was going to take time. She had to take back control of her life or live forever like this—in a world without color, without depth, without memories.

Turning off the television set, Anna grabbed one of the many books stacked on her closet shelf, drew a hot bath and ordered herself to settle in and read. To focus her mind on something else for a while, to think about somebody else's problems. She made it through only a couple of pages before realizing that she'd read the story before. She couldn't remember how it ended, but she knew she'd read it.

And several hours later, as she lay in the middle of the pullout bed, snuggled in her nightgown under the covers, and finished the book, she couldn't help replotting the ending. And that was something she'd done before, too.

HE SHOULD HAVE learned his lesson, but Jason couldn't seem to stop himself from spending most of his free time with Anna. She was like a drug, an addiction, had been since the first time he'd ever met her. He was also thinking about her too much, preoccupied when he should have been focused—on the racquetball court, at the station, out with Sunny. But he couldn't just desert Anna. Not now. Not when she needed him. Not when her eyes lit up every time he walked into the room. Not when she said his name in that husky voice. Not when he…

It couldn't lead to anything. She had other priorities, people who came before he did in her life, in her heart. But where was the harm in helping her? He was a strong guy. He could handle it, he assured a couple of his buddies from California when they phoned. He was fine, he told his mother when, for once, she remembered to call to wish him happy birthday.

What he couldn't handle, couldn't accept, was walking away from a friend in need.

And Anna was a friend in need, he told himself the following Saturday. She needed a day out of the city. A day of freedom when she could be the same as everyone else around her, carefree, enjoying herself. A day at the beach. He wanted to take her somewhere that might spark a memory—of him, of the love they'd shared. They'd been on a beach the first time they'd made love. And the last time.

His Jaguar was waiting for him, sleek, its white paint gleaming, the leather seats cool in the dark of the garage. Flipping the switch to put the top down, he waited for it to curl into the back of the car, securing the leather cover around the entire mechanism. Jason counted on very little in his life, invested his heart stingily, but he cared about his car. It was the one thing he'd really wanted that he'd had the power to get, to keep. He'd worked hard, demanding from his career what he couldn't demand from his personal life, fighting for the top spot in a competitive field, settling for nothing less. The Jag was his reward. And his reminder.

Anna had loved his car. She'd loved the wind blowing through her hair, unconcerned when the long strands became tangled because of her refusal to pull it back, laughing out loud when he pressed the accelerator to the floor, the thrill of speed turning her on.

"What a gorgeous machine!" When he collected her Saturday morning, her eyes lit up just as they'd used to. "Why haven't I seen it before now?"

She had. And she'd run her hands along its smooth contours just as she was doing now. "The closest garage I could find is fifteen miles away from my apartment," he said, opening her door for her.

She climbed in and he shut the door, asking, "You have your swimsuit?"

"I'm wearing it." Pulling down the top of her dress, she showed him.

Yep, she was wearing it. A tight-fitting one-piece black affair that showed him the cleavage he already knew intimately. Suddenly it was his turn to appreciate a sleek body. Except that he couldn't run his hands along this one the way she'd done moments before. Not anymore.

"You'll let me drive it sometime, won't you? After I get my new license?"

Jason froze, halfway around the car, staring at the back of her head. She finally turned, frowning at him.

"What?" she asked. "I'm a great driver." And then, "Aren't I?"

"Yeah, growing up near L.A. you have to be, but what makes you think I'd let you drive my car?"

She shrugged. "You're a nice guy."

Giving some inane reply, Jason continued on to his side of the car, sliding into the driver's seat with the ease of practice. For a second there he'd thought she'd remembered. In the old days, back when they loved each other, her driving his car had been a standing gag between them. She always wanted to. He always let her—and was nervous as a ninny sitting beside her the whole time. But she'd always made it up to him in the most glorious ways. More than once, before they'd ever made it out of the car....

"I met this girl in the hallway yesterday," Anna said, breaking into his thoughts as he headed out of the city. "Maggie Simmons."

"Someone you knew before?" He downshifted, trying to ignore the feel of his hand brushing against her leg. He moved over to the right lane.

"Not well." Anna frowned. "Like all the others she said I kept mostly to myself."

Jason nodded, content to listen to her. She'd been giving him hour-by-hour accounts of her day ever since she'd left the hospital, sharing more of her thoughts with him in the past two weeks than in the two years they'd been lovers. He would gladly have spent the rest of his life listening.

"Has it ever occurred to you that I'm not a very friendly person?" she asked.

Keeping his speed moderate so he could hear her, Jason considered her question. God, he hated the secrets between them. Not just the things she couldn't remember, but his lies by omission.

"You were always private, honey, but never unfriendly," he said, weighing his words. He wasn't a doctor. How the hell did he know how much he should tell her? And how, loving her as he had, did he stomach keeping the truth from her?

They drove silently for a while, Anna's expression smoothing as the Jag ate up the miles, putting more and more distance between them and the city.

Anna at last broke the silence. "Maggie told me something kind of odd."

"What's that?"

"Well, she's pretty sure I haven't worked in the past six weeks because I was always home."

"Nothing too odd about that if you were having troubles finding a job you wanted. It's not like you couldn't afford to take a little time off."

"My money isn't going to last forever."

Jason acknowledged the truth of that with a shrug. She was getting a settlement from the city, though not enough to live on for the rest of her life. But she had lots of time to worry about earning her keep and more pertinent things about which to worry.

"Anyway, Maggie said sometimes I'd come home carrying full garbage bags like some kind of bag lady." Anna said the words hesitantly, stealing a glance at him as if to assess his reaction.

Jason chuckled. "Surely you aren't thinking you were a bag lady."

"Of course not!" Anna said indignantly. "But you have to admit, it's odd."

"Only because you don't seem to have several garbage bags worth of stuff in your entire apartment."

"Oh, well, that's the other weird thing." Anna's hair flew about her face, brushing his shoulder as she turned her head toward him.

"Apparently, after bringing in the bags, I'd be home all day, sometimes several days in a row, and then I'd leave again, carrying the same full bags."

"And what do you make of all this?"

"I did people's laundry?" She grinned at him.

Jason grinned back. "Where, in the tub?"

"I had a bird-sitting business and was smuggling in birdcages?"

He hooted with laughter. "You're afraid of birds."

She frowned at him. "Why on earth would anyone be afraid of a poor defenseless creature like a bird?"

"You saw Alfred Hitchcock's movie *The Birds* when you were little."

"And?" she prompted.

"Swarms of birds practically take over a town, and they attack people. It gets pretty ugly."

"I wonder why a little girl would be watching such a thing?"

He'd asked the same question when she'd first confessed her childhood fear. It was the first time she'd told him anything about growing up with only her sisters for guidance. The three had spent hours in front of the television watching programs they never should have seen, waiting patiently for the parents they adored to get home from work. There had been times when they'd fallen asleep, still waiting.

She wouldn't like the answer any better than he had.

"I wasn't there," was all he said. "Anyway, it wasn't birds. What else can you suggest?"

"I liked to shop, but suffered from buyer's remorse?"

Her stories got wilder the farther they drove. She was the bagman in a smuggling ring. A drunk—the bottles empty when she carried them back out, of course. A thief with a conscience, stealing and then returning what she stole. By the time they'd parked and gathered the cooler and blanket from the trunk, Jason had almost forgotten the troubles they'd left behind. For a moment out of time he had his Anna back.

Following Jason, Anna took a deep breath of the salty ocean air. "I love the beach, don't I?" she asked, but she didn't need the confirmation. Something else she just knew. Like she knew she was a good driver. Things were coming back. Too slowly, to be sure, but how glorious to begin to know herself. To really know the person in whose body she lived.

"You had a cottage on the beach," Jason told her, coming around the car.

Had she stayed there alone? she wanted to know, but didn't ask. She wasn't going to ruin this time with him by worrying about things she had no control over. Not today.

The sand felt like heaven between her toes. So familiar. So good. She could imagine herself lying in it, the grains closing around her body like a glove.

"Let's build a castle," she said suddenly, plopping down close to the water.

Dropping the blanket and cooler, Jason joined her. "Watch out," he warned, settling in as though he expected to be there awhile.

"Whatever for?" Anna asked. How difficult could it be? Anyone could see that all you needed was the right mixture of water and sand to construct just about any shape you wanted. It didn't take a memory to pile up a bunch of sand.

Jason pulled off his shirt, threw it down and stretched out on it, his elbow in the sand, his hand supporting his head. "Just wait and see."

He looked resigned, expectant. And gorgeous.

"Did you play sports in school?" Anna forced her eyes back to the job at hand. The sun was hot enough without her thoughts making her even hotter.

"Quarterback of my high-school football team," he said, clearly pleased with himself.

She wasn't surprised. His body was a work of art.

"Did you go to college?"

He nodded. "On a swimming scholarship. Care to race me?"

Anna grabbed a cup out of the cooler, packing it with sand. "In a minute. Let me finish this," she said.

"That'll take more than a minute."

She didn't care if it took all day if it meant he'd still be lying there beside her. Her stomach was doing flip-flops just looking at him. But she couldn't make herself stop stealing covert glances.

"What school'd you go to?" she asked, making room for the small tower that had to go on one corner of the castle.

He'd gone to USC, had a masters degree in communication, could ski as well as he swam, spent summers playing beach volleyball and had lost his virginity when—

"What?" he snapped, sitting up when she asked that last question.

"Sorry," she said, using both hands to dig her moat. "It just slipped out."

When it came to Jason, she had sex on the brain. She was praying that was because she didn't have much else there at the moment. But she wasn't convinced.

"Sixteen."

"Hmm?" she said, trying her best to concentrate on the sand castle.

"I was sixteen. She was a present from my father. He was supposed to have taken me skiing for my birthday, but had to fly to New York on business at the last minute."

"Some present."

Had that woman been worth being ditched by his father? To some guys, probably so. Anna wasn't so sure about Jason. His priorities were different. People were important to him. Commitment, loyalty were important to him. This was perfectly clear to her, even after having only known him less than two weeks. Why else would he be continuing to help her if not for his loyalty to her family?

Remembering what he'd told her about his youth, Anna wondered if he'd ever come first in his parents' lives. Hadn't they seen what a special person they'd created? She couldn't imagine not wanting to spend every minute she could with her baby as it was growing up, whether he was a model child or not. Life passed so quickly.

"She was actually kind of nice," Jason added almost as an afterthought. "I dated her for a while, until I realized that just because she was seeing me didn't mean she wasn't also working as a prostitute."

Anna didn't want to hear any more about it. She was sorry she'd ever asked.

"I'm sorry, Jason," she said, knowing the words weren't going to do anything to dispel the memories she'd roused.

"Don't be." He filtered a fistful of sand through his fingers. "It was a long time ago. And hey, for a kid with adolescent hormones, great sex isn't anything to scoff at."

"That's some castle!" A young couple strolling down the beach stopped beside them, interrupting just as Anna was getting jealous of a seventeen-year-old memory.

"One of her more basic attempts," Jason said.

The girl leaned down, marveling at the nooks and crannies. "Basic! She's an artist!"

Anna dug her moat a little deeper, hating the attention she'd inadvertently drawn to herself.

"Gee, lady, you're good!" a little boy said.

One by one, people of all ages came over, little kids who wanted to make a castle, too, their parents, assorted couples, several teenagers, even an old codger down on the beach with his metal detector, looking for Lord only knew what kind of treasure. But they all had one thing in common—shared amazement at Anna's creation.

Jason being Jason struck up a conversation with just about every one of them as they wandered over. Anna, feeling tongue-tied and uncomfortable, marveled again at his charm, his talent for making people feel at ease.

Embarrassed by the continued attention, she finally suggested they break out the lunch he'd brought along. But before they opened the cooler, she insisted on moving as far down the beach as she could get from the castle she'd made.

"I had no idea I was going to cause such a stir," she said. Looking back at it, she couldn't help but be proud of her work. She really was good. She'd had no idea.

"I did."

"I've done this before, huh?" she asked. She should have known something was up by Jason's reaction when she'd first sat down in the sand.

"Your sand sculptures have won prizes," Jason said, helping her to spread their blanket.

Anna laughed. "Get out of here."

"Kids used to knock on your door just to ask you to come out and play in the sand."

She froze, her hand half in and half out of the cooler. She

couldn't tell if he was pulling her leg or not, and it was suddenly important to her that he wasn't. For the first time since she'd awoken in this nightmare, she was discovering something about herself that she liked—a lot. She wanted to be the kind of person little kids knocked on the door to play with.

"Did I?" she asked.

"Of course."

Satisfied, feeling better than she had in days, she tucked her sandy damp dress beneath her and sat down to lunch.

She'd discovered a talent. She'd made a sand castle. She'd had fun.

CHAPTER NINE

BEDRAGGLED BUT SMILING, Anna climbed the steps to her apartment late that afternoon, meeting Maggie in the hallway.

"Looks like you had a day at the beach," Maggie said, pointing at Anna's damp and sandy dress. In spite of the bathing suit she had on, she'd never taken the dress off. She'd been too aware of Jason's half-naked body to be comfortable undressing with him so near, and too self-conscious of the fact that, though she wasn't yet showing, there was a baby growing inside her. She'd also seen that look in his eyes again.

"Jason took me," Anna said, smiling shyly at the other woman. She'd told Maggie about her amnesia when they'd met the day before, and also about Jason's rescue of her from nowhere land.

"You guys have dinner?" Maggie's short curls bobbed as she spoke, giving the impression that she was always on the move.

"No." Anna felt her stomach rumble even as she said the word. She may not feel pregnant yet, other than the occasional bouts of nausea, but she was hungry enough for two. "I imagine Jason had a date."

Maggie grinned. "It's so cool that you know him," she said.

Anna nodded, a little uncomfortable with Maggie's brash way, not sure how to respond. But she welcomed the woman's friendliness just the same. Especially when again faced with a lonely Saturday night of trying not to picture Jason with another woman. Anna and Jason spent days together. Never nights. She assumed he had less platonic ways to spend his evenings off than with a pregnant, confused family friend.

"So how about dinner? I made spaghetti and there's plenty," Maggie offered.

Anna shook her head instinctively and then stopped. "I'd like that,'' she said. "If it won't be too much of a bother."

"No bother at all. I'd love the company."

THE TWO HAD DINNER together twice more that next week. Once at Anna's. The other time at Maggie's. Maggie wanted to be an actress and waited tables four nights a week to make ends meet while she spent her days traipsing from one audition to the next. Anna didn't see what Maggie saw in her, a woman with no past, and feared sometimes that the only thing that kept Maggie coming back was pity. And yet Maggie's friendship felt genuine.

"Do you know if I was dating anyone?" Anna asked Maggie the following Thursday night. They were sitting in Maggie's apartment, and though she itched to tidy up some of the clutter, Anna liked being at her friend's place.

Maggie nodded, helping herself to another piece of the pepperoni pizza they'd ordered. "You mentioned having a date once or twice."

Suddenly not hungry, Anna asked, "Did you ever see the guy?"

"Yeah." Maggie frowned. "Once. I'm not even sure if it was the same guy each time. I just assumed it was. You weren't quite as easy to get to know back then."

"From what I can tell, I was a really private person," Anna admitted. "I'm not really sure how to go about the friend thing."

Except that she knew she wanted Maggie's friendship. She looked forward to their evenings together, to having another woman around to talk to, laugh with.

"Relax." Maggie grinned. "You're doing fine."

"WHAT DO YOU DO during the day?" Maggie asked on Wednesday of the following week. They'd gone to a deli around the corner for dinner and were on their way back to the brownstone.

"I walk in Gramercy Park." She might have hated her apartment, but she adored the gated park, she'd discovered, which was for residents' use only. "And I read a lot." Hearing herself, Anna was embarrassed by how boring her life must seem to her actress friend.

"That's all? I'd go nuts." Ever dramatic, Maggie rolled her eyes and pressed a hand to her chest.

Anna supposed to someone like Maggie it sounded like a prison sentence, but to Anna, this time was a gift; she could feel herself growing stronger with every day that passed—although she suspected it wouldn't be long before she was going to have to find something to do. One could only sit around getting strong for so long. Then you had to do something with that strength. Trouble was, she had no idea what she wanted to do. What she *could* do. Other than sew—and build sand castles. She didn't want to sew, and building castles was a bit difficult in the city.

"I also see Jason," she said, hating that she was actually trying to win Maggie's approval with the admission. It was more important that she approve of herself.

"Now that I could handle." Maggie grinned. "You guys an item yet?"

Anna laughed, embarrassed. "Of course not."

"Why not? He's gorgeous. You're gorgeous. A match made in heaven."

"I'm pregnant." Anna couldn't believe it when she just blurted the words.

Maggie stopped in her tracks, staring openmouthed at Anna. "Pregnant?"

Anna nodded, watching her friend, wishing she'd kept quiet. But she was going to be starting to show soon, and if she planned to continue this friendship, Maggie was going to have to know.

"How?"

Anna shrugged. "The usual way, I suppose," she said, echoing words she'd heard from Dr. Gordon.

"You mean you don't remember?" Maggie's eyes widened, her New York accent more pronounced than usual. "It happened before…?"

Nodding again as Maggie's words trailed off, Anna started walking again. Maggie followed.

"Then you don't know who the father is?" Maggie asked, turning to watch Anna.

It sounded so horrible the way Maggie said it. Anna shook her head.

"Wow."

Exactly. But at least now Maggie knew.

"So how often you seeing Jason?" Maggie asked a few moments later.

"Almost every day."

Maggie stumbled. "You're kidding!"

"It's nothing, really," Anna said. But it was. She cherished every moment of her time with Jason. "We're just doing the tourist bit. He's only been in this city three months and with the new job and all hasn't done any sight-seeing yet. And it's not like I remember any of it even if I have seen it."

"You're touring the city with him and you call that nothing?" Maggie screeched. "You know how much I'd give for one lunch with someone like him?" She clearly thought Anna needed some brain readjustment. If only she knew. Anna was glad to see their brownstone just up ahead.

"It's completely platonic." If you didn't count the way her body had a mind of its own every time she was with Jason.

Maggie harrumphed. "Maybe you simply haven't figured out yet that he's nuts about you. A guy doesn't spend that much time with a girl unless he wants in her pants."

"Maggie!" After several days in Maggie's company Anna was still sometimes shocked by the other woman's New York bluntness. "And he's not nuts about me," she said. He couldn't be. Period. "He's just a friend. I think he feels sorry for me."

"Real sorry," Maggie said sarcastically. "Has he asked you up to his place yet?" Her question was accompanied by a sly lift of her eyebrows.

"I lived there for three days."

"I mean since then," Maggie said with exasperation.

"No. And he doesn't come to my place, either," Anna said before Maggie could ask. "We go out in public, in broad daylight. That's the way one tours the city."

"Just wait," Maggie said. "He'll ask you up to see his etchings."

"Trust me, he saves his etchings for other women, Maggie. I never even see him after two or three in the afternoon."

Maggie gave a disappointed sigh. "Have it your way."

"It's the way it is." The way it had to stay.

"So what's he like?" Maggie asked, stepping sideways to avoid a little boy on a bicycle.

Anna smiled. "I don't know... Charming. Intelligent. Nice."

"You go out with a man like that and you call him *nice?*"

Anything else she might see in Jason she couldn't admit to herself, let alone Maggie. "He *is* nice." He was still taking pity on her, wasn't he? Although, if she was to be honest, there'd been more than one time since that night in his apartment when his interest in her had seemed like anything but pity. There was that peculiar look in his eyes...

"He's also to-die-for gorgeous, every inch male—even his eyes can knock you for a loop if you let them."

So Maggie had noticed. "He's just a friend, okay?" Anna couldn't think of him as anything else. To do so would be emotional suicide. If not now, then certainly when she regained her memory of the man whose child she carried.

"And he takes you out every day?"

"Not every day, but a lot." Anna was growing more and more uncomfortable with Maggie's questions. "We're seeing Manhattan one block at a time."

"You're in love with him, aren't you?" Maggie said suddenly, stopping at the steps of their brownstone.

"Of course not!" Hadn't Maggie been listening? "I'm not, Maggie," she added when her friend still looked unconvinced. "We're just friends."

"Well, if you're not in love with him, you should be." Maggie persisted. "Take a chance, girl. A relationship with that man would be...*incomparable.*"

Somehow Anna knew that, her lack of anything to compare it to notwithstanding. But that changed nothing. "Maggie, I'm pregnant."

"So?"

"So, the baby's not Jason's."

"Does he know?"

"Of course."

"Then what's the problem?"

"The problem is that there's a man out there I don't remember right now, but who I loved enough to make a baby with."

"Maybe. Maybe not."

Anna prayed every day that she'd loved her baby's father. She didn't want to be the type of woman who'd get pregnant for any other reason. If she hadn't loved the man... The very thought terrified her. Because if she hadn't loved the man, she could be carrying the child of a creep like Roger. Or a man who'd forced her...

"Besides, what would Jason want with someone like me?" she asked, wishing she'd just stayed home that night. She'd really been having a good day.

"Have you looked in the mirror lately, girl?" Maggie asked. "You're nuts if you don't try to make it with this guy."

And suddenly, as much as Anna loved having her new friend around, she felt the strongest urge to turn and run. To get as far away from Maggie as she could go. Her chest felt tight, every breath a struggle as, standing outside in the balmy New York evening, walls started closing in on her.

She couldn't let herself be talked into something she felt was wrong. She had to make her own decisions. Even if it meant that Maggie didn't want to be her friend anymore.

And as for what Maggie'd suggested, what kind of man would Jason be if he was willing to settle for someone like her? Someone who came to him, not only memoryless, but pregnant with another man's child?

A man who didn't love her, that was what he'd be. Because with the way he'd grown up, never coming first in his parents' lives, there was no possibility he was going to allow himself to settle for second place again. And second place was all she had to offer.

WAITING TO DRIVE across the Verrazano Narrows Bridge onto Staten Island Saturday morning, Jason smiled to himself. Life had a way of slipping in surprising little twists and turns that made the impossible almost seem possible. He would never have believed a month ago that he'd be joining a queue of summer tourists with Anna at his side. He wouldn't have believed she'd ever be at his side again, period.

As usual she was wearing one of her lightweight, sexy-as-hell dresses, though one Jason had never seen before—something she must have picked up on one of the shopping expeditions she'd told him about. He approved of her choice. The colors were bolder than she usually wore. So many little changes.

"I saw Dr. Gordon yesterday," she said, her long hair wind-tousled. "His wife had her baby last week—a little boy. Both are home and doing fine."

"Good for them!" Jason tried to inject the same enthusiastic note he'd heard in Anna's voice into his own, in spite of the surprising flash of jealousy that flared in him. So the doctor and his wife shared something he and Anna didn't share—a child. The best of both of them in one package. He could almost picture the little towhead he and Anna would have had. But it wasn't to be. Still, he had more today than he'd had a month ago. It should be enough.

"So what did he have to say about you?" He stole a sideways glance.

"He says my confidence is growing."

"It is." Three weeks ago Anna had relied on him for everything. The sun highlighted the gold in her hair. "I asked him about calling Abby."

Jason froze. So the bond the triplets shared *was* reaching her even now?

"What'd he say?" Not yet. He wasn't ready yet.

"That to rock the boat at this point could very well cause a setback," she reported. "He still says it's best if I remember on my own."

"And he's confident you will?"

Anna stared straight ahead as Jason inched his Jag closer to the bridge. "Absolutely. According to him all these little things coming back are just the beginning."

"Like the sand castle."

"Yeah." She paused, frowning. "You know, I had the oddest sensation last night, almost like a memory, but it wasn't that tangible."

"A feeling?"

He wanted so badly for her to remember their love. And dreaded the day when she did. He didn't really hold out any hope that he and Anna would ever be together again. So much more than her sister stood between them now.

"Yes, a feeling—that describes it as well as anything," she finally said.

"What happened?"

"Maggie was nagging me and suddenly I got really claustrophobic." Anna was still frowning, still watching the traffic inching ahead of them. "I mean, I really resented her for a minute there. I enjoy Maggie's company a lot, but I've got to make my own decisions."

If only the old you could hear yourself now, my love.

"There's nothing wrong with that." Jason pulled the Jag closer to the suspension bridge.

She shrugged. "I don't know, maybe I overreacted, but I've got precious little control over anything right now. At least let me control my decisions."

"You're not overreacting, Anna. It's just like Dr. Gordon said. Trusting yourself means trusting your own decisions."

"You're right, of course." She twisted in the seat to face him. "And a good friend. Thanks."

Hold that thought, he urged silently. He wasn't so sure how happy she was going to be with him when she remembered everything.

"You know, it's odd," she said a few minutes later. "But lately I've been more at peace with my amnesia."

"Yeah?" So she was okay with this, too, the two of them living in the here and now, in their own little world?

"It's just that when I get these feelings, they're so strong, you know? I didn't simply not appreciate Maggie's nagging. I had to physically restrain myself from running away from her. For a second there I thought I might pass out or something."

Looking her over carefully, Jason asked, "Do you feel okay now?"

"Of course. Fine." She brushed her hair back from her face. "But it makes me think that maybe I do need this time to heal from whatever happened. The intensity of some of my reactions scares me."

"You're afraid of remembering?" *Oh, Anna, if only I really knew the extent of our problem here. If only I had all the answers.*

She looked away, out her side of the car. "Sometimes."

Thankful for the traffic that kept them at a standstill, Jason turned her to face him, holding her chin in his hand, forcing her to look at him. "That's nothing to be ashamed of, Anna."

He could see the tears welling in her eyes as she searched his gaze. Relaxing his hold, he moved his thumb along her jaw, needing to kiss her more right then than at any other time he could remember.

"Thank you," she whispered.

"For what?" Wanting to kiss her senseless?

"Knowing me so well."

Oh. That. In her other life she'd been able to read him just as clearly. "It's the truth, Anna. Fear is natural."

"Are you ever afraid?"

Her eyes implored him for the truth, looking for reassurance. Dumbstruck, Jason sat there staring at her. He used to be afraid sometimes, back when he still counted on his parents to be parents. He could remember being at a football game, afraid as the quarters went by that his father wasn't going to make it to see him play again. Afraid that he'd go to his mother's house, after four days at his father's, only to find he'd lost his bedroom. But sleeping on couches hadn't been so bad, and that was all so long ago, back when he'd depended on other people for his happiness.

And fear?

He continued to stare at her—until a horn sounded behind him. Jerking away from Anna, he put the car in gear and shot forward. He was concerned. Concerned she'd remember everything. Concerned she wouldn't. Concerned about the baby she carried, about the man who'd fathered it. Concerned she was going to see his own misrepresentation of their relationship as a betrayal, in spite of the doctor's advice. Because parts of him saw it that way, himself. Concerned he'd never again be able to hold her in his arms, lose himself within her honeyed depths. Concerned he'd never be home again. That he'd carry the ache of her loss with him to his grave. Yeah, he was concerned.

He was not afraid.

CHAPTER TEN

STATEN ISLAND deserved better. Its beautiful shorelines, magnificent rolling hills sprinkled with grand homes, and miles of trails waiting to be explored didn't receive even a tenth of Jason's attention. He was too distracted by Anna's nearness. They visited Conference House, a stone manor that had served as the only site of a Revolutionary War conference. But while noteworthy, if one cared to take notes, the Revolutionary War was far in the distant past—and Anna was the present.

He took her through historic Richmond Town, visited the Staten Island Institute of Arts and Sciences and debated with her about the exhibits, comparing them to pieces they'd seen at the Museum of Modern Art earlier in the week. He was challenged by her thinking, pleased with her new openness—telling him what she thought rather than leaving him to guess—and entranced by her laughter. At her request, he walked with her through innumerable gift shops. She pointed out trinkets, commented on likenesses to things they'd seen, bought a deck of cards. All he saw was Anna. All he heard was Anna. All he wanted was Anna.

And she wanted him, too. He'd been her lover for almost two years, her friend before that. He knew when Anna was turned on.

They toured the Alice Austen House Museum that afternoon and then it was time to go home, to get away from Anna before darkness spread over the city, cloaking them in its intimacy. To avoid temptation.

"Let's stay for dinner," he heard himself say, instead, as they climbed back into the car.

After a full day of being with Anna, Jason wasn't ready to reenter the real world, temptation be damned. "I saw a pamphlet back there." He indicated the cottage that housed the pioneer photography collection they'd just viewed. "It advertised waterfront dining just a few miles from here."

Anna stopped, her seat belt pulled out but not yet fastened. "Don't you have a date?"

The question sounded so wrong coming from her. "No."

"Why not? It's Saturday night."

Because, after a two-year commitment to her, one he'd expected to last forever, he had no desire for other women. "Never got around to asking."

She studied him closely. "But you *are* dating someone, right?"

For a woman who wanted him, she was doing a damn good job of convincing him she didn't. "No, Anna, I'm not currently dating anyone."

"But you have to be!"

He wasn't sure it was panic he heard in her voice until he turned and read it in her eyes loud and clear. Just then a family walked by the convertible, staring at them; Anna looked down at her lap. Starting the Jaguar, Jason roared out of the parking lot and sped along Hylan Boulevard past the Gateway National Recreation Area, turning off at the first semiprivate cove he found along the shore. He stopped the car and stared out at the ocean.

"Now, you want to tell me why I have to be dating?" he asked.

Anna hadn't said a word since he'd left Austen House. She still didn't.

His gut turned hard as a rock when he saw the hunted expression on her face. Reaching over, he took her hand. "Anna?"

"You get this look in your eyes sometimes." Her words were a mere whisper on the ocean breeze.

He waited for her to continue, fully aware she hadn't pulled her hand out of his grasp.

"I recognize the look, Jason." Her own eyes burned with heat. *Shit.*

"And?"

She gazed at him, shook her head and got out of the car. A breeze from the ocean whipped her dress up, swirling the thin material about her thighs, reminding Jason of the first time he'd seen her. As then, he had no choice but to follow her. Down the small copse to the beach beyond.

But the laughter that had been in her eyes when he caught up with her that first time was nowhere to be found now. Sandals in hand, she just kept walking, her face a mask.

"I feel like such a fool," she said.

"Why?" He was the one making a royal mess of things. He had the facts. He knew better.

"Because if I'm wrong..." She stopped walking, turning to look at him. "Except I'm not, am I?"

He shook his head. "I want you, Anna, if that's what you mean."

Looking away, she started to walk again, silently. Jason could only keep pace with her, waiting, watching. She had to make the decisions.

"Why now?" she asked suddenly. "Why not when I knew you before?"

Okay, Dr. Gordon. What now? "I can't answer that, Anna," he said, carefully weighing his words. She was going to remember their past someday—along with today. "Except to say that I see things in you now that weren't there before."

"What things?"

"You're more independent," he said, strolling slowly beside her on the deserted stretch of beach, the late afternoon bringing a chill to the air.

"Really?" She seemed pleased.

"Really." He smiled at her. "And stronger, too."

"I don't feel very strong."

Grabbing hold of her hand, Jason stopped her, reaching up to brush her hair back from her face, his hand lingering on the softness of her cheek.

"Is it so very wrong to admit that we're attracted to each other?" he asked.

Winning her heart a second time hadn't been what he'd had in mind at all, but what kind of fool would turn his back on this chance?

Jason withstood her gaze as she stared up at him. He wanted her. She wanted him. And for now, he and she were all that existed.

"Yes," she finally said, breaking eye contact with him. She took his hand and held it against her cheek. "It's very wrong, Jason."

"Why?"

She dropped his hand and continued her trek up the beach. "You know why."

She wasn't talking about her amnesia. "Because you're pregnant."

"That's a start."

"I'm sure you're not the first pregnant woman to have a romance."

Dropping her sandals, Anna plopped down in the sand, scooping up a handful and letting it run through her fingers. "And when my memory comes back?" she asked, her voice stronger, bitter. "What if I discover I love someone else?"

"And what if you don't?"

He sat down beside her, and took her hand. "Anna, would it help if I tell you that I won't hold you to anything? That you call all the shots? That if, once you remember, you choose someone else, I won't stand in your way?"

The longing in her eyes as she stared silently up at him was all it took. All reasoning, all conscience vanished. With the familiarity of having loved her before, he lowered his mouth to hers.

ANNA WAS LOST at the touch of his lips. He felt so right in a world that had been nothing but wrong. Her mouth opened to his automatically, as if possessing a mind of its own. And because her body seemed to know exactly what to do when she hadn't a clue, she listened to it.

Easing her back onto the sand, Jason moved over her, sliding one leg between hers, molding their bodies to a perfect fit, his lips caressing hers all the while.

Like a starved woman, Anna returned kiss for kiss, finding in Jason's arms everything she'd been looking for—a sense of home, and a strength beyond anything she'd ever be able to muster on her own. Fire, too. Fire that ignited a matching flame in her veins. One that threatened to consume her if she didn't have more of him.

His hands, never still, caressed her body, pleasuring her in ways she'd never imagined until finally, blissfully, they found her breasts. Not just cupping them, as she'd longed for so many times over the past weeks, but moving back and forth, back and forth across her hardened nipples, sending shock waves of sensation through her.

"So perfect," he whispered against her lips, continuing to torture first one breast and then the other with his light caresses, only ceasing when Anna arced her body, pressing his hand more firmly against her aching breast.

"So full," he said.

Anna fell back to the sand, turning her head, breaking the kiss, pushing him away with both hands. Yes, they were full. Fuller than normal, or so she'd been told. Because she was pregnant.

"Anna?" Jason's voice sounded drugged, or as if it came from far off. "What's wrong, honey?"

"I'm sorry," she said when she could speak. Rolling away, she sat up a few feet from him, hugging her knees to her throbbing breasts.

It took him a minute. She saw his struggle, saw the cords in his neck tense as he tried to compose himself. Eventually he, too, sat up, his hands on his knees as he stared silently out at the ocean.

"Did you remember something?" he finally asked, his voice level, resigned.

Not in the way he probably meant. "Yes."

He flinched, but gave no other indication that he'd heard her, strengthening Anna's resolve to let things go no further between them. Because Jason wasn't going to protect his heart. With his eternal optimism he would enter into the relationship with high hopes. But if the worst happened, if she suddenly remembered another man, one who already had her undying love, Jason would simply allow her to walk away from him.

Even though he knew that doing so would kill him.

"I remembered the baby," she said. She owed him complete honesty. If they were going to salvage their friendship, one that had become as essential to her as the air she breathed, they had to talk openly about this.

"And his father?" Jason asked, still deadpan, still gazing at the ocean. If he hoped to convince her he didn't care, he'd failed miserably. Or maybe it was himself he was trying to convince. One thing was clear, he wasn't going to try to urge her to forget whatever it was she'd remembered.

"No, Jason." She shook her head. "Just the fact that I'm pregnant."

He looked at her then, relief in his eyes. "That's all?"

Nodding, Anna gave him a sad smile. "I don't know what I did in the past, Jason, but the person I am today, the person I'm learning to live with, the person I have to like, can't make love without commitment."

"I don't have a problem with making a commitment," he said.

"I know."

He shifted over until his thigh pressed against hers in the sand. "So what's the problem?"

"*I* can't make any commitments, Jason," she said, not bothering to hide her pain from him. At least it told him she cared. "Until I know what promises I've already made, I'm not free to make any more."

He didn't move away. Didn't move at all. Just sat staring out at the ocean.

"I'll understand if you'd like to take me back to Manhattan and forget you ever knew me."

He was silent so long she wasn't sure he was even still listening to her. Not that she blamed him. All she'd done was take, take, take since he'd first walked into her hospital room. Strength, money, peace of mind, time. He'd given them all freely. And she had nothing to give in return.

"No chance of getting naked, huh?" His outrageous words dropped into the silence and suddenly Anna felt giddy with relief. He was going to get them through this.

"None," she lied.

"Then my next choice is dinner on the waterfront."

"But what about—"

"Anna," Jason interrupted, taking her hand, "look at me."

She did. When he gazed at her like that, she couldn't look anywhere else.

"I understand, and it's okay," he said, enunciating every word. "When your memory returns, we'll have this discussion again. Until then, I'll wait."

Her eyes wet with tears, she touched his sweet handsome face. "What did I ever do to deserve you?"

"Someday, when I have you in my arms, I'll tell you."

She prayed that someday she'd be able to take him up on his offer.

HE CALLED ABBY much later that night. He'd finally dropped Anna off sometime past midnight, walking her to her door but not asking to come inside. It wouldn't have taken much to get her to acquiesce and, once inside, to bed her. But then he'd have been as bad as Abby, overriding Anna's decision with his own. He had no choice but to respect her judgment.

But damn, doing the right thing felt like hell.

All things considered, they'd had a great evening, almost like the old days—laughing, simply enjoying being together. Being able to feast his eyes openly on her had helped. There was more honesty in their relationship now. And for the time being, he could live with that. Was determined to have this chance—and to be prepared to walk away.

Abby's phone rang so long he was ready to hang up, a bit relieved to see that Abby had found something to do with her Saturday evening besides sit at home.

"Hello?"

The voice that answered, just as he was putting the receiver down, barely resembled his old friend.

"Abby?" he asked, frowning.

"Yes?"

"Am I interrupting something?" Did Abby have a man there? Wonder of wonders. He'd never known the oldest Hayden girl to bring a man home.

"No. I'm just sitting here."

"Alone?"

"Yeah."

Oh. "Something good on the tube?" He remembered some cozy evenings back when Audrey was alive. Abby would make popcorn and coerce everyone to sit down and watch some show or other she was sure they'd all enjoy. And they usually had.

"Nah."

"You working up something spectacular to introduce in the fall?" He wasn't sure how Abby kept coming up with ideas for her children's-wear designs fast enough to keep her growing clientele happy.

"No. Just sitting."

"Anna saw the doctor yesterday."

"And?" She sounded almost afraid to ask. Suddenly Jason wondered if he and Anna weren't the only ones frightened of her memory.

"He's happy with her progress, her growing confidence."

There was another long pause and then, "How is she, Jason?"

"She misses you."

"Oh, God, I miss her, too..." And that was when Jason heard the tears Abby had been trying to hide. She'd been sitting in that cottage on the beach all alone on a Saturday night, crying.

FIFTEEN MINUTES after hanging up the phone Jason was still sitting on his couch in the dark—his thoughts far from pleasant. While he'd been convinced that Anna would only be free to live a full life if she could separate her identity from Abby's, he'd also honestly believed that in the long run Abby, too, was going to be happier. He was no longer so sure.

Hell, what did he know? He'd never been a part of a relationship of the sort Abby, Anna and Audrey had shared from birth. Had never really been part of a family.

Maybe being together was the way the sisters were meant to be, the only way they could be happy. Maybe there was a greater reason for their multiple birth than simple genetics, a connection stronger than physical resemblance and blood ties. A connection beyond understanding.

A connection that threatened him more than anything else in his life.

He'd been so sure that he'd had all the answers, that he knew exactly what the problems were between Anna and him. But looking back now, he was seeing something else. Something that sickened him. Could he possibly have been jealous of the closeness Anna shared with her sisters? Had his New York job offer merely been an excuse to make her choose, once and for all, between her sisters and him? Had he been so shallow, so immature?

God, he hoped not.

And if he had? And Anna had seen through his righteous indignation to the selfish man beneath? And Anna remembered?

Breaking out in a cold sweat, Jason dropped to the floor. One. Two. Three…

CHAPTER ELEVEN

JASON WAS ON THE PHONE first thing the next morning, Sunday or no. He couldn't wait anymore. He had to know what he was up against. He had to find the father of Anna's child.

She may have to remember on her own, but nothing said he couldn't find out in the meantime. Not only would he be better prepared to help her deal with the memory, especially if it was distressing, but he, too, would be better protected. Knowledge was power. And Jason needed all the power he could get.

Calling his contacts in California, as well as the fact-finding sources he'd encountered since coming to New York, felt good. Right. At least he was doing something. He couldn't fight what he didn't know. And he planned to fight.

Unless it turned out that Anna truly loved the man who'd fathered her child just weeks after Jason moved out of her life. In that case he'd walk. A thing much easier done sooner than later.

Again, he had to know.

He also put down a retainer on one of New York's best private investigators. If anyone could find out who Anna Hayden had been sleeping with, Smith Whitehall could. A Harvard graduate, the man not only knew how to turn up dirt in a bottle of glass cleaner, he was smart.

And then Jason set out himself, visiting all the places he would expect Anna to visit upon arriving in New York, showing her picture around, asking questions. He'd have sent out an all-points bulletin on the evening news if he could have found a way to do so without humiliating Anna.

"Yeah, I've seen her," a clerk in a bookstore close to Gramercy Park told Jason late Sunday afternoon. "Not lately, though."

"Was she ever with anyone?" Jason asked casually, his heart pounding. *Say no. Say yes. Say she didn't love him.*

"Nope." The clerk shook her head. "Always came in alone. Always bought a lot of books, though. Fiction, but nonfiction, too. Art-history stuff. I suppose she could've been buying for two."

Nodding, Jason thanked the clerk and walked out. He was getting nowhere. New Yorkers were a tough bunch to crack, too concerned about their own backs to notice other people. He'd spent an entire day traipsing the town for nothing. An entire day he could have spent with Anna.

Shit. He was losing it, big time. And all for a woman who'd already sent him out of her life once. Once home, Jason changed into cotton shorts and a T-shirt, grabbed his racquetball gear and headed for the club. He'd stay until midnight if that was how long it took to beat some sense into himself.

He knew better than to look to anyone else for his personal happiness, to need to be the most important person in another's life. Knew all the inherent dangers of doing so firsthand. Had, as a boy, lived with the fear of rejection as his constant companion. He wasn't going to be afraid again. Not ever.

ANNA INVITED MAGGIE to go secondhand-clothes shopping Tuesday evening. She'd seen Jason that day and was too restless to be content with her own company. Being with him was better than ever—and worse. It was ten times harder to keep her desire under control when she knew he wanted her, too.

"What do you want with used stuff?" Maggie asked. She was sitting on the only counter in Anna's kitchen eating Anna's last apple.

"It's got character," Anna told her. Besides which, it was cheap and she needed some more dresses. With the baby on the way, Anna was growing more and more aware of the limits of her bank account.

"You've already got plenty of character," Maggie said, surprising Anna with her praise.

"You think so?"

"You might've lost your memory, but even you have to know that much," Maggie said. "And you've got looks, too, dammit. If I didn't like you so much, I might have to hate you."

"So you'll come?" Anna asked.

Begrudgingly Maggie followed Anna into three different shops, grumbling when Anna bought exactly what Maggie told her not to buy, more of her "flower child" dresses as Maggie called them.

"You need some shorts, girl," Maggie said. "Show off your legs."

"I need dresses," Anna countered. "To hide my belly."

"No kidding?" Maggie looked at the part of Anna's anatomy in question. "You're starting to show?"

"I don't know. I'm three months along and I'm starting to look bloated. It's embarrassing."

Maggie laughed. "What're you gonna do when you're big as an elephant?"

"Don't," Anna groaned. "Let me get used to bloated, first." And let her not think about four or five months down the road. Who knew where she'd be then, who she'd be, or with whom. It scared her witless every time she thought about it. So she tried not to.

"I sure wish I knew what I used to do," she complained to Maggie on the walk home. "I'm getting restless."

"Which means you're getting better," Maggie said. "You've got that computer on your dresser—can you type?" she asked. "You could get a part-time job as a secretary or receptionist or something. Lord knows you have the looks for it."

"I'm not even sure how to turn the thing on," Anna admitted. And she hadn't wanted to admit to Jason yet another failure, another thing she no longer knew. Plain and simple, she'd been too proud to ask for help.

"Even I know that much," Maggie said over her shoulder as they climbed the steps of the brownstone. "Come on, together we can figure it out."

ONCE MAGGIE HAD the laptop open and on, Anna suddenly took it from there. There were no conscious memories, but she knew how to move about in the first couple of programs fairly well. She spent the rest of that evening fooling around with the computer, surprised to find how many things she just automatically knew to do.

She'd just discovered her personal financial file the next morning when the telephone rang. Assuming it was Jason, she grabbed it up on the first ring.

"Hi!" she said. She couldn't wait to tell him that she had an account in a bank in California with enough money to see her through a couple of years, baby expenses included. Then she'd have to go to work. But, God willing, by then she'd have regained her memory.

"Hello, yourself, sexy lady."

Anna froze, wanting to drop the phone back in its cradle and pretend she'd never picked it up. But as horrified as she was to hear Roger on the other end of the line, she had to know why he was calling her. Was he going to claim his child? Expect visitation rights?

"What do you want?"

"You know my voice," he said a little less enthusiastically. "Does this mean you've recovered from your unfortunate affliction?"

He made her sound like some kind of half-witted freak. "My memory hasn't returned yet."

"It's been three weeks and one day since you were so naughty and ran out on me, Anna. Are you ready to kiss and make up?" His voice was oiled with sickening innuendo. "I promise to take good care of you."

"Never."

"I see you've still got a lot to learn, Anna. Lovers' tiffs aren't meant to last forever. Come back to work, let me take care of you, and you won't have to worry your pretty little head anymore."

"Never," she repeated. Still fighting the urge to slam the phone down, Anna hung on. Did he know about the baby? Surely, if he was the father, she'd have told him about the baby. The woman she was now certainly would have.

"But, Anna, it's summer! We can go to the beach," he said, as if coaxing a child. "I'll take you down the coast, just you and me. No one will know about you." His voice lowered. "You won't have to use your mind at all."

Yeah, but she could guess what she would have to use. She'd rather die.

"I'll make you happier than you've ever been," he said confidently, as if he actually thought there was a chance she'd go away with him.

"I'm pregnant, Roger."

"Son of a bitch! You threatened me with a lawsuit for stealing a little kiss and here all along you were screwing some other man?"

"I didn't sleep with you?" Anna asked, almost dizzy with relief.

"You aren't going to pin your bastard on me, you little bitch. Other than that one kiss, I never touched you—"

Anna clicked the off button on her mobile phone and laid it calmly beside her computer.

Two seconds later she picked it back up, dialed automatically and held her breath, praying he was home.

"Jason? He's not the father!" she cried the minute he picked up his phone.

"Who isn't?"

"Roger. He called just now. I never slept with him."

"Why'd he call?" Jason didn't seem to be sharing her joy.

"He wanted me to go to the beach with him."

"If he calls again, you let me know," Jason said. "We'll get him for harassment."

As thrilled as she was at the protectiveness in his voice, Anna stomped her foot.

"Didn't you hear me?" she practically hollered. "He's not the baby's father."

"I didn't think he was, Anna. You'd never sleep with a jerk like that."

Anna was grinning when she hung up the phone after promising to be ready to accompany Jason to lunch in half an hour. He'd had a lot more faith in her than she'd had herself. She was damn lucky he'd been in New York when that subway crashed.

A WEEK PASSED and there continued to be no word on a man in Anna's life. Jason hung up from his daily call from Whitehall, frustrated as hell. No news was supposed to be good news. But in this case, it was still just no news. Because it was beyond doubt that somewhere out there was a man who'd impregnated Anna. She was starting to show. Not obviously, probably not at all to someone who wasn't as intimately acquainted with her body as he was. But when he'd slid his arm around her on their walk through Gramercy Park the day before, he'd felt the difference.

It had bothered him so much, this evidence of another man's having touched her, he'd dropped his arm, then contented himself with simply holding her hand. And for the first time since Staten Island, he'd broken his promise to himself and to her. He'd kissed her goodbye. He hadn't lingered, just a quick peck. Because he'd had to leave his mark on her like some macho jerk. An insecure one at that. The fact that she'd clung to him made him that much more of a heel. That kiss hadn't been about loving. It had been about jealousy, plain and simple.

So for the fourth time in three days it was back to the gym for him. To things he could control, things he was good at, things he could count on. But for the first time in months he lost a match.

JASON WAS LATE. Which wasn't all that unusual. Anna, on the other hand, had been pacing her small apartment since fifteen minutes before he was due to arrive. It was this way a lot recently, her nerves stretched tight with impatience. It had been two weeks since the night she'd finally admitted to the restlessness that was slowly consuming her. She was sick and tired of sitting around storing her strength and waiting for her mind to heal. She needed something to do.

When Jason called, saying that he'd gotten caught on the phone, that it would be another forty-five minutes before he'd be by to take her to Chinatown, she almost snapped at him.

She sat down at her computer, instead. Jason was a saint, and there was no way she was going to take her growing tension out on him. But she'd already played the few games installed on her computer a hundred times apiece. She was bored as hell.

Desultorily flipping through the directory of her hard drive, she found several files she didn't recognize, having really explored only program files to this point. She clicked on the first unfamiliar file. It contained only a series of unreadable formating codes. As did the second, third and fourth.

She clicked on the fifth file, surprised when her word-processing program opened up. What she saw was entirely readable. And there was a lot of it, paragraph upon paragraph. Her heart started pumping furiously, butterflies swarming in her stomach as she scrolled through the pages.

She closed her eyes, frightened suddenly, wishing she could turn off the machine, return to the tedium of sitting and waiting. Something safe. Something she was sure she could do.

But the words continued to flow in her mind, words she recognized. Exciting her, balancing her panic. She couldn't exit the file, couldn't turn off the machine, couldn't get up and walk away. She had to read.

Starting with the first page, she read every word, knowing some of them *before* she read them. It was a story. A compelling one. Of a young man...

And Anna knew this man better than she knew herself. Knew his desires and goals. Knew his fears. Even his hobbies. She knew because she'd admired him most of her life.

The pages were the beginning of a book, a biography. The story of John Henry Walker, a nineteenth-century New York artist whose tragic life was filled with triumph. A man who, orphaned at a young age, grew up in squalor, an unwanted ward of the state. A man whose first wife was killed by outlaws, whose baby girl died of tuberculosis. A gifted impressionist. A loving husband, a revered father. She'd come to New York to research his story.

She was so engrossed in her reading, she didn't hear Jason's knock on the apartment door. Until his knock became a pounding accompanied by his voice calling her name.

"You won't believe it!" she cried when she threw open her door.

"Are you okay?" He looked her over swiftly.

"Better than okay. Magnificent! Terrific! Oh, Jason, I know why I came to New York!"

His face drained of color and he shut the door behind him. "You remembered everything?"

"Yes. No!" she grabbed his arm, dragging him over to the computer. "I haven't regained my memory, just a small part of it. Look!" she cried exultantly, pointing at the screen.

Jason looked from her to the computer screen and back again, as though wondering if she'd finally flipped her lid completely. "It's a paper of some sort," he said.

"It's a book, Jason!" She could hardly contain her excitement.

This book was a huge part of her, of who she'd been before the accident. "I remember writing it!" She tapped the computer screen. "This is why I came to New York!"

"You wrote it?" he asked, clearly shocked.

"Yep!" She *did* have a worthy endeavor. "It's about an American artist—an obscure American artist—named John Henry Walker. Some of his work is still on display here in New York."

"John Henry Walker?" Jason asked, frowning. "You had a print of his hanging in your cottage in California."

Anna was so relieved to hear that she almost cried. She wasn't losing her mind. She was remembering. "I think I like art."

"You minored in it in college," Jason said.

"I have a college degree?"

Jason's glance was shuttered suddenly, as though he was remembering he was supposed to be watching what he told her. "You earned a B.A. in English," he finally said.

Leaning over, he looked more closely at the words covering the computer screen. "Is this finished?"

"No." She shook her head. "I don't remember how far I was into it, but judging from the number of pages, it's only about half-done."

Scrolling through the pages, he asked, "You haven't read it all?"

She grinned, shaking her head again. "I just found it half an hour ago."

After reading a couple of paragraphs, Jason went back and read the first two pages.

"This is really good," he said, turning to look at her.

"You think so?" She'd thought so, too, but she still put more stock in his opinion than her own.

Jason straightened, pulling her against him and kissing her full on the mouth. "I know so," he said.

As if suddenly realizing what he was doing, where he was, the temptation that was even now blazing into flames between them, he set her gently away. "If you'd like, I can take a copy of this with me and print it out for you at the station."

Though she missed his warmth, Anna was too grateful for what she'd discovered to mourn for things she couldn't have.

"Great! Sure. If it's not too much trouble," she said, still prac-

tically dancing with excitement. She couldn't wait to immerse herself in the life of the man she'd admired most of her life. To read
the whole book, or the finished portion of it, anyway.

Finally she had a little piece of the real Anna Hayden.

THERE WAS A MESSAGE from Smith Whitehall waiting for Jason
when he stopped home to change before work that afternoon. The
man had a lead, was chasing it down and would call back. Jason
flipped off the machine, the day suddenly bleak. This was not good
news. And yet it was the news he'd been waiting to hear. The
question was, was he ready to hear it? Was he ready to give Anna
up?

But then, how could he give up what he didn't have to begin
with?

HAVING GONE into the station early enough to print out Anna's
manuscript, Jason was sitting on the couch in his dressing-room-
cum-office reviewing the day's stories.

"You're here!" Sunny came into his office without knocking.
She was wearing one of the short tight skirts she always wore on
the air, her white silk blouse displaying a fair amount of cleavage.

Jason nodded, continuing to read, hoping she'd get the hint and
leave him alone.

"What's the occasion? Lately you've barely gotten here in time
to go on," she said, her tone a little resentful.

"I've been busy, Sunny. You know that." He wasn't in the mood
for a showdown with his partner. ￢

"I know." Her voice softened as she sat down close to him on
the couch—too close. Running one perfectly manicured finger
along his arm, she laid her head against his shoulder.

It wasn't the first time she'd cuddled up to him. In fact, he'd
probably encouraged the closeness a time or two. But it wasn't
enough. He had to resist the urge to shrug her away from him, to
jump up off the couch and put as much room between him and
Sunny as he could. He didn't want her touch. He wanted Anna's.

Still, a small part of him wanted to wrap his arms around Sunny,
place his mouth on hers and ease the ache that had been burning

inside him for weeks. Maybe even find a moment or two of forgetfulness.

But although she might be able to ease his physical ache, it would only be momentary. And the self-loathing that was sure to follow would be far worse than the original problem. If all he had was himself, he was damn sure going to be someone he could be proud of.

"Why don't you come back to my place after the last show tonight?" she invited softly.

"Sunny—".

"I'll even make breakfast in the morning," she interrupted. For Sunny that was major. She hated to cook.

"I need to get home tonight." He had a manuscript to read.

"Why?" Her finger strayed higher, moving toward his chest. "Don't you think it's time our relationship progressed a little?"

He braced himself against her practiced seduction. His body had been too ready for too long not to be tempted by the beautiful woman beside him.

"We're friends, Sunny. Good friends. I never intimated that we'd be more," he reminded her.

"It's because of that woman you're helping, isn't it?" she asked, sounding jealous.

He didn't want to think about Anna. Thinking about her only made the ache worse. The ache Sunny was offering to ease. One she wanted to ease.

"I'm not seeing her tonight, if that's what you mean," he said.

"Then why not come home with me? It's not like you two have anything going, right?"

He shifted slightly away from her before he threw good judgment to the wind and drew her onto his lap. "We're friends." Unfortunately the new position had her breast pressing against his arm.

"But you don't owe her anything."

She was right of course. The person he owed something more to was himself. He had to look at himself in the morning. He wanted to like what he saw. And using Sunny for his own selfish release wasn't something he'd be able to look upon too fondly, no matter how he tried to rationalize.

"She has nightmares sometimes," he heard himself explaining. "I told her she can call—"

"She calls you in the middle of the night?" Sunny sat up, her eyes reflecting her hurt as she pushed away from him.

Jason wondered how a face could be so beautiful and make him feel so uncomfortable at the same time. "Once or twice."

"So how much longer are you going to be at the beck and call of this poor family friend?" she demanded.

All trace of desire fled. "You make her sound like some dim-witted hanger-on," he said, biting down on his anger.

"Your words, not mine."

Jason stood, walking to the door. "Let's get one thing straight," he said. "Every woman should hope to be as smart and courageous as Anna." He held the door open for Sunny to leave. "If you can't accept that, then we have nothing more to say."

Sunny rose—graceful, classy and way too disappointed as she walked slowly toward him. "You *are* involved with her, aren't you."

"No," he said. "I've just known her a long time, and I admire the heck out of the way she's handling this whole thing."

But while Sunny seemed to accept his denial for now, Jason wasn't so easily convinced. He might not have fallen in love with Anna all over again, but if his instant defense of her was any indication, he was starting to care more than he wanted to. With that in mind and considering the call from Whitehall that afternoon, he needed to take a serious look at what he was letting himself in for.

LATE THAT NIGHT, after two hours of engrossed page turning, Jason set Anna's manuscript carefully down on the coffee table in front of him. She was good. Better than good. Anna possessed a talent for pulling the reader so completely into the story, that Jason actually thought the man's thoughts, hoped his hopes.

As he put down the manuscript, Anna's earlier words rang in his ears. She'd come to New York to sell this book—not to see him.

CHAPTER TWELVE

EXCITED, NERVOUS, a bit frightened, Anna stood outside Jason's apartment building at nine o'clock the next morning. She'd never just popped in on him, hadn't really planned to do so now. But she was on her way to an ultrasound appointment, and she didn't want to go alone.

Her fear wasn't logical. Seeing the child growing within her wasn't going to tell them anything about the conception. Still she was frightened. She really wanted Jason to go with her. But could she ask him to do this? Considering their encounter on the beach on Staten Island, was it fair of her to ask?

And yet, considering his willingness to accept her, pregnant and all, was she really out of line to want him there?

Time continued to tick away, people stared at her as they passed her on the street, and still she couldn't make up her mind. Looking around her, she noticed a phone booth a couple of buildings down. She'd call him. Should have called him before she'd ever left home.

He answered on the fourth ring, and the first thing Anna could tell was that he'd been asleep. The second was that he wasn't in the best of moods, though he did try to cover that up.

"No, Anna, don't apologize," he said quickly. "I told you to call me anytime. Is something wrong?"

He sounded concerned. Anna felt a little better.

"Not really," she said. She still had an hour before her appointment. There was time for him to get dressed and accompany her. But should she bother him?

"Did you remember something?"

"No." Should she ask? Would he want her to? "I just…"

"What?" He still sounded sleepy.

"I have an ultrasound appointment this morning. I just wondered if you wanted to come along," she said quickly.

"Are you having problems?" he asked.

"No, not at all. It's strictly procedure." This was a bad idea.

"It doesn't hurt, does it?"

Not unless you considered her uncomfortably full bladder. "No."

"What time's the appointment?"

She heard the hesitancy in his voice. As if he wanted to come. And at the same time didn't. She should never have called.

"Ten-thirty."

"I'm sorry, honey, but you'll have to go without me," he said. He didn't sound sorry—more like relieved. "I have a meeting at the station at eleven."

"That's all right, Jason. It was no big deal," she said, embarrassed, trying not to feel hurt. Jason had already gone above and beyond the call of duty. She'd been wrong to expect him to step into the shoes of a man he'd never met, a man who might very well appear at any time and claim them. And her.

THE LIGHT on her answering machine was blinking. Dropping the bag of groceries she'd carried in, Anna hurried to the machine. She'd been so busy writing the past several days she'd hardly seen Jason at all. She missed him. A lot.

Jabbing impatiently at the button, she waited through three beeps to hear his message, hoping he wanted to take her to lunch. Monday was broccoli soup day at the deli. Not only was she lonely, she was starving, too.

"Hello, Anna dear." The unfamiliar deep baritone startled her. "I'm sorry to have missed you. Business is going to keep me here much longer than I expected. I'm in Italy this month and part of next, and then back to London for more meetings." More than his words, the regret and genuine affection in the man's voice spoke to Anna. With both hands she rubbed the swell of her belly. "I'll be in touch the second I'm back in New York, my dear," the voice continued, "with great hopes you'll still be free to take up where we left off. Until then, happy writing."

The machine re-wound, clicking off, and Anna stood there staring at it. She had no idea who the man was or where they'd left off. Remembered nothing, felt nothing at hearing his voice. But she was suddenly, sickeningly afraid he'd fathered a child he knew nothing about. By the sounds of things he'd been in Europe awhile. Possibly before she'd found out that she carried his child?

Oh, God. Her unattended groceries scattered, the frozen foods melting on the hardwood floor, Anna sank to her knees and wept.

"YOU LOOK like a rag."

Anna chuckled wanly, taking the chain off her door to admit her friend. "Thanks, Mag," she said dryly. "I can always count on you to cheer me up."

"Hey." Maggie held up her hands, sauntering over to sprawl on Anna's couch, her feet resting on the arm. "You're the one who invited me to dinner." But Anna saw the concerned glance her friend gave her on her way past. She sat down in the chair at her computer desk, needing the support for her back.

"You cry when you're preggie and the kid comes out a grouch." Maggie grabbed an apple from the bowl on the coffee table that Anna kept specifically for her.

"There was a message on my machine today from some guy in Europe," Anna blurted. "He's there on business and says he hopes we can take up where we left off." She had to tell someone, and she couldn't bring herself to talk to Jason about it. "I think he might be the father."

Maggie sat up. "Yeah? Wow, that's great!"

Anna nodded, wishing she felt half as excited as Maggie about the news. What she felt was a bone-deep dread.

"So you remembered? Recognized his voice? Something?"

"No." As hard as she fought them, tears filled her eyes again. "Nothing happened, Maggie."

"It's okay, kid." Maggie's voice was uncharacteristically gentle. "You know the doc said it'll take time. When you're ready, you'll remember this guy."

Anna shook her head. "I don't want him to be the father of my baby," she whispered, ashamed, frightened, as lost as she'd felt in the hospital after the crash.

She needed Jason.

Maggie set her half-eaten apple back in the bowl. "So what makes you so sure this guy's it?"

"He almost has to be, doesn't he?" She rested her chin on her hands. "There's nobody else beating down my door."

"Still doesn't make him the daddy."

No, it didn't. But this man, whoever he was, was the only logical choice. She'd apparently been seeing him. And she was sure she wasn't the type to date two men at once.

"He must have money if he's got business all over Europe," Maggie surmised.

"Yeah." But though Maggie clearly saw this as a plus, Anna didn't care.

"He's probably that guy I saw you with," Maggie said, frowning. "He was always wearing natty suits. Seemed real important."

"What'd he look like?" If the man had fathered her child, she should at least learn the color of his hair.

Maggie shrugged, picking up her apple. "Tall, thin, dark hair. Fortyish."

Twelve years older than I am. Seven years older than Jason. Old enough to have a nearly grown family of his own. Maybe past the time in his life when he wanted to start a new family. She started to cry again.

"Buck up, kid!" Maggie said. "You don't owe the guy anything."

"If he's my baby's father, I do!"

"That's a big 'if,' and no, you don't. He took off for Europe without you, right?"

Anna nodded.

"And he only *hopes* you'll be free when he makes it back, right?" Maggie took another bite of apple, chomping contentedly.

Anna nodded again. It all seemed so hopeless. The baby didn't even seem real yet, and here she was, having to accept a complete stranger as its father.

"There you have it, then." Maggie tossed the apple core in the trash. "You guys obviously don't have a commitment at all."

"We have one big commitment," Anna said, rubbing her stomach. "He just may not know about it yet."

"A baby's a responsibility, Anna, not a commitment," Maggie said, her voice more serious than Anna had ever heard. "Say you get your memory back, you remember the guy, the baby's the result of one night with a little too much champagne, a little too much loneliness—no love. You gonna marry the guy?''

''No.'' Surprised at how quickly the answer came to her, Anna suddenly felt better than she had since she'd listened to that wretched message. No one could force her to do anything she didn't want to do.

''He may not want to marry you, have you thought of that?'' Maggie tossed out the question.

She hadn't. Feeling incredibly stupid, Anna realized she'd never even considered the possibility that the man wouldn't expect her to marry him.

Jason's image as he'd kissed her on the beach on Staten Island filled her mind. He'd wanted her then, baby and all. Was it possible that things could work out for them? Someday?

''Of course, when you get your memory back, if it turns out this guy is the father and you do love him, it's good that he called,'' Maggie said cheerily.

Maggie's words plummeted Anna straight back into the depths. She had nothing to give to Jason. Not while there was still a possibility she was in love with a man she couldn't seem to remember.

OTHER THAN BRINGING HER a new printer, reams of paper and extra diskettes, Jason stayed away from Anna for six days. Long enough to win a racquetball tournament at the club and to drink himself into a celebratory stupor with the guys afterward. Long enough to convince Sunny he hadn't fallen in love with his old family friend. To gather his defenses about him. To drive himself completely crazy with wanting Anna, with worry.

She was pregnant and virtually alone in one of the most dangerous cities in the world. And she had no memory of her life prior to the past seven weeks.

He'd planned to wait until he heard something concrete from Whitehall before spending any more time with Anna, but the lead the man had mentioned was on simmer because a contact was on vacation. Finally Jason couldn't stay away any longer. He still hadn't come to terms with her pregnancy, with the other man in her life. Still wasn't certain he could stop himself from falling for her all over again. But he was sure of one thing. The past week had been hell. So while he still could, he wanted to spend as much time with Anna as possible.

Feeling guilty, he rapped on her door Tuesday morning. He'd been wrong to leave her on her own so long.

No answer.

Jason rapped again. Harder. She didn't usually leave the apartment in the morning. Though she'd never outright admitted it, he knew she was still suffering from occasional bouts of morning sickness.

The vacant look on her face when at last she opened the door changed to instant welcome when she saw who was standing there.

"Jason!" Throwing her arms around him, she hugged him tightly. His arms came around her automatically as he gloried in her softness, ignoring for the moment the evidence of her pregnancy.

"I'm sorry, Anna," he felt compelled to say. "I didn't mean to desert you." But he *had* meant to. And he'd been wrong.

"No, Jason, don't be sorry." Her sweet smile tore at him. "I understand. You have things to do." Smoothing the frown from his brow, she said, "It's okay, really."

"How are you?" he asked, still holding her. He couldn't seem to let her go.

"Fine. Especially now that you're here. I've missed you."

"I missed you, too."

Looking into her big brown eyes, seeing the desire there, he either had to kiss her or get away from her.

He couldn't kiss her. He had to keep enough distance to retain his sanity when they eventually found the man who'd slept with her.

Seeing her computer blinking over her shoulder, he let her go and crossed to it. "You've been working?"

She chuckled. "All the time."

"It's going okay?" His gaze met and settled on hers. Damn, she looked good. Her hair was tousled, her face was devoid of makeup—exactly as she'd looked waking up in his bed.

"Ideas are flowing so fast I'm afraid of losing them," she said, grinning.

She was doing fine. Just fine. Jason was glad, relieved. Whatever happened, Anna was going to be okay.

"You want to go out for breakfast?" He had to get out of her apartment. She was too close, too tempting. He couldn't stop thinking about Staten Island.

"Sure." She grabbed her purse. "So, what've you been doing besides working?"

What could he tell her? That racquetball had been more important than seeing her? That he'd taken Sunny out several times?

As easy as Anna was making it, Jason couldn't just pretend that there hadn't been a problem, that there wasn't still a problem. She might not remember their relationship, but he did. And the one thing that had made it so different, so remarkable, was the complete honesty between them.

"Staying away from you." The words were out of his mouth before he could stop them.

"What?"

"I've been avoiding you."

Anna's purse hit the floor. Her face white, she sank onto the couch, her eyes stricken. She didn't say a word. Just looked at him.

"I was wrong." The confession didn't make him feel any better. Her either, apparently.

"To the contrary, your reasons were probably quite valid." Her calm impersonal tone cut him to the quick.

This was Anna when she was hurting the most. She'd perfected the art of covering up. *Don't let it show.* He could almost hear the ingrained words repeating themselves in her head.

"Valid or not, avoiding you wasn't the answer." He sat down beside her, taking her hands in both of his, holding tight when she tried to pull away. "But we have to talk about this, Anna."

"Why are you doing this?" she asked. "Why do you hang around, keep coming back?"

That was easy. "Because I care."

Her gaze searched his relentlessly. "As an old family friend?"

"No."

"Oh." She looked down at her lap. He looked, too, and was surprised to see how much larger she'd become in just six days.

"I tried to stay away. It didn't work."

Anna nodded, feeling stupid. She'd had no idea. All the while she'd been working, content with the knowledge that Jason was just a phone call away, he'd been contemplating changing his number.

Jason's hand suddenly moved, and Anna flinched as it covered the swell of her stomach.

"Don't." She pushed his hand away, embarrassed. She would have given anything for Jason to have been the man who'd put the child there.

"Do you want me to go?"

Her gaze flew to his. "No!" she said. And then, more softly, "I care, too, Jason. A lot." Frightening as the admission was, it was also a huge relief.

Bringing his hand back to gently caress the baby again, Jason said, "We have to talk about it, Anna," He tapped her stomach with one finger. "This little guy's a part of you."

"She's a girl." He was right. They couldn't keep pretending the baby didn't exist.

His hand stilled. "You know for sure?"

She nodded. "I found out last week during the ultrasound."

Not only wasn't it fair to either of them to keep pretending the child didn't exist, it wasn't fair to her daughter. Something shifted in Anna's heart as she finally allowed herself to acknowledge the tiny being inside her. She was bearing a child. And a part of her was very very glad.

"Was everything all right?"

"Fine." The baby was growing right on schedule—which made Anna about fifteen weeks pregnant.

"I'm sorry I let you down." He was troubled. And that troubled Anna.

"Oh, Jason, don't," Anna said, laying her hand on top of his. "You've done so much for me. There's no way you've let me down."

Jason's gaze held hers, seeking what she didn't know. But she knew when he found it. He smiled at her, squeezing her hand.

"Have you thought of names?"

Hell, no. She'd barely thought of the child as real until two seconds ago. She shook her head.

"What happens next?" he asked, rubbing her stomach again, staring at it as if he could actually see the little girl growing inside.

"Not much for a while," she said, her eyes misting with tears as she watched him. Oh, God, why couldn't it have been him?

"I continue my monthly checkups clear up until the last month," she continued. "Take my vitamins, get fatter."

"This isn't fat," Jason said, almost sounding like a proud papa for a moment as he continued to rub her stomach. One thing she'd learned about Jason over the past weeks, something she greatly admired, was how completely he jumped into everything he did. He'd decided to acknowledge her baby, and now she couldn't get him away from it.

Unfortunately his fingers weren't just communicating with the child in her womb; they were sending erotic messages to her.

She forced herself to concentrate on his original question—the months ahead. "If I can find a partner, I'd like to take childbirth classes."

If she'd been looking for a way to stop Jason's attentions, she'd found it. He pulled his hand away, sitting stiffly beside her, not touching her at all.

The ensuing silence screamed with the offer he wasn't making.

"What about after she's born?" His quiet words fell into the awkwardness she'd created. "Have you thought about what you're going to do?"

Anna shrugged. "I guess that all depends on where I'm living."

"Where?" He turned to look at her, shocked. "You're thinking about leaving New York?"

If his stiffness a moment before had hurt her, his dismay now made up for it.

"I meant whether I'm still living in this vacuum or in the real world."

And there was the crux of their problem. The past weeks, the time they'd spent together, the relationship they were building—none of these were real.

Taking her hand, Jason pulled her up and into his arms. "I want to be a part of that world, Anna."

No more than she wanted him there. Still... "Nothing's

changed,'' she whispered. She wasn't free to make promises, no matter how badly she wanted to make them.

"Just tell me you won't disappear without a word. No matter what happens, what you remember or when, you'll come to me first? Talk to me about it?"

His request was fair. It was even one she could grant. "Of course."

He smiled at her, kissing her lightly. "Then there *is* a commitment we can make."

"Yes?" She was desperate enough to listen, even knowing he was wrong.

"We can promise each other the present."

It wasn't at all orthodox. It solved nothing, as the present became past with each new minute. "I promise you my present," she whispered, her eyes welling with tears as she looked up at him.

"And I give you mine."

Jason offered to attend the childbirth classes with her.

WHITEHALL'S LEAD turned out to be nothing—wrong person, wrong place. They knew from questioning Anna's landlord that Anna had been accompanied by a man on at least one occasion, but hadn't managed to find out anything about him. Jason had already questioned all of Anna's neighbors himself, knew what a dead end that was. On a hunch Jason had Whitehall check every literary agent in New York, but a month later, nothing was still all they had.

Sitting in Anna's apartment one Tuesday in mid-September, waiting for her to finish getting ready for their lunch date, Jason wasn't even sure he wanted Whitehall's answers. Anna was nineteen weeks pregnant. In all that time, no one had shown up on her doorstep. Maybe their luck would hold out for another fifty years.

"Jason! Come here, she's awake!" Anna called from the bathroom.

He was up in a flash, striding across the apartment as fast as the cramped quarters allowed. He'd missed the last two times. He wasn't about to miss a third.

"Where?" he asked, reaching for her belly the second he was in the door.

"Here." Stretching her dress across her stomach, she took his hand, placing it just under her left ribs.

Jason waited, feeling Anna's heart beat, but nothing else. Damn. Did the little girl somehow know it was him? Had she recognized his voice when he'd walked in the room?

Waiting impatiently, refusing to budge until Anna's daughter gave in, Jason continued to cup Anna's stomach. *Come on, darling, move for me,* he encouraged silently.

The flutter against his hand startled him so much he pulled back instantly. Shocked, he looked up into Anna's laughing eyes.

"Put it back, silly." She grinned, guiding his hand to the right spot.

"It's amazing!" Jason said seconds later. Until that moment the life forming in Anna had been a source of pain to him. Suddenly the child was nothing but incredible joy.

His gaze met Anna's, the wonder, the awe of life's creation passing between them there in her cramped little bathroom.

"I wish she were yours," Anna whispered softly.

Not as much as I do, sweet Anna. Not nearly as much as I do.

Unable to say a word, Jason broke his own rule and leaned down to kiss her.

THEY WERE FINALLY READY to leave the apartment when her phone rang. Still tingling from the shock of Jason's kiss, Anna fumbled with the receiver, nearly dropping it before getting it to her ear.

A woman's voice greeted her in German. It sounded harried, apologetic and wonderfully familiar.

"Rosa!" Anna said. *"Guten Tag."*

The older woman spoke rapidly, apologizing profusely in her native tongue for disturbing Anna, aware that Anna was writing, that Anna would call if and when she had some extra time for sewing. But Rosa was in a terrible bind. Just had two seamstresses come down with the flu and had a whole series of jobs due out that week. Please, could Anna help her just this once? She didn't have anyone else to call.

Anna assured Rosa that of course she'd be glad to help and was halfway through her commiseration with Rosa's predicament before she noticed the odd way Jason was looking at her. That's when she realized she herself was speaking fluent German.

And just as suddenly she knew that she'd studied German because she didn't want to study Spanish. Though what relevance that piece of information had was completely lost on her.

Quickly explaining her condition to Rosa, she asked for directions to Rosa's shop, saying she'd be by later that afternoon to pick up a batch of jobs. Rosa started to cry when she heard what Anna had been through, trying to retract her request for help fearing that she was putting too much on Anna's shoulders, but finally giving in when Anna assured Rosa that she'd welcome something extra to do.

Rosa did, however, insist on bringing the sewing to Anna. She couldn't get away that day, but she'd come by first thing the next morning.

"Rosa?" Anna asked, just before she hung up. She just had to know one thing, she explained. Did she pick up her sewing in garbage bags and return them the same way?

"*Ja.*" Rosa went off on another spurt of German, worrying about Anna, assuring her she'd do anything she could to help.

Maybe Rosa would know who Anna used to consort with. Maybe she'd be able to help Anna find out who'd fathered her child.

CHAPTER THIRTEEN

ABBY NEVER CALLED anymore. Jason dialed the beach cottage for the third time that week, frowning when he realized he was the only one keeping in contact these days. The past months were taking one hell of a toll on Abby.

She answered on the fifth ring. "Yes?"

"What, you can't say hello anymore?"

"Jason!" There was a little more life in her reply as she recognized his voice. "Nothing's wrong, is there? You just called two days ago."

"Everything's fine," he quickly told her. He knew it was hell for Abby being so far away when Anna—the sister she'd spent her entire life caring for—was going through such a difficult time. Jason understood, which was why he called so often.

"I felt the baby move today," he told her.

"No kidding!" It sounded like Abby might even be grinning. "Is Anna getting huge, then?"

"Not yet, but she's definitely showing."

"Will you send me a picture?" The wistful tone was back.

Jason agreed readily, then said, "She had a call today from some German woman who owns an alterations shop. Anna had been doing piece work for her."

"That's one mystery solved."

"Anna spoke to the woman in fluent German."

"She remembered her German?"

"Not only that, she told me over lunch that she remembered studying it because she didn't want to study Spanish."

Silence thrummed over the line. Jason had expected Abby to find the news encouraging. Slowly but surely Anna was remembering.

"I never knew she didn't want to learn Spanish. I just thought she liked German," Abby finally said. It sounded as if she was crying again.

"What's wrong with her not liking Spanish?" Jason asked, lying back on his couch, exhausted. Tired of trying to find answers that didn't seem to exist.

"I made all three of us sign up for it," Abby finally said. "Living so close to Mexico, with so many Spanish-speaking people, I thought it would be good for us to be fluent." She stopped, took a deep breath.

Jason waited.

"Both my sisters agreed, but the first day of class, Anna didn't show up. She'd gotten Mom to change her schedule at the last minute. They just told me she really liked German."

"Maybe she did."

"Or maybe she was trying to get away from me even then."

"She wanted to think for herself, Abby," he said softly, the back of his hand over his eyes. "Not to get away from you."

"I'm not so sure."

"I am."

"Because she wouldn't leave me to move to New York?"

It hurt to hear her say it even after all this time. "That's one sure sign."

"Did you ever think that maybe we're the real reason for Anna's amnesia?" Abby sounded as worn-out as he felt.

"That she needed to find her own identity, you mean?" he asked. Of course he'd thought of it, they'd all discussed it—he, Abby and Dr. Gordon. But while the doctor had seen that as a contributing factor, he'd been sure there was more going on with Anna than an identity crisis. Something far more disturbing.

"No. I mean, maybe by forcing her to choose, we forced her to escape, instead."

Sitting up, Jason frowned. It was past midnight. He was beyond playing mental gymnastics with Anna's sister. "I don't follow you."

"Think about it, Jason. If Anna loved us both equally—shared an equal though different bond, an equal loyalty—we both betrayed her by forcing her to choose one bond over the other. To make one of us happy, she had to desert the other. For someone as intensely loyal, as deeply committed as Anna, it was an impossible situation.''

Abby had had a lot of time to think. And what she said made sense.

"So how do we get her back?"

"Wait. Just like the doctor told us," Abby said, sounding more like the bossy woman Jason had grown to love. "It's when we have her back that it's our turn to go to work. We can't make her choose anymore, Jason."

"You're prepared to give her up?" Jason asked.

"Are you?"

"Of course not."

"Then how can you ask it of me?" Her voice was barely above a whisper. But Jason had no trouble hearing her message. *Or of Anna?*

"I'm an ass," he said, finally seeing what he'd done all those months ago. He'd let the insecurities he thought he'd left behind years before overrule his good sense. Anna was an identical triplet whose bond with her sister had grown as necessary to her as breathing over the years. Moving her to New York wouldn't have changed that. It would only have made Anna miserable. Just as miserable as Abby was now.

And because he was a jealous fool, feeling shut out by a bond that was stronger than anything he'd ever known, anything he could ever share, he'd laid down an ultimatum.

"I'll quit my job, move back to California," he said, surprised to find that he wasn't as upset as he should have been at the thought. He'd been so proud when the offer had come in.

Or had his excitement been charged with the knowledge that he now had a legitimate excuse to force Anna's hand, to make her prove she'd forsake all others for him? To get her away from her sister?

He didn't know. But one thing was for sure—the job alone had not made him happy. He needed Anna. And although he'd sworn he'd never again allow himself to come second to a woman he'd committed his all to, wasn't second still better than nothing? If he knew going in not to expect any more than that?

"Jason?" Abby's voice was oddly hesitant.

"Yeah?"

"Don't quit your job yet."

"I'm not going to lose her again, Abby."

"You may not have a choice."

He'd thought Abby was on his side. All these weeks she'd been encouraging his involvement with Anna. "We were meant to be together, Abby. She may not remember our past, but she's fallen in love all over again."

"And how's she going to feel when she remembers the choice we forced on her? Do you think she's going to be fond of either one of us?"

He didn't know. Dammit, he didn't know. "The move back to California should settle that."

"Maybe. But where's her guarantee it won't happen again?"

"She'll have my word. Besides, life never carries guarantees. Anna's smart enough to know that."

"There's another possibility. What if, when she remembers, there's another man she loves more?"

Her words sliced into him and he couldn't answer her. *God, did she hate him this much?*

"I'm worried about you, Jason," Abby finally whispered. She was crying again. "You're the best there is and you're getting in too deep."

"You'd rather I just walked away?"

"No." She sniffed. "I'd rather you just marry her before she comes to her senses."

The thought had crossed his mind.

"But I know you. You won't do anything even remotely so dishonest."

"Thanks for that, I think." God, he'd never felt so weary of spirit. Why did he go on? But with Anna still within reach, how could he not?

"I wish you weren't so damn honest. Because when Anna remembers who the father of her baby is, she may very well choose him even if she loves you more. And knowing you, you're going to let her go—and that just might kill you."

"You think letting her go now is going to hurt any less?"

"Just be careful, okay?"

"Yeah." He'd be careful.

If only he could figure out how.

"OH MY! HOW DID THAT happen?" Rosa exclaimed in German, standing in Anna's doorway the next morning. The plump gray-haired woman was staring at Anna's stomach.

Anna looked down, too, as if she might find a spot on her dress, something she'd spilled. But her head remained bowed. "I don't remember."

Rosa didn't seem nearly as bothered as Anna was by the humiliating admission. "I'll bet it was that nice man you brought with you sometimes," Rosa said pleasantly, her old-fashioned brown dress crinkling as she walked by Anna to set her bag of sewing down beside the couch.

"I brought someone with me?" Anna asked. Her embarrassment fled in light of possible answers to questions she'd almost given up asking.

"A man, yes," Rosa nodded. "He was tall, nice-looking, if you like them skinny. Older than you."

Sounds just like the man Maggie described. Anna looked blankly at Rosa; she didn't remember this man at all.

"Clark, you called him," Rosa told her.

Clark. Anna felt sick to her stomach. She didn't want him to have a name. She'd wanted Maggie to be wrong, to have imagined the man. *And the voice on the answering machine?* She'd erased that.

"He had dark hair?" Anna heard herself ask. But she didn't want to know. Didn't want this man to exist.

"Yes, he did." Rosa's heavy, flat-soled shoes against the hard wood floors sounded like cannon shots as the woman approached Anna again. "You remember him?" she asked.

Anna shook her head, shame washing over her. Not only did she not remember this man, she didn't *want* to remember him, didn't even want him to exist.

Rosa clucked when she saw the stricken look on Anna's face. "Oh, he'll understand, dear. He was always so nice to you, carried your bags, took you nice places."

Anna tried to smile at the older woman, all the while feeling more and more trapped. Tied up in so many knots she'd never get out, never be free.

"Sounds like I spent a lot of time with him," she said, and knew she hadn't hidden her distress very well when Rosa took her hand and led her to the couch.

"A bit, I think," Rosa said. "But don't you worry about it now, dear. You just rest here." She pulled the blanket off the back of the couch, laying it over Anna's legs. "You've got that little one to think about now."

Yes, she'd think about the baby. And Jason. The past was past. She was living in the present. A present she'd promised to Jason.

BECAUSE DRIVING in the country was one of Anna's favorite things to do, Jason took her out most weekends. He loved to see the smile on her face as they sped down quiet country roads.

"I feel so free out here," Anna confessed one Saturday in early October.

He glanced over at her, seeing her hair falling about her shoulders in a golden halo. "You don't feel free in the city?"

Shrugging, she said, "My problems are there."

"You shouldn't worry so much, Anna." Jason frowned. "Dr. Gordon gave you a great report just last week."

"I know." She nodded. "And it's not even worry so much as it is feeling trapped by my own mind."

He was happy with their present. A small part of him wished she, too, could be satisfied with just today, although he knew he was asking the impossible.

And were he to be completely honest with himself, he'd have to admit he was only happy with the present because he refused to consider the future. But ignoring it was getting harder and harder.

"Do you want to start asking questions? Call Abby?" he asked.

Anna took a long time answering him, telling him without words of the battle taking place within her. He needed to do something to help her. But he sat beside her, instead, completely helpless.

Finally, shaking her head, she said simply, "No."

"Then we'll wait."

"Are you disappointed in me?"

The car swerved as Jason stared at her. "Good Lord, no!" How could she even imagine such a thing?

"You don't think I'm a coward for wanting to wait?"

Jason pulled to the side of the road and stopped. Then he took both her hands in his and leaned over to kiss her gently. "You're the farthest thing from a coward, Anna Hayden," he said, kissing her again. "You're brave—" another kiss "—and strong." He brought his lips to hers one more time.

"Strong enough to hear the truth?" she asked when he finally pulled away from her.

"Strong enough to make your own decisions." He sat back in his seat, still holding her hand. "And for the record I think you've made the right one."

Her eyes clouded. "Because you don't think I'm ready?"

"Because I trust Dr. Gordon, and he thinks you're going to remember on your own."

Jason's heart jumped when she pulled on his hand and planted a big kiss on his mouth. "Thank you," she said, smiling as she let him go.

"You're very welcome." Jason ran his finger along her cheek. She was so beautiful, his Anna. Except that she wasn't his Anna. At least not yet.

"TELL ME MORE about Jason Whitaker," she said later that afternoon when the Jag was headed back toward the city.

"What do you want to know?" This was one of the hardest parts for him, looking at the woman he'd shared his heart and soul with and having her act as if she'd only known him for a few months.

"Why are you still single?"

The flippant answer that came automatically to his lips froze when he glanced at her earnest expression. She cared about his answer.

"You know about my last relationship," he reminded her.

"The woman who turned you down?" She was frowning.

Guiding the Jag around a curve, he studied the landscape. "Mm-hmm." Such a beautiful day—and so filled with land mines.

"What about before her?" Anna asked. "You're thirty-three—

you had to have had some other relationships.'' Her husky voice drew him.

"I lived with a girl my last couple of years of college.'' Which was something he'd never told her before.

"What happened?'' Her eyes shimmered with ready understanding.

"She could never get over her first love, a guy who left her at the altar to marry a woman almost twice her age.''

"I'm sorry.''

Jason shrugged. "I was young,'' he admitted. "Just made a bad choice.'' He grinned at Anna. "I didn't really love her, anyway— at least, it only took me about a week to get over her.''

Anna smiled back at him, connecting with him the way she used to when they'd had entire conversations without ever saying a word.

"So what about after her?'' Anna asked.

"There was only one other serious relationship....'' One the old Anna had known all about. In fact, he'd met her the day it had fallen apart. He'd only spoken three words to Anna that day, but her smile had carried him through a very difficult afternoon.

"She wasn't in love with someone else, too, was she?'' Anna asked.

Jason shook his head, welcoming the lights of the city ahead. "Nope. The law was her first love.''

"She was a lawyer?''

"A defense attorney.''

"Oh.'' Anna sounded almost intimidated. "So what happened?''

"My grandmother died. Sheila chose to bail a new client out of jail rather than accompany me to the funeral. The guy didn't want to wait a few hours. I decided then that I didn't want to wait around anymore, either.''

"I can't believe she did that!'' Anna's eyes were wide, just as they'd been the last time he'd told her this story. "Did she know your grandmother?''

"My grandmother introduced us.''

THE INSTRUCTOR Anna wanted for her childbirth classes, a woman who came highly recommended by Dr. Litton, already had a full roster during Anna's last trimester, leaving Anna the choice to take the classes during her second trimester or take them from someone else. Anna chose to take the classes early, starting in mid-October.

His leather jacket over his arm and nervous as an expectant father, Jason showed up at Anna's apartment half an hour early the first night of classes, extra pillows in hand.

"These okay?" he asked, thrusting the pillows, still in their packaging, at her when she opened the door.

"Fine." Anna grinned. "Any pillows would have done—I only have one."

She looked great, her long-sleeved brown flowered dress matching her eyes. She was going to be able to get through her whole pregnancy without having to buy maternity clothes. Her loosely cut dresses came in handy for more than the freedom of movement she'd always claimed from them.

"Where's Maggie?" he asked, looking around when Anna disappeared through the open bathroom door. Maggie had laughingly promised to send them off with a glass of champagne. Jason had hoped to have more than one.

"She got a job!" Anna called, coming out of the bathroom with a tube of mascara in her hand. "She's playing a female cop in an NBC pilot. She flew to California this afternoon."

As happy as he was for Maggie, Jason was sorry to see her go. She'd been a good friend to Anna. And he'd really been counting on that champagne.

HIS FANTASY WORLD shattered the minute they walked into the classroom. It wasn't until he saw the size of the stomachs of the women who were in their third trimester, saw how far Anna had yet to go, that he was forced to acknowledge the dangerous pretense he'd embarked on. And the small hope, that chance in a million that Anna was carrying his child, that the doctor had been six weeks off on Anna's due date, died a very painful death.

But because everyone, Anna included, was watching him, waiting for him to take his place beside her, Jason didn't give in to the impulse to bolt. Like the mature grown man he was, he sat down beside her on the mat and proceeded to learn how to help her bring another man's child into the world.

Unfortunately mature grown men experienced agony right along with the rest of them.

THAT FIRST CLASS introduced a new intimacy into a relationship already on the verge of becoming far too personal. Feeling like a wanton woman, Anna started to flood with desire at the merest glance from Jason, at the unexpected sound of his voice on the telephone. And every time he helped her practice for the birth of her daughter, every time she lay back and lifted her pelvis for him to shove a pillow beneath her, she ached with the need to pull him down on top of her. More than one time she had to bite her lip to stop herself from begging him to make love to her.

Instead, she directed her emotion into the biography she was writing, pouring her longings onto the page, her frustrations, her desires, knowing that if nothing else came from this nightmare time of her life, she was writing a good book.

In the evenings she sat, drained, watching Jason on the news and sewing for Rosa.

Then one afternoon toward the end of October, a letter came in the mail from a literary agent in Manhattan. It seemed she'd sent three chapters of her manuscript to the agency back in June. They liked them. Enough to want to see the entire manuscript as soon as she could send it.

It wasn't a sale. But it was more than she'd even dared hope and her spirits soared.

Coming down long enough to dial Jason's number, Anna hung up in disappointment when he didn't answer. He'd been invited to take part in a celebrity touch-football game that afternoon to benefit homeless shelters in the city, and she'd hoped he would already have arrived home.

She tried again between newscasts that evening and finally reached him when she was half-asleep late that night. He was as delighted as she'd known he'd be, and more, he sounded proud. Even invited her out to dinner on the Upper East Side the next night to celebrate. But only after she promised that when she was a famous celebrity, she'd still remember him.

As if she'd ever forget him.

Anna hung up with a huge grin on her face. Amnesia or no, she felt good about herself. She'd built a new life. A happy life.

Lying on her side in bed, cradling her unborn child, Anna finally had the courage to admit what she'd been hiding from for months. She didn't want to remember anymore, didn't want to find the father of her child. She didn't care if she'd loved him before the accident—she didn't love him now. And the reason she didn't love him was that she was passionately in love with Jason Whitaker.

But the admission didn't bring her relief. Instead, she started to cry, stopping herself only when she remembered Maggie's words about crying women having grouchy babies. Not that there was any truth to that. Still, her sobs couldn't be good for her daughter, this tiny being who was a hundred percent dependent on her, Anna, to give her a good life.

Could she do that? Her chest tightened. Until she found out who she was, what did she have to offer this child? Not even a father. And what if, when she remembered her past, she found herself irrevocably bound to another man?

What if the past she was running from turned out to have been immoral, or so painful she couldn't face it?

Until she knew what she'd done, what she'd been, she wasn't free to love Jason. Nor fully equipped to be a mother to the child who'd be arriving in less than three months.

Tossing and turning, Anna finally drifted off, but only after forcing herself to practice the breathing techniques she and Jason had been working on. But sleep, when it came, brought, instead of relief, only more nightmares.

HER HEAD POUNDING, she called Dr. Gordon first thing in the morning. Wasn't there something more he could do? Because until she got her life back, she couldn't go forward.

No, the doctor told her. The most she could do for herself was just relax. Allow her mind whatever time it needed to heal itself. Getting upset was only going to slow the process. She should take heart from the memories she'd had, resting assured that the remainder would follow. In the meantime concentrate on her book, on shopping for baby things—on relaxing.

Unfortunately the doctor saying so didn't make it happen.

LIKE SOME DIRTY TRICK, more than three months after he'd hired Smith Whitehall, Jason finally got some answers on Halloween. Jason was sitting in his office an hour before he was due on the air, going over the day's stories, when his phone rang.

Whitehall had a name for him—Clark Summerfield. The eldest son of a family with old money, a New York businessman with fingers in numerous financial pies, he'd been dating Anna for several weeks before being called out of the country on business. There was no evidence that Summerfield and Anna had ever slept together, no indication of nights spent at each other's homes or records of any hotel stays. However, Whitehall was certain Summerfield was the only man Anna had seen on a personal basis since arriving in New York—and there was no one in California at all, not since Jason.

Cold with dread, Jason spent the next half hour calling several of his New York contacts, needing factual and frank character assessments of Clark Summerfield.

The accolades came in almost immediately. Clark Summerfield was a prince. A widower for many years, he had no children, worked hard, although he didn't have to, and attended every family get together. He donated heavily to charities. Before Anna, he'd often been seen escorting his mother or unmarried sister to business functions. He'd celebrated his fortieth birthday the previous spring. His only fault, if you could call it one, seemed to be his workaholic tendencies.

And the fact that he wasn't the least bit athletic. Anna loved sports. Or at least, she'd always been eager to watch Jason's various athletic ventures.

So, his rival had a name. A damn good name. A damn good life. One that in other circumstances, he could see Anna being happy with. Summerfield was a man Anna could love.

Jason went on the air, he exchanged quips with Sunny, even had dinner with her in between shows. And he did it all with a frozen heart.

For the first time in a long time that night Jason went home and did some serious drinking. He hoped the alcohol would warm him up a bit, make him feel again. And maybe it did, because by the end of the evening he felt as if he had died and gone to hell.

But if he had, his rival was there with him, taunting him. Clark Summerfield. New York's number-one catch. Hell, maybe America's number-one catch. And, it seemed, Anna's sweetheart.

Sometime around three o'clock in the morning, six or seven whiskeys under, he started to think. If Summerfield was the father of Anna's baby, wouldn't she have told the man? And wouldn't he, respectable responsible man that he was, have stood by her? Married her?

Or was this guy's image a sham? Had he simply used Anna and then deserted her in her hour of need? Conveniently finding it necessary to wheel and deal in Europe for the next several months.

Had this been the blow that had done her in?

No, if Summerfield was that much of a jerk, someone would know. Anna wouldn't have been the first scorned woman. Men like that left a trail of them.

So maybe he'd left before Anna had known she was pregnant. Maybe she hadn't had a chance to contact him before the crash had wiped away all evidence of his existence.

And maybe Summerfield wasn't the father, after all. As good as Whitehall was, wouldn't he have found some evidence if Summerfield and Anna were lovers? Even if they'd only had sex once? Of course, they could have done that in the car or on the beach....

It was also possible, based on the lack of any other evidence, that Anna's mysterious lover had died. Perhaps that was the tragedy she was running from. No. Whitehall would definitely have been able to determine that.

Perhaps the guy was running from something himself, purposely covering his tracks. Maybe he'd been a swindler, a professional crook who changed identities and ate nice girls like Anna for bedtime snacks.

So what if the man never turned up? What then? Jason couldn't base his future on what ifs. Was it wrong for him to want to come first in someone's life? No matter how hard he'd tried, he'd always played second fiddle—to his father's career, his mother's second marriage, her new daughter, his college love's other man, the law, even to a prostitute's career. He'd been eating leftovers his entire life.

But weren't leftovers better than starving? And the bottom line was, did he have any choice? He'd been in love with Anna Hayden since the first moment he'd seen her. He had a pretty good idea the feeling wasn't going to disappear now, just because his head told him he'd be safer not to care.

Dizzy with the circles his thoughts were running, Jason finally fell across his bed, still half-dressed, just as dawn was breaking over the city. One fact remained. The father of Anna's child wasn't here. Jason was. And possession was nine-tenths of the law.

HE WAS GOING to lose her. In the cold light of day, his head pounding in protest, Jason had to face the truth. Clark Summerfield was the only logical choice for the father of Anna's baby. He simply wasn't aware of the child he'd created. When he was, a man like Clark would ask her to marry him immediately. And Anna, loyal as she was, would marry him out of duty. Wouldn't she?

Or would she?

Anna had changed, was sticking up for what she wanted. Would that new determination extend to rejecting what she didn't want?

Summerfield was in Europe during Anna's greatest hour of need. Which meant he must not know anything about the crash or her amnesia. Had he known, he'd have flown home to see her through this difficult time. But if there was commitment between them, wouldn't there also be communication?

And if there were no commitment...

Jason had won her love once. While the field was clear, he at least had to try again. But he'd do it with his eyes wide open, knowing the risks. No more pretending.

CHAPTER FOURTEEN

JASON SENT HER FLOWERS. They arrived Saturday afternoon just before his phone call asking her out on a date. An official date. Dress comfortably, he told her. They were going on a cruise around the harbor.

At six and a half months pregnant, Anna didn't have any idea how she could feel sexy and romantic, but when she opened the door an hour later, when Jason looked at her as though he'd like to make love to her right there on the floor, she'd never felt sexier. Dressed in a long-sleeved ankle-length flannel tent with a thick cardigan sweater on top, she felt like every man's dream centerfold. Maybe pregnancy made your hormones rage.

The cruise was idyllic, quixotic—and deserted. No one else was crazy enough to cruise around the harbor at night on the first of November. But snuggled against Jason in the wool blanket he'd brought, Anna couldn't think of anything more romantic.

They ate assorted cheeses accompanied by a homemade French loaf and grapes, popping them into each other's mouths, licking the juice from each other's fingers—and lips. Jason drank wine, Anna, mineral water. And they talked. About the world. About people. About life. Jason believed in so many of the things she found most important. Family. Loyalty. Commitment.

After they'd eaten he pulled her back against him on the secluded bench. The blanket enveloping them in their own private world, he linked his hands beneath the swell of her belly, holding her and the baby both.

Happy, drugged with the night, the romance, she snuggled into him, content to remain as she was forever.

The baby moved, her little foot dragging across the bottom of Anna's stomach.

"She's awake, Mama," Jason whispered in her ear.

"It's 'cause she knows you're here." Anna was convinced that the baby recognized Jason's voice, his touch. These days she seemed to become active whenever he was around.

Jason laughed, following the baby's progress with one hand, poking her gently, playing with her. Anna didn't see how any moment could be more perfect.

"There's a daddy position open if you're interested." The words slipped out before she could stop them.

And she wished she had when she felt Jason stiffen behind her. "I'm not her father."

She was spoiling the most perfect evening of her life, but she couldn't stop herself. When she'd awoken in that hospital all those months ago, she'd had to start fresh, fill the horrible void that was all she knew. She'd created a new life for herself, a good life, and that hadn't come easy or without a fight. If convincing Jason they were meant to be together took another fight, so be it.

"Not biologically," she said, placing her arms over his, keeping his hands on her belly. "But in every other way—in my heart and, I believe, in hers—you're already her father."

"And what happens to me when you find out who her father is, when he returns to your lives claiming what's rightfully his?" Jason's words weren't an accusation; that wouldn't have hurt so much. They were resigned.

It was time to speak up or lose him forever. "He doesn't matter anymore." The confession was difficult to make, not because she wasn't completely certain of its truth, but because it left her so vulnerable. "He can't matter," she continued, her voice breaking. "Because I'm completely in love with you."

Jason's heart soared. Which made the plunge to despair that followed all the more painful. He didn't doubt that she believed what she was saying. But how could she possibly be sure of her feelings without a yardstick to measure them by?

Then, too, she'd claimed tearfully to love him when he'd asked—okay, demanded—that she come to New York with him. Yet less than two months later she'd become pregnant by another man.

"You don't know how desperately I want to believe you," he finally said, her honesty deserving the same from him.

She turned to face him, clearly shocked. "You don't believe me?"

Jason kissed her slowly, tenderly. He'd always been able to show her so much more than he could say.

"I believe you feel that way now," he said when he raised his head.

"You don't think I know my own heart." Her head fell against his chest, and her gaze turned to the bay.

"You know what's there now, Anna, but what about when it fills back up with all the emotions you've forgotten?" He couldn't believe her words, couldn't count on them. He'd only get hurt. And he couldn't go through that again.

Her silence wasn't a good sign. He had to help her see that they had to know for sure. "I'm here," he said quietly into the darkness. "I'm the only one here." He chose his words carefully, needing her to understand. "But we have to face the fact that somewhere there's another man about whom you could have felt the very same way."

"How do I convince you he just doesn't matter anymore?"

"Until you remember him, you can't, Anna," he said, his voice strong. He wasn't going to let her sway him on this. He couldn't. It would kill him to believe her now, only to have her regret her decision when her memory finally returned. "Until you remember what it is you're giving up, you can't know if you want to."

"And what if I don't ever remember?" Her question fell between them, a question they'd both asked themselves a hundred times. A question neither one could answer.

JASON CALLED Dr. Gordon first thing Monday morning. He rushed through pleasantries, assuring the doctor that Anna was fine, the baby was fine, he was fine, and then got straight to the point.

"What are the chances that Anna will never remember?" When was it time to tell her the truth? At least about them. To tell her that she'd opted not to marry him when he'd asked her last spring. To give her at least those facts and then let her decide if she still wanted him to be the father of the child she carried. If she still wanted him.

The doctor was silent so long Jason was almost afraid to hear his answer. "You know something I don't know?" Jason finally asked him.

"No," Dr. Gordon said, the word drawn out. "I'm just not sure I can give you any percentages, Jason." He paused. "Of course there's always been a possibility that Anna won't ever regain the memories she's lost."

"Does it grow stronger as time passes?"

"No."

"So five years from now she could be sitting in a restaurant or driving down the road and suddenly have it all come flooding back?" Five years' worth of living, of loving, only to lose it all?

"Or it could come in little snatches, just as it's been doing."

"I want to marry her, Doctor."

"I'm not surprised." Dr. Gordon sighed. "But I can't tell you I think it's a good idea right now. Too much still rests in the balance."

"It's not fair to Anna, is what you're saying," Jason stated flatly. He'd already reached that conclusion himself. It was just convincing her he was having troubles with. "How can she make such a lasting commitment when she doesn't know what she's leaving behind?"

"Exactly."

The doctor was only confirming what he already knew. And it sounded just as hopeless coming from someone else.

"It also wouldn't be fair to you, Jason," Dr. Gordon continued.

"I'm not worried about that." He brushed the doctor's words aside. He'd given up on fair a long time ago. Now he simply kept himself safe. If he didn't count on anything, didn't look for things that weren't there, he'd be fine. "I'm just not sure I can convince Anna to wait another five years to start living her life."

"You'd have a hard time convincing me if I were in her position."

"She says she isn't going to wait until she's eighty and then, when she's too old to do anything but die, decide that her memory isn't coming back." They'd been her last words to him the night before when, in her apartment, they'd had a replay of the conversation from Saturday night. Jason had a feeling that they'd continue to replay it until he gave in.

"She has a point."

"So you think I should tell her about her past? At least about my part in it?" he asked, hopeful for the go-ahead. It was his only chance.

The doctor took a moment to think, but his answer was disappointing. "I really believe it's too soon, Jason. She's a strong woman, stronger now probably than she ever was before, but we have to remember that none of us knows what she's running from, what prompted her amnesia."

"And you don't think she's strong enough to handle whatever it is even now?" Because Jason did.

"Probably she is strong enough. But if she no longer wants to remember, if she no longer has any reason to try, you might be committing her to permanent darkness." He took a deep breath. "She's growing increasingly more frustrated. Her determination to know her own mind is becoming all-important, her need to make her own decisions stronger than ever. These are all signs of imminent recovery. I can't urge strongly enough that you give her more time."

Jason could find nothing in the doctor's words he could fault. "I'll give her until the baby's due," he said. "If she never remembers who fathered her child, if she never remembers the circumstances that led to her amnesia, I can live with that. But I'll never be able to live with myself if we bring this child into a relationship based on a lie."

There would be no argument on that point.

THE NIGHT SUNNY argued with him on the air, Jason knew he had some other decisions to make. His co-anchor, knowing he'd been seeing a lot of Anna, was trying to get his attention.

"Lighten up, Sunny," he said softly during a commercial break. Cameramen were milling around, someone from makeup came over to blot the perspiration on Jason's brow. Now wasn't the time for a showdown, but he hated to see Sunny humiliate herself on the air. She was a damn good newscaster. And she'd been a good friend.

"I don't know what you're talking about," she said, her voice sweet enough. But she wasn't as relaxed as she sounded. He watched her tap the end of her pencil on the desk in front of them.

"Will you at least agree to wait until we're in private?" he asked.

Sunny's assistant came forward to adjust the collar on Sunny's blouse. "Wait for what?" Sunny asked when the girl stepped away.

"I promise we'll talk, Sunny. Tonight. Right after the show." He smiled at the technician who adjusted his mike.

"The show. Sometimes I wonder if that's all you've ever cared about," she said. "Well, don't forget, I helped make you, Jason. And if all it took was my opinion, my acceptance, to gain your entrance into this town, then my opinion can just as easily guarantee your exit."

"Five seconds!" The voice boomed from the darkness in front of them.

Feeling sorry for Sunny, Jason braced himself for a difficult second half. His ability was one thing he was sure of. If she thought she had any power over his career, she had an eye-opener ahead of her.

ANNA WATCHED the news that night, Friday, almost a week after her cruise with Jason, feeling restless and bothered. She'd become used to Sunny Lawson's proprietary air with Jason, or told herself she had, anyway, but that night, either Anna was even more insecure than she thought, or Ms. Lawson had turned up the heat.

Busy with the little overalls she was stitching—a pattern she'd drawn herself and cut from an old newspaper—Anna hadn't noticed anything all that unusual about the first half of the newscast, other than an occasional uncharacteristic barb from Sunny. But during the second half of the show, Sunny not only touched Jason, she actually rubbed his arm a time or two. She was acting like a woman confident of her man's affection, confident her overtures would be accepted.

Licking her lips, Sunny smiled sexily at Jason as she told him they'd have to discuss their differing opinions on a recent parochial-school levy in a more private venue. Everyone watching was meant to know that the last thing Sunny and Jason would be discussing was school levies. That they'd be too involved in more…physical pursuits to discuss anything at all. Anna stabbed herself in the thumb.

Jason had explained about Sunny months before, assuring Anna that any personal relationship he and Sunny pretended to share was just that—pretend. He'd told her about the publicity campaign the station had devised to introduce him to his New York viewers. He'd told her how Sunny had become a friend, someone who's company he enjoyed. Not someone he wanted to have as a lover.

Anna knew all this. She even believed it. So why did Sunny's hand on Jason's arm make her feel so small, so insignificant?

SUNNY FOLLOWED HIM to his dressing room. Shutting the door behind her, she helped herself to a drink from the sideboard, fixing him one, too. Liquid courage.

"Lillie's having a mystery party next weekend on the yacht," she said, settling back against the smooth leather of his couch. Lillie was Sunny's best friend and a bit too shallow, too materialistic for Jason's taste.

He stood at the desk, the drink she'd brought him untouched. He didn't loosen his tie and didn't remove his jacket. He simply stood, not saying a word.

"It's from four on Saturday till whenever on Sunday."

He remained there, unmoving, unbending, by the desk. In his professional life, at least, he was in control. Always. He'd accept nothing less. And he had the feeling Sunny was actually trying to issue him an ultimatum.

"We're invited." She was no longer looking at him, drinking her martini more quickly than she should.

He still said nothing. Did nothing.

"If you pick me up at four-thirty, we should get there late enough to make an entrance."

He wondered where Sunny had gotten the idea that he'd ever change his mind about them. He'd been clear from the start that a friend was all she could expect him to be.

"I'm sorry, Sunny, but I can't go."

Her gaze shot up, locking with his. "Of course you're going," she said with an attempt at a laugh.

"No, I'm not." Jason enunciated the words carefully.

"Don't be stupid Jason." She set her glass down, stood, came over to the desk. "Didn't you hear me earlier?" She placed her hands on his shoulders, leaning her body into his. "The show's mine. You want it, you take me."

"Don't do this to yourself, Sunny," he said, pleading with her to come to her senses before she did irreparable damage to their relationship.

As she pulled away, the look she gave him was a mixture of desperation and hurt. "I'll have you moved to weekends," she blustered.

"I don't think so."

Picking up the phone, Jason dialed the station manager's office. And less than two minutes later hung up.

"You play nice or take weekends," he said. "The choice is yours." He didn't wait around for Sunny's reaction—or her decision.

DURING THE LAST childbirth class they watched a movie of a woman giving birth. Anna decided one thing instantly. Jason definitely wasn't going to be there for the birth. There was no way his first sight of her naked was going to be like that. She couldn't get out of the class fast enough, away from the chattering couples, the cheery instructor.

Wonder if she'd be feeling that cheery if it were her going through the ordeal, Anna thought sourly, her head bent as she walked out to hail a cab.

"Wasn't that the most amazing thing you've ever seen?" Jason asked, catching up with her at the curb. "Here, honey, put this on before you catch a chill." He handed Anna the coat she'd left behind in the classroom.

Amazing? She snuggled into her coat. "Thanks."

Lifting her chin and looking into her eyes, he asked, "You okay?"

Anna's glance fell. Hell, no, she wasn't okay.

"Anna?"

His gorgeous blue eyes were warm with understanding. He knew.

"I'm scared," she admitted, her breath misting in the cold air between them.

Silently cupping her face with his hands, he lowered his head to kiss her, the touch of his lips a distraction, a reassurance, a reaffirmation of how far she'd come, how strong she really was.

"I'll be there with you, honey, every step of the way."

"You promise?" She held his gaze. "No matter what happens between now and January?" She was asking a lot, but dammit, this was one thing she couldn't do alone, no matter how badly she wanted to.

"I do."

His words were promising far more than his attendance at her daughter's birth. They both knew that.

CHAPTER FIFTEEN

JASON WAS IN HIS KITCHEN when the phone rang Thanksgiving afternoon. Anna, having lain her increasingly cumbersome body back against the couch for a minute, reached lazily for the receiver. "Hello?"

"Is this…" A young woman rattled off Jason's phone number. Instantly on edge, Anna sat up. "Yes."

"Is Jason there?"

"Who's calling please?" She had no business asking, no right to monitor his calls. Suddenly she felt ill.

"Is he there?"

Anna didn't answer. She was too busy trying to see through the haze that was enveloping her. Sunny wouldn't be calling; Jason had told her his co-anchor had taken a cruise for the holiday weekend— with the new man in her life.

"May I speak with him please?" The woman was determined. Anna just wanted to hang up.

"Just a moment," she said, setting the phone down. She felt awful, light-headed. Must have overexerted herself in the kitchen, but she'd been so determined to prepare a perfect holiday dinner complete with all the trimmings for Jason.

"Anna? What is it?" Jason asked, coming out of the kitchen where he'd been lifting the Thanksgiving turkey out of the oven for her.

"Huh?" she asked, looking up at him. "Oh, nothing… I mean, the phone's for you." She couldn't think, didn't want to think.

"I didn't hear it ring," he said, looking first at her and then the phone.

She lay back, suddenly afraid she was going to be sick. "It did," she finally said.

Forcing herself to concentrate, she listened when he picked up the phone.

"Hello?" A pause during which Anna's stomach clenched again. And then, "Oh! Hi!"

Did he have to sound so cheerful? "Uh, yeah." This with a furtive glance her way.

Intending to lay right there and figure out what this mysterious woman could possibly want with Jason, why he was suddenly uncomfortable with her listening in, Anna was forced, instead, to bolt for the bathroom—giving him plenty of time to have whatever private conversation he wanted.

JASON DIDN'T TELL HER who'd been on the phone. And she refused to ask. He didn't owe her any explanations. Except that she needed one. She fought with herself the rest of the afternoon, barely touching her dinner, right up to the moment he dropped her off at her door that night. She didn't want to know, didn't want to be hurt. And didn't see how she could go another minute not knowing—loving him as she did.

He'd said he was bringing her home early because she was tired, because she'd been so violently ill earlier in the day. And he seemed genuinely concerned. But Anna couldn't help wondering if he had somewhere else to be. Someone else to see.

Not that she'd blame him. She just had to know.

"Who was she?" she finally blurted as he slid her key into the lock, her proximity to her own apartment giving her the courage to face whatever might be coming. If the news was devastating, she only had to make it a few feet to her bed, then slip under the covers and escape.

Jason didn't look at her or even ask who she meant. He obviously hadn't forgotten the call, either. "Nobody," he said, flipping on a light before standing back to let her enter.

Anna's nausea returned. For "nobody" the woman really bothered her, though Anna figured that was understandable. No matter how much she wanted to, she couldn't promise Jason anything, not yet. Maybe never. The phone call had brought home to her just how untenable that made her position.

He had every right to find promises elsewhere.

"There's no reason to lie to me, Jason," she said, standing in front of him, feeling like a beached whale as she imagined how beautiful the other woman surely was.

Helping her off with her coat, he stopped, looking down at her, his eyes serious. "Yes, Anna, there is."

He couldn't have surprised her more if he'd slapped her. "Why?"

THE DESPAIR IN HER EYES finally decided Jason. This had gone on as long as he could let it. If the past needed to be buried, that was just too bad. He wasn't going to let it interfere with the future.

"Come," he said, drawing her over to the couch, aware of how reluctantly she followed. She'd been through so much, his poor darling. And he had a feeling things were going to get worse.

"Anna, how did you feel when you answered that phone today?" he asked. He'd been worried about Anna's violent reaction to the call. And he wasn't the only one who'd worried.

"Well, if she hadn't evaded me so obviously, it probably would have been okay," Anna said defensively.

Oh, honey, if only you knew. He'd never felt so helpless, watching her, not knowing what to say, what *not* to say.

"It's okay, Jason, I understand," she said, obviously misreading the look of pain in his eyes. He hurt for her, not for himself.

He shook his head slowly, brushing her hair back from her face. "No, honey, you don't," he said, ready to take the plunge, and yet not ready.

"Yes, I do, Jason, and it's really all right." She was trying so hard to mean what she said it broke his heart. "I won't hold you to your promise to hang around until the baby's born," she rushed on. "You've been wonderful to stand by me this long, but you don't owe me anything."

"It was Abby."

Anna's eyes went wide, blank, and she started to shake.

"Oh, God." The words were anguished.

Pulling her against him, rocking her as he held her, Jason told her about the call and the two others he'd made later in the day, both times when she'd been in the bathroom, reassuring Abby that no harm had been done. Abby had miscalculated the time when she knew Anna was due at Jason's. And then realized what had happened and been terrified, knowing that hearing her voice could very well have risked Anna's future health.

What he didn't tell Anna was how devastated that call had left Abby. To have actually spoken to Anna, to have had her on the phone, hearing her voice—and still not be recognized had shaken Abby to the core. Nor did he tell her how worried they still were. Both from Anna's first nauseous reaction to having spoken with her sister, and the fact that Abby's voice hadn't sparked any memory at all.

"I could have talked to her—" Anna's words, thick with tears, broke off.

"You can always talk to her, honey."

She swiped at the tears on her face. "Dr. Gordon says I should wait."

But the doctor's way wasn't working. "And is that what you want to do?" This was Anna's show now.

"I don't know what I want." Her voice broke again. "Hold me, Jason," she begged. "Please, just hold me."

He did. But his arms couldn't take away the fear. For either of them.

AUDREY. ANNA SAT straight up in bed, looking around at the pre-dawn gray of her apartment as if she'd find someone there. Audrey. She wanted to name the baby Audrey.

Although not knowing how she knew that or why, Anna had never been more sure of anything in her life. *If the baby was a girl, she was to be called Audrey.* Anna was having a real live honest-to-goodness memory. A resurgence of a thought she'd had before she knew the sex of her child, a thought she'd had before the accident.

She'd been walking in Gramercy Park, and she'd just found out she was pregnant. She'd decided to name the baby Audrey if it was a girl. And she'd hoped it was a girl. Surrounding the memory was a feeling that someone would be very pleased about her decision— once she was free to speak of it.

Still frustratingly locked away was why she couldn't speak of it or who would be pleased.

Tempted to call Jason, in spite of the hour, a new worry held Anna back. Something—or someone had been calling out to her more and more often lately. Before it had only been in dreams, like the nightmare she'd had at Jason's just after she'd left the hospital. But in the three days since Thanksgiving, she'd been experiencing the oddest sensations while wide awake, almost as though someone else were there in her mind, calling her name, needing her.

Terrified, she had no idea what to do—and half suspected she was losing her mind, after all. Which was one reason she didn't tell Jason. She couldn't bear to have him see her go crazy. To place such a horrible burden on him.

But there was a second reason she didn't call. She was horribly frightfully suspicious that she was remembering someone—and that the someone was the man who'd fathered her child. Who else would have such an intense emotional hold on her? A bond that was reaching out to her even through her darkness?

Queasy, shivering, Anna burrowed beneath her covers, her arms cradling her child, holding on by the barest thread to logic, to reason.

She only had one thing to focus on right now. One thing that mattered. In only seven weeks she was going to give birth to her daughter. To Audrey.

TO SAY JASON WAS SHOCKED when Anna told him what she planned to name her baby was an understatement. Fortunately she did so over the telephone and he was able to hide his reaction. She was remembering. She had to be remembering. And for that reason alone he didn't tell her the significance behind the name.

He was achingly aware of what the return of her memory would mean. Every day as her baby grew, so did the tension between them. They were living on borrowed time. They both knew that.

Jason was sitting with Anna in her apartment the first Saturday in December, his leg bobbing swiftly and almost imperceptibly as they watched another movie. They'd been spending most afternoons that way since Thanksgiving, and he had to get out, to do something besides wait quietly for his world to come crashing down around him. He was spending far too much time watching Anna's expression, waiting for the light of memory to come into her eyes. Dreading what would happen when it did.

And today was worse, knowing as he did that, since it was a weekend, he didn't have to leave for work in a matter of hours. That he could stay right there with her as darkness fell over the city. And stay. And stay. Now, before her memory came between them.

"Isn't it about time to buy her some stuff?" He asked, his hand resting on Anna's stomach, waiting for Audrey to wake up.

"I've been looking through catalogs," Anna said, grabbing one from under a pile of books on the coffee table. "I found the furniture I want, but as small as this place is, I figured I'd wait until I was a little closer to my due date before I started getting any of it. I was thinking about looking for a larger place." She'd received her settlement check from the city the week before.

Flipping through the well-worn pages of the catalog, she found the nursery ensemble she'd chosen.

"All that color's great," Jason told her approvingly. The crib and changing table were white with colorful balloon motifs. The baby would only have to open her eyes to be entertained.

"See, there're sheets, receiving blankets, hooded towels, sleepers—everything to match." She pointed to the next page.

Standing up, Jason said, "So let's go get 'em."

"Now?" She looked up at him. They'd just finished lunch. She usually rested after lunch.

"Sure now." He suddenly wanted to do it all, to take part in everything that was yet to be done to prepare for Audrey's imminent birth, and to do so as soon as possible. Because he didn't know from one day to the next if there'd continue to be a role for him to play.

"But where will I put it all?"

Looking around the cramped apartment, Jason could see her problem. And suddenly he had the perfect solution. Or at least as close to perfect as he could get, considering his limited options.

"We'll set it up in the downstairs bedroom in my place. I'll move back up to the loft."

"Your place?" she asked. But she didn't sound at all displeased with the suggestion.

"Sure," he said, grabbing her coat. "I've got the room."

And if he had the baby's things, didn't he stand at least some chance of eventually having the baby? And her mother, too?

"But won't it be a lot of trouble to move it all again?"

Jason shrugged. The possible trouble would be worth the chance to have her stay. "Your chances of finding a place you want before she's born are pretty slim," he said, which was one thing they both knew to be the truth. Waiting lists for New York apartments, at least ones she'd want to raise Audrey in, were a mile long. "You guys can room with me until something comes up."

Neither examined the plan, knowing that to do so would only borrow trouble. Instead, avoiding each other's eyes, they locked hands and went on a shopping spree.

"WE DID GOOD, don't you think?" Anna looked around Jason's spare bedroom on Sunday night, tired but happy.

"We did great!" he said, the pride in his voice sending little thrills clear through her. This was how expecting a child was meant to be. A man and woman, their love electrifying the air between them, filled with anticipation as they surveyed the crib that would soon bear a tiny body, the changing table filled with tiny T-shirts and sleepers, bottles waiting to be filled, diapers to be worn.

"You don't think we went a little overboard?" she asked, looking around them. They'd bought out half of New York in less than twenty-four hours.

"This little one's worked damn hard to get here," Jason said, wrapping his arms around her from behind, his hands spreading over her stomach. "She deserves to have her necessities waiting for her."

Anna grinned at him over her shoulder. "I'm just not convinced that a life-size bear that plays nursery rhymes can be considered a necessity." She covered his hands with hers, leaning back into him, loving the solid strength of his body. A body she'd not yet discovered, and yet felt as if she knew so well.

"Sure it was," Jason said. "He matched the crib."

"And the curtains?" She looked at them, hung at the window to pull out the creases. They were playing a dangerous game. But curtains could be rehung.

"You want someone peeping in at her while she sleeps?" Jason asked.

"On the tenth floor?"

Her gaze locked with his over her shoulder. He'd never actually asked her to move in with him, but they were both talking as if such a move was a foregone conclusion.

"Anna?" Jason's voice was hesitant, unlike him. "If, after the baby's born, we're still where we are now, would you consider making this her home?"

If we're still where we are now. If she was still without half her senses, he meant. If she still didn't know who Audrey's rightful father was.

She should tell him no. She had to tell him no. None of this was fair to Jason, but moving in with him, being a family, was downright cruel.

"For how long?" she whispered when she'd meant to decline his offer. "Not just until I can get into someplace bigger than what I have now?"

She felt him shrug as his arms fell away. Cold, suddenly bereft, she took his hand gladly when he offered it, following him out to the living room.

He sat down on the couch and pulled her down beside him, still holding her hand. His gaze locked with hers.

"I want her here," he said. "I want you both here forever."

Her heart flip-flopped. She'd been living to hear those words since she'd first come home from the hospital with Jason, maybe even before. And then reality set in. "But..."

"Shh. Hear me out." He placed one finger against her lips. "I want to marry you, Anna."

Tears sprang to her eyes. She didn't think it was possible to hurt so much. "Oh, Jason, I want that, too, so much."

He nodded. Swallowed. And then started again. "I can't ask you to do that, Anna. It wouldn't be fair."

"To you," she said, her tears still welling as she held his gaze. "I know."

Shaking his head, he said gently, "To you." He reached up and dried her eyes. "I'd be taking advantage of you if I married you now when you're at your most vulnerable. When you have no idea what you'd be giving up.''

''You mean Audrey's biological.'' It was how she'd come to think of the man.

''Her what?''

''Her biological, as in the biological source of half of her existence.''

''He's a man, Anna,'' Jason said, although she could see what the words cost him. ''He's her father.''

She couldn't allow him to go that far. ''No, Jason.'' She shook her head. ''He's not a father.''

As if he knew she was prepared to argue semantics with him all day if that was what it took, he nodded slowly. ''He exists. Someplace in your memory he exists.'' A pause. ''And there's more.''

Frowning up at him, she asked, ''What?''

''You have no idea how you felt about me before, but if your memory returns, that will come back to you, too. And whether you believe it or not right now, that memory could very well change how you feel about me.''

Anna's stomach clenched. She hated the sudden turn the conversation had taken. ''Didn't I like you?'' It was something she'd never even considered.

''Yes.''

But his eyes told her there was more.

''Was I angry with you?''

''Yes.''

Frightened, she grasped his hand more tightly. No. She didn't want there to be any problems between them.

''Did I have reason to be angry?'' she whispered, her heart thudding.

She'd pretty much decided that she was ready to deal with whatever it was she'd been avoiding remembering now that she was stronger, now that she had Jason by her side. She'd never once considered the fact that he might be part of the problem.

''Yes.''

She pulled away from him and then, seeing the pain in his eyes, grabbed his hand back again. ''You wouldn't ever have hurt me deliberately, Jason, I know that,'' she said, the conviction in her words coming straight from her heart. There were just some things a body knew, no matter what.

Jason acknowledged her trust with a nod, a slow smile spreading across his face. "Never," he said.

"Do you want to tell me this horrible thing you did?" she asked, trying to make light of it.

Jason studied her for a long moment. "Do you want me to?"

No. She didn't. She didn't want to know any of it, to have had a past at all. She was happy with the present. A present they'd promised each other. Why couldn't they just leave it at that?

"What do you think Dr. Gordon would say?" She knew she was copping out even as she said it. But while she'd been convinced she was strong enough to handle the return of her memory, she'd also planned on having Jason to turn to, to help her pick up the pieces.

"He said you're probably strong enough to hear what I have to say."

Her fear increased. "You've already talked to him about it?"

Jason nodded. "I'd planned to tell you, anyway, before the baby's born."

"And he agreed?"

For the first time Jason looked away, and Anna breathed a small sigh of relief. He wasn't sure.

"He advised me to wait. Going by what you've already remembered, your chances of complete recovery are excellent, and so anything we might tell you could hamper that recovery." He said the words in one breath.

"Then I'd like to wait."

"Okay, we'll wait." He didn't even try to convince her otherwise.

"Will you tell me one thing?" she asked, missing the emotional closeness they'd been sharing these past weeks.

"I'm ready to tell you whatever you want to know," Jason said, sounding resigned.

"This thing that made me angry, was it something horrible enough to make me run from myself?"

"Not by itself, no," he said, choosing his words as carefully as he had those first few days she'd been with him. He was going to honor her decision not to be told about her past. "We had a nasty quarrel. The stance I was taking was unfair. But that was all."

Anna started breathing easier.

She grinned up at him. "I can live with that."

"Here? After the baby's born?" Jason asked, his eyes serious.

Anna nodded. She'd learned to trust herself these past months, and Jason's home, in his life, was where she wanted to be. "But if six months after the baby's born I still haven't recovered my memory, I'm going to be expecting a marriage proposal, anyway."

Shocked by her own boldness, Anna nevertheless held his gaze.

"I'll do better than that," Jason said, pulling her into his arms. "You have it now, due and payable six months after Audrey's born."

She wanted the proposal more than anything else. And yet, as part of her rejoiced, another part shivered. So much could happen in the next seven and a half months.

CHAPTER SIXTEEN

JASON HELD ANNA for a long time, reluctant to let her go, knowing that every minute of his time with her was to be cherished as though it was his last. Knowing that every moment might very well *be* his last.

She felt so good in his arms, so right, even pregnant by another man. This time was his. His and hers. And if, with the regaining of her memory, he lost it all, he at least would have had something he'd never had before. Unconditional love. Total commitment. An acceptance of his proposal of marriage. Even if just for today.

Pulling Anna closer, Jason inhaled her natural scent. Anna. His woman. He couldn't get enough of her.

"I love you," she whispered against his neck.

And because this was his moment, he answered her. "I love you, too, Anna." He raised her face, kissed her deeply. "Please remember that."

Her eyes clouded, almost as if she'd heard the desperation he'd thought he'd concealed. Before she could delve into things better left buried for now, he kissed her again, lifting her, settling her on his lap, on the aching hardness he'd grown almost accustomed to these past months.

Or thought he had until she moved against him, creating a friction she'd created so many times before.

Her dress slipped up her body, bearing thighs firm and long and so painfully familiar. He knew every freckle, every shadow there—and other places, too. He ran his hands along one smooth thigh, back and forth, up and down, caressing her, remembering. Until her long legs wrapped around him, straddling him, cradling him.

And he was lost.

With the ease of exploring familiar territory, Jason seduced Anna, knowing where to touch, how to caress, how hard and how soft, how much to tease. He knew because she'd taught him; he'd insisted she teach him. And he'd taught her, too.

Breaking off a long satisfying kiss, Anna drew her tongue down his neck, unbuttoning his flannel shirt as she went. Artfully flicking his sensitive flesh with the tip of her tongue, she ignited him as she'd done so many times in the past, the only difference being that, instead of laughing up at him as she'd done in the days when confidence had made her bold, her eyes were shyly downcast.

And even this turned him on. To seduce Anna all over again, to relive those shockingly erotic days of teaching her how to give him love, how to take it for herself. A gift few men were honored with twice.

Then, as she settled herself more completely against him, things were suddenly different. She didn't fit as she used to. Her stomach protruded between them.

Oh, God. He let go of her thigh. What in hell was he thinking?

"We can't," he said, unable to hide the agony in his voice as he pulled away from her.

She stared up at him, her eyes clouded with passion. "What?"

"The baby." He could barely get the words out. He was struggling to breathe, to hold her calmly, to not lose his control in an agony of want.

Pulling herself farther up his body, she traced his ear with her tongue. Hadn't she heard him? He had to stop. Now.

"It's okay." He barely heard the whispered words through the roaring of his blood.

When he didn't respond, didn't do more than sit there holding her, holding on, she whispered something else, her words sending the blood straight back to his groin.

"I asked Dr. Litton when I saw her last week."

Her announcement stunned him. She'd been that sure? Or, his body throbbing harder with the thought, just that needy? Jason held her firmly away from him, watching her as he demanded, "And?" His hands were shaking with the effort it was taking not to carry her upstairs to his bed.

"I'm still seven weeks away," she said. "As long as it's not uncomfortable and we're careful..." Her voice trailed off as she lowered her eyes.

His own sweet Anna. Bold yet shy. Needy and yet not wanting to ask anything for herself. Even in love. He was going to enjoy teaching her how to ask all over again.

"Then let's be careful, my love." He was already carrying her up the stairs to the loft as he said the words.

ANNA HAD NEVER BEEN so thoroughly loved. Even without a single memory of anything to compare it to, she knew making love had never been so good. Not only did she catch fire everywhere Jason touched, she sensed his love, as well, and a reverence she wasn't sure she deserved but knew she returned with every fiber of her being. She was his totally, completely.

When she sat astride him, lowered herself down on him, she found not only a physical joy beyond anything she'd imagined, but an emotional release she felt she'd been craving for as long as she'd lived.

At first, when it became obvious to her that she knew what she was doing, that a man's intimate touch was achingly familiar, she worried that she might be remembering another place, another time. Another man's touch.

But soon, as Jason stroked and kissed and encouraged her to do the same, she had no thoughts other than Jason. Loving him.

"You're so beautiful," he whispered, every muscle in his body straining with the obvious effort it was taking him to be gentle.

The truth of his words were reflected in his eyes. And in that moment Anna felt beautiful.

"I could get real used to this," she said, watching him, the concentration on his face, the love in his eyes.

"Good."

He held her motionless on top of him and Anna frowned, eager to reach the destination she'd been climbing toward for months.

"Just giving us a minute to slow down," he said, his words coming with an effort. "To prolong the pleasure." Then he gasped, thrusting so deeply she felt the sensation to her fingertips and toes.

There was nothing slow about their loving then.

JASON HAD TOUCHED heaven, confirmed not only its existence, but that it was everything he'd hoped it would be. He held Anna, rolling with her until she was lying on her side facing him, his body still connected to hers. He was home.

"That was incredible," he said, needing her to know that what they'd just experienced hadn't been ordinary at all—not even for them.

"Mm-hmm," Anna said, moving her body against his, getting him aroused all over again.

"You're sure?" he asked, his body already fully hard within her.

She moved with him, giving herself to him completely. For now, this one night, this one time, he knew there was no part of her already reserved, already spoken for. For this one night he was first.

As Jason moved slowly within her, holding her gaze with his own, speaking on so many levels and connecting on every one of them, he couldn't help thinking that their lives would always be like this if she never regained her memory. And for just a second he hoped for exactly that.

But only for a second. Her beautiful brown eyes were filled with love but only a present love. His love had its roots in their past, had a depth hers would always be lacking. It would never be enough. For either of them.

He loved all of Anna—before and after. For both their sakes she needed to know herself, to love herself, too.

SHE'D STEPPED OUTSIDE *herself again, was watching as she walked in Gramercy Park, stumbling because she hadn't seen the uneven sidewalk through her tears. She even knew why she was crying. What she couldn't figure out was why she was there all alone.*

She'd never been alone before in her life.

And then there were two of her. Only she was in a different park, the ground covered with soft white sand, instead of grass. There was a sand castle nearby and she was laughing. Both of her were laughing at something beyond the castle. Something she couldn't see.

No. Wait. She'd miscounted. There weren't two. There were three of her. And all three were crying. They must know about Jason, she thought. They're all crying because I can't remember anything so I can't marry Jason.

Except that Jason hadn't asked her to marry him yet. This was before the crash. But the tears didn't stop. Had Anna caused all this pain? She wanted to tell them she was sorry, but all three ignored her. They'd reached the end of their endurance, found a hurdle they couldn't vault.

She was losing her mind—but not the pain. It wasn't ever going to go away. No matter how hard she cried, how hard all three of them cried, they couldn't change the—

With a start Anna sat bolt upright in bed. Remembering wasn't the shock it should have been; it wasn't even surprising or new. It was a solid wall of agony. An agony so familiar she knew she'd never forgotten it, not for an instant. Had been carrying it with her every day since the accident. And before.

Dr. Gordon had told her an incident, something deeply important, could very well trigger her memory when she was ready. Making love with Jason must have been that important. But she didn't think she was ever going to be ready.

She was Anna Hayden. Of Abby, Anna and Audrey Hayden.

Oh, God. Memories assailed her. Audrey. And Abby. ''Abby!''

Her voice startled her, scaring her, bringing the nightmare to life. She felt arms steal around her, allowed them to hold her only because she hurt too much to fight them off.

They weren't three anymore. ''No!'' she shouted, shaking her head, refusing to accept the picture in her mind. She couldn't bear the memory. Couldn't go back to living with the pain day in and day out. But the memories continued, pouring in so quickly she thought she might collapse from the onslaught.

Audrey. Beautiful vibrant laughing Audrey. Still. Terrifyingly unnaturally still. Covered in blood. Her face. *Oh, God.* She saw her identical sister's face. No one else. Only her. She'd been the one to find Audrey out on the beach. Had gone there to build a sand castle.

She'd screamed, could still hear her screams even now. They deafened her, sickened her. Covering her ears, Anna rocked from side to side. No! Stop!

But the pictures, the sounds, the smells just kept coming. She hadn't been strong enough, even then, to handle things on her own, to call the police, to spare her sister Abby at least that much. Instead, she'd stood there shaking and screamed for her. She'd thought that was all she'd done. All those months after the accident, she'd thought all she'd done was stand there and scream, the smell of Audrey's death enveloping her. But that hadn't been all. First she'd rolled her dead sister over. She'd rolled her over so Abby hadn't had to see her face.

"Ohhh nooo, please!" she cried. "Please stop!" She shook her head again and again, trying to dislodge the pictures. Anything to make them go away.

The funeral had been closed-casket. At the time she'd been too thankful to question the decision her parents had made without even seeing their daughter first. Now suddenly she knew why. They'd probably been told...

Rocking, crying, holding herself, Anna was no longer aware of the arms that held her, couldn't feel anything but the agony. A pain so deep there was no way to recover, to ever be again the innocent woman who'd walked out of the beach house that day.

And Abby. *Oh, God, Abby!* It was Abby who'd been calling out to her these past weeks. Abby who was hurting, who was needing her. Abby, who'd also had a part of her soul destroyed. "Abby!" she cried. She needed her sister. Needed that part of herself.

JASON JUST HELD ON, sweat running off his body as he listened to Anna's anguished cries. He'd never witnessed such suffering, had no idea what to do for her, how to help, how to reach her. He just knew he couldn't let her go, couldn't let her be alone when she came back out of this hell of hers. If she came back. His throat dry, his body starting to shake, it hit him that he might be losing her forever.

She'd remembered. Though she'd still said nothing but Abby's name, nothing else could have rent this much pain from her. But as he sat there holding her, the memories no longer mattered. Anna mattered. And her torment was breaking his heart.

His helplessness rendering him powerless, he just held on.

"Shh," he whispered over and over, rocking her, brushing the tangled hair back from her face. "I'm here, honey. I'm right here," he kept saying.

Whether or not she could hear him, he kept repeating the litany, hoping that even a trace of the comfort he had to offer would reach her, help her fight her way back.

"Oh, God."

The anguish in her voice tore at him. It was so hard to believe it was only hours ago he'd heard her crying in ecstasy. Their love-making must have triggered her memory. Subconsciously she'd remembered loving him before.

Anna continued to cry out against whatever visions she was seeing, locked all alone in a world he couldn't share.

Why? he asked over and over. *Why her?*

Fighting him again, she kicked the covers away.

"Anna! What is it, honey? Talk to me." He spoke firmly, urgently.

She continued to wrestle with no direction. Then one arm wrapped around his, holding him in a death grip.

"Talk to me, honey," he said again. "Let me help."

Pushing frantically at the hair tangled about her face, she continued to sob.

"I saw her!" she cried suddenly. "I saw her face." And then, as if the admission drained the last of her strength, she went limp in his arms.

"Whose face, honey?" Jason hoped to God he was doing the right thing in making her talk.

"Audrey's. I saw her face." The words were mumbled, as if she'd finally given up.

Unsure whether she was speaking of the baby she carried or the sister she'd lost, Jason asked, "When? Where?" Had Audrey visited her in a dream? He'd never been a big believer in the supernatural, but Anna couldn't be imagining whatever horrors were playing themselves out in her mind.

"That day—" She broke off, started to sob again. "On the beach..." More gasps. "I saw her face."

"What day?" he asked softly. When Audrey was killed, she'd been found facedown in the sand. Anna was remembering something else. If only he knew what.

"The blood!" she cried, and then moaned, burying her face against his chest. "Her beautiful face."

Jason held Anna more tightly, as though by sheer force of will he could erase her mind once again. Anna had found Audrey, but the police had made her leave—made Abby leave—before anyone had touched the body. Neither had seen the extent of the damage caused by the murderer's knife. Unless...

Jason swallowed, took a deep breath. "Tell me about it, Anna," he said, his voice gentle but commanding. He had to get it out of her before she escaped back to a place where nobody could reach her. "Tell me what you saw."

"Her face—" She broke off, sobbing. "I c-couldn't even r-r-recognize her." A spasm of hiccups choked her words. "But I saw her neck...her neck...her necklace..."

Cold to the bone, sickened, Jason knew. Audrey hadn't been found facedown. Anna had seen her and then wiped the sight away. But the vision had remained in her subconscious, preying on her without her even being aware of it, waiting.

"Her n-n-nose was g-gone."

Sick to his stomach, Jason had heard enough. "Shh," he whispered. "I'm here, honey," he crooned.

"Her ch-cheeks and m-mouth..." She tried to breathe, couldn't, tried again, her voice shaking with sobs. "So much b-blood."

Oh, Anna. Beautiful strong silent Anna. You didn't have to do this all alone. We would have helped you.

Suddenly she stopped. Stopped crying, stopped speaking. Stopped breathing. Panic shot through him and he sat up, intending to force his own breath into her lungs until she was ready to take over on her own, a part of him trying to devise a plan that would allow him to be in two places at once—breathing for Anna and on the phone getting help.

He lay her down, her closed eyes scaring the hell out of him. But before he could do more than prop her neck with pillows, a shudder tore through her. She was breathing again. Tears running down her face, she lay completely still and cried.

Unable to bear her pain, Jason reached for her again, and her eyes opened. She looked at him as though only just realizing he was there. "Oh, Jason!" she cried. "Her eyes, they were open and glassy and they weren't laughing at all." Her husky voice was thick with tears, but sounding more like her own.

"Anna. Lovely Anna." He swallowed, exerting every ounce of

control he had to hold back his own emotion, cradling her against him.

And then, leaning back to look up at him, she asked, "You knew Audrey, didn't you Jason? Were you our friend back then, too?"

He nodded, unable to speak. Hadn't she remembered him?

"I'm glad," she said, smiling through a fresh spate of tears. "Oh, God, Jason, how could I have forgotten something like this?"

He didn't have any answers for her. Only platitudes she'd heard before. Leaning back against the pillows, he held her close, surrounding her with strength, with love. It was all he could do.

She cried quietly now, speaking little. "Thank you," she said at one point.

Brushing his hand gently across her cheek, he said, "You don't have to thank me, love."

She nodded, as if accepting the truth of his words.

A long time later, still crying but much calmer, she pulled away just enough to look up at him. "I rolled her over," she said, as though confessing a crime.

"You did the right thing, Anna."

She shook her head. "I couldn't bear to look at her."

"There was no reason to."

She started to cry harder, still so full of raw anguish she overflowed with it. "Death smells awful."

Jason had smelled death once, during his early days as a reporter. He'd never forget the sickly sweet stench that had permeated the air, choking him. He'd been so violently sick to his stomach he'd had to leave the scene.

"I love you, Anna." The words were torn from his throat. He'd take her pain, her memories, upon himself if he knew of a way.

"I love you, too," she said, sitting up and gazing at him, the love in her eyes still fresh, still new. There was no recognition of the former love they'd shared.

NUMB, ANNA LAY in the bed with Jason, her head on his chest. He'd made her get up, put on one of his shirts, afraid she was going to catch a chill. But he'd taken only a brief moment to yank on a pair of cotton shorts himself before pulling her right back down into the comfort of his arms, the covers close around them.

But still she shook. Her whole body trembled as her mind wandered, stumbled, shied away and wandered some more. So many things, so many memories to revisit. Her childhood, growing up with her sisters. The time she'd broken her arm and Abby had been the one to sit up half the night with her, trying to take her mind off the pain of her broken bone setting in the cast. She remembered the jokes they'd played on their teachers, on their long slew of baby-sitters and nannies. But never on their parents.

Desperate for time with them, the girls had always been perfect angels whenever their parents were around. Except of course when they'd done some stupid kid thing, like the time their parents took them out to dinner at the Beverly Hills Hotel and Anna had spilled her drink on the table and into their father's lap. Or when Audrey had gotten lost at an amusement park, and the nanny of the week had panicked and called her father out of an important meeting.

Anna remembered the time Abby had bloodied Jimmy Roberts's nose for calling Anna a bookworm. The year her mother had surprised them with three birthday cakes—for her three little angels, she'd said. And Anna remembered Audrey, always hugging everyone....

All of these memories and more she shared with Jason, talking long into the night, one memory resurfacing after another. But every memory was tainted with bone-deep sadness. It was over.

"Poor Abby," she said, her eyes welling with tears as she thought of her older sister. Older by twenty minutes chronologically, older by years in every other way. "She grew up so fast." And had lost so much.

"Too fast and yet not unhappily," Jason said. "Abby's a born caregiver."

Anna had to remember that he'd known them before, that some of what she was telling him might not be new to him. But then, why was he still new to her?

She sat up, frowning. "There're still some blank spots."

He nodded. "Dr. Gordon said there might be, that your memory probably wouldn't come back all at once."

Anna started to shake again. "I can't take any more, Jason." She'd rather die than go through another night like last night.

"You're a strong woman, Anna, stronger now than ever before," he said, his hand rubbing her arm, warming her.

And in some ways she knew he was right. She was stronger now. If nothing else, these past months had given her that.

"It's funny," she said. "I remember leaving California. It was just like Abby said—I had to prove to myself I was a complete entity on my own." She chuckled without humor. "I guess I've done that, huh?"

"Absolutely," Jason agreed, his breath brushing the top of her head.

"The shop," she said, suddenly remembering the business she'd built with her sisters, the reason she was such a good seamstress. Knowing, too, that the overalls she'd been sewing for her baby were Abby's design. "I left her all alone with the shop."

"And it's doing just fine," Jason said. "Abby hired a couple of women who love her designs almost as much as she does."

Anna was glad. She'd hated spending her days sewing when her own creativity had been clamoring for release. But she'd owed Abby and hadn't begrudged her sister her chance. Or herself the opportunity to do something for Abby for a change. Even Audrey had done her share at the shop without grumbling.

Frowning, Anna said, "I even remember making my family promise to leave me alone for an entire year." She could picture the scene as if it had happened yesterday. Her parents had been stunned, Abby devastated.

But in the end they'd given her the promise she'd demanded.

"I just can't remember why it was so important," she said weakly. How could she remember hurting her sister so horribly and not remember why she'd done so?

"It'll come back to you, Anna," Jason said. "You just need to be patient."

"And you?" Anna sat up again, staring at him. "Why can't I remember you at all?"

Jason shrugged, breaking eye contact. She couldn't blame him for being uncomfortable. How must it make him feel for her to claim to love him but to have forgotten him so completely?

And then there was the other person she'd forgotten....

"I still can't remember the biological," she said softly. She was frustrated and frightened and so damn tired. What horrors remained to jump out at her? And would she be able to cope when they did?

CHAPTER SEVENTEEN

DAWN WAS BREAKING over the city when Anna finally fell silent. Believing she'd fallen asleep, Jason lay completely still, cushioning her head on his chest. And although he had a lot to think about, to consider, to accept, at the moment only one thought occupied his mind. Anna hadn't run for the telephone—for Abby. She'd remembered and had come through her emotional crisis without her sister.

And then, as if his mind had conjured the action, she sat up, slipping silently from the bed.

"You calling Abby?" he asked, resigned and maybe even a little relieved. She'd made it through her crisis. That was all that mattered. For the rest he'd been wrong. Wrong to expect her to leave a bond that was as necessary to her happiness as food and air. One that had been forged long before she'd even known him. One that had seen her through her entire life, made her who she was. The woman he loved.

Surprised when Anna shook her head and walked past the phone, Jason climbed out of bed and followed her. She'd turned her purse upside down and was shaking out the contents, sifting through them. Pulling an envelope from the pile, she opened it, dumping a chain and locket into her hand. He recognized it immediately.

"I thought it was such an odd shape," she said, holding the locket lovingly in her slender hands. "It's odd because it's only a third of a whole. Put together, the three parts form a heart."

Jason nodded silently, although he knew she wasn't looking at him. His throat thick, he watched Anna, seeing her—all of her—for the first time. He'd thought he'd wanted her to be whole, and all the while he'd been the one tearing her apart. Refusing to see an important part of who she was simply because it was a part he couldn't share.

"Our parents bought the original locket when we were born,"

she murmured. "They had it cut into three and then made into three separate lockets."

Even with her head bent, Jason could see that she smiled.

"They made us wear them always so they could tell us apart." Her finger brushed over her name.

"As we grew up, the lockets were a sign of our loyalty. We agreed never to take them off." She shrugged. "Other girls had best-friend necklaces. We had our lockets."

He ached to hold her, but didn't.

"It was also a symbol of our own separate identities," she said, telling Jason something she'd never told him before. "We were always part of a whole and yet different, too. I can remember Abby telling us that once when we were little. Audrey had been crying because Abby's locket was bigger than hers. Abby explained that hers was biggest because she was the oldest. Mine was next, and Audrey's was the smallest. That we were the same and yet special in our own ways."

"I didn't know that." Jason spoke for the first time since following her out of the bedroom.

She glanced from the locket to him, as though surprised to see him there. Frowning, she said, "You know, it's funny, but I don't think I've thought of that in years."

She handed the locket to Jason. "Would you help me fasten it?" she asked, holding her hair up off her shoulders.

She wanted him to fasten around her neck the symbol of what had driven them apart, asking him to give her back to the relationship he'd tried to take her from. She was asking him to share her, to know he was never going to be the single most important person in her life.

He fastened the locket.

MONDAY MORNING, just as soon as she was alone in her own apartment, Anna called Maggie.

"Hey, preggie, what's up?"

You were right about Jason and me all along, Maggie. We're lovers now. And it was even better than I imagined. Better than you'd probably imagined. And...I remembered some things. "Your apartment was rented."

"Yeah, well, I don't think I'm coming back."

"You got the job?" Anna asked, happy for her friend.

"Don't know yet, but the pilot's finished and it looks great."

"Oh, Maggie, that's wonderful!"

"I got me an agent, Anna," Maggie said, her usual sardonic attitude slipping. "He says I'm good."

"You *are* good, Maggie." Damn good.

They talked about a couple of other auditions Maggie had been on, and Maggie actually made Anna laugh when she told her about the job she'd lost for a cookie commercial. Maggie as a life-size macaroon Anna couldn't see.

"Where are you staying?" Anna asked when she could finally get a word in. She'd had a crazy idea during the cab ride home this morning.

"A dump on Sunset Boulevard."

Anna paced her apartment, her phone pressed to her ear. "You got a car yet?"

"Yeah, you could call it that. It used to be a compact sometime before the last wreck or two."

"Does it run?"

"Of course. You think I'm throwing my money away on something that isn't reliable?" Maggie demanded. "It's not pretty, but it works."

Crossing her fingers, Anna plopped down on the couch. "I've got a favor to ask, Mags."

"So ask."

"It's my sister, Abby."

"You talked to her?" Maggie asked, suddenly alert.

"No." Anna paused. She was afraid to call. Not until she remembered why it was so important that she left. "But I remembered her."

Maggie's silence spoke volumes. "Not everything," Anna answered the unspoken question quickly. She wasn't up for an interrogation, not yet. Maybe not ever. But this was something she had to do.

"Abby's all alone, Maggie. I want you to live with her."

"Whoa!" Maggie was probably backing away as far as her telephone would allow. Her New York friend was not used to California's laid-back ways.

"She has a three-bedroom cottage on the beach, Mags," Anna said before Maggie made up her mind once and for all. Once she'd done that, there was no changing it. "And she's only about forty-five minutes from the city, depending on traffic."

"I'm not worried about traffic, Anna. It's your sister. You ask her about this?"

"She won't mind, Maggie," Anna said. "I know she won't." Abby would never turn away a person in need, whether she wanted to or not. And Abby needed Maggie much more than Maggie needed a decent place to stay. "You can have my room."

"Your room?"

"Yeah. The cottage is half-mine."

"You and your sister lived together?"

"Yes, until I came here." Anna took a deep breath. "She's all alone, Maggie, and not, you know, doing all that great. She could use having you around."

"Right."

"You kept me sane, didn't you?"

"You're easy Anna."

"Abby's a lot like me." Well, okay, maybe not in some ways. But she had a feeling Maggie and Abby would hit it off. And couldn't bear the idea of Abby being alone one more day.

"I don't know, Anna."

She was losing her—she could hear it in Maggie's voice. "It's right on the beach, Mags. Think of all the beachboys."

"I'm getting enough pretty boys in the city."

"You can have my room at no charge."

She'd hit a chord there. She could tell by Maggie's silence.

"Please, Maggie, for me?" she asked.

"I'll go meet her," Maggie said grudgingly. "How do I find her?"

Anna rattled off the number at the shop. If Abby wasn't in, someone there would know where to find her.

"And Maggie?"

"Yeah?"

"I don't want you shocked or anything, but when you see her...?"

"What, she looks like Godzilla or something?"

"No." Anna smiled mistily. "She looks exactly like me."

ANNA SPENT the next couple of days making herself crazy. Every waking moment was eaten up with remembering—and searching for the lost pieces of the puzzle that had become her life. More and more frightened by the number of things still unknown to her, she became desperate to discover them, to get the ordeal over with once and for all. To own her life before her baby was born.

And for every memory she had, she conjured up an imaginary one that could explain the gaping holes still left in the picture. The largest hole, the one that mattered most to her, was Jason. Why couldn't she remember him? What was so threatening about an old family friend? She didn't know why it took her so long to come up with the answer—not when it was so obvious. Her only explanation was that she'd simply been too self-absorbed to see.

Sitting with Jason at lunch on Wednesday, she worked up the courage to confront him.

"Tell me about you and Abby."

She watched him put down his sandwich, her stomach a mass of knots. She'd been feeling poorly all morning—ever since she'd figured it all out.

"What do you want to know?"

"Whatever you need to tell me."

"We're friends."

"And?"

He splayed his hands, then dropped them to the table on each side of his plate. "That's all."

She believed differently. And her subconscious agreed—which was why it wouldn't allow her to remember Jason, especially since they'd spent the last three nights together in his bed.

"She was the one you went to see before you left town," Anna said.

"I had something to say to her." His sandwich still lay untouched on the plate in front of him.

"What?"

"That Audrey was gone, you were an adult, and it was time she concentrated on her own life."

Anna frowned. That sounded more like a friend than… "What about that phone call on Thanksgiving?"

"You know about that, Anna." Jason was frowning. "She was alone, it was a holiday, and she wanted to connect with you in the only way she could."

"You're sure that's all it was?" Because there had to have been some reason he'd grown so close to her family, something that kept him coming back. And she already knew it wasn't her. She'd have remembered loving Jason. She was sure of that—especially now that she knew what loving him was like. And besides, if they'd been lovers, he'd have told her. The pain he felt because he wasn't Audrey's father was too real to ignore.

"Of course I'm sure," he said impatiently. "What else could there be?"

"You two could have been in love."

The shock on Jason's face alone drove that suspicion from her mind. "We could have been, but we weren't," he said calmly, staring her down.

Bowing her head, Anna felt herself blush. Okay. She'd missed the boat again. Apparently that was something she was good at.

Light-headed with relief, she actually giggled. At least her beloved and her beloved sister weren't lovers.

ANNA HAD EXPECTED to feel better after her conversation with Jason, but as the evening wore on, she only felt worse. She wanted—needed—to call her sister. She hadn't heard from Maggie, didn't know how Abby was doing, if she was all right. And yet, Abby knew Anna's memory had returned. Anna could only surmise that Abby was respecting Anna's original request, her stipulation for silence between them. She just didn't know why. Her head hurt from trying to make sense of it all.

What was still out there for her to know? What had happened between she and Abby? Why had she extracted the promise in the first place? Why couldn't she remember Jason? And where in hell was the biological? He had to be that Clark guy. But why couldn't she remember him?

Audrey kicked her so hard she doubled over on her couch. She was waiting for Jason's second newscast to come on so she could admire his thick blond hair, the way his mouth curved when he smiled, his eyes. All the while knowing she'd be admiring the rest of him the minute he got home.

The baby kicked again, stealing the breath from Anna's lungs. She lay still.

The third kick scared her a little bit, coming as it did so low in her belly and in her back at the same time. Either the baby had turned miraculously fast, or she had six legs.

Halfway through the news, her water broke. Jason spoke to her from the television set, his blue eyes warm as they gazed straight at her. She could do this. That was what he was telling her. She was sure of it. She could do this. Never taking her eyes from his face, she reached for the phone.

Twenty minutes later Jason was at the door, a cab holding downstairs. The wait had almost killed her. Especially the last ten minutes when those steady blue eyes had been missing from her television screen.

CHAPTER EIGHTEEN

THERE WAS NO TIME to tell her the truth, in spite of his vow to do so before they had the baby. Jason threw Anna's coat around her shoulders, lifted her off the couch and carried her down the stairs. Six weeks early, Audrey was one determined little girl. *God, please get us there in time. Let them both be okay.*

"We've got plenty of time, Anna. Just relax, honey," he said, helping her into the cab. His heart thundered in his chest.

Please let them have found Dr. Litton. Have her waiting at the door.

"That's it Anna, one, two, three." He breathed with her, holding her in the backseat as the driver swerved in and out of the Wednesday-night traffic.

There was nothing else he could do. Nothing else but worry.

"We have to move my stuff to your place," Anna said after what seemed to Jason a particularly long contraction.

Stuff? Who the hell cared about stuff? How could she think about that at a time like this? They were having a baby here.

"Sure, honey," he said. "We'll do that."

"Right away, Jason." Her voice was stronger. "We'll probably be ready to come home tomorrow or the next day."

Okay. Fine. Whatever. "I'll move everything in the morning." *Now would you just concentrate on what you're doing, please?*

"I can't believe I'm finally going to get to see her," she said, resting her head against Jason's shoulder. She sounded as if she might be going to sleep.

They were having a baby. He was scared to death and she was going to sleep. Nobody had said anything about sleeping during the childbirth classes they'd taken. Sleeping wasn't in the job description. But sure enough she was actually going to sleep.

Right up until the next contraction. That was when Jason went back to work. At least he knew what to do. "One, two, three," he breathed. "Easy now, honey."

"I want to paint her bedroom red," Anna panted through the pain.

Red. Right. "Breathe, Anna."

"And the ceiling blue with a bright yellow sun."

"Uh-huh." And they thought she was actually going to have this baby? Why in hell had they gone to the classes if she wasn't willing to do anything right?

She chattered on about the room as the spasm passed, her voice getting drowsy again. Jason was almost glad this time. If she could just sleep until they got to the hospital, he'd have Dr. Litton to assist him in getting this job done. He didn't think they were going to get much help from Anna.

"I'd love a burger, Jason," she said suddenly. "You think we have time to stop for a burger?"

A burger! She just didn't get it. Giving birth was serious stuff. So much could go wrong...

"With pickles on it, please?" she asked sleepily. "Lots of pickles. Tell the driver to stop."

Jason wasn't sure how much more of this he could take.

But once they got to the hospital, Anna seemed to get more with the program. Dr. Litton was waiting for them in emergency, quickly checked Anna and determined they had time to get her up to a birthing room. Jason was doubtful. However, bowing to Dr. Litton's greater experience, he kept his opinion to himself and pushed Anna's wheelchair silently. And prayed for all he was worth.

THINGS MOVED so quickly Anna didn't have time to be afraid. She smiled at Jason when he appeared, garbed in a green surgical suit, in the door of her birthing room.

"This where the party is?" he asked.

She nodded. "Mm-hmm." They could get on with it now. He was here.

"Anna?" He looked as if he had something important to say.

"Yes?"

He paused. Glanced at the IV in her arm, at the monitor hooked to her stomach. "I love you."

That was all she needed to hear. "I love you, too."

She couldn't believe how excited she was. Soon, very soon, she was going to meet her daughter, see her, hold her.

"I'd expected to be scared," she confessed to Jason. "But with you here I just know everything's going to be fine."

He smiled at her. "Of course it's going to be fine."

It must have been a lot warmer in the room than she thought. Sweat was darkening the cotton surgical garb Jason wore.

Watching the monitor for her, Jason handled labor like a pro. He could tell from the lines on the screen just when her next pain was due and had her already breathing properly by the time it hit. He counted. He cajoled. He offered his arm for her to squeeze and ignored her when she yelled at him to shut up.

A nurse wheeled in what looked like a portable incubator just as Dr. Litton stopped by for one of her periodic visits. Anna looked from the machine to Jason, and then up at the doctor.

"What...?"

"She's close to six weeks early, Anna," Dr. Litton said calmly. "We have to be prepared."

"Jason?" Anna cried, fear choking her as she reached for his hand.

He held her, but looked at the doctor. "Have you any reason to expect trouble?" he asked.

"None at all. We wouldn't be in this room if we did."

"What's the immediate danger?"

"Probably none," the doctor said, smiling at Anna. "The baby's been perfectly active, her heart's strong, everything looks good. But with an early baby I like to be extra careful."

"You worried?" Anna asked Jason as soon as the doctor left the room.

He shook his head, smiling as he smoothed her hair out against her pillow. "Not at all. She knows what she's doing."

That was enough for Anna. If Jason wasn't worried, she had no reason to worry, either.

Jason's scrubs were drenched by the time she'd fully dilated, and by then she was pretty hot herself. And exhausted beyond belief. As the worst pain yet subsided, she wanted nothing more than to go to sleep. They were all going to have to take a break.

"Come on, Anna, it's time to get to work," Dr. Litton said from the end of the makeshift bed.

After she had a little sleep. Then she'd do all the work they needed.

"Now, honey. Push!" Jason instructed, watching the monitor.

She pushed. And wished to God she'd gone to sleep.

"Again!" Jason said.

She pushed again. Jason wasn't watching the monitor anymore. He was keeping company with Dr. Litton, both of them at a party she couldn't get down to attend.

"I see her hair!" Jason said, his eyes glowing with a light she'd never seen before. It made her want to push again, harder.

Jason's face her cue, Anna did her job, pushing when she was told, holding back as she had to. She watched the birth, not from the mirror they'd mounted for her, but through her lover's eyes.

Then, just as the baby surfaced, as her body found a relief so powerful she cried, she saw an expression on Jason's face she'd seen before. Once. In another life. The intensity of his yearning, the look of pain that resulted from unrequited longing, was completely familiar to her. It was an image she'd been carrying in her heart every day since she'd sent him from her life. She remembered him.

She remembered everything.

"Seven pounds!" a nurse declared, holding the newborn on a scale to one side of Anna's bed.

"Seven?" Dr. Litton was still working on Anna, but glanced over her shoulder at the nurse. "That much? Are you sure? Better check it again."

A pause fell over the suddenly still room.

"Still seven," the nurse said.

Clearly surprised, the doctor checked the scale herself.

Ignoring Jason completely, Anna was vaguely aware of the doctor and nurse, but her gaze was glued firmly on her baby girl. Audrey. A new life for one lost.

A baby born right on time.

Jason stepped back, his ears buzzing, his heart thumping heavily. He had answers to all his questions. As long as Anna and Audrey wanted him in their lives—in any capacity—he would be there. Period. Being someone's first priority was nothing compared to being needed, to being part of a family, to loving. He'd been playing second fiddle all his life. Was good at it. Memories, other loves, be damned. The past, the future. Nothing mattered except being whatever, whoever, his two girls needed him to be for however long they needed him.

SO MANY FEELINGS exploding inside her, so many thoughts clamoring for attention, she wondered if she'd ever see clearly again. Anna lay in her hospital bed the rest of that day, assimilating all that had happened before her accident, all that had happened since and what was yet to happen. And holding Audrey. Almost constantly holding the baby girl who was everything she'd ever hoped her to be and more. So much more.

She'd already made the decision to breast-feed her daughter, and so she'd had Audrey moved right into bed with her, feeding her when necessary, holding her while she slept. Keeping her close. At times throughout that long day, she felt as if Audrey was the only person she'd ever be close to again.

Anger, pain, guilt, all cascaded down on her until she had to send Jason home, telling him to go ahead and go in to work, that she needed to sleep. Unaware she'd remembered, he wanted to talk. She didn't have any idea what to say. Playing for time, she insisted, that she had to rest as much as possible before they released her the next morning.

Except that, of course, she didn't rest after he kissed her softly goodbye and left. She watched Audrey. Cried over her. Nursed her even though her milk wasn't in yet. Loved her. And thought. She'd bought herself one day. It didn't seem nearly long enough.

BEFORE SHE KNEW IT, before she was ready, she was back in Jason's apartment firmly ensconced on his couch, a blanket tucked snugly around her and the baby she held.

"You're sure you're comfortable?" Jason asked, hovering at the other end of the couch, almost as though he was afraid to touch her—or the baby he'd yet to hold.

Nervous as she was, she couldn't smile at him, but she tried. "Fine."

He nodded, then hovered some more, moving pillows out of her way, the coffee table closer. He was aware that something was wrong. He'd been avoiding her eyes all morning. And now that she'd combined the Jason she'd known before the crash with the

Jason she knew now, she could read him like a book. Just as he'd been reading her all these months.

"You should have told me." So many emotions roiling inside her, and anger won out. "I can't believe you didn't tell me."

He stopped dead, just stood frozen beside her.

"All these months and you never said a word."

Pale-faced, he sat down, no longer avoiding her eyes. "When did you remember?" he asked simply.

"Yesterday, the second she was born."

He nodded. "The birth brought it all back."

"No." She shook her head. "You did. I was watching your face." Anna sighed, her anger draining away. He'd done what he'd thought right. Jason always did what he thought right. If only his thinking wasn't skewered by his upbringing. He'd done what he thought right, yet he'd been so wrong, too.

"Dr. Gordon knew," he told her, but not in way of defense. "He said it was possible I was somehow mixed up in whatever you were running from, and so telling you who I was could force you to deal with a relationship you weren't ready to handle."

"After all we'd shared, Jason, you didn't know me better than that?" Her anger was back, but maybe just to camouflage the pain.

His jaw tightened. "We hadn't shared anything in quite a while," he reminded her. "And you were pregnant."

The words hung between them, his unasked question underlined by her silence.

"When are you going to stop being a martyr, Jason?" She couldn't look at him, couldn't bear to hurt him. Yet the words had to be said. Should have been said seven months ago.

"You mind explaining that?" He was angry.

She looked down at her sleeping daughter. *For you, my darling. For all of us.* Then she took a deep breath and spoke.

"You settle, Jason. Always." She glanced at him, saw the stoicism settle on his face as he prepared, once again, to take whatever was handed him. "You make it damn near impossible for people *not* to put everything else first, to think of you last. You're so undemanding one could almost believe you have no needs at all." Almost. But not quite. She'd seen the longing on his face.

He remained silent. She wasn't even sure he was listening.

"Think about it, Jason. Did you ever ask your father to be at a

game?'' She'd had so much time to think those two months she'd
been alone in New York. Time to figure it all out, to see where
she'd been wrong—and where he'd been wrong. She just hadn't
had the faith in herself to know that she could do anything about
it.

''He knew when they were.''

''But did you *ask* him to be there?''

His silence gave her the answer. ''And what about that girl in
college? Did you ever try to win her love away from the guy who'd
dumped her?''

''You don't win love.''

''Yes, you do, Jason.'' She forced back tears. ''Sometimes without doing anything more than being yourself.'' Which is how he'd
won *hers*. He'd certainly never asked for it. ''Love isn't easy—it
doesn't just fall in your lap and stay there happily ever after. You
have to work at it, grasp it with both hands and be determined to
keep it, or it's going to just slip away.'' Her last words were barely
more than a whisper, her throat thick with unshed tears. This was
a concept he had to understand.

The room fell silent again. Finally Anna couldn't stand it any
longer. ''And what about your lawyer friend?''

''What about her?'' Jason asked, sounding suddenly confident.
''I asked her to go to that funeral.''

''Yes, but in all the years you'd been with her, had you ever
before asked her to put her job second? Or had you given her the
impression that you *expected* her job to come first?''

Again his silence spoke volumes. ''Don't you see, Jason, not
only are you living proof of self-fulfilled prophecies, you actually
make people feel that they're pleasing you by doing as they please.
That to be lavished with attention would turn you off.''

Another glance in his direction. If he couldn't understand this,
couldn't see it, their life together was over.

But even if their relationship was going to end, she owed him.
Because she'd been wrong, too. The woman she'd been before had
never even tried to communicate this to Jason, had never dared
voice her doubts, her fears. She'd been too much of a coward to
speak up, too afraid of being a problem. Swallowing back her tears,
she held Audrey close to her heart and faced Jason head-on.

''I'm just as guilty as you are, Jason,'' she said. ''I did you—

us—a terrible wrong, and I don't know if I'll ever be able to forgive myself for that.'' Once again she pictured that look on his face. She'd seen it twice. The first time, when she'd walked out of his life in California, refusing to leave her sister and go with him. And the second she'd brought a baby into the world, a baby he'd so very much wanted to be his own.

''There's nothing to forgive,'' he said softly, gruffly. ''I never should have asked. It was unfair, cruel, to expect you to leave Abby so far behind.''

''Leaving Abby wasn't the problem, Jason. Or at least, not all of it.''

His shocked gaze collided with her sad one. ''Moving away wouldn't have made any difference to the bond I share with Abby. What we share isn't dependent on physical closeness.

''And that was the problem, wasn't it?'' she asked, still holding his gaze. ''Neither of you was willing to share the part of me you each had.''

He nodded. ''If it means anything to you, we've actually both realized that. We know how wrong we were to expect you to sacrifice one for the other.''

''You and Abby have talked about this?''

''In depth.''

''And you're friends again?'' She could hardly dare hope.

''Closer than ever, I think.'' He paused, looked down, and then met and held her gaze unwaveringly. ''We were wrong, Anna, insisting that we wanted all or nothing. Abby swears—'' he stopped, swallowed and continued ''—no *I* swear never to do that to you again. To love you is to love all of you, including the part that belongs exclusively to your sister.''

That was one hell of an admission coming from Jason. And a prayer come true for Anna. She was free to love both of them. If only…

''Do you know why I chose not to come to New York, Jason?''

He looked away. ''You're going to tell me it was because I led you to believe I expected you to say no.''

So he had been listening. Had heard. ''You did, but that's not why I said no.''

His gaze flew back to her. ''Then why?''

''Because I honestly didn't believe you loved me. Not completely. Not as wholeheartedly as I knew I was going to need to be loved if I was going to sever my relationship with my sister.''

"After the two years we spent together?'' he asked, scowling. "How could you not know I loved you? I told you so all the time.''

"Because you didn't need me, Jason. Not really. You always held a part of yourself back, relied only on yourself, protecting yourself for that moment when I'd let you down.'' She paused, looked down at the child in her arms. "I needed you to need me as much as I needed you.''

"And if I'd let you know that I needed you, you'd have come with me?'' he asked, even now expecting a negative answer.

"I did come, Jason.''

His eyes were pinpoints of steel, boring into her. "You came to sell your book.''

"I came to be with you.''

JASON WANTED to believe her. More than anything in his life, he wanted to believe her. But his heart couldn't accept what she was telling him. He'd been a selfish jerk. Why would she have come here to be with him?

"You were here for more than two months,'' he reminded her.

Her eyes filled with tears, and a full minute passed before she managed to get any words out. "After you left California, I hated myself. I hated you and Abby, too, but mostly just myself for not being strong enough to stand up to either of you.''

Jason was hating himself pretty thoroughly at the moment, too.

"And I was terrified,'' she continued, her words making him hate himself more. He'd done this to her. "I was afraid that I couldn't get along on my own. When I reached deep down inside, looking for some imaginary well of strength to draw on, I found that there wasn't one. Not in me alone. Not without Abby. And I knew you were right. As painful, as terrifying as it was, I had to get away from my sister. I had to know I could rely on myself alone.''

She stared down at the baby, and Jason looked away. He couldn't look at the child. Sooner or later she was going to tell him about the father. And that she was returning to the man.

"When I broke your heart, I broke mine, too,'' she said now, crying softly.

Reaching over, Jason brushed the tears from her face, then handed her a tissue. The baby didn't so much as stir.

"I came to New York to be close to you." She wasn't giving up on that one. He still didn't believe her.

"But I didn't contact you, couldn't contact you, until I'd proved to myself that I wasn't just transferring my dependence on Abby to you. I had to come to you whole or not at all."

After a lifetime of disappointment Jason had no idea how to handle anything else. Stunned, he just sat there, listening as two months of anguish poured out of Anna.

Those first days were harder than she ever would have imagined, but Jason could imagine it. She'd done this for him? She told him about being forced to quit her job when her boss tried to put the moves on her, how she was desperate to work—not because she needed immediate cash, but because she needed to be permanently independent for her own peace of mind. Independent of Abby. Of the shop. She told him how she'd always wanted to write, that working on John Henry Walker's biography was the only thing that had kept her going at times. She told him about finding Rosa and how much she'd liked the older lady.

And Anna saw him on the news. Saw him enjoying Sunny's attentions, saw how easy they were together. She knew she was losing him and that it was her own fault. And his, too, for not fighting for her, for their love. For letting something so wonderful slip away.

She was out walking one night less than a week after she'd left California, afraid, lonely. She walked for hours and still had to hail a cab to take her where she'd been wanting to go for weeks. The television station. That was the first time she'd seen him with Sunny off the air. Seen how close they were. She'd followed them to the Central Deli and Restaurant. And though she told herself to forget it, she started almost a daily ritual, taking a cab ride down to the deli between newscasts. And each time she saw him with Sunny, she died another death.

"If only you'd come to me." The words were torn from Jason.

She looked at him, her lips trembling. "I couldn't."

Of course she couldn't. He'd moved on—or so she'd thought.

"I met a man, Clark Summerfield, coming out of the deli one night shortly after I first saw you and Sunny there." *Here it comes, the part I've been waiting for.* And suddenly, with the truth at hand, he knew he never wanted to hear it.

"You want something to drink?" he asked.

Startled, Anna looked at him, shook her head and continued. "I was crying, and Clark saw me, came over, insisted on having his driver take me home in his limousine."

"You cold?" Jason asked, standing. "I can turn up the heat."

"I'm fine, Jason."

"What about her? Maybe she's cold." He still didn't look at the baby. Clark's baby. Twenty-four hours ago he'd been willing to settle for that.

"I spent a lot of time with Clark," she said. "He was nice. Mostly he was a much needed balm to a broken heart."

Okay, okay. He got the picture.

"I tried to convince myself I'd be happy without you," she said, her voice thick with tears.

Jason's own throat was uncomfortably tight. They'd made such a mess of things. Both of them. And ruined something beautiful in the process.

"And then came the day I couldn't avoid putting off doing the home pregnancy test I'd bought," Anna said. Her words were like a knife in Jason's heart. "I was getting sick every morning."

Was this the penance he was to pay for not fighting for her in the first place, this cruel blow-by-blow?

"When it was positive, my first instinct was to run home to Abby."

Why not straight to nice, balm-for-the-heart Summerfield?

"But as much as I was hurting, as terrified as I was, I couldn't run anymore. For myself, but also for her." She smiled down at the baby in her arms. "Then, more than ever, I had to know that I was a whole person. How else was I ever going to face raising a baby by myself?"

By herself? Jason stood frozen, every nerve ending tuned to her, listening intently.

"What about Summerfield?"

She frowned. "He'd left for an extended business trip to Europe." She sounded as if she couldn't have cared less.

So he didn't know yet?

There was hope. Not a lot. But enough to speak up.

"Anna?" He sat down, gently taking her free hand in his, his thumb running along her palm. He brushed the hair back from her face with his other hand, his eyes trained on hers.

"You were right," he said. "I do settle." The admission cost him. Far more than he'd expected. Because once made, he couldn't take it back. Couldn't allow himself to settle ever again.

"Growing up as I did, it was just easier."

She nodded, her eyes brimming with tears. "I know."

"I guess it just became habit. I didn't even realize I was doing it."

Anna nodded, waiting.

"Habits are hard to break."

"I know."

Her eyes shadowed with fear, she waited for him to continue.

"But I can't settle for a life without you."

She smiled, her lashes wet with tears.

"I love you, Anna, so very much."

"I love you, too, Jason." Her whispered words drove him on.

"But there are some things I have to have."

She nodded again, still smiling through her tears.

"I have to know that I'm the only man in your life." He couldn't live with the fear that Summerfield may one day return, discover he had a daughter, insist on a place in her mother's life.

"Absolutely." Her reply came swiftly. "You always have been."

"And always will be." This wasn't negotiable.

"As long as we both shall live."

He needed to kiss her, to hold her close to the heart he'd just bared for her. But there was a seven-pound baby lying between them. He knew she was there. Just couldn't bring himself to look at her.

"I'll gladly raise your daughter, Anna," he said, still holding her gaze, holding it almost desperately. "But only if I have your word that you'll allow me to be a *real* father to her." He stopped. Looked away, then back. "If I'm to love her, I have to do so as though she was my own."

He wouldn't settle for any less.

Tears pouring down her cheeks, Anna said, "I never slept with Clark, Jason."

He stared at her, sure he'd heard wrong.

"I'm not saying he wasn't interested, but he travels so much he knew he couldn't make a commitment—and I couldn't settle for anything less."

She really hadn't slept with him?

"Besides, he knew I was in love with you. He told me before he left for Europe that if, when he got back, I was still single, he was going to set out to steal me away from you."

"You never slept with him?" Jason couldn't quite grasp the gift she was giving him.

Anna snuggled the baby briefly, then held Audrey out to him.

"Take her," she whispered. *"You're* her biological." And then she grinned.

Jason stared at Anna for another full minute, then down at Audrey. His baby. His daughter. His and Anna's.

"She's *mine?"* he asked.

Anna nodded. "Even ultrasounds can be wrong. She's small, but she's all yours." Jason's heart full to overflowing, he took the sleeping baby from her mother's arms.

"Hello, Daddy's darling," he said, tears in his eyes as he gathered his daughter to his chest.

Audrey stirred, opened her eyes, then fell back to sleep with a little sigh. In that instant Jason knew he was never going to have to settle again.

His gaze left his sleeping daughter only long enough to run lovingly over her mother.

"Will you marry me, Anna?" he asked.

"I'd be honored to marry you, Jason," she answered softly.

After a lifetime of loneliness Jason had a family.

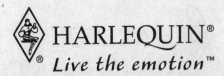

Harlequin Books presents

LEGACIES . LIES . LOVE .

An exciting, new, 12-book continuity launching in August 2003.

Forrester Square…the elegant Seattle neighborhood where the Kinards, the Richardses and the Webbers lived… until one fateful night that tore these families apart.

Now, twenty years later, memories and secrets are about to be revealed as the children of these families are reunited. But one person is out to make sure they never remember….

Forrester Square… **Legacies. Lies. Love.**

Look for *Forrester Square,* launching in August 2003 with REINVENTING JULIA by Muriel Jensen.

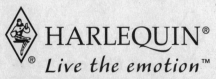

HARLEQUIN®
Live the emotion™

Visit us at www.eHarlequin.com

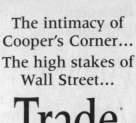
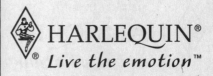

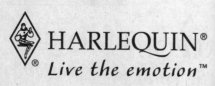

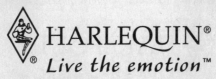

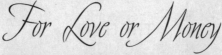

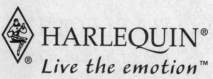